MT Ceres is the pen name of Louise Ceres, the author and creator of the Gaiadon Universe. She has a Bachelor of Arts in English Literature and is an avid reader of SFF.

Shadow on The Other Shore is the first book in the Bloods Bane series. A novel which Ms. Ceres began writing almost a decade ago when she left her role in the English Civil Service to care for her father who had Alzheimer's Disease.

Ms. Ceres is now a full-time writer, with further works of epic fantasy fiction published independently, and her poetry published by Lothlorien Poetry Journal. She calls the North Lake District her home where she shares her space with two cats and two kids.

You can visit her online at:
https://www.mtceresauthor.com/
https://www.facebook.com/mt.ceres
https://twitter.com/LouiseCeres

To Mia and Theo.

One day I hope you find me in these pages, long after I wake from this, our shared dream.

MT CERES

Shadow On The Other Shore

MT Ceres

Austin Macauley Publishers

LONDON · CAMBRIDGE · NEW YORK · SHARJAH

Copyright © MT Ceres 2023
Cover: The Other Shore. Digital Art and Design, Copyright © Louise Ceres 2022

The right of MT Ceres to be identified as author of this work has been asserted by the author in accordance with sections 77 and 78 of the Copyright, Designs and Patents Act 1988.

All rights reserved. No part of this publication may be reproduced, stored in a retrieval system, or transmitted in any form or by any means, electronic, mechanical, photocopying, recording, or otherwise, without the prior permission of the publishers.

Any person who commits any unauthorised act in relation to this publication may be liable to criminal prosecution and civil claims for damages.

This is a work of fiction. Names, characters, businesses, places, events, locales, and incidents are either the products of the author's imagination or used in a fictitious manner. Any resemblance to actual persons, living or dead, or actual events is purely coincidental.

A CIP catalogue record for this title is available from the British Library.

ISBN 9781528904339 (Paperback)
ISBN 9781528957670 (ePub e-book)

www.austinmacauley.com

First Published 2023
Austin Macauley Publishers Ltd®
1 Canada Square
Canary Wharf
London
E14 5AA

In memory of my late father, Clive, Kin 34, White Galactic Wizard, RIP, and with deepest gratitude to my mother, without her help it would not have been possible, Elizabeth, Kin 198, White Electric Mirror. Out of the deepest sorrow… To whosoever buys and reads this, my heartfelt thanks. To my kids…rations for everything, except love and fresh air. To their dad for the support, he gives. Mia for being the best sound board. Theo for showing me Minecraft and the sheer joy of creating a new world. FiFi, everyone should have a friend like you. For strong women seeking spirit and soul in all that we do, Devi Kaur, and Clare Bevington. Rosemary Stephenson, without the spiritual quests you lead, this would not have been possible, and for the moment I connected with the Cosmic Heart, everything is exactly Right On, Right On. Betty and Al and all the other folk I met when out with my father – kind hearts and coffee in supermarket cafes. Austin Macauley Publishers, it means more than I can ever express here, especially Chris and the production team (my timescale for this work was 'longley' and then some), and the graphics folk, thanks for your patience, and Vinh (take all the time you need) Tran; I did, I pray it was enough. And finally, summertime Ralf, for the Selgovae and Novantae, and swimming in wild water.

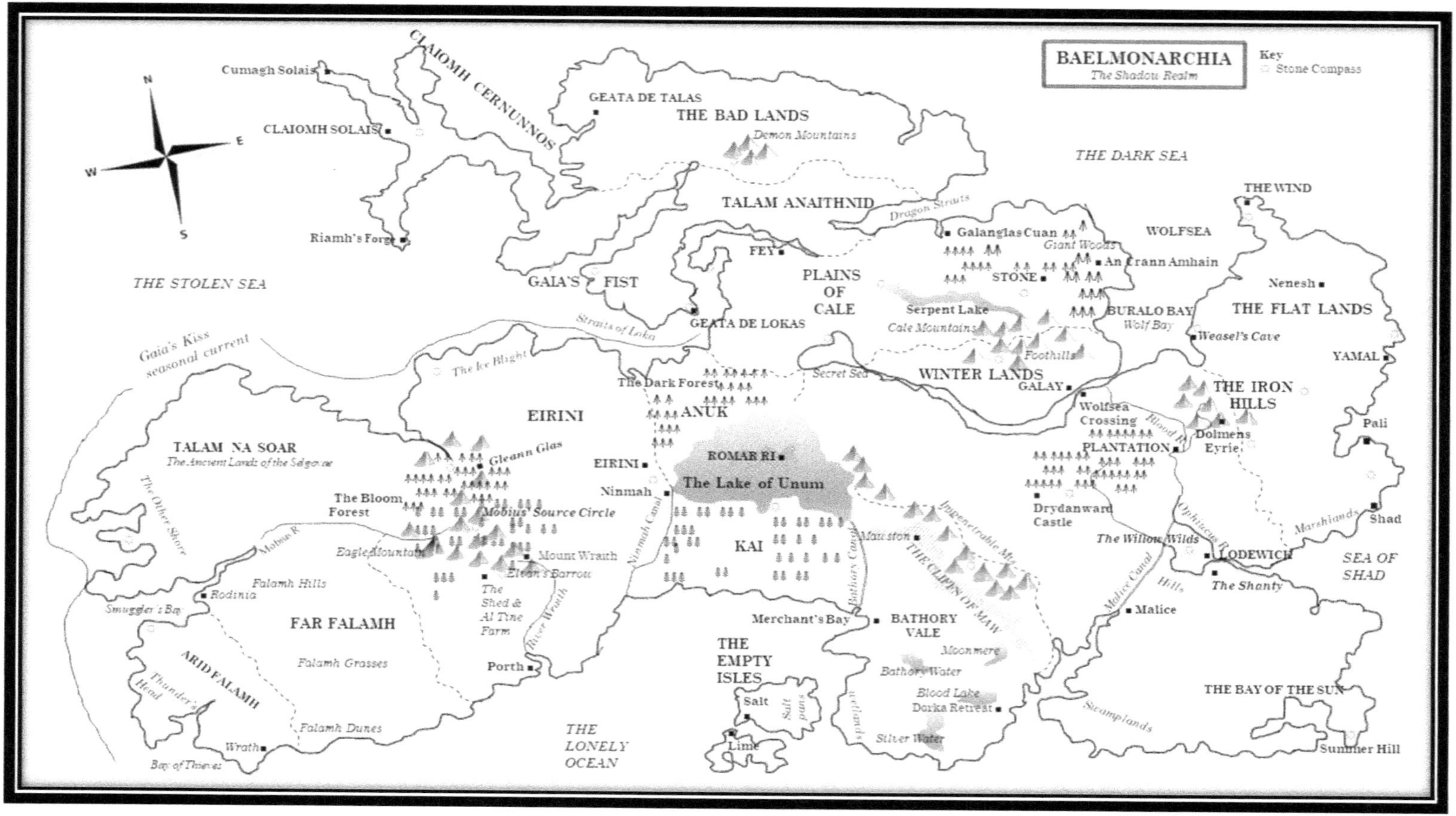

BAELMONARCHIA
The Shadow Realm
Key
Stone Compass
N
E
S
W
Cumagh Solais
CLAIOMH SOLAIS
Riamh's Forge
CLAIOMH CERNUNNOS
GEATA DE TALAS
THE BAD LANDS
Demon Mountains
THE DARK SEA
TALAM ANAITHNID
Dragon Straits
THE STOLEN SEA
GAIA'S FIST
FEY
PLAINS OF CALE
GEATA DE LOKAS
Straits of Loka
Gaia's Kiss
seasonal current
The Ice Blight
Galanglas Cuan
Giant Woods
STONE
An Crann Amhain
WOLFSEA
THE WIND
Nenesh
THE FLAT LANDS
Serpent Lake
Cale Mountains
BURALO BAY
Wolf Bay
Weasel's Cave
YAMAL
Foothills
Secret Sea
WINTER LANDS
GALAY
THE IRON HILLS
The Dark Forest
ANUK
EIRINI
Wolfsea Crossing
Blood R
Dolmens Eyrie
Pali
TALAM NA SOAR
The Ancient Lands of the Sedgewae
Gleann Glas
EIRINI
ROMAR RI
The Lake of Unum
PLANTATION
The Other Shore
The Bloom Forest
Ninmah
Drydanward Castle
Mobius' Source Circle
Impenetrable Mts
Shad
Marshlands
Mobius R
Eagle Mountains
Mount Wraith
Ninmah Canal
KAI
Maulston
The Willow Wilds
Ophiucus R
LODEWICH
SEA OF SHAD
Elvan's Barrow
THE CLIFFS OF MAW
Bathory Canal
The Shanty
Falamh Hills
Rodinia
Smuggler's Bay
The Shed & Al Tine Farm
River Wraith
Hills
Malice Canal
Malice
FAR FALAMH
Merchant's Bay
BATHORY VALE
THE EMPTY ISLES
Moonmere
ARID FALAMH
Thunder's Head
Falamh Grasses
Porth
Bathory Water
Blood Lake
Dorka Retreat
THE BAY OF THE SUN
Salt
Salt pans
Swamplands
wetlands
Falamh Dunes
THE LONELY OCEAN
Wrath
Bay of Thieves
Lime
Silver Water
Summer Hill

THE SOUTHERN ISLES
TE TONGA MOTU

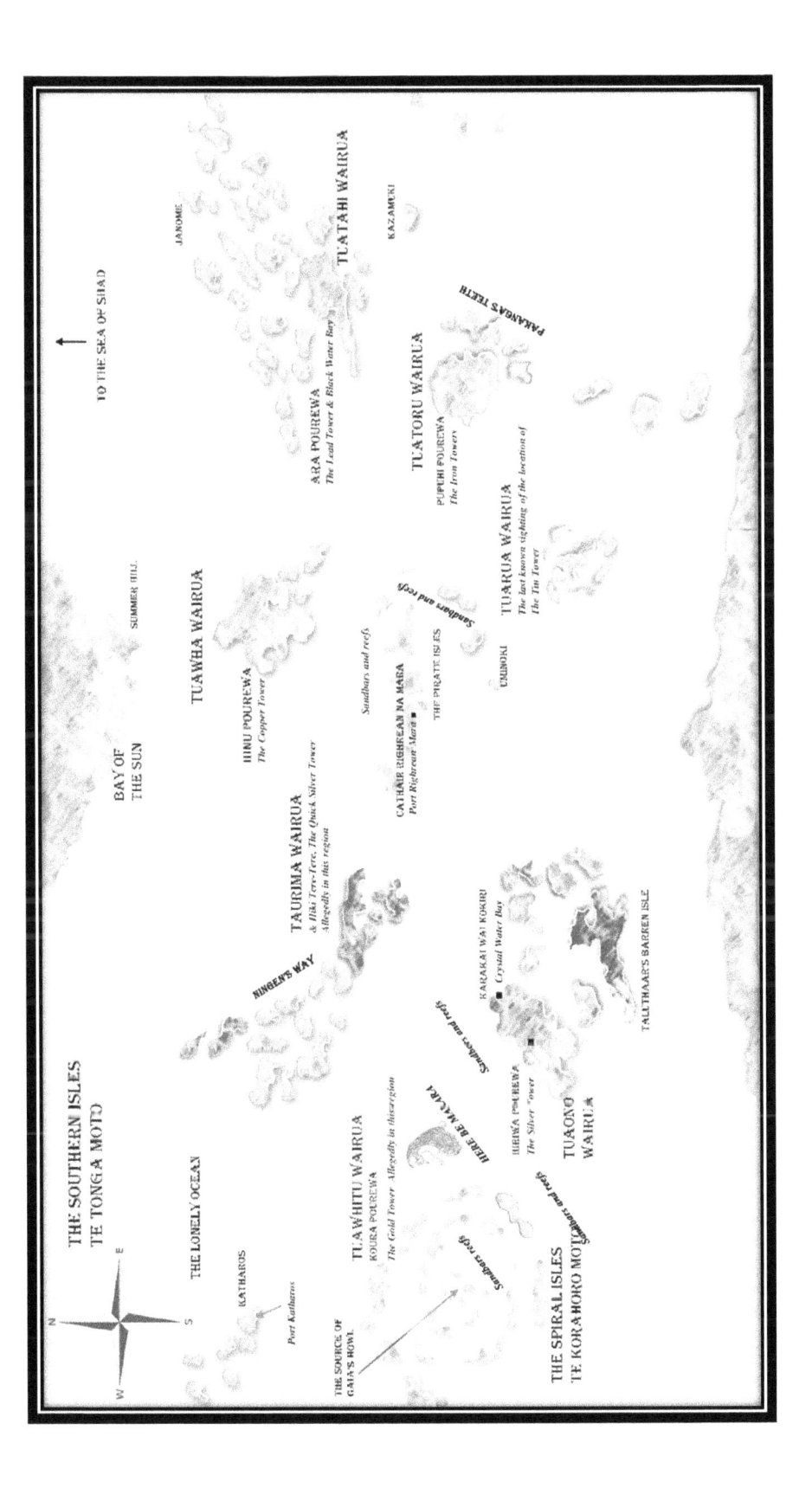

THE LONELY OCEAN

KATHARDS
Port Katharos

THE SOURCE OF GAIA'S HOWL

TUAWHITU WAIRUA
KOURA POUREWA
The Gold Tower. Allegedly in this region

MERE BE MACATA

THE SPIRAL ISLES
TE KORAHORO MOTU

HUEWA POUREWA
The Silver Tower

TUAONO WAIRUA

KARAKAI WAI KOKIRI
Crystal Water Bay

TALITHAAR'S BARREN ISLE

NINGEN'S WAY

TAURIMA WAIRUA
& *Riki Tere-Tere, The Quick Silver Tower Allegedly in this region*

CATHAIR RIGHREAN NA MARA
Port Richrean Mara

THE PIRATE ISLES

UMINOKI

TUARUA WAIRUA
The last known sighting of the location of The Tin Tower

BAY OF THE SUN

SUMMER HILL

TUAWHA WAIRUA

HINU POUREWA
The Copper Tower

Sandbars and reefs

TO THE SEA OF SHAD

JANOMIE

ARA POUREWA
The Lead Tower & Black Water Bay

TUATAHI WAIRUA

KAZAMUKI

PANANGA'S TEETH

TUATORU WAIRUA

PUPUHI POUREWA
The Iron Tower

Table of Contents

Prologue: In The Dead of Night 13

Part One: Eirini Zone... 15

Chapter One: Star 17

Chapter Two: Horse's Whispering 24

Chapter Three: Of Fire 29

Chapter Four: Rise... 38

Chapter Five: The Volpi 48

Chapter Six: Troy Valoroso-Wyburn 55

Chapter Seven: Rodney Weaselton, The Bastard 67

Chapter Eight: Empty Wrists and Bags Of Blood....................................... 80

Chapter Nine: Bang-Bang You Are All Dead 89

Chapter Ten: Curtain Twitcher 99

Chapter Eleven: Decisions 113

Chapter Twelve: Mad As a Hatter 132

Part Two: Lodewick The Capitol of Baelmonarchia 139

Chapter Thirteen: An Act 141

Chapter Fourteen: Why Would Weasel...163

Chapter Fifteen: Here Be Nightcrawlers 173

Chapter Sixteen: The King Is Dead 187

Chapter Seventeen: Big Fish, Little Fish 192

Part Three: Pale-Mouthed Prophets...211

Chapter Eighteen: Dearly Departed...213

Chapter Nineteen: Broken-Hearted 239

Chapter Twenty: Dark Dreams And A Black Sun Rising 247

Chapter Twenty-One: The Crone. Arianrihod 253

Chapter Twenty-Two: Saying Goodbye 272

Chapter Twenty-Three: Sonii Romarii...283

Chapter Twenty-Four: Miserable Folk..296

Chapter Twenty-Five: A Change Of Direction..309

Chapter Twenty-Six: Travelling Light 316

Chapter Twenty-Seven: Well Met Sonii..332

Part Four: Troy A Galactic Cycle In The Life Of… 345

Chapter Twenty-Eight: Tranquillity...347

Chapter Twenty-Nine: Bon Voyage..370

Chapter Thirty: Nightcrawlers Remixed 382

Chapter Thirty-One: Elgenubi Zuben 444

Chapter Thirty-Two: Murzim 464

Chapter Thirty-Three: Worldbridgers Are A Funny Old Lot...................477

Chapter Thirty-Four: The Ophiuchus 495

Prologue

In The Dead of Night

In the dead of the night, when the world was muted with shades of charcoal, and filled with fuzzy white particles of light that tremored and vibrated through air that was somehow more alive because of the lack of light; that was when she believed Tara. That…was when she believed she could shape a world from naught but air and imagination. Even though she knew the particles, floating like dust and dander in a shaft of sunlight, were not supposed to be there, she only had to hold her hands in front of her face – a pale cup in the palsied dark – to know it was true. When she made her own chalice, the light, and the shadow she caught within it were tangible. Then she could draw the particles, that made the shape and the shadow of the night, to her questing fingers and open palms, she imagined that they were like clay but lighter than that, a pliable thing in her hands that had no name she knew, but she could feel it wielding to her desire to make something out of nothing. Then the night was not an unknown void, a fear without a name skulking in the corner of her eye but a thing she could embrace, a thing waiting to be fashioned to whatever she desired. With a little effort, she was sure she could mould the fabric of the night, bend it to her will, but she never tried. Instead, she chastised herself, a fragile mind would think such thoughts. A mind like Tara's would think it so.

Part One

Eirini Zone

Chapter One

Star

'I just think you should listen to what I say, the power in the words and how I set my intention.' Tara put one hand on Celeste's shoulder before she said, 'Magnetise. Illuminate. Charge. Reveal.' Her voice was filled with an energy that rippled through the air; her breath misted in purling clouds of translucent white while the fingers on her other hand wove an intricate pattern before her face. It was an unseasonably cold evening, as if a tongue of winter had travelled from the far north to taste the air in Eirini.

The moon Lilith disappeared. Tara strained to keep her breath steady. Her heart thudded in her chest, but she could see quite clearly that only one moon remained. She had cast her own illusion, small as it was, to prove to Celeste that it could be done, she just needed Celeste to see it.

'No, I don't see anything, Nan,' Celeste replied, and shrugged impatiently. There was a strange feeling in the air that had her tensing her shoulders against its chill. An oppressive but fleeting sort of energy had set her teeth on edge, but she brushed it off as a drop in temperature. She could see her own breath misting the air, it was cold. Why are her hands always twitching and weaving? Is that part of her madness too? Celeste thought while she pulled her attention away from the sky.

'You do not see because your own power has not activated. I cannot tell you, or explain anything to you, because you cannot see…and it is not enough, it will never be enough that you just believe me. To just believe me is to enable what you think is my madness.'

Tara flinched when Celeste took her hand in her own and removed it from her shoulder, but her granddaughter squeezed, then released it, an apology of sorts she supposed as they both watched while it fluttered and hovered in mid-air just like the butterflies she painted. Tara studied her hand intently. 'I am sorry you can't see or feel it. It is one of the marvellous things about coming to this place. The power inside us that the demon accidentally activated when he brought us to the other shore,' she paused and turned her hand back and forth, ignoring Celeste's sharp intake of breath. How she hates the mention of demon's and dark magic she thought but said instead, 'Blue Planetary Hand. For manifesting healing and, erm,' she paused then said, 'the application of the imaginative arts.' She touched Celeste's arm and said in a hushed voice, 'Yellow Spectral Star, but I do not know what purpose it serves.' She stepped forward and met Celeste's gaze fully. 'They would not tell me and now I have left it too late to share anything with you. Sometimes, I even believe I have gone mad myself and this place is naught but my own psychosis. Sometimes I believe I have died and my other shore, the promised land, is this hell.'

'Oh, Nan-'

Tara cut her off. 'But know this, I love you, and I will protect you, if I can.'

Celeste dropped her gaze, she felt thoroughly ashamed that she thought her mad. Tara had not raised her voice, nor was she behaving too erratically, the hand weaving was strange, but she had seen worse, much worse. It was the way she spoke; Tara's words, the tone of her voice and a strangeness in the air had found something inside of herself, a place that longed for the truth, the part of her that needed to make sense of the world and her place in it. She rubbed her wrist and gulped down a sudden urge to sob before she said in a voice made gruff with emotion. 'About tonight, it was such a kind gesture. I know the extra rations to bake must have,' she paused. Then continued in a softer voice. 'You must owe Dorothea. Do you owe Dorothea?' she asked, while she hoped they did not?

'I don't owe Dorothea nor Padrain Al Tine anything child, never have and never will. I don't owe anyone on this rock, well no one that possesses a human soul, the rest can go screw themselves after what they contrived,' she said, and her tone was run through with a hard and haughty anger.

'Nan, really.' Celeste faked shock before she said, 'Then there was no need to make a special day up for me, like I'm his divinity Lord Lucas Abrecan himself. We'll be shot if anyone finds out. Official festivities only,' she half jested. 'Anyway, Spectral Star is a grand enough power even if we don't know what it's for. As long as it's not for soil singing, don't you think?'

Tara's face was overcast, her eyes suddenly darkened by a fleeting pensive shadow, her mouth opened as if she were about to say more but Celeste stepped forward and kissed her on the top of her head. 'Be back before you even know it.' She turned to bolt out of the yard.

'Celeste, it's about that, about the Spectral Star, you can't tell anyone. I know we never discuss galactic signature nonsense in rural zones, our power, such as it is, is either Seed or Earth, the occasional Hand but, from now on, you shouldn't mention it at all, not ever do you hear me.' She held her granddaughter by the sleeve of her linen tunic.

'You won't believe any of it until you see it…but you are close to the age where the devil's own spawn,' Celeste frowned, and Tara changed her tone. 'I mean an Acolyte of Anuk.' She shrugged apologetically and tried to keep her voice from screeching with fear. She took a deep shuddering breath; I hate the air here; I am sure it's how he showers us with falsehoods she thought as she composed herself.

'The Acolytes of Anuk should be sending messengers to the area soon. They will call your classmates to Ninmah. I think that you may escape the call, but you need to have something in place. A plausible story for the others, so that it will not seem suspicious when you are not called. I doubt the Acolytes will come as far as Mount Wraith what with the temple being nothing more than a ruin, but they will want to know who is fit to carry out soil singing. Whatever you do, do not say you are a Seed or an Earth power.'

Tara rubbed her forehead as if that would help her spiralling panic, her scattered thoughts. 'Have any of the girls at school mentioned their powers yet?' She cupped her chin thoughtfully while she studied Celeste.

'Not to me directly, but they dislike me…we hardly talk to each other, maybe that's why. I know Melaine Merilyn,' Celeste's mouth puckered as if she had taken a gulp of vinegar, 'and the Oarfish twins have been named as soil singers because their galactic signatures are similar, and they all have types of Earth power. I saw the puncture holes in their palms where they had been attached to the Acolytes', blood chalice. You would think it a badge of honour the way Melaine walked about holding her hand so all could see the vile thing.' Celeste screwed her face up in disgust.

Tara nodded, her frown deepened while her brow bunched into tight knots, but she held her tongue. I need to know how bad it is she thought and gulped down a wave of nausea while she kept her face calm and her breath steady.

'They only got assessed recently. I think Melaine actually sought the Acolytes out. She went early because her father's crops were faring so badly, she wanted to give her blood to the soil on her own farm. Some others went forward to support her. The twins, Raife, and Sirena Oarfish, although I think Raife went to keep an eye on them. He loves Hel Croce but won't tell her, and him and Bran Muntor tried to talk them out of it. Margeride Shroude, Sarlat Penroe and Hel Croce went too. Seemed it was easy enough to go down Ninmah and have the work done at one of the temples…because' she paused, tilted her head to one side and pursed her lips before she tutted and said, 'they all actually have Nano devices Nan, unlike me.' She waved her empty wrist in the air, then turned and leapt through the gap in the hedge next to the gate before Tara could reply.

'Light above! They do not understand child, they walked into the demon's lair and as for that chalice, it will never be full…and I thought the Shroude girl was a Resonant Hand. She should be learning healing and hedge craft, who in the hells is going to help her mother when the time comes?'

'I don't know and don't bloody well care. They're a coven of little witches and deserve to have a hole put in their hands.' Celeste shouted over her shoulder. Though she did think that being bled was a waste of a good healer. Hedge witches were always an important part of village life and Goodwife Shroude was not a young woman. What would they do without a replacement? The acolytes could use it as an excuse to reopen the Temple of Anuk at Mount Wraith she realised and felt her feet turn to lead. It was a ruined stone Guratt, but they would soon put that right if it meant they could establish a small temple there. 'No,' she groaned and ran faster.

Tara's voice faded away.

Celeste sighed and felt her tension tear away in chunks and a cloud of relief settle like a silk cloak with every stride she took, but it was short-lived when she heard Tara yell, 'It is all a lie; do you hear me?

'He is sifting through the population, looking for something…or someone, but worse, he needs blood to sustain his lie because that is how he casts his dark magic…BLOOD,' she screeched to Celeste's retreating back then took a deep gulp of air and shouted again. 'I need to give you another galactic signature, the day before or after, but not that day – NOT A STAR.' Walking stiffly towards the gap in the fence, she looked up the lane, but it was too dark to see so she continued listening to Celeste, and the sound of her feet, running light and quick like nimble fingers pattering on a small drum to Al Tine's farm.

Tara shuddered. 'There is little I can do to stop that relationship…Not if I value my own life,' she whispered as she stepped carefully over a clump of grass to lean on the rusted gate. She paused to listen to the last birds come home to roost, tweet, and flutter in the adjacent hedge as they settled.

She thought she saw two large eyes watching her from the depths of the branches. Making her way slowly to the hedge she parted the foliage but there was nothing there. 'Is that you Nympts, in there? I need to get away from this place. Can you help me?' she whispered while she peered into the hedge.

~ ❋ ~ ❋ ~ ❋ ~

An owl hooted somewhere in the forest behind their cottage which they fondly called the shed, followed by stealthy wings that barely stirred the air and then, a small squeak. So final, I wonder if it hurt? Tara thought while her breath shuddered as she took a deep gulp of the evening air and returned to lean on the gate. She cast her gaze toward the two moons and said in a voice cut through with determination, 'One day someone will destroy you, and all that you stand for will be ground beneath another's heel.'

Bringing her gaze back to the lane, she said, 'Good evening Foxbury. I thought I wouldn't see you again.' Tara did not conceal her surprise and felt her heart lift suddenly while she smiled at a large animal as it came padding along the lane from the direction of the Bloom Forest. She once thought it was a fox cub, and had hand raised it. Well, at least until it became apparent it was not a fox, but something much larger. A Volpi and want to do its own thing. Foxbury had come and gone intermittently over the years, with no pattern to his visits, but now he was back; full grown and as large as a Falamh Lion. He sat patiently while he waited for Tara to feed him.

'How can I tell her the truth, where do I even begin? Dare I go against Padrain's wishes?' She muttered to herself. The Volpi whimpered. 'No, I dare not, you're right, it isn't wise, he's kept us safe all these years, and he will kill, to protect his own. I know what Padrain and the Romarii are capable of.' She clasped her hands about her waist and shuddered while she studied the creature who eyed her much the same as a lion would gaze upon its prey, though she was not worried. He had always been gentle with her.

Flinty magenta eyes sparkled in the moonlight when he tipped his head to one side. 'I know, I know,' she agreed with the Volpi who remained mute and hungry. 'I can't endanger the community. I won't tell her anything else, apart from the thing about her galactic signature, Spectral Star – we need to hide it, but who bothers with such nonsense in rural zones, not like the barren elite in Lodewick,' she gripped the gate, 'but if it is God's will…then, I'll end up like the rest of them, amnesic, believing everything around me is real. Pah, it's come to this.' She spat on the dry earth.

The sound of Celeste's feet had faded, leaving only the noise of the night, a chill frigid wind that whispered dryly through the nearby hedge like shallow fast water rushing over gravel, a Volpi that stunk, and a slightly mad women who still gripped the rusted gate. She looked at her hands and released them, then she wiped them absently on her legs, not that it mattered one bit, she never wore anything other than baggy work dungarees.

They were military issue, and she knew they were the very same style as those given to land girls. Although, the originals had run out more than twenty years ago, the ones she wore now were made from robust homespun Fustian fabric, usually as thick as moleskin, a thinner linen or hemp in the summer with a linen tunic beneath and woollen jumpers in winter. Most folk, well those who could afford them wore hobnail or ranger boots, a combat ankle boot with a leather high top cuff, some had two buckles, them being the sorts of boots that were available when the humans were brought to Gaiadon. Others wore clogs or went bare foot depending on the circumstances in which they found themselves. The lady loose-skirts down Ninmah wore brightly coloured silk slippers. What need did they have of outdoor footwear.

She stroked the Volpi. His pelt was soft but, his large ears were bald along their edges but like a new fleece behind. His head was chest-level. A regal head, dark, golden-red fur with light copper crystals running along his muzzle, they shimmered across his temples, and around his eyes, then they ran in iridescent twinkles towards his ears and along their edge. The back of his ears was a similar colour to the fur on his head, although they were a pale lilac inside, but the colour mutated along his neck, the rest of his large muscular body was a deep copper green, almost brown, and dappled with dark, red-gold patterns that mimicked the way the sun would fall through the canopy of the Bloom Forest.

'You are a beautiful animal now that you have your new coat,' she talked and fussed a little more as they meandered back to the cottage.

She sniffed the air, her eyes smarted and her nostrils stung with a sneeze that threatened to explode, then disappeared again. 'Was that smoke? Pipe smoke? Surely not now.' She looked hesitantly at Foxbury as he slunk confidently across the yard before her. Whose side is he on…light above. I am even suspicious of animals now, though to be honest I should be she thought and pushed aside a sudden surge of fear.

'We're perfectly safe – do you hear me you fiends…you bastards, we're safe here and I'm not going anywhere,' Tara shouted at the moons, her hands balled into tight fists rested on small defiant hips, 'and don't think I don't know that you're listening behind that hedge because I do know. I know you can hear, and I know you can talk – I'll prove it one day, you wait and see.' She stomped away back over the yard to her haphazard cottage where the Volpi waited at the door.

Chapter Two

Horse's Whispering

Nellie? What was noise from aged woman?' Hossy asked, as he munched a last mouthful of sweet grass. The moons were up, and it was time to make their way back to their stable, but there was always time for another bite to eat he thought while he waited for Nellie to reply.

'It was woman-Tara making war with words at the demon-moon that should not be there. Then she talked to the Volpi, who is back from his wanders, Volpi growled at the woodshed and sniffed the tree where the drake returned to roost.' Nellie brought her head back from the gap in the hedge she had been looking through and rubbed it along Hossy's neck. Blowing softly, she left a patch of silvery snot on his ebony coat.

'Volpi back, and drake. Rats in the woodshed? Winter breath on the air? Things changing, eh. Wonder if Volpi will go see Cissy…' Hossy trailed off.

'Winter's breath is a wrongness,' Nelli replied and watched her own breath leave her nostril in shafts of silver mist that curled at their ends. 'Volpi not safe up there near Padrain, he's wise thing, he will stay away, but Tara…She say, maiden-Celeste be safe here. I hope she right, Hossy, I like maiden-Celeste. She joys itself and always have carrots or apples. She takes us nice places, on long rides with nothing tied behind. What say you, Hossy?' Nellie's eyes glistened like deep indigo pools framed by large, voluminous lashes.

Hossy Black stopped chewing. His ears pricked while he considered carefully what he would say to Nellie. 'I say you right, Nellie. I like best when we make frolics, race over fields like we warrior horses, like Roma-ranger, eh. Me, like Lord Nimrod, his own-self,' he neighed, and stamped his great hoof bravely on the soft grass. 'Always she has own nosebag, only small times she bites my carrots and apples, is true. I like she, much, not so much man-child. Think he own us, like he and his grandsire own the smelly Foss machines.' He paused while his lips quivered. His tail twitched nervously, and Nellie watched him with concern in her eyes. 'Be biters, Nellie,' he said before he continued,

'Soon man-child honour the Romarii trade-off. None escape The Calling, then The Becoming…then they own him, eh.' Hossy curled his lip back as if he was grinning. 'Then we speak. I say silly man-child with no ear holes, no nose, only eyes that are closed, this is what I say to him, Nellie. Then I say, you owned now, man-child, even we more-free than you.' Hossy nickered, then nudged Nellie, while they made their way back up the Long Field and to the open door of their stable. He paused once and breathed the air, not as humans breathe it, all unconscious and desperate to get it into too shallow lungs, but in the way a Romarii horse does.

'The crone, Arianrihod, know that man-child's blood too thin. That's what me think,' Nellie said softly while she turned to follow Hossy.

'The crone break Dorathea's heart if she say he not fit for the Calling,' Hossy said absently before he began gently reading the many things that made up the silence of the night, it being the only way to read what was true.

Everything Hossy needed to know was all held in the Silent Thing an invisible shroud of energy, memory and action. The Silent Thing was the sum total of all living things' thoughts, in a particular area, while they moved through space and time. Hossy turned his attention to it, his eyes focussed on the middle distance while he sensed the wealth of information withheld in the Silent Thing.

A fair night, there were no unusual taints to the air. Although, he disliked the smell of the hidden Poiten distillery and the state-owned Foss silo, they had become part of the Ever-Was. Therefore, they did not clang like a great bell all dissonant and raw with wrongness. Yes, they smelled foul, but not like the smell of demon-made predators, stinking of sulphur, blood, and dark magic. But they are not here, Hossy reminded himself nervously while he recalled an unpleasant smell at the woodshed. Volpi piss, he thought and felt his fear settle. He smelled Romarii far off in the Bloom Forest. Making their way here but he would not know until he read the Silent Thing again tomorrow. He thought it was Yumni with the Koma Ranger, Inola.

'Did you read it all?' Nellie asked, knowing full-well he had probably gotten bored or distracted. Hossy was not much of a reader.

'Enough.' Hossy snorted, dropped to his knees, then rolled onto his side. The ground shook as he turned on to his huge ebony back and rubbed his fat neck into the ground. 'It good itself,' he grinned at Nellie, 'You try?'

She ignored his invitation. I may as well read it myself she thought. Then. It will be man-child who grooms him, although he hopes it's Celeste. Silly Hossy.

'Is Maiden-Celeste safe here, Hossy, like moon-mad Tara say, is what I ask,' Nellie pressed him. She valued Hossy's opinion although he was younger. She watched him roll around in the dirt and rolled her eyes. *He has come from good Romarii stock, same as I. We aren't like the human-bred horses, rare and weak. Donkeys be better but are bothersome folk, easily annoyed.*

Hossy regained his feet, a sleek mountain of glossy coat and rippling muscle rising like a great black shadow inside the cool shades of a moonlit night.

'Well, she safe?' Nellie blew contented thoughts about life on the farm out of her nostrils and into the night. She sent an image of Ganaim Al Tine coming to the end of his man-child years. Padrain and Dorothea stealthily moving contraband and rendezvousing with smugglers at hidden places not marked on any map. Cissy manufacturing weapons in the secret factories, hidden in caves deep in the vast Bloom Forest. *It is same as it ever was*, she reassured Yumni and Inola as she meandered back up the pasture.

'No, Nellie, she not; sooner she gone, we better,' Hossy replied sadly.

'When she goes…we will move too. Our own story here will soon end. Lately, I see winds of death from the moon, lunar winds followed by dragon fire, Hossy. I feel the mother-father tree die, and armies of the dead gather in the land of shadows. Wind, fire, and death, is what I see.' Her flanks twitched and Hossy rubbed himself against her to comfort her. She was afflicted with the gift of sight. He waited patiently until the milky hue of prophecy left her gaze just as quickly as it had appeared.

'Your gift has given…this I know for true. Nellie, we will speak of it to the Ever-Was. Our Kinsfolk will smell it and know it for real. Did you feel the ranger in the Bloom?'

'Yes, I felt Yumni, and Ranger Inola. There are still Romarii ways there. We still have our ways and our hidden places,' she replied proudly.

'Our way from this place. Will be soon-come.' Hossy cast his senses through a vast distance, seemingly empty, but it was not. It was filled with under and over currents of silence, some thick like velvet, others soft as silk or thin as smoke, they took the form of many streams and rivers, sometimes spreading like the branches of a great mobile tree. A gigantic network of invisible synapsis that the horses called the Ever-Was. The Silent Thing of a place, of all places was a vital part of the Ever-Was that remained hidden from humans and Romarii alike, unless they were exceptionally gifted or had been trained to find and read the currents therein, but hardly any knew how to access the Ever-Was, apart from the forbidden galactic power, Worldbridgers, and some of the Brotherhood of Morrigan.

'Tell it to the Ever-was, Nellie,' Hossy said while he rubbed her neck with his head. They were Romarii horses, involved in a trade deal with the farm, and oath bound to perform their duties as part of the trade agreement the Romarii had made with Dorothea and Padrain Al Tine, but their loyalty remained with their kin, other Romarii horses and their rangers.

Their breath misted the air with puffy clouds of pale-grey, while night, and ice, settled in around them. Nellie steadied her breath, opened the space at her forelock, the inner eye that sat between her ears and cast her perception outwards. Tenuously she sensed a branch of the silence that was receptive to her questing senses. It was open for her, no more than a thin ribbon of imperceptible silk that meandered towards the Bloom Forest, it had been cast outward by the Romarii horse, Yumni, who waited there. Nellie began to whisper her message while she released her thoughts in a wealth of images, essences, scents, and feelings.

Volpi has returned, Nellie sent the image of the creature sitting at Tara's feet and was pleased when it threaded its way into the night. *The drakes come roost in the blossom tree with news of death on the Isle of Uminoki.*

Hossy, not to be left out, he knew he was not much of a reader, but he could send a strong message or two when he wanted, so, he cast the smell of the drake lime as well as an image of Cissy Al Tine collecting their acidic waste and his feelings about the strange smell at the woodshed. He thought Nellie rolled her eyes. 'Smell is important, Nellie. I give the tale flavour.'

But Nellie did not reply, she was far away, into the embrace of the Ever-was. It wrapped about her, it caressed her with invisible fingers, it drew her further in. *Silas Al Seamist is come to Smugglers Cove, with Moe Moema cats and Fairmist Al Mara, all dressed like a minstrel fair, with tales of horror from the Southern Isles, and a burden afore his ship that breaks his heart. There is a wind coming. A lunar wind on black wings of death, followed by dragon fire. The moon-mad woman descends, the girl does not believe.*

Chaotic images wheeled and spun like fireworks; thoughts and feelings tumbled erratically through the thin ribbon of communication. Hossy nipped Nellie on her flank, her eyes had gone moon-white and her breathing was laboured, her nostrils flared...*Woman-Tara lies under a mound of evergreen boughs, crushed and breathless she will fall into the void of her madness, where the Fae seer will kill her anew. Maiden-Celeste, hands blaze with fire, and a shadow-boy, hungry and dangerous, hunts.*

It was too much, Hossy realised. Nellie had the gift of foresight, but she did not have permission to enter the Oracle. He leaned forward and nipped her firmly on the buttock.

Nellie whickered and bucked, then shook out her ink black mane. Her heart hammered against the inside of her chest. 'You sense the story in the silent thing?' she asked though her voice was shaky.

Hossy did not answer until her eyes had run clear. 'It is done and gone. It will find ears and be heard. I was afeared you lost inside the Ever-was, Nellie, else I would not bite' he added then lipped at her neck.

'There are more rangers out in the Bloom, Nellie. Not just Inola and Yumni, but I sense more,' he said proudly, then whickered and rolled his eyes until she could see the whites. 'They hunt wraith from the Lake of Unum.'

'By Llamrei, the wheel turn fast, and the time come,' she exclaimed.

Hossy nodded and waited for her to continue. 'Rovander and Niyaha, Alfie and Vana, and I think Sonii and Nimrod. But is imagine, running in my head. Nimrod, eh. Here? We will read the silence tomorrow, Hossy. There be a song for us there. We wait for Volpi?'

'Yes, big Nimrod there, but far away, with Morrigan, Sonii. He knows our song' he said. 'Our folk will whisper our way; things are all a-changing. The wind is nipping.' Hossy shuddered. 'Volpi will stay with women-Tara, he thinks she his mother,' he snorted.

'And so, he should. She save his cursed life. He a stupid Novantae Fae. He curse-bringer, troubles, always trouble follow him, but' she paused and flared her nostrils, 'he brings terrible tales from faraway.'

Chapter Three

Of Fire

She cupped her hand in her chin and eyed the informatics monitor. It was on a box at the bottom of Ganaim's bed. The monitor was a strange brown colour, like dry kelp and the anxious light in her eyes. It smelled like iodine and its shell looked as brittle as her hold on her sanity. Weaving her hand in the air like a madwoman she thought but held her tongue and watched while the screen glittered as if it had been dusted with ice crystals. A black line rolled hypnotically from top to bottom. She was underwhelmed and failed to see what all the fuss was about, but she did not say that to Ganaim, he had been talking of nothing else for more than a moon, the monitor, and Micah Apollon.

'Why do you want to watch Micah Apollon so desperately?' she asked and moved her feet onto the bed when a cat, easily the size of a mountain lion, prowled into the room. It bellied under the bed and disappeared.

'Rats,' Ganaim said by way of explanation.

'Ah, we have some too, in the old stable. The wood pile attracts them, but the drakes will see to them. Where did you get it?' she said while she pointed to two large paws, black as soot, while it pulled itself out from beneath the bed, followed by a tatty ear and the palest emerald eyes imaginable. It sat on its haunches and stared, then thrummed in the back of its throat like it was trying to talk. Celeste reached across and held her hand out; the cat bumped it with his head. His ears pricked suddenly at a noise from the kitchen below. He gave one last growl and left the room to patrol the rest of the house and farm.

'Fairmist Al Mara stopped by a short while ago, that one's called Francis,' he shrugged, 'no idea why, Padrain said so and there's a tabby called Marley and another black one, a queen, called Shabba, according to Dorothea. They are on loan but came all the way from the Southern Isles, that is why they're so big. Seems there are more rats than there should be at this time of year, especially up at Elvan's Barrow.' He frowned and dipped his head as if to avoid her gaze.

'There's a minstrel, will he be playing for his stay?' she said. Now, that was something in which she was interested.

'No, he's gone already. Fairmist Al Mara, just dropped them off, had a bite and away he went.' They listened to the cat thud down the stairs.

'Oh, that's a shame, he is really good. I saw him once, at market at Mount Wraith.' Celeste paused, then said quickly, 'Tara says rats spy for the devil and his kind.'

Ganaim pulled her gently towards him. 'Then we should be well enough. We have a bunch of cats here. Never mind what Tara says, does she want to give you nightshades?'

Celeste laughed while she made herself comfortable next to him on the bed. 'Tara is a bloody nightshade at times. Anyway, why are we watching Apollon? I do not like anything from Baelmonarchia. I prefer a minstrel playing a proper instrument.' She tried to sound disinterested in Micah Apollon but had heard plenty of gossip about him, from people she knew, folk who went to the capital of Eirini, Ninmah, and thought themselves cosmopolitan because they did. She tutted and screwed her lips into a tight scrunch, Melaine, and her little coven.

Ganaim interrupted her thoughts. 'Because he's living as his latest 'alter', The Son of Sophia. Can you imagine that Cel? Just turning yourself into something more than you are, you know, better than this.' He looked around the room while he scratched absently at his temple. Miniscule scrolls and patterns in shades of gold, red, and polished pewter caught the light and twinkled like the skin of a fish as it flits beneath sun-dappled water. They trailed delicately around the tips of his pointed ears. Some people thought they were scales but if you looked closely, they were pinpoints of crystalline light.

He shrugged again. 'Can you imagine? Something, anything better than this?' He cast his gaze around his sparsely furnished bedroom then felt the emptiness in the pit of his stomach like a bottomless pit, an absence of something that had nothing to do with hunger, but at the same time, it did. It felt like a longing but if someone had wagered him, name it in exchange for everything Micah Apollon had, he could not name what it was that was missing.

'Anukssake, Gan, he's the elite of the elites and can bloody well afford to be whatever he wants. He lives in palaces, wants for nothing, and is only here to entertain us bumpkins with his brilliance and beauty, so for a little while at least, we forget we are bled to death or carted off to The Wind. Micah Apollon is nothing but a creation of the academies in Baelmonarchia.' She pulled a sour face and continued. 'You know, to the elites that live in Lodewick, we are worth less than the beasts we rear, and that is what our nano-assessments will recommend; soil singing until there isn't a single drop of blood left. We,' she tutted and swung her finger between them, 'do not have fantastic 'alters' and a celebrity life in high society. We don't even have the freedom to fertilise our piss poor soil when we die. No, we have to do that while we are still alive' she finished bitterly.

'One day it may be different. We should listen to what he has to say. Anyway, I am glad Tara let you come. Though, I can't believe you said yes.' He smiled slyly, kissed her on the top of her head before he got off the bed and walked to the box where he fumbled about with the monitor.

Whether Tara liked it or not, Celeste had come tonight, a small victory. I got her away from the mad woman he thought while he tuned the large knob on the monitor. Padrain had forbidden it be anywhere in the house, but they had to have it installed by law, though the law did not say where. He volunteered to have it in his room which had satisfied Padrain – almost. The monitors were the talk of Ninmah, some people even thought they were magic boxes. Idiots, need to know a bit more about crystals and alchemy he thought wryly.

The black band wavered and an image of his divinity Lord Lucas Abrecan, snapped into place. His dark hair was combed flat, and his red beard was trimmed neatly to a point below a thin smile that did not reach his cruel eyes. In the background someone sang his praises, exulting him as the divine descendant of the One-God Anuk. Then, the picture faded and a row of people swinging from a hangman's scaffold came into view with the notification of their crimes below. Stealing food, removing their nano device illegally, hiding a natural birth, and lying about their galactic signature power. 'All crimes made against the State of Baclmonarchia are a theft from the One-God Anuk and are punishable by death, including not reporting a crime to the relevant bureau's,' a disembodied voice reminded them.

Celeste shuddered and turned her face away from the screen while she massaged her empty wrist. Then she said in a voice made short with tension, 'It was an easy yes to you, Gan, otherwise it's another night in, listening to the scanner with Tara, and that is always the same old thing. Trouble at Ninmah, especially at the canal border. Light knows why she does it, it sends her into such dark moods, especially when they mobilise anti-grav flyers, and don't get me started on what they've done to the people of Kai. Disgusting, there can't be a living soul left,' she finished on an angry note though her eyes were wet with unshed tears.

'How is Tara?' Ganaim asked, casually changing the subject while he made his way back to the bed, rubbing his pointy left ear. He sat on the edge and kept his eye on the monitor. I can't meet her eye he thought while he balled his hands into tight fists. He hated asking about Tara, it always felt like the beginnings of a sneaky interrogation oiling off his tongue. In fact, that was what it was, but she never seemed to notice.

Celeste swallowed, surprised to find a sudden lump in her throat. 'Tara?' she sighed heavily. 'Odd as usual. She made cakes to celebrate the day I was born, and she was pointing to the moons, and acting strange, shouting about blood and sorcery…' she trailed off.

He held his tongue just like he had been taught. It was, according to Dorothea, the best way to get information from someone without them knowing it, but he did turn to study her. Light of the flame, she's worried sick he thought and hated that he couldn't do more for her.

'It's worrying, especially with our assessments coming soon.' Celeste massaged her empty wrist, no Nano device, but looked sneakily at Ganaim's, the pip on his wrist protruded slightly, like a small piece of bone. 'Why do they even bother with them?'

'Not for anything other than keeping a tally on their bags of blood,' Ganaim replied.

She worried quietly, Gan was right, what was the point of the assessments, no one got out of the zone they were born in, unless they went mad and were carted off to work the wind. Why has Gan got a nano, why haven't I she thought but said instead, 'I'll keep an eye on Nan. Should I tell you and Padrain still…you know…if she goes outside the box?' Celeste turned her face from his gaze and fluffed the goose feather pillows roughly.

'Aye, definitely, Cel, an' you be careful you don't pick up anymore of her bad habits.' He eased off the side of the bed. 'Remember, we do not celebrate the day we entered this hell, we only celebrate the day his divinity, our Lord Lucas Abrecan was born, the day the One-god Anuk defeated the Romarii and Spider King, and…' he waggled his finger in the air – Celeste laughed, as he mimicked their teacher, Carter, 'anything different is considered outside the box and that means that most wonderful of rewards, Working The Wind.' Ganaim made an invisible noose which he pretended to tie around his neck. He gagged and let his tongue lol out of his mouth. He gave the informatics monitor a gentle tap on the side, then he jumped on the bed beside her.

She laughed nervously, pressed her empty wrist as if her anxiety would implant the nano device for her, while she thought of Tara's own empty wrist. Neither of us has one. Is that why she's a bit loopy. Is that what will become of me…I am off to work the forsaken wind, she thought morosely, though she did not really have any idea what that punishment really meant.

He slid onto the bed next to her. 'As for your galactic signature? Power?' he raised one eyebrow and tutted, 'Who bothers with that pile of dung, apart from the elite who buy their babies their galactic signature days? Apollon's got some crazy expensive galactic signature. Now, that's what gold can buy, a day of birth when the galactic energy was a massive two hundred. And the power, a stonking, Golden, Overtone Sun. Imagine the kinetic energy from that?'

'You mean sorcery?' she said.

'No, I mean kinetic energy. Sorcery is different, I think, but humans have the ability to draw the kinetic energy from the day they were born. Say you were little Lugh Muntor, and you were born on a Resonant Wind day, then you can access that kinetic power and bind it to your voice, no one has a singing voice like his, but I bet he couldn't kill someone with it. Whereas sorcerer's may draw power inside but then they wield it however they like,' he replied while he fussed about with the pillow behind his head. Then, he pulled her to his side while he spoke casual and soft into her ear. 'What's yours anyway?'

'Blue Hand,' she lied easily as she waved her hand in the air to hide the sudden tension in her body. 'Artistic like Nana, probably, but yes I understand, I'll be careful.' She smiled and its insincerity was thinner than a rapier through the gut. Her reply had taken her by surprise; she had lied to him so easily, but there was just something off about her birth. Not just knowing who her parents were, it was something else that Tara was trying to tell her, but it was stuffed in among her madness, and try as she might, it was hard to fathom, but she was not going to take any risks, even if it was Ganaim. A loose tongue led to the noose, that was how the saying went and Ganaim had a runaway mouth. He looks wounded, he knows I just lied.

'And what is yours?' she whispered in his ear, then kissed it lightly. 'I assume it's not rude to ask a gentleman his signature?' She smiled sweetly as she moved away from him and propped her own pillow against the wooden headboard.

'Don't know. Not even sure if anything will manifest for me,' he replied while he tugged at his pointy ear. 'Probably Magnetic Seed or Rhythmic Earth, it is what we mainly are in the rural zones, isn't it? Nowt special, just bags of blood for the infertile soil, definitely not a Sun.' He cleared his throat. 'Hands are better than Seeds.' He nodded towards her curtly and shrugged.

'There aren't any better than others, well, there shouldn't be. We should all be proud of what we are, what we can accomplish and not be so limited by a silly galactic signature. It's only the elites who put any value on it anyway,' she replied with a surprising amount of heat in her voice.

'Are we in a rebellious mood this fine evening, Celeste Melsie?' he teased her while he reached forward and planted a kiss on her lips. 'Some are better, no, not better but...' he paused giving himself time to find the right words. 'You know, they've got real power with them, strange, dangerous powers,' he dropped his voice dramatically and widened his glacial eyes, 'There are some that kill the mother, which is why there aren't any of that type of signature anymore – outlawed, they are.' *She lied to me and now I want to know why. What is she hiding* he thought.

He was sure that this was the missing piece, the small thing that would make sense of who Celeste Melsie was. She might not know it, but he had spent all his life knowing that she was hidden. His task had been to make sure it remained that way, and that she did not ask too many questions which was easier in remote rural zones, for now at least. He pushed a wave of unease away only to find that empty space within him. His own place where something was missing.

But hidden or not, Padrain and Dorothea knew it would end. His pointed Fae ears and crafty Fae nature had been useful when he had eavesdropped on them while they talked in hushed tones about their problem at The Shed. 'We need to be done with the pair of them, Dorothea, the deal was time-sensitive, you know that. One of them could pop at any minute and bring a bloody shitstorm of trouble to our door...what was Aindreas thinking when he dumped her here, and where is he now?' Padrain had reminded his wife, Dorothea, that the terms of their deal, concerning Tara, and her offspring, with the Romarii was coming to its end. Ganaim shook the memory off and tried to focus on the monitor. *She never lied to him – ever.*

'What are they, then? The dangerous powers,' she asked and tried to hide the interest in her voice. *If he mentions Star, I will not be able to lie about it again.*

'I think they're Worldbridger or something like that.' He searched her face, then bored into the pit at the centre of her eyes with his own. She shuddered but managed to keep the ripple of fear under her skin. 'Seriously though, Cel, we need to be careful, until you get this done.' He massaged her empty wrist. 'Let one of us know if it gets too bad. Tara can always come and talk to Dorothea, she understands stuff like that, how the life we have to live can, well, you know…' He let his words trail away, they all knew what life in a farming zone could do to the faint-hearted and thin-blooded.

She pushed a sudden wave of tension back down to her chest and shoulders. It would wait until she got home, then she could scream into her pillow until she fell asleep; tomorrow would be another day. Tara's madness did not usually last for days on end, just a few rabid hours at a time – she would sleep it off, it was not bad, a bit of hand weaving and shouting about bad blood and demon magic – not at all bad.

He let his arm linger deliberately against her thigh. Celeste did not object, so he began to smooth it back and forth, across her leg, small gentle strokes. He had had a gut full of talking. Of listening to her lie. *She never lies to me, never* he thought and felt her untruth like a sharp stab through the heart.

They had kissed before, many times. Not regular like lovers or even delicately like courting couples, but with enough occurrences to suggest that they had begun to like each other – more, as they grew together, despite her Nana's warning and his family's dismay as they became the closest of friends.

'Do you want to go all the way, Cel?' he whispered. 'I've, er, been chewing Neemna seeds and got a blue sponge, down Ninmah. 'In the pleasure district.'

'Yes, I do,' she replied. Her words caught in her throat, and she gulped. A strange sensation travelled through her body, a wave of energy that she mistook for pleasure while she thought *it's now or never, I love him, he loves me.* They were meant to be together. All of their childhood together, in her mind at least, was an unspoken promise that they would never be apart. Nothing and no one would come between them. She had no other friends, male or female, only Ganaim and that was the way she wanted it. That was the way it had always been.

He visits the pleasure district and has started chewing Neemna seeds? How long for? A sneaky doubt whispered in her mind, but her suspicions and train of thought became lost as she pulled him towards her and kissed him hard on the mouth. He tasted of apple pie and honey, like Summer and sweet expectation all rolled into one. They kissed hungrily while she threw all thoughts of blood and magic, of mad women, to the back of her mind. Finally, she felt his fullness inside as they lost themselves in a vacuum of sensation, where nothing else existed, only them, their exchange of sweat, bodily fluids, and soft moist breath, broken only by his whispers, his throwaway promises which threatened to overwhelm her with their mounting intensity.

Then, their mutual agreement, a vow, and a promise to love each other. Forever.

~ ❖ ~ ❖ ~ ❖ ~

Afterwards, they turned their attention to the monitor. It was clear, and the images were colour even though the black line rolled down the screen every now and then. Micah Apollon stretched his lithe body across a red velvet sofa. Then extended a long thin arm across a low glass table and picked up a strategically placed glass of water, he drank it in one go. He waggled the glass in the air above his shoulder; someone out of the view of the crystal box that was recording the event took it and a fresh one appeared on the table.

'He's called the golden mouthed prophet, the voice of the youth, Cel. It's about time someone started to ask the questions he asks.' They sat on the bed, propped by lumpy feather pillows.

Celeste had put her clothes back on carefully; she had not wanted to disentangle herself from Ganaim. After making love, she knew he was hers and she was his. 'He's a fake. Not authentic like Fairmist Al Mara, who actually goes into the world and gather's real stories,' she said, then folded her hands under her chest.

'I know what you mean, but Micah doesn't have the threat of the poet's curse to protect him, like Fairmist has, Micah has to do what he is told.' He put his arm around her, and drew her close to his chest, reluctant to let her go. This is what it will be like when we are living together properly, hand-fasted, not taking any other, just us, he mused while he pushed images of the Ninmah pleasure district to one side, but plenty of time yet for that sort of commitment he thought while he turned and tousled her hair. He pushed the sudden surge of emptiness he felt, firmly away but not before he thought, surely Cel is enough to satisfy me.

He was grateful when Micah began talking about his work. A project in consciousness, he called it. Then added he would make attempts to collaborate with other artists from other countries, adding that music could bring down the borders around Baelmonarchia.

'Light of the flame,' Celeste huffed, 'how out of touch is he. Who, in any of the free countries, would want to see a bunch of soil singers being bled to death and the rest of us half-starved? Not to mention bones in gibbets and necks stretched on scaffolds.'

Ganaim muttered, 'It's the same in Baelmonarchia, Cel, just a different kind of hell. I think there may be more food, for the elite at least. But what I want to know is how did he get the permission for this? He has already committed treason, at least twice. Bring down the borders? He'll have to hurry up, it'll take more than a tambourine and a drum to take down what they've got at Ninmah,' he said, and his voice was filled with disdain. 'Look, Cel I'm loyal to Lord Bucky, secretly, most folk in Eirini are, you know we would see Micah on the throne at Galay, before anyone else, but he will need to do more than rattle his drum at the proc if he's to rally us to his cause.'

He shifted his weight and blew on her hair. 'Apollon's Lord Bucky's favourite bastard you know, he must have kissed some elite arses to get his son's gig past the censors.'

'Will you shush, I'm missing it...'

Ganaim smiled. 'You may not care for Micah's music, but a hint of rebellion and you are made of fire,' he teased.

'No,' she retorted and elbowed him in the ribs, 'there is only one Al Tine on this bed.'

Chapter Four

Rise

Srondall Smite had a bad feeling. Not a gut shrinking feeling but the kind of persistent niggling that ate away at one's inside until all that was left was guts and gore, but she could not quite put her finger on the source of her unease. Who was she to say no to Lord Bucky's favourite son? She did what she was told. Said the lines she was given. Whether they were an eye-watering fabrication or not, she made them real. Yes, her eyes filled with tears when the scaffolds swung with carrion, not because the people were dead, but because she liked her own neck, unstretched. Her steely-eyed revulsion when she named the rebels who were sent to work the wind was not because she cared a damn about what they did but because she liked her life. There had never been a knock at her door in the dead of night and the strange whipping sound the protectorate orbs made while they hovered above, full of guards and laser fire? Silent. She had been chosen to host this show because she was good, she was a state-owned mouthpiece, careful of her words, the way she said them, but also, she wanted to know where her father was, what had befallen him…but more than that, she wanted to make sure she avoided a similar fate.

'The recording is available soon, depending on the Bureau of Artistic Moderation,' Micah frowned, 'their censors will have to assess its suitability.' He sucked air between his teeth, his irritation clear before continuing with more than a hint of bitterness. 'My voice will be alchemically cast into a silver disc, depending on who you are or where you live you will be issued one. A listening device should be available,' he finished while a tight frown which set the scrolls of light beneath his skin twinkling. Then added, 'If you are poor,' he paused then said, 'If you are rural or mining then maybe a minstrel will be able to,' he looked set to say more but cut his words short before he hid his anger by adopting a louche attitude. He took a red lip balm and smeared it across his full lips while eyeing Srondall Smite, his interviewer, in an altogether disarming manner that made her cough then take a large gulp of water.

He smiled sardonically though the heat had not left his eyes and a vein in his neck thrummed. 'We are happy we got permission to record the song. It is called The Song of Sophia, a project in the expansion of consciousness.

'We hope to free the people of Baelmonarchia from the physical and mental borders we find ourselves ensnared in.' He rubbed at the nano device implant on his right wrist.

Srondall eyed it too. Anukssake, what is he up too? she thought with a sudden sinking feeling in her gut. 'Would you like to elaborate on that, Mr Apollon?' She shifted uncomfortably in her chair as she cast her eyes about the box-like studio. It was not unknown for any of the Bureaus to test the citizens of Lodewick, the trick to survival was working out which one of them was on your trail, baying for blood, and one-up-man-ship on its rival bureau. Worse yet, she realised with a sudden lurch, it could be an investigation from one of the temples of Anuk. Would they dare ambush, Lord Bucky's son during a live transmission? Yes, she thought and felt a rush of fear run along her spine.

She cast her eyes quickly over Micah's shoulder, way past the rickety old crystal boxes that alchemical devices which caught and transmitted images, and past banks of bubbling, cylindrical, crystal power-packs that lined one wall from floor to ceiling; the band stood before them like a row of gaunt silhouettes. Copper wire twisted through the middle of the different coloured cylinders, just visible through the silvery white, translucent, conducting liquid inside.

Micah continued to describe a chant on one of the songs and urged people to listen to it, to sing along, while Srondall, suspended in the moment, could not help but think, it is an alkaline, rubi-something or other? No, that was not it – rubidium! Mined in the Flat Lands somewhere to the North, along with other things, she shuddered.

It all looks like a liability, Apollon included. A massive risk, perhaps if it all just goes bang…we might get some new equipment, she pondered, there isn't ever any new equipment, no innovation – we've used the same pile of junk since I left the academy and started here, she sighed, scanned the audience, no acolytes, non that she could see, then took her full attention back to the sparkling Micah Apollon, adjusted her earpiece and smiled like a snarl at Baelmonarchia's most eligible bachelor. 'Mr Apollon?' What had he been blethering about.

'Falsehoods are in every part of our lives. This…' He waved his stick thin arm in the air, his bony finger pointed like a wand. 'This is all wrong, do not believe anything you see around you – we are all being bombarded with codes, with little lying illusions, sent to blind us to the truth of the reality in which we live.' He screwed up his lips while his brow knotted. 'We are being fed falsehood on a scale that is beyond your worst nightmares, Srondall. And yours too.' He swept his arm to indicate the audience. On an invisible cue, they made a noise like the wind.

'When we wake, we will emerge into a living hell none of us will believe or can escape from. They are bleeding people like pigs and if you believe it's to fertilise the soil…it isn't. It's for sorcery, magic that is blacker and more soulless than the void,' he rambled.

Srondall Smite's jaw dropped open. 'Anukssake, where's my cue to shut him down?' she bent her head and hissed into her mic, discretely hidden behind her lapel as Micah continued to talk. He sat on the edge of the low settee like an animal waiting to spring from a trap. A sparkle of sweat glistened across his face, as if he had been misted with dew, but he was too animated, like a wind-up toy, frantic initially, but waiting to wear down, so it could for a brief span of its momentum, exist at a normal speed.

He is off his face she thought and clenched her hand into a tight fist.

'Worse still,' Micah grimaced and looked around like a paranoid thief, unaware or not caring about his host, 'is this. We are not even supposed to be here on Gaiadon!' He smacked the arm of the settee just as someone in the audience said, 'Easy for you to say, Lord Fae, with his noble blood.'

Srondall jumped, visibly but said in her most condescending tone as the offender was carted out bodily. 'This is a music session not a debate about ethnicity.' But she need not have bothered.

Micah continued, 'It is wrong, things are wrong with this reality, only we are being born, on the day allocated to us, so that the demons can have a bunch of galactic powers at their disposals. Have you ever wondered why Seeds and Earths are born in rural areas? Nights and Storms for the mines. Why do we believe every damn thing we're tol—' he stopped suddenly, seemed to change his mind about the speed of his delivery while he sensed the hush, now a suffocating wall of inertia, fall over the studio. People around him were frozen to their various spots. Wide-eyed with terror; they could not move their gaze from the madman, Apollon.

They had all heard of people going outside the box, but here, in the capitol Lodewick, you just kept your head down and got on with it. The hangman's scaffold was never empty. The spying-eyes never closed. They liked to believe it happened elsewhere. Whole villages of rural peasants taken to Work the Wind, large tracts of the outer areas that housed the Lowers were frequently cleansed, and to be honest, the Elites were always happy to see it was being taken care of; somewhere over there. But to see the madness, and from one of the most elite, was an entirely different thing. It was manic with oily rebellion, an incendiary device ready to blow, full of grotesque paranoid fantasy that made law-abiding citizens grind their teeth and whisper behind their locked doors of an evening. Mostly, it was full of all the forbidden things that one could hold secretly in one's mind but never in your mouth, words like that would get you killed.

Srondall quickly checked her own knowledge of interventions into people who went outside the box. Did the witnesses to the event get interviewed? No. Why the hell would the interrogators bother with that nicety? Bystanders just disappeared; they were never seen again, along with the nutters who shouted about alternate realities, devils, and veils of lies. She snarled as she strained to control her own emotions at the sudden threat to her career. Why had she agreed to this? A favour.

She would kill him herself first before they took her to Work the Wind. The absolute twat, she thought. Last time I do a favour for an old friend from the Academy of Entertainment. She studied Micah and chewed the inside of her bottom lip. Your own fault she thought and felt her own acid sour her mouth; he was always a bit of a rebel rouser. She had considered herself lucky to be selected by the bureau who took care of entertainment, then sent in the same batch of candidates as Micah Apollon to the Academy. Her mother had only half-teased when she suggested a royal engagement which had made her cringe. She briefly recalled a happy hour or two, spent in the intimate dusty dark of the broom cupboard; Mr Apollon pressed firmly against her willing flesh. He was as prolific in love as his father Bucky.

Is that it? Did I expect I was going to get a monumental fuck out of this? I am, she thought bitterly, only not the one I expected. She pushed the thought away quickly. He had used her, she realised, repulsed by what he had become…he was clearly unhinged. Oh hells, I hope he is not really outside the box. 'Is this a stunt?' she hissed into her earpiece.' Still nothing.

'Mr Apollon, Micah, perhaps…if I could just bring you back to your work, and especially the eponymous son—'

'Free your mind, protect your brain from their manipulation and your DNA3 from their harvests.' He took a skeletal index finger, tapped the side of his temple, turned to Srondall, winked, then leaned forward and whispered, 'What is your galactic signature, Srondall? Where has your power gone?'

'Absolute bastard,' she whispered back.

'Yes, I am that.' He smirked while he watched her squirm while she waited for her direction. They were all caught by his perfect machination. Who here would challenge Bucky's favourite bastard? The small audience had started to shuffle and talk loudly amongst themselves while Micah continued to stir them up.

'What galactic signature are you? Where is your power? When was the last time you had an idea that was not stolen from you before it came to be yours?' He had risen to his feet and stood in front of the audience. Some were whispering behind their hands, others were nodding.

Fuck, fuck, fuck she thought, did I invite him here? No, he had the permissions for the broadcast already before he approached me. Does that mean I am in the clear? Srondall rose and motioned to security behind her sheaf of paper as she approached Micah, determined to get him to sit back down. Was this supposed to happen? Was it a test? Was she being evaluated for loyalty? What in the hells was she supposed to do? She wanted to kick him in the seat of his leather breeches but fumbled with her earpiece instead, nothing.

'Please, Micah, please, I need you to sit down so we can discuss your music, we really should focus on that.' Micah followed her back to the sofa, picked up his glass and drained it. Srondall relaxed. 'Thank you.'

'You want to talk about my songs,' he said in a voice that carried to the furthest corner of the studio. 'I want you to Rise before it's too late. RISE,' he shouted.

He looked around and sneered down his nose at the dithering security, while the light in his eyes flashed like the fire at the centre of a diamond and he dared anyone to approach him, to put their hands upon him. His long platinum tail of hair, bound with leather, swung from the crown of his otherwise shaved head. The skin on his skull glittered with the tiniest pinpoints of gold and red that cast about his flesh like rune-light and arcane symbols made of small jewels. There was no denying that once upon a time, one of his parents was a descendent of the

Novantae Fae. When he smiled his teeth were white and even and bared like an animal snarling. He was delighted that everything around him continued to turn to stone – to freeze. He let his power run through every blood vessel, he let its heat emanate out, he felt the urge to burn and destroy, to tear it all down cascade through him like gigantic waves rolling to the shore.

Srondall began to stutter into action, she reached for him, but he shrugged her off, stepped forward and gazed into the bulbous lens of the crystal box while it continued to record.

In the black pit at the centre of his eye, a furnace roared, inside its inner fire, was a mirror of death. 'I am anarchy,' he mouthed into the lens while he bared his teeth in a smile that was full of self-mockery and a secret that only he knew.

Should I just kick the crystal box over and be done with it? The thought of the punishment for that made Srondall's eyes water.

Just then Micah took a step back from the crystal box but before he did he said, 'Maximum impact…is the only way… I can get you…to rise.' He turned from the camera and took his seat once again, folded his arms across his chest as if nothing had happened, as if nothing bothered him.

Party time is over…wind him down Srondall, it is, not a stunt, we have had a call.

'And thank you, for this evening's entertainment from the ever so nearly, marginal Mr Apollon. I'm sure your collaboration, although not to everyone's taste,' she paused and filled her voice with vinegar, 'will get the success it truly deserves.' She resisted the urge to stuff her papers down his throat and instead turned her back to him and cast her eye over the papers that shook in her hand. Wind him down, why not pull the plug? They cannot risk it, too many viewers. They have left it to me to control the freak. I will be screwed after this. Fucked she thought and pushed down a whimper.

'And now,' Srondall gulped, but rolled her eyes to cover her discomfort, 'people, on to our next guest, the violin virtuo—'

'Srondall, I haven't finished with you yet,' he said in exactly the kind of velveteen voice he used in the dusty broom cupboard before he stood up, reached around her shoulder, and knocked the sheaf of paper from her hands.

'You think I am pretending to be marginal to promote my music. You think that is what any of us are doing? People are disappearing, being killed – for what? Doesn't that bother you? How many Dog Soldiers do we need when we are not at war? What do they really produce in the Flat Lands…why aren't you asking these questions, Srondall Smite?

'I always thought you were a decent reporter. Report on what I've just told you,' he ordered her, and his voice carried his birth right inside it like a rod of iron. He was an elite, Lord Bucky's heir, destined to sit upon the throne at Galay, if not for Lord Abrecan manipulating him that was where he would be.

And this, Srondall Smite realised as she felt her bladder loosen, is the beginning of the revolution.

Her father's brother, Sohon, told her it would come to this, but she had not believed him. Even when Sohon had vowed to avenge his brother's death and had even gone as far as the Silver Tower seeking answers. She did not know if he had found any there, but he had returned to her mother, once, in the dead of night. He had one white eye and a huge cat-like animal with him. Light I do not know what happened to Sohon either, she thought while she blinked back tears. It was all out of control.

Micah ignored the movement of people just out of its line of sight. His band had packed their equipment and quietly left during the interview. The tension in the studio had swollen to a taught maximum. They were only waiting now for the crescendo, the last act, whether it was a knife in the back or a blade to the throat they did not care. They only knew it was not likely to be a happy one. I have marked them all with the Crimson Stain, the kiss of death, he thought regrettably but pushed the feeling away. I am doing what I must, to free us all.

Srondall waved frantically to security, who stood discretely towards the back of the set, glued to the far wall, still not sure whether they should manhandle Lord Bucky's heir. Was it even in their permissions to accost an elite?

Micah swayed in front of the lens, his platinum tail swished like a gilded serpent, rune-light sparkled in rippling shades of fire and his skin was suffused with a golden light while he looked into the eye of the lens and kept looking. Way past the bulbous glass, further than the blue alchemical light in its depths, beyond the studio and out, out toward everywhere he could reach and while he cast his consciousness far and wide he let his power shaft from him like the rays of a distant sun while he mouthed repeatedly, 'RISE.'

Micah looked through the lens while he lifted his right arm, making sure the outside of his wrist was forward, then he made a fist, and shouted defiantly, 'I WILL DIE TO WAKE YOU UP! COME, RISE WITH ME.'

The flash of metal in his left hand was mercurial, the cutthroat razor moved like a beam of light. He slashed. The cut was clean and sharp; the tiny nano protruded slightly like a small bone-yellow boil waiting to be lanced. He threw the blade behind him, where it clattered, then skittered noisily across the low glass table.

Srondall reached the back of the studio where she grabbed at security and dragged them towards the closest thing Baelmonarchia had to royalty. 'Get over here you monkey's and move his elite backside out of here,' she screeched as Micah's blood spurted, then hit the lens in a fan of hot crimson.

The letting of blood broke the spell he had woven over them all. Micah dug his claw-like fingers in and pulled at the head of the nano device.

The lensman, behind the crystal box, adjusted his bulbous, dark optics, nodded once, then said, 'Superbly done, fàidh òir.' He waited until Micah snorted his agreement then stepped from behind the crystal box and slipped out with the rest of the panicked audience.

Micah was incandescent. He radiated a supernatural light while trails of a lesser light made up of miniscule orbs and strange geometric shapes trailed behind the nano while he pulled it out of his wrist.

It gave up its hold suddenly then evil looking roots left his body, they glittered with malevolent codes of light suspended in gossamer threads of ectoplasm.

'Wake up. Come, rise with me,' he said in a voice that was no more than a whisper, but carried in its tone a command, one that could not be disobeyed by any who had the ears to hear it true.

~ ❈ ~ ❈ ~ ❈ ~

'Arghh, he's hit a vein,' Ganaim shouted and retched.

'Did you see that…Gan, did you see the lights?' Celeste jumped, pointed at the screen while her hands shook, and her heart pounded like a fist against the hard bone of her ribcage.

Ganaim gasped for air and rubbed his hands against his temples. 'I knew he'd be out there somewhere but seven hells that was totally extreme, my guts are heaving.' He sat on the end of the bed, running his hand through his hair which erupted like flames blazing up a chimney.

'GAN…AIM!!' They both jumped while Dorothea banged on the ceiling below with a brush. 'Ganaim Al Tine, keep all that noise down. That damned fool boy has got them rioting in Ninmah. Bucky will kill him, if Abrecan doesn't get there first. Keep it down, we need to hear the scanner.'

They waited, frozen to the spot, staring over the bed at each other, while Ganaim held his hand to his mouth and tried not to laugh. Celeste turned beetroot red.

'AND it's time Celeste was away home.' They jumped a second time. Cissy stood in the doorway, a black cat at her side, and her face screwed up in distaste. 'There will be heads on stakes down the canal district tonight. Not to mention the purge the people in Lodewick will suffer. Apollon won't feel the backlash, but everyone else will.' She folded her arms stiffly under her chest.

'Get her home as soon as you can, boy, then you've the horses to see to…making nests up here…with no thought to the proper order of things.' She stared down her nose at Celeste and raised her top lip in a sneer.

'You need to see to your own this night, Celeste, and the dark nights soon to come.' Cissy pointed, and Celeste felt her chest cave under the stern accusation of her finger. 'Can't you feel how cold it is? The stench of sulphur on the air, the sorc-'

Ganaim cut her off before she could say anything further. 'What are you doing? Spying?'

Cissy turned towards him. 'No, Ganaim, that's what rat's do. Spy for the devil. I am doing what I can to protect us all. Shabba and I are patrolling the shadows,' she pointed to the glossy black cat with yellow eyes. 'While you make nests, and dreams for potential hybrids beyond anything we can imagine, you let cat-folk do your work for you.' Celeste thought Cissy would spit, but she did not; she turned and left before either of them could say anything.

'Francis patrols the inner boundary. Marley patrols the outer boundary of the farm; you will aid him after you have seen to the horses. Pay particular attention to Elvan's Barrow. We need it cleared, it's overrun, and freezing cold up there,' she said coolly over her shoulder while she made her way down the stairs.

'Bloody rat catching, in the pitch dark, just because she doesn't understand what it feels like to be young,' Ganaim moaned.

'Are they that bad, the rats? Celeste asked, but he only shrugged and put his hand across her shoulder as they moved silently to the foot of the bed and stared at the chaos on the screen until the transmission cut suddenly.

The last thing Celeste saw and heard was Micah still bleeding from his wrist. He reached forward and smeared it like crimson oil on the lens of the crystal box while studio security restrained him.

They held him gingerly by the waistband of his trousers as they tried to move him, but the diminutive Srondall Smite clung to his back and hung around his neck like a small doll, desperate to regain control of her career, and save her sorry skin while Micah shouted, 'Wake up, slaves.'

Chapter Five

The Volpi

They sat on the edge of the bed, and watched while anonymous stars glimmered with promise like unsaid wishes, distant and cold, and the dark night filled the small window in his bedroom with the colour of eternity. It was the year of the Blue Resonant Storm and by the goddess' breath Micah Apollon had set the sky afire Ganaim thought, while he got up and closed the wooden shutters; on the distant horizon he saw shafting rays of green stab through the dark and knew that the proc had launched their orbs. The overhead rubicity light sputtered, and he reached into a cupboard under the window and brought out a tallow storm lamp. 'They'll cut the rubicity and the lights will go, no doubt punishment for Apollon's outburst. It'll make it easier for the procs to clear Ninmah district if they're the only ones with power.' Sometimes he hated living in a rural zone but not tonight.

'Are you taking that ratting?' Celeste nodded to the lamp deliberately changing the subject.

'No need. I will be taking these,' he pointed to his glacial lilac-blue eyes, and she half-laughed when he enlarged his pupils until there was hardly any iris left. 'The lamp is for you. I would walk you, but Cissy is right, I need to go around the outer boundary with the cat.' He shrugged, then dropped his gaze while he busied himself with the lamp.

They are obsessed with rats she thought while she finished pulling on her boots. 'They are like Micah Apollon's; your eyes are like his. Fae's Kiss, probably.' He grunted, but she continued, 'I'll wager it is, and I don't need the lantern. I know every rut, pothole, dollop of shit, and weedy hillock all along that lane.'

He smiled while he rubbed his jaw thoughtfully. 'Well, we'll remember our first time after that.' He smoothed his hands over his head.

'Understatement!' Celeste blew through tense lips. 'I still feel a bit shaky. You know – inside.' He sat beside her; concern clouded his face, but she held her hand up. 'No, not the blood, silly. Believe it or not, that was not a life-threatening slash. It was the wrong side of his wrist for a start off, nowhere near a ve—' she stopped abruptly while Ganaim frowned and the space above his nose bunched into a tight knot while he peered closely into her eyes. The overhead light flickered off suddenly, and he reached forward and drew her to his chest.

'You shouldn't think about things like that, Cel.'

'I know, but sometimes, I just wonder where they went, how they died.' Taking their own lives was the only thing that would explain their absence, how they had abandoned her. Surely, they were not so important as to have been taken by the procs. Had they been involved in any accidents? She ruled both out, she knew someone would have said to her, 'Bloody procs taking our loved ones to Work the Wind, or how tragic that your parents died in so and so a way.' Her mother had not died in childbirth; she realised if that had been the case it was likely that Tara would have told her, or she would have a Worldbridger galactic signature, whatever the hells one of those was. Worldbridger, she rolled the name round in her head and sighed against the warmth of his chest. I am secluded here, surrounded by Seeds, Earths, and Hands. Worldbridger? Star? This is the first time I ever heard of them. She pushed the thought away, even though it still bothered her along with all the other things that bothered her, things she was an expert at pushing away while she kept her attention on the mad woman she lived with.

No one spoke of her abandonment. Her Nana refused to discuss her mother, Ganaim avoided or changed the subject, and she did not have the courage to ask Padrain or the heart to ask Dorothea. So, she had reached the conclusion, that they must have taken their own lives. Why? Sick to their empty stomachs of their life here, rations, living in what was once a cow shed, a mad mother to deal with – was Tara always mad or did their death make her so? Hard winters and a general lack of most things, a new baby to care for. It was too much for them, she reasoned as she imagined a death pact made as an act of love to spare their innocent infant but still, that hardly resonated. Things were bad but there was always a way…it must have been suicide, the big secret.

*

'He's a presence all right.' She lifted her head off Ganaim's chest as she fished for something to say rather than focus on her dark thoughts. Still looking at the screen, she pushed her auburn hair out of her eyes; macabre thoughts of her parents trailed away with it. 'I can't believe what I just saw, Gan. What was he on about? Sounds outside the box – is he like that?' Agitation crept into her voice and made it tremble as she stood and paced in front of the shuttered window. 'We maybe shouldn't have watched him, the procs could be watching who watched him…can they do that?' She pointed to the monitor screen. 'They could be on their way now to question us.' Celeste panicked; while she continued to worry that if they could, they may check on her Nana. She side-eyed Ganaim. Does he know the full extent of Tara's madness?

'Who are the "things" he was talking about?' She sat heavily on the edge of the bed, her eyes adjusted to the dark. Her mind still raced as she tried to piece together what Micah Apollon was trying to say. 'What have I just seen? The shapes and lights sprang out of his wrist and then out of the monitor towards us, Gan.'

Ganaim brought her back from her thoughts when he said, 'He's a prophet, Cel, a voice for the youth, for us.' He half-wished he had not invited her over; she was not supposed to see any of that. Why couldn't the madman just sing his song and be done with it? May be incite a little rebellion but light of the flame he'd set the world on fire.

Given time, I can show her our way of life too, our proper ways. I am sick of hiding things from her and now this too. He would have to be careful. How he acted and what he told Celeste. It was not his place to tell her too much and the truth be known, he did not have anything of substance to say anyway. Nothing, that he could just say, then leave alone without creating more questions. Padrain was up to his neck in the black market, the appearance of Fairmist Al Mara, the minstrel-spy, was testament to that, but it was something more than that which he was afraid of. He saw it in his real mother Cissy's eyes and Dorothea's too. They were sad to their marrow about something they did not talk about, and he was sick of their deceit, let alone his own. The secrecy and lies that surrounded her had somehow leeched into his own life. Sometimes he hated his grand-folks Dorothea and Padrain, who he thought of as his parents and his mother Cissy, like an older sister, who told him nothing about the big picture, despite his constant asking and prying. Recently, he had been told to keep a closer eye on her. Padrain had not said why, or what he was supposed to be looking for and he had found himself doing it without question. It was only now, after Apollon's outburst that he had actually paused and recognised the faraway voice of doubt, stronger because Micah had been strong enough to stand up, to rise. But was it always like that, was he so easily led?

Once over, Padrain and even Dorothea had encouraged him to be her friend, her closest and only friend, then – and he could not remember the exact details, but it had changed – he was encouraged to think of himself as her protector. Was it when they started school? Was that when he had started to filter potential relationships. Until only he remained. Then what? A reporter of what she did or said, what happened at the shed, her relationship with Tara – he had become a spy. All dressed up, casual as you like, and done over time. They groomed me and trained me like an animal he realised while sour bile made his stomach clench; the truth coupled with fresh spattered blood was a bitter pill to swallow. He pulled his pale cream homespun shirt on roughly while he skewed back and forth between disgust at himself, the role Padrain had thrust upon him, and the need to protect Celeste. Finally, he knew, though it did not make him feel any better, that he had to carry out Padrain's requests, if he did not; then he risked Celeste's life, her Nana's, his and his family and probably the whole of the community where they lived. There was something about Celeste Melsie, something that they had all agreed to hide, whether he had vocalised it or not, he was up to his gullet in the mire along with everyone else.

'Come on,' she pulled away, 'you have to see to the horses. I bet Black's been rolling again.'

'Aye, I'll just get my boots. I swear he does it on purpose. He'll have to wait till the morrow for a comb, whether he's pitted or not, I've other stuff to do. Pass me that bow, Cel?' He pointed to a compound bow, it was what he used for close quarters killing, and a quiver of cruel looking silver arrows tipped with black tourmaline that hung on the wall next to recurve and longbows, assortments of arrows and different sized bodhran drums. They did not have any other type of weapon on the farm, apart from Padrain's gun but even that could be passed off as a tool for hunting. 'The traps are downstairs by the back door. Take two. If the drakes kill anything from the woodshed, but don't eat it, can you put them in the traps? Dorothea needs to see what kind of rat they are,' he replied while he bent down to retrieve his boots from under the bed.

It was hardly surprising they could hear in the kitchen below; the rush matting was worn almost bare and there was a chink of light between the floorboards.

'I didn't think there were different kinds,' she said and frowned, but did not follow her own reason, did not ask him to explain. 'What about the rat blood?' she asked, suddenly worried he was about to spend his night, cold, cramped, and vomiting.

'They won't have any,' he replied. His voice was cold and flat, hard like the surface of a frozen pond while he took the bow and quiver full of silver arrows from her hand.

~ ❈ ~ ❈ ~ ❈ ~

The air was fresh and sparkled with hints of ice crystal not yet formed, her breath fogged before her, purling away in small misty clouds as she emerged into the night. An unseasonably cold breeze swept lightly down the land from the great glacier Amnasia in the North; Celeste shivered.

'What was that?' She pointed towards the stables at a large shadow that was suddenly illuminated by the moons, only two glittering magenta eyes with a lilac cast to them, were visible in the shadows like two shards of ice.

The animal emerged into the moonlight fully, its own breath vented from its wide jaws as if it had run hard and fast. Silvery purple ears like fragments of moonlight twitched inquisitively, a thin trail of scales about its temples that caught the light of the baleful Lilith twinkled like golden-red stardust. It stopped, placed its head to the side, then with a quizzical expression that seemed too human on the Volpi face it studied Ganaim. Before it turned to leave, it lifted its nose like an acknowledgment while it sniffed the air, appeared to grin, then slunk away on large feet which padded silently across the yard. Then, the Volpi disappeared through the opposite hedge.

'It's a Volpi. I have to go and tell Padrain; he said I must if I ever saw one. It must be shot on sight. I, I, I' he stuttered, 'have to…did you hear it speak? It said pack, or was that you…' He was anxious, almost childlike with panic, but Celeste knew that he would not be the one shooting the Volpi. He disliked killing anything. Although, why he was being sent to hunt rats puzzled her, but she did not have time to dwell on it.

She put her hand on his arm and asked him gently, 'Does he need to know? Who saw it but us, and now it's gone?' She hated the hold his family had over him. He was as much a prisoner to their eccentricities as she was to Tara's.

Ganaim shuddered. 'You're right. Anuk only knows what his problem is with it anyway. It's probably the last of its kind, and Padrain's after its head for the wall, bloody disgusting.' He pulled Celeste to him and hugged her hard until his heart stopped hammering. 'Thanks, Cel, I don't know what came over me, hearing animals talk,' he huffed through his lips before he continued, 'Padrain's got me terrified of a creature that's supposed to not exist anymore, probably because of folk like him, but I've no idea why he's got this thing against them. He once told me they bit off babies' heads, and small boy's faces, and if I ever saw one, I had to tell him straight away. Then Cissy and him had a huge row later that night but Dorothea took me outside to check on the chicks, so who knows what that was about?'

'Don't say anything to him – he doesn't need to know,' she met his gaze fully until he nodded, 'and we got to see a Volpi, together. It was beautiful; it could be a good sign, you know.' She studied him, drinking in his otherworldly beauty, thinking herself lucky that he had chosen her, his eyes were full of an iridescent light, the same light kissed the delicate pointed tip of his ears, and the glittered like freckles just visible beneath the soft flesh. 'You have Volpi ears, and Micah Apollon eyes,' she teased. 'I wonder who your…' she let her words trail away at a hard look from him.

'You have eyes like pits of darkness,' he teased back awkwardly, 'I mean nice darkness, you know, like soft…' he flustered to change the subject. The matter of his sire was his business, his alone.

'Please shut up before I throw up.' She pecked him on the cheek then paused, she felt reluctant to leave him. A strange sense of unease stirred something inside her as if the Volpi had been a portent, not a good sign like she had first thought but a bringer of change. He had been so panicked by the presence of the Volpi she had made light of something that had set in her stomach like a ball of lead.

'See you on the morrow,' she said in a voice full of false candour. She watched while he made his way to the stables, just to be sure the Volpi had gone. Although she knew she could have done little to help if it had attacked them. Turning she walked out of the farmyard and began her run down the lane, softly lit by a cold silver moon and a moon run through with red, the texture of the light and shade reminded her of the times when she had tried to mould the dark in her hands.

    A shudder ran through her, from her toes to the roots of her hair as if she had run through a waterfall of ice, it settled somewhere in her centre but curled like a snake next to her spine where it continued to vibrate softly. She pushed the feeling to one side and leapt forward, pushing against the cold thin air while she ran past the far end of the stables, then the outbuildings where she heard cows lowing, smelled their manure and the pungent sulphur smell of what she assumed was Volpi spoor, it was strong thick smell she could almost taste like a cloud of warm gases trapped beneath the frigid, sterile air. Cissy was right she thought, it does smell of sulphur. The orchards were silent, dark silhouette's against the sky. Large domed beehives, made from rye straw and willow sat beneath the trees, ready to be moved come quota time, else that produce would go to the cities of Baelmonarchia too. There was even a hidden Still. Fields full of growing crops, and others dotted with beasts grazing. Just now they were all Romarii beasts, healthy and fat with the vital essence their earth provided, but they would be returned to the nomadic Romarii come harvest time, and the scrawny animals that were kept in the North would be brought down and collected by the quota men who descended like locusts from the Protectorate Administration centres. It was just as the Romarii said, bad meat makes bad meat.

    The lane disappeared under her swift light feet. The single dirt track eventually meandered away to nothing but an invisible hint of a way, more like an animal track as it approached the cottage that still looked like a stone cattle-shed, especially from a distance, sitting almost hidden by trees and shrubs, the gentle arboreal beginnings of what would become the vast Bloom Forest and mountain range beyond.

Chapter Six

Troy Valoroso-Wyburn

Like everyone else, he had been frozen to the spot while Micah Apollon, the self-anointed Son of Sophia, seemed to possess the power to operate in another timeframe. Then, when everyone else had begun a panicked stampede, Troy remained where he was, poised and still. He processed the carnage on the screen, waited while a sudden rush of adrenaline from the shock of seeing the nano erupt out of Micah's wrist, slapped him hard in the face, about the same time he had seen strange colours and shapes, trails of snowflake light that could not be there, yet still they were. Malevolent particles that signed his death warrant as surely as his stupid friend had, but whether it was the droge waere and liquor, or something else, he was not sure, but he knew he could not mention what he had seen to another person, his shallow life of luxury and privilege depended on it. He stepped into a cupboard and pulled the door gently to, almost closed while his heart hammered in his chest, and he watched an assistant producer run into the greenroom. Sweat ran from his brow then mingled with tears that ran down his face, currently a vivid shade of puce while he talked furiously into his palm com. Then he gathered the crowd together and herded them like animals, away from the monitors and out of the door, to the canteen on the floor above.

Troy waited. How many steps until it is safe for me to move? he thought, and he began counting. His fingers twitched uncontrollably as if all of his fright had found its way to their tips. So, he balled them into tight fists before he rubbed his knuckles with his thumbs. The silence was broken only by his own breathing and the dry sound the pad of his thumb made while it moved rhythmically over flesh stretched taut over knuckle bone. He pushed the door ever so slightly ajar with the toe of his boot and waited while a wave of fear moved through him. He gulped but his tongue cleaved to the roof of his mouth, while he imagined his future unfolding in a blaze of torture and hate. Abrecan will not kill us, that would be too quick. He will use us like whores first to prove to everyone in

Baelmonarchia that he can, that he can use the heir to Galay as he pleases. Anukssake, Micah's that now. He banged one fist into the palm of his other hand. He will take it all until we have no self-respect, dignity, or identity left.

Troy studied the screen through the crack in the door while he chewed his knuckle and watched Micah wipe his bloodied wrist across the lens of the crystal box. 'Rise?' he said in a soft voice that burned at its edges with ire.

'Abrecan will bury us alive,' he groaned as he sprung lightly out of the cupboard. He took the droge waere from his trouser pocket, wiped the bag of marching powder down, so named as it was a stimulant favoured by dog soldiers, himself, and of course, Micah. Then, he held the small bag in the fabric of his jacket while he made his way to the unit on the wall near the cupboard. He elbowed the flap open and chucked it in. Then, he moved to the door and pressed his ear against it; not yet, he thought, but it will not be long now. Micah first, security will dump him like a contagious disease. Followed by the proc. Aerial orb-unit rather than a foot patrol because they will have the numbers, and kit, in case the sheep in the canteen decide to riot.

At least it will not be dog soldiers, Troy fretted. Suddenly, he leaned his head against the wall while another vibration passed through him, travelling from the soles of his feet to the roots of his hair, he felt his body being yanked back and forth by gigantic invisible hands, hands that were trying to wake him up, while his vision spiralled into shades of black and grey. He gulped and pushed bile back into the pit of his stomach, hoped it would drown his fear, and still the terror that oiled around his guts like a snarl of snakes.

At least the guard will be semi-normal. What will they be? Monkeys. Yes, they will be Monkey's on the lookout for illegal droge ware, if found, we can deny it belonged to us. He felt a fleeting pang of guilt. Just say they find it, and we deny the droge is ours, the families that were in here will get questioned. 'Hells, what should I do? Do I even care enough?' he whispered to himself as he studied the waste unit and recalled the tiny girl who was going to play the violin after Micah had been on. Her parents had been herded out of the greenroom, their pride at their daughters' achievement burned off the face of the earth by Micah's rebellion. They were minstrels, judging by their clothes he thought and wondered if they would escape Abrecan's acolytes questioning them. Would the acolytes fear the poet's curse? Would a Baelmonarchia minstrel dare utter words that always came with a price to be paid. They would not he thought and knew that the threat of the poet's curse was the one small thing that let poets, bards, troubadours, and minstrels have the right to roam across Baelmonarchia. They would not lose that right.

He rummaged in the unit, found the bag, then ran lightly to the window; it opened after he gave it a good hard push. Rust flakes spattered on the sill. He put the bag between his thumb and index finger, flicked it like a missile and watched it disappear into the night, he wiped rust deposits out of the open window and closed it carefully. Then he cursed inwardly, I am not fast enough, but he forced himself to be careful. 'Evidence, evidence, leave no trace,' he muttered under his breath, while he checked the area again; no debris remained. His hands shook, his palms were slick with sweat while his skin continued to crawl in wave, after creeping wave, up his spine. In the corners of his vision black wings beat slowly, rhythmically, marking time.

I am paranoid, he thought while he rushed back to the centre of the room; he tripped over a low couch and cursed again. What can they do to us? Surely, we…the elite's, own Lodewick, although this is not the time to test that he thought while he surveyed the area. His heart pounded blood through every vessel as if they were rivers in flood, inside his ears, the sound was an intense pressure from an unbearable drum, in the corner of his eye the shadow was a dragon lifting up and away, it's wings pushing air down. The pressure at his chest was building, hot like a freshly forged sword, it pushed through his jacket which had become unbearably tight then released something inside, a strange sort of melting sensation at the top of his sternum but hotter than the sharp edge from a flare of blue alchemical fire. He fell to his knees and clutched at his heart. 'No,' he stammered, 'no', but he did not know what he was denying and could not control the vibration that rattled his spine and moved his body as if it were a sapling facing off against a mighty wind. Eventually, the feeling subsided, although he still felt shaky, deep inside, while his chest burned white-hot. He had no idea of how much time had passed while something greater than the entire sum of his small existence had held him in its hands and shook him like a small animal in the jaws of a predator.

He got to his feet slowly, not trusting his balance or the absence of the energy that had completely overwhelmed him. He patted down his pockets. 'Nothing incriminating,' he said to himself while he found his mo. 'Breathe, just breathe. You had better keep it together or they will destroy you…was there anything else?' he whispered as he took a final feverish look around. 'No!' He retched, then forced himself to calm down, but his breath came in gasps, short painful stabs that hurt his chest as the hidden fire dissipated, he felt his resolve slip and a sneaking fear cloak him like a shroud of lead. He knew that the procs liked nothing better than panicked prey.

Where the memory came from, he was not sure, as the two separate situations could not have been more different, but still it chose that moment to surface, like the sun had risen on that other day, soft with gentle muted grace. He recalled being on a hunt in the Winter Lands, in the foothills that led to the Cale Mountains. Micah, wrapped in white winter fur, stood by his side, the pale light caught him just so, not a sharp light that angled off his flesh but a light that blessed, a light that brought every particle of crystal to the surface and made his skin glow. Then all at once he knew, Micah was the Sun in Winter, and no other could claim that name or the throne at Galay. He recalled feeling a sense of loss, of all that had been taken from them. Not for himself but for his friend, and Micah's father, Lord Bucky. Bucky was further along the ridge, a dark smudge wearing golden bear and night fox, their sleds were in the valley below.

They had no alchemical or crystal weapons with them, Bucky did not allow it. 'Man, and nature, animal against animal, or you will lose your instinct to survive, and only develop an instinct for war, destruction, and a perversion of the natural order. You want to end up like Volsunga?' he spat the words as he handed out bows, arrows, and spears but held Troy's gaze until he replied. 'I will never be like them. Especially Volsunga, he perverts everything he touches.'

The memory was a soothing balm that calmed his nerves and settled his soul, he exhaled just like Bucky had taught him. He imagined that he felt the snow-wet air tickle his nostrils while he pictured he was about to take a shot with his crossbow. He recalled the stag on the ridge as if it were before him while it twitched its small wings, a remnant of a time long past when its ancestors could fly, its nostrils had quivered, once, before it caught their scent and darted.

Recalling the day helped. Suddenly his own breath had steadied, and he held it a little longer, deep in his lungs, until he felt his heart steady, then he released it slowly.

His breath was calm now, and he brought his attention back to the present. With eyes full of mist and a heart struggling to contain a sudden flush of emotion, he pulled his mo out of his pocket. Poor Bucky, poor Micah, they will pay for this. Lords above will he make them pay, whether by pound of flesh or foul deed, the will pay. He rubbed at his temple, aware of tension in his neck and jaw, a side-effect of his analytical ability, droge waere, and fear. He felt a tremor pass through him again, but it was like an echo, its source far away and the vibration made of naught but a memory.

'Mother?'

We saw, why are you there with him? I forbade it; you were not supposed to be there. Your father…he is on his way now. Do not let your friend leave that room with the guards. Stall until your father gets there, do you understand? I will not have you brought into this debacle. I will not have you harmed.

~ ❋ ~ ❋ ~ ❋ ~

'Watch how you handle him; he needs attention for that. Where's the medi-kit?' Troy shouted at security as they bundled through the swing doors, carrying a limp and bleeding Micah.

Troy grabbed the silk cushions from the couch, small blobs of overstuffed luxury that cost more than some people made in a Moon. He slid it under Micah's neck as he turned him onto his side.

'I feel weird, Troy, really not myself, but I showed them – took it out,' Micah whispered between clenched teeth while he tried to lift his arm. Indentations ran under the pale flesh of his lower arm like dry riverbeds. Twisting like vines, they meandered up his forearm, disappeared under the rolled-up sleeve of his shirt; then they emerged again at the side of his neck, then they disappeared at the back of his neck where his spine met the bottom of his skull. What are they? Troy thought as he watched the dry riverbeds in Micah's flesh slowly fill with bodily fluids and the skin smooth itself out.

'If I just reach one person, if they see it, then I've done eno—' he stopped short when a convulsion passed through his body violently yanking him back and forth. His back arched into an unnatural position while white foam flecked the corners of his mouth.

Troy shouted, 'Stay away, give him air, he's gone into shock.' He cut his words short. His own voice vibrated strangely and the air around them trembled as if it were alive with an unseen current. He put his hand over his mouth and prayed no one had heard. Although there was no need, studio security had sneaked off and while they lingered outside in the corridor, they were not about to come and investigate.

The green room door kicked back violently, and a city unit of Protectorate Guard marched in efficiently. Their hand scanner read the room while it made a series of metallic clicks that began to grow in intensity and frequency. 'He's gone outside the box, vibration building like a wind generator, we need to take him, NOW!' The unit commander ordered his unit with the sort of gleeful fervour of a man on the edge of exhaustion while he waved the scanner in the air. 'Someone, check the area for illegals. You there, Seft, get the sniffer, start with the bin.' He ordered the nearest guard as the others assumed position at the windows and door. Satisfied, Noble stood over the two men, what an absolute coup he thought while he studied the scanner in his hands. Plain as day, whacked, wobbling, out of the box and dancing a jig on a table he thought while he felt a wave of satisfaction warm him to the soft marrow of his bones.

The sniffer was brought from the rear of the party. Troy groaned and his insides lurched with the sense of wrongness that emanated from the humod. Had he been a man once? Was he a machine? His eyes were covered by a dark visor which protruded from a metallic skull cap. A thick mesh mask covered the lower part of his face, from under his eyes to just under his jaw. His breath rasped while they led him mechanically to the bin. A series of reports rolled across the visor, listing the contents of the bin, by item then by chemical structure. A light flashed green. The bin was clear of illegals, but the humod sniffer pulled away to the window, again the report on the goggles said nothing. 'Is it broken?' the commander asked gruffly. 'Replace it, before we go back out tonight, Seft.'

'Nah, this has been a good unit. I think it has been overused, Commander Noble, sir, but I will get another one sent immediately. It might need a rest, that's all.'

Commander Noble pulled a face. 'Rest? Are we a bloody infirmary, Seft? Do it now. Lodewick is alive with Nightcrawlers and the stinking filth that follow them. Then, on top of that, this little prick has incited a riot. Not just here mind, but right across Baelmonarchia. Because the skinny shit knew that all the monitors would be installed an' he had a captive fucking audience.

'Get me some new kit as soon as,' he scowled at the guard. 'Right. Now where was I – that little panty-waisted elf is outside the box.' He pointed a large stubby finger towards Troy and Micah.

'He's a fae. Well, not a fu-' Seft cut his words short, then shut his mouth and dropped his head when Noble gave him a look that could ignite a cold fire from three leagues away.

'Panty-waisted-fae,' he said before he spat on Micah.

'He is not a panty, whatever it was you said…nor is he outside the box.' Troy said while he met Noble's gaze full on and felt a wave of anger tense every muscle tight.

'Give me a look at the scanner. YOU BLOODY LIARS.' The words flew out of his mouth with such force, he toppled off his knees. He righted himself and knelt next to Micah. Then placed his hands firmly on his friend's shoulders, determined to push the vibration back into the earth if he had to. He looked around with wild, dark eyes flashing angrily. Do they know who I am. Better if they don't. If he doesn't die tonight, I might kill him myself, Troy thought while he held Micah and studied the sniffer.

The humod repulsed and saddened him in equal measure, but it did not frighten him like the rest of the guard did. It was not programmed for anything other than sniffing for illegals. He could see how the man had been modified to become a sniffer unit, but the guards? They looked normal, no modifications that he could see which meant it could be something hidden. 'Prove it. Show me your report,' he barked angrily at the commander.

'I'm forgetting myself, of course, sir.' Commander Noble inclined his head. 'Let me give it to you now.' The commander pulled his lips back into a thin smile, a purple-lipped slash against his grey-stubbled chin.

Troy relaxed. They knew not to mess with an Elite. Good, they do know who I am he thought arrogantly, while the unit commander stepped forward with the scanner held out, lifted his foot, and kicked him hard in the face with the sole of his boot. He put up his hand but was too late. A flash of white light followed by a sharp intense pain across his cheeks, then heat that seared deep into his skull while he heard his nose crunch. Before he could say anything else, Commander Noble kicked him again, in the stomach, then for good measure, right in the ribs.

He made a happy contented sigh while Troy crumpled like a discarded cloak across Micah's body. 'See that?' Noble nodded to the nearest guard. 'They fall like us, and bleed like us, it's as red as ours. Now, someone tell me why they think they are elite. Bet their shit stinks the same, or worse, what with all the food they stick in their gobs – fucking in-bred the lot of them,' he chatted away.

'I'll remember that. You, churl,' Troy gurgled at the unit commander.

'No, you won't, puffball,' the commander spat back and made ready to thump him in the head. He snorted when he saw Troy try to get his hands underneath him, then he nodded, once, satisfied, when he saw him slip toward unconsciousness.

You feel it when you go outside the box. It is a feeling, not a madness of the mind but a sensation that rises, followed by invisible hands shaking you awake Troy thought as he spiralled into the dark. Was that it, the first stage on the road to madness was a vibration outside of yourself, you felt it enter your body through the soles of your feet, travel upward, until you were on your way to the glittering prize, torture, correction – death. What in the hells would they modify Micah to? He was not solider or guard material, although Micah was called an iron fist in a velvet glove by some, and he knew that to be the truth. He was strong, quick, and could survive in the wild, and he was beautiful beyond natural; there were few people who looked like him or were made the same way. He had heard of poor people in the North who were supposed to be descended from Fae, but they were said to resemble serpents or toads, not the elaborate designs that traced across his golden skin. He was unique. Troy shuddered and thought bleakly, what would they do to corrupt that at The Wind? He pushed dark thoughts of empty-eyed, toothless brothel boys, to the back of his mind where they collided with rolling clouds of unconsciousness. Lords above protect him from that, what would they do if they discovered he was not one, but two sexes in one body. It did not worry Micah and it certainly did not bother him, but he knew Abrecan would use it to make him appear a freak. By any means possible they would manipulate the situation, they would blame Lord Bucky because he had created Micah without permission from the population bureau, because he had chosen the day of Micah's birth and because he would not reveal who the Sun in Winter's mother was. Abrecan had already captured and interrogated every likely Fae woman it could have been, and still he did not know what gave Micah the right to be the fabled Sun in Winter, what gave him the right to claim the throne at Galay and with it all of the North of Baelmonarchia.

~ ❃ ~ ❃ ~ ❃ ~

'I'll take that.' Reynard Wyburn held out his hand. Commander Noble reluctantly handed the scanner over. Reynard had quietly materialised next to him. Anuk only knows how long he has been there Noble thought, then pursed his lips in irritation.

Reynard wore a suit of deepest russet, the same colour as his hair. A gold and cream brocade waistcoat was intricately embroidered and just visible between the lapels. Below this a plain dark shirt, open at the neck, but delicately embroidery along the collar identified him as belonging to the Elite class. However, he was so much more than that. Reynard Wyburn did not need much of an introduction. If you lived in Lodewick and valued your life, you made it your business to know who was in power. You either needed the knowledge to climb the greasy pole, or you needed it to avoid the elites. Reynard was the man who once upon a time had been promised eternal life, which was progressing quite nicely so far, when he married a demon of a woman, who he loved and did everything and anything to protect, including managing the affairs of the in-laws, in a society they ruled but could not reveal their true natures in. Reynard was human, just.

He was not what you would call tall. He was average really; his distinguishing feature was his practiced disdainful façade. There was nothing in his face, mannerisms, or behaviour that would let you know if this man liked or feared anything or anyone, if he cared at all. It was perfect and flawless ice, completely at odds with his shiny autumnal hair, cropped close as was the fashion in Lodewick. It was neat like his beard which angled sharply across his cheekbones to end in a precise deep red goatee. One thick russet eyebrow twitched slightly, not enough for anyone to notice, but he felt it and made a mental note to eradicate the tick – something like that could cost him his life and the cherished contents of his brain.

'Do you see what this says?' He pointed to the screen.

'Sir! It says elite, sir.' Noble chewed off his words while he studied Micah and Troy with regret. He had been looking forward to interrogating them.

'It does indeed, and we all know the rules concerning the elite. Commander Noble, you are out of your permissions framework. I'll take it from here and I do hope that you haven't broken anything.' He nodded towards Troy. 'His mother will be most displeased. You are dismissed.'

Commander Noble held out his hand and nodded towards his scanner.

'No.' Reynard looked down his nose at the machine and ignored the commander.

Noble turned quickly on his heel, his back was stiff with anger, and his face was suffused with black rage which he struggled to control, but he knew he was in danger, so were his men. They all knew it and with a visible effort he brought his voice under control and barked, 'Let's be having you, we've a report of another illegal gathering to investigate. Nightcrawlers.' He circled his hand in the air, indicating that they needed to move out.

'Sir, area's clean, sir. Replacement sniffer unit is ready. What should we do with this one?' Seft indicated the humod, who now stood motionless, his visor blank, his mask still in place. A faint rasp, rasp, could be heard while it breathed.

'You're sure it's just overuse?' Noble asked as he stepped closer to the unit, his eyes narrowed while he studied it. There was something about the unit that bothered him. You really should not be able to discriminate between them, but it felt familiar – when they should all be the same, but he could not think what it was. He stared at the humod again; was it the way it held its head like it was listening, or the way it walked on its leash? There was always tension. Was that supposed to be there? If he had the time, he would check it out, but he never had the time to do anything other than hunt for rebels and reprobates. He scratched thoughtfully along the stubble on his jutting jaw. 'How many times has this unit been with us, Seft…have we wor…can they wear out?' he asked while he scratched his head as they made their way to the door.

'Can't be certain, sir, but it's been dependable till now. Probably started out up at The Wind.' Seft studied the sniffer. 'Too small for dog soldier if you ask me, probably not enough signature power,' Seft tapped the nano on his wrist, 'to make one of them new Ash Warriors that's been the talk of the barracks, that's why it'll have ended up in the city. Good for nowt but sniffing bins.' He shrugged.

'Hmmm, I haven't the time to report this. The paperwork,' Noble paused while he thought about it, then said in a hushed voice, 'You can push this one out of the back of the orb. We'll say it was standing too near to the door; an accident, understood?' Noble met Seft's eye full on, the look in his own left no room for any doubt.

'Aye, sir,' Seft replied. He maintained eye contact with his superior while hiding the hesitation in his voice with care. He pulled the sniffer through the door on his lead but Noble lingered defiantly. He made sure he left last, his square jaw set, and chest puffed out, while the garish light glinted off a chin covered in steely grey stubble. It had been a long couple of days and nights, and more to come too, but he was determined to destroy the Nightcrawlers. If he could find them first. They were as elusive as the nomadic Romarii, but he was closing in on the nest of disruptive rats – he could feel it. *What is the point of my permissions if I can't exercise them on people who are outside the box and inciting riots? There will be a rebellion before we know it. I would love to show the elites up, do that one the world of good.* He took one final look at Micah's prostrate skeletal body; the spasm had passed. He was sprawled across the floor, a dishevelled pale golden god, waxen beneath a crumpled Troy who lay on his friend like a shadow. His eyeliner was smudged, his lips a garish red, his shaved head sparkled with fine jewel-like lights, which undulated beneath his skin in patterns like ancient ciphers. A tail of platinum hair snaked from his crown. He turned on his heel but not before he thought, I hate Nightcrawlers, but I know what they are, filth inside and out, but Fae, I detest.

Reynard Wyburn watched Noble retreat, heard the clunk of boots disappearing down the polished corridor. Then the orb, a thick whip sound as it ascended into the night sky. He placed the scanner on the floor, crushed it resolutely with his heel. It had detected outside the box, but it was not Micah, he had already pulled his Nano Device out of his wrist; he was not readable. Reynard allowed his lips to pucker into a thoughtful grimace. Bucky will have already seen to his son's education, no doubt. There is only Troy who we keep in the dark, and quite rightly so, we would not want him running away. He sighed and raised his eyes to the ceiling, then shuddered while he regained control of his emotions. What is Leleth thinking? Protecting it. He studied Troy again. It is no more than a tool, a thing to be used. He pushed him with his foot; there was no response.

He walked to the wall and tossed the pulverised scanner in the bin before pulling a crystal clear mo from his inside jacket pocket, where it had been vibrating politely. Then he walked back to the two unconscious bodies, a small crease of what could be anxiety attempted to crawl across his forehead but was quickly controlled. He turned away from the bodies of Micah and Troy. He pushed down a sudden wave of fury and resisted the urge to give them both a good kicking. What had possessed them? He had made it clear to Leleth that on no account should Troy accompany Micah tonight. *Let Apollon light the blaze that burns him and his father Bucky to the ground*, that is what he had said. Can't the skinny bitch get anything right? He scowled fully now, spat on them both, then with a satisfied sigh composed himself.

Lord Abrecan would make Bucky pay for this little debacle, with what Reynard did not know, but he knew it would not be with Troy. Although...he smiled thinly, while he let the mo vibrate a little longer, Apollon can take care of himself, an iron fist inside a velvet glove if ever there was one, Bucky had seen to that. He studied Troy's hands, has he spent too much time with them? He wondered as he clicked the receive button.

Request for visual contact incoming Reynard, the phone asked politely.

'Reject visual, voice only.' He could not stand the sight of the prick on the other end of the line.

'You're enroute? You saw? Nothing that cannot be handled. Issue a press release forthwith and an accompanying nano download. Content: to inform the public that Micah Apollon has entered a period of restorative reflection, following a stress-related outburst on the state owned and popular entertainment channel, a gift to the people from His Divinity which Apollon abused. Micah faked the removal of his nano device to enliven his flagging career, and to distract from his poor musical ability. Express his immediate and heartfelt apologies, his absolute loyalty to our exalted leader, Lord Lucas Abrecan, his unceasing support of the Nano Programme and our great nations Protectorate Administration Bureaus…etc. I'll leave the rest of the detail to you.' He remained silent as the listener repeated his instruction.

'Yes, correct. A few other matters, a bio on Captain Noble, aerial orb unit commander, city area one. Take out the rubbish and give the area a wipe. Pick them up from here, they will need medical intervention, a patch-up in one of the outer zones, which I will leave to you. I do not need or want to know where. Make it discreet. Finally, inform Leleth that Troy won't be dining with us this evening.' He slipped his phone in his pocket and without looking back, he left.

Chapter Seven

Rodney Weaselton, The Bastard

'Come on, your highnesses. Your carriage awaits.' A man in serviceable clothes, a single-breasted jacket with mandarin collar and tight breeches, toed Micah, and Troy with one carefully polished boot. Weasel was wealthy enough to afford the finest clothes, but he did not buy them, nor did he flaunt his wealth. The occasional untraceable indulgence he permitted himself, safe things that would not draw undue attention. His suit was understated, it blended perfectly with the social strata he should come from, and his current role; that of a gentleman's aide. He had made not just a living, but a career out of deception and discretion. Wealthy? Yes. But the money had ceased to excite him a long time ago. He was in with the Elite's for an entirely different reason. The Shadow sat upon the throne in the North of Gaiadon and called itself King of Baelmonarchia. The only resistance to speak of were the Romarii, diminished secretive horse-people with naught but bows and arrows. They were old-Gaiadon, not like the demon's, they had tech weapons and dark arts that set his teeth on edge and lit a greedy light in the pit of his eye: he knew where the real power was. He had once rubbed shoulders with Yalan Daboath, but he was only One, and the demons were becoming legion. There were a bunch of old witches in the Southern Isles but as far as he was concerned, they were always at war with each other. I am right he thought, and pushed a subtle niggle of doubt away, while he pressed the tip of his boot a little harder into Valoroso's upper arm, the real power is in Lodewick.

'Weasel?' Troy groaned and tried to frown but that felt like his face was about to peel off, so he asked instead, 'Where are we going?'

Even as he regained consciousness his mind was already analysing myriad probabilities. It will be the outers and he will want Micah's nano, damn, he thought while he held his ribs as if that would somehow knit them back together. He used his other arm to heave himself up. He sat heavily on the couch and breathed through his mouth, pain was still exploding across the front of his face and nestling like lava in the centre of his forehead. He touched his nose gingerly, and it squeaked. It might not be broken, just a bit of a crack that is all, he hoped while he continued to watch Weasel but push his awareness inside himself. There were no vibrations. Did I imagine it? Droge, probably.

'Outer zone,' Weasel said, 'There's a community quack there who'll do a patch-up on his wrist and look at your ribs and, er, nose.' He studied Troy's face and nodded. 'I'm no expert, but that looks broken…hurry up, car's outside, it's charging – we'll have enough ruby to get us there and back, that's if the powers on long enough for a full charge. Anywhere there's rioting, is being shut down, and that will be most of Baelmonarchia,' he said conversationally while he prodded Micah with his toe. 'O Son of Sophia…is there anyone there? What a stupid name,' he commented dryly. 'C'mon, Micah, we gotta go. You have been ill-behaved, naughty, spoiled little boys. The plebs are rioting, and Anuk only knows what else, but everything will be just fine for you two, Now that there's is an adult here to escort you out of the shit storm you just crapped all over our fair city. Best be sharp about it,' he clicked his fingers, 'Troy's Daddy said so,' he antagonised them.

'Got any droge waere, Weasel?' Micah opened one eye and groaned. He shut it, then shuddered violently.

'Are you feeling sick?' Troy asked and did not keep the concern out of his voice despite a sneer from Weasel. Ginger prick he thought while he watched Micah prop himself up on his stick-thin arm, muscle, sinew, and vein were visible through too translucent flesh that had turned a sickly yellow.

'Tut, tut, Micah, haven't you had enough already?' Weasel scrutinised him wryly. 'Here. I'll put it on your bill for the moons end.' He reached into an inside pocket and retrieved a small bag of marching powder which he tossed to Troy. 'Help his lordship up,' he flicked a finger at Micah, then turned and said, 'I don't know how you're going to get that up there, Valoroso.' He pointed to Troy's bloodied nose before he turned and began to busy himself. 'Hurry up we need to get out of here, lest your fans be brave enough to venture out of the canteen to seek your signature or your blood.' He grimaced while his shrewd eyes scrutinised the room. 'Here, pass me those.' He pointed to the blood-soaked bandages, cushion, and medi-kit. Then he removed a small and carefully folded pouch from a leather shoulder bag that crossed his body like a sash.

'Where's the nano?' he asked slyly and held out his hand to Micah who frowned but shrugged nonchalantly, reached into his pocket, and held out the small golden pip.

'Here, you're welcome to it,' Micah replied, and his voice was undercut with an indolent tone while he met Weasel's gaze. He lifted his shoulders in a nonchalant shrug.

Troy took Micha's other hand. 'You need to sit down,' he said while he pulled him onto the couch. A peculiar looked passed between them but Micah shook his head imperceptibly. Troy lifted one eyebrow while he took the nano off Micah and placed it in the centre of his palm. He studied it intently, making Weasel wait, before he handed it in the flat of his hand to Weasel. He felt like deliberately dropping it on the floor just as Weasel reached for it, but Micah put his hand on his shoulder and gave it a gentle squeeze. 'Not now,' he whispered, and his words were full of exhaustion.

Weasel frowned, then said, 'I've never seen them removed quite like that, nor I suspect has anyone else. You put on quite a show there, O Son of Sophia.' Weasel bowed while he retrieved the nano, then he slipped it into the small pouch and put it neatly in his outside jacket pocket. 'Right. You two wait at the door, I need to take out the rubbish.' He placed all the debris that they had created in the bin, then taking a bottle of clear liquid and a wad of thick white cotton cloth from his neat leather bag, he soaked the cloth and wiped what blood he could from the surfaces.

'Don't look so worried, I've come prepared. Wound liquor.' He waggled the bottle at them. 'And we've got our professionals coming in after I leave. We don't want to be leaving your precious elite DNA3 just anywhere,' he said with a carefully masked belligerent tone in his voice. 'Although, if you ask me, you two are tainted with a whole lot of bad. Who would pay good Crollar to have that in their petri dish – must be all the in-breeding, that, and the Fae blood – crazy makers?' He smiled slyly at them, but his eyes were two slits of contempt.

Micah ignored him. Rodney Weaselton had a sly tongue and eyes like a hawk, but he knew he would rub Troy up the wrong way, he always did. He studied Troy out of the corner of his eye. *I heard the proc guard say outside the box, but how could they read me? I had taken the damn thing out; they should not have been able to read anything from me.* He worried while he looked casually at Troy and gave him a thin, concerned smile. *Will they take him away? Will Abrecan want to interfere with him before he needs to? But why is he* scanning us too? There was no need for the proc to do that, it was completely outside of their permissions. Has the Star activated? He rubbed a knot of tension that had set like granite in one shoulder and turned to Troy. 'Are you well? It all went a bit off course there.' He put his arm around Troy's shoulders and squeezed.

Weasel snorted. 'Well? He'll never be that.' He was about to say more but Micah gave him a sour look, one that could curdle lead.

Troy resisted the urge to scratch. Weasel made his skin crawl, but he followed Micah's lead. He mistrusted Weasel with a passion. Where in the hells did my father go? Why put this little prick in charge? 'Let's just get to the car, Weasel, get the patch-up while the night is young. Here, do you want me to carry that?' Troy got up from the couch in one easy move and stepped forward quickly, grabbed hard and sharp at the bin bag.

Weasel snatched the bag back, dragging Troy with it. Troy fell heavily against him. 'Get off me,' Weasel shouted and pushed him away.

'Watch it, whore-son, I nearly fell – clumsy churl!' Troy snapped haughtily; his eyes narrowed as he looked disdainfully down his nose. He enjoyed a moment of cruel pleasure when he watched a cloud of rage suffuse Weasel's face in shades of purple and black. It was gone in a moment.

Weasel pulled the bag sharply from Troy's hands and steeled something inside of himself to a tight ball of simmering hatred.

Troy let go of the bag suddenly and watched while Weasel stumbled a step backwards. If he was an inbred elite, then Weasel was an oaf, chattel of the lowest order, no better than the filthy peasants from the rural zones.

'Leave it to me, your father trusts me with this. Not you,' Weasel replied sharply, his face was schooled carefully into a mask of disdain, as complete as Troy's had been, while he aimed his barb exactly where he knew it would hurt most. He was Reynard's favoured assistant. Better yet, he had worked his way into favour with Lord Lucas Abrecan himself, and he was not about to let anyone forget it, especially Troy. He clutched the bin bag greedily to his chest and turned on his heel. He took a deep slow breath and pulled his shoulders away from his ears, they were stiff with rage, he felt it sheet up his neck and pound his temples. Spoiled, indulged whoremongers, he thought, Apollon's bearable, but Valoroso is just a massive cunt. He marched stiffly in the lead while Troy and Micah walked slowly behind, each lost in their own thoughts as they made their way down hushed corridors, and eventually outside into the clammy damp evening.

Three orbs whooshed past overhead, the thick-whip sensation of their passage vibrated in ears and rattled chests, then shortly after laser fire pinged and hissed in the distance. The ground trembled gently; a stickle bomb had been fired somewhere close by. Orbs continued to move overhead, the alchemical light from their rubidium engines, shone like pale-blue stars through a blanket of smog which obscured the night sky.

'Your encore, my Lord of Galay,' Weasel said sarcastically over his shoulder while he lifted his arm, then swept it theatrically in an arc.

Drizzle coated everything with glistening drops, sparkling parts of a poisoned night that was only just beginning. Troy said in a hushed voice, to Micah's back, 'Lodewick burns,' but it was not an endorsement of what he had done, rather he let his accusation hang between them. He did not need to say innocents would die; Micah already knew that.

Micah dropped behind Weasel and paused, then he put his hand on Troy's arm and pulled him closer. 'It's not enough,' he said, and a deep frown furrowed his brow while fire blazed in the pit of his seafoam eyes and the rune light beneath his skin rippled like the edge of a flame running along a fresh log on the fire. 'It will take a lot more than what I possess to flush them all out. They are like a canker, growing insidiously under our noses. Steal our memories, walk as we do, talk as we do but they are not of the Light. The only way to finish them off is to kill their King.'

Troy met his gaze, and his look was as fiery if not hotter when he snapped, 'Stop talking like a bloody madman. You are not making any sense.' He shook his arm off his shoulder and turned to follow Weasel reluctantly. His nose throbbed, waves of pain coursed and throbbed across his face. He regretted speaking harshly, but Micah's words settled like a snarl of unease in his gut. He could not forget seeing what he had or deny feeling the vibrations that had coursed through his body, the fire at his chest or the dragon wings, beating.

~ ❋ ~ ❋ ~ ❋ ~

Weasel waited for them beside the scrid, while the night popped and burned behind him. His face was a mask of contempt and every time something blew after a laser had been fired, he tutted and shock his head, a charade of mock disgust. The scrid sucked in the light around it like a piece of shadow resting in the muted glimmer of a sodden night. Beneath the undercarriage a faint blue glow reflected off the cobbled road. Troy studied his nose in the blacked-out windows and winced. Weasel got inside and turned on the lights, a soft sickly yellow that pooled into the dark, just in front of the single front wheel. He tapped on the dash and the nav-screen shimmered into life, then he entered an address. He was about to pre-programme it when a wave of unease settled in the pit of his stomach, it emanated cold fear like a lump of frozen meat pressed against the base of his spine. He shuddered, then deleted the information, refreshed the screen, then entered the address of a nearby infirmary, it was attached to the Temple of The Saviour's Salve, which was for the sole use of the Elite's. He pressed programme, then turned the transmission from auto-driver to manual. I will not be going within a short step of that place he thought and felt a tremble of fear creep along his neck. He was not an easily frightened man, but it was a revolting charnel house where Volsunga regularly experimented with demon evolution, and modified men, and woman, for the pleasure garden called Bliones Tun. Once, he had taken a satyr there, on Reynard's orders, game for the forests inside the Tun, that is what it was for. The satyr had been a rebel once, but had ended up half man, half animal, and even though they had done away with his tongue they could not take away the accusation, and the knowing look in his eye. A look which told him he would be next. The rebel was weak and had picked the wrong side, he deserved it, he thought and felt a hot rush of hatred tighten his hand into a fist. Then with a satisfied little nod, he left the scrid and went to retrieve the bag of rubbish from the edge of the road.

    He would drive manually tonight. He liked to secretly pretend he owned the scrid, basking in the admiring glances he got as it purred along the Silver Seaf. He could afford one, maybe at a stretch, but scrids like this were not for sale. The scrid was state issue and only a handful of the Elite had them. Once, Abrecan had even had it lowered to the marina so he could drive it through the elite areas on the east side of Lodewick. It was a precarious journey on the way back to the plateau at the top of the city, sometimes through too narrow streets, but Abrecan was making a point. He had alchemical orbs, and antigravity flyers, he had the first scrid ever made, while everyone else had a rickshaw, carriage, or solar.

    He had sweated rivers while he navigated each twist and turn with care. Driving slower than pond ice melting, it had been a difficult drive, even though the streets had been cleared of dross for His Divinity to pass through on his way to the silver-grey dome of Abrecan Castle. They had driven through the avenues, parks, and gated streets of the elite areas, the Bealdras Landar where Micah

Apollon had a residence, then the Estmere Scir where the temple Matriarchs and Patriarchs had their mansions. Following this they made their way along the shores of the Seaf reservoir. The Whitestone bridge called the Silver Seaf spanned the reservoir to his right and led to the Bliones Tun, but they had gone Westward through Boho, then over the Merewif Bridge. Sisters of Bloodgita had lined each side of the massive black bridge, and each had ripped their left sleeve from their ochre robes and had cut seven lines into the soft flesh of their forearms. They let the blood run freely onto the stone at their feet while they ululated like banshees as the scrid sped past. He had kept his eye fixed on the middle distance before him and pulled what he thought was his soul into a tight ball and hide it deep inside.

Abrecan's whore tapped on the black glass that divided the driver from his passengers and he let it down. Abrecan and the loose skirt were both naked, but he did not look, he kept his attention focused firmly ahead, until Abrecan said, 'My sisters are beautiful are they not?'

'My lord, yes,' he had replied while the last thing he had eaten roiled around his stomach.

'Seventh from the end on the left. Stop and help her in, there is room for three in the rear. Are you hungry?' Abrecan asked the whore.

Before he heard her reply, or met her eye, he closed the glass partition and did what he was asked. He would clean up what he could afterwards, then take the scrid to be deep-cleaned elsewhere.

Once they left the Merewif, they headed into the outskirts of the Cheapside and towards the Snide. He did not care who saw him in it here, he did not need to impress anyone from Cheapside, the Seegda Seed, or the Shambles, nor the fat wealthy merchants and dealers that proliferated on the Snide. Though that is exactly where Abrecan had him drive along. Not content with his charade through the elite areas he had made him take the scrid along the Snide, then through the Seegda Seed, fondly called the Seedy Seed. He had driven carefully through the narrow labyrinth of streets, filled with pride while those who had been forced to line the ways with their pentagram banners and snaking red flags in hand, waved with a forced joy that he pretended was for him, while Abrecan and the sister of Bloodgita fucked and fed on the whore in the back, their grotesqueness hidden behind the blackened glass.

He was relieved when they left the twisted route and dropped the sister of Bloodgita off at The Temple of The Needful Scrip, she looked younger and far prettier than she had before, to be honest, but the stench of offal when the scrid door lifted was overbearing. He averted his gaze and held out his hand to assist her. She swiped it away roughly and snarled, 'Do not touch me, unclean thrall.'

The scrid was almost ovoid in shape and had a single wheel at the front and one at the back. There were a further two wheels in the middle, the driver seat rotated like a carousel to face whatever way the scrid faced. Theory had it, that the scrid could be manoeuvred on naught but a Baelmonarchian Regal, but theory was a liar. He had hit a couple of solars, small domed cars with solar wings on top, and a small rubidium alchemical chamber behind. He was lucky he had not caused an explosion but was still trying to stop himself from vomiting, still trying to wash the scene of carnage from his eye when he ran into them. They were like fat red beetles ready to take flight. He wished they had. He had scratched the paintwork and slightly dented the body on the scrid.

Abrecan was almost incandescent with energy, he always was after he had sated his lust on the power of another. He wondered what galactic signature power the whore had been but pushed it to the back of his mind. What did it matter now? What she had been was gone, consumed by a couple of demons who looked like a man and woman.

His punishment turned out to be a like for like skinning of his flesh and a broken wrist. Abrecan had hissed at him, 'Did you think I would not see you bask in your pride. You took your attention from the task I set afore you. You vainglorious fool, be grateful you do not lose an eye. Be grateful I do not wed you to a Sister of Bloodgita, you would make a fine bed-thrall for them.'

It was the Demon Sleek, Velig the Butcher, who conducted the work, with all the precision of a master craftsman. He put the wad of leather in his mouth, and he bit down, he knew he would survive, while he thought of the glory and sense of safety that came with absolute power and rule, and the cunning of Demonkind.

They did not reveal themselves to the general populace of Gaiadon. They would lose the fight if everyone in Lodewick rebelled against them, instead they fed them a stream of lies. Gaiadon was a steppingstone for Abrecan. One where he had little time and limited resources to spend on quelling rebellion when the falsehoods he spun, worked just as well. He kept his train of thought on that while Velig cut, sliced, and peeled his flesh. Besides, it was not as if he was a stranger to torture, what were a few well-placed incisions in a hide that had once been almost whipped from his bones.

*

'Ah, there it is,' Troy whispered to Micah as he bent down and picked up what looked like a bit of rubbish.

'Huh?' Micah replied softly, out of earshot of Weasel, who was opening the scrid storage.

'Our stash, I threw it out of the window. I didn't want any fall-out…you know, for the others.' He shrugged and stepped back while the door lifted while Weasel put the bin liner full of rubbish in the boot of the car.

'You have a good heart, Troy,' Micah said gravely while he moved across to let him in.

'No, just lucky that's all.' Troy replied misunderstanding what Micah was saying while he watched as Weasel closed the storage.

Troy leaned into Micah and whispered while Weasel struggled with the charge cable, it was only meant for rickshaws and solars, but Weasel had managed to take some power from it. He replaced it back into the portal of one of the units and held his wrist under the scanner and waited while the meter deducted the necessary credits due for a rubidium charge. 'Here, look what I found.' Troy winked and covertly showed him the nano he had just pilfered out of Weasel's pocket.

'You always were such a good thief, Valoroso.' Micah grinned.

'I know, Mr Apollon, I know. Did it when I offered to carry the waste bag. I fell against him just enough so that I could slip my sticky fingers into his jacket pocket while he was busy being a gigantic *werhad* stuck right up Reynard's backside.' He gave the nano to Micah. 'Here, do with it what you must.' He smiled, then grimaced. The effort hurt his nose and knotted his brow into a nest of pain.

'When we get to Tota, that's where he'll take us, get him to leave us there, alone,' Micah whispered while he took out his mo. 'I know someone who'll meet us there with dud nano's. We cannot have this,' he waved the nano under Troy's nose before slipping it back in his pocket, 'put back in. You need to have yours replaced too. They aren't as inactive as Abrecan wants us to believe.' He looked set to say something else but turned his gaze away from Troy. He focussed on his mo while his eyes hardened, and a steely resolve set his spine straighter. I cannot risk Abrecan finding out that he has started to activate, he thought while he rubbed at his forehead. The sooner he had a dud fitted, the better chance he had of surviving, and not just a trip to The Wind either, there was far worse fates than that. Especially the one that lay in wait for Troy. Micah's eyes welled with emotion, lords of the light flame save us, he prayed.

'Agreed,' Troy said and found his voice was weary. He pulled himself straight, and pushed his tiredness, his pain away, the chance to bait Weasel always had that effect on him. 'I'll send him on a fool's errand. I will message Mother now and demand something outrageous for dinner; he will have to pick it up and deliver it. No, actually…there is a minstrel in town, quite popular in her circle, and he has the permits to play and travel because he has the Lady Leleth's approval, not to mention the poets curse, he paused and waggled his fingers in the air. They both laughed but it was full of nervous energy. 'I will demand his entertainment after dinner this evening. It will help ease me. She will do it as I am traumatised, of course,' he patted his heart dramatically, 'but I will need to get the timing right. He would quite happily die trying to please her, little titstrel…who is meeting us?' Troy whispered as he pressed his thumb into the groove at the bottom of his mo, waited until he felt it take its charge from his own lifeforce, then he sent a short message to his mother. He watched the symbols scroll onto the glassy screen the fade away, while Weasel brought his wrist from under the scanner.

'Quick, he's here now.'

'It's a Romarii,' Micah whispered as he took a red lip balm out of his breeches pocket and smeared it across his lips.

'You've always got to do this, haven't you?' Troy shook his head, running his hands through his hair. He studied himself in the glassy surface of his mo. Do I always end up worse when I go out with him? Bloodied nose, blackened eyes, he felt his ribs emit blasts of pain every time he breathed and hoped he did not have to sneeze or cough. A Romarii, he thought, perplexed, how does he know a filthy Romarii? Although, he wondered, while he studied Micah out of the corner of his eye, it was rumoured Bucky's amorous adventures did not stop at the Tun, or the salons and boudoirs of the bored elite, but still, a Romarii? He shuddered. They lived like animals, didn't they? In make-shift camps, moving like bands of vagrants from one place to another. A scourge, his father called them, in league with demons and devils – not to be trusted. Their camps, when they were located, were destroyed and they were to be arrested on sight and hung without trial if they were ever found in Lodewick. How in the hells has he got a Romarii to come into the city? He glanced sideways at Micah who stowed his mo in his jacket pocket, rubbed his palm casually across the scrollwork of crystalline runes at his temples and brow before he undid his hair. He combed it through with his fingers, then retied his platinum tail with the strip of leather. 'Pour a brandy.' Micah smiled nodding towards the drink's cabinet on the opposite side of the interior of the scrid.

The driver door opened. 'Right, that's the ruby done. Off we go. They are expecting us, so it should be straight forward. Even for you two.' Weasel got in the scrid, pushed his thumb onto the ignition pad and waited until the alchemical transducer took the charge from his pulse, then the scrid purred into life before slipping away. Troy sipped his brandy; it was a fine vintage. It warmed him and slipped down his throat like spiced honey.

He narrowed his eyes while he stared at the back of Weasel's head. Prick, he thought. He could see a thick dark purple welt just above Weasel's collar. It ran all around his neck. Years old now; it was not the sort of scar that would fade over time. It had done all the fading it was going to do. It still looked fresh as a whip slash across bare flesh, and he wondered why Weasel had been hung. He wondered how he had escaped.

~ ❋ ~ ❋ ~ ❋ ~

When the Romarii had discovered they had been infiltrated by a pretender, hell-bent on spying on them as they in turn returned from a mission to deposit spies at The Wind. They tortured then hung Weasel. Then, as was their way continued with their journey.

He had been hanging in an ocean cave, far to the east of the Palace Galay, across Wolf Bay and north of the mining zones, for almost two days, fighting to survive as he dreaded the tide that came and went, waiting for the high tide that would eventually drown him, while the special leather noose chewed at his neck and shrunk a little tighter each time it dried out between tides.

His hands had been manacled and joined by a chain that ran through an iron ring embedded in the cave roof; the iron ring in turn supported a length of something that looked like whale bone – hard and white. The cruelty of it was that you could use the strength in your arms to hold yourself up, releasing the tension on the noose at your neck, but once it got wet, then dried, it shrank a little more. They must use this execution spot regularly, he had thought at the time, it is perfect.

Weasel let his body rise with the first tide, elongated it, and forced his muscles to relax. Even though he felt stiff and tight with fear, he was determined to survive, and he imagined not just relaxation in his body but a softening that reached to the marrow of his bones while he bobbed about on the leather leash. He worked his boots off, shortly after the had Romarii left him to his fate, knowing that they would hinder him when the waters rose.

Then with a calculated need to survive that bordered on the feral, he used his toes to find purchase on a small ledge that sat towards the top of the cave wall, close to the high tide line and close enough to his hanging spot that he could carefully guide his body towards it, but only when the water was at the right height; too low and he would choke trying to gain the ledge, too high and he would drown.

That is where he crouched, pissed, and shit, for two days while he waited for the tide to rise so he could rest his body in the cool salt water – let it clean some of the filth from him while he made peace with himself, which was a lot easier than he thought. He had no regrets. He had been paid to carry out work no one else would. He had killed rubbish, he reasoned, as he prepared for his imminent death. There would be no one looking for him, no one who would bother to save him because no one would miss him. The only surety he had in what was to become his last moments on Gaiadon, was the genius behind his death. It was imbibed with a level of cruelty he doubted even he could have managed. He was sure of the skill employed behind the design of the execution chamber and sure of his own slow death, but he had seriously underestimated the lengths the Romarii would go to, to torture someone, then not stay to watch. He found it quite unbelievable – he would have seen it through to the fascinating end. Although he would have preferred a quicker end for himself, you accepted in return what you took from life, and he had always been careful to take the most he could, he supposed as he bobbed about in the saline water.

Their message was clear: his life and the information he held was worthless to them. He had possessed nothing to trade with and they had been toying with him when they tortured him. He knew the high spring tide would take him and so did they. He imagined their captain, Rovander, enjoying the light of the full moon that brought the ocean to its highest swell, the tide that killed him. He knew she would have taken pleasure when the knowledge of his coming death rose with the clarity of a winter sun on a frosty morn. She even knew the very day it would occur. Of course, it had taken two agonising days and nights trying to save himself, before it had suddenly dawned on him that they knew the very tide that would kill him. The one where he would relax his weakened hungry body in the water, again; only this time the water would not recede, it would push him against the cavern ceiling until there was no space, no air left. But despite all that he had endured, he survived.

Chapter Eight

Empty Wrists and Bags Of Blood

Carter narrowed his eyes and studied the class, he could not put his finger on it, not exactly, but there was a strange feeling in the air. It set his teeth on edge and turned the soft flesh on his rotund gut, taut, and uncomfortable. Trouble. He could feel trouble coming, long before it had even considered brewing. He would be glad to see the back of the year of the Blue Resonant Storm, look at the trouble Bucky's lad had caused. Although it had not affected them here in the arse end of nowhere, Ninmah had gone supernova. He checked the papers on his desk and smiled inwardly while he thought, now that is a coincidence. The day was Kinetic One Hundred and Fifty-three, and the power from the cosmos was Red Planetary Skywalker. It was Ganaim's mothers' galactic signature, but he and Padrain Al Tine had made sure that was kept off the records. Earths and seeds, which was what rural folk were supposed to be, drew less attention. Skywalkers were never birthed, but he supposed Cissy Al Tine was a rare creature herself. Earths and seeds, bags of blood to water the soil, he thought dryly and recalled he had put Cissy down as a Blue Overtone Hand, it was a healing energy rather than artistic or musical. Although, to be fair she had no real talent for anything a Hand did, she was far too insular, still it saved her from being carted off to The Wind, and whatever fate awaited the poor sucks who ended up there. He itched at his forehead, all she had to do was pretend to be a hedge witch, which she did well enough, her potions and salves were popular at market, whereas she was not.

He felt an unnatural vibration charge the air and send pressure into his ears like a large bird's wings banging against a window. He shook his head, then shuddered while he pushed his unease to one side and gulped. His mouth tasted of copper and salt, and he coughed to clear his throat before he said, 'The nano device assessments are nearly on us and while they are important, there is nothing to fear from it. A reading from your DNA3 will be taken via the nano device. The assessment will consider the potential power of your latent galactic signature. The gift the cosmos bestowed on you on the day you were born.' Carter sounded efficient and bored, like he had practised the speech beforehand. He looked once or twice at the broken surveillance crystal box in the corner of the classroom and his pale steel-grey eyes narrowed. They called them spy-eyes because that was what they were. He snorted and barely hid a contemptuous sneer.

Meanwhile, Celeste took her thumb and rubbed at her wrist while she looked at Carter's empty wrist, then back to her own; they were the only two in the room who had not been implanted. She sneaked a glance at the group of girls surrounding Melaine Merilyn, who for whatever reason, stared at her and Ganaim with a knowing look in her eye and a curl to her top lip. Melaine lifted her chin and tutted, her tiny bud-mouth puckered while she looked down her little snubbed nose and whispered something to Bran Muntor, who nodded his head while Melaine laughed behind her hand, the one on the end of her nano chipped wrist. Bitch, Celeste thought. Then, flaming lady loose-legs. Light, has Gan told Bran Muntor? She returned an equally sour look towards Melaine. 'And?' She mouthed while she raised indignant eyebrows, dark and thick like thunder clouds. She kept her eyes on them until Bran had the grace to lower his head.

'Right, before we hear from Lord Abrecan's, Governor General of Lodewick, Reynard Wyburn,' Carter paused and tapped the film canister next to him while he swept his gaze around the gathered people, 'we need to cover the memo for the forthcoming nano assessment.' He folded his arms across his chest and said sternly, 'And for those of you who ran off to the temple of Anuk at Ninmah because you could not wait for Headteacher Muntor and myself to carry out the assessments here, I will read the list of Soil Singers who have been allocated to Merllyn's Farm for Arable Crops, Blood Fertilization.' He sighed and ignored the sense of wrongness that prickled up his spine. It happened every year when he had read the damn list. He rustled the paper and began to read. 'Soil Singers are, Melaine Merilyn, Sirena Oarfish, Hel Croce, Margeride Shroude, Sarlat Penroe.' Carter paused and raised his eyes above the top of the sheet of paper; he flicked it angrily with his index finger. 'And was anyone else as stupid as the people whose names I have just read out?' The class remained silent, and a couple of the girls chewed their lips while they stared wetly at a small doughnut of metal that circled the puncture hole just below the heel of their left palm.

Carter snorted then continued harshly. 'As we all know, rural stock stays in rural zones, seeds for seeds, earth for earth. Why waste that blood in the city when you can be here helping the crops to grow. Light knows they need it…and I don't see any superstars here today, would you agree? Here, on the day of Red Planetary Skywalker, do you think any babes have been born? No, they have not, because that gate is shut, because we need bags of blood not folk who allegedly trip the light fantastic between worlds.'

The class shuffled nervously, some nodded in agreement, but most held their tongue. Carter pulled a document folder from his top drawer and blew a layer of thick dust from it, then began to read, his lips pursed as his face began to flush. All a load of bull dung he thought, thanks be I did not bin this pile of lies, state propaganda the lot of it. He looked briefly at his own nano-free wrist. Only a matter of time, although who pays much attention to the old and almost retired, I may get away with it yet. He smiled wryly and coughed.

'He's having to read that this year,' Ganaim whispered to her, 'the replacement head teacher's here and old Muntor wants it all done properly.'

'What about me?' she hissed back pointing to her own empty wrist.

'They'll cart you off if you're lucky,' he joked, while her heart hit the floor and Carter frowned at them as he flicked the paper in his hand and began to read.

'For those without an implant, and in the final year of state education, in any of the support zones which includes, but is not inclusive to, mining, manufacturing weapons and military hardware. Manufacturing paper, technology, plant-based food, livestock, all rural endeavours including animal husbandry and crop production.'

The list seemed endless. Carter continued to drone, his eyes glazed over, and his lip curled with hatred, '…a paper assessment will take place, and an appointment will be made for an implant forthwith at the nearest administration centre.'

'Well, there you go, Cel, think yourself lucky you're not one of Padrain's herd – that would be chipped right under the scrag of your neck and worse, you would be meat that belonged to the elites.'

'Instead, it will be chipped into my wrist,' she huffed crossly at him. For once, could he just be a bit more supportive? She tensed and her hands clenched into fists. She tried to hide her anxiety, but he replied, 'Relax.' then tried to grab her neck, anything to touch her; he was still very much under the spell of their shared intimacy.

'And the Fae?' Melaine asked and made it sound like the worst insult while she narrowed her eyes at Ganaim.

'Do you mean The Fae or just Ganaim?' Carter responded quickly and cut her with a glare that was sharper than the edge of a knife. 'The Fae and Ganaim all have nano devices; they are no different from you or I.' He waited until she lowered her gaze.

Ganaim winked and waved his hand in the air then said, 'As if I give a rats arse about what Melaine thinks.' There was a wave of laughter which Carter subdued with a raised hand and a stern look while Ganaim stretched like a red and gold mountain cat preparing to hunt, sinuous and strong as he reached his muscular arm over and draped it around Celeste's shoulders.

She tried to shrug it off. Her hair concealed his finger as he ran it gently behind her ear. He smiled, and his eyes sparkled in icy shades of lilac blue, flecked with green and gold, glittering hints of mischief, and a promise. Then he felt her tremble. Followed by a change in the air, like an updraft of something thicker, hotter; it reminded him of a heat haze shimmering across a field of ripened oats, it stole the breath from his mouth when it hit him right in the face. His nostrils flared and he inhaled deeply while every hair on his body tingled. It was all he could do to stop himself taking her by the arm and marching her out of the school and into the nearest secluded woodland. He groaned at the thought while Celeste turned to him innocently. 'Are you well?' she inquired, her head tilted to one side, her deep brown eyes were soft with concern, while a cascade of dark auburn hair fell in luxurious waves across her right shoulder, as if it wanted to cup her right breast with thick dark tresses. Just like fingers he thought and coughed. 'Yes,' he managed to squeak as the last shivering tremble passed between them. What is that he wondered briefly but said instead, 'We should bunk off tomorrow, Cel…go to Ninmah, it's lively down there. You'd love it, and you would be safe with me there,' he said with a flourish of bravado. 'It's like a carnival, honest it is. Romarii trading, herbs, elixirs, horses, if anyone can afford them, foretelling, the future and the past.' He paused for dramatic effect, waving his hand in front of his face like a magician.

Celeste harrumphed and raised her eyebrows, then shook her head. She was forbidden to go anywhere with him that was not the school, his farm, or the shed. Why? she thought but pushed the question away when a strange sensation oiled up her spine like a trickle of icy water running.

'Best-ever though.' Another pause as his eyes skirted the class. No one was listening, they were all engrossed or pretending to be engrossed in what Carter was saying. 'They take bets on bare knuckle bouts with the procs and anyone else willing to give it a go. One day I'll be able to do that.'

Celeste felt tempted. She did not doubt that one day he would be able to take a proc guard out or anyone else for that matter. He was far taller than anyone in the class; broader and stronger, easily the most confident and the most attractive there. He reminded her of Micah Apollon, though there was something more elegant and graceful about Bucky's son, he and Ganaim wore their blood on the outside, proud of what they were, where they came from. She smiled triumphantly; she knew that Melaine had settled for Bran Muntor when Ganaim made it quite clear that she was not his type.

The Fae curse had been kind to him. Ganaim Al Tine had been kissed with crystalline points as fine as gold and ruby dust, light that ran just beneath his skin at his brow, his temples, and the top of his cheek bones just beneath his eyes, then along the cuff of his pointed ears, like rivulets of precious metals and gems. They were beautiful and sparkled when they caught the light. Not all who had Fae blood were so lucky. Although, his luck did not end there. She would be quite safe down Ninmah canal district with him, despite it being the roughest part of that town because he had the light's own luck and an uncanny knack of avoiding danger, usually because he had created it and knew when the subsequent fall-out would arrive.

She smiled. I bet he has been loads of times, he got hold of sex-safes, Anuk only knows how long he has been active for. She shuddered; again. Where in the hells is that coming from? It is not cold, why am I trembling? 'Yes, I'm sure I'd be fine down there with you, as long as the proc guard didn't get a nose-bleed and you didn't faint at the sight of spilled blood.' She replied though her voice sounded far away, and the room suddenly felt airless, and cloying.

He pulled his arm from behind her neck. 'Get stuffed, Cel.'

She half-smiled, an unconscious effort to be present, to make it seem like everything was all right, but it felt thin and cruel. Suddenly she was overcome by a sense of unease. He was not what he seemed to be, and as for his arm about her neck, it was too familiar, possessive, he did not own her, she thought acidly as another tremor passed through her body. It felt distant like the first tingle of a fever, but still it was there, lingering like a suspicious cloud on the horizon, a bad mood waiting to hurl a lake of ice-cold water on her sweet summer love. 'An adventurer,' her Nana said when she was being polite about Ganaim Al Tine and when she was not, 'To be avoided like the plague, and if you cannot avoid him, then you manage him like you have caught it anyway.'

Carter continued to drone on, 'Here in rural zones, we know what we are, Seed and Earth, no one pays attention to their galactic signatures here, but the nano assessment changes that. We have been bred to stay in our lanes, if you are assessed as rural farming stock…the majority here are Seed and Earth, then that is where you stay, folks. However, it is not unheard of, and I have had a couple of very bright girls who were assessed for the arts and state literature, but their galactic signatures were Rhythmic Hand, rare in these parts. If there is a shortage in the administration centres then some of you may be suitable for duties there, depending on the tone of your signature and if the land can spare you, or perhaps…' he trailed off. He hated this next bit, but he had to ask it, the new head could ask anyone if it had been said. He pulled himself upright and smacked his lips together. 'Perhaps the guard for some,' he paused while it sunk in, and he saw some of their faces turn ashen. He continued, 'But we don't have any suitable signatures or personalities for that type of work. Now, do we?' he thumbed the paper in his hand while a murmur of unease subsided. Not that I know of and if I did, I would not be sending any of these kids to that, Carter thought wearily, unless Padrain said so.

She knew the colour had leeched from her face, it felt green and when she looked at her hands, they seemed pale and waxy. I need to talk my Nana, again. Does Carter know about my signature? How could he, I have not got a device so there would be no way to find out. She ran her hand through her hair, it felt dirty, and she shuddered while she struggled to grasp her own thoughts. They think I am Seed or Earth because that is what we are here. I should have told Gan that, why did I say Hand, it is artistic, and she is – I suppose.

'No one for the glitterati,' Carter said ironically which raised a laugh from some of the boys. Little more than courtesans and whores, she had heard Ganaim say that once, and sighed deeply while she thought of Micah Apollon. I wonder how they will make an example of him. I doubt his head will grace a spike down the canal district. She recalled the bodies swinging from the scaffold just before his interview, what was he thinking, she wiped absentmindedly at a sudden tear. Light, but he was too beautiful to be tortured, though a head that pretty was bound to draw the crowds she thought gibbously and looked around to see if anyone was watching her. She felt strangely ungrounded and the sensation in her spine felt as though it had stretched something deep inside of her that was connected between the here and now, and a place that was neither in the future or past, but both at the same time. Something that was pulling at her with a constant and measured effort. She studied her hands again; they were shimmering and opaque as sea glass.

'Is my madness leaking out of my skin?' she whispered and caught Ganaim giving her a peculiar look. The others were all watching Carter, thankfully, and she sighed though her breath felt like the last exhale of the dead when it juddered past her too tight throat.

Carter continued. 'Nil for the centres of excellence in entertainment or sport; you don't run donkeys with what the elites call thoroughbreds, more's the pity.' Carter and some of the others laughed. His voice was muffled, like he was speaking through a thick wall. She dropped her head and yawned behind her hand. He sometimes had fits if he caught anyone yawning. She raised her head and took a deep breath.

'Tired?' Sour-faced Melaine mouthed across the class to her, then looked deliberately at her groin, with a judging look in her eye and her mouth screwed up like she had just drunk a beaker of vinegar.

I swear I will get up off here and punch her in the mouth if she so much as looks at me again. Celeste scowled back and the challenge in her eye was a smouldering ember waiting for the fuel to make it burn. Melaine tossed her bouncing golden curls defiantly and turned her head to whisper something to Hel Croce. Hel leant forward; her black hair framed her gaunt face like crow's wings. She shrugged her shoulders then sat back. Miserable as Hel they called her, and she was. Just like a rain cloud at a picnic.

~ ❖ ~ ❖ ~ ❖ ~

Celeste watched while a shaft of sunlight pierced a cloud of chalk dust, it pooled in a lazy oblong on the wooden floor. The windows were open, and a breeze danced daintily through the stuffy room. It made no difference to the still heat that cloyed at her insides as it sought to rest in anything fresher than the torrid air. She blinked, the world felt like it had stopped turning and she could feel time snake about the room, in unpleasant currents that felt like tongues of fire seeking new wood. A tremble passed through her body. Then another followed, but a little stronger. It travelled down her spine into her buttocks then though her thighs and lower legs to where her feet ached with the heat, trapped in her awful school clogs as they rested on the dusty wooden floor. She preferred her ranger boots, but they were for farm work. She hated her ungrateful thought. Light, what am I thinking, I have two pairs of shoes. Some of the people here are in bare feet. I am going to give these away after class, she decided suddenly. Why was it so unfair?

Skin-crawling shudders ebbed across her flesh in waves. 'What the hells?' she hissed as she straightened herself and looked around at the blank faces currently turned towards Carter. Even Melaine Merilyn was staring at the dented old film canister. Celeste harrumphed. Ganaim continued to ignore her, still angry at her for calling him out on his dislike of blood. She frowned and pulled her chair ever so slightly away from his.

Curse the lot of them she thought angrily but did not know why her mood had changed while she slipped her clogs off. They were oxblood red leather tacked to a light wooden sole. They looked like an instrument of torture, and she hated them, if only they would walk off and lose themselves. 'I am giving you away, today,' she whispered to them, and her nose crinkled in disdain.

The Governor General of Lodewick looks like a fox she thought as the film juddered to its end. Melaine and her little coven watched intently, their arms folded beneath large breasts, and loosened at the neck tunics, showing far too much flesh in Celeste's opinion while they fluttered eyelashes from lowered gazes and made eye contact with those boys in the class who did not need to say anything; a slight smile and a nod said they definitely would. And it is not even the Fecund Harvest feast day yet, Celeste thought dryly.

'Are you ready, Cel?' Ganaim whispered as he turned to her.

'For what?' she gave a start and hugged herself tightly as another vibration hit her suddenly. A wave crashing into a cliff face that was not stopped by the wall of stone, instead it continued through, rippling away to eternity and she felt the pull, and the push of fate and destiny followed by a stretching of the fabric of her being. She had not been listening, she had been too busy watching the others as they paired up. He frowned at her while she held herself and rocked back and forth as if she had a stomach cramp, when all she wanted to do was feel her body, stay in touch with the solidness of flesh and bone. She shook her head at Ganaim, which he took as a sign to continue.

Light, why is she so bloody odd at times? he thought while a moment of silence took on form and shuffled across the classroom, dry and bored, desperate to go home.

'Any questions?' Carter asked; secretly he hoped Al Tine did not have any.

'Over here.' Ganaim waved his hand stiffly in the air. Carter moaned quietly under his breath. 'Is it not true, that if we all have a nano, then I should be able to trace the Romarii who left me Ma pregnant and get myself some Roma-tatt by way of compensation, considering I'm half-starved to death here.'

Carter cut him off, 'Not today. Sit down and shut up, Ganaim. Has anyone got a sensible question about the nano device?'

Celeste felt a quick and indignant heat rise. The final tremor had hit the floor. Seemingly repulsed by her blood red clogs, it had gathered what it could of the previous waves that had passed through her, then returned through her body like a stampede of bulls running from the slaughterhouse. Somewhere in the pit of her stomach it exploded.

It detonated something inside that had been hidden for far too long, it went BANG. 'Why should we shut up? Why have I got two pairs of shoes? Why am I here?' she screeched and watched Melaine and her little band of witches guffaw. A faraway version of herself, the sensible part of her who agreed with her sentiment but remained silent, watched from behind her skittering eyes and knew there was no way to stop the unleashed beast, she may as well try to damn the River Wraith with a yard of silk as stop a lifetime of frustration and anger. She thought she had it all under control while secretly it boiled inside, while it waited, more patiently than she, for a chance to vent.

'I hate them, do you hear me, I hate my clogs.' Then she pointed at Melaine and screamed, 'If you don't stop laughing at me, I am going to come over there and throttle the bloody life out of you. You big-titted siursach.'

Before she knew what was happening, she was on her feet, and trying to leap toward Melaine, but it did not matter the vibration had rooted her to the spot while the blast of her rage spread like a corona around the room. She stood alone in the crater of her desolate insanity, hardly able to focus on the scene before her, even her ox-blood clogs had been flung to where Raife Oarfish cradled his sister in his arms, beneath a heap of debris.

Chapter Nine

Bang-Bang You Are All Dead

Her hands clenched the sides of the sticky desk, fingers bent like arthritic twigs while her nails clawed at lumps of resin-hard chewing toffee, now devoid of any flavour, and stuck like sea mussels beneath the ledge. Salt water assaulted the backs of her eyes, and a sudden swell of hot tears that she struggled to control, rendered her momentarily blind. Chairs scraped while people righted them, and themselves. No one spoke; but they all knew that the snarling pit of madness she had created in their midst, was all hers.

'I want to know WHY…I want…why…WHY…?!' the vibration tore the words from her mouth while she continued to spasm. 'Why no one seems to care where our parents are Mr Carter?' she screeched and spat the words angrily. The vibrations she felt increased her fury and tried to knock her sideways while her face contorted, and she clung on to the sticky school desk like her life depended on it. No, no, no she howled inside as she clung desperately onto the desk. I am going outside the box and there is not one person here who can hide or deny it.

No one moved to stop her once they had righted themselves. Witnesses to her unravelling as their fragile safety, so cunningly constructed by those elders in the community who knew about such things, was torn apart by the appearance of a screeching mad woman who used to be Celeste Melsie.

Carter looked nervously to the door, then to the inoperable spy-eye on the wall. His eyes turned hard like polished metal, and lingered for a moment, too long on Ganaim's, in what seemed a casual glance that took in the whole class. Wait, they implored, do not move, it will pass. The sun beam had travelled further round the classroom; it pierced the muggy air, illuminating dust motes and particles of chalk. A stray hair that the lazy breeze had lifted to inspect, now hung in the golden light – suspended.

Her classmates looked on stiffly. Melaine and her circle of friends were astonished and afraid. Some of the girls had family who had disappeared. Gone to Work the Wind; Hel Croce had lost her uncle Fionn. They held back tears while they stared at Celeste, their fear, and their hatred was a pool of seething water. Carter kept one eye on Ganaim. He shook his head imperceptibly and waited until Ganaim lifted his chin once by way of acknowledgement.

Carter remembered former pupils, some hazy and distant but not Fionn Senones, the Croce girl's uncle, athletic and nimble, bright, and sharp, quick as a whip, too quick for some and gone for so many years now. Then he recalled others, the ones who would have already reported Celeste's outburst, the ones who would have run from the room before she had even finished her last breath. A clutch of dangerous boys who thought they were going to bully and control everyone around them, that he had had the unpleasant task to teach. He, Padrain Al Tine, and Muntor, arranged for their assessments to recommend the Protectorate Guard, on the mainland. Although to be fair Padrain had wanted to kill them but off they had gone, their cruel superior sneers confirming what Carter had suspected all along, but the oily bastards had done what damage they could before they went. He rubbed at his chin thoughtfully. Fionn had gone to Work the Wind, they had made sure of it. Now what was that bully called, the leader of the pack, Noble the knobhead? He was lucky he had talked Padrain out of killing the lot of them. In those days, it would have been no trouble to arrange an accident while they were being transported to the base at Malice, Carter recalled, while he studied Celeste. She had stopped. He sighed while he raised his eyebrows imperceptibly towards Celeste, then looked pointedly at Ganaim.

'Cel! Light! Where did that come from? Sit down or we are all finished.' Ganaim hissed, reached out and pulled her sharply back to her seat while he pulled his own chair upright and placed it firmly next to hers.

He looked around at the class, gauging their reactions and pulled his jovial mask firmly about his face. He turned, shook his head, and grimaced painfully while he raised his shoulders and indicated that he – her only close friend – was as baffled as everyone else. He looked to the lads nearest to him: Raife Oarfish, Chrissem Shelvocke and Albar Hattley. He had sold them some Erbal this morning but had not taken any coin. They nodded, and took their fingers to their lips, 'Closed,' Raife mouthed. Then turned casually back about his business. Ganaim made sure those further away could see him as he mouthed a silent 'moon time.' Bran Muntor, Caul Clements, and Origen Harea, they shrugged and nodded. Bran Muntor cast his dark eyes, deep-set, and smouldering beneath heavy thick brows towards Ganaim and an unspoken knowing passed between them. He turned and took Melaine's chin in his deeply tanned hand and drawing her face close to his mouth, he tilted her head gently and whispered in her ear. A frown knotted his forehead, and his eyes narrowed when she tried to pull away, but he moved his hand behind her neck and gathered her even closer. When he had finished, she was flushed red as a sunset with something he had said, and stared balefully at Celeste through slitted eyes, but she nodded to Bran and gave him a stiff little smile all the same, then she turned to her group of friends. Their heads came together while she whispered. Margeride Shroude held her chin in her hand, her forget-me-not deep blue eyes studied Celeste, and they were filled with pools of sadness. She nodded to Ganaim and went back to the whispering group. It was acceptable they all had sisters, girlfriends, and mothers; female moon cycles were hardly a mystery to them. It would be good enough. The class exhaled while the circle of distance between themselves and Celeste dissipated and something like normality resumed.

'I don't know, Gan, I don't know,' she whispered wetly, her face flushed, and hands trembling. 'I just don't feel right, things are changing…it's inside of me…I think…and I don't know why.' She could hardly speak. It felt like her insides were going to vibrate out of her mouth. The classroom had become shimmery and rippled back and forth. Ganaim kept a firm hand on her arm. She looked at it briefly; the short nails and stubby calloused fingers suddenly seemed too real, solid, and heavy. She tore her eyes away and the surface of the wall before her became illuminated with white light. Her mouth gawped open, and she pointed weakly while a rainbow of strange geometric shapes, some like snowflakes, others like spheres of light made of intricate patterns, cascaded out of the wall directly into her eyes.

Ganaim kept hold of her arm, squeezing gently at first, but then with increased pressure as he said under his breath, but with the force of a thousand stinging insects, 'Cel, do not do it. Do not dare go outside the box, or we are all finished.' He gripped her harder while the rest of the class seemed to be busy doing anything else rather than witness what was going on. Carter had turned stiffly to a stack of papers on his desk that had been blown over by the vibration. He busied himself gathering them; he knew when a cause was lost, you only had to look at her, ashen green-grey, and slinked with sweat.

Ganaim continued, 'Listen to me…everyone here now, including me, my folks, your Nana, all of us will fucking disappear if you don't stop it, right NOW!' He squeezed her arm, hard. She yelped and her eyes snapped back into focus.

*

Easy does it, Colin. Last thing you need here is the new head reporting this, he's an outsider, a proc man that's for sure. We have managed to keep under the radar for this long. I have kept my end of the deal, to keep a watch on her and the boy. I'll be screwed if I'm going to let it slide now and have those proc snits all over my reports, thought Carter while he shuffled papers. Then he wiped sweat off his brow with a cotton rag, the one he had recently used to clean the board. He peered over the top of the papers once or twice, before placing them neatly to one side.

He looked sadly at the class, owlish and wise from above the rim of his wire framed optics. He sighed a little, hoping to cover his sense of alarm, while he patted the papers and cleared his throat, but only when he sensed Celeste was calming down.

The lad has done well, he thought as he used a stubby nicotine-stained finger to push his optics further up his ale-infused nose. He ran his finger around the neck of his shirt and gulped dryly. She'll be what, thirty-two, maybe thirty-three galactic cycles, maybe her moon cycle, maybe her galactic signature but Anuk only knows…she's intense, is that one, not like the other girls. Padrain was right to ask me to look out for her and for Cissy's boy, but am I glad this will be me last lot. Only the goddess would know what her Nano Device Assessment result would be if she had an implant, Thank the light she did not, she was on a dangerous trajectory there, already a bit of a loner – Marginal if she was lucky, Outside the Box if she was not…we will have to give her something stable and hope she is never selected for inspection. He looked at Melaine and her friends. Too late for that bunch of young fools.

'Celeste, Ganaim, stay back for you both, report to me here at two-hora past noon please. The rest of you stay out of trouble, you cannot tell me you have not all got an afternoon's soil singing to do. Especially you, Melaine, Hel, Sirena, Margeride, and Sarlat. After the foolish stunt you pulled down Ninmah, you are lucky you got out of the temple with your lives, never mind a quart less of your blood.'

The group of girls hung their heads, embarrassed at being chastised but it hardly compared to what their parents had said to them. Whether their intentions were good or not, they had marched innocently into a temple of Anuk, it was the

Temple of The Children of Bloodgita. They may as well have offered themselves as sacrifices. It was fortunate indeed that Bran Muntor had informed his father of what they intended to do. They were in time to get them out of the temple but not before the heel of their palms had been permanently punctured and a ring of steel cast about the hole. Then their nano devices had been updated with their new status of active Earth, and Seed galactic signature power, bags of blood for evil doing, known fondly as Soil Singers.

'All of you remember this: seeds and earths, nowt will grow till you get out in those fields and channel your blood into the piss-poor soil. We are not Mirrors and Suns adorning Lodewick with our beauty. Our life is short and violent, the soil is red with our blood, our iron…now get out of my sight.'

The class filed out, abashed at his sharp words. He glanced questioningly at Melaine and her friends. His eyebrows knotted into a tight frown that wrinkled across his forehead and set his mouth in a hard line while he looked at their tunics. They blushed and tied them up. He did not lose his temper often and never reminded them of their need to channel their own energy and blood into the soil so that crops would grow. They felt foolish and selfish. It was Melaine and her friends' turn for the next couple of nights to enter fields that needed the energy most. Easy to tell – you just needed to know where the crops were failing the worst.

'Light above, it is getting harder every day,' Carter spoke to the empty classroom while he rubbed at his optics with the chalky rag he used for the board and his sweaty brow. Best to keep them two back a bit and from further trouble today, and that boy does not need to be going down Ninmah either. Dorothea and Cissy would have a flying fit if they knew.

He had taught Cissy. She was an exemplary student he had hoped would go to one of the Baelmonarchian state universities. He had certainly made sure her assessment recommended it; in those days, it seemed easier to do so. Leave Mount Wraith and make something more of herself, even get a position in one of the administration cities. Eirini itself or even Ninmah, not the canal district but the administration district where things were more civilised, or even the capitol Lodewick, bright enough without a doubt. Now that would have been something. Although he had to admit it was hard to get any of them a position out of the rural zones. Seed and Earth belonged in the rural zones. Nights in the mining districts. Storms in the tech zones.

What a shame for Cissy, and for him too; poor kid thinks it was one of the Romarii. No, that was not who it was, Cissy was not the type, either for their tastes, or hers. A few people knew she had taken a cleaning job on Limi for the new Acolyte of Anuk, in town to help the aging Patriarch rebuild the ramshackle stone Guratt, in mount Wraith. Light, he could see where Ganaim got his Fae blood from but then again, he was another one who just disappeared. Carter tutted then thought wryly, as if a descendant of the Fae would give himself to Anuk and as for the Guratt, it was still a heap of stone.

He sighed loudly and smacked his lips together, wet, and thick with anticipation, as he opened his desk drawer and pulled out his flask of rini-cheen chicory, a hot drink made from the root of roasted and dried chicory. He had bought it from Dorothea, who added honey and herbs to the roasting process which made it far more palatable than some of the roasts you got in Mount Wraith. Dorothea's roast had proved popular on market days at Mount Wraith with the other goods she and Cissy made and sold. The brew was dark and woody, sweet with blossom honey, infused with aromatic notes of rosemary and cedar, and with a kick like a mule, especially when you added a large slug of Paddy's Cheen, as it was called locally.

Carter poured a generous serving into a ceramic beaker, raised it to the sunbeam that had travelled along its certain path and now rested on the pile of papers on his desk. 'To my forthcoming retirement and the sins of Anuk's sons.' He took a large drink. 'I don't know how – in the seven hells – they've managed to keep it from that lad. He knows everything about everyone, nosey little shite.'

~ ❅ ~ ❅ ~ ❅ ~

Later, they watched while the dusty school bus idled in the yard. Celeste squinted through her right eye; her left was swollen closed where Melaine had punched her in the face, after they had come to blows in the yard, about how useless Celeste was, and why she was not in the fields with the other girls. Did she think she was too good to soil sing? Bran and Ganaim had let the fight rumble on until Celeste nearly knocked Melaine's teeth out. Then they held them apart while Ganaim spoke loudly to the gathered throng, 'She's a Hand galactic signature, not suitable for soil or seed work.'

Sarlat had sneered, 'Just what we bloody well need, another artist.'

The girls had turned and stomped away. Bran shrugged by way of apology then said to Ganaim, 'And what about you, Fae? Does your blood carry a signature power?'

Ganaim replied coolly though his eyes flashed like flame beneath ice and the crystals on his face sparkled like pinpricks of fire. 'We use ours on our own farm, you know how remote we are. Think yourself lucky we don't have to ask you lot to stop by there as well,' he lied, though it was enough for Bran who grunted and sauntered after Melaine and the gaggle of girls who flapped and fussed about her.

She rubbed the knuckles of her right hand which were red and sore, but at least the teeth marks had stopped bleeding. The bus shook as pupils clambered aboard. The body of a single-deck tram sat atop tractor wheels, too large for its narrow shell. It filled slowly with pupils, who squashed together on wooden benches or stood holding rails; some took the small ladder on the side of the bus and sat precariously on the luggage racks on its roof.

Ganaim raised his hand, half wave, half salute aimed at the lads who sat on the top of the bus – lanky Raife Oarfish pointed to his pipe then blew lazy rings of pungent smoke at him. 'He's such a goit, face like an empty milk sack,' Ganaim said to Celeste as she returned to her seat, while he made a rude gesture towards the bus.

'His sister Sirena isn't any prettier. Did you mind what Bran said, you know, about the Fae thing…' Celeste replied sourly as she rubbed her tender fist and peered out of the window.

'Bran is a good friend, but he has to be something else sometimes, it's the only thing that will keep Melaine's girdle loose. If she sees or hears that he is being the thing she wants him to be…anyway, he knows Padrain, and Dorothea take care of our farm. We let them think we have to use soil singing but we don't, we are lucky our land is better than some of the other land around here, like the taint has missed us, though we would never put it to crops, it's too high, so better for pasture.'

'But don't you ever wonder why that is?' she asked.

'No, not at all, it just is,' he lied and sighed with relief when Celeste said, 'O look, there's the Muntor kids. Is that little Lugh gathering dung into sacks to take back with them? You would think they had plenty owning the Nag and all.' She pointed to a group of children of varying age as they gathered manure from the field. She smiled when she saw one of the girls step carefully to avoid getting her almost new, ox-blood red clogs dirty.

'They have, but there's a whole tribe of them. The Muntor clan breed like rabbits. They don't waste anything, that will probably be spread on the kitchen gardens. Then we can all eat donkey shit eventually!'

'Well, we seem to be eating one another's blood so it may not be that bad,' she retorted dryly, and Ganaim was about to laugh, but became serious. 'See those clogs? They'll go north or her old one's will, depending on whose need is greater.'

'I know,' Celeste sighed. 'It's just that I had two pairs, and it didn't feel right.'

'None of it is right or fair, Cel, that's just the way it is – we have to do what we can.'

Celeste's hand curled into tight fists behind his back. 'I'm going to remember this day, Ganaim. I gave away a pair of shoes, that is all. It's nothing compared to what some of the others are expected to do, but it's a start and I'm going to change, if I can.' She pulled away from his chest and looked at the bus chugging pale blue Foss fumes that smelled of cheap paraffin and hot wax into the summer-blue sky.

'I'll call me Da if you want. If I can get on the airwave.' He put his hand into pocket and pulled out a mo, then waved it under her nose while he tried to assess what his next move should be. *How did I miss it building up like that? What if I started it? Should I have had sex with her? Oh no, Dorothea knew what we were up to. I will have to tell Padrain. I might have caused it.*

Celeste interrupted his thoughts and he jumped when she said, 'No, Gan. Do not call them. He will tell your Ma and she'll tell Tara and I don't want her to know how I feel. It's not fair, not fair on her, she would just worry.

'Is that a real portable mouth?' She changed the subject, not wanting to dwell on her earlier outburst, and as for the fight, she blushed every time she thought of it. Thank the light Ganaim had told everyone she was a Hand. She was still terrified she was going mad. She chewed at her knuckle then winced, it was too painful for that.

'A portable mouth? Are you older than Dot and Pad?' he teased. Then said, 'No one calls them that anymore. They just call them a mo. It's a Romarii copy, look,' he turned it over and showed her the back. A single eye was etched on the smooth silicone surface with the name Rawa underneath. 'I think it's a Romarii copy of a Tuaono. The seller told me it has genuine Tuaono Recordkeeper Crystals in it. Got it at Ninmah, canal district, of course,' he laughed nudging her. 'It uses the energy from my thumb to activate the crystals then proc waves to transmit an' receive, so once I've paid for the unit, it's free after that....'

He rubbed her arm, smiling gently and she half smiled back but when she turned to meet his gaze it seemed as if a glacier were about to melt behind his eyes as if he had been given the worst sort of news. News like the imminent death of a loved one. She was about to ask what was wrong but then thought everything is wrong, where would he begin when he said, 'Carter's here, see if you can manage not to claw his eyeballs out. Here, you can have a look at my erm…mouth.' He pushed the mo gently into her hand and laughed along with her though it sounded weak and forced. Then, he glanced through the glass door of the classroom to where Carter stood talking to old Muntor. He looked over Celeste's shoulder, while she was busy studying the mo, nodded imperceptibly before taking the seat next to her. Carter raised his eyebrows slightly in response and said something to old Muntor, who clapped him on the arm, before turning to leave.

Celeste tried to blink but it was too painful, and she winced when she touched her eye. Light, it was sore, not as sore as her knuckles. How could such a smallmouth, it was like a doll's, have teeth like a wolf? She thumbed the mo open. A squat crystal with three raised triangles on its surface lay between two quartz points. One was pointed upright; the other was inverted. They were wrapped in sticky threads that looked like a thick spider's web.

Ganaim leaned over. 'Record keeper,' he pointed to the squat crystal with the raised triangles on its surface, 'transmit and receive,' he tapped the quartz points to either side. 'You put your thumb in that indent and wait for the alchemical transducer to take a charge from you.' Then he added, 'Wrapped in organic silicone connectors. The unit is sea-silicone, like the informatics monitor. Stinks like fish guts if it gets too warm.'

'You are wasted in agriculture,' she teased. He took apart most things to see how they worked, as did his grandfather, Padrain Al Tine. "Life's tinkerers" is what Tara called them. She frowned then said, 'Should you be using this?' while she thought, does he know anyone else who has one, let alone their sequence? 'Can't they listen,' Celeste broke off as Carter entered the room.

'Ah, Gan, Celeste, just you two this afternoon.' Carter nodded quickly to Ganaim. 'Let us see, a quarter should do. I will give you a lift to Al Tine's. I need to see Padrain. Er, I mean Mr Al Tine – so I'm going that way.'

'Oh. Just. Bloody. Great,' Celeste moaned under her breath.

Ganaim sighed and relaxed visibly which Celeste thought must be due to relief at not having to walk home from school. He watched her slyly out of the corner of his eye, while she turned the mo over in her hands. He was happy to let her believe that he was relieved at Carter's offer of a lift, when really, he was relieved that Carter would be the one who would relate Celeste's outburst to Padrain. Decisions would be made, decisions with dire consequences, he thought, as he took the mo back from her and squeezed her hand gently. 'Won't be needing this after all.'

He bent down while he pretended to fasten a strap on his ranger boot, waited until the tightness at his throat passed and he defeated the sudden prickle of tears that nettled his eyes.

Serious decisions. In the end, I lose her. The knowledge hit him in the chest like an iron stake through the heart. She is all I have that I really love, and I will defy Padrain. If I must, I will, but even as he thought it, he knew he could not.

Chapter Ten

Curtain Twitcher

Celeste's retreating anger was replaced with an acutely painful embarrassment, of the type and intensity that only the young can feel. 'Thank Anuk, it's over,' she whispered under her breath as Carter pulled his old car to a halt at the farm gate and she got out quickly. She could hardly meet his eye while they exchanged hurried thanks with their teacher. He was reaching eagerly for his Foss lighter. He wound down the window, puffed quickly while the dry herbs in his pipe caught the light from the blue Foss flame. Finally, after taking a long draw, he asked them through a cloud of thin, brown smoke.

'What you two going to do…you know?'

~ ❋ ~ ❋ ~ ❋ ~

Ganaim recalled when he used to beg Padrain to sponsor him, let him leave the suffocating education system. 'I'm a wild bird,' he said to Padrain, 'I need to fly free, I'll be working here anyway, it's just daft.'

To which Padrain replied with a resounding, 'NO. And do not get poetic with me, lad…a wild bird? Sport for the procs, that's what wild birds are.'

He then reminded Ganaim that sponsorships attracted the attention of administrators who were duty bound to report them. Asking "why" questions brought inspectors out, skelfy bureaucrats who earned points through paperwork. Desperate to find the next cell of resistance, they elaborated the truth to gain favour and reward from their superiors, lower ranked elites who governed each bureau or the powerful few who ruled over each support zone. Lord Bucky himself was Lord Governor of Eirini and although no one wanted to be told what to do by an elite, there was worse than Bucky.

'We don't need that sort of attention, there's a system in place, son, a game to be played, but more importantly, you're forgetting your duties…family first and that includes community. Look, I am not being hard on you, Gan, you just need to do your duty. Which is to keep an eye on Celeste. The Romarii have asked us to do that. Even if we wanted to refuse, we couldn't dishonour our contract with them.' He patted Ganaim on the arm then waited for his response, his own reply already formed and ready. He knew because he had been told plainly, by The Crone Arianrihod, that Celeste did not belong with them, or Tara for that matter. Celeste, when the time came, belonged to the Romarii. The trade had already been agreed regarding her, much the same as the trade involving Ganaim had.

'I'm sick of it, Dad. What if she finds out…she is my…my friend, and I, I love her! Sod the Romarii, I will not go with them. When it is time, I'm not going.' He had gotten himself all hot and bothered; he had even surprised himself when he blurted out that he loved her. He studied Padrain's face, it was harder than granite and craggy with age, the lines around his eyes and across his forehead etched by countless nights of planning and scheming, silver-grey badgered away from each ear like lightning strikes through a tumble of dark curly hair, which moved when he talked like a rough and choppy sea. He must have been handsome once, but that had almost disappeared under the mountain of responsibility he had found himself obliged to shoulder when he met then married Dorothea. Who had told him plainly what the nature of her reality was and whose side he was on?

'You know, son, I'm sure you do love her, but it can't be, and I won't have you hurt. I am not forbidding you to love her, or any of the other lasses down Ninmah you may want to love, but you remember you cannot have her – it can't be…and…you are goin' with the Romarii. Whether you like it or not.' He chopped the air with his hand. 'There's no arguing, Ganaim. Dorothea made the deal; you will do as you are told and there will be no sponsorship. You will wait for the official assessment result, like the law-abiding good citizens we are. Final.'

Ganaim had turned and walked sullenly to the farmhouse; once there he tried to persuade Dorothea that he was a wild bird who should be sponsored by her and Padrain. Her response, while different from her husband's, asked him to, 'Have a mind where my loyalty must be placed, a war is coming whether you believe that or not,' she said, 'and it will be the insignificant things that matter the most. It is always the small unseen things that make all the difference, the decision to be patient, for example, such a small thing…' Dorothea ruffed his hair and gently touched the tip of his ears while she sighed and steered him toward the table. She served him chamomile tea, homemade honey and apple tart drowned in fresh cream; unsavoury news should always be delivered with something sweet she thought, as she took the chair opposite and began to talk with him about what was expected from him when he went with her folk, the Romarii. She watched him eat as if she wanted to remember every detail of this meal. Heavy sadness weighed across that afternoon and seemed to slow time, as the once upon a time first Crone of the Romarii watched her grandson while he slowly accepted his fate. 'Would you like some more?' She could barely meet his gaze, so she looked at the scrubbed surface of the wooden table and made ready to rise from her seat.

'No, I'm sorry, it was good, but I have had a gut full,' he replied as he gulped down unexpected tears.

'I know, dearest boy, we all have, but it will end; I promise you that things will change.'

~ ❋ ~ ❋ ~ ❋ ~

He brought himself back to the moment with a bitter, 'Aye.' Then added, 'Not long now, is it…hardly another cycle at school then it will be life on the farm – I mean, that's if I'm recommended for agriculture. Not like I need a Nano Assessment to tell me that I was born in this dirt, I eat this dirt, and one day it will cover my rotting corpse?' he said tersely while he lifted his wrist and his eyes filled with fire.

Carter did not respond, nor look him in the eye. He knew of Abrecan's intent through the Romarii spy network. He knew more of the young would be falsely recommended for soldiers or guards regardless of whether they had the right signatures. What did that matter when Volsunga could modify them to whatever he needed? Young healthy people were beginning to disappear by whatever means Abrecan invented; if they were not blowing villages on Kai to pieces, then they were emptying them of the young men and women, on the pretence that they were rebels.

Celeste glanced quickly at Ganaim, surprised by his sudden sharpness. It was not like him, he sounded so bitter, but then her own empty wrist drew her attention, she frowned and gulped while her heart skipped an anxious beat.

'And you, Celeste? What do you think you'd be recommended to do?' Carter looked pointedly at her wrist; it helped keep his attention from her bare feet. Where the in the seven hells had her shoes gone – she was a strange kid.

'You'll have to have one fitted at some point. There'll be stringent checks in place in the remote rural zones soon, and you won't get gainful employment if you haven't one,' Carter said.

'Erm,' she held up her palm and said, 'Hand.' It sounded so stupid, but she continued, trying to hide the lie, 'So, I expect, what do Hands do? She thought quickly then stuttered, 'midwifery, healing or writing, literature, depends on the galactic tone I suppose, maybe…ermm, I think, Mr Carter,' she said listing off the jobs she thought Hands did. Staring into the half distance, she wished the ground would swallow her – her bare feet, and her shame whole.

'Aye, the written word, would suit you, lass. The artistic temperament from that Nana of yours, no doubt. Yes, that would be an exceptionally good decision indeed. The paper assessment will focus on your strengths, and I hope when you get your nano fitted, it suggests that too. There are generally opportunities for writers of the known words of the world.' Carter nodded reflectively. Yes, plenty of room for writers of state propaganda, a risky job for little pay…you put something out there that was not palatable, and you disappeared, he thought.

'Col?' Padrain shouted from further down the yard. 'Bring her round the back.' He pointed to the car.

'Aye, Pad, on me way.' He nodded to them both and they waved while Carter pulled his Ensign away. The car chugged off towards Padrain and a bunch of squat outbuildings at the bottom of the large farmyard.

'Ganaim, what's gonna happen to me?' She grabbed his arm. 'I haven't got a nano; will I be in trouble?'

'Of course not. Your Nan will have to go into school, talk with old Muntor and Col…then they will do a paper assessment. You might have to go to one of the medi-centres for an implant but that's all – nothing to worry about,' he lied and found that he almost gagged on the words while he remembered his lines perfectly.

If she were found now, after being hidden for all these years, there would be a huge investigation with the result that many people would disappear, not just

Celeste, who, if she were lucky, would be killed with the rest of them; if her luck failed her…he studied her deep red hair then took his gaze to her dark eyes and looked deep within the pit at their centre. How had she been this lucky, why was she hidden? He shook himself when a sudden chill crept through his flesh and pulled the tiny hairs at the nape of his neck upright. If her luck runs out, she will be taken and experimented on – they would want to know why she had been hidden? He reached forward and took a strand of her hair in his hands; it felt like silk ribbon. She was about to pull away but put her head to one side, a puzzled look upon her face. Suddenly he realised, he did not fully know or understand why she was hidden either. He suspected that Cissy, Padrain, and Dorothea knew more than they let on, but Dorothea had an uncanny knack of knowing where he was; she always discovered him when he was lingering or hiding while he tried to listen to her private conversations.

'Cel, all will be well, we're at the arse end of the universe, half the teachers haven't got one.' He found himself lying again, it was only old Muntor and Carter who did not, another bunch who had retired a few years ago, most of the new ones had them, some were from the capitol Lodewick and were not to be trusted. 'No one will care, honest.' Lie.

'You're right…I'm sorry, it's been a very weird sort of day.' She shook her head as a flush of embarrassment crept up her neck.

'Don't I just know it, but you're fine now, it was actually not that bad. Cel, you know what they're like in school,' he lied easily. 'You had a twist, shouted some stuff an' those stiffs thought you were going outside.'

He took hold of her hand, pulled her closer to him. 'I'm right, aren't I?' He put his hand under her chin, and his violet-blue eyes sparkled with an iridescent light while they locked on hers. He tilted her mouth to his and kissed her.

He stepped even closer, hugged her tight, and was reluctant to let her go. I could stay here and smell her hair forever he thought as he glanced furtively at the farmhouse. A curtain twitched, his eyes became hard, dangerous, but he knew it would only be Cissy watching from her bedroom window. *Nosey hag*. His slight head movement had broken the spell.

Celeste pushed her bag at him. 'Here, take this. I'll get it tomorrow.'

She kissed him lightly on his cheek, ruffled his sticky hair and laughed. 'Yeah, you're right, nothing ever happens here – was about time someone livened the place up.'

'That's the spirit…' He grinned. His eyes flashed like boreal lights on ice as he reached for her hand. 'Cel? Wait a bit, come here.' He pressed her close to his body again, and kissed her full on the lips, parted her mouth gently with his tongue. I will kill anyone who harms her, he thought. He did not care if anyone on the farm saw him, damn them all to one of the hells. He released her reluctantly but kept her close.

Celeste asked, 'Is everything…' she trailed off. He was acting odd.

He looked set to speak, then lowered his head and huffed through his lips. 'I'll be…ermm, I'll be going.' He was suddenly solemn; his bright eyes were full of silver water. Then, thinking better of it, he said harshly, 'I'll be going through all your private stuff, then.'

'You're welcome to. Who has secrets from you anyways?' She squinted at him, with a puzzled look on her face. Since they had made love, they had both been acting strange, and she more than half-wished they had not. She punched him lightly on the arm and waited until he laughed. Then without another word she turned and made her way through the farm gate. She lifted her hand once, a half-wave and set off.

He watched her run away, her lithe body and strong legs eating up the distance. She is fast, he thought as he ran his hand through his hair. His brow creased with worry and his heart lay heavy in his chest that was already brim full of dread.

'Where are you going?' He jumped when Cissy came around the corner of the whitewashed farmhouse wall.

'None of your business. Were you spying on me, again?' he said, and his voice was run through with heat.

'Perhaps. You should not be so easy to sneak up on,' she retorted dryly before continuing. 'Where are the Fear Me's from the stone circle?'

He pointed towards the outbuildings. 'Padrain's got them down there. How many did you and the other cats get?'

She fell in beside him as they walked towards the distant outbuildings. 'Another seven in all.' She brushed her hand through her golden curly hair as she looked up and continued, her own eyes were as startling and glacial as her son's. 'They are being sent to block the ways, although there are so few of us who can use them to travel it seems pointless.' She stopped and put her hand on his arm. 'What is the matter?'

'I don't know how I'm going to tell her, Cissy, but I need to tell her I'll be gone for the summer, right through to harvest, but how can I? She will want to know where to. If I tell her it is with the Romarii, she will ask too many questions. Questions that I am not allowed to answer – I hate this, it is not going to end well. I can feel it,' he blurted as they made their way slowly down the yard to the outbuildings and the inquisition that waited.

'I know, Ganaim. Come we don't have to rush to see Padrain, let Col tell him what went on, and as for Celeste, if you tell her too much and she gets caught, they will be merciless in their torture, but if she does not know anything…' Their voices trailed away while Cissy led Ganaim towards the new building she was constructing, and a group of crofters who were busy finishing the thatching on the long low roof.

'Come on, the cob has dried, and you can help apply the render, which will keep you busy and out of Padrain's way.' She smiled then reached up to squeeze his shoulder, she noted proudly how tall he was and how muscular he had become. It was a fleeting moment that showed how beautiful she could be when she was happy, then, just as quickly her mouth set into a thin miserable line and ice set behind her eyes.

~ ❁ ~ ❁ ~ ❁ ~

Picking up her pace, Celeste smiled. The lane was quiet and familiar, suddenly, she was grateful for that, and the smell of the dry dusty soil as it rose when her bare feet disturbed the earth. The strange cold snap had passed during the night as if it had never happened. The horses smelled earthy and solid, and the meadow grass like the scent of a summer breeze. A small group were finishing the thatch on a large communal building that would house the refugee crofters that would come south during the winter; the sounds of their chatter and the noises they made as they were about their work lifted her heart. Just a normal day she thought and continued on. The dirt track soon disappeared, then the springy grass felt cool under her feet. She ran on and was glad when joy spread through her heart like a small sun rising inside and she pushed the day's events away. It is going to be a good summer and I am going to spend as much time as I can with Ganaim, I will offer to help on the farm too, I will see more of him that way – Dorothea asked me if I wanted to last year. Her heart lifted and her feet skipped in time with the hoofbeats from over the hedge.

'Who that?' Hossy and Nellie ran along the edge of the field next to the lane, their work for the day completed; they were free to graze and roll.

'It Woman-Celeste, Hossy. She makes joy in the lane, she jumps at the sky, even the stars hear her happy heart,' Nellie replied to Hossy.

'Woman? Yes, she woman now, I smell it,' Hossy Black said a little sadly. 'We right, he not to be trusted, only interested in own-self, silly little stallion.'

'Man-child, take that happy heart and make it dark with sad…when he gone with Romarii?' Nellie asked, lipping the air in concern.

'Very soon. They come now.' Hossy Black sniffed the air, reading the information, feeling the scents.

He and Nellie absorbed the picture of a group of riders making their way silently through the Bloom. Their cloaks hung long from their shoulders, then draped over their horses' flanks as they shimmered under the canopy and oiled through sunbeams, hardly disturbing the motes of pollen that were like the tiniest golden orbs in its light. Then horse and rider disappeared in mottles and dapples of light and forested shade. Before them, a dark warrior scouted, lost in shades of ink blue-black, his eyes flashed yellow gold while he made his way beneath the trees. A woman with a large scar across her face that had almost taken her eye and had marred her arrogant beauty with something hard and cruel beneath, stared straight ahead while she led the rest of the Roma Ranger party. Her amber eyes and that of the rest of the group sparkled in the gloom, as if a pack of wolves were on the scent of their prey.

Hossy pricked up his ears. 'Nel, Nel,' he whinnied excitedly. 'Let's be up the field, webby-fingered Selgovae be scratching their fiddles and hoofing at their drums.' He and Nellie turned from the lane and cantered back up the field to put their noses over the hedge where the crofters had stopped for tea and song.

A man as lumpy as an old toad, with a low brow frill, weathered and green like mossy wood, had hold of a harp, and a young woman who was iridescent and silver-green like a sea serpent, circled her hips and spun around. Her skin caught the light, not to mention Ganaim's breath in his chest, her hair a mohawk of the deepest brown, cascaded like sea kelp about her shoulders. She stopped twirling and picked a flute out of a case at her feet, put it to her lips and began to play. The young man next to her, picked up a small set of drums. Ganaim wished he had brought his own bodhrán when the young man's hands teased out a gentle rhythm and his broad easy smile lit up the day. They began to play, a quiet introduction at first. Then a woman with large swinging hips and full skirts, sashayed into the circle. She had patched her skirts with coloured strips of rags, cotton, silk, and wool, which assaulted the eyes and stomach, soft boots reached to just below her knee, and her dark blouse billowed, loose and flowing over her ample chest. She twisted her arms through the air and swayed her hips back and forth, seashells and sea glass woven into a wide belt tinkled while she ululated softly. Taking a scarf of blue from about her shoulders, she moved it through the air and around her body and it shimmered like an azure sea. She moved around the people at the fire and pushed air through her teeth while she made a shushing noise like waves moving across a pebble beach. They started to move their hands, one against the other in a motion that was half clap and half rub which sounded strangely like the wind, and then she began to sing.

Cissy stood near the fire and lifted the kettle off the boil. She nodded her head and smiled as she made herself busy making tea and dividing sweet bread into generous portions. The woman sang the ballad of the two tribes of Fae. 'The tale of the Kissed and the Cursed,' she announced and bowed to the audience with a well-practiced flourish. The gathered crofters greeted her announcement with ululations and stamping of feet, but she continued dancing and singing, which sounded folkish and raw.

Ganaim sat with the others, his bucket of render at his feet, drinking tea and eating bread. The fire crackled and pushed warm air his way. The sun hung low in the sky, ready to give birth to the night, and duster drake's spun overhead on sparkling wings that caught the last light on their way to their roosts. Two of the cats lay on the newly thatched roof, they looked down at the gathered throng, and eyed two Crofter Curs, one cream and brown, the other silver-grey and black, disdainfully. The curs lay near the children watching the cats curiously, but they did not growl or bark, there was no danger here. Smoke tickled his nostrils and made his eyes smart, but he could not think of any other place he would rather be.

The gnarly woman, had a wide fat nose, and skin thick as hide at the knuckles of her hands. Nails like black claws drew pictures in the air, as she sung of the two tribes of Fae. Selgovae, Master of Water and Earth – she opened her fingers wide to reveal webbed skin between them while she sang. 'Who here can burrow beneath the sea caves in the north, who here can swim in the frozen sea to find

Ningen spawn, lost, lost, lost – since the breaking of the dawn?' she chanted and clapped her hands rhythmically.

The crofters returned the chant. 'We master the Earth, and we master the Sea, it is me, it is me.'

Following several verses about the deeds of the Selgovae and their heroes of old, all taken away by a white wizard, leaving only those who were out at sea, she moved into the next round. The Novantae, Master of Air and Fire, who were the stewards of the mighty Ningen, who according to the Lady Minstrel, were Lords of the Five Realms. 'Who eats the crystal catkin, who can feed it to a Ningen and watch while it dies in ice and flame? Who will set it free, its soul to soar to the skies, who can fly, fly, fly?' She twirled around the circle while the crofters clapped and tapped their feet to the tune. The woman continued to spin.

Ganaim noted how precise her steps were and how light she was on her feet, the ululating sound she made keened like an animal in flight far above. The men think her beautiful, he thought, as she began to point at different crofters. She came before Ganaim, halted abruptly, and stamped her foot, the music stopped, and she pointed. He flustered with his bucket of render and then picked up his mug and gulped his tea. The woman frowned as did many of the other crofters while they waited for Ganaim to finish the verse.

Cissy stiffened while she sat at the fire and shook her head imperceptibly at the singer.

A child sitting with his mother sang in a reedy voice, 'It is not me, for I am not Novantae, they are gone into the wilds, with their curse on their backs to seek Igi Ekun the weeping tree, it is not me, it is not me.'

There was a palpable easing of tension, and the music began again, then the woman spun on. She named herself Key to the Legend of the One to Come, chosen by the split-in-two King of the Five Realms, Taluthaar. She sang sadly then, and the music was slow and whining, the *One to Come* was not of her tribe the Selgovae, the beautiful Fae, but was of the tribe Novantae, the plain and ugly Fae who did not have the embellishments that were so desired and thought so beautiful by Selgovae. She fussed about with her green and brown scaled hands, clasping them romantically to her heart, then she stroked two large, heavily scaled barbs at the top of her ears, which she waggled at the children who feigned terror. The crofters fell about laughing, even Cissy raised her eyes and shook her head, but she laughed.

Ganaim ran his hand gently along his temples. He had a puzzled look in his eye when the silver-green girl with the flute smiled at him with her head to one side and mouthed, 'Novantae?'

'You do not know the old songs?'

Ganaim gave a start. The youth who had played the drums stood before him, a bucket of render on his arm. 'Come, I will render where you are.' He nodded to the long wall of the building and smiled by way of invitation; Ganaim rose and followed him.

'I'm Ganaim Al Tine, what name do you have?'

'Gaoth ar Muir,' he bowed his head and touched his heart, 'Wind upon the Wave, but just Gaoth will suit me plenty.' They put their buckets down and began applying render. 'I like your running friend; she is very pretty,' he said quietly and raised his eyebrows.

Ganaim laughed. 'Yes. She is that, and the flute player?'

'Is my sister.' Gaoth replied and sensed relief from Ganaim. He was about to say more but the willowy girl approached and interrupted him. 'His sister can speak for herself and is named, Solas Airgid ar Muir, Silver Light on the Sea, but please call me Airgid.' She curtsied and her brother snorted. Then she said, 'I think your running friend rather plain.' They all laughed loudly which earned them a hard frown from Cissy. 'You are not Romarii, yet still they come for you, Ganaim Novantae.' She sounded perplexed and stood with one hand on her hip, while the other cupped her chin.

'How do you know that?' Ganaim hissed.

'I am the troupe's seer. I scry or am given sight by Gaia. We seek the Ningen we are to guide to the Southern Isles in the hope that the Novantae break their curse and await us there with the elixir from the crystal catkin. Raweni came to me in a dream and told me it was time, so we have come,' she replied matter-of-factly.

Ganaim half-decided Airgid was mad. He looked to Gaoth for help, but he had turned his back and was rendering. He frowned then said to Airgid. 'I don't know what you mean.' Just then the older woman shouted, 'Airgid, will you leave them to be about their work.'

Airgid tutted then asked her brother Gaoth, 'Can you tell him what he needs to hear before the sun kisses the horizon and the night is born?' Gaoth nodded and replied, 'And if his ears are not ready?'

'They are pointed and Fae, they will be ready to hear the truth of his blood.' Then Airgid touched Ganaim's arm lightly. 'I will see you again, Solas Nua Novantae, but' she studied the air around him, 'But not until Cernunnos blesses you.' She pursed her lips, turned on her heels and walked away. She wore sea breeches tucked in soft suede boots to her knees and her shirt sleeves billowed out of a leather waistcoat as favoured by sea faring folk.

Ganaim studied Gaoth, a question formed in his head, but he could not find the words. They returned to their work but a brief time later when Gaoth was not forthcoming, he asked, 'Well?'

'Solas Nua Novantae. New light of the Novantae.' Gaoth shrugged and added, 'She has named you according to an ancient prophecy. We are recently put ashore from a stint at sea with the Galanglas pirate, Silas Al Seamist.' Ganaim drew in a sharp breath through his teeth, but Gaoth continued, 'I will speak freely, Solas Nua, as my sister has charged me to pass on this message. We and a few others in the Southern Isles, are all that remain of the Selgovae. We are not much more than a travelling troupe of minstrels and jugglers, but our wise one, Ceann Cialmhar, Caorran is a Key, a holder of sacred knowledge, and my sister has some seer talent. It is our duty and our heritage to find the Ningen and bring them to the Southern Isles. We travel the seas with the Galanglas but unfortunately the seas have become full of Demon to the South after the fall of the Crystal Court. To the North the seas are thick with Gaia's ice.' He shuddered and stopped rendering. 'You have heard of it. It is not exactly like ice should be, it is thick, cold, and slow moving not hard and crystalline. We cannot find traces of the Ningen beneath it to lead them south. Though Raweni shared with my sister a vision he had in Silver Tower and because of that we head to Geata de Loka, but first we seek Riamh's Finger, a magical spear,' he added when he saw that Ganaim was confused. 'We are Selgovae, Masters of Sea and Earth. But you are Novantae. Master of Fire and Air. Do you know who your sire is?'

Ganaim scratched his head. 'No,' he lied. 'And I think you minstrels love telling a tale to any who have the time to listen.'

Gaoth laughed. 'Aye, we do that, but you will see. I have passed the message on, keep it well. We will meet again.'

'Well, yes,' Ganaim replied dryly, 'It will be at supper this evening, no doubt.'

Gaoth shook his head. His eyes sparkled intently in shades of ocean green and old gold. 'You jest, it is good. We are only come down from the forest to help finish this. We are all too heavily kissed by Selgovae blood to remain here. We would not bring trouble to Dorothea and Padrain for a lack of care on our part. The spying eyes are too many, so plentiful in Eirini they would outnumber the barnacles on the bottom of a ship.'

Ganaim nodded. He understood what Gaoth meant. He was dressed like Airgid, attire favoured by sailors, and from a distance, he would easily be taken for a seafarer. But his skin glittered with pale-green iridescent light. Tiny scales that sparkled like jewels beneath his skin could not be explained away. The barbs he had at the bottom of his ears spiralled like a shell, and his nails were black. They were different enough to have folk talking, and if they were on a mission to find mythical beasts, then he imagined they would not want that.

Most of the crofters sported a mohawk of sorts like his own. A full length of hair that covered top of their skull to the nape of their neck. Strands of hair grew from patches on their skulls above their pointed ears. The Selgovae had plaited them into intricate whorls and spirals that reminded him of a seashell, the hair was then attached to the large mohawk with combs made from whalebone and tortoise shell. 'I see what you mean, you, Ningen, and the Galanglas giants are not supposed to exist.' He nodded towards the rest of the Selgovae as they packed away their things ready to leave for the evening. Cissy was handing out bundles of supplies.

'And yet, here we are,' Gaoth said while he clapped him on his shoulder, 'and before me a Novantae our seer has named, Solas Nua.' Gaoth touched his heart then waited for Ganaim to return the gesture of farewell. When he did not, he took his hand in his own and shook it. He let go and flexed his fingers. 'For the sea and the earth,' he said while he held up his hand towards the setting sun. The light made the webbing seem thin as silk. He took his hand and put it on Ganaim's arm. 'Your blood carries too much of the old magic, you must change. If you do not, you will die of it. We…' he pointed to the departing troupe and patted his own chest, 'have already quickened, our adults see to that. We are masters of our aquatic form, and that is how we seek our Ningen. You lack the correct guidance, I do not see other Novantae here, only thin blooded Selgovae,' he nodded to some of the other crofters, 'Romarii, and humans.'

He paused and watched while Ganaim frowned intently. 'You do what?'

'We change our form, we become Mara-folk.'

Ganaim stepped back but hid his shock while he thought, He is a flaming lunatic. Anuk, he looked so normal too. 'You are saying I will change into a merman?' Ganaim retorted incredulously.

'No. I am telling you that I change into a maraman. If you have enough Novantae blood in your veins, you change into something else, but it is not for me to tell you what. That you have missed their curse so far is unusual but not unknown. The Romarii will help, but do not leave it too late.'

Ganaim folded his arms about his chest. 'The Romarii do nothing without trade and I have nothing to trade with.' He screwed up his face.

Gaoth turned. 'I must be on my way, we depart for Wolfsea Crossing, where we hope the inns are well kept, the inn keepers are fat, and the customers are drunk enough to believe we are in costume and in need of a song and dance, and that the sea is not full of Gaia's ice. Until we meet once more.' He bobbed his head once, almost a bow, then turned and walked away, leaving Ganaim staring slack-jawed at his back, dumbfounded, until a crofter and his cur came and stood next to him. The tamed wolf sat next to him and leaned heavily against his leg.

'Come on, lad, or we'll never get it finished.' The crofter touched him lightly on the arm. Ganaim nodded. The crofter's skin was unusually coloured, almost green, but it was unscaled and though his ears were as pointed as his own they did not have barbed flesh at their ends.

He saw Ganaim studying him and said, 'They're pure Selgovae, son, returned from far away to take the Ningen to their awakening.'

Ganaim shuddered. 'I thought that was just a story, a myth from Thomhas' Phantasmagoria.'

The man laughed. 'The truth of every age gets lost in myth until the wheel turns, then up it comes again. The truth of the new age.'

Chapter Eleven

Decisions

Padrain stood at the shed door and whistled softly. Carter had pulled his Ensign to a stop over a pit in the floor. The engine rumbled loudly, the chug-a-whug-whug-grhuuug echoed around the empty space like an old man clearing his throat in an empty tap room. As the door hushed closed, it cut off the song and merriment of the crofters about the fire. Padrain frowned. Fairmist Al Mara was right, they are the worst marked Fae I have seen in an age – I hope they are not staying and putting fancies in that boy's head, he grimaced and then turned to Carter.

'I got your message, Col.' Muntor contacted Dot. 'Is she likely to blow at any minute? You know, go outside?' Padrain asked intently.

'Not sure, it's not in my experience. But I don't think so, Gan was closest to her, but if you ask me, she is just hormonal. It happened to me sister when she was around that age, but then it settled down, there was no madness. So, what do you say, Padrain?'

'Aye, decisions, decisions. First Ganaim. Fiddle the paperwork to recommend agricultural labour, not soil singing. Say there is no evidence of any galactic signature power.'

Carter replied, 'Lad has too much Fac in him then.' Padrain snorted in irritation. Carter rubbed at tension knotted in the back of his neck like a frozen mole hill while he quickly changed the subject. 'I thought a Hand recommendation for the Melsie girl. She reckoned that was what she is,' he said and moved his head around until his neck cracked.

'You're right, Col. Why not some sort of arts for her? The written word, she is a Hand, so it would be the right choice.' Padrain laid out his tools on a wooden bench that ran along the wall and started polishing them with an oily rag, polishing the same spanner twice while he thought, it will give us the option of relocating her, hiding her if we need to. Poor Colin, I'm glad he's retiring. It's getting too risky – one thing to make sure our own don't end up working the wind, but this carryon with the Melsie girl, it's getting too dangerous.

'How much this time, Col?' He put the spanner down.

'Ahhh, just the usual. Look, Pad, there is always plenty of spaces at the proc universities for people who are good with the written word, an' the girl is good, but…' Carter trailed off raising his eyebrows in a knowing way.

'Aye, I know, it'll be a death sentence for her if she puts a foot wrong. A misplaced word or the wrong inflection is all it takes, but she will be away from here…I've a community to think of, Col, not just one person, but generations, whole families, and things are changing. You understand?'

'All too well. It's me last lot, Padrain. I'll be gone soon; they are bringing in new blood and I'll be glad to go.' Carter nodded reflectively before continuing, 'Aye. Things are getting tighter, they're introducing new tech, all the latest recording gear. Farewell to fiddling paper records and wrist scans, there'll be no room for error, if you know what I mean.' He looked meaningfully at Padrain and moved his eyes towards the door. 'They were marked heavily with Fae blood. I noticed when I passed. One of them looked like a barnacle covered rock playing a harp.' He shrugged and took a seat on top of some bales of straw left over from making the cob wall of the outbuilding.

'They're not staying,' he paused surprised to hear the relief in his voice. Then he said, 'They travelled with Fairmist Al Mara, came off the Realta Siar, be making their way north and east from here.'

'The Western Star has been to shore? Smuggler Seamist is back?' Carter sounded intrigued.

'Aye, but only to drop them off and out she went again. Now what were you saying about the records at the school?'

'We've to input all paper records from the last twelve years onto computation devices, starting on first day back, a galactic signature of Kinetic Two, White Lunar Wind, it's the day after the Day of the Dead which incidentally is Kinetic One, Red Magnetic Dragon, at least it is in this galactic cycle…it's not a good omen, not a good omen at all. The power of fire and air around the day of the dead, it will not mix well.' Carter was pensive, he removed the cotton cravat from around his neck, then used it to mop at his brow.

'Seven hells, Col, I didn't think you'd be the type to be bothered by superstitions.' Padrain looked bemused. 'You've too much time on your hands.'

He leaned against the oily work bench, took his chestnut brown leathery arms, and folded them across his broad muscular chest while he studied his old friend.

'Aye, probably, but I soon won't have. The machines have letter keys like a typewriter. It will take ages to input all those records, but much better than looking for information in stacks of paper or so the new head says. He has me paranoid. What is he looking for? He has a full school to run. Why is he rustling about in old papers? He should be focussed on the future not the past.' He waved his hand at Padrain, clearly agitated.

Padrain shook his head and shrugged. 'There are a lot of questions that need answered there.'

Carter seemed relieved at Padrain's response and finally stopped muttering as he got off the straw bale and walked stiffly over to the car, where he lifted the bonnet of the Ensign, shutting the conversation down. He did not like the omens, but he did like admiring the sparkling engine – it was a passion of his to regularly strip it down and clean it, which was one of the reasons it had lasted so long. But he was only a tinkerer; it was Pad who knew what to do with her. He sighed. 'I'll miss her, Pad, I wish there were a way to keep hold of her.'

'You're right, she'll be a miss. She has been a good motor on the smuggling runs, and this new system…well, it's a young man's game, but the community know the good work you carry out for all of us. We will not forget it. Right then, I'll sort her out.' Padrain leaned over a heap of machinery piled neatly on the wooden bench, reached out a muscular arm and patted it.

'Got a nearly new engine and some top-flight Foss, she'll go like a proc anti-gravity flyer. You thought of replacing her?'

'You mean you've got a piece of scrap that's only just better than what we've got now and some of your home-made Cheen-fuel,' Carter said wryly before continuing, 'Maybe if I was an elite, but even if I was, the supplies never on long enough in these parts to get a full rubicity charge, and who can get a Foss-only motor these days or the fuel? Vehicles in the cities run on alchemical batteries charged with rubicity.' He paused and waggled his thumb in the air before he added, 'But the transducer requires a spark of lifeforce.'

'It's not natural,' Padrain whispered but when Carter gave him a puzzled look he flapped his hand for him to continue.

'I am only getting away with running her now because Old Muntor signed her off as an essential school vehicle that I had to repair and fuel myself. Good luck finding that in the paperwork. I might have to hand her back yet, wait until they find out she's been running on Cheen,' he guffawed, and Pad laughed aloud too.

'I would like to see the proc alchemical orbs and anti-grav flyers running on Cheen.' He grinned sardonically. 'Or Lord Bucky, filling his airship up. Light! It is something to behold. He must crap gold to be able to afford that.'

'Aye, that's true. Although after the stunt his boy pulled. What was he thinking?' Padrain grimaced. 'I've seen some expensive proc kit down Ninmah canal district, and more sophisticated flyers too, not just alchemy either, some of them have a magnetic beam into the earth, like a green stinger it is. They are getting tighter at the borders too. I pity the clans on Kai, that I do. They'll be fried alive, especially after Bucky's bastard went stellar on the bloody information channel.' Padrain shook his head then pointed to the car. 'Let me know if you've to give her back, I'll remove the engine. If they want her back, they can bloody well tow her.'

Padrain stopped and reached under the bench where he had half buried a medium sized keg of beer in the cool earth. Lifting it up easily, Padrain took two ceramic pint pots with large handles, from the shelf above his work bench, checked to see if they were clean, shrugged and blew out a couple of dead spiders. 'They'll do. Come, share a pint with me, friend, it's been a long day.' He turned the tap on the barrel, watched as a steady stream of beer frothed into the pint pots; it smelled of sweet grain while the amber liquid poured.

'Aye, it has.' Carter took a long drink of the beer while he leaned against his car. 'That's a good brew,' he said contentedly.

'The pigs love the bags of grain after it's been fermented.' Padrain smiled.

'I'm not surprised, good beer, good bacon…Pad?' He paused, then studied his beer while he thought about Celeste's outburst in class. I am not a fool, it wasn't just something hormonal, it felt like an earth tremor he thought, then took a long draught of beer and asked, 'Is there something I should know about the Melsie kid?' Carter wiped froth from his top lip on the sleeve of his homespun tunic, then took another drink of the frothy ale.

'No, old friend, there isn't. The less you know, the safer you are. There's a little something for you and that sister of yours.' Padrain put his beer down then went to a side door that led to a long narrow scullery that had a variety of slaughter implements hanging from the eaves at the far end. They jangled and glinted above the stone basin where he collected the blood from the pigs he slaughtered.

He heaved out a large wooden crate filled with cheese, butter, fresh and dried meats, handmade soaps, and fancy goods like tanned leather insoles for worn-through boots and skeins of yarn and wool, honey, bottles of Padrain's finest Poiten and roasted rini-cheen chicory root powder.

'There's another two dozen besides this one in the outhouses up the yard, they'll need shifted soon, so I best get her running like a young buck.' He nodded at the car. 'Dorothea wants you to have a good supply before harvest is upon us, then we'll sort out the fruit and grain. I've managed to hide pigs and goats from the quota counters, and there is plenty of deer and game in the forest too. The northern crofters will drove the scrag herds down through The Bloom soon, when they come to take refuge for the winter, and the Romarii will be here as usual, for the stock swap.' Padrain watched while Carter made a mental note of the forthcoming activities. 'At least the Fae will be away, did they say anything of their origins, Pad?'

'Called themselves Selgovae returned from the Southern Isles, got Dorothea in a right spin, trust Smuggler Seamist to send them our way, but I've left it to her and Cissy to sort. I am not encouraging them to stay nor am I denying them aid, we are all in the same resistance. Now, can I rely on you and the lads from the Nag to help when the time's right?'

Carter investigated his empty pint until Padrain took it off him and refilled it. 'Of course,' Carter said while he took his replenished pint, 'we will help with the stock swap, bad meat makes bad meat, it's always been the way. Tell Dorothea thanks. The council of elders will make sure the crates are collected by the crofters and sent to where they are needed most. They will find it harder this winter, the lands to the North have barely thawed out. That damned glacier Amnasia is encroaching more each year, soon we'll be farming bison or bear for their skins – it's bloody worrying, Pad.'

'Aye, it is, Col. I've heard that some of the crofters in the far north, up near Anuk, have had trouble with wolves, as well as other things…seems they're travelling across the ice and over the land bridge. The clans aren't doing much to stop them either – their faces are turned to watch the shores around the dark water of the Lake of Unum. They're barely surviving themselves, truth be told, predators on the ground, procs in the air looking for sport…' he trailed off as he supped his ale.

'And all manner of foul things crawling out of the Lake of Unum.' Colin looked owlishly over his ceramic pint jug.

Padrain nodded. 'Here, this is what we've been hunting in the shadows, we've had to get help in.' He pointed to a pile of traps in the corner; two were full of oily black bodies, about the size of a large black rat, but their tales were like spears, hard and flattish like a beaver's.

'Anuk, they're bloody Fear Me's from Unum, they spy for the devil and his kind,' Carter exclaimed then spat. Both men shivered despite the warmth of the afternoon, then turned their attention to the car and their ale.

~ ❈ ~ ❈ ~ ❈ ~

'Ah, that'll be Ganaim now.' Padrain went to the door and opened it when he heard the crunch of boots outside. The yard was awash with a warm light and the sky, cloud-patterned, like a mackerel's skin while the bottom arc of the sun dipped lazily toward the horizon. 'Come on in, lad, we're just having a pint.' Padrain nodded slowly letting Ganaim know that all had been decided.
Ganaim was not sure whether to be relieved that he had avoided the inquisition or worried that he had missed what had been decided about Celeste; he wanted to express his opinion as regards to what should happen to her. He had decided, following his strange encounter with the Selgovae troupe, on his slow way down the yard, that he would offer to marry Celeste and they would both settle down immediately.

'What's going to happen?' he asked Padrain quietly at the door. He could see Carter bending over the open hood of the old ensign, drink in hand.

'That's none of your concern, son, you know, you've always known that this day would come.' Ganaim was about to argue back that it did not have to be that way, he would care for her, he would keep her safe. 'What's up with Colin?' he asked as he pointed to the car. Carter had dropped his ceramic mug and was holding on to the car while an invisible force was moving him back and forward as if two pairs of large hands fought over him.

'This is a Standard Ensign,' he moaned between clenched teeth, and he pointed a shaking finger at the car as if it would turn into a dragon and eat him alive. 'It was manufactured in a city called Coventry. It was my first new vehicle, for my new job. My parents bought it for me…there was a girl I was to marry,' he retched violently, brought up warm frothy beer that spattered across the oily floor. 'Where in the hells am I? Padrain,' he shouted, then 'What the fuck's going on?'

'I'm coming, Col. Gan, you get Dorothea, tell her to bring her apothecary bag.'

He felt like he was running on the spot, such was his haste to get away from the scene. This was a dangerous time; if Padrain could not talk Carter to his senses and the acceptance of what had happened and where he was, they would lose him to screeching madness and episodes where he flitted from one reality to the other – a bit like Tara, he thought and felt a wave of panic run through him.

'Quickly now, Gan, the scales are falling from his eyes, at bloody last. Col, I need you to calm down, I have some explaining to do, old friend. Dorothea is going to give you a tonic that she brewed specially for the job.'

'I hope she bloody well hurries up, Padrain, my head is about to pop off my shoulders, and my stomach is going to join that.' He pointed at the floor while he shook violently. Padrain took hold of him and said, 'Just keep talking, Col, it will help you make sense of it.' He put his arms around Carter, kept them there and absorbed some of the tremors while they waited for Dorothea to arrive.

'I remember it…I was driving to school – Christ Almighty, Pad, I was a young man, I was in love…' He could not help the sob that escaped his mouth. Where was she? he wondered briefly while he pulled himself together for one fleeting second and skewed to madness the next. Whatever was happening, he was not going to let it destroy him. Outside the box? This is it, he thought while he steeled himself to ride the storm to its end. He gasped, grateful for Padrain's arms around his shoulders. 'I was driving to school, there was a moment of blackness like a fainting fit which did not materialise into anything, so I kept driving,' he shook his head. 'Incredible! Then I was driving to school here in Mount Wraith, it was my first day at my new school. Hells below, Padrain, it was seamless! All my memories taken and replaced with a load of lies. Suddenly I did not have a girlfriend and never had any intention of wanting one, that had been erased. My parents? Dead and gone. By the light, what evil bastard did this?!'

'I know, Col, I know,' Padrain comforted him. Then said, 'Abrecan, did it. He is the Lord of the Dark Flame, Conquest. I know how cracker's that sounds but it's still the truth.'

'Why didn't you tell me, Pad, why?' he continued to shake violently.

'Because when we tell you all there is to know, once Dorothea gives you her tonic, you'll know that you wouldn't have believed a word we said, and you would've thought me the crazy one, friend.' Padrain hugged him, then sagged with relief as the door opened and Dorothea entered followed by Cissy.

Cissy took in the scene. I hope he makes it back to his senses. Lords knows what we will have to do if he is not able to ground the differences in the two realities. Surely, we will not put up with another liability like Tara, Cissy thought while she scrutinised Carter. There was no doubt what was happening.

'Bloody hell, Fear Me's and Fae, the stuff of nightmares and dreams. Galactic signatures and people being taken to work the wind – fuck! How did I accept it as the truth for so long. How long have you known?' Carter asked between bouts of tremors, while Padrain led him towards the bale of straw he had been sitting on. He was as glad to see Dorothea as Padrain was.

'Since the beginning, I came here fully conscious. I was a young youth with the whole of my future before me, though my folks did not survive the dimension jump, they were dead in their chairs, when I opened my eyes,' he replied softly.

'And you, Dorothea?'

She met Carter's gaze, then to ease his fright she smiled gently as if he were a child and touched him lightly on the arm before she said, 'Col, concentrate on steadying your breath. Not too many questions, try not to ramble so.' Then she took a small vial of liquid from her bag. 'Open up and touch the roof of your mouth with your tongue,' she instructed as she let the tiniest drops of liquid fall onto the frenulum beneath. 'I'm from here, Colin. Gaiadon is my home world.'

His jaw dropped. 'What? Of course, how could I be so stupid, your eyes are almost purple, and that hue to your skin, well, it is too shining, like pale sandstone glittering beneath the sun. There is light in the fabric of the folk from here. It runs in their blood and illuminates their flesh,' he said incredulously. Then added while a snarl of tension crinkled his brow, 'We must seem so lack lustre.'

'You seem anything but. You are so resilient. Now, hush. Be quiet, just for a while until the elixir modifies the wave vibrations. Cissy love, fetch the chairs from the scullery.' She nodded to the slaughter area Padrain had retrieved the crate of goods from. Then smiled when she saw that Cissy was already bringing an assortment of faded garden chairs through. 'It won't be long now, Col, then we have much to talk about. You will stay for your tea, until I am sure the spasmodic wave vibration has subsided.' Dorothea smiled and patted him on the leg.

'The light?' Carter asked.

'It is called Eleri Imole,' Dorothea replied, then added in a voice wrought through with grief, 'It is a supernatural light, one that the lords of the flame continually make war over.'

'Are the Selgovae gone, Cissy? Padrain asked interrupting Dorothea while he met her eye and shook his head imperceptibly. Carter had enough to contend with.

'Yes, they've gone into the Bloom. The Romarii make their way here,' she gulped quickly, 'for…Ganaim,' she finished abruptly.

Padrain pulled an old cane chair next to where Carter sat on the bale of straw and watched while his friend's vibrations subsided. 'It can't be any other way,' he replied coolly to Cissy over his shoulder. Then he changed the subject and nodded to the traps with the black Fear Me's inside. 'Take them and burn them. Then you, the boy, and the cats are to clear the shadows again this twilight. One of them wants to use the stone compass to travel. She is taking something to Lodewick, you are to escort her.'

'I'm not taking the horses in there, Dad, and I will not enter the demon spawn city,' she snapped to Padrain while she looked at Carter. There was no point hiding anything more from him, he was aware now and seemed to be settling well, at least for now. Who knows what poor Colin will do, when the full extent of this living hell is revealed, she thought sourly?

'No, you certainly are not taking the horses, and you are to guard the stone circle on the edge of the Willow Wilds, while the Roma-ranger enters the outer zones of the city.' He looked sternly at Cissy and her heart sank. They want to use my galactic signature she thought.

But Dorothea spoke before she could. 'It is for our people, love, they need you to take them back; to last night,' Dorothea said gently while she stood behind Carter and lay her healing hands on each side of his head, which twitched involuntarily for a few more times before it became still.

'Thank you, Dorothea, the anxiety has gone. It is all right, resolved, if you get my meaning.' They all looked relieved, Padrain especially.

Cissy pursed her lips while she pulled at the lace tie at the neck of her tunic. 'I do not like using it, it is not a gift, it is an unnatural curse, and I will not be used,' she snapped, then moved stiffly towards the two traps that were full of Fear Me's. She picked them up just as Francis the black cat appeared, a low growl rumbled in the back of his throat.

'Take a cat with you,' Padrain said to her retreating back.

'A cat?' She could hear the screech building in her voice and tried to remain calm. 'I would need a colony,' she retorted dryly and tried to slam the heavy shed door with one hand, but she failed. She was too laden with dead Fear Me's, the cat hurried through before her.

They walked with purpose up the farmyard, Cissy cursed under her breath while Francis stalked next to her, occasionally growling at the dead Fear Me's. He was large and sleek, similar in size to a mountain cat, and unlike Shabba who was inky black. Francis' coat shone under the setting sun as if it were burnished with dark orange-black, like the deepest bronze.

Ganaim and two other crofters were finishing the last patch of rendering on the cob walls. They stood back to admire their work and wiped sweat from their brows with bits of rag. The crofters, Abhhain and Moin, put their homespun tunics back on, their hard bodies were sculpted, as if they had been carved from grey-green jade and when they moved or walked it was quick and easy like acrobats and tumblers. They tucked their shirts into cotton trousers, baggy but cuffed at the ankle – typical summer wear for crofters. Moin held out a leather waistcoat to Abhhain. 'Too hot… leave it on the bales, next to your fiddle, I'll get it after tea.' The fire was still blazing hot, although the green wood that the children had put on it before they departed sent sparks and hissing flame spiralling toward the dusky sky. Cissy stopped by the fire and opened the first wire trap and started to pull out the first oily shapes, ready to give them to the flames. Her hand twitched and her face was contorted with anger.

'Here, let me help you with that, lass. I'll get some more wood, it'll need to be hotter and bigger to send them back to the hell they came from,' Crofter Moin said as he brought dry logs to the fire and removed the big kettle and tripod to one side. 'I'll deal with them until they've faded if you've stuff to do.'

She nodded. 'Are you able to watch them, Moin? The fear visions they release are not pleasant.'

'Aye, I know. We're plagued with such beasts in the north,' Moin said as he dropped the first black body into the centre of the flames. It popped, and they gagged as an acrid puff of sulphur hit them in the face and a strange chill passed through the air. An image of a terrible beast with the body of a man and the head of a misshapen creature, like a lizard, loomed out of the fire and made its way towards them, trying to stab and slash with an awful, curved blade. Cissy jumped back and reached for her waist, but the Moin just built up the fire more.

'That,' he pointed to the creature as he took a flaming stick and stabbed it through the chest, 'is a vision of a demon drudge who has eaten too much animal flesh, favouring reptile brain, by the looks of it. Though I see you used black arrows on them, it leeches the spell power away. They are not a threat even though the shadow-manced form remains. This is just an illusion, trying to put doubt and terror into our hearts. But without death by black crystal, like tourmaline and obsidian, it would embrace us and suck us into the world from which this vision came, what with the membrane all ripped asunder.'

Cissy nodded. 'All manner of creature will fly and crawl between worlds where they do not belong when the demon utters the words that fragments the dome of the sky, and the All-There-Is will weep and fall.'

The crofter nodded as he knelt by the cage and pulled out another Fear Me. The fire cast his pale greenish skin into shades of lurid orange and brown, but his eyes sparkled with the quick diamond light of curiosity and like a diamond there was a fire and something hard underneath their strange beauty. Although, he had a kind face with plenty of lines to suggest he smiled and laughed a great deal, despite looking like what folk would say was a demon, he was not. His eyes were large with a narrow lid and although dark like a seal's when the light caught them in a certain way, they twinkled with glacial lights, luminescence's of seafoam-green, silver, violet and aquamarine that marked him as a descendant of the Fae as much as his ears did which were very pointed. 'You know Cassandra's Chronicles?' He smiled.

'Some,' Cissy replied cautiously. 'Other foretelling's are hard to decipher; the language can be difficult to understand.'

'You let me know if you need any help. It may be in the old tongue which would mean you have an ancient copy. Does it have the story of Cassandra leaving into the west on the back of a unicorn at the setting of the sun on the longest day?'

Cissy looked puzzled. She did not have that edition even though her copy of the book was ancient. It had been a gift with the other books and manuscripts she had, held in an ornately carved chest in her bedroom. She was about to share that when the Fear Me rose in a last terrible vision before it disappeared into a cloud of smoke and drifted away to nothing more than an acrid smell on the wind.

'See that vision there?' Crofter Moin pointed as the smoke dispersed, 'Now where that image comes from, now that be real. Fear Me's are rats turned evil by black magus. They take the water of Unum and when the dark eye looks upon it instead of the light, it brings forth shadow, but mark my words, the Willow Wilds are full of the real beasts the Fear Me's copy, monstrous chimeras, with no other thought than killing. That,' he nodded towards the remaining bodies in the traps, 'is what demon drudges gone wrong are. He don't want them in the city of Lodewick, there still be too many powerful humans there, hard men, evil men, part of a secret society run by the Brotherhood of Perpetual Pain. He needs to hide his kin and his true self from them.' He snorted then said, 'The devil is cautious of the evil he brought with him an' he don't trust Volsunga neither.' The others nodded their agreement, they all knew that some of the human governors of the bureaus could show a demon how to be darker than pitch.

'He cannot send the drudges to the Flat Lands where they would band together like renegades and maybe try to take the cities for themselves. So, when he finds them that's been eating brain flesh, he kills them, but some escape to the Willow Wilds. Living and hunting there, making a sacred place, another hell. Demon beast, they're called, bloody filth they are.' He spat and picked up another Fear Me and waggled it in the air before throwing it onto the fire. It popped as it hit the flames. They both stepped back and covered their noses and mouths, but their eyes smarted all the same.

'Walking dead, Abhhain,' he shouted to the other crofter who leapt nimbly forward with his large thatching spar hook in his hand. He twirled gracefully and sliced the head off the zombie before he kicked the shadow back into the flame.

'Aye, it was that Moin. What a nasty bag o' tricks we have here.' Crofter Moin turned to the traps. 'And plenty more nightmares for you to be twirling and slicing at before the night's done.'

Abhhain jumped in the air and flipped over backwards. 'If it weren't for my tumbling, we would have gone hungrier than my stomach could have borne, Moin, your fiddling being what it is.'

Ganaim smiled at them, although he was sad that he would not be here to share the merriment they had brought since Fire Feast. A celebration that was strictly forbidden but as Abhain had pointed out, 'Burn the demon effigy, get a skin full of ale, Ganaim. I won't tell if you don't.'

But that was earlier in the year, there would be more arriving for the harvesting, then they would stay for the winter. They had a hard life, but if there were more like Moin and Abhhain, there would be plenty of entertainment and fun. I would like to learn how to tumble like that, he thought, as both Crofters laughed and began to take wagers on what the Fear Me's would release next.

Fear Me's were physically harmless after being killed by black arrows, they were just remnants of dark magic and whispers of ill intent, but they could still drive fear into the minds of the hardest of warriors. They were the black clouds the shadow sent on the eve of destruction, before the storm broke.

Cissy turned away from the obscenity in the fire and said a silent prayer to Gaia that they had not infiltrated Elvan's Barrow. That was where the paths she would use were hidden. They led to other ancient stone circles. Paths she had to take carefully without the distraction of nightmare visions to worry about. 'Ganaim, come with me, get the other cats and bring the obsidian and tourmaline arrows,' she called to him as she left the heat and light of the fire and walked towards the back of the farmhouse. 'We have a job that needs doing before the night takes hold.'

'What now? More hunting?' he asked as he tore his eyes away from the fire and a bear-headed monstrosity. He moved alongside Cissy and said quietly, 'I am only pleased they have no blood.'

She nodded. 'A silver lining, I suppose,' she replied dryly as he walked beside her. 'Yes, you will hunt, but I have to use the stone compass to take a Romarii to Lodewick; back to last night.'

He took hold of her arm, bony beneath the soft linen tunic she wore. 'Why? Why do they let you do it? I will come with you. I can tell you what we did yesterday, what we ate, how we hunted last night? Even you, spying on me through the curtains,' he said in a hushed voice while his fingers dug into her arm.

She shook her head as she pried them lose. 'No, you will not, you will go to my room and bring me my journal then we will enter what we did in there; perhaps if I put my memories on paper, they will return to me one day,' she said sadly.

'But they do not.' He clenched his fists tightly and folded his arms about his chest. 'You will lose that day. What other days have they made you throw away, so they can take your power and walk like gods through Time? One day you will not have to do it, Cissy, I promise you. I will forbid it,' he finished through clenched teeth.

'You will forbid it? When did you get so brave?' Her mouth remained straight but he could almost see the flutter of a smile there.

He sighed. 'I didn't, we will do as we are told, or someone, somewhere, will die. Who?' He held out his palms in mock query. 'We do not know. Lord above help us if we dare to ask too much, and we are never told, but death there will be…' he trailed off and nodded in satisfaction while she guffawed. 'You read them so well, you are not such malleable clay after all.'

'I am not,' he nodded vigorously, his red and gold hair aflame from the light as it pooled out of the kitchen window while they approached the farmhouse. The rune light about his temples and across his forehead glittered momentarily and the light chased the luminescence across his face and cheeks, all the way to the tips of his ears. Cissy smiled inwardly, sometimes she felt fit to burst with a mother's love, but she pushed the feeling aside and resisted the urge to reach out and smooth his cheek.

'According to the Selgovae, I am Solas Nua Novantae.' He waggled his eyebrows in what he thought was a superior way, setting off another cascade of twinkling crystal light across his skin. They stood before the big dusty oak door at the back of the farmhouse. Smells of wax, newly shaved wood, and herbs that were hanging to dry in the eaves of the porch wafted around them. Beneath them a row of hard leather work boots stood regimentally inside the porch. Padrain's overalls and Cissy's favoured dungarees hung above them. On the opposite side of the porch, a couple of crossbows hung next to several unstrung bows of varying lengths which were secured in wooden brackets, designed so that they would not warp; the strings, some made from sinew others made from hemp – even one or two from silk, favoured by Dorothea – lay in neat circles beneath them on a shelf of dark wood.

Cissy stopped suddenly and placed her hand on his chest. 'If you are that, if you are named true by their seer, then fly away from this cursed place, Ganaim, fly far and fly fast, then set the sky aflame for there will be little that will put out the first light, the new light of the Novantae, when it rises in the west, as red and gold as any dawn from the east.' She quoted the prophecy from Cassandra's Chronicles and noted with disappointment that it was lost on Ganaim while she took the sleeve of her pale-yellow, linen shirt and wiped her eyes with it.

'I…I upset you, it was just them, they were being strange…I didn't mean to make you cry.' He was shocked, he had never seen her cry before so openly. 'This talking in riddles, lords it must be catching, Cissy. How am I supposed to set the sky on fire?' he exclaimed as he took down a couple of crossbows. 'And…' he paused while he steeled himself, 'they asked if I knew who my sire was?'

'Hush, I am just being overly sentimental. Now, get that journal. We will record the day I will lose when I travel back in time with the Romarii, and you will hunt tonight because you must. Listen to me, Ganaim, to survive we must remain focussed, we must remain in the now, not the past full of regret, nor the future full of anxiety. Airgid and Gaoth should not have…' she trailed off then stopped. 'No, perhaps they should have. Who am I to try to stop the wheel as it turns? As if I could,' she finished reflectively, then took his hand in hers. He almost wept himself; he could not remember a time when she had been gentle with him or displayed any emotion to anyone. She was efficient, ordered and commanding. Her sudden softening almost undone his resolve not to love her either; she had shown so little to him, none that he could remember.

'Listen, I cannot discuss it with you, because I have no knowledge on what they have shared with you apart from ancient and illegal copies of Selgovae, Novantae, Ningen and other Mythical Beast, and Prophecies of the Age of Man and Shadow Yet to Come. One was written by Fae, the other is a series of verses and visions by an unknown mystic called Cassandra, claiming to be The Stone.' She noted his frown. 'The Stone is a mystical creature, someone who holds the law and lore of worlds in their form. If I have translated the text correctly. If you must delve, I will leave them in your room but,' she squeezed his hand tight, 'promise me you will not reveal what the Selgovae said…it is not the right time…please?' She continued to wipe at her eyes with her free hand while she resolutely ignored his question about his father.

'If it is important, I promise.' He frowned and checked the anger that rose suddenly. He removed his hand from hers. There was no point in prodding her now, she was going into the stone compass and back a whole day too. She would hardly remember any of it. He grimaced sourly as he made his way towards the door. The other two cats brushed past him as they came out of the kitchen; the black female's tail swished at his bare arm like a whip, but she ignored his 'ouch' and slinked past. They both came to sit next to the outer wall, still warm from the afternoon's sun, where Cissy already had an array of equipment waiting for her forthcoming journey.

Cissy listened as Ganaim climbed the stairs heavily. 'Oh, to be able to go back and kill the bitch,' she said to Shabba who stared at her as if to say, you should. The brown cat hissed lightly at the sleek black female who ignored him; it seemed as if Francis looked the other way deliberately.

'But my blessed gift is a curse. Skywalker,' Cissy spat. 'Some bloody good that is if there is no one alive to show me how to use it properly. Then if there was, what would I do? Slippery Selene disappeared before Ganaim was born. If I go back to the last time, I saw her and kill her, Celeste would not be born, and although I was heavy with Ganaim, I will not remember a single day of my life with him, nor of anything I had experienced since.' She laughed hysterically. 'Perhaps that is it. I will wipe myself bloody clean of the lot of them and free the world of the tainted saviour.' The brown cat padded softly towards her. His large tail swished across the dusty ground; he met her gaze and his wise eyes glittered.

The dusky evening faded into shades of grey and silver, but she could see in the pools of yellow light from the farmhouse that his coat was intricately patterned. They were Moe Moema cats apparently and according to legend the witch queen of the fabled Quicksilver Tower called Hiki Tere Pourewa made them. Marley was like one of her favourite sketches in a book called Navigating the Southern Isles by Captain Charyia Sea Storm. It was an eclectic captain's periplus, with three chapters on how to avoid the seven mythical isles of Wairua, which, according to the book, disappeared and reappeared at will anywhere in the massive southern archipelago; and how to pass tests set by the witches who ruled them if you ever had the misfortune; notes on mythical eels called Eternity Eels, and delightful recipes on how to prepare them for dinner; beautiful illustrations of fantastic white birds in cages and the instructions for preparing them, although Cissy was not sure whether it was to eat them or not. It involved crystal seeds and quartz fingers and the instructions seemed more like a scientific dissection than a recipe. The translation of the text had been arduous, and she had left it incomplete. Although, she thought she knew the location of Makara and had enjoyed just looking at the excellent charts and maps of the archipelago, the stars, tides, and sea passages.

Marley studied her and brought his eyebrows together in consternation. *You must not use your galactic gift in such a way, pale daughter, who is sad inside the sun, it is forbidden. We will accompany you along the ways of the stone compass and protect your memories from loss. We can learn something of the sky walk you do and from this we may be able to teach you more. Together, we fight evil, we do not need to add dark into an almost full vessel.*

'I hope it works, Marley, for I am heartsick of doing what I do not want to do,' she said sadly to the cat who turned and blinked at the large black female. She rose gracefully and sniffed the air. Cissy gathered up her pack and placed several stickle-bug bombs she had made from drake lime and saltpetre carefully in the bottom. Padrain had a Storm galactic signature and he had put a spark of lightning inside a tiny glass sphere blown by the glass-smiths from the north; once the stickle-bug was thrown, the lightning released and blew the powder and nitrogen preparation sky high. Then Cissy took a small crossbow and attached it to a sling across her back, and checked her throwing knives at her boots, wrists, and neck just as Ganaim came down the stairs.

He came slowly through the neat kitchen; the large table had been set with many places by Dorothea earlier. He could still smell scones as they cooled on the side of the woodburning stove, next to hams and cheeses. She knew they would be expecting guests. It is like a tea party for my departure, he shuddered and held tightly to the quivers full of silver arrows; their heads glinted like glassy black death, light oiled across their heads like silver water. Cissy's leather-bound journal was tucked under his arm; it did not have anything else in it other than the memories of the days she had lost when she had been sent sky-walking in the stone compass up at Elvan's Barrow. He knew because he helped her write the entries down, then after she had travelled, he sat with her and read to her the things she had done the day she entered the stone compass. He had, also, on more than one occasion, sneaked in her bedroom and had gone through her things. His need for answers had incorporated a full sweep of the entire farm; no room, bedroom or property had escaped his investigations.

'I am going to Elvan's Barrow. The Romarii I need to escort will meet me there. You wait here for the others. Ask Moin and Abhhain to be ready to stable their horses, put the kettle on, and the bread in the oven, and if you have time, you could always fill in that journal for me before you go hunting.' She smiled with a warmth she did not feel while she gave him plenty of tasks to keep him occupied and away from the stone circle.

'Francis can stay with me and hunt?' he asked hopefully.

Cissy tilted her head. 'You recognise his need for vengeance well.'

Ganaim frowned. 'Not sure about that, he's just sleek and fast that is all. The Fear Me's didn't know what hit them.' The other two cats stuck their noses in the air and turned their backs on him with a swish of their tails.

Cissy pointed to the black female. 'Shabba, she is their Witch Queen and illusion weaver, she has placed wards within the shadows,' then she pointed to Marley. 'He is their mystic, their spiritual leader. It was he who approached Fairmist Al Mara and shared his vision of his need to journey here. They have come a long way to help us fight. They are all psychic, to protect us, and destroy the dark where they can.'

'And I thought they were here to kill rats and Fear Me's,' he retorted cheekily while he passed her a quiver full of silver arrows with jewel black heads.

'One day they will tell you exactly why they are here,' she said and nodded brusquely to him while she turned to make her way to the topmost field of the farm, where the ancient stone circle stood.

'Mad people think they can hear animals talk,' he half-jested to her retreating back. She shrugged but continued walking, across the farmyard and away from the house, in the opposite direction to the crofters around the fire who were still exclaiming about the inventiveness of magicked rats.

'In my experience, it is mad people who cannot hear them talk,' she replied loudly.

He tutted but held his tongue as she cast a final word over her shoulder, sweeping her arm regally about her. 'It is all communicating, all of it, The Silent Thing, breathes and sings…can't you feel it? The very breath of the Ever-Was speaks. At least the Romarii will show you that,' she paused and turned to face him. She was a small lithe woman in her prime, not a pound of spare flesh or humour anywhere about her, her curly hair sprung around her head in a mass of corkscrew curls that looked like the rays of the sun. 'You be careful you do not make a trade and a contract you cannot get out of. Be careful of the hands you shake while you are with them. They are not like us, not really.' She sounded almost amused at something she said as her voice faded, and she disappeared through the hedge into the field. The two cats blinked at him then bounded after her, leaving him with Francis who stared after them. He sniffed the air once before he walked to the porch wall and stood on his hind legs to swat at a small crossbow with his front paw.

'Kettle and bread first, like a bloody goodwife. Away to the Romarii on an adventure? Well not before I bake the bread and put the kettle on.' He stopped and brought down the weapons he would need for later that night before he turned and walked a little way out into the yard. He called down the yard, 'There will be horses to be stabled shortly. Moin, Abhhain, will you stop playing around?'

The two crofters finished off the Fear Me vision in the fire and Abhhain shouted back, 'Aye, we're nearly done here. I had to stop Moin proposing to the last beauty out of the trap; it was a sea siren, clever little buggers, one kiss from that…'

Ganaim hesitated before he walked back to the porch and thought should I go to the shed? He knew that once Cissy started to sky-walk the paths inside the stone compass, Fear Me's would be attracted to the vibration. 'I'll leave Celeste, she will be fine,' Ganaim muttered. The large cat brushed past him, almost knocking him aside on its way to the kitchen. He put one hand under his chin and narrowed his eyes while the black tail disappeared around the door. 'I do not know if I like cats, you seem too clever by half.'

Chapter Twelve

Mad As a Hatter

She walked across the yard with something that felt like relief making her steps lighter, her earlier encounter with her nana almost forgotten. Although, there was always that gnawing worry that Tara would do something that would draw attention to them. One thing pretending she had made a moon disappear to an audience of one, quite another if she started telling folk at market she could. She shuddered and felt another strange but weak wave of vibrations pass through her, she paused before she pushed the door open.

'Nana…I'm back…sorry I'm late, we got held back, Ganaim was being a…well he was being himself in class…' Celeste lied as she opened the old stable door that served as a front door to the shed. She wiped her bare feet on the small rug, out of habit. So easy to program someone she thought and curled her toes into the rough matting until the wave of frustration she felt subsided.

'Nan, where are you…I want to talk – please. It's about the nano assessment, I've given my clogs away too…I'm not having two pairs of shoes when people in my class have bare feet.' She paused and tilted her head to one side. 'Nana? Where are you? Also, about this galactic signature thing, we need to sort it out, get our stories straight, if I've to go to Ninmah or even Eirini…' Celeste trailed off while she walked slowly towards the living room. Tara was not there.

The kitchen, she thought, but when she got there, Tara was not there either. A pan of boiled eggs on top of the old stove had nearly burned dry. She reached for a cloth and removed them; taking them to the sink where she hastily pumped water over them before she wafted steam that smelled faintly of sulphur away. Turning from the sink she made her way to the adjoining room. Tara called it her artist's studio, but it was really a chaotic mess where dust and oddments gathered. Plants in varying stages of life, and death, stood in pots on the floor in front of the window, different sized panes of glass were dusty and cobwebby, festooned like an old potting shed, shells and fossils, and lumps of spiky green fur which looked like evergreen tree foliage, fought for space. Tara insisted the fur belonged to imaginary creatures called Nympts. All of it crowded the bench that ran along one wall. Dry wood stacked next to the old wood burner in the corner nearest the large window, had a layer of dust atop it like a cap of grey snow. There was paper everywhere, paints and pots, a rickety old easel. This was the place where Tara said she could 'think straight.'

Tara was sitting on an overstuffed armchair, staring out of the large, mismatched windows, towards the cobbled yard and her small cottage garden to the right.

'Oh, Nana. Are you well?'

'I remember the days of the week,' she said as she pointed to the white-washed walls of the studio and a trail of lettering, not her usual delicate shades that brought butterflies or roses to life, but a trail of bold dark letters, ominous in shades of black, dark purple, and crimson. 'The days of the week are Monday,' she shouted as she leapt to her feet, 'Tuesday, Wednesday, Thursday, Friday, Saturday and God's Day was SUNDAY.' She clapped her hands as she sat back down. 'I remember them,' she said proudly. 'The butterflies have shown me today, they have shown me the days of the week…I knew someone would hear my prayer and send me help – God has answered me, do you hear, God has sent me help.'

'Oh no. Nana, please don't,' Celeste implored the wild-eyed Tara, 'Please, Nana, we'll sit down and talk, you can tell me all about them.' She pointed to the graffiti that trailed and danced across once pristine walls. They had been the only uncluttered place as Celeste had refused to put shelves up – it was bad enough keeping the floor and the bench clean.

'Yes! We will talk, Celeste. I will talk, you write…quick, get paper and pencil while I remember…my name is Tara Melsie, I lived in a place called London, I was a visiting artist at a college or a university, it was a place of art and literature…oh dear, my memory of that is not complete, but I met Aindreas Sackeyfio. It was…was in the 1950s. One day I woke up, and everything had changed.' She stopped, then looked angrily at Celeste. 'Quickly, girl, I told you to write this down, it's important.' Tara jumped up again, grabbed paper and pencils, and threw them at Celeste. 'Write it down, hurry, before I lose it again…before the veil descends…' She sat down and drew a ragged breath.

'My name is Tara Melsie. I lived in a place called London. One day I woke up and London had gone; the London I knew had gone. I was in a place called Lodewick.' She paused. Celeste began to scribble. 'It was…' she clicked her fingers, 'Aindreas said the new anchor site was the centre of the Hawksmoor Pentagram and that was the only part that was like London. The demon put the top of the Fifth Tower right in the centre and called it Abrecan Castle.' She wove her hand furiously in the air while she said, 'Of course we all believed it, we all believe whatever he wants us to believe. Write it down,' she shouted.

Celeste jumped but it felt as if it was not her body, not her skin that had fled from her bones, though the heart hammering in her chest and the tongue cleaved to the top of her mouth were hers. She retched but taking a pencil and willing her hand to stop shaking she wrote it down while she howled inside.

'But Lodewick,' Tara continued, 'below the flat plateau where he had lifted the pentagram to, was tier on tier of stone and rock, like it had been punched through the planet from below. London is not here, that is not what I am saying, how could it be...but the handful of buildings that make the Hawksmoor Pentagram, are.' She stopped to rub at her forehead as if she were amazed at a sudden revelation before she said, 'It was like I had been lifted out of one place and time and put into another.'

Suddenly Tara gasped, and clawed at the air with one hand, as if her memories needed to be retrieved from an invisible breeze, while Celeste cried silently inside, and her vision blurred in and out of focus as she pretended to write down all that Tara said. Hot tears spotted the white paper, but still she continued, knowing that she had to humour her until she could get back to Ganaim's, to Dorothea, and Cissy, they would know what to do, if she could not get Tara to stop – Dorothea would know what to do.

'The people were the same, some of them, but they'd had their minds altered. They believed everything around them was true. They were completely wiped clean then filled with lies – but some of them were missing, including my Arthur.' Tara wiped at her eyes making them red rimmed while tears of grief and insanity rolled down her face.

'I don't know why, but when I shouted at them that something was very wrong, they looked at me as if I was mad, then took me to a rest room...Aindreas Sackeyfio came – he was a poet who collected ancient stories, but I digress – he came and explained,' she stopped suddenly and turned to Celeste, stared her full in the face with a black look that filled her eye sockets with shadow. 'Are you writing this down? It's important – don't you let me down.' She banged her hand on the side of her armchair. 'He, Aindreas Sackeyfio, was a poet, a collector of stories and things, sacred things, he told me...I don't know what he told me, I don't fully remember, but he was expecting it, he knew it would happen. His wife and he were on the lookout for people who retained their memories after the calamity, after that demon had taken the sword and invoked the ritual hidden in the Ars Notoria. If it was not for them…' she shuddered then whispered, 'They brought me here to safety.' Tara hit her forehead with the side of her hand curled into a tight fist. 'It's the thing about here though, something I don't remember' she gulped at the air and her eyes skittered in their sockets while she rocked back and forth. Then she brought her hand down hard on the arm of the chair and shouted, 'We've been lifted up the axis of reality.

Celeste dropped her pencil, but did not retrieve it off the floor, instead she slowly reached out her hand and retrieved a new one from the table. Her eyes never left the face of the mad woman before her.

'I know, I know it…not all of us, he couldn't bring all of us here. Abrecan was not that clever, he could only control those with the right DNA3, or the wrong DNA3, depending on how you look at these things. He only brought those with the taint…it's something to do with the…the…' she screwed her face up and made a grunting noise as if the memory would need to be birthed. As if the information was a painful thing to be brought into the light.

'It's the Ancient Law of Evil Sharing,' she shrieked with glee, 'but he doesn't understand what that is, the stupid demon doesn't know the full design, he does not see it, his very nature obscures what it really is, and now I can't remember what Aindreas told me.' She could hardly draw breath when she ran out of words and her hands shook and her lips trembled.

Celeste groaned quietly but sat still her breath held deep in her lungs. Muted by a strange sort of silence that had permeated her to her marrow like insidious fog, and as thoroughly saturated as Tara's madness had soaked her in its hysteria. She observed her Nana and supressed a shudder, bit down on the inside of her bottom lip, and groaned inside while she waited for the all too familiar.

'This!' Tara jumped to her feet and pointed to the ground. 'All of THIS isn't real, it's not real for us, not where we're supposed to be. The fire mouthed prophet was right. Apollon is right. We have fallen through the looking glass into a nightmare of his making…and anyone who remembers, he kills or adjusts. It is perfectly evil – don't you see the genius behind it?

'Even though I know the truth, which sometimes drips into his illusion like a leaky faucet, everyone around me thinks I'm as mad as a hatter.' She slumped back down and breathed deeply before she added in a voice hushed with fear,

'Well, not everyone. Not the Al Ti-' She cut off what she was going to say, then just as quickly as her madness had erupted it was over. She composed herself as she ran her fingers through her silver hair, patted it down absentmindedly then straightened her tunic. She looked calmly at Celeste. 'Did you get it all down, Celeste dear? Tomorrow I will go through all we have gathered, then we can make plans to go home. I know there is a way back.

'I have been practicing, honing my galactic power. You saw what I did with the false moon Leleth. If I can make something disappear then I can create something out of the fabric of the All-there-is. I know I can,' she said, and her words were full of determination and a resolve that crackled through the air. She met Celeste's gaze until Celeste dropped her eyes and pretended to scribble something on the paper.

'There will be a tree portal and the Nympts will help me if I can remain calm enough for them. They are very shy creatures – sensitive to human emotion. Now, stash the information.'

'I'll put it in the draw with the others, we need to keep it safe from prying eyes,' Celeste replied and heard the dead tone of her words fall flatly to the floor while she walked slowly to the adjoining kitchen. Then she opened a cupboard drawer in the large wooden dresser that Padrain had made. It was one of many drawers and cupboards already stuffed full of bits of folded paper, where she had written down all the ramblings of a mad woman, who she could not shut up.

There were notes about artists Tara knew, who did not really exist; many ramblings about a god called God; partial conspiracy theories that were treasonous and included everyone. His Divinity, most of the elite families were mentioned; even Padrain and Dorothea were included, who according to Tara, were in cahoots with creatures who were made of soil, horses that talked and collected information from the song of a place called the Ever-Was. They were spies, she said, and black magic that leaked from the Lake of Unum, took on the form of horrific creatures who worked for the devil. Butterflies communicating something she called the days of the week was completely new – the days of the week were Dali, Seli, Gamma, Kali, Alpha, Lima and Silio, not whatever nonsense Tara said they were. The Ancient Law of Evil Sharing was new too, the tainted stream she had mentioned only yesterday.

Celeste banged her hand gently against her head. Of all the madness, this has got to be the worst, but still it was all there, tucked away inside the huge wooden dresser, all of it completely outside the box. Every bit of paper, with every sentence scrawled in haste was a warrant for their deaths. All of it written in Celeste's own hand. She did not dare throw any of it out or burn it, in case Tara asked for it, but she never did, humouring her this way usually meant she calmed down and so Celeste acted her part and screamed silently while Tara spiralled further in her insanity.

She pushed the drawer shut and leaned against the dresser with a heavy sigh. She will forget about it again – it will not be long until she needs to sleep, Celeste thought. Then walking back into the studio, she said, 'Why don't I make tea, Nana? You go and put your feet up for a while, I'll shout when it's ready.' She placed her hand softly on her Nana's shoulder. Good the shaking is almost gone; her madness is leaving.

'You know, dear, I could do with a rest, I've been busy today…so busy.' She pointed to the walls.

'I see that, they're extraordinary. What are they, Nana?' Celeste asked gently.

'Why they are my interpretation of the flight path of butterflies, how they move from one flower to another, the patterns they make – it's their dance around the garden outside. Nature here is sentient and she is trying to tell me something – I've studied them since they first arrived in Solar Moon, round about Yellow Silio if I'm not mistaken.' She smiled and her face lit up, and she was beautiful, and gentle, and Celeste felt her chest heave with grief and her eyes fill with tears.

'Will you put a bit of meat out for the drake too? Make sure they eat it as there were rats in the outbuildings. They have gone now but best not encourage them to return.'

'Yes, Nana, I'll feed the drakes, and Ganaim was rat catching last night.' She soothed the older woman. 'What a beautiful way to fly!' Celeste said gently as she guided Tara from the room towards the kitchen and the sitting room beyond. She studied the band of painted words on her way out. They trailed without break, circling the walls of the room twice.

ThefirstDAYisMONDaythesecoNDisTuesDAYthethirdWEDNESdayTHursdAYtheNFRIDAYSATUrdaYthelastGODSdAySUNDday…BEwaREtheWizardontheWINDandDRagonFire. What new madness is that? Celeste thought while she glanced at the words and felt her world spiral once more towards madness and death.

Part Two

Lodewick

The Capitol of Baelmonarchia

CHAPTER THIRTEEN

An Act

The clouds hung so low, and the drizzle was so fine, Troy could have sworn he was only getting wet from the waist down. 'You, did it?' Micah said quietly. He kept his head lowered and his shoulders pulled up to his ears, while he and Troy meandered slowly down a dark alley towards the venue. It was just past dusk. Most citizens of Lodewick would be heading home before the curfew sirens sounded, apart from those with permits; and those without permits, or the good sense to be off the streets before the Protectorate Guard started their patrols.

The night promised to be rank with city stink, and clinging damp. They were three moons into the year of the Yellow Cosmic Seed, but it was the last day of the galactic cycle, it was Kinetic Two Hundred and Sixty, the day of the Yellow Cosmic Sun. Absolutely no one will be born today but a good day for Micah's event, Troy thought and studied his friend out of the corner of his eye. He looked well, different somehow, there was even an air of resignation that hung around him, almost tangible like an unpleasant smell. *I wonder if the threat of a spell at The Wind put his fire out*, he thought while he flapped his hand at a cloud of steam.

The Pipe regurgitated blasts of steam like an animal smouldering and belching poison from vents in the streets. The vents had been grated over with iron bars, which were slick with green and yellow slime. It was as if great metal mouths released fetid breaths of sulphur, and ammonia, which hung in the air like clouds filled with the promise of a fatal bout of yellow lung. There was another smell Troy could not place. *It is from his leather cloak* he thought while he studied Micah again. He wiped at his nose and followed at Micah's elbow. There was a tight feeling deep in his gut, a snarl of unease, which stopped him from settling his thoughts, Micah felt flat, as if there was something amiss. *Did something happen when he had to rehab in Eirini?* he wondered while he eyed the crown Micah wore. It was an exquisite piece, from one of the artisans who lived and worked around the Copa Nordende, the silk and textile district which also housed some of the most talented carpenters and cabinet makers. The antlers looked real and were set in carved wood that twisted like vines, small flowers carved from pearls and berries from semi-precious stones glistened like dew. Micah wore his hair loose, shiny waves of platinum cascaded like streamers of light to his shoulders. They all but hid the scrollwork of fine crystalline lights on his scalp. However, his face still twinkled like light on water when rivulets of jewel-like brilliance all around his eyes and temples, caught the sickly light from the marsh gas streetlamps. It was why he usually shaved his head apart from a long warrior tail at his crown. He was proud of his crystal markings; they were like diamonds and specks of gold. He was different, descended from something older, and more powerful than Abrecan, and he took a care to remind the dark lord of that.

'You look good, Micah, hair suits you.' Troy nodded to his friend.

'I know,' he agreed humbly. 'I need to make them believe I have emerged from my rehabilitation as something else. That I killed the Son of Sophia and stamped all over his rebellious nature.' He paused and thumbed to his chest then swept his hand over his clothes. 'This, he inclined his regally, 'is somebody new. Somebody we will not forget after tonight. But the data?'

'I have the data,' Troy patted his breeches pocket while a worried look creased his brow. Is he up to something he thought but said, 'He will kill me if he finds out – I doubt if even Leleth could stop him?' Troy fiddled with the Spider King eye mask he had pushed back on top of his head. Large arachnid eyes looked towards the dark muggy sky, black glassy lenses that reflected the water above them as it drizzled weakly down, coating everything in a layer of mist which only made Micah seem more ephemeral, and Fae-like, a beautiful creature from the realms of myth and magic, dusted with diamond dew and crystalline tears that luminesced like a borealis trapped beneath his skin.

Micah studied Troy and replied seriously, 'I don't believe they would kill you. You are far too precious,' he paused, then added quickly, 'To your mother. I think she may actually have developed feelings for you.'

Troy guffawed and rubbed an annoying drop of moisture off the tip of his nose. 'Feelings? Will you stop making me laugh.' Then he cursed the wet night. 'If I get any damper, I will not be able to get out of these damned breeches.' He pointed to tight leather breeches he wore.

Micah smirked and arched an eyebrow. 'If anyone sees you wearing them and walking with me, everyone will want a pair.'

'Seriously? Then let us hope every dung stinking Ostler and coal dusted Farrier is ready for the demand, as that is what they are,' he retorted dryly. He did not care about pleasing others or dressing to impress. The breeches had come with the Spider King jacket. He could swear it was for a much thinner man, someone like Micah.

'Costume looks good. You should wear tight breeches more often,' Micah said dryly. Troy harrumphed but let Micah continue. 'How did you do it then. Are you allowed to divulge trade secrets?'

'It was not easy. I stole an alchemical formula from Volsunga. I overheard him bragging about it at dinner. So, when they retired to the drawing room, I snuck into the room where he was staying for the night and copied it. It is ancient, for crafting something called a Passerine matrix. A thing that mimics-'

Micah interrupted him, 'I know what a passerine bird is. A mynah bird. I had one as a child and I taught it every word I knew for stick and slit. Do you want to hear some?'

Troy chortled. 'Not right now, we haven't got all night. Anyway, I used the Passerine Matrix to create a replica of their security system. It was like a blanket overlay, a sheet of blotting paper. Then I went in and retrieved my passerine and took the data it had copied with me.' He enjoyed the look of utter confusion on Micah's face. Crystal technology and some of the alchemical practices needed to programme the devices were beyond what Micah could do. Troy beamed proudly, sometimes it was hard being in the shadow of the sun, although mostly, he preferred it.

'It sounds impossible. So…' he let the word hang. He did not want to risk putting words into Troy's mouth. Whatever he said, had to come from him. He wanted him to discover for himself how The Shadow had taken hold and what they really were.

They stopped and hung further back into the shadows of the alley, hugging the shadows next to a leaning wall. The brickwork was running with moisture and streaked with mouldy growths. It stunk and Troy brought his hand to his mouth and took a breath from his cupped palm. There were Shroom Plates, large fungi growing out of the wet brickwork like steps that led nowhere. Eaves loomed high above, barely discernible through the dirty mist. The old but recently refurbed warehouse venue was just in sight across the cobbled road.

Troy's brow knotted and his shoulder hunched but he said hesitantly, 'They are definitely transmitting something from the dark moon, but I need to have a closer look, analyse the intel if I can.'

Micah nodded. 'I'll see what I can arrange.' Then he inclined his head towards the end of the alley. 'Hells, even their parties are a charade. It is all controlled, Troy. This should have happened last year before that stupid debacle – and, it should have been underground. In the Cheapside district proper, that is where the wave vibrations would have the most effect, not here.' he thumbed down the lane. 'They will have installed wave disruptors,' he said while he tapped at his wrist.

Troy nodded solemnly. 'I know. Light knows how we will disable the transmissions from the black moon if they are as bad as you say they are.'

Micah nodded thoughtfully then said, 'But we will keep trying. Let us just show up and get it over with. This will be an entirely safe and boring evening. We are several streets from the Snide, too close to the Temple of the Needful Scrip. Surveillance, disruptors, and patrols. Pah.' He spat and pointed a white skeletal finger to the warehouse. 'That was used for storing silks and fine cloth from the Southern Isles. It is hardly the grime, filth, and drama, I wanted. I wanted it down there. Right in the gullet of The Shambles.' Micah moaned while he pointed to the oily looking cobblestones.

Troy studied him through narrowed eyes. 'Seriously? Dry up, Micah. You've managed to launch it on kinetic two sixty, Yellow Cosmic Sun, an exceptionally good omen, especially for a creative project,' Troy replied shortly.

'Yes, you are right. Light, I am nervous, Troy. Tonight, is important for me. I suppose if you believe in the portents, then the galactic signature is perfect, but' he trailed off and screwed up his face while he thought, it is not what I wanted; I want to be far away from this night. How do I tell him? 'Oh, never mind, I am sure it will suffice.' He waved an elegant hand in the air, gold and silver bangles about his wrist chimed flatly.

'No buts, just be grateful we are actually here, and this is happening at all. We are fortunate we escaped a spell at The Wind that night…and how we got away with the Romarii is beyond me.' Troy stood further under the eaves. At least it is dry even though it stinks, fish guts, it must be the stink from the docks.

'Weasel must be losing his touch. Or he is storing what he does know for use, or sale, later,' Troy said dryly.

Micah nodded. 'You have to admire his mercenary soul. Can you imagine what he knows but has not shared because no one has thought to ask and enter into a transaction with him?'

Troy frowned. 'Perceptive of you, Micah.'

Micah smiled thinly. 'Some people are easier to read, easier to understand than others. You know, you should try putting yourself in his carefully considered shoes, you may discover something about yourself.'

~ ❋ ~ ❋ ~ ❋ ~

Whenever Troy thought about that night he broke out in a cold sweat. The Romarii woman had materialised silently out of the glittering dark just as Weasel sped away, leaving them in the outer zone called Tota. She ignored him which he hated but then again, he was used to being overlooked; it always happened when he was with Micah.

Her cloak reflected the evening perfectly, like it was made from the fabric of the night. He did not move but puffed his chest out, even though his nose throbbed and trickled with snotty blood, and his ribs made sharp but fleeting stabs of pain in his side that made him want to gasp, but he would not show weakness before her. She did not move around him but brushed past, catching him with her elbow, as if she knew a sharp jolt would hurt him.

Then she put her hand to Micah's heart. 'You agree to the terms of the trade, Lord of Galay?' Her voice was warm and dark with a thick foreign-sounding accent. He started to pay more attention then. It was earthy and powerful, with a hint of haughtiness, not at all like he had expected. She was arrogant, like the elite women in Lodewick who had real power, like his mother, Leleth. Unlike their perfect skeletal faces, she had an ugly slash mark across hers that travelled from her left eyebrow, across the bridge of her nose and down onto her right cheek where it had left the deepest scar, an uncomfortable-looking gouge marring her smooth red skin. Even marked like that he had found her attractive, a dangerous beauty, and hated himself for it. Light, I pity the poor sod who gave her that, he thought while he studied her, without looking her way. Her athletic build and confident manner, the way she had not acknowledged him but in doing so had taken in every detail of what he was, told him that she was military trained and held a position of command. He watched her eyes, never still, always searching the surrounding area, and listened to her talk in hushed tones to Micah while he thought, my first encounter with a Romarii...How did I expect her to be? Poor, downtrodden, gutter-filth, like I was taught?

'You know how far I have had to travel, and what it costs the one who brought me here?' She waited while Micah nodded then continued. 'This is not something we do lightly. We do this for your father, but there will be a price. Are you willing to pay it? You must be sure that you will enter that place.' Then she touched a place in the middle of her forehead. 'It has been seen in Silver Tower; therefore, it is so. On your heart you must make the vow,' she whispered huskily. Troy inched a little closer while he wondered just what kind of deal Micah had made.

'Yes, Ro, I agree it on my tri-fold heart which is mine to give.' She smiled but it held no joy; it was thin and hard. The deal was done. Her eyes glowed with orange-red fire as she presented Micah with two dud nanos then bowed slightly.

'Three times I ask if the conditions of the trade suit?' she said softly.

'Yes, yes and yes, they are agreed,' Micah almost sang his reply, although his head drooped, and he sounded sad.

The woman took a small throwing knife out from under her thick dark ponytail, where it had been hidden in a small scabbard at her neck. 'Blood?'

Micah nodded, and she closed the few steps between them quickly then untied his tunic, exposing his chest without taking her eyes from his. Something passed between them, a peculiar look that held a secret at its heart, and she lifted her chin to acknowledge the thing they held between them. Then, she pressed the tip of the blade quickly into the centre of his chest, drawing a short line of dark blood. He did not speak but Troy knew that it would have taken him by surprise. She had been quick with the blade; the small cut was no surface scratch and the first drops of blood soon turned into a thin rivulet that meandered down his body. She pressed the blade to her thumb, drawing an unequal few drops of blood, as a cruel knowing smile twisted across her mouth, then she pressed her thumb to his chest.

'Is it done?' Micah whispered and his eyes dilated, while his nostrils flared. Troy looked up and down the deserted street. The sign above the door squeaked when a light wind caught it, he jumped and hoped the Romarii woman had not seen him. *What are the lunatics doing? If guards come now...we are fish food.*

'My Lord of Galay.' She inclined her head. Micah nodded curtly in return, then she turned towards Troy, like a lioness stalking her prey, and met his gaze fully while she frowned and gazed deeply into his eye.

He thought the ground would swallow him whole, while his tongue stuck to the roof of his mouth, and he found himself paralysed beneath the weight of her gaze. She tutted and looked him up and down in such a way, he felt himself blush, embarrassed, that she had looked deeply into his core and found him lacking in something. What? He did not know and while the heat travelled from the roots of his hair to his feet, he lifted his lip into a sneer and did his best to stare her down.

Her eyes narrowed briefly to two shards of contempt while she tutted. 'Only time will tell the story of your days. Dark eyes, and light eyes, seek you for themselves, while clouds form around your fate the choices you must make roil and slither, nothing is yet decided, changer.' Her eyes narrowed to slits of fiery amber her skin feathered at the corners when she said, 'Masterless, you will be mastered, but who will it be?' Then without another word or a single look backwards, she turned and disappeared into the night.

'What?' Troy asked as he pointed in the direction she had taken. 'Is she going to the Willow Wilds? By the light, she must be mad.' He shuddered when he heard faint howls in the distance that only confirmed his suspicion. The outer zone Tota tumbled from the city and sprawled beneath the debris of broken bridges and aqueducts that ended abruptly on the edge of marshland that bordered the Willow Wilds. A dull thud, and a slight tremble set his teeth on edge. 'Another grenade,' he said to Micah accusingly. Then added, 'You have set the night afire.'

Micah bowed and said sardonically, 'Then I succeeded.'

He frowned. 'I hate it here, it's a bloody shithole,' he cursed and tensed his gut so tight he could almost feel his spine when two orbs sped overhead. He did not have to look; he knew when he heard their lasers burn and hiss through the air that the people in the outer zones were rioting too. There was a loud explosion and one of the orbs exploded and fell through the inky night, scratching at the sky like a comet. Bazooka he thought and changed the subject while he moved closer to the door. Then asked, 'Lord of Galay?'

'It's just their way. Leave it, we haven't the time, and we need to get you done first,' Micah replied impatiently while he pulled the bell chain that glinted dully in a niche next to the thick wooden door. Above them, a plaque with a pestle and mortar, and a dark snake entwined about a winged staff squeaked on rusty chains in the light wind. A light went on behind the frosty glass panel which turned it sickly and green, as the shadowy shape of a woman walked slowly towards the door.

'We were sent by—'

'Make haste. I am expecting you. This way please,' she replied, and her voice was filled with urgency. She turned and walked gracefully off into the depths of the room. Troy looked at Micah and raised his eyebrows.

'No idea,' Micah mouthed silently back.

I do not believe you, Troy thought but said, 'Will it be long? Weasel, you know?'

By the time Weasel found out Troy had fooled him and returned in a rage that put the fires in hell to shame, they were both standing innocently outside waiting for him. Micah pulled the bell chain a second time, while Troy wondered if he should just ask him if he knew, had he heard the Unit Commander say his scanner had registered someone as being outside the box. But he did not; he rubbed the incision at his elbow and followed the trail of aching pain where the apothecary had pushed the nano through his subcutaneous layer of fat; both ways. Out with the real one, then in with the dud. 'This way, you will pass an inspection, there will be no scar on your wrist, and the ointment will deal with signs of bruising, although you will feel pain deep within your flesh,' she said in a hushed voice while he balled his hand into a tight fist and prayed, he did not pass out. He caught Micah watching him gravely but did not know who the sorrow in his eye was for.

The scrid had a dent the size of a medium sized human in its roof. Troy smirked; it must have been uncomfortable for Weasel to drive. But he shouted instead, 'What the hell?' How are we going to open the doors? That is a pile of scrap! Light, to be in your shoes when you have to explain that.'

'Shut up, you spoilt little prick. Something fell out of the sky on to it, then rolled off into one of the storm drains,' Weasel replied in a voice that was taut with anxiety, but he still managed to bristle with anger. His heart had almost left his mouth, he was sure it would have if not for his immediate need and uncanny knack to survive the most bizarre of circumstances. He had not only crouched low in the seat, but his body had taken on an elasticity and speed that redefined what flesh, blood and bone could do. He had only just missed his head being caved in when he had pressed the button to move the driver's seat. Following that, instinct brought his hands to the spinning wheel, though he could not see anything from his prone position, he steadied the spinning and avoided a near fatal smash with a bridge, scraping the side of the scrid recklessly along the brickwork before he managed to right it. Around about the same time, he realised he was on a fool's errand to find the minstrel Leleth wanted.

Shortly after he had stopped shaking, a quick call to her confirmed it was for Troy. He was seething with rage but managed to say in a calm but tense voice, 'Troy, has changed his mind, my lady.'

Leleth did not reply, and he knew she had dismissed him. He studied the wreck while he pulled himself together. Then he reminded himself that at least it was Reynard's scrid, and he had escaped the toll the demon sleek, Velig the bloody butcher would have extracted from his hide. He was getting too old. His bones ached if the weather was wet, and his skin was getting too thin.

'Something fell out of the sky!' Troy guffawed and pulled him back from his memory.

Micah pulled the bell again. He stared into the small panel of frosted glass, no more than a viewing portal on the front of the door while he stifled his laughter and thought, the fire between them does not need further fuel.

Troy had had his nano replaced. It was only a small matter for him to put the other dud back in Weasel's pocket. He chipped away at Weasel while they made their way to a large table-come-counter at the far side of a room that was not unlike a harbourmaster's parlour. The tallow oil lamps were turned low, and a small coal fire crackled in the grate while it cast a nimbus of light and heat into a large open space in front of the hearth. The table stood before a door, covered with heavy drapes that led to the room the apothecary used for dispensing potions and extracting teeth and the like. It had several instruments on the wall that seemed more for torture than healing and smelled of pine and lavender.

It will not take much more prodding, Troy thought while he looked at Weasel's over-tense back and stiff shoulders, he is already fragile. He smirked wickedly and did not dare meet Micah's eye. That shell is about to crack.

'Something fell out of the sky, Reynard, honest, it did. I think the sky may be falling down.' Troy leaned on the table and whined in Weasel's ear, which was immediately followed by a shouting and shoving match that ended up as a wrestling bout on the hearth in front of the fire. Troy screamed when Weasel, frenzied with rage, wriggled from beneath him and taking him by the hair he pulled his head back and bit him hard on the chin while he shouted, 'Why waste my energy on breaking a nose that's already broken. Why waste my time fucking over a thrall.'

Micah watched the fight from a comfortable armchair before the fire with his feet pulled up to avoid the scuffle, and a wide grin across his mouth. If only they could get on, he thought, they would be extremely useful. Then with a loud sigh he grabbed them both by their collars and pulled them apart as if they weighed no more than children.

'I had to make it a convincing length of time,' he whispered to Troy, while Weasel made his way back to the table, smoothed himself down and glowered at Troy. 'You cur – enjoyed it, more like,' Troy accused him, while he rubbed his chin. 'Vicious little prick bit me like an animal would,' said Troy, while he took a seat.

Micah whispered, 'You underestimate him, at your peril, Troy.' Then he went to stand with Weasel while he talked to the olive-skinned woman who had let them in. She greeted him by name. 'Mr Weaselton.' Then asked casually, 'are you on Lord Abrecan or Mr Daboath's business.'

Weasel pulled a face, as if he had stood in fox entrails. 'Anuk's sake, woman, I don't run for that fool anymore. It's for Wyburn, Lord Abrecan's governor.'

She gazed into the middle distance, then looked directly at Troy while Weasel retrieved the dud nano from his pocket, and almost threw it across the counter. He continued to be rude, while she calmly ignored him. Troy's eyes slid away; but he raised his eyebrows quizzically. How interesting, Mr Daboath. Who is Mr Daboath? Micah sauntered over and grabbed him round the shoulders, pulling him back from his thoughts but not before he had stored the name, Daboath.

'It was funny. Seriously funny, I have never seen anything wriggle that fast. It was like his spine was made of snakes.' He smiled and said with mock seriousness, 'I wonder if he's rabid.' Then turned and said a little louder, 'I have never seen anything move that fast. He could have been in gentlemen's tournaments when he was younger.' Micah nodded towards Weasel who turned and although he looked surprised, he managed to smile at the unexpected compliment. Gentlemen's tournaments were anything but gentle.

Troy bristled. 'He could not be, he is a lower, good for a bout on the village green at Winter Begone or another peasant pursuit. Beltane Feast Day around the pole, or fuck the village pig, something like that. An earthenware cup, not a goblet of gold for him.' Troy sneered while he watched Weasel stiffen with rage.

Micah frowned, then turned from Troy, he would have no part in his silly baiting game. Then he walked towards Weasel but stopped halfway between them and turned and put his gaze on him, meeting him eye to eye. 'That's enough for this night,' he said with such weight to his words it hardly sounded like him at all.

He thinks he's Lord of Galay already, Troy fumed.

~ ❋ ~ ❋ ~ ❋ ~

Troy brought himself back from his reverie. He always defends Weasel, he thought sourly but said in hushed tones, 'You are on to something, Micah, but' he paused and blew air through clenched teeth. 'This is dangerous. The people involved. You know what they are like. How it is.'

Micah nodded. 'Yes, but we need to do something about this, Troy, and we are in the best positions to make the change. What did you find out?'

'I found the blueprint for the black moon. It is as you said, artificial.' He heard the fear and the disbelief in his voice, but even he could not deny what he had found. It was what it was. 'The crystal matrix Cronos uses to bring it into reality is state-of-the-art. I certainly did not learn the craft in the Institute of Alchemy and Crystal Craft. If I had known that this is what I was going to steal, I would never have set out to do it.' He whispered.

'I know,' Micah replied and squeezed his shoulder.

'How I managed to get it at all is nothing short of a miracle. I put the passerine matrix into the system, it shut down for a micro-second, if that, then I retrieved the data. I thought I would have to wait.' He shook his head while he waited for Micah to reply.

Micah retorted dryly, 'They really ought to be more careful.'

Troy scratched his head then rubbed at his neck; hard knots of muscle crunched under his fingers. It would play hell with him later, causing headaches and popping visions of colour and noise. They had become stronger since he had had the dud nano fitted, despite his attempts to modify it himself. 'Here, I put the data onto this.' He struggled to get his hand into his tight breeches pocket then handed Micah a dark obsidian pendant with a small star carved at the centre and seven diamonds set at irregular spaces in a silver mount around the edge. 'It's the Sky Sisters formation.'

'Did you copy or cut the data?' Micah asked softly while he turned the pendant over in his hands. If he took it all, then the Selgovae seer Solais Airgid ar Muir was right, and Rovander too. What did she call him? Changer. Light above he got into their crystal matrix as easily as he walked into the shop for that outfit. This is really happening he thought, while his heart flipped in his chest, and he does not really understand what he has just done.

'I took the whole lot, Micah, like you asked. But because I used the blotter' he made a patting movement with his hand. 'It left their system matrix there, but it will look like it crashed, and burned.' Troy replied haughtily. For once he felt like he had achieved something that Micah could not, and although he could not share how great he thought he was with anyone else, because that would get him killed, he was determined to crow about it to his friend.

'I asked if you would look into something for me, Troy, you on the other hand cannot keep your light fingers to yourself.'

They both laughed and Troy said, 'They must have something that keeps the moon manifestation substantial. A stabiliser of some kind.'

Micah frowned then said, 'Explain?'

'I would say, and this is only a guess, he is using some sort of geomagnetic device or two devices. The flux between them is keeping the moon manifest and stable. The device has to lock onto something large, like the planet and the holocast becomes real, if you like,' Troy waved his hand in the air, 'because enough people believe it to be true. There has to be a device, definitely.'

'Like two rings?' Micah asked gravely.

'That would work. One for the North Node the other for the South Node,' Troy replied while he studied his friend. 'Are you regretting being selected for The Glitterati, now?'

'We both know I did not have a choice, but even if I did, I doubt I would have followed you into alchemy and crystal craft,' Micah replied and pulled a face. 'This is very well made.' He ran the pendant through his fingers and held it towards the nimbus of light from the gas lamp. Then he brought his attention back to Troy and said, 'How in the hells do I get it off here?' Micah put it around his neck, pushing it into his open tunic which was as transparent as a cloud and hardly worth wearing, but he had been told to wear it, and because he was newly reformed, he had. The pendant rested low down, against his skinny pale chest, which had been decorated with henna tattoos of trailing vines and a perma-tatt of a tri-fold heart design in the centre of his sternum. Delicate filigrees of crystalline light scintillated beneath his skin and followed the trailing vines as if they had been kissed with dew.

'Blind man at Cheapside docks. It was the right crystal combination, obsidian, and quartz, which is all I am saying. What are they?' Troy pointed a gloved finger to the tattoos.

Micah dipped his head and hid his surprise. Light, Yalan gave him the pendant to store the data on. I do not know who pulls which string anymore, and Troy? He does not even know he is being used. Afterwards, I hope my father can help him. He lifted his head and studied Troy while he replied, 'I'm supposed to be Oberon, The Faerie King. It was Bucky's idea to give a royal finger to Abrecan, small as it is, Bucky's still fuming that he had to hand over a whole library at Ninmah so the Sisterhood of Bloodgita can establish their temple there and had promise to open the ruined Guratt's in the rural zones. All my fault,' he said in a hushed voice while he pushed aside a stab of guilt.

'These tatts are supposed to be evocative of elemental realms, you know, natural like the kingdom of Oberon was,' he pointed to the woodland vines then thumbed towards the end of the alley. 'Not like this wasteland, a ruin which will probably be the death of me.'

Troy spoke in a quiet tone when he said, 'I miss the Winter Lands. That Romarii was right, one day, you will be the Lord of Galay.' Troy tried to reassure Micah even though they both knew the chances of that happening were becoming remoter as Lord Abrecan tried to establish his own man on the throne at Galay.

Micah shrugged then said thoughtfully, 'And the Sun in Winter will rise.' He continued, 'This,' he pointed proudly at the heart, 'is a tri-fold…a Gaiadon heart, I had it done recently.'

'I like it,' Troy replied.

'I hope everyone does,' he said while he indicated the gathering crowds outside of the venue. 'Time for me to meet my obligations,' he finished sourly. 'Later,' he said, and slouched elegantly away.

'See you at the door,' Troy whispered to Micah's back while he pulled his spider eyes over his face. He cursed when he stumbled then took them off and wiped the dewy drizzle off the lens. He turned and walked quietly in the opposite direction, blending into the shadows – invisible, all crystal boxes and eyes were focussed on the newly re-habilitated Micah Apollon. A gasp escaped the crowd and a wave of media pushed forward, held back by thick red rope and even thicker necked security.

'Micah…Lord Apollon…this way, this way…over here…What are you? Who is your alter ego this time? Does this mean the Son of Sophia is dead?

Following last year's mental breakdown, did you feel the need to reinvent? Did you kill the Son of Sophia?'

~ ✻ ~ ✻ ~ ✻ ~

Troy waited silently for Micah near the entrance. The dark jacket he wore was a little too tight under the arms, it had bones sewn along the front panels. They were like real ribs but painted gold. Green jewelled eggs rested between them, like clusters of spider eggs. He shifted from one foot to the other, the leather breeches were sweaty, and the dark leather boots he wore squeaked, but he knew he looked shadowy. He grimaced; he quite liked the idea of looking shadowy. He had taken as much care on his appearance as he could, he wanted to look as elegant as Micah did, and he had put his hair back in a single plait; though some hair had escaped, and it framed his face like black wings. He had considered using his mother's cosmetics but could not find any that were like what Micah wore, so he left them where they were, but he had painted his nails with black lacquer which had already chipped. He chewed at his thumb and removed some more. He was on edge. Stealing had seemed such an adventure. Uncovering Volsunga and Abrecan, showing them as the villains they were, but it was only afterwards he had realised he did not know anyone more powerful than they. He took a layer of black gloss off his little fingernail in one go. Then folded his hands under his arms, they were shaking. He took his attention to the crowd and studied them intently, anything but think about what he had just done. He had put on a show for Micah, all the swagger of a successful thief, when really, he knew if he were caught, he would be hung, drawn, and quartered. He was not like Micah; he did not have Bucky to protect him.

'Micah! Sign…here…Micah.' Micah swaggered over and asked, 'Why?'

'It's worth more if it's signed…I got an orig…before it was pulled…you know, last year…know it off by heart.' She thrust the silver disc at him.

He glanced casually at it. It was one of the state-produced copies that the entertainment bureau had released when he was rehabilitating at his father's castle in Eirini Zone. The frequency of the tones used in the song, and the power of the incantation had been disrupted on the orders of Lord Abrecan, who on hearing the vibration had vowed to kill him, he was not sure how Bucky had stopped him, the establishment of the Temples seemed too meagre a punishment, though Bucky had been furious.

She does not even know. It will not matter how many times she sings along to it now; its effect has gone. It was all for nothing. We will never free them, and they are all going to die. 'Tell me what it's about,' he asked coldly, staring down at her. She was young and inelegant, but very pretty. She was too buxom to be elite, who were insect thin by design, and competition, with one another. She was not rural either, not scrawny enough. Far from home and too well fed. Domestic class, he thought, eating her fill of what was left from the wasteful tables of the elite. He continued to look into her large delicate brown eyes and hoped to see some glimmer of knowledge that she understood the message in his songs. Why am I troubled by her? He narrowed his eyes. Her top lip was dewed with sweat, and while he watched it seemed that something was slipping beneath her skin, or the skin itself moved, it was never still. Light above, he thought, is this it? Is this the thing they sent for me? A shifter-assassin? Surely not, he frowned and stared even harder.

Suddenly flustered, she blushed furiously. He smiled, he found it utterly compelling while he noticed her hot sweat condense in the cleft of her breasts. He continued to scrutinise her. He ate her with his eyes and wanted to remember this moment for as long as he lived. Her life rhythm was not held in blood and bone, no it was something else, oily, and slinking beneath a skin that could take on any shape the Rodinian wished for. I will miss Gaiadon he thought and licked his lips.

The girl fought to control an urge to run. She felt troubled; there was something not right about him. His presence was overwhelming, oppressive like the heat from the centre of a thunderstorm. The air was charged with an unnatural energy that emanated from him in waves, and his eyes were a vacuum, they held nothing warm, not like Lord Bucky's did. Only cold contempt while he peeled away layer after layer of her being.

She gulped. He can see right through me. Light! He is looking for what I am. He knows. I could be in danger. She gulped again. The tension hurt her throat and she resisted the urge to wipe away the sweat that was building up under her hair. I should have tied it up, I don't care if it's how scullions and servers wear it, it's sticking to my neck and making me even hotter. Hells, how do I get away from him, she thought, while she turned her head slightly, looking for her friend, only to be greeted by a wall of people…listening…waiting. She stared at them. Her eyes flickered to the back of the pack. Then, she took a gulp of air and turned to face Micah again. Will he kill me before a crowd? She did not have time to answer her own question and was glad when he hissed, 'Well?'

'I, er, well, I err…it's about your life…isn't it?'

He looked deflated when he took the disc case from her. Gently, he opened it and made an elaborate show of a simple enough action, while he thought, why hasn't the shifter killed me? What is it waiting for? I did not think they would work for the shadow, surely, they are creatures of a lighter consciousness. He pushed his manic thoughts to one side with a grunt, and whipped a small knife out of his sleeve, licked his lips and smiled as he looked at the corpulent shelf of glistening coffee coloured flesh and sighed.

It happened so quickly; those fans who were close enough to see, gasped in horror as the blade flashed down. A wicked smile cracked across his mouth while he pressed the disk firmly on to her chest, pushed its hard, silver surface into her yielding flesh then scratched across it – VEIL SLAVE WAKE UP.

The crowd retreated a step. Horror had made jaws drop and eyes pop, while Micah leaned closer to her. He put his arm around the back of her shoulders and drew her towards him. Lifting her hair to one side with his hand, he paused briefly to feel the back of her neck. Her hot sweat slipped like oil, and he rubbed it between his cold dry fingers. Such life he thought while he stooped and found her ear, then he whispered in a voice wrung dry with urgency, 'It's about your life, isn't it?' Suddenly, he released her, turned towards the door, and strode off while she fumbled to catch the falling knife. The silver disc remained glued with sweat to her chest.

The crowd of elites folded behind Micah like a wave of flesh while he stomped towards the entrance with fire in his eyes. The press, eager for something, rushed to the girl, who had been caught by her friend. 'What did he say, what did he write? Veil Slave? It says VEIL SLAVE…It's his new alter…it's his ne—' The circus of people chirruped.

The girl regained her feet. She felt stupid and ready to throw the disc as far away from her as possible. She felt sullied, touched by something unpleasant which she could not put her finger on. It was the strangest experience, as if they were both waiting for the other person to make the first move, for the other one to deliver the killing blow. Her resolve hardened as she pushed angrily past the crowd and grabbed her friend. She dragged her along and whispered, 'We need to get out of here, now. There is something wrong with him. Lord Apollon is not quite himself and I, feel out of sorts myself.'

'What do you mean? Not quite himself?' Her friend took her arm and slowed her down while they walked away from the venue, and over the street towards the small alley Troy and Micah had previously occupied. They stopped at the entrance to the alley, under the glowing nimbus of a streetlamp that sputtered and hissed softly, the marsh gas smelled brackish and raw, but they hardly noticed it. It was just another stench to add to an already stinking city.

'Light, Tranquillity, he felt wrong…how can I say it – flat. Like his light had been doused. His hand was freezing cold but felt like it burned, here, have a look.' Homily lifted her hair. 'It was horrible. His eyes seemed empty of soul. You know I am not one to scare easily, but that took me by surprise, and a smell, something I know, something unusual, but, I have come across it before.' She shuddered and pointed towards the venue. 'What in the hells is wrong with him?'

Tranquillity looked under Homily's hair, even in the poorly lit alley she could see how bad it was, it was red raw like it had been exposed to wind chill. 'We should head back to the outer, get some ice or some heat, I'm not sure what. It looks wind burned, or blistered; not sure which under this poor light…what do you say?' She squeezed her friend's hands between her own.

'No, not our base zone, Tranquil, we'll go back to our quarters at his, we need to be quick with the information we have gathered. Lord Bucky ain't in residence in the city just now, he is at Autumn Hill, making ready for the carnival at Ninmah. We should give the nightcrawlers a miss, there will be other times, eh? How many spies did you see? I spotted Rodney Weaselton behind the crowd while that freak was stripping me naked with his dead eyes.'

Tranquillity lowered her voice and said, 'Hydra the Cup selling hot pies to the crowd, looking like a grandmother; Eschamali Zuben on the door, hardly disguised, but I detected a sonic disruptor set on low; I was sure Alcyone Sun was there disguised as an Elite, sporting a Mirror galactic signature and her electric whip, but I did not see any others from The Ten. I missed Rodney Weaselton completely. You did well, Hom – Weaselton is a slippery bastard.' Tranquillity hugged her friend and kissed her softly on the forehead.

'Don't know who that elite shit is.' Homily tossed her head towards the entrance of the venue at Troy; even though his eye mask was down, she knew he was staring at them. She gave him the finger and stuck her tongue out. Then linked Homily and they turned away. She hoped that ice would cool the blistered flesh and that her friend would stop trembling by the time they walked back to Bucky's city residence.

*

'Are you sick, poor bitch thought you were going to slash her,' Troy said angrily.

'And thank you for waiting for me, friend. It's for show,' Micah said bitterly. All of this is for show,' he paused then drew a long deep draught of air before letting it out slowly, 'Even she was,' he said in a voice that full of ire, but he dropped his gaze and would not meet Troy eye to eye.

Troy set his mouth in a hard line. For show he thought while he took in the scene that Micah had created. It would get them skinned alive, he just knew it would, but he still followed his friend as he made his way up seven steps covered in fine red carpet and waited while Micah sat down on a gilt throne. The throne was huge and had a large crown at the apex of its elaborately carved backrest. Furs of the ancient royal line of Galay, snow leopard, winter fox, silver night wolf glistening like hoarfrost and brilliant white ermine, were casually strewn over it as if they had no more value than tissue paper.

Troy gulped and hissed, 'The only difference between us and those dead animal hides is they were dead when they lost theirs. Abrecan will bloody skin us alive.'

Micah turned slightly but would not meet his gaze, instead he whispered, 'Will you just enjoy the act, Troy. You are in danger of becoming a wet blanket not a valuable hide.'

He had never felt more like kicking Micah up the arse, but instead he gritted his teeth and followed in his wake. He gawped while the security guard opened one massive door. The crowd gasped as it swung into place; the dais and throne were dwarfed before it and painted on the interior of the door was the crest of a bright yellow-gold sun, rising. Its rays shafted through a midnight blue background, which was full of stars and planets fading gradually towards the celestial horizon. There was no mistaking who rode the deep red dragon that curved along the crest of the sun as if it were a corona of fire. It was Micah. Fingers of flame cascaded like red, orange, and gold rain from the dragon's mouth. Micah wore armour of platinum and gold but rather than a helmet, he wore a crown. Exactly like the one he has on now Troy thought and felt his insides turn to jelly while he dropped his head to hide his frown when they ascended the final steps.

In the image, the City of Lodewick lay in smoking ruins below the might of Micah and the dragon he rode. It was obvious from the painting that the message he projected was that he was The Overtone Sun. To Micah's left, the West, Troy supposed, a golden dragon flew in the distance, spouting shafts of light; to his right, a black dragon spouted stars, and small galaxies, and at the bottom of the image a river ran silver-blue, and its current was the back of a gigantic sea serpent. He had seen the four dragons before though that did not make him feel any better, it only reinforced the tight ball of dread that the snarl of his guts had turned into. Their carved wooden heads were the finials on top of his four-post bed. He even knew one of their names. The black dragon was Taluthaar. The name had been carved onto one of its ear barbs by the craftsman who had rendered its image long ago. It was common enough knowledge that there was a mythical black dragon. There was even an isle called Taluthaar's Barren Isle, faraway at the other end of the world, but what Micah had done was something more than a lesson in mythology. He had crowned himself King, and rode a dragon made of fire above the desolation of Lodewick.

He tore his attention away from the image and took it to the other door which remained closed, its external surface carved with a multi-pointed star, like that of a compass. "Pakanga Te Hiki, Silk Road and Spices from the Southern Isles" trailed faintly about the perimeter of the star in faded black, almost charcoal script; an equally faded golden banner had been painted across the star. Each end of the banner was wrapped about a large red tower; in it was written: "Wairua Tuatoru Motu."

Troy took his attention to the guard on the door. He had a pleased look on his face while Micah sat on the throne beneath his own idol. 'Stand at my right and slightly behind,' he whispered to Troy and beckoned regally with his hand.

'I, fucking, hate, you,' Troy whispered back through clenched teeth, but took his place anyway. His eye mask was still firmly in place, and he knew that he would not be easily recognised, but the stunt Micah had pulled would be the talk of Lodewick for moons to come. He put his hand on the back of the throne and leant forward, one hand rested confidently on his chin, as if he were giving advice on the crowd as they filed past. 'Was it for them?' he hissed indignantly. 'Is that what they like, your public suicide? Is that what you have to do to keep them happy? What are you up to?'

Micah ignored him while he waved at the crowd of elites, with a thin smile frozen on his face, and a noble nod of the head. This will send Abrecan catatonic with rage, one last delicious dig before I go, he thought and turned his head slightly towards Troy and said, 'None of it is real. It is all an illusion. It is not just my sovereignty that he has stolen, it is everybody's.'

Troy ground his teeth and wondered if he would get away with punching him in the head, but he knew without looking that the huge guard had not taken his eyes off them. He made sure his spider eyes were firmly in place and lowered his head before he said, 'I know what this looks like. Spider King, at your right-hand side. I swear I will kill you if Abrecan does not get there first. You madman.'

Micah leaned towards Troy and whispered, 'Will you lower your voice and play your part?'

'When are you going to drop this flesh-circus, expose them, like you did with the nano device?' Troy whispered as he tried to calm down. He did not usually feel anything towards the lower status humans who served them. They were invisible mostly, but what Micah had done to the girl disturbed him; it was beyond cruel. It reminded him of his Uncle Abrecan. Although, he would have cut her head off and harvested her stem cells too. As for Micah involving him in yet another debacle. He shuddered with the effort to control an urge to tip him off the throne.

'There's Srondall Smite…doing airwave broadcasting? I thought she had her own show?' He diverted his own and Micah's attention to Srondall, who scowled darkly at the gilt throne, then thinking better of it, she narrowed her eyes and tossed her head back while she called over a man carrying a portable crystal box and began pointing out the crowd, then Micah seated on the throne, then the backdrop behind him.

She gave them a look that would burn the fires of hell into submission, and he felt a growl rumble in the back of his throat, while he feigned interest in what Micah was saying. She will end us, he thought and tried to keep his eye on her while a stream of elites entered the venue. They bowed and simpered to Micah who lapped it up. Light, I need to get that recording crystal out of that box before it is beamed across all Baelmonarchia, and our sorry souls are flying from a mast at The Wind.

'Srondall is a bitch.' Micah hissed out of the side of his mouth while he continued to beam at the crowd. 'She lost her show then took an injunction out on me. I only tried to apologise, she said I had ruined her career…then she said I tried to molest her…a slight misunderstanding, she used to be a lot easier to get on with. Anyway, I should try to be careful now, Troy. I'm screwed if I have to do another rehabilitation. I certainly won't be allowed to languish in my misery at Bucky's castle in Eirini.'

Troy shook his head, and coughed into his fist while he said, 'More careful? This charade is a death wish.' He pulled himself upright while Micah blew a kiss to a group of young men dressed as Eagle galactic signatures. They wore leather kilts in bronze and gold, hard military boots, and had large bronze and gold wings strapped to their back, held by leather harnesses that crossed over muscular smooth chests that were slick with drizzle. They bowed back and a few used small pulleys on the harness to flutter their wings. Micah puckered his lips at them and winked while he said to Troy in a hushed voice. 'They'll say rehab is clearly not working and I'm only fit for proper correction. Only Bucky saved my ass from the wind last time. Besides, if I exposed this lot, there would be nobody attending this event. Everyone here is hungry for a bit of fame, a little taste of the allowed underground. So, I have given them it.' Micah watched as the last of the elite youth entered the venue. Brightly dressed men, and woman, with planets in their hair and about their clothes. 'Skywalkers,' he said dryly but forced a smile for them. 'It is all fake,' he sighed imperceptibly, but Troy caught the sudden shift in his act and the wave of sadness that coursed through the air.

He knows he will not escape without punishment, lords above I am watching my friend commit suicide he thought. Then said, 'They all look like gigantic plebs if you ask me. I include myself in that too.' He thumbed at his own costume even though his mind was racing. How can we get out of our immediate arrests and imminent correction at The Wind? Steal the recording crystal, buy off Srondall Smite, manipulate the influencers in the crowd, paint over the idolatry, burn the warehouse. Impossible he thought, while a surge of bile cramped his stomach into a knot of fear.

Micah rose from the throne, and before he knew it, he had fallen in behind him, while Micah flashed his enigmatic smile at door security. 'Thank the Light. My fuck off to Abrecan is done. Now, I need wine,' Micah said softly while he blew out of the side of his mouth. 'Just follow my lead, Troy.'

'Nano scan,' a gruff voice commanded.

'What for?' Troy asked before he could stop himself. Micah tensed and raised his eyebrow at him but held his tongue.

'You know who he is, it's his gig for Anuk's sake.'

'Sure, here.' Micah held his wrist out and whispered, 'What did I just say, just do as I do, Troy. It is fine, I need to be seen having my nano scanned. The Bureau insisted on it.' Crystal boxes flashed in agreement.

'And you?' The huge security guard, growled. His dark skin shone like it was made of some sort of resin that had been chiselled and angled over bone. He had deep-set indigo eyes with a shimmering cast to the lens like a creature from the deep. He stared dispassionately at them as if they were a pair of minnows. A mane of black and silver hair, dreadlocked and twisted like galleon rope, hung about his face, some were tied with a leather thong behind. It looked heavy; Troy doubted if he would be able to carry it as he stared past him into the half distance while he read the sign on the door again. The security guard remained solidly emotionless while he ran a scanner lazily over Troy's wrist. The tail of a bright red dragon etched on his skin and implanted with small jewels, twisted around his index finger, and disappeared into the cuff of his coat.

'Lord Micah Apollon and Troy Valoroso-Wyburn,' he said their names a syllable at a time, as if he were showing a child how to do its letters. Troy resisted the urge to laugh and bit his tongue instead. You can go too far with folk like that and not realise you had until your nose was broken in two places, he thought.

Micah replied, 'The last time I looked, I was the Lord Bucky's favourite bastard, Lord Apollon, if you please.' He bowed with a flourish then said, 'Although it is hard to keep up with oneself…one of these days I am quite sure I will be in danger of disappearing up my own arse, but only if I can get past the hordes on their knees hell-bent on kissing it first.'

'Ha. He makes jest.' The guard laughed roughly but cut it short. Then growled, 'No trouble here tonight.' He pointed his tattooed finger at each of them in turn.

Troy felt a shiver of threat pass through him in a frigid wave; he was glad that he had kept his eye mask in place. The guard put him on edge, not in a tight gut sort of way but in the way the threat of lightning did. It was a build-up of something, an intangible force waiting to be felt.

Chapter Fourteen

Why Would Weasel

Weasel watched while Micah and Troy slipped away from the warehouse, exactly on the midnight hour, riding away from the carnage they had created on the back of Kinetic One, Red Magnetic Dragon. It was the beginning of a new galactic cycle and the first energy just happened to fall on the day of the dead. Not a good omen Weasel thought and ran his finger around his collar. Apollon had made his appearance and put on a show, just like he was expected to, but had he gone too far? Probably, Weasel thought dryly while he wondered how they would kill him. They had informants everywhere. Although, while he doubted that the spy-eyes in the eaves above the warehouse worked, he did not doubt that Abrecan already knew what had happened. He was only glad that there were no live transmissions from the event. He had hidden himself in the yard knowing that they would sneak out the back. There was a sea of people still trying to get in and several gangs of guild apprentices had shown up too, most notably the apprentices from the Elleadern Weatende. The night, he decided with a sigh, was as explosive as the surface of the sun, but then again, it always was when Micah was around. Not that he had wanted to be here personally, but there were some people you did not refuse when they called in a favour.

'Like I said, wearing a crown and a huge idol behind him, riding a dragon. Valoroso dressed as Spider King standing at his right-hand side, next to a throne covered in winter furs...' Weasel spoke in a hushed voice into the wafer-thin, crystal device in his hand. 'I know what it looked like. The Lord of Galay and his Hand, Spider King. He may even kill Valoroso yet, depends on whether he can make another.' He nodded while the voice on the other end spoke.

'Yes, for a price, I could do that for you. It is a tinder box in there. They had boles of silk hanging from the ceiling like pennants, mountains of cushions, and a lake of alcohol, no doubt,' he said and pulled a disgusted face. He hated the excesses of the elite.

He waited with one hand bunched into a tight fist and a knot of fear in his gut, still hidden behind the barrels and wooden crates stacked near the warehouse wall. He was still trying to keep his anger in check, and wondered how Yalan Daboath had gotten hold of his private sequence, never mind access to his brand new mo; worse still, the small screen had flashed, *Incoming, His Lord D.*

He had thought briefly about ignoring the call, but greed and a love of his sneaky little life had persuaded him otherwise. 'That will suffice.' He hid his surprise at the considerable number of creds Yalan was going to pay for the job. 'Anyway, they have left.' He waited then replied, 'Just now. Yes. I sold him the Aurora, you supplied me…errm…I imagine Nightcrawlers. It is The Night of The Dead in case you forgot…Yes. They will go. They were dressed for it, it's what the young do.' He finished with an irritated tone to his voice. He had never celebrated anything in his life. Yes, he had felt a sense of completion at a job well done, but he certainly did not get himself dressed up like an imbecile, and drink, or droge waere himself into oblivion. He sighed when he realised, he had never felt young. He had never been young, he was sure he had been born old and knowing, cynical, and hungry for power.

'No. I can't go,' he hissed in disgust at the assumption that he would attend such a filthy gathering. 'I've repaid my debt, Yalan. I will torch the warehouse and get the recording off Smite, then that is it. No more – I'm out.' He made to end the call then stopped. 'You are not serious, flowers! Where to? Right, that is it – after this job, it is the finish – and do not remind me of what you did for me, it is years ago, ancient history.'

He paused while the other person continued. His forehead creased into a bunch of knots above his brow, while he glowered at the night and pressed the mo to his ear. Fuck, fuck, fuck he thought while his hand clenched, and his knuckles shone like hard white moons against the otherwise pale pink flesh of his hand. 'Right. Consider it done,' he snapped, then ended the call while the finger of his free hand ran round the mandarin collar of his shirt. It felt damp despite the chill, and he groaned, not at the expense of replacing it but at the behaviour the sudden call had initiated. Though, he knew he could not tolerate a dirty neck and he could only stand the best fabrics against his skin. It was good cream cotton, spun so fine it was like silk, but softer, and cooler. He wore it beneath a deep maroon jacket and well-cut trousers in the same colour. He waited until his skin settled. It always felt like it was crawling over his bones, when he had any dealings with Yalan he thought, while he itched gently at his neck. The dark purple scar was unusually hot and tight. Then he straightened his suit and stepped carefully from his hiding place behind the barrels and crates. Struggling to remain focussed and in a fit of spiteful pique, he dropped the mo and crushed it beneath the heel of his handmade boots. The silicon and clear quartz crystal sounded like ice cracking in the silence of the yard. The dull thud of music and raucous voices echoed dully, muffled by the walls of the warehouse. After standing for what felt like eternity, his nostrils flaring against the chill night air, and his breath misting in delicate curls, he gathered his thoughts and made additional plans to move his special things from the place he had found along one of the paths inside the stone compass. He thought it was a secret place, an ancient village, no more than ruins, but it obviously was not. Yalan knew about it, and he was the last person he needed going through his things.

Satisfied, he picked up the pieces of the mo and deposited them in a small bag he retrieved from his leather satchel. 'Go there?' he spat. 'I will be bloody well sacrificed if Abrecan finds out I'm here talking to him, never mind enjoying myself with the Nightcrawlers,' he muttered under his breath while he rubbed furiously at his implant. He did another quick check of the delivery yard for spy-eyes; there were none. His breath felt ragged in his chest, and he was sure his movements were being monitored. He ran his hand through his long fringe of strawberry blonde hair, then paced back and forth, and chewed nervously on the side of his thumb. His head twitched involuntarily while he flicked his fringe like an anxious horse tossing its mane. Grateful for the privacy to let his anxiousness run its course he took gulps of chilly air. Lords above knew he could not put his emotions on display at The Fifth Tower. Sometimes he regretted his decision to work for either party, but it was a small regret that lasted no more than a moment, and his anxiousness soon subsided, while he began to plan. 'Damn,' he hissed as he patted his leather bag. I should have used that mo for this, he thought while he retrieved another mo from his satchel and pressed his thumb into the transducer.

'Ah yes, good eve...I mean morning. I need to order some flowers for delivery to Baelmonarchia.' He stood against the chilly wall and rested the back of his head against the brick while he studied the black moon.

His thoughts drifted while he waited. 'Why?' he moaned before he could stop himself. Out of all the people who could have found him, why would it be Yalan Daboath? He could not shake him, nor did he dare try to kill him; it was impossible anyway. Yalan turned up like a seasonal virus; just when you thought you would not catch it, there it was – it had been waiting, watching, ready to take advantage of your weak moment.

I am being paranoid, he thought, it was for the money, plain and simple – he had a never-ending supply of creds, a mountain of gold and crollar that would have had the Matriarch of The Temple of The Needful Scrip wetting her pants, and he paid extremely well. Though, deep inside, he knew it was not really for the coin.

Weasel was a whoreson and although it seemed as if his pretty, young mother, distributed sexual favours for money, she did not. It was the power, and like her son, she was hell-bent on using what she had to climb as far as she could. The one pregnancy, and subsequent babe she decided to keep to full-term was her strategic attempt to get out of the inn called The Buttered Leg, which was a whorehouse at Wolfsea Crossing. Her plan to escape had ended successfully, but unfortunately, with her death.

'Yes, they must be those particular flowers and half a dozen crates if you would…I am aware of the price, it will not pose a problem. Are you able to meet the delivery date?' Weasel waited while the person on the other end of the line went to check on stock.

Why Daboath? I wanted to make something more of myself, he thought and felt an uncomfortable prickle in the corner of his eye. He had been thinking more about his beginnings lately. It was always an uncomfortable memory, one where he tried to find love, and a sense of belonging but found nothing but a resolute determination that his mother's fate would not be his own. It had been a hard climb from the whorehouse at Wolfsea Crossing. Then to the desolate shores of the Flat Lands, where he stole a mule from one of the mining towns and made his way to Rubric Volsunga, and the screeching horror of the correctional colony, The Wind. He rubbed at his forehead and massaged his eyes, but he would never shift the memories, he had buried them under a mountain of other horrors instead. 'Yes, I'll hold.'

~ ❖ ~ ❖ ~ ❖ ~

He shuddered, he disliked recalling when he had been captured by Roma Rangers, but the memory of being stripped to the waist, tied to a tree on the cliffs overlooking Wolfsea Bay, and whipped until their Captain, Rovander, had almost flayed the skin from his back, was a constant companion.

He had kept his mouth shut; he was a dead man anyway. Shut apart from his cries of agony which the spring wind tore from his mouth and cast out to sea, just another fire drake screeching, until they grew bored and left him to die strung up in the sea cave below the cliffs.

They should have cut his throat, but they did not realise he had an uncanny knack of surviving. Driven by greed, he knew where the real power lay, he knew if he survived, he was closer than he had ever been of securing a place within the hallowed circles of the Elite of Lodewick, and commanding fees he had only ever dreamed of before. Dreams of selling himself, and the information he had gathered, to the highest bidder kept him going. The Romarii had their own men, and women, in place at The Wind. How and where? He did not know. While the water in the cave tried to leech his life away, and the salt from the cold sea washed like acid over his exposed flesh, he repeated to himself, while he imagined walking up golden steps of power, to sit upon a throne of purest white crystal; Volsunga first, then Reynard Wyburn, then His Divinity the Lord Lucas Abrecan. Volsunga first…

Weasel did not believe in the One-God Anuk, his brethren or any of the forbidden religions at that time. Weasel believed only in himself, and the evil men do. Now, it was different. Now, he knew that evil was incarnate, a demon calling itself a God, and even if he wanted out, it would be with a bite to the neck and his brains served pumping and raw to whatever abomination Volsunga and Matriarch Smite was working on at the Temple of The Saviour's Salve. He had no desire to let any of them know what he had inside his skull, so he kept his secrets hidden under a mountain of thoughts, and actions, which would thwart the worst interrogator Volsunga could throw at him. It was something Velig had told him when he tortured him the first time. The time when he had stuck his chest out and lifted his chin defiantly, while he kept his mind clear, and his mouth closed. Surely, the stupid demon knew he had survived The Romarii? Velig no longer looked like a demon. He was rumoured to be hundreds of years old, but regularly ate another victim and was an expert in evolving. Velig the Butcher was a slightly overweight man with a too small nose, and metal rimmed optics that gave him an owlish and wise look while he broke his thumb with a mallet, then said, 'They think that by keeping their minds blank that they are thwarting the interrogation. Better to not expend the energy it takes to keep a mind clear unless you have set the protective wall there with a spell. Keep your mind busy with daily dross if you want to hide what you are really about. You, I think, are a cunt. Feel free to correct me if I am wrong.'

Did he believe in fate? He had come close that day when Yalan, the bumbling fool, had stumbled upon him. Harsh weather had driven his boat off course. Weather which was beginning to push the swell of the spring tide to record levels, levels that the Romarii bitch knew would drown him, towards the cave where he was hanging on for his dear, desperate, corrupt life. A fortuitous encounter at the time, but now. Now, he found himself between the devil and death with no way out, so he played his part and looked for his escape route, constantly.

Yalan had been in a small skiff, which had lost its sail. It was at the mercy of the spring tides and the changing currents that pushed furiously into Wolfsea Bay from the Dark Sea to the north. A churlish wind swept Yalan into the cave like an apple bobbing on top of rapids. He was soaked to the skin but seemed to be bereft of any protective clothing and wore what could only be described as swim wear. A full-piece bathing suit that cut off above his knees and at his wrists; it was made of seal skin and a tight-fitting swim cap of the same shiny silver material that fastened under his chin which made his head seem too large and bulbous for his scrawny exposed neck. He still had a wooden pipe clamped firmly between his lips. His dark optics looked like googling seal eyes and were still pulled firmly over his own eyes while he struggled to row the tiny boat to safety.

Weasel had shouted weakly, no more than an inhuman croak. 'Man ho, over here.' He had started to cry as Yalan manoeuvred the boat towards him.

Yalan did not flinch nor comment when he cut Weasel, who looked like a skinned salmon, loose from his leather manacles and noose. He grunted an apology when he tumbled through his arms into the boat and landed with a thud.

How had he managed it? Weasel did not like to imagine; it was better if he did not. He had seemed too weak and stupid to have survived himself, let alone rescue another. He regained consciousness slowly, brought back to the surface of reality by screeching pain that tore about his body like claws raking flesh from bone, and the foul stench of a pipe that was desperately burning too-damp tobacco. He reluctantly left a dream where he was walking through hell to save a golden eagle whose feathers were on fire. Groaning, he found himself wrapped in rough blankets, loose around his back, in the foetal position on top of coils of rope that at least saved him from the bilge water in the bottom. Sharp waves rose from the black water, their curling tops illuminated silver-white, the air was crisp, and every star looked down upon them from the deep blue velveteen dome of the sky. The oars were at rest and Yalan had hoisted a small sail.

'A spare, the other was blown away,' he explained as he sat puffing away on his pipe at the tiller. 'Fortunate for you, young sir, that I was out here searching for the Ningen Chief. Alas, I lacked a Selgovae, and my expedition has been fruitless.'

Later, Weasel devoured damp rye bread and gulped weak wine Yalan had retrieved from a leather sack tied to the mast. Yalan studied Weasel shrewdly, then muttered, 'There is no mistaking where you are from.'

Weasel frowned, his strawberry hair and the odd smattering of crystal light, like metal freckles, no more than that, and not visible – thank the Light – marked him as being from Wolfsea Crossing as easily as if he had signed its name on his forehead. He knew that Ningen were a mythological race of sea giants, who lived beneath the icy waters of the Dark Sea. Weasel thought he had been saved by a madman. Ningen? A horror story that was common in Wolfsea Crossing; parents told it to children to keep them away from dark water and from messing about on the shores of Wolf Bay at night – a myth, nothing more, and that fool was out there in a rowboat looking for them. He must have been storm tossed hundreds of miles from the Dark Sea into Wolf Bay, then dragged by the current into the cave where he hung. How fortuitous, he had thought at the time.

He suggested getting to the shore then moving east from the cave, overland towards the mining zone where he knew he could get a message to Lord Rubric Volsunga faster, but much to his chagrin, Yalan had insisted on sailing his boat to the garrison town, Wolfsea Crossing, where they sought aid from the local quack, dried out at an inn, which Weasel thought only marginally better than a flop house, and not more than two dirty streets away from The Buttered Leg whorehouse where he had been born. The quack was the inn keep and mouth surgeon too. He was a large man with a round belly and shining head. Although the inn left a lot to be desired, it was as clean as most inns were in the country, and certainly cleaner than the rest of the inns in the town. Outside, a sign swung above the door, a regal image of Lord Bucky with a crown like the rays of the sun atop his head. Benevolent Bucky was the name of the inn. A fitting name for an establishment just over the water from the Palace Galay.

Yalan watched with interest as the inn keep sewed what he could of the ripped skin and tissue back onto Weasel's back.

'Salts kept it clean, otherwise we would be considering mercy,' he said to Yalan.

Weasel half-shouted, half-croaked, 'You will not kill me, you bloody oaf. I have to live; I have to survive this.'

Yalan studied him thoughtfully then nodded to the inn keep, while he said, 'Do what you can, never mind the cost. Use the salve.' He pointed to an earthenware jar on the chest next to the pallet bed while Weasel vowed, 'I will never return to this shithole, do you hear me, if it's the last thing I ever do – never. Not unless I am at the head of a fucking royal procession in my honour, where I am named as his right Royal Highness the Lord and cunt of the Palace Galay. Are you listening, old man?'

'Now there is a wish desperate to be spoken.' Yalan smiled sardonically while Weasel raised his eyes to the dirty ceiling and cursed his luck.

The inn keep said, 'Best be careful what you wish for, lad.'

But Weasel did not hear. Instead, he bit down on a filthy rag while the Innkeeper threaded his needle, before he sewed the last ragged piece of skin into place. The inn keep marvelled at how the youth, obviously close to death's door, was still conscious enough to be so vitriolic, but then he reasoned it was a hot fuel that kept a person going, long after it was necessary, or even safe to be conscious. He shrugged when Weasel finally succumbed and passed out. Yalan caught him and lay him on his side on the rough mattress. 'I can only thank the heavens, at last, he is silent.'

The inn keeper blew air from his cheeks and replied, 'Aye, you can say that again – what an unpleasant prick.'

Following his survival, he made his report to Lord Rubric Volsunga who had given him the recommendations he needed, then he had begun to do the odd contract for Fox Enterprises. The city suited him. Weasel by name and nature, he had gained a reputation for being very discreet but vicious in the execution of his duty, leaving no trails behind, and not afraid to get his hands dirty with whatever stain was required – whether it be poison, blade, or, and it was only the one time, laser.

He turned and pressed his forehead against the cool damp wall, then gave the name and address for delivery, pressed the nano implanted in his wrist against the receiver on his mo, heard the whirr on the line as the machine prepared to take payment for the flowers. 'No. Not personal debit, use my Fox account.' It will get lost in the multitude of expenses that run through the system he thought while he replied to the voice on the other end.

'How in the hells…why would I keep getting myself indebted to him, bumbler yes, but still more dangerous than Abrecan and Reynard put together. Soonest opportunity I get, I am off this godforsaken rock. Ningen! By the Light, the madman was right. They were real.'

~ ❋ ~ ❋ ~ ❋ ~

Their large white heads had risen like a swarm of moons above the dark water. He thought they were moonlit crests on curled waves at first, although the wind had long since stopped chopping at the surface of the sea. Deep-set circular eyes studied them intently. There were set like spheres of shiny black jade inside elaborate frills and barbs that moved back and forth like fish gills. Alabaster flesh, tufted ears high on their heads and elongated snouts, were all he could see above the waves. One approached the skiff, and its head was at least twice its size.

Yalan hid him under a blanket while he talked to them in a bubbling sort of voice, snatches of conversation he heard and understood, as if they found it difficult to speak the common tongue to Yalan. 'Do not insult us by trying to speak our language. You are not Selgovae. We cannot move without them, nor without the Novantae to meet us there,' the Ningen rumbled. 'We will send a scout to Lodewick and wait for our own prophecies to be fulfilled when the time is right. Solas Nua Novantae is to come again. He will be the sun that rises in the west. Where is the Sun in Winter, why is he not on the throne at Galay?' the gigantic creature hissed and bubbled. 'You must send for our Selgovae, blind man. The Witch Queen, Mordeana, knows of their whereabouts.'

Yalan mumbled loudly, 'I will try Puaka. I give my word.'

Weasel hated himself for being as terrified as he was, but they were the scary monsters from the tales he had been told as a child. Puaka sniffed the skiff. 'You carry interesting cargo, Yalan. It smells of fresh blood, and yet, faintly of the winter sun, but it is not that. Besides, it is almost carrion.'

Weasel met Yalan's eye with his own and his plea was plain, *spare me*, it said. Yalan studied him for another moment which felt longer than the moon took to wander through its twenty-eight houses.

'Anything,' he croaked.

Yalan inclined his head in a short nod. A strange energy filled the air, then something passed between them that caught Weasel right in the centre of his shallow, shifty chest.

That was the moment I sold my soul he thought, while he pushed the memory away and sighed deeply. That was the moment he had me. He was going to throw me to the Ningen or have me in his pocket. 'One gulp, which was all it would have taken, and it would have been over for me,' he whispered while he punched lightly on the wall with one hand while he pushed the mo back into his satchel with the other. Then he slid quietly out of the yard, keeping close to the wall of the warehouse. He slunk away in the opposite direction from the entrance to get some incendiary devices. A couple of stickle-bug bombs ought to be enough to take the warehouse down, especially with all that fabric inside; one on the obscenity Apollon had had painted on the door, the other where the alcohol was. Better make it three he thought and smacked his lips together when a sudden well of saliva surged like expectation into his mouth. He enjoyed blowing things up. It was the stealth, and the precise placing of the devices, then the thrill of getting out. Sometimes, he left it so that he made it out just in time. More often he waited just outside of the blast zone and let the flaming debris fall at his feet. Powerful, untouchable, even if it was only for a short while. The tantalising memory of the thrill sustained him, especially when he had to knuckle his forehead, protect his neck, and bend his back like a serf before those who would call themselves masters.

Chapter Fifteen

Here Be Nightcrawlers

Micah led the way along the dirty streets and filthy alleys of the Seegda Seed, avoiding Proc Patrols with all the slink and cunning of an old rat. They hugged the shadows, and were strangely quiet, afraid that any words they uttered would be tainted and sour, while they crept along the tiers of Lodewick, then made their way down onto the Snide, and across towards the headland. At the headland end of the Snide, Hol district sat like a festering sore. Dilapidated buildings had fallen into ruin, skeletal frames and fallen walls revealed the caves, quarries, and pits of sunken rock behind their facades. They ran with dark water as if the stone that made up the tiers of Lodewick wept inky mineral tears. They spirited past disused warehouses and along broken streets where shifty people wove in and out of the shadowed wasteland, some were even making their way to the tribal. The night had turned chill, and their breath purled from their noses while the icy air caught sharply in their chests. It was Micah who broke the silence. 'Can we just forget about the silk warehouse?'

Troy shrugged then said with a certainty in his voice that froze Micah's marrow. 'Yes, if you want, but I know there is something you aren't telling me.'

Micah stopped and took his arm. There was something hard, something dead in his gaze. 'I can't, Troy.'

'Can't or won't? You do not have to protect me. I can keep a secret,' he replied gravely, and studied his friend while he forced aside his growing sense of unease. Micah felt his nerve waver, but he gulped a mouthful of air and replied, 'I know, but in this matter, I need you to trust me.'

Troy hesitated then scrutinised his friend as if it were going to be for the last time. 'Another act?' he asked harshly then regretted it when he saw sorrow lance through Micah and pain set behind his eyes, as if he had already betrayed him.

Micah broke their gaze and turned from him, then spoke lightly while he stared into the middle distance. 'Yes, I suppose it is.' His voice held such a note of finality that Troy took him by the arm. He waited until he met him eye to eye before he said, 'We should just turn round, right now, and go home.' He tapped at the pendant on his chest. 'I will put it all back. They will never know I took it.' He knew when he finished speaking that it was too late for that. Too late for them both.

Micah removed the pendant and ran it though his fingers, then he slipped it into his breeches pocket. 'No,' he whispered, and the word was hoarse with emotion. They had started something that they could not stop, and they both knew it. Micah tilted his head to one side and said, 'Have you heard of the Dagger Path? It is what the people seeking the Silver Tower walk. It's a journey here, and here.' He tapped at the centre of his head, and then his heart.

Troy nodded and replied with a note of interest, 'I have read about it and seen the white-eyed mendicants begging along the Snide. But they are just beggars swapping false prophecy and fortunes for food. I am surprised Abrecan does not have them killed. Why?'

'Because that is what we are on, right now. Don't you feel it?' He put his arm around Troy's shoulder, and they walked further into the night. Micah changed his tone and lifted the mood. 'You know, they say that when you are separated on the Dagger Path, then if it is meant to be, you will meet those you love again.'

Troy exhaled; his steamy breath was full of relief. He replied, 'And tonight, where does our Dagger Path lead.'

'Tonight,' Micah paused for dramatic effect, 'We are going to a slaughterhouse.' Before he could protest Micah added, 'It's abandoned. It is an illegal tribal. The Ten are holo-manifesting using crystals to collect thought patterns and wave vibrations. I want it to be, you know…' he trailed off. Leaving fantastic, unsaid, but hanging in the air like a glittering promise.

'I know,' Troy replied and wondered how long he would be taken away for this time.

The last time he had rebelled, Bucky had taken him to his Castle Gairdin in Eirini. Micah was forbidden visitors or contact with anyone for an entire year. Bucky would not let him be corrected at The Wind and had enforced his solitary punishment rigorously and had bought Micah's penance with a temple for the Sisters of Bloodgita and a promise to reopen the Guratt's, but he would have to do something more to appease Lord Abrecan this time. Micah had crowned himself King, not just any old king, but the King of the Fae, and the young Elites of Lodewick had flaunted their Galactic Signature power, even though it was a pale imitation of what it should have been. Then, they had bent the knee and bowed before the Sun in Winter.

He will lose Galay to one of Abrecan's men Troy thought and felt a wave of fear creep along his spine. He pushed it away, but he will manoeuvre his way out of it, he always does he reassured himself. They were on the Dagger Path, not a couple of scullery's strolling in a park he reminded himself sharply and was almost glad when the old slaughterhouse came into sight.

He read the cracked and flaked sign above the door and a sense of unease dried his mouth so that he could not swallow or say another word. A strange feeling like the pull of lodestone on iron pushed through the air and a sensation of huge wings, beating, almost stopped his heart.

The sign said, Athanasius Blood. Purveyor of Meat.

He put his hand on Micah's arm and met his gaze fully. Studying the pit at the centre of his eye he waited until he saw the flash of something bigger than them both in its depths.

'Follow me?' Micah said, and the words rang through the night, clear as a bell, a question, and a command.

~ ❖ ~ ❖ ~ ❖ ~

'Who's on tonight?' Micah asked the dead bride who stood just inside the old wooden door. She was giving advice and directions to stragglers.

'We've got The Ten here tonight and supporting artists from across the realm…it will be a long one, so pick your floors carefully, some of the holo-cast experiences can be quite dark.' She paused and tilted her head thoughtfully. Troy got the impression that she was scrutinising him, that her warning was directed for his ears. He bristled but held his tongue, even when she turned her head towards him and said, 'You should be prepared for that, be prepared to hold your fear in check lest you create something unpalatable with the vibration of your thoughts and feelings.'

He wanted to tell her he knew all about that, that he had studied alchemy and crystal craft at the finest university in Baelmonarchia, but she turned away sharply, tutted loudly at two men, then rattled a tin a quarter full of coin.

The men were overly interested in the dullest of things. Pointing to the smooth thick walls and the windows set high in them, marking the exits and the stairs. While he watched, their heads came together in heated discussion. Their faces were covered with elaborate sugar-skull decorations, and they did not walk, they strutted, agile as mountain cats, heads together, one had his arm about the other who laughed uproariously, then said, 'Light Abhhain, this city stinks worse than the mire.'

They wore shiny stovepipe hats that were pulled down over pointed ears but still they did not hide the silver-green skin on their necks which was the colour of seals and the green-grey shade of water when it absorbed shafts of light and lost them in its depths. Colours found in wild oceans, and skies to the north. Troy studied them from the corner of his eye while deep in his gut a strange feeling gnawed, then grew a mouth and a voice. *Go home*, it said but he pushed it aside. This was the Night of The Dead, a night not to be missed, it was supposed to feel edgy and dangerous. Only the old or the infirm would sit before the embered hearth and wait for sleep to come.

From Wolfsea? he thought while he eyed the men from the corner of his eye but then recalled that the people from Wolfsea had smatterings of crystal light, like scales. When they were dull, they were like freckles, like Weasel has he thought. Beneath their elaborate face paint, he knew their skin was smooth, while he marvelled at their Night of The Dead costumes. They made him, and Micah, seem poorly dressed. They wore lined velvet cloaks above tailed jackets in dark wool with shiny skull buttons. Smart breeches were tucked inside long riding boots, gloved hands carried shiny black canes topped with silver skulls that looked more like fighting staffs than walking sticks. They are like any other person here, and though his thoughts seemed reasonable; they did not stop the sense of unease he felt when his stomach squeezed tight against his spine. The one called Abhhain turned his way and caught him looking, he smiled, but there was something set hard as stone in the set of his face and a calculating look in the pit of his eye that had his inner voice shouting a warning. Troy inclined his head by way of greeting and was the first to pull his gaze away and was glad to turn his attention to Micah. The sugar-skulls stopped and bowed their heads and dropped their coin into the tin. 'Where should we position ourselves?'

The bride replied in a hushed voice, 'I need you to keep the way clear to The Wilds, Moin. Once it is done, we need to be out quickly and away from here, and with the child,' she whispered. The man named Moin nodded once then hissed, 'I want to go back to the point we entered by. The exact one mind you. It's bloody unnatural.'

She agreed dryly. 'I am aware of that.'

Abhhain took her hand and squeezed it then said, 'Look on the bright side lass, at least you'll forget your night with the new head.'

Troy steeled himself, he hardly dared breathe and wondered when the fight would start. Even though Dead Bride wore a veil, she had an air about her that sparked and crackled like dry wood full of pockets of resin, there was something incendiary about her, a short fuse atop a bucket of fuel. Besides, he realised, they would hardly put a wilting weed on the door, not here.

Instead of the thump Troy expected, she guffawed and said, 'Aye, there is that after all. Now off you go, not a moment more than necessary will I spend in this hell-spawn pit.' The men nodded and moved away gracefully.

She studied Micah for a second too long then said, 'Top floor, below the spice attics, Markab Storm and Homam Wind.' She pointed to a bunch of revellers dressed in dark clothes and said with a note of caution, 'More to their tastes, I think.' They wore thick trousers made of small squares of dark leather; muted colours, in shades of grey and brown, a patchwork of animal suede, joined together with tiny circles of metal that shone like the best Solais steel. Even the short jerkins they wore over their woollen tunics, were laminated leather, like breastplates, and they walked as if they had arrived from a far-off battle. They sported feathers in their hair, eagle, and nighthawk, which they wore in long crests, even the women. Their facial tattoos, although delicate, were arcane and inked in black.

Their breeches are wet to the knee. They have come over water Troy thought and realised with a lurch that they were from The Shanty. She ushered the Shanty tribe away to her left and up some stone stairs with a flap of her hands and a final instruction. 'Remember to mark the exits. Choose your experience carefully, this is the night of the dead, and be prepared if you have to leave suddenly.' She folded her arms over her chest and sighed. She knew they would take no heed of her.

'Well, aren't you the lively one.' Micah laughed. 'Who else dear dead bride?'

She sniffed disdainfully. 'Homan and Markab are alternating with El Nath Night and Alcyone Sun.'

'Alcyone Sun?' Micah looked puzzled.

'Yes, it is an unusual combination, but we need her to bring in the dawn up there. El Nath Night will be no good for that. He will collect the shadow and negative patterns.'

Once more Troy felt as if she was talking to him. 'If you should have anything you need to let go of, and the light knows there will be plenty of that to do in this shadow-spawn hell.' She grimaced and looked like she was about to spit. Her thin lips were painted black like she had died, and kohl had been painted, then smudged around her too bright eyes. They narrowed and took the measure of Troy and Micah. Then she said, 'Alcyone will create more than one of the dawns. She will float between floors if you're desperate to experience her set, and I recommend that you do. She is attempting a mass consciousness acceleration.' She looked briefly at their wrists her then continued. 'Just look for an incredibly tall woman who shines with shafts of light, coming off small mirrors fastened about her clothes.'

Micah interrupted her. 'Do you think they will get the consciousness shift they need.'

She paused and sighed. 'I do not know. All we can do is try. It has to start somewhere.' She reached over the counter and touched his hand. 'Last year was a beginning. Now? We must keep going.' Something passed between them, and Micah tensed his jaw before replying. 'That is the thing, I suppose. A small wave, sometimes, it becomes the tsunami.'

'I pray it is so,' she replied gravely then turned to Troy and said, 'Himalia Skywalker is casting an alchemical set.'

'I would like that,' he replied and was glad that he had somewhere to begin.

'I know,' she said softly, and though he should have been worried that she did know, instead he heard sorrow and something else in her voice, something that sounded like resignation.

She turned to Micah and continued. 'Middle is Hydra the Cup, Acumen Sting and Alnilam Seed,' she paused and nodded to a small girl who had appeared behind them. 'Next floor up Vye, they're expecting you. I'll get you out afterwards.' The girl nodded and pushed between Micah and Troy. She placed her hand on the bride's arm. 'Thank you for offering to take me.' The bride fluttered her hand at her as if to shush her away. 'It is no-'

Troy cut her off. 'Gods above what are you doing here?' he sputtered while Micah looked on puzzled. 'It's the violin girl from that night…the night at the studio.' Micah shook his head; his eyes were dull and filled with confusion.

'Not that it's got anything to do with you two fuck ups,' she replied angrily, her dark eyes narrowed to slits. She wore face decorations layered in frills like those around a dragon's eyes and they glittered in gold and green. She was more elaborately scaled than Micah but beneath the glitter and paint there were deep shadows in the hollows beneath her eyes. Testament to sleepless nights, sudden change, and too much sorrow. 'I'm playing a set with Hydra the Cup,' she retorted proudly and removed a thin violin from where it was strapped across her back like a longbow. Four strings stretched across a bridge, taught from neck to base, the bow was shorter and hung from a scabbard at her waist like a stiletto, just hidden beneath a sparkling minstrels coat of deepest green velvet, lined with golden silk. Violet's cloak was boned like a corset, and when it opened it would resemble dragon wings, her costume beneath was scaled and tight to her small body as if she were a dragon whelp. 'I will be suspended from a vine trapeze created by Alnilam Seed, while Hydra and Acumen Sting fight it off beneath me. Snake versus Scorpion is the experience they will provide. They will harvest any memories people have associated with any fights or acts of violence they witnessed or were told about as the holo-cast progresses. Anyway, I should be asking what the fuck are you two doing here? How come they let 'you' out – screw-up.' She looked Micah up and down, her face contorted with rage. The jewels around her eyes threw off scintillant beams of light. Her tail of black hair swung back and forth like a scorpion's stinger.

'For lights sake Micah, this is the violin player who had to go on…after you sliced yourself up.' Troy spat at him while he thought what in the hells is wrong with him. 'I think we should just go Micah,' Troy said and put his hand on Micah's arm to lead him away, outside, then home. The dead bride paused momentarily, a minute stiffening across her body, followed by a wave of tension, which she covered quickly and rattled the tin at another bunch of late comers. Maidens dressed as Marama Rawa, one or two had painted themselves blue, one wore almost next to nothing beneath her dark cloak.

Micah gave a start and put his arm about Troy's shoulders. 'What? Light, no. I cannot leave.' He squeezed Troy's arm and pulled himself upright with effort before focussing on Violet. 'Yes of course it is you, I apologise, Viola, I hope it didn't scare you too much?' he waggled his hand in the air.

'Scare me? What is left of my family will never recover from Abrecan's interrogation.' She held up her tiny hand when Micah gawped at the air as if he were going to say something. 'We were professional musicians,' she looked down her nose at him and sniffed. 'Highly thought of minstrels, and in demand.' She brought herself to stand in front of Micah, and dead bride laid a hand on her shoulder, gently, while she stood on her toes and hissed, 'We played at the tables of the rich, many times at Abrecan Castle, but still, he thought we were spies. Despite the threat of the poet's curse, Velig the butcher killed my father to make us confess to a crime we knew nothing of. Then Abrecan changed his mind about the charge just as I was about to lose my fingers, and cast us out of the dungeons, stripped us of our permits and our livelihood. They took my mother's left hand and two fingers from her right. Shortly after we were released, she threw herself from the highest bluff into the Ophiuchus.' She gulped at air, then rasped, 'And that is why I'm here…now piss off out of my way. There is a revolution happening, you pair of blind idiots.' There were no tears, she had cried herself dry many moons ago. She spat vitriol at their feet. Just like a baby dragon Troy thought.

Then she said as she turned, 'That cloak absolutely stinks of the fish wharf.' Then she shrugged the bride's arm from her shoulder and pushed past, rigid with hatred.

The bride said pointedly to Micah as Violet disappeared. 'We all have sacrifices to make this night.'

As if she had uttered a spell Micah suddenly regained his common sense and bobbed his head stiffly. 'You may inform them; I am prepared.'

She lowered her gaze and said in a tone heavy with resignation. 'My Lord.'

Micah met her gaze fully and something secret passed between them, then Micah turned and stomped off down a dark tunnel into the bowels of the warehouse, his stinking leather cloak flapping behind like a pair of tattered wings.

Troy watched his friend depart and felt a mantle of dread settle upon his shoulders. He turned to Dead Bride, but she met his gaze with a look full of fire and said in a tight voice, 'The Nightcrawl waits for no one. You, had better go and meet it full on.'

~ ✦ ~ ✦ ~ ✦ ~

Troy trailed after Micah like a shadow chasing the sun. Meat hooks beckoned like clawed fingers, chains and pulleys tortured and contorted with age were suspended from the lofty ceilings. Rusted in place, they smelled of oxide and metal decaying, and glistened wetly while blood-red iron dripped like fat oily rain from the edge of a storm. Below, heat from bodies full of blood and brine evaporated, and condensation from a thousand mouths rose. The smell of blood, like slaughter and murder, was stained across the walls and the floors, its essence ingrained greasily in the fabric of the air while an animal spirit in the shadows watched, and waited, hungry to see if the Night of The Dead would earn its name justly, while Micah Apollon, King of Nothing, soared into the dark.

Troy caught up with him and put his hand on his shoulder. 'Wait,' he said and wanted to say more but the words would not come.

Micah sensed he was troubled, stopped and turned. He looked set to say something else then shook his head and let something hard set inside him. 'I value your friendship above everything I have Troy. You are a good person, inside where it matters.' He pointed to Troy's heart and searched his face, his seafoam-green eyes were no longer dull and flat but were keen and shrewd. They shone like a predator in the dark, suddenly clear of the fog that had come and gone all night with his skewing mood. The scaling about his brow and temples scintillated like the smallest points of gold and burnished copper; distant stars caught under his skin which glowed like the chest of a song thrush in summer. Light trailed away in scrolls and symbols that said something in a language that no one knew or understood anymore. He smiled lopsided and adjusted his crown, then wiped absently at a film of dewy moisture on his top lip. He rubbed it between his fingers then frowned.

Troy studied Miach while he wondered what he was doing. Even his sweat seems blessed. Micah is golden, he thought, while I am not. 'Above everything? Even Galay?' Troy asked and narrowed his eyes; their lids were heavy with worry and the gnawing sensation in his gut was full of anxiety.

'Even Galay.' Micah half-laughed and the wisdom behind his eyes was a dull light which said that all hope of Galay had gone. He put his hand on Troy's arm. 'Let him have it. He will find it more trouble than it is worth. It will take more than his pox ridden garrison at Wolfsea Crossing to manage the Winter Lands and the folk who live there.'

Troy curled his top lip into a wry acknowledgment; he knew how wild, and free, the folk in the Winter Lands were. Then he replied, 'I didn't think you would give Galay up so easily.'

'I haven't,' Micah replied, and a determined look settled on his face and relit a fire in the pit of his eye. He caught Troy by the arm and met his gaze fully before he said, 'I am only just beginning. Now, let us just go and enjoy the holo-manifestations. See what we can conjure out of the dark.' He let Troy's arm go and tapped the side of his head.

Troy heard the plea in Micah's voice but held his gaze, and his tongue, while he nodded once more and pushed a building sense of unease away.

'I have to look for someone, if we get separated, I will call you.' He waved his translucent mo at Troy. Then said, 'Remember,' he emphasised the word, 'Be good, and mark the exits.'

Troy replied gravely but with a smile and a mock knuckle of his forehead. 'I am a thief, my Lord of Galay, I always know where the exits are.'

Micah snorted and hurried off into the night with a last word over his shoulder. 'Come look for me, Troy. When the time is right.'

Troy took the other direction towards Himalia Skywalker. He did not want Micah to think he was following him or was acting like his keeper. Although that is exactly what he wanted to do. Instead, he walked into a low-lying cloud of hazy sweat. Droplets of perspiration coloured like blood, pattered from the rusted machinery strewn across the ceiling. Organic movement like the heave of the ocean carried him further into the night as crowded bodies shifted together fluidly, a single thing in the dark, massive, and of one consciousness. Troy went with them. I will join my will to the body of the beast he thought.

The night unfolded in pulses of light and waves of flesh, maidens dressed as the Witch Queen, Mordeana Never Dead, rattled their gold bangles and twirled chains seductively on their fingers, chains which hung from pierced ears, eyebrows, noses, and navels. Their costumes in part, were gossamer thin, though a waistcoat of thicker cloth, cut low, and tight, about pert high chests. Troy grinned and fell in with their steps and circling moves. They thronged to his bug-eyed Spider King and took him by the hands. He swung one of them round by the waist. 'Who is it?' he shouted into her ear.

'It's Himalia Skywalker.'

At least I found her he thought, while he put the maiden back on her feet. She pointed to the woman with the flat black crystal matrix that hovered before her, an oblong of night that thrummed with a luminant potentiality, a dream waiting to explode into existence. 'Wait until she moves, she is a giant,' she shouted. Then spun quickly away, a scented cloud of sweaty fluidity that moved like an enchantment across the dancefloor.

Himalia Skywalker was visible from the waist up. The rest of her body was submerged in a pool of liquid light. A projection she had cast with her matrix. It appeared as if she floated in the dark, disembodied below. She moved her hands over the crystal matrix and wave after wave of sonic vibration cascaded through the air like a song that spun thoughts and feelings into shape and form.

Suddenly, Troy felt something heavy leave his chest. He watched while his hatred was torn away; like a black cloud being burned off the face of the world by the blistering eye of a quicksilver sun. He cursed himself for a fool. Why did I begin with an emo-psych he worried? Then watched with his jaw hanging loose while Himalia lifted the dark and bared the fear within. 'All brought to the light,' she whispered, and her voice sounded as if it came from all around while streamers of dark oily matter entered her matrix and were evaporated. Troy rubbed the condensation from his optics. At lease I did not begin with El Nath Night. This I can cope with, he thought while he patted his chest, it felt light, but fragile as porcelain and he knew that a kind of calcination had taken place.

Time danced on; spiralling away into a future they could not see, though they created it with every movement they made. No action they took, lacked a distant consequence that layered heavily onto a reality yet to be lived, and the first galactic signature made its power felt in fire and flame. Kinetic One, Red Magnetic Dragon, was spun into existence by Himalia Skywalker. It roared above their heads in hot clouds of billowing purple smoke, and tongues of curled flame, which flicked and lashed in green and red when they roiled like anarchy along the ceiling. The dragon slithered above illuminating rows of large meat hooks that suddenly became claws hungry for flesh, chains and pulleys arranged to look like the enormous, wedged head, of the great red and gold beast angled starkly as the holo-cast followed their line.

Following the dragon holo-cast there was a moment of complete silence and pitch dark. The crowd were thrust into a nowhere space where they became insubstantial as feathers; weightless, while Himalia Skywalker changed the vibration. Troy felt his tongue stick to the roof of his mouth then it filled with the tang of copper and salt when his saliva began to flow. The air was strangely charged, and he felt the alchemy grow. The dragon had departed and plunged everything into black. The crowd paused as if they were one thing and inhaled like one mouth, they held their breath and waited for the plunge into the abyss. Then, a platinum light, like wisps of ectoplasm, silvered out of the dark. The etheric power of Kinetic Two, White Lunar Wind twisted and turned all around, building shape, and form, created from naught but the thoughts and feelings of the crowd below.

Micah. The thought slipped through the far reaches of his mind and refused to be pushed away. It oiled towards the surface, and he muttered 'Where is he?' Troy took his attention from the manifestations above his head with a sigh when seven fantastic water dragons slid past. The crowd roared their appreciation, but he elbowed his way through them. Himalia Skywalker smiled down at the crowd from the platform she sat atop, cross-legged on a cushion, her gown pooled around her like a silver pond, and she did seem as if she was hip deep in water. Her eye caught Troy's, she frowned and narrowed her gaze, there was something in her look that pierced an empty place in his heart and made it thud erratically against his chest. Her hair was a nimbus of tight curls, silver and cropped close to her head. She was old but had an ageless face and while she continued to play, her eyes never left Troy as he elbowed his way through the crowd, while worry built in his chest like temperature rising.

Himalia levitated out of the crystal pond, and her gown pooled around her feet while the crystal matrix floated before her. She wove her hands through the air. Then taking them above her head she made two fists and opened them slowly while a triumphant light glittered in the centre of her eyes and her jaw lifted determined and proud. Thousands of white orbs descended like gigantic snowballs then stopped two paces above the heads of the crowd who had all turned their faces upwards expectantly, they gasped when the orbs opened like a child's fist uncurling to reveal hundreds of white owls. The vibration had a life of its own. It breathed steadily rising while the lunar wind rose, a movement of air that moved like the ocean until it fell in crashing waves, and every mouth welcome it and every lung moved with it, every heart marked the same time while hundreds of owls began to beat their wings.

'Soul bird is the gatekeeper to your freedom, Soul bird is the door to your Will,' she intoned then said sharply as if she cast a spell, 'I protect yours now.' The intention was a whip of energy through the air while Himalia continued to chant in a language that had no meaning, only sound and power. Then the owls descended and disappeared in effervescent light. Troy rubbed the back of his neck, it burned like an alchemical ward had been place there, and he wondered what a soul bird was and what manner of incantation Himalia had sung. It was not anything he knew or had been taught. Himalia Skywalker stood above him and scrutinised him with a look of disdain that had pulled her top lip into a sneer. He tried to move but was hemmed in by the crowd and by her gaze which burned like augers not on his flesh but through his soul. Her spin was at an end, she studied him down her long nose, it was sleek and angled as sharply as her cheekbones were. Her eyes were judging, not soft and full, but tilted and shaped like almonds, cold as the deepest blue sapphires. Her mouth was full lipped and soft but set in a hard distasteful line. She twitched her gown into place impatiently. It was hooded, and the platinum material fell to the floor like a waterfall of quicksilver. She was tall and hard. Not matronly but muscular. Haughty as well as wise, and she knew it, her head moved to one side as if she waited, as if she listened, and her eyes never left Troy's. He was entranced and stared right back while a space opened around him and he felt her judgement like fire held against his bare flesh, with a start he realised she saw into his inner-self and found it empty. Then her eyes narrowed while she sought his spirit and found only a dark thing growing there.

She lifted her chin and sniffed just as a voice rang in Troy's inner ear. 'Your friend is in danger,' it said. And he heard danger, danger, danger, thump into his skull and hammer at his heart.

I knew it. Why did I not stop him? The huge dragon manifestation came back to his inner eye and roared 'DEATH.' He felt his heart shudder and flip; then its golden forked tongue struck him in the centre of his forehead, and he fell backwards and landed heavily on his behind. He came to his knees slowly holding his head in one hand, while his brain pounded, and his vision reeled.

A firm hand cupped his elbow and pulled him to his feet. 'You know not what you kneel to. So quickly do you prostrate yourself, spawn. Get up and move.' Himalia snapped while she stripped Troy's skin off his bones with a hard stare. He was grateful when one of the sugar skulls approached.

'Himalia I am to escort you away now.' She nodded at Moin and narrowed her eyes disdainfully at Troy.

Troy stumbled away to find Micah on legs made of water. He was not sure whether the voice was part of the experience the Nightcrawlers had spun. How could it be he thought bleakly. Why would I want to imagine my friend's death? I avoided El Nath Night for that reason. Who would want to holo-manifest their worst fears and on a festival too? he thought gibbously and staggered on. Though he knew that certain people enjoyed the Night of The Dead for that very reason. It was an opportunity to exorcise their demons and ghosts, shake out their worst fears so they could kick them in the teeth and pretend that the death of a loved one did not worry them at all. But not me he thought and tried to push harder through the crowds, while the events of the evening coalesced into the source of his worry.

Violet? Part of a revolution? Although, she hardly seemed old enough to be out unchaperoned, and the sugar skull men, pointed ears and skin the colour of seals. They were a long way from home, but here, preparing exits, why? Where to? They said the Wilds! The dead bride, saying sadly, 'my lord,' and Micah replying, *'I am prepared.'*

Prepared for what? Where is he going? Troy thought anxiously while he stumbled and slipped and wiped tears of sweaty iron rain from his face.

Chapter Sixteen

The King Is Dead

Troy pressed his body against the wall of the corridor and pushed past a group of people dressed as demons, they had curling black moustaches and hooked noses that touched turned up chins. Horns twisted from their heads and were hung with chains and bells. They wore black and red capes with stiff collars and tight stripped hose, with forked tails hanging behind. He wished he could brush his unease away, but it bunched his forehead into a tight knot above his brow and chewed relentlessly at his gut. He did not emerge from the corridor but was expelled before a swell of people into the dawn Alcyone Sun had created. He gasped and for a time Micah was driven away by the orb of the morn. He had seen sun rises in the Winter Lands that defied the ability of language to describe them; when nature the artist showed the depth, and the breadth of her majesty, and the intricacies of the wealth and nuance of colour on her palate. Perfectly capturing the time when the sun kissed the sky tenderly like each time was the first time, making the morn blush in every shade of love.

Alcyone Sun stood on a platform above a sea of black leather. Raised about her on other platforms were musicians invisibly dressed in black, apart from their hands and instruments which were outlined in sulphur yellow, and lurid green, like the colours of Shroom Plate fungi. He pushed aside the thought of Violet losing her fingers and her mother, a minstrel left with one hand that only had two fingers and a thumb. Alcyone's crystal matrix hovered in the air above her chest; wires and tubes extended out of the oblong box and attached to devices at her crown, ears, and heart. An electric whip hung at her side, and the small mirrors and jewels on her clothes, shafted light like laser beams as if she were the evening star, lancing through the deepest dark, an inorganic thing floating in the void of space. She retrieved small silver discs from a bag at her side and flipped them into the matrix. Then inverted pyramid crystals in shades of green, silver, pink, and black. A large crystal teardrop, fluid like liquid gold, another that contained liquid night and starlight.

Suddenly, an orb of light floated into the space above their heads, light shafted off her mirrored clothes and a great central sun exploded into being, surrounded first by planets, which grew smaller as her design expanded. The sun remained the same size, always central to her holo-manifestation, and it began to pulse, white at first, then yellow, then green. The cosmos exploded into fourth-dimensional life, and she chewed her bottom lip while she moved her projection down into the crowd and all around. Planets and galaxies spun beneath feet and comets trailed past until the people too became naught but stars. Troy felt a vibration on his hip and while the crowd cheered and roared, he pulled his mo from his pocket. He felt relief wash his heart with warm gentle hands and ease the knot in his gut like thick liquid slowly pouring. He kept the device in his hands and left the splendour of Alcyone Sun's dawn.

The slaughterhouse was a labyrinth of corridors and pits, cold stores and holding pens. He took the stairs down and found himself on the ground floor, not exactly where he had begun his search for Micah but close. He was in what had been the holding pen area, but the dividing wooden fences were gone, and the place was full of the creatures of the night of the dead instead.

'Eschamali Zuben,' someone said as they moved past Troy. Then he turned his head towards the spinner and recognised the guard from the silk warehouse. His dreads swung back and forth while he flipped disc after disc into his crystal matrix. Sweat sheeted his face and light alloyed his skin as if it were resin coated in oil. Drumbeats pulsed like blood pumping through veins, and it began to rain elemental light; hundreds of large teardrops descended from the sky, then hung in the air above the revellers where they began to flicker and spin. Then the teardrop spun and turned into a tiny cosmic warrior which bowed and raised its fists to its chest.

Troy was transfixed and his mouth dropped open. The tiny creature was an exact copy of him. It spun and bowed again. Then, it oiled its thin wicked lips, into a lover's bow of a smile and the pit of his stomach roiled. This is not possible he thought while he met its eye with his own, but they were empty and black. It sneered and it felt like he was looking in a mirror, then the strange little imp began moving through a martial arts sequence. 'What the hell. This should not be possible,' Troy shouted and tried to flick it away. To his right, he saw one of the sugar skull men copy his holo-manifestation while he moved graceful and fluid as the wind and the dance spun on. He swatted at it again and it stood in an aggressive pose, then turned in the air and kick him in the face. 'DEATH,' it shouted, and Troy felt its words like the kiss of a hurricane, but cold and empty as the void. It is the white lunar wind he thought, while his knees buckled then gave way. He heard his voice come from faraway, distant as the top of the highest peak, but raw like a blizzard, shout, 'No.'

~ ❋ ~ ❋ ~ ❋ ~

Micah's crown was strangely neat just like he had put it on. But his cloak was hanging open and draped like a funeral cloth over the edge of the gurney. Someone had ripped his tunic open, and it hung in threads like tissue paper and mist, exposing his thin golden body that glittered as if tiny diamonds had been cast upon his flesh and scattered among the vines and woodland animals that suddenly seemed small and afraid. The pendant had gone. Troy's heart leapt into his mouth, and he began to run towards him. Then, a weight in his gut and tatters of memory than hung like lead stopped him. Instead of rushing to his aid, and his own death, he recalled that he had put the pendant in his pocket. The tattoo that he had proudly called a Gaiadon Heart, oiled desperately with cold sweat that shimmered like waxy dew.

Troy bent forward and emptied the contents of his stomach on the floor as a wave of shock punched him hard in the belly, his vomit burned like an acid scream up through his throat and out of his nose until he took deep hacking breaths and righted himself.

He remained spellbound with horror and hung back while the crowd surged forward. They had stolen from Abrecan, and Micah had called himself King, he had stood at his side, at his right like his Hand. His punishment had been swifter than either of them had imagined. Troy studied the scene. Had he been knifed or poisoned, was the killer still here. Was he even dead? Thoughts ran like fast water through a twisted ravine while he waited. Is this another act he wondered. He had said it was an act. He thought he would feel relief, but he did not while he watched the medic move the crowd away. Demons dressed in black and red, with curling moustaches and noses hooked like beaks, maidens dressed as Mordeana Never Dead, goblins and imps, ghosts and ghouls, all manner of the dead parted, and an angel of death glided over to stand at Micah's side. Her eye burned with malice and the crowd thinned, holding their arms to their suddenly shivering bodies. A sense of wrongness filled the air and a sting of dread hit him in his heart, thin as a needle. While a voice screamed in his head, run. But he did not. Troy dreaded the sudden movement that would catch her eye. Instead, he slid quietly to one side and half hid behind a stone pillar.

A crown of blue-black bird feathers circled pale ochre hair, which fell down her back, and a large brooch, an eye with two wings, one at either side spread out like fingers, clasped a long black cloak around her neck. The eye blinked, and a membrane of pale skin passed over its surface, oiling it while the orb slid its sight back and forth across the crowd, looking, scanning. A sharp but fleeting pain lanced through Troy, when it passed over where he hid, and he felt it lance to the marrow of his bones. It was chill and thick with the weight of death.

Death crouched next to Micah sheathed in black and gold. Its face was lacerated with crimson welts as if a beast had raked talons across its pale white skin. The feathered cloak folded behind its back like large wings come to rest. It scanned the crowd again and its lips twisted with contempt, and its nostrils flared while it fed upon their fear.

A wizard wearing a cloak of deepest blue, patterned with alchemical symbols, bobbed manically in front of it until it looked away with a shrug and took its focus back to Micah.

Troy waited. Is this the act? he thought while he watched it lean in and speak to Micah who looked regally at its face, he nodded, and smiled. Troy felt his knees wobble and he leaned on the pillar and brought his hand to his heart. It is the act he thought and felt relief wash over him like a curtain of warm water. His bottom lip trembled. He hated Micah for not telling him the act would look so real. But it is the night of the dead it would have to be extreme he thought while he waited quietly for the act to be done and the crowd to cheer on their hero. He pushed the dread that eddied and swirled around the edges of his consciousness firmly away and whispered, 'It is an act.'

Act or not, I should still be cautious he thought and wondered what Weasel would do in this situation. Kicking Micah's backside apart, what would he do. If it is real danger? I just must get him, and the pendant to safety. He felt his hand leave the cool smooth surface of the pillar and his foot take the first step when it suddenly dawned on him what Weasel did for them both, and what it must have done to his patience and their dignity in his eyes, while every self-indulgent act they ever committed, and there were hundreds, was cleaned up by their strawberry blonde nursemaid. Damn aftereffects of the emo-psych he cursed while he dropped his head and his breath shuddered in his chest. He did not know what shamed him more, his cowardice and inability to act or his own reluctance to grow up. His mo vibrated on his hip, and he ignored it. Then he set his lips in a hard white line and stepped out of his hiding place. Act or not, he was going to pull that thing off his friend. It is not there to help, and this is not a mummery, he just knew it, anger clawed his hands into fists and set fire running through his veins.

Micah's eye met his while he shook his head. A small movement that was barely noticeable, but anger looked out from his eyes, and the sort of knowing, and soul wrenching resignation that stopped the World turning.

Troy felt the muscles at the front of his legs bunch and his knees bend. He leapt forward with murder in his heart, and death was a fire he felt build in the palm of his hands. The creature would not take Micah from him. It would have to kill him first.

The wizard leapt at the same time and placed his hand lightly on Troy's shoulder. It rooted him to the spot.

Micah's sparkling skin had turned greasy ash-grey, while his tight jaw strangled the life from his smile and turned his lips vein-blue. Troy fought against the wizard's hand but could not move, nor turn his head, and so it was, that when Micah turned his own head towards him, they met eye to eye. A single connection that spanned space and time, as if lodestone and iron had drawn together when Micah looked into the cave of his soul with seafoam-green eyes that blazed with a celestial light, and his heart was open, and his spirit was knowing, and vast like the sky.

Tears streamed down Troy's cheeks their salt water all stained red with iron, and rust. Then he gazed into pit at the centre of Micah's eye, and he saw the eternal life that resided there. He saw the Sun in Winter and he was riding on the crest of a wave, and dancing atop wild water, like he did not have a care, not even then, like death did not frighten him, while mist rolled across the eye of his soul.

A veil of sodden sorrow descended between them, vaster than the cosmos, deeper than the bottomless ocean of Time, on it spread, separating them further, until Troy's grief was silver-grey though it seared like a vortex of flame from the heart of the Sun while it suffocated his spirit in a cloak of bleakest despair.

Chapter Seventeen

Big Fish, Little Fish

Yalan Daboath, attired as the greatest wizard of all, Myrddin Emrys, pushed Troy towards the exits like a tin soldier. Although Myrddin Emrys was lost on the crowd at the Night of the Dead, the wizard in question belonged to Yalan's own dimension, he respected the ancient alchemist and bard's principles, and he had done decent work for Yalan in the past, as well as having a flair for theatrical costume which Yalan sometimes indulged in. He smiled thinly; so far it had been a good night out. He was pleased he had made the effort with the costume, the design he had taken from one of the original robes too. He flinched his fingers slightly when Troy tried to move his head. Yalan sighed, it would not do to let the Valoroso boy know who was behind him. Yalan did not trust Troy, not fully. Sometimes an empty vessel was anything but.

Troy's heart hammered in his chest, followed by intermittent sharp pain like lancing needles as if glass had fractured in the cavern of his heart and was trying to make its way through the meaty walls to the surface of his skin, cutting through muscle, slicing tendon, and scoring against bone. Suddenly, something twanged, like the elastic thread of reality vibrating following a faraway explosion. Troy stumbled.

Ylan had been expecting it, he righted Troy with a strong arm and muttered, 'That ought to do it, just enough space and time for the exit.'

They made their way through a sea of faces, bone white Calaca's, skulls decorated with flowers, hearts and twisting whorls of colour, top hats and silver canes, demons dressed in red and black stripes, and devils with forked tails, angels and imps, and Witch Queens aplenty, parted as if a fleshy curtain had been drawn back while the wizard pushed Troy onwards.

Eschamali Zuben, had been replaced by his sister, Elgenubi. She was at the silk warehouse Troy thought as he continued to sob uncontrollably. Out of the corner of his eye he could see the rickety leather gurney being pushed from the building, in a procession that marked time with his own surreal departure.

Elgenubi Zuben watched the two men briefly while Troy stared at her, his eyes begged for help, but she turned quickly away, lifted another disc, and continued to spin her holo-experience for the exhausted crowd. Her music changed the mood like a blanket of snowy sorrow falling. The tempo was slower, more melody and grief, heartbreak vocals, a wailing violin, lyres, and harps – too many strings that keened like desolation while they lamented the death of love. The night was ending; small specks of emotion lifted like teardrops from the people below and ascended towards the ceiling which oiled above them in whorls of midnight blue and deepest green. Then a million stars began to sparkle and shine, silvered teardrops hanging like jewels from the fabric of the night.

'Ah, it is most beautiful, Elgenubi,' the wizard sighed, and Troy tried to speak though his words when they came were muffled and trapped in a throat constricted with grief. 'Let me go, let me go.' It sounded like he had something stuffed inside his mouth that was thicker than his sorrow and heavier than his shame.

Elgenubi Zuben's holo-manifestation intuitively connected her to the death she could not see but felt was there, a sad shroud hanging all around, as the teardrops turned to stars, glittered, and trailed past in intricate spirals, carried on a breeze that smelled of autumn leaves while they rotted on the ground, to the centre of a single many-faceted purple heart, which pulsed with three coronas of light. Crystalline white and sharp, three times faster than the gold corona that was filled with amber fire, warm and liquid, it pulsed three times as quickly as the outer red corona whose light washed the slaughterhouse in waves of diffused crimson blood.

~ ❈ ~ ❈ ~ ❈ ~

The day dawned like misery herself, the half-sister of sorrow, and nothing Troy could do would ever change that. Yalan led him from the warehouse, towards a new morn and the first of his future without his friend; a square of grey ahead marked the exit, and the regret that waited for him there. Yalan halted him at the door and turned Troy to face him. Lifting his bulbous optics, he looked down into the dark ironstone of Troy's own eyes, which were swollen and rimmed red.

'You will not remember me helping you out, boy, but this you will remember when the time is right. You are flawed...but that is the very thing that may save you in the end.' With that said Yalan turned Troy around and pushed him through the door and into the waiting storm.

Suddenly, Troy found himself outside, acidic residue still stung his nostrils, a sour taste coated his tongue and stripped the enamel from his teeth, and his throat hurt – burned. He staggered. 'No, no, no, no. Light, please let him live, please,' Troy begged while he looked about for the medic. They must be here somewhere, he thought. How can I steal a pendant from dead body, is he dead? Please let him live.

He gathered himself together as best he could, his earlier encounter with Yalan forgotten. In a cloud of exhaustion and self-loathing he thought he had made his own way outside when he followed the rickety leather gurney as it wheeled Micah away. He retched again, bringing up foul air and a horrifying noise, a wail of despair and anger bubbled at the base of his throat as it threated to strangle him. He shuddered violently but stopped himself from falling to his knees and howling. Then he spotted the back of the departing medics to his left, and the tall dark thing that followed. He rubbed at his eyes but could not shift the perception that reality folded away from the strange procession. Troy bit into his jacket sleeve. Hells, I cannot steal anything…the only thing I could or should do, is get help, and confess my crime to that line of proc guards.

He rubbed his head and watched while a line of City Guard made their way slowly towards the warehouse exit, a thick thread of law and order, armed to the teeth. Behind them sonic canons hummed, ready to discharge while the proc edged along stealthily. A tsunami of pain waiting to break across the people inside. He stood with his jaw flapping while people ran back inside, to safety, to raise the alarm, but he knew the Night of the Dead had had its fill. It had eclipsed the Sun in Winter and now nothing would ever be the same.

'How long?' Troy asked a weary-looking sugar skull in a black velvet cape, filthy and wet at the hem, he held his cane like a fighting staff. 'Over two days, nearly bed-time for those who aren't able to make the diversion,' he rasped at Troy before speaking rapidly into a com he held in his hand. 'We will draw the fight here, all to the doors on the south facing tier, the cave exit is clear, get them out that way.' He pushed past Troy and spoke harshly. 'Move it, or fight. The time for spectators has long since passed.'

'Over two days!' Troy sputtered as he realised that whatever had happened was something beyond anything he understood – not just his friend's death, but the data Micah had asked him to steal. The evil angel with wings that were real, the malevolent eye at her neck was no jewel, it too was real, and it scanned souls and found them all wanting, the hand on his…Light, I have no memory of leaving the venue, shock, I am in shock, and I need to get away from here.

The sonic canon began to hum and vibrate loudly while Troy made his way past a random pandemonium of revellers who began to push back to the warehouse. A molly whistled half-heartedly over his head and hit a shield the proc had only just activated. A thin flash of blue flame and it was gone. Then a small stickle-bug incendiary device thudded somewhere in the distance to his right, the smell of smoke snaked acrid and dry through the wet miserable morning. Night of the Dead sugar skulls and demon masks yawing in contorted agony, imps and ghouls, flocks of the dead in cloak and cape, flapped past in an organised wave, soldiers of the damned retreating towards the warehouse. Troy felt a large hand between his shoulders, immense pressure then he was catapulted forward, through them.

He stumbled and skittered on splayed legs, desperate to get away from the scene of Micha's death and to have no part in the uprising. He fell through a final wall of people who launched a volley of incendiary devices, over his head. They were no larger than an egg and they cracked when they hit the ground and filled the air with thick black smoke. Then they turned and fled back to the warehouse or disappeared down small alleys or over waste ground as if they were ants returning to their nests, leaving Troy stranded and alone in a thin strip of empty space, a sliver of no-man's land.

The Night of the Dead still felt greasy and alive, a predator at his back. Smoke cleared in tatters to reveal a line of proc with their helmet visors down and blue electric shields that buzzed and flickered. Black shiny boots crunched, halted, crunched, halted, ready to charge, kick, and trample; the sonic canon behind vibrated and whined and its gaping mouth yawed hungrily at the air while tendrils of heat hissed like hot tongues through the drizzle. To the left, behind the line of proc guards, the medics were still resuscitating Micah, surrounded by a flurry of black feathered wings.

'For Anukssake,' Troy shouted, and waved his arms about manically while he pointed at the guards, then at the angels of death. 'There's a flock of them around him. Look! Look there! Can't you see? Urghh, what are they? Get them away from him.' His throat was raw but still he managed more than a croak through teeth that chattered beneath cracked warehouse-dry lips, contorted into a snarling rictus.

A flock of dark angels surrounded Micah. The medics turned away from the stretcher in a daze and made their way back to the warehouse as if on another errand while the flock of darkness lifted Micah off the stretcher and started to spin. Then, they began to elevate with Micah's limp, skeletal remains in their arms.

The Memitim commander turned to Troy. 'Empty dragon,' it hissed directly into his skull. Then it lifted its chin defiantly in a challenge that made Troy's guts melt and unfurl. The Memitim took a dagger from its boot and made ready to throw it, but then it hesitated and looked at the line of guards, spat in their direction, and laughed as if something was hysterically funny, while it spun off in a flurry of black wings.

~ �֍ ~ �֍ ~ ✯ ~

'Commander Noble, sir, we have a crawler leaving the warehouse. He is approaching at speed, foaming at the mouth, and seems agitated, aggressive – over.' *Click.*

'Well, don't wait around for him to introduce himself, Seft. He could have a stickle-bug or a shield disruptor – take him down – taze the little shit, then check his body for discs – over.' *Click.*

~ ✯ ~ ✯ ~ ✯ ~

The grim day accosted Troy with the force of a lightning bolt to the heart, Kinetic Three, Blue Electric Night was upon them, and it promised to be as portentous as it forebears.

Baton to the head, landed with a thud and flash of white light. Tiny silver darts on the end of glistening wet chains found their way past his open jacket and punctured the thin costume below. He fell to the floor heavily and landed on his side. His ribs popped and the pain was sharp but fleeting like a stiletto had been slid through the slats between them; they had never been the same after being kicked-in by Commander Noble.

'To the King, to Spider King!' someone shouted, and a rocket launcher hidden behind the warehouse, fired. A flurry of duster drake screeched as they flew into the air, a small colony late to migrate South, headed that way now, raucous as a gale full of screeching wind while the rocket found its target and blew the sonic canon apart, just as it was making ready to fire a volley of green light. A line of pre-charged explosions erupted to the right, destroying the cave exit, and protecting The Ten as they made their escape. The sandstone tier screeched like two continental plates rubbing together, then it cracked with a sound like thunder directly overhead. An avalanche of rock slid from the cliff behind the warehouse and rumbled across the wide street. It gained momentum and cascaded onwards over the tiers and cliffs below, tumbling and carving a path of destruction on its way to the muddy-brown River Ophiuchus, which slugged along hundreds and hundreds of feet below.

Sickly green laser fire erupted like a volley of arrows while the line of guard moved into small fists of two dozen men apiece. They fanned out around the venue and crept slowly into the rubble of the tier where Athanasius Blood's abandoned warehouse stood. Their shields melded above and around them, and they scurried like many-legged scarab beetles over the ruined tier where they searched for and killed anything that moved. A stickle bug found its target and latched its oily black ball full of explosive to the side of the shell of one melded shield. It blew it apart as if a fist had punched through a paper bag; and tatters of translucent green and blue were carried away by a desolate wind that tore relentlessly up the estuary and raked the swell of the sluggish Ophiuchus into spumes of frothy white.

A severed hand landed next to his face; the wedding band on its finger was slicked with blood.

A distant whipping-whirr, thwuck-thwucked but not fast enough, and the warehouse exploded like a great beast roaring. It burst into flames that vortexed into a column two hundred feet high, setting aflame the tithe barns on the tier above.

The final revellers scattered then disappeared behind fire and smoke, and the wind drove a volley of hard rain that rattled stones loose from the deserted road, as if they had not been there at all. As if the night of the dead never was.

Troy lay in a puddle of filthy water, mud, urine, and litter…he gasped for air while he held his ribs tenderly. He faded to black and wished he were dead. The taser hooks were stuck in his flesh and the wires extended, to the leader of a fist of protectorate guard who were creeping the last few paces towards the burning warehouse. It stunk like burning meat while the flames hissed and spat like a fire from the belly of hell while Troy flapped and twitched in the mud.

''Ere Seft, should I just put a laser slug in the back of his head, say he got hit running?' a heavily armoured guard asked.

'Best have a look at the rubbish first,' he said wearily and lifted Troy's head up by his hair. 'Light, no, wait until Noble hears who we landed. Might put a smile on the miserable bastard's face.'

~ ❅ ~ ❅ ~ ❅ ~

'You listen to me, and listen good,' Reynard hissed across the table. They were in a small anteroom and sat on red velvet chairs at opposite sides of a marble and gilt table. 'Is there anything else I need to know about?' He had never seemed so fox-like. His pointed red beard made an already sharp face a sharp mask of cunning, his auburn hair brushed back and tied in a tail behind with a single thong of dark leather. Reynard's eyes glittered while he waited, dark like fruit dried in the sun, against his creamy complexion. Nothing moved, all seemed immobile and perfectly composed, but Troy knew that every muscle beneath his expensive suit was taut as skin pulled across a drum.

'In the water closet, ther—' Troy hung his head and mumbled to his father who cut him off.

'Shut up.' He held his hand up and Troy stopped, ashamed he hung his head while he fought back tears. Reynard thumbed his mo in his hand under the table. To Weasel, no doubt, Troy thought, and his cheeks reddened, he will be sending my nursemaid to clear out my room. He studied his filthy hand while it rested on the table; the cold green marble was veined with black and gold, it reminded him of Micah's eyes and wings of death.

The grey day had eventually faded to late afternoon, and then early evening while he waited to see if his father would show. He had been offered food and drink but touched neither; he knew what the guard had done to it. He heard half a dozen of them shout, 'Spider King, all hail Spider King the fuckwit,' as they marched past the room, he was being held in. Eventually, a commander had forbidden anyone speak in that area. He had not been held in the usual gaol, small windowless cells, carved out of the rock of the tiers, deep beneath the old mansion that was Hol Protectorate Guard Central. It was situated on a tier just below the Snide, a remnant of a merchant family who had increased their wealth and moved up a tier or had even bought a place on the flat plateau above. It was the only protectorate guard base on the western side of the tiers of Lodewick.

Below, the merchants hired mercenaries to protect the contents of their warehouses. Dockmasters and assistants were all paid for from the fat purses of the Merchant Guilds, who did not want the heavy-handed protectorate city guard sniffing about their wares; they were better suited to herd the population to their respective zones like sheep, when the curfew sirens sounded.

Troy shuddered when a stab of sorrow pierced the fog in his mind, a hot needle of emotion into the heart of senses numbed by grief, shock, and taser volts. He knew that the Hol Guard Base was only there to stop the riffraff from the Shambles and the refugees from the shanty across the Ophiuchus River from making their way unchecked to the pristine areas of the elite on the top of the plateau. Hol district was a lump of derelict land, abandoned quarries, and disused buildings. It had been left and forgotten when newer, more profitable areas became available. Hol nestled against the headland like a wound festering below the east end of the long wide road called The Snide, and four tiers below the Seedy Seed, the common name for the shitty underbelly of the city which skirted the bottom of the Temple of The Needful Scrip like a whores filthy, frilly underskirt.

'I have got to go and identify a body now, Troy. You will be out as soon as the protectorate guard are satisfied with their enquiries which should not be too long,' he said flatly as he made his way to the door and indicated to the officer outside, he was ready to leave. 'Rodney will be waiting for you; he will escort you home.'

'There's…there's a body?' Troy croaked.

'There usually is when someone has died, Troy. That is what happens, the dearly departed leave their corpse behind. And, when you get home…all of this,' he waved at the air then pointed a disgusted finger at his Spider King costume before he snarled, 'is over. You can start immediately at the Waste Corporation. I need someone with analytical ability to look at the sewer maps to input into the maintenance programme – gutter work, will be a good enough start for you. You seem to like to hang around with filth,' he snarled with utter contempt as the guard opened the door. They nodded, shook hands without speaking and Reynard Wyburn left.

*

Weasel waited for Troy in a sombre mood. His strawberry blonde hair was like spun straw against his immaculate grey suit, which was the colour of a storm cloud, heavy with rain. He leaned casually against an ovoid, black and gold scrid, with Reynard's sigil on the door – a bright red fox, holding its tail in its mouth. He pushed his hand against the door and stepped out of the way when the door lifted, its silent motion matched his mood and he did not say a word but kept one eye discreetly on Hol Central and a group of hard-faced guards, who were still dirty and blood-stained. He knew that they were depleted of energy, they were ash grey because of the lasers they carried. Each shot fired would have cost them dearly. He had used one, only once, to kill one of Bucky's bastards and found that he hardly had the energy afterwards to deal with the corpse. He was primarily a thief, which was what he had started his illustrious career as for the madame of The Buttered Leg, so, he knew deep in his gut when he was being robbed. He felt it as soon as he put his finger to the transducer, there was a pull, not from him, but from the machine and the sensation that a root had travelled through his finger, up his arm and into a space at the top of his sternum, a centre of energetic activity, the place where instructions were made, and power was channelled. It was no more than a second, he aimed and put pressure on the trigger. He felt the pool at the centre of his chest pull, then drain the energy from his vital organs. His heart palpitated, and his liver moved like a serpent under his skin. His spleen kicked, and acidic bile pushed into his throat, then a sharp but fleeting pain hit his kidneys hard. The energy, his own life force, travelled down his arm and the green beam fired a single silent ray of death. Feill, one of Bucky's eldest sons, fell to the floor, but so did he.

Weasel studied the guards, Droge Waere he thought, it is the only way to keep their organs firing and them upright when they use those weapons. Marching powder. He never used a laser weapon again, not if it meant supplementing his own life force with marching powder. He hated intoxication of any kind, except the thrill of a mission completed and the high that power gave. He hated being vulnerable and he had lain unconscious for longer than he cared to remember while his murder victim lay only paces away. He had been fortunate it was the dead of night, and they were in a discreet inn, for gentle folk, called The Well Met Stranger, on the outskirts of Wolfsea Crossing. He was disguised as a whore, a siursach, and although it was the last thing he wanted to do, and the irony was not lost on him, do it he did. He had been paid a fortune by Abrecan to take care of Bucky's son, Feill Sgaoilte, who was gaining popularity in the north. Like several of Bucky's sons Feill was an incorrigible brothel moth. He had worked his way into his favour over months, finally earning his trust, and the offer of a rendezvous, and a night to remember. It was certainly that, thought Weasel while he continued to study the guards, discreetly. They had been fighting riots all day and their life force was beyond depleted. A fist of twelve men had gathered at the top of the steps to watch Troy depart. Their eyes were dull black pits in sunken sockets, their hollowed cheeks full of shadow, but their fingers rested too tightly on the black hand lasers at their belts and the veins in the side of their necks were full and pumping. One or two mustered the energy to spit when Troy walked past. The consensus being, that it was Troy who had incited a riot when he ran into the thin strip of neutral land, flapping his arms and, according to the guards, shouting 'To the King. To Spider King.'

Troy walked with his head held high and all the arrogance of a king in his jutting jaw, until Weasel narrowed his eye at him, and he dropped his head and got into the scrid clumsily. Weasel closed the door with a too hard push and hoped he had clipped his foot, hoped he had hurt him, while he kept his attention focused on the job at hand. He got into the scrid and pressed his thumb into the ignition and waited until the alchemical transducer took the charge from his thumb. 'They searched your suite of rooms for Droge Waere, bathing rooms, and water closet. Turned it right over, but they didn't find anything,' he informed Troy dryly.

Troy gave a ragged sigh of relief that raked like hot fingers of grief past his heart while he watched Hol disappear. Instead of heading toward the headland and the twisting chicanes that would take them to the top of Lodewick they went west and north. 'We will have to take the drovers route out of Lodewick, through the Shambles, then towards the docks, along the river, and skirt the edge of the Willow Wilds. Fuck only knows how I'll manoeuvre this through the streets,' Weasel said over his shoulder and Troy could feel the heat hidden in his voice. 'Then we'll head back in by Tota. The headland route was cut off by avalanche debris, and unstable structures, not to mention the burning buildings, the casualties, the fists of guards. The general fucking pandemonium.' He took his attention back to the drive but not before Troy heard the accusation in his words.

His grief had dried his own mouth and coated his tongue with sand, he could find no answer, no clever comeback or put down, he just wanted to die and join his friend.

Troy stared out of the window as they made their slow way along the narrow cobbled roads that edged the Shambles proper. They always led down, and out towards the docks and river. They skirted the docks, then descended again onto what could be described as the thin end of a wedge of rock. Once Live and Dead Stock Wharf had disappeared, the last breakers yard, and the rickety old wooden wharfs that were used by cockle fishers and crab men, he knew he had left the city and all that remained was an air of abandonment and decay before nature took back what was hers.

The Ophiuchus to their left, swept past, its course was wide, and the Wyrm currents that carried the experienced quickly to their destinations, and killed the unwary, wove like glass streamers on its surface, but the river looked pregnant and slow. There were no docks or breakers' yards here, just scrubby bushes and marshland. Dark esturial water whipped at the bank as it rose in sandy white plumes. Over the water, the cliffs had all but gentled into a semblance of a riverbank. On the horizon dark coniferous forests spread towards jagged bare peaks. The cobbled road became rough and bumpy, a wide drovers road made of packed dirt and potholes, that Weasel had to follow in a sweeping arch to head back into the city, and on towards the flat plateau of Lodewick. The sun orbed towards the horizon, a brief flaming ball between gaps in dark clouds, it watched the scrid with its flaming eye, while the last rays of its light lanced and cut at the overcast. The scrid bumped and swayed over the rough road, each jolt like a stab to the heart while it crawled toward home and a life without Micah.

It was almost dark when the scrid crept cautiously along the edge of the Willow Wilds. Troy looked despondently out of the window. Water channels and dark pools of brackish water lay across marshy fields to his right. Short scrubby gorse and thick small willow bushes grew in copses between the channels, they crawled like fingers towards a forest of gigantic willow switches, growing close together and as impenetrable as a stockade. Beneath them a tangle of willow scrub, ivy and thorny bushes frothed and wove like a prickly green net. Above, evergreen vines canopied the crown of the trees. It was rumoured that there was another river channel at the heart of the Willow Wilds where a mystical weeping willow grew alongside a beautiful and sacred river. Troy doubted anyone one could get through the thick undergrowth to find out if it were true, and his eyes stung with molten tears when he recalled it was Micah who had told him about the magical tree, Igi Ekun and the sacred water. He wanted to throw open the door and run into the Wilds, but Weasel had locked the door from the main control. My nursemaid, my protector, and gaoler he thought but could not get his anger to rise, the fire in his belly had been put out by an ocean of grief.

The scrid crawled along while Weasel manoeuvred it around one pothole after another. Willow switches hit the body and he cursed his luck and his lack of an aerial permit, also the stupidity of the people who had destroyed the southern route on the tier where the warehouse had been, it being the best way to get along the tiers from Hol to the Seegda Seed, then to the top of Lodewick, without having to manoeuvre through the wasteland behind.

This was easier on the way here; I swear it was he thought with a sting to his heart. He had driven like the devil to get there because he had hoped that Micah might still be alive. He had hoped to find them worse for wear and had even memorised a barrage of insults for Valoroso. He had even kept aside the best night poppy this side of the commonwealth of Turanga, in case the pair of them were really hurt, it had never occurred to him that Micah might be dead. Reynard's message said, sweep the house for Droge, then get to Hol Central.

Troy continued to stare into the depths of the forest. The bars of switches thinned momentarily while the scrid crawled by. Troy stared into the dusk while he thought of Micah and let the pain in his chest burn and score a charcoal wrought guilt across his soul. Suddenly, he came eye-to-eye with a large animal that sat on its haunches in the shadows at the edge of the trees. It had flinty magenta eyes and a scaled muzzle, pulled back to bare large sharp teeth. He jumped back from the window, but the beast continued to snarl. Then he saw Himalia Skywalker remove a longsword from the body of something from a nightmare. It was large and partially armoured with a single tusk coming from its scaled forehead; she had speared the beast to a tree.

He groaned and leaned back on the seat while the Volpi's opened their throats and howled their hunt song. 'Light, can you go any faster,' he snapped at Weasel who had jumped at the sound of the howls, but hid his shock just as quickly. He flicked a button on the dash and the scrid suspension lifted to accommodate the uneven surface. It began to move a little faster and he gave control over to the auto-driver before he turned his attention to Troy.

Weasel took a thin translucent sheet from a leather satchel that rested neatly on the floor next to the single driver's seat and began reading efficiently, barely hiding the tension that twitched along his jaw. 'Your father will establish that any involvement you have had with Micah, was an error of judgement on your part, and that you had been led astray by the wanton youth, Micah Apollon. He will inform the necessary channels, that Micah Apollon was a young man hell-bent on causing an uproar wherever he went,' his voice cracked, and he turned away for a second to compose himself. The auto-driver had increased speed and Troy warily cast his gaze to the retreating Willow Wilds – nothing.

'He will then go on to say, trouble followed Micah everywhere. He will insist that everyone knew that, citing the incidents and the stunt he pulled last year, where he alarmed children, and sickened adults, in every town and city of our great nation, Baelmonarchia. The Night of the Dead revolt was led by him, and he was killed in the battle between rebels and Protectorate Guard, who were protecting the citizens of Lodewick, and merchants from the Snide from kidnap. The ransoms he aimed to demand are used to fund the rebel movement. Ransom notes and freed kidnappees will be provided.' Weasel kept his body forward while he read; the first spans of bridges that led into Lodewick could be seen in the distance. His eyes glistened wetly; he even risked a stray tear as his hands gripped the edges of the translucent sheet tightly while he thought of the cave he had been tortured in and wondered if he could lure Valoroso there.

'Are you happy now?' he growled. There was a crack in his voice that pierced the final shard of Troy's heart like a rod of hot iron. He crumpled to the seat and curled into a ball, a heap of filthy green and black, his hands felt oily with death, and his face was streaked red and brown. He stunk of old iron and greasy slaughter, and he knew it would take a lifetime to clear it from his skin and out of his lungs. He knew he would never be able to wash it from his heart. 'Fuck off, Weasel,' he croaked and began to weep.

'I wish I could, Troy,' Weasel spat over his shoulder, 'but even more than that, I wish it had been you, instead of him.'

He switched back to manual when the dirt road suddenly gave way to large cobble sets and the first viaduct that led into Lodewick approached. The outer zone Tota, cascaded and spread outwards and down the embankments at the back of the monolith. Buildings, and small plots of land with thin soil which had been turned to growing things grew out of the hinterland of the city. Houses were even built beneath the arched viaducts and bridges that seemed to lead everywhere and nowhere at the same time; most had fallen into disrepair, the top of their spans ending in thin air. The bridges were fantastical structures that seemed to have been dragged into the air by a gigantic fist and left there like sticks and springs that pointed outwards at jaunty angles. The twin river Ophiuchus hugged the base of the cliffs, docks on the Cheapside, marinas, and pleasure zones on the Side of Light before it snaked away on either side of Lodewick northwards to its source in the Iron Hills. Roads suddenly ended as if they had been chewed or broken away, and the wilds grabbed and clawed at the earth tumbling towards the city in fingers of scrubby willow that destroyed everything they touched.

Weasel closed the privacy screen but not before Troy saw that Weasel was weeping too.

~ ❖ ~ ❖ ~ ❖ ~

Troy escaped a spell at the correctional colony, The Wind, in a dazzling display of illusion orchestrated by his father Reynard, who had insisted the debacle be beamed on the newly installed informatics monitors. He would appease the masses, and he would make an example of Troy, who he had portrayed as an innocent bystander, a handy scapegoat to the madness that swirled from Micah Apollon like a maelstrom. The Lord Apollon had clearly gone outside the box. An awareness campaign, and how to report your nearest and dearest dissident was launched at the same time. He even showed footage of Micah, a little too distant, being shot and killed in a battle with the protectorate guard. Micah was only recognisable by his fair hair and antlered crown; he had a child under one arm who he had kidnapped and was using as a human shield. Other rebels who were caught were executed, beheaded on the steps of Abrecan Castle and their heads placed on spikes in the white marble square, blobs of black and red before the great red tower as it loomed towards the sky. A national holiday was declared, and the well wrapped crowds gathered, prepared to picnic, it being a fine dry day, although a little on the chilly side. Rumours abounded that bank upon bank of snow clouds were howling down from the north, and the storm yet to come was quickly named, Bucky's Revenge.

Hot food, pies, roasted nuts, stews, and pastries were free, bringing far more people to the spectacle than there should decently have been. Minstrels played, albeit their dulcimers and harps sounded strained, their flutes and pipes sour. Jugglers threw balls and hoops in the air, afraid to drop a single item as they kept one eye on the spy-eyes that monitored the festivities. Tumblers tumbled as heads did the same and were caught in baskets below the slicing arm of the execution scaffold. The Protectorate Guard had cleared their gaols on the orders of Lord Abrecan; the people, still dressed in costumes and masks, had clearly been prisoners for longer than a week, any one with eyes and a brave stomach could see that, but most had the sense to look the other way.

Two demons were among those picked for execution, sugar skulls painted over bumpy flesh; the male looked very much like it had a sheep's muzzle, the other, a woman, had a hawkish nose that was yellow and hard. Both had sad confused eyes. They were demon beasts who had come from the Willow Wilds into the outlying zones, sick of animal brain and flesh, and afraid of the Volpi hunt.

Elites sat in a canvas covered grandstand and who could tell who had crawled, slithered, and lumbered up the axis of reality from hell, who had been brought from Earth and who had been born on Gaiadon.

Troy was shown to have gotten off lightly, in one sense. He was given a warning because of his previously good character and behaviour and had been given a menial job with the Waste Corporation; pictures of him down the sewers waist deep in sewage were beamed across Baelmonarchia. It was heard that his uncle, the Lord Lucas Abrecan, had written a character reference for him, with the assurance he was soon to accept a position of gainful employment at the headquarters of his company Cronos Industries, but only once his punishment was complete. Those with the common sense to see through the charade expected he would disappear without a trace soon after.

As was fitting, Micah's body was burned on the galactic signature of Kinetic Twenty, Yellow Resonant Sun. He had arrived on the planet on Kinetic Two Hundred, Yellow Overtone Sun, one of the rarest galactic signatures, no one was born on that day, ever, but Lord Micah Apollon was destined to be the Sun in Winter and his fate had been written in more than the stars. He would sit on the throne at the Palace Galay and set the Ningen free, according to a Ningen prophecy that was ancient, but the Sun in Winter had set for the last time, taking light, and life, and the hope of freedom with it.

Micah was cremated on the nearest similar galactic signature gateway to the one on which he was born. It was a lowkey family affair. Lord Bucky would retire to Eirini to mourn. Only the closest of family attended. His mother was thought to be dead, leaving a smattering of Micah's half-brothers, who thought it was safe to enter Lodewick – some even managed to leave alive. The few elites who dared show support to Lord Bucky were Reynard Wyburn who was only there to keep an eye on Bucky, one exotically dressed merchant from the Southern Isles, and a dignitary representing the Witch Queens, alongside the servants of the city residence. Lord Bucky cried and cried, well into the "After the Tears" party, held to remember all the good Micah had done, which was as embellished as the golden bier upon which he laid prior to his incineration.

The invite had not extended to Troy, just his parents. Lady Leleth had declined. 'The missing data?' she asked Reynard and he shrugged. 'Gone.'

She paused. 'Cover it up, Reynard. I will need to be at the Fifth Tower with *Him*, he must be distracted.'

Reynard studied her gravely while he wondered when she had discovered she had a heart. The boy was nothing more than an instrument put in their care, and he doubted Lord Abrecan would destroy it.

'Despite your best efforts, he may still come seeking revenge. There are many ways to torture that leave no mark. He may even send Velig the Butcher. I will not have that here.' She pointed above her, and Reynard's frown went from a furrowed brow to a tight knot of tension. What is wrong with her he wondered but held his tongue.

Troy stayed in his rooms, surrounded by maps of the sewers Reynard had thrown at him. 'Look at these it will take your mind off it, then tell me the order we need to shut down in, for cleaning and repair – use that bloody superior brain of yours I paid a damn fortune for,' he had shouted before he turned and left.

Troy watched him walk through the door and pull his mask back across his face before he left his suite of rooms. Light, did I break him too? he thought and reached for a hookah and a vial of Memorigi oil.

He shaved off his hair with a cut-throat razor, which he held against his jugular while he imagined Himalia Skywalker and a pack of Volpi coming for his blood, but he could not make the cut. He remained the coward who had killed his friend, the pathetic fool who had thought he stood in the shadow of Micah's sun, when all the while he was the shadow. It was my fault. I killed my friend and the others. All those who had been executed in the wake of the riot. It was all my fault. When I ran into that ribbon of empty space, shouting and pointing as if I had two lasers in my hands. His thoughts were rabid and worried at his mind, night and day, and the machinery of his grief was oiled with self-loathing.

He did not pursue his line of enquiry about the body. Not only did it seem perverted and morbid, but his experience at how thorough Reynard was at manipulating the truth stayed his hand. In his own head he swayed from one version of the truth to another as he tried to resolve his guilt and punish himself in equal measure. Sweaty, greasy nights where his sanity seemed to ooze from every pore, and surreal days, cogs grinding in his head reminded him of rust and alchemy, of slaughter and death, over, and over, again. Eventually his eyes stopped leaking and he realised his denial that he had had a part in Micah's death, had sent him crazy; it had manifested into an imaginary kidnapping by strange creatures. Angels of death, no less. At least in the light of day that is what he thought, in the pit of night he stalked about his rooms, where he ruminated over the details of how Micah had disappeared that night. Fantasy, mental, outside the box, hallucinations…still, he could not believe Micah was dead, but that was part of his grief. He did not believe he was dead because he thought he was coming back.

He put his thumb into the indent at the bottom of the mo and waited until the alchemical transducer took energy from his thumb, while the translucent data spun around the screen. He selected the crystal pips he needed then keyed in the sequence. The pain in his heart was not fleeting but heavy and intense like a vice was squeezing until he pressed the mo to his ear.

'Remember what I said. You look for me, Troy. When the time is right.' He was sure he heard him sigh before the recording ended as if he was going to say more but had changed his mind at the last moment.

When the time is right, he thought and knew that Micah was trying to tell him something.

~ �֍ ~ �֍ ~ ✷ ~

Kinetic One, Red Magnetic Dragon, would be a decent galactic signature, desirable even, if you liked to be a bit different. There may have been an increase in bio-baby implants two hundred and sixty days ago, at the end of the last galactic year. Elites paying vast amounts to artificially sire a babe that would emerge on the auspicious day, Kinetic One, but that year, the year of the resonant storm, it fell on the Day of the Dead. No matter how rich you were, you would not throw your money away on that sort of vibration – you may as well try to create a Worldbridger signature, it was that ill-fated.

He had been born on Kinetic Two Hundred and Forty-one. His galactic signature was Red Resonant Dragon, and it had fallen on the Night of the Dead. I was born on the Night of the Dead eh thought and felt a shudder creep along his spine, he felt it caress each bone with a finger made of ice, then tingle across his skull.

'What were they thinking? Light, Micah, if you were here now, you would know this. What were they up to?' Troy spoke to the mo in his hand wishing that his friend waited on the other end.

He sat on the edge of his canopied bed and shivered. It was a white-out across Baelmonarchia, the depths of winter had descended colder and bleaker than ever before, snow beyond measure had fallen, which his father blamed Lord Bucky for, while he shouted at his mother. 'Why did we not foresee this? We should have kept Bucky in the city. He has stopped the world. The man's grief is going to bloody well freeze us to our marrow.'

Leleth placed a thin pale hand on Reynard's tense arm. 'Let him grieve. What is a bit of weather when he has lost his son?'

Reynard nearly gasped in surprise but hid it behind his hand. Where did she learn about empathy? He checked that the surge of emotion he felt in his chest had not rippled or moved his face or body in any way while he held his demeanour in a carefully constructed pose, swallowed his anger, and marvelled at his demon wife, and the danger she was courting. Feelings would get her killed.

'He cannot keep it up. Only Gaia had the power to cast permanent ice and it is not even that. Ectoplasm.' She had sniffed and arched one elegant brow.

'And his galactic signature power?' Reynard let the question hang between them until Leleth replied, 'You only have to look out of the window to see that it is off the scale, but a storm is a storm, and this one will eventually blow itself out.'

~ ❋ ~ ❋ ~ ❋ ~

What are they up to? He thought while he pulled the goose down quilt around his shoulders. Deep-red velvet drapes were half closed around the bed to keep off some of the chill. The bed was raised on the centre of a black and white tiled platform. Soft light pooled from underneath, cast from charcoal fires beneath the tile dais that heated the room and the bed, though not enough to quell Bucky's icy howl.

The Spider King costume lay next to him, he poked it with a finger and sighed. Then he ran his hand across his badly shaved scalp. A scab fell off and he felt a thin trickle of blood run past his ear which he ignored. He chewed at his thumb while he thought, two hundred and forty-one out of two hundred and sixty, it is almost at the top of the range. Why that kinetic, why a dragon? Why on the Night of the Dead? Did they really want to give birth to hell? I have brought nothing but dark with me, so much dark, I put out the light of the Sun.

He thumbed the mo once more. One last listen to his voice he thought and felt the pressure on his heart rupture a new wound there. He jumped in surprise when it vibrated. He almost dropped it and gazed at it while it pulsed in his hand.

'Who is this?' he snapped.

'My name's Tranquillity Maegdelan…you don't know me, but we need to talk…'

Part Three

Pale-Mouthed Prophets

Chapter Eighteen

Dearly Departed

It should have been my night she fumed silently, mine and Ganaim's but said instead. 'At least we have a seat near a brazier, it being as cold as it is,' Celeste commented dryly while she pursed her lips disdainfully and met Cissy's glacial stare. The three women were wrapped in long cloaks against the chill air while they sat at a wooden table in the back courtyard of the Nag. Metal braziers like barrels of fire dotted about the yard provided pools of warmth and golden light. Celeste eyed Cissy over the top of a beaker of cider. The other woman narrowed her eyes and folded her arms beneath her small bosom, her lips puckered into a distasteful sneer. Celeste tutted. I hope she knows I mean her, frigid old sow.

Dorothea nodded. 'You can follow me indoors after the elders have finished their meeting and the tap room is free, it's locked doors on that room until then.' She smiled and nodded to the row of windows that faced the courtyard. 'There won't be a seat in the Long Room at all. Cissy, put another log on the brazier, there's a love.' Cissy took a log out of a willow basket next to the wooden table and stood to reach over and place it in black metal brazier; sparks flew from the top like fireflies and curled away, into the crisp night. The fire glowed through a pattern punched in the metal, a single oak tree with wide boughs and scattered leaves that glowed red and orange.

The River Wraith rushed noisily somewhere in the distance, as it tore across rocks and chewed frothily at stone banks, sounding more like wind than water, as if it blew relentlessly down a ravine. The night was dry and crystalline with the promise of a light frost. Stars had begun to twinkle against the sepia backdrop of the sky, soon to fade to deepest blue, then black, while the twin moons hung like imperfect pearls – black moon Lilith, pewter and slashed with streaks of red, hung before her sister Luna, a pale lilac ghost behind.

Chopped wood scented the air from willow baskets full of logs, their ends pale gold, and round as fresh bread rolls while they awaited the flame. An assortment of tables nestled around the edge of the courtyard beneath the balcony of the floor above. It had been strung with old coach lanterns with cracked glass that had been painted in translucent shades of rose, ultramarine, viridian, and raw sienna. Meat roasted on spits on the huge fire at one end of the Long Room, and tables heaved with food, the last of the crates of provisions had been distributed, harvest was in, quota met, and inspectors were happy and away back to Ninmah. Aromatic pipe smoke, not just herbal blends but also Turanga Tobacco from the most northerly and eastern of the Southern Isles. Fairmist Al Mara had come ashore four moons ago and that meant a ship had been to Smugglers Bay. Romarii would come too, so there would be more than tobacco, tea, and coffee, traded at the inn this night.

Dorothea smiled and inhaled. 'Ah, tonight does smell good, like home and hearth. Peat fires have been banked high tonight, Celeste.' Celeste smiled and nodded while Dorothea continued, 'Some will be here till the early hours of the morning, even later. Did you manage to take a room?' She turned to Cissy who sat next to her in what looked like her best clothes. Her dungarees and hunting garb put aside, she wore an intricately embroidered waist coat, covered with fantastical animals in silver thread against a deep blue background, winged deer, unicorns, white peacocks with ruby red eyes, dragons and even a Volpi, which Cissy drew her cloak across when she saw Celeste pay too much attention to her needle work. The waistcoat was over a plain linen shirt; she still wore breeches, but they were deep forest green, and the warm moleskin fabric was tucked into leather riding boots. Her velvet cloak shimmered like light mottling beneath a canopy of trees when she moved, which was often as she fidgeted anxiously in her seat.

'Yes, it is done,' she snapped sourly. Celeste sighed quietly, not wanting to draw Cissy's attention to her. Dorothea's jaw tightened slightly but whatever she was about to say, her jaw loosened, and a softness came to her eyes when she asked, 'And the other?'

Cissy scowled. 'Yes, Moin and Abhhain will come meet me here at dawn, then we will depart.'

Dorothea met cissy's gaze full on; her eyes were feathered with tension at the corner. 'Where?'

Cissy cut her off and said too sharply, 'The small compass near the disused Guratt, you know the one? It is hardly more than boulders.' She nodded over her shoulder then grabbed another log as if she wished to strangle it before she pushed it into the already full brazier; sparks hissed.

Celeste jumped. Dorothea shook her head but said no more, although Celeste itched to ask them what they were talking about.

Cissy and Dorothea sipped their damson honey-wine. Celeste looked morosely at her small jug of cider with even smaller alcohol content. Ganaim had not come back in time to escort her to the Night of The Dead gathering, but Tara had eventually given in to her pleading and had given Dorothea her permission to chaperone Celeste on her first night out. Celeste sighed loudly. She suspected it was because Tara knew Ganaim Al Tine would not be there. Cissy frowned and turned her back to the two women at the table to watch the back door of the inn. Dorothea smiled at Celeste but made no attempt to make further conversation as she too seemed to be watching the inn.

Romarii horses clopped into the stable yard, too far away for her to see properly. Cissy and Dorothea paid no attention to them although their eyes narrowed, and their bodies stiffened while they continued to pretend not to care. The distant voice of the Muntor boys travelled up the yard, stable hands' talk that found a quiet space in the bubbling conversation on the surrounding tables.

'Aye we'll see to that, cooled and stabled...' Celeste recognised one of the Muntor boys' voices when several shadowy figures appeared. They wore long cloaks like Cissy's own, which rippled with the colours of the night as they disappeared around the side of the inn.

Celeste shuddered even though the heat from the brazier had warmed her chest and heart, but the cold she felt was an icy finger running along her spine. 'Was that Ralfe Oarfish?'

The two women dismissed her question with a shrug, and silence. She took her own rough woollen cloak, plain as a field of bare earth compared to Cissy's, caught it in her fingers then pulled it over her knees but not before she had tutted loudly, which Dorothea and Cissy ignored. I am sure it was Raife she thought while she wondered how he fared.

*

Tara had laid out a beautiful crimson velvet dress, trimmed with creamy seed pearls and matching slippers for her to wear. Celeste, intrigued by the quality and the idea that Tara possessed something that was obviously expensive, had tried it on. The red velvet was as smooth and seductive as the lady it must have been made for. She had run her hands over the fabric while she stared into the looking glass, both embarrassed, and fascinated, while the fabric clung like a second skin to her figure. Cut low at her milky white throat, into a deep plunge that showed too much bosom, she thought, it was snug around her waist and skimmed her hips, before it fell in luxurious shades of red, scarlet, and deepest crimson.

She had wrapped the dress and slippers up and given them back to Tara. 'I am not going dressed like a loose-skirt.'

Tara replied coolly, 'Clothes for a lady, yes, but a loose-skirt could not afford them, no matter how talented she was with her tongue, nor, or how wide she could spread her legs.'

Celeste had blushed furiously and stomped out. On her next trip to market, she traded three brace of Coney, four Pheasant, and a pile of furs she had saved, one from a dead mountain cat, it was the palest gold like ripe barley, and she had wished the animal were still alive. The hide had not been damaged by predators, but the animal had been old and starved; she had happened to stumble across it while out foraging and hunting. The hide would make decent leather or suede if treated properly, and she had been keeping it for new breeches for the winter. Reluctantly she had traded it and the other skins for the trousers she wore now. Darkest brown, oiled and waxed to ward against the rain, with more than a dozen pockets and cuffed with a silver buckle at the ankle which she wore with her black boots, high at the ankle and thick of sole.

Slippers and clogs, velvet, and seed pearl! What does that woman take me for? Her eyes were full of envy when she studied Cissy's waistcoat; her own was plain soft suede over a deep green plain knit tunic, the same colour as her cloak, something else Tara had produced for her out of a chest that smelled of lavender and cypress. The courtyard was partially sheltered by the overhang from two wooden balconies that stretched out like arms from each side of the back of the wide tavern building. Enclosed in their embrace it seemed warmer than it was. Small doors on the floor above led to rooms that Carter's sister, round and jolly Chessie, the innkeeper of The Nag, rented out. The rooms sat above stores, kitchens, and workshops that were used by a carpenter, a farrier, and blacksmith.

The two arms of The Nag ended at a sandstone wall and the beginning of a large kitchen garden. Beyond that the stables faced the back of the inn. The ugly school bus was parked at the end, next to a pile of scrap metal, as if a child had discarded it in messy tangled heaps, Padrain's motorbike and sidecar hidden just behind.

The entertainment was beginning to get louder as people talked above the music. The musicians played harder, and folk whirled and danced, inside, and outside of the inn. The tap room doors had been unlocked, though few headed that way, not unless the elders had invited them, and only then if Padrain had given them the nod to do so. There were jugglers, fire eaters, dancers with tambourines, a makeshift stage had been made ready at one end of the Long Room for bards and minstrels to take their turn. Celeste looked at Cissy out of the corner of her eyes, not daring to draw her attention. *I will not let that sour little pig spoil this. "This" is as exciting as my life has been, even though Gan is not here – I will enjoy this night.*

~ ✦ ~ ✦ ~ ✦ ~

It was indeed almost perfect, exciting, but normal. Celeste had left her madness at home, sketching butterflies in front of the fire with a cup of strong valerian root tea. She had learned about such things from Dorothea during her time helping her. She was not sure when, but at some point, over the last few moons, she had stopped feeling guilty about drugging Tara with the remedies Dorothea suggested while she pulled packets of powder and vials of essences from the depths of her apothecary bag. It was probably when Celeste realised that the herbs were working; Tara was stable, lucid, and for the first time in what seemed an age, Celeste felt happy, though perhaps a little lonely. Still, she was content to wait for Ganaim to return, they had promised to love each other, and that sort of vow should be borne through solitude and separation. At first his absence had made her heart ache with longing and filled her head full of golden memories and what-ifs, while the halcyon shades of perfect summers she had created in her imagination, blinded her to the waxing shadows that were never far away, and the winter nights as they drew in, were a deeper shade of black.

She sighed then smiled, while a man with a bodhran drum accompanied by three women, one with a tambourine, danced and twirled before them. Smatterings of crystal light scattered across their faces like metal freckles as they caught the glow from the braziers while they moved through the steps of, *She*

Who Spins and Weaves. Their long crests of hair had been thinly plaited, even the man wore his the same, and they were all adorned with jewelled beads that shone like specks of rainbow, and made a chinking sound, like glasses raised to good health when they turned and spun.

'Dorothea.' A small boy skidded to a halt beside the table. He stopped then cleared his throat. His bushy black eyebrows waggled while he looked around the table, Cissy frowned at him. 'Light, sorry, me manners…Mrs Al Tine, your people are here, you are needed in the tap room.'

'No need to be so formal, Lugh. I hope it's quieter in there than in the Long Room, or out here,' she replied gently just as a cheer went up from the tables when a plume of flame sputtered out of one of the dancer's mouths and the two others spun so fast their silken skirts lifted to an indecent height.

'Light of the flame,' Lugh said while he goggled at them. He had never seen so much flesh, well not on a beautiful lady. Bathing in the river Wraith with his sisters and his ma' did not count.

Dorothea coughed. 'You were saying, Lugh?'

'Aye, Light, the council are waiting for you. I've been told to be on me best behaviour. Uncle Col thinks the new head may make an appearance later – he's fair flapping about it, wants the business done now,' he said hastily, his voice dropping to a whisper before he began to move off. Then he said, 'I'll tell them I've told you.'

'Wait, Lugh, you tell them I'm following after you, as I'll never keep up! Are you singing tonight, dear?' Dorothea stood slowly and ruffled his hair, while she smiled.

'Aye, I am if I get the tankards cleared. I'm to go on before Fairmist Al Mara and the Romarii fiddler, Rowa Hellfire. Light, I've to sing the Departed Dirge. Fairmist said he would play for me.' Lugh's eyes were big as saucers as he continued, 'Fairmist Al Mara, playing for me,' he shook his head in wonder. Then dropped it and frowned before he said in a hushed voice, 'It's to be done and gone, before that new head gets here…he wouldn't understand about such things, him being a city man.' He turned and sprinted off shouting over his shoulder, 'Me nerves are on end, Dorothea.'

Cissy chewed at her bottom lip while she watched him leave. Then turned her attention to her beaker of honey-wine and pulled a strange face, not sour, nor a scowl, but something that looked heavy with resignation, while a shadow passed over her face that looked like dread.

Dorothea turned to them and said, 'I will be back soon. It is usually the same trade agreements and contracts as it is every year. I am sure they only invite me out of courtesy. You two enjoy yourselves.' Cissy snorted, and Dorothea gave her a hard frown before she made her way after Lugh who had slipped and pushed his way through the crowds. People moved aside to let Dorothea pass, even though she was hardly taller than Lugh, as she followed the path he had made. Celeste groaned inwardly while she searched for something to say and found nothing. She gulped at her cider while Cissy watched her like a mountain cat watching a fat, stupid, slow rabbit. Celeste started to cough.

'Are you well, Celeste?' she asked dryly.

'Mm, it went down the wrong way that's all – I'll be fine,' Celeste replied using the sleeve of her new tunic to wipe her mouth and the tears from her eyes.

'It helps if one takes one's time drinking, especially at events like this…didn't Tara want to accompany you?' She put her glass to her lips gently, no more than wet them with the wine, screwed up her mouth, then returned it to the table.

'She felt…out of sorts, well, not really, she's a bit tired that's all, it's not really her thing,' Celeste stuttered as she realised Cissy knew she had been drugging Tara with herbs to keep her quiet, malleable to her request to go to the Night of the Dead, sedate and stupefied while she slipped away to have fun. Suddenly it felt like the most selfish thing in the world as Cissy continued to stare at her disdainfully.

It's not fair, how can he look like her? It is like his laughing eyes have been taken and put in her face, then turned hard and hateful. Celeste turned her back to Cissy and began watching a juggler who threw hoops and balls into the air while an older man sat by a brazier and began to play a lyre, and sing, *Naked Cassandra Novantae*, much to the delight of a group of young men – it was very explicit, and she wondered at the number of words there were to describe just one nipple.

Celeste was glad Dorothea had gone. She only half listened and wondered how she had survived the summer with Cissy, 'Her Sourness or sour puss,' she had begun to call her. In stark contrast, Dorothea was lovely to work with. She had so much love and generosity, not just with her goods but also her spirit and patience, all packed into that small body. Everyone knew her, they all stopped to speak to her, they shared a little bit of the life they were having that day. It made taking the stinking cheeses to the quota warehouses a bit more bearable. Where, on Dorothea's instruction, they remained neutral while the quota men took what was required by law and a little of what was not, leaving the bare minimum to be taken to what passed as a market in Mount Wraith. 'There is no need to cause trouble over light fingers and a bit of cheese, let them have it, Light knows they'll need it with winter coming.' Dorothea whispered.

After the quota, it would be off to market, no more than rows of tables and dusty stalls that sat around a market square with a large statue of his divinity Lord Lucas Abrecan at its centre. He held aloft a sword with carved wings shaped like shoulder blades at the handguard. His foot rested on the neck of a man, whose body was contorted in agony, his mouth snarled, and spider fangs protruded and dripped with venom, all beautifully cast in the most expensive bronze. There were other similar statues in all the squares of every town and city, with even more in the cities of Shad and Pali, where large temples housed the religious orders of Anuk. The largest was at Shad where it was rumoured there were more Acolytes of Anuk than there were slaves at Copper Tower. Most of the statues depicted the One-God Anuk, in the image of His Lord Lucas Abrecan, killing the monstrous horrors that had risen to defend the false goddess, Gaia.

They had their own place at market, outside in the square under a small wooden veranda that Dorothea hired from the market council. On the first day, Dorothea had nodded to the statue and hissed, 'Abomination. I am only pleased we face the back of the hideous thing.' Then Dorothea and Cissy had cautiously removed the boards hiding the false bottom of the cart and lifted out their other wares.

Where Dorothea was open and warm, Cissy was guarded and closed. She rarely passed the time of day with anyone, and seemed to be constantly fretting about something, seeking out the paper merchants when they arrived every three or four weeks, so she could buy paper and charcoal or lead pencils. She made the paper into small leather-bound journals which she sold or swapped. She carried her own with her everywhere, always scribbling away as if she were afraid she would forget the days as they spun past, into a future that Celeste could not see clearly. But still it festered on the horizon, a cauldron full of madness, ready to boil over, a melting pot ready to blow. Clouds of golden dust began to rise from fields, trees bent their boughs under the weight of fruit, bees droned, and fought for space as the late summer sun fattened like the deer in the woods. The harvest moon Luna bloomed behind black moon Lilith as if she would devour her, if only she would, and more crofters from the north arrived; although none were as heavily kissed by Fae blood as the Selgovae Fae had been.

Celeste stared into the distance, ignoring Cissy while she cast her mind back to her first week helping at market. 'How is Ganaim getting along at his cousins?' Celeste had asked Dorothea and Cissy, the first day of that first week, on the way to quota count and market, sitting on the back of the flat wagon, surrounded by produce.

'His cousins?' Cissy replied snootily, then whispered angrily to Dorothea, while she pushed the long reins into her hands, before she jumped from the moving cart, as agile as a mountain cat. 'We'll all be bloody well killed before we know it. Why do you not tell her?' She pointed at Celeste as she shouted angrily, 'Cousins!' Then she made her way towards the Bloom Forest. Her hat flew off and her hair erupted as if a firework had exploded. Celeste watched her go with her top lip curled and hatred bubbling inside. *Cissy sour puss, acid and alone, empty…and her hair is a disgrace, like a dried stack of hay gone wild. Miserable old sow.*

'She's in one of her funny moods again, never mind her…can be just like Padrain at times, all overcast and stormy. Come, Celeste, you sit up front with me, I'll show you how to drive.' Dorothea waited until she made her way over the produce to the front of the cart. It was uncovered today as the weather promised to be bright and sunny, according to Dorothea who informed Celeste, 'I can read the sky as well as Cissy reads those books of hers.'

When Celeste was seated comfortably, she put the long rein correctly in her hands. 'You know, Celeste, we're lucky to live where we do, Lord Bucky is a fair and decent governor. Once the quotas are met and the mainland is fed, we are reasonably free to trade and go to market.'

'I heard it isn't like this on the mainland. That there is plenty of food in Lodewick.' Celeste watched the dusty old road ahead rather than pay attention to Cissy who had almost disappeared. She did not want Dorothea to know how much she disliked her daughter.

'No, it's not like here, they have a little more food but a lot less freedom. Everything has changed and still, it will change more. Abrecan will not tolerate the freedom we have much longer. Not after Micah Apollon's outburst. We will all be in danger then.' Dorothea paused and her usually violet blue eyes became distant and shadowed with deep indigo. She shook her head and continued.

'Over the land bridge to the north, lay the lands of Cale, where the last battle took place; beautiful highland meadows, rolling hills and gentle plains, under the watchful gaze of majestic skies, but they are no longer populated as they were. We know that the glacier has covered much of what was there, whether permanently or not we do not know, perhaps some of the crofters will know better.' Dorothea's face lit up as her eyes cast about a landscape she recalled from her past. 'Now you may not believe me, but a race of magical beings once inhabited a city there called, A'chiad aite Fae, which is called first place of the Fae in the common tongue, and was named for their race, but of course it was not the only place they inhabited. There were other places where the ancient race lived, especially along the Straits of Loka, which were their lands. Their ships had sails that bristled with light like the purest white wings, as if swans floated on an azure sea as they sailed about the Bay of Loka all the way to the city of A'chiad aite Fae. They could trace their blood back to two tribes, Novantae and Selgovae. The Novantae seer Cassandra lived in her cave high above the town called the Gate of Loka, and she foretold of shadows yet to come, and the warriors of light who would stand afore them.' Dorothea sighed and moved Celeste's hands onto her lap and loosened her fingers about the reins.

'Another race also lived then, a race of warrior giants, all with flaxen hair plaited into warrior tails that hung long down their backs. They lived in a forest-city called One Tree in the common tongue, or An Crann Amhain, which as legend would have it, is the first seed from Gaia and Cernunnos' first tree. There is a town we called Stone, in the common tongue, but it was known as Tearmann an Cloch Cosmai. A sacred place, that none knew the way to, but rumoured to be somewhere past Serpent Lake.' Celeste smiled as the tension in her arms released and she listened intently to Dorothea. When she told stories of all the forbidden myths and legends, they seemed like the truth, whereas when Tara tried to tell her, everything she said was tainted with madness, every word she uttered filled her with fear.

'But the Fae, and the magical creatures who spun about their psychic and spiritual spheres, like planets spin around a sun, faded.' She paused, then turned to Celeste and said, 'It is why the magical light on their faces is dim, they are diminished, though some myths say that Cassandra Novantae shone like crystal glass so full of Eleri Imole legend said she did not bleed at all but that the fluid in her blood vessels was silver light. His Lord Bucky loved them so…' Dorothea trailed off thoughtfully as she passed an earthenware jug filled with rosehip cordial and spring water to Celeste, who frowned but took a drink while she politely ignored Dorothea's mistake. Surely Lord Bucky could not have been alive then? Dorothea means an ancestor of this Lord Bucky, Celeste reasoned.

Dorothea took a sip then replaced the cork stopper and put the earthenware jug under the wagon seat. She took a small square of cotton from her sleeve and dabbed at her forehead and neck. The sun hung above the horizon, a bright yellow ball, almost white in the bright sky – it would be a sweltering day. She offered Celeste another piece of cotton, then continued.

'The Fae and the Galanglas Giants, with their ancient lore, had to leave this land, for the white wizard could not promise he would or could protect them from the shadow that Cassandra Novantae foretold would come, and now all is ice and dangerous starvation as our goddess Gaia holds onto her lands in the North with what she can. The fair folk and giants are gone and with them their particular power and magic, a precious thing that was part of the Ever-Was. When they left, their power went with them, and by the goddess I miss that every day. The light fades and the shadows deepen.' Dorothea dabbed at her eyes with her cotton kerchief. Celeste felt her own prickle then fill with salt but did not dare reach down to her knee where Dorothea had laid the cotton square; she blinked and the wet subsided.

Dorothea nudged Celeste gently in the ribs. 'Give Hossy a bit more head love, he knows the way.'

'Now where was I…they will not tell you this in school, it belongs to them, so it is full of their falsehoods. To the East lies the barren waste of the Flat Lands where all of nature was exploited and laid bare by the lord governor, Rubric Volsunga, he that is War.' She screwed up her face and shuddered, her voice was tense and hard, and Celeste began to pay more attention; this felt real, threatening. Rubric Volsunga governed The Wind too, and she needed to know if the threat she felt crawling behind her, the eye of evil that had set its gaze upon her spine, was likely to come and kick in the door.

'Volsunga has control of the fortress cities where heavy industry is carried out, weapons of war are made there, although we are not at war.' She paused. Celeste nodded and recalled what Micah Apollon had said. Something about dog soldiers when we were not at war. Dorothea continued, 'They are desolate hungry places, barren areas, where natural resource has been stripped away to the very bedrock and the wind picks up speed across the flat land as if a steel blade were scything souls from the earth, but not all support that sort of exploitation. Volsunga has enemies; Lord Yew Drydanward would kill him if he could for the crimes he commits against nature, and the desecration of the forests there, and Lord Matthias Dolmen would like nothing better than Volsunga to wander into the Iron Hills. We feed the cities, not enough, and their rations are small, compared to ours. Our animals eat better, so we are lucky to be here, under Bucky's governance, and Cissy should remember that, sometimes she thinks she has it bad, when we do not.'

Celeste bit her lip, while she wondered how she would ask her question. She could hardly bring herself to mention the name and at mention of Volsunga, her stomach had flipped, and bile rose suddenly in her throat, then her tongue went dry. She was afraid that the name she uttered may bring the ominous curse that lingered like a shadow over her life into real existence. 'And The Wind?' she stuttered. 'Where is that?'

Dorothea's hands clasped tightly where they rested in her lap, but she maintained her steady gaze as she replied, 'Now who would want to know about such an awful place? It's not the type of thing young mai…young women would need to concern themselves with.'

'They don't say in school…yes we know about the fortress cities and that the glacier Amnasia takes more of the land each year, but we've never been told about the people who live there. Despite what you say, Dorothea, it is not the best here, so what must it be like in the Flat Lands, or at Shad, or Pali, the workers must be frozen or starved to death and…and The Wind…is used to terrify us. What is it really, Dorothea? I think I'm old enough to know.' Celeste sat up straight, a determined frown nipped her eyebrows together. Dorothea could not escape, like Cissy had. She wanted answers, she shifted her attention between Dorothea, the reins, and Hossy's plodding back. The large quota silos loomed like a low bank of grey cloud on the horizon.

'The Wind is a correctional colony that lays on a peninsula of land to the far north of the Flat Lands. It is across Wolf Bay, and to the north and east of the Giant Woods. Is that what you needed to know, Celeste?' She turned her head and stared hard at Celeste who nearly wilted under her gaze, her violet eyes were hard as crystal and just as cold.

Celeste steeled herself. 'If I wanted to know the geography of the area then yes, Dorothea. What do they correct, how do they do it?' Celeste finished sharply. Her tongue felt thick with emotion; she needed to know what they would do to her nan, and to her, if they were ever caught. 'I'm sorry, I didn't mean,' she trailed off, and dropped her head while a sheet of red set her cheeks aflame.

'I know, dear heart, I know, but why spoil the day with talk of that place. Tara is doing well with the herbs. You must not look to the dark lest it see you studying it and think your gaze a challenge. We're almost at the quota warehouse, chin up, and be nice to the guard.' She smoothed Celeste's auburn hair into place and adjusted the pretty blue ribbon she had insisted she tie round her hair. 'Straighten your skirts and apron, there's a love.' She smiled and Celeste obeyed. She hated the "goodwife" clothes they wore to market; full linen skirts in lichen green, with a white apron on top, a cotton bodice in blue wool with too many buttons and a plunging neckline over a linen blouse, which she thought was cut too low, and too tight. The whole outfit made her want to gag and she hated the way the flesh of her breasts jiggled like jelly whenever she moved, while she wished for her breeches or her dungarees. Cissy wore nothing else but dungarees, but then again, Cissy was not a decoy she thought dryly as they rounded the corner of the dusty old road and passed through the open gate in the high wire fence. Black pulled the cart and its wares easily towards the quota complex, five large grey barns for livestock and six squat silos for grain behind. The anti-gravity craft landed behind the silo when they came to collect produce come harvest time. Livestock was shepherded down to Porth on the drover's road, then by ship to the mainland.

'Here you are, dear, a little bit of this won't go amiss either.' She passed Celeste a small pot, made a satisfied "harrumph" in the back of her throat and nodded approvingly when Celeste sighed but dabbed the waxy cherry-balm on her lips.

~ ❦ ~ ❦ ~ ❦ ~

'Here,' Cissy said shortly, and Celeste jumped back from her memories while the other woman she pushed a couple of thin silver bars, no bigger than the tip of her small finger to the first knuckle bone. 'It's your pay for helping out.'

'I err…I didn't expect anything – it's not why I agreed to help.' Celeste blushed but took the money anyway. A couple of silver bar was as much real money as she had seen in a long while – although Tara always had money, she had no idea where it came from, and had always assumed she sold her paintings for a reasonable sum, folk-art like that could be exported to the cities she supposed. A family of four could live, quite frugally mind, for a week on one silver bar. It seemed too much. But I have been working from sunup to sundown for over three moons and putting up with old misery guts most days – actually, it is not enough.

'I know it's not why you did it.' Cissy's voice softened. 'Celeste, it's about Ganaim. He's gone with his cousins.' She tilted her head to one side and shrugged, then said, 'He's been away for moons now, and well, you know how lads are, things could have changed. He may not be the same. You know,' she paused, and Celeste took immense pleasure in witnessing her struggle to find soft words, words that did not hurt or sting. Intrigued, she leaned forward and tried not to smile at the other woman's discomfort.

Cissy continued. 'He may not feel the same…when he comes back…I'm not sure if it will change him…sometimes it does.' She shook her head, perplexed, then picked up her drink; her hand trembled slightly as she took a large mouthful and grimaced. 'Actually. I am sure, and if you've any sense, you will bear this in mind – he will not be the same. None of us ever are,' she finished sharply, and put her beaker on the table with a bang.

'What?' Celeste was startled and hurt. It was the most she had ever said, conversationally that is, and as usual it was as sour as a cooking apple.

'What do you know anyway, Cissy sourpuss?' Celeste replied. She winced inside, her voice was too loud but matched the sudden rush of temper she felt. She got to her feet, banged her own cider jug on the table, and turned to stomp off. Cissy reached forward and grabbed her wrist. The few people who remained at the tables glanced over once, then ignored them, while they stood and took their own tankards in hand and headed inside – it was nearing time for the Departed Dirge.

Cissy laughed, then threw her head back, and laughed again, loudly, gaily, but she hissed at Celeste quietly. 'Oh, Celeste Melsie, you'd be surprised at what I know. Leave my son alone, do not take him into danger and I will tell you what you want to know. About slippery Selene – the sneaky little deal she struck – how she slid away, and I had to stay.' She picked up her beaker and drained her wine in one gulp while Celeste watched, horrified. 'The things I gave up…it's a sad tale if you want to hear it.'

'Get lost.' Celeste pulled her wrist out of her grip and stormed off. She was away in her cups, all caution to the wind with too much honey wine. Always spying on us, sneering, and scowling any time she saw me or Nana, and now this,

this sabotage. *What is she trying to do, poison my thoughts and feelings, while hers are already as acidic as drake shit? It is because we love each other, and she has none in her.* 'She's got a problem with me and Gan, stuck in her bloody cups that's what she is,' Celeste muttered angrily and continued to walk, not really bothered about which way she took, she just wanted to put distance between them.

She made her way through the gap in the stone wall, and into the large kitchen gardens beyond which had been lit with rainbow-coloured lanterns that hung from stakes in the ground, immobile giant will-o'-the-wisps, hanging in the sharp air like balls of brightly coloured promises. They bathed the whole area in elemental light that cast soft nimbuses of colour in pools at her feet – it was beautiful. She sighed and felt a stab of loneliness like a dagger made of ice, right in the centre of her chest. *I should be stealing kisses with Gan, right now.*

The raucous noise from The Nag suddenly muted as she stepped further behind the sandstone wall. The river was louder, water rushed like the sound of the wind from winters heart. It slapped against the stony bank where the short jetty behind The Nag was. Row after row of dark green leafy veg, squash, garlic, leeks, and rhubarb lay, waiting harvest. She could almost hear the damp earth crusting beneath a thin coat of frost, and the scent of slow growing things that cast their aroma into the dark, thick tendrils of life that crept like fingers along the surface while the air above continued to freeze. The weaving rows looked like end-to-end dead bodies, hessian sacks laid over lumpy shapes of vegetables that snaked away neatly, but that was not what interested Celeste. A single tent sat expectantly in the shadows, just on the other side of the wall, but tucked away in the far-left corner. *How will anyone know this is here?* Celeste thought as she made her way to the Romarii fortune-teller. The small silver oblongs in her pocket clinked, dully.

Little Lugh had begun to sing a folk tale about the giant warrior caste, Galanglas. They were Masters of the seas, and songsmiths to the trees, protectors of people, animals, and a sacred stone. Dorothea had told her about the Galanglas. They once lived in a forest-city, An Crann Amhain, now abandoned like the city of Fae. *We are never told this* she thought, and a suspicious kind of fear set her nerves on edge.

Lugh began to sing, softly at first, then his voice gained strength and confidence, a high wind that keened sharply across the bubbles of silence that hung around the crowded tables, while each person looked into their glass, and their eyes were wetter than the liquid within.

Celeste halted and leaned against the chill wall to listen. Fairmist Al Mara strummed a mountain dulcimer, soft and slow, and Rowa Hellfire, the Romarii fiddler made his instrument cry, softly; background sadness that flowed like a full lazy river into the chill night as she heard one person after the other rise.

'They took my son, Conor an Mhorn, gone to work the wind,' a gruff male voice stated.

'My daughter Afric, her husband Enda, and their bairns, Aine and Alma,' another voice said as if she read a list of things to do, though her voice was thick with emotion.

A woman defiantly said, 'They took my betrothed, my beloved, Fair Fionn Senones, and I will have my recompense, in this life or the next.' She raised her voice. 'When the war comes, I will go.' People banged their hands and glasses on the tables – the dulcimer never lost a note, the violin wailed, and Lugh sang the names of the dead like a chorus of angels.

Celeste hunched her shoulders to her ears and covered her mouth with her hand when Raife Oarfish stood. She would recognise his voice anywhere. There had always been the hint of laughter there, lilting but deep, and honest, though that had gone, and it was taut with grief this night. 'My sister Sirena, Melaine Merilyn, and Hel Croce, all for saying no to the blood sucking parasites, the Acolytes of Anuk.' His voice strained and cracked, and he sobbed loudly, but only once. Then he took a deep breath and said, 'My friend Bran Muntor taken from his community, thought of as dead by you folk here, and thrust upon the dagger path because of the deed he had to do.' There was a moment where the only sound was that of the River Wraith speeding past and it sounded like a mournful wind. Then Padrain said into that space, 'They were gone, our daughters were gone, and from this night hence Bran Muntor is remembered as a demon slayer.'

Then Raife's mother began to ululate like an injured animal and the men, and women alike, banged their fists upon their chests or the tables before them and said as one, 'Demon Slayer.'

Celeste crouched down and sat on her heels, her back against the wall while she wrapped her arms round her knees and moaned, then wept in guffawing sobs that were full of fear, and frustration; it would be her and nana Tara next. She knew it would.

*

After their first visit to the Acolytes of Anuk and subsequent modifications, the girls had refused a summons to return to the temple at Ninmah. It seemed that their developing galactic signatures were of interest to the acolytes there, a branch of The Sisterhood of Bloodgita, called the Children of Bloodgita, who were governed by an Aldhelm. They were a mixed order and were beginning to monitor the rural areas around Ninmah, especially after Bucky had had to repair the ruined Guratt's. Perhaps if they had not gone, perhaps if they had not been so naïve as to bring themselves to the attention of the Children of Bloodgita in the first place, perhaps they would have lived. When they said no, a half dozen acolytes arrived in a copper orb, that pissed rays of blue alchemical light through the overcast, and landed in one of farmer Merilyn's wheat fields, where the crops were failing, and the three girls were soil singing.

At first, they screamed for help when the acolytes moved in on them. One punched Melaine in the gut, and another kicked Hel Croce's legs from under her and kneeled on her back while he caught her hair in his hand and pulled a blade from his belt.

Sirena, panicked, and her fear rose through her body like the sharp edge of a blizzard. It brushed aside the false hold the nano device had on her power as if it were a mote of dust before its fury. The nano device exploded out of her wrist and her full power, when it came, was a river of fire, a spuming geyser that the earth beneath her feet gifted her, from deep within its sacred belly. It cascaded through her body until she was incandescent, until she felt it light every cell, and harmonize every atom of her being to a frequency that was beyond sound and a light that was beyond vision, and behind it all she heard a song, and in her heart, she knew her galactic signature was more powerful than she had been told, and at its centre a platinum Eagle soared.

'Cernunnos,' she cried and ran to the centre of the field to aid her friends. Another force lifted her hands above her head, though she did not really know what she was doing, she called on a power more ancient and potent than any of them knew or understood. 'Cernunnos m'hathair, an domhain. Cabhair liom.'

'My father, Cernunnos, aid me,' she howled the words into the sky, and they took on shape, and form. Blood poured from her wrist while she made wings with her hands. Then eagle, and raven, answered her call, and the crows came flying down like black hail, and all manner of hawk circled and keened overhead and from their midst a lightning bird appeared, resplendent in black feathers that shone like oil and white feathers that shimmered like fresh snow. It screeched and bolts of white light crackled then speared through the hearts of two acolytes before they hit the ground. The other birds flew at the acolytes, herding them back towards the orb under a storm cloud of feather, sharp claws, and hard beaks.

Melaine and Hel were Seed and Earth galactic signatures and when they got to their feet, they emptied the contents of a nearby stream on the acolytes' heads in a glassy shaft of water that broke a collar bone and shattered a skull. Then they called to the vegetation that ran under the ground and tied the acolytes' feet up with roots and vines. The earth beneath the orb yielded like sinking sand and the craft began to disappear.

Their families saw the birds gathering and the lightning bird discharging its fury while they ran to their aid, but as far as the acolytes were concerned, it only proved their suspicion, that the girls' nano implants had not dulled their galactic signature powers, and that Sirena Oarfish had hidden her birth date and had somehow hidden the majesty of an Eagle power behind the lowest Earth resonance.

Their black blood had run to ice when she called on Cernunnos and their craven hearts quaked. Surely, he was dead and gone their Aldhelm thought, but he knew that times were not just changing, but had changed and that they were here, at the eve of destruction where light and shade was balanced on the edge of a single hair. He saw Cernunnos' power rise from the earth and enter Sirena in molten, liquid light, which was redder and more golden than a phoenix feather. He heard the lightning bird and his innards turned to ice; how can it be he thought. Then, he crawled on the ground while the girls were distracted. He rolled to his feet behind Sirena and pointed his laser weapon into her back. 'I will end her,' he shouted, and Hel and Melaine dropped their hands. The roots dispersed, then the earth became solid, the birds lifted and circled overhead.

It all happened at once, quicker than the eye could follow, but her family heard her when Sirena screamed, 'Keep fighting, we are dead anyway.'

She spun quickly and faced the Aldhelm down. Then she raised her bloodied hand and used the last of her life force to send a beam of fire, a shaft of fury so raw it had come from the raging heart of a volcano, straight into his chest, at the same time, he pushed the transducer on his laser baton.

According to goodwife Oarfish, who had been told by goodwife Merilyn, the acolytes then used a device in their hands, a black rod about a hand's length long with symbols on the side, which interfered with what Melaine, and Hel were doing. They broke their connection to their power and the birds flew away and the earth became soil again.

After that, Raife Oarfish, Margeride Shroude, Bran Muntor, and Sarlat Penroe disappeared. Celeste had heard the goodwife Shroude whisper to Dorothea, when she came to market all harrowed and scarlet rimmed about her eyes, that Margeride and the others had gone to run with the Romarii, it being the only safe place left. Bran Muntor had left on a smuggler boat to seek the Silver Tower. Dorothea had patted her arm and whispered, 'They will be as well as can be with my people, your Margeride was a good hedge witch, her healing skills will be valued highly. Hiriwa Pourewa, will be the right place for Bran.

The goodwife Shroude threw her hands about Dorothea's neck and cried for the longest time. When she pulled away, she said in a voice thick with grief, 'Dot you don't understand. Bran followed them to Ninmah, and the first time Melaine and Hel walked out of the temple wearing the ochre robes of the Children of Bloodgita, he put an arrow through each of their hearts.'

~ ❀ ~ ❀ ~ ❀ ~

Celeste pressed the back of her skull into the wall and snorted her salty grief back down her throat. She knew it to be true. Bran had killed his betrothed, Melaine Merilyn, and took the life of his friend, Raife's, heart's desire, Hel Croce. Raife had turned up at The Nag this very night along with the Romarii, though he was much changed from the lanky youth she knew not more than a few moons ago. He had filled out, and was tall and strong, but the laughter had gone from his warm eyes and the mist of his sorrow had turned his gaze to stone, and his anger flared amber bright. He wore the shimmering cloak of a Roma Ranger like the mark of his maturity, as surely as he wore his grief at the loss of his twin like a shroud.

Voice after voice stated the names of their dead and bushy browed Lugh lamented each departed as if he sang of the great deeds of long-lost warriors. 'They shall atone,' Celeste heard the gathered throng say together as she wiped her nose on her sleeve and regained her feet slowly. She peered, wet-eyed and sad beyond belief, around the corner of the gap in the wall towards the emptied yard. All the people had made their way indoors to listen to Lugh's angelic voice, to let the Departed Dirge break their hearts. As the dirge came towards its end, those who had instruments accompanied the small group on the stage with pipes, small drums, a lyre, and harp, and a list of the dearly departed – not one person left nor raised their voice until everyone who had gone had been recalled to hearts and minds.

Then Lugh said, 'Thank you, one, and all, for the remembrance of our dearly departed. After a short break, Fairmist Al Mara will sing the long version of Charyia Al Farraige Stoirme's shanty, accompanied by Tintean Ramah.' The crowd gave thunderous applause for Lugh, but also because Fairmist Al Mara and the fiddler Rowa Hellfire, also known as Tintean Ramah, who sang like a god as he played the fiddle with all the fire from the seven hells behind him, would sing with Fairmist. The Romarii troubadour was not a small man as Romarii go, but Fairmist Al Mara was half as tall again and easily head and shoulders taller than Padrain and Ganaim Al Tine, who Celeste thought were the tallest men she had ever met.

Celeste took the rough stone path that skirted the kitchen garden and headed towards the stables. She had no desire to be with anyone. The departed dirge had left her feeling wretched, and afraid. Seeing the horses stabled there was the only kind of company she wanted. She passed within a hand's width of the tent which seemed deserted. She paused and her breath felt too wet, still too full of sorrow while it curled out of her nostrils and misted away in the chill air. The gold scalloped edge around the crown of the dome of the tent glittered warmly when the light from the lanterns caught it just so, and the intricate symbols and images of gods she was not familiar with shimmered. As stealthily as she could – it looked deserted – she put her ear to the canvas; nothing, not a sound from inside. She reached out to touch an image of a woman, a goddess red-brown, tall, and strong, who appeared to be marrying a gigantic snake with the face and upper torso of a man who looked kindly, but sad; a single tear had been embroidered onto his earthy coloured flesh in bright blue. He was speared through the heart and his hands were tied. They were surrounded by three different coloured eggs, amber, green, and violet, which were held aloft by large spiders. Hundreds of other woodland animals as well as birds and insects cavorted about the walls of the tent, a scene which was filled with joy and sadness.

'Why don't you step through the veil, child?' a soft voice enquired into the dark. Celeste jumped and turned hastily. 'Don't you want to know what the god of love has in store for you?'

'How much does it cost?' Celeste asked as she parted the thick velvety material that hung across the opening of the tent.

The fortune-teller was dressed in what she thought must be traditional robes, garish and carnival bright, heavily embroidered with geometric shapes and symbols which reminded her of the things she had seen when she had a fit at school, but the Romarii seer was completely veiled.

'Silver is what I seek.' She extended her arm, a long brown index finger slipped out of the robe, waggled once to indicate Celeste should sit on a leather pouffe, opposite the one she occupied; miscellaneous occult objects lay on a low wooden table between them.

Damn it Celeste thought and pressed her hard earned silver bars together in her pocket. 'Here.' She took out one of the bars and slid it across the small table. 'Is that right?' She sat down heavily and started to cough. The inside of the tent stunk of mouldy damp, which snatched at her breath. Thick smoke poured from ornate silver censers that hung from supporting joists above their heads and made her eyes sting and nose pour with fluid. She wiped her eyes on a corner of her cloak just as she saw the silver bar shushed away into the folds of the seer's heavy cloak. There was no way to tell what she looked like under there, so she studied the seer's hands: rough, nails short, and dirty, a pad of hard skin on the inside of both thumbs, weapon, and tool calluses.

'More than enough, but gratefully received all the same. Your hand please.' She took it and placed it in hers. Then using her other hand, she removed a black cloth from a large egg-shaped violet crystal that sat on the low table between them. Celeste felt her palm tingle, then she began to sweat, and her stomach fluttered uncontrollably while more smoke belched from the censer into her eyes.

'Daughter of the moon, this night has many portents.' The Romarii seer waved her hand above the crystal which remained opaque and thoroughly unimpressive.

Celeste sighed heavily and muttered, 'Oh I see, it's a night with many portents that just happens to be the Night of the Dead, wouldn't take a wise man to figure that out.' What a waste of a bar, she thought as she tried to retrieve her hand from the seers, but her grip tightened, and a small flurry of fear crept along the flesh at the nape of Celeste's neck. She knew little about the mysterious

Romarii, only what Ganaim told her – which focussed on bare knuckle bouts and dangerous tales of villainous acts. Light, does she have a dagger under there?

'Pay attention, child…you've paid after all,' the seer scolded her and tutted before continuing. 'I see a liar, a thief, and a prince, all forbidden unless his prophecy comes to pass, had you, wants you, your heart belongs. The hour of the witch has passed, she rode the dragon to hell to make way for the new dawn. Now,' she paused and lifted her finger, 'we bend to the will of the white wind. Tonight, we say goodbye to our dearly departed, the prophet, and the crone, both killed by the blind man who stands alone. He can be anywhere he wants to be, only he controls the creation storm, or his kin…not the first, but the second born. The darkness comes for you,' she hissed, and Celeste felt her spine turn to water and waited for it to run between her legs such was the weight of the seers' words.

'It will write it across the palms of your hands.' She paused while she opened Celeste's hands and bent her head towards her palms as if she sought the dark in them herself. 'Then, the journey you must make will take you to strangest lands.' She released her hands.

Celeste stared at them, then at the thickly woven veil over her eyes. 'I err…I thought you were going to tell me about love.' She was surprised at how whiny and desperate she sounded, and she wondered whether she risk asking for her silver bar back. The seer had told her nothing; it was just words with an excess of dramatics and meaning that was as clear as the smoky interior of the tent.

'I just did,' the seer retorted coolly, then shrugged.

'Oh…I thought it would be different.' Celeste remained seated, not sure what to do, when suddenly she felt the urge to rise. She did so slowly and bowed out of the tent. She could hear Dorothea calling gently for her as she reached the veiled entrance and was glad that there was someone close by who would come if she screamed.

The Romarii seer stood and moved gracefully around the table. She was at least two hands taller than Celeste. She placed her calloused hand on Celeste's chest and her words were rough, her throat sore with censor smoke when she said, 'You won't know what love is until your heart has been broken, Celeste Melsie. Be prepared tonight, to experience love.'

'Thank you,' Celeste muttered as she stepped back, turned, and pushed through the curtain. Ganaim's on his way back, she thought, completely misunderstanding the seer's warning. At last, the horrible emptiness she had felt since he left, would be eased. He always made everything better. The stabbing ache in her lonely heart, was the ache of a broken heart about to be mended by the return of her true love.

She paid no attention to how or why the Romarii seer would know her name, she took the seers words and twisted them to her own desire to fulfil her own selfish need while she hurried along the path next to the garden. The gap in the wall was a dark square and the stone was coated on top with hoarfrost. Her breath purled like steam from a kettle, and she pulled her cloak tight to her chest, just as Dorothea walked through.

'Coming, Dorothea. Are we ready to go? Is Cissy with you?' she asked and knew her voice had been too tense. She ducked her head rather than meet Dorothea's eye while she made her way alongside the rows of dark shaped vegetables towards the courtyard. The lanterns had grown dim although the noise from the inn was still merry. She could see folk taking their young one's home, carried asleep in strong arms or across backs like small sacks of grain.

'No, you'll be glad to hear just you, me, and Padrain. Cissy is getting along famously with the new head; she will be using that room no doubt. Come, it's well past midnight now, it's the time when the young men and women take part in the oldest dance, time us old folk and bairns were away to bed.' She put her arm around Celeste's shoulders. 'Have you been crying? What were you doing in the gardens, dear?'

Celeste glanced back, but the small pavilion had gone. 'I was looking at the last of their rhubarb,' she lied.

Dorothea studied her a little too intently while they made their way along the stone path next to the wall. Then she nodded sagely and said in a hushed voice, 'The dirge gets longer every year. It is always hardest to bear when it is the first time you hear it. The first time someone you know is named.' Celeste wiped at a sudden sting in her eyes. Dorothea paused and took her hand in her own and squeezed it while she met her gaze. 'Longer, and a whole lot sadder,' she said quietly, and Celeste bobbed her head once and gulped back a wave of raw emotion. She recalled Raife's single sob, full of grief, anger, and hatred, and she knew that she did not trust herself to speak.

They made their way past the heaps of scrap to the motorbike and sidecar that they had arrived on, a luxury compared to what most had. Pushing her grief to one side she focussed on the rickety old sidecar and sucked air from her cheek, it would be her job to light the way home. She was glad that Cissy was staying at the inn, not just because of her sour disposition, but because there would be room in the sidecar now; she had been squashed tightly next to her all the bumpy way to Mount Wraith from the farm.

Celeste jumped in and arranged her cloak tightly around her. It would be freezing on the journey back; a pile of old sheep skins was stuffed inside the sidecar which she pulled around her too. Dorothea got nimbly behind Padrain; her long gown had split skirts that had been sewn as if they were trousers, so she did not have to ride sideways on. Padrain kicked the old machine into life, a cloud of blue smoke burst from the exhaust, it smelled warm and of alcohol like the hidden still. Celeste happily picked the lantern up and held it in place on the front of the sidecar. She watched the lamp light pool on the ground in front of her, before adjusting the small, mirrored discs to direct the light beam, so that it was focussed down and a few feet in front of them.

'Right then, goggles on…are we all ready?' Padrain asked and they both checked their goggles then nodded as the vehicle stuttered out from behind the school bus and onto the road, she heard the horses whinny and stamp their feet as the bike picked up speed on the road that ran next to the stable wall. Suddenly the world turned dark when they left the inn behind and the yellow light that pooled on the road, did not seem bright or big enough while they gained speed and left Mount Wraith behind. The wind whipped at her hair and stole her breath away, moths pattered on her googles and the road ahead seemed liquid in the lamp light. A fast brown river flowing too quickly for her eyes to follow but still she shouted while they tore along country lanes, keep her centre, pothole left or deep ruts to the right while they hurtled along in the pitch dark, on a khaki green machine from another planet that Padrain said was "almost a whole Norton", though none of the lights worked, and it ran on Cheen now.

A quarter of a mile away from the farm, Dorothea put her hand up, 'Stop!' she shouted to Padrain above the noise of the engine. Anything that ran on Cheen fuel was smelly and noisy, but he heard her and turned his head sharply.

'Are you sure, Dot?'

'Stop, Pad. Something is wrong. Hossy is out, he is on the road.'

Celeste turned towards Dorothea, while Padrain brought the bike to a stop. Her usual dark red skin looked pale and misted with dew, her eyes were wide and bright, they glittered like ground amethyst, more purple than Celeste had ever seen them. She clung to Padrain's back, craning to see over his shoulder, and to Celeste's eye she was suddenly small and frail, and it seemed as if something about the Night of the Dead had begun an earnest unravelling of what she thought she knew, a dissolution that had begun when Lugh sang. Then Raife Oarfish's lament, and his mother's ululation had pushed her to the seer's tent, she had walked through the veil and now a knowing in the pit of her stomach greased its way into her thoughts. Nothing would ever be the same again.

Her attempt to stabilise Tara, would not work. It was a bandage across a split in the earth while the molten rock pulsed and burned below. It was like pushing the tide back with a sieve, a useless action, against the hand of fate and Tara's certain destiny. Celeste knew it and felt the certainty settle in her gut like a ball of lead, when she saw fleeting terror cross over Dorothea's face and though she tried to hide it, it was still there in her eye, and in the tremble on her hand.

The mask Dorothea had worn for all of Celeste's life slipped. Her other worldliness made it seem as if Padrain carried a changeling strapped to his back. Her age and her vulnerability were stripped away, revealed as the lie they were, lambent purple irises in large, slanted eyes, too large for a heart-shaped face that was forever young, and eternally wise. Dorothea was both young and ancient – timeless. Celeste gasped and blamed it on the cider, the grief, the heady rush of freedom while she pushed her nonsense to the back of her mind and put her hand on Dorothea's leg. She was not a strange creature, she was Ganaim's grandma.

'What is it, Dorothea, what's wrong?'

'How…?' Padrain trailed off then said, 'Oh, never mind, where is he?'

'Right there.' Dorothea pointed into the dark.

'Celeste, shine the lamp where I point.' The weak lantern light revealed a sleek patch of night that was blacker and shinier than the dark around it. Hossy Black blew softly, and his breath steamed like curling dragon smoke while he hoofed at the ground, he looked at Dorothea and lowered his head.

'There's something wrong at the shed,' she cried.

Celeste pushed the lamp at Dorothea and leapt out of the sidecar, as if the white lunar wind had lifted her and propelled her on to Hossy's back in a fluid motion that left Padrain gawking and Dorothea shouting, 'No, child! You must not go there; I will handle this.' Black did not shy away or rear, it was like he knew what to do as Celeste grabbed his mane. She did not have to heel him to get him moving, he was off before she even thought about it.

'Celeste, wait! Let Padrain go…it could be dangerous…'

'No!' Celeste yelled back. 'There isn't anything faster than Black, follow me if you must.' She rattled away, sitting back on her seat bones, her lower legs close to his neck, and hunched over – a bit like a lumpy sack of grain, as she rode clumsily bareback toward the shed. They tore past the gate to Al Tine Farm and on down the grassy lane. Nellie ran alongside, thundering down Long Field over the hedge. How are the horses out, light, what is wrong?

Chapter Nineteen

Broken-Hearted

Hossy Black skittered to a halt next to the rusted gate. The shed was quiet, a pool of light spilled from Tara's studio. Tara would often be in there, sometimes working. Though usually it was doing odd things, at odd hours. Why should tonight be any different, Celeste reasoned as she slid off Black's back and rubbed her buttocks. The large horse snorted, and plumes of vapour purled from wet nostrils. His flanks quivered but he settled to wait patiently at the gate as she stepped through the gap in the hedge. She may be still awake, did I put too much powder in her dinner, she may not have drunk the valerian tea, did I make it too strong? Light above, let her still be awake, let her not be mad, let me not have poisoned her.

Celeste walked stiffly over the yard; a rustle near the outbuildings startled her, and a knot of fear had her clenching her stomach tight. The cider she had drunk, frothed up her gullet and left a sour taste as it reached the back of her throat. Rats. They must have come back after the Duster Drake had gone south. I will have to tell Ganaim to let Cissy know; I will not be telling the old hag that we have rats again, she thought as she began to hurry over the yard. Black whinnied but stood patiently at the gate, looking up the lane, waiting for Dorothea and Padrain while Celeste reached the door and let herself in. She walked quietly through the house, but her heart hammered in her chest and sweat oiled down her back. She could feel a strange vibration, a tremor and was not sure if it were her fear or if it ran through the air. She gulped, the taste of salt in her saliva had thickened on her tongue and was tangy and metallic, but she refused to rush. If she was asleep, the last thing she wanted to do was wake her, especially if it was mad Tara who opened her eyes. The kitchen felt steamy and damp, the kettle on the stove was boiling and was starting to mist the window; two cups waited next to the teapot.

'Nana, I'm back, I'll just bring the tea through, shall I?' Celeste called quietly, just loud enough not to wake someone who was asleep, and in as normal a tone as possible.

'Yes, bring it through, I heard you come in…Celeste, then we need to have a talk.' She sounded lucid and Celeste felt her chest cave in. Her relief was so strong she had to hold onto the table to steady herself while she bit back tears and took deep breaths. Her hand shook while she began pouring the water onto the tea. Then she pumped water that they did not need which did nothing to stop her hands shaking, and her silly heart from racing. It is fine, what had Dorothea been so worried about?

'This isn't about "the talk," is it?' Celeste shouted playfully from the kitchen. She bit back a giggle. The cider had been stronger than she thought. Then she gulped and continued, although her voice held an unnatural tremor. 'I'll read a book if you don't mind,' she finished as she prepared herself to enter the studio. Please let it not be more paintings on the wall, I will not have time to remove them before Dorothea and Padrain arrive.

'Not that, silly,' Tara replied lightly. 'I'm sure you and that Al Tine boy have been doing plenty of homework where that's concerned, regardless of what I've said on the subject of giving Ganaim Al Tine a wide berth. Nooo, this is more important.'

She talked a little more loudly as Celeste put her teacup on a saucer. Light, I thought I had poisoned her with valerian. That, is, it, no more sedation, she worried, then she whispered, 'Dear lord or lords or whatever the heck's up there, please don't let her be crazy when I go through with this tea – not tonight, please not tonight.' Her head ached and buzzed. She stopped to gulp down a cup of water, the taste in her mouth was strange and set her teeth on edge. No more cider she thought. The night had been odd in a way she was not used to, at least the strangeness on the other side of the kitchen door was hers, familiar.

She poured tea into her mug and added honey, then some into Tara's cup, plain hot tea, it was from Janome; Dorothea had given them it. She took a handful of dried mint and put that in too. We will get proper Turanga black tea too, she thought and recalled the smell of tobacco at The Nag earlier that night, and the mention of coffee, real coffee not Chib, and goodwives talking of spices, nutmegs, and cinnamon for flavouring instead of herbs and berries. She took a gulp of sweet tea, pleased to be rid of the sour taste the cider had left on her tongue and embraced her relief fully while she wondered if Dorothea had not been a bit reckless to startle her so.

Tired, she was in no mood to deal with Tara's erratic behaviour tonight, especially since Dorothea and Padrain would arrive soon. *I hope Dorothea can explain what just came over her.* Resigned to an end to the evening that was bound to be as sour as the cider tasted in the back of her throat, Celeste took another two cups from the cupboard, then left them next to the kettle before she opened another cupboard and brought out sweet bread buns.

'I need to tell you about things…Oh dear Lord, where to start…you need to know about your mother, Selene, as well as your galactic signature,' Tara raised her voice, clear and determined, there was no hint of the usual range in tone and mood, waves and crashing depths as her madness helter-skeltered. *Thank the Light she sounds lucid,* thought Celeste.

'Who's that out there? Who is in the yard…Don't you dare point at me – not now? Quickly, CELESTE…' Tara shouted then was suddenly cut off. Celeste groaned, pulled open the kitchen cupboard and found the tin where she had hidden the small packets of sedative powders.

~ ❈ ~ ❈ ~ ❈ ~

From the kitchen to the studio was mere steps away and directly through the door, no winding corridor or other room to walk through, only the gap in the wall. They lived small lives in a tiny cottage that used to be cattle shed. They stepped from one room to the next like people turn a page in a book to read the story. It should have been that quick, but it was not.

Celeste felt as if she walked on the spot while Tara called to someone in the yard. The tea tray was glued in her hands, like some grotesque prayer bead, a penance that should not be dropped or discarded, like the one the Acolytes of Anuk carried. She walked slowly and carefully towards Tara while she thought, *at least she has stopped her rambling.* A wave of tension tightened her jaw, but she was determined to keep everything as normal as possible, even though a strange thrill of excitement fluttered in her stomach…*Selene? The name Cissy had used earlier.* With a heart full of trepidation, she sucked at the well of her cheeks, her saliva tasted of copper and salt, but she gulped it down, walked with deliberate ease into the room, and sighed with relief when she saw the top of her silver hair just above the back of her favourite chair. She still watched out of the large window, into the inky dark beyond.

    Celeste blew her hair out of her eyes; it was just another one of the strange things Tara did. The one where she would just gaze at an invisible thing that only she could see, which existed in the middle distance, somewhere over there. Celeste half-smiled and wondered at her earlier alarm. Here, all was peaceful and still, a moment in time caught in the kaleidoscope of her life. She made her way to the small table next to the chair when suddenly, the tray slipped from her hands, and fell away. She watched the china scatter, then tumble in a slow weary motion, as the lovers on the bridge beneath a giant willow tree, were suddenly turned upside down. The tea, a tattered ribbon of hot liquid, was suddenly solid, suspended in mid-air like a ribbon of translucent-brown glass, while everything else dropped to the ground, and her heart followed them and she tried to move faster, but the air was thick with invisible power, and she could not.

    Scalding liquid splattered across sheets of paper laid out in neat rows on the floor. They were scrawled with all her conspiracies, ordered by category of madness, while Celeste felt her life end, over, and over, again, and the sound of a motorcycle in the distance sounded like the orb that had come to take Melaine Merilyn, Hel Croce, and Sirena Oarfish away.

    She stifled a scream while she read the headings. Missing people, the Nympts know the way home, dark magic used, Romarii spies are The Brotherhood of Morrigan, the name of the beast and his kin, the tyrant King is conquest, war and famine are here, she had scrawled across one page, who is Bucky, where is Death, across another. Dorothea is the queen of the soil people, The Romarii are not what they seem, the Al Tine boy is Novantae, sired by the Volpi Lord. Neat rows that stretched from her feet to the windowed door of her studio. The tea had marked them like drake shit and splotches of lichen on white gravestones; her madness lay like a death sentence at Celeste's feet, but as usual it did not bother Tara while she sat in her comfortable armchair, silent, and free, at last.

    Celeste felt her heart flip and lurch greasily in her chest. It garrotted her words while it ran sorrow like hot oil down the interior wall of her ribs. Then, it shattered into a million fragments of despair, and still it broke again as love made itself known. A storm of a thousand shards of grief like small sharp knives stabbed her again, and again. Abandonment, failure, hate, rejection, and anger ripped her insides apart.

Death for those who still live is a torture inflicted from the inside out she realised, opened her throat wide and screamed. A torrent of black emotion spewed forth from the lungs of a mad woman, that on Tara's death, Celeste was destined to become.

A voice in her head asked, I thought you were going to tell me about love, and another replied, I just did.

~ ❋ ~ ❋ ~ ❋ ~

There were no more beats left in Tara's heart, her last precious breath, like all the others, wasted, the final shudder of electricity passed along her spine, the cord cut, and Celeste wailed like a banshee while waves of power moved through the air. Tara's powder-blue, empty eyes were open, looking upward and outward, oblivious to the despair her sudden departure had created. Limpid pools of light that cloudily reflected the colour of the dark night sky, while a peaceful smile frozen in time and flesh, caressed her limestone lips which remained firmly closed.

All of time slowed and the night suddenly thickened. The temperature in the little room boiled, seethed, took on a life of its own. A torrid strangle-hold that stifled Celeste's senses, but her broken heart still beat furiously, and continued to flee her body, by way of her mouth. She retched and brought up acid-sour cider. Then taking her hands she put them under Tara's arm's and tried to lift her, to drag her to her feet, to pull her out of her favourite chair and the hands of death.

'Wake up, wake up, Nana...' She got her to her feet. Tara slumped against her chest. In death as in life, she was a too heavy burden, one that she struggled to hold. She thumped to the floor, taking Celeste with her. Celeste screamed and pushed the dead woman away. She staggered to her feet and threw the studio doors open, scattering paper and knocking over dusty piles of books and withered plants as she ran into the dark.

Padrain arrived first, a dagger taken from inside his ranger boots flashed silver in his hand, leaving Dorothea to switch off the engine and see to Hossy. He found her in the middle of the cobbled yard shouting to the departing night and the two baleful moons. They slipped toward the crest of Long Field, and illuminated the top of the stone circle, just visible in the distance like a graveyard on a hill full of derelict tombstones. Celeste continued to yell, madder than Tara had ever been. 'Don't leave me alone! Just you dare leave me. This is somewhere I don't believe in. Don't leave me here.'

The drakes had been gone a good moon and a half at the autumn equinox, the blackthorn was bare, the moons hung lower, full of malcontent, and a wolf howled in the distance while the sky to the east ran with a thin silver light. She slipped easily past Padrain, a shadowy figure who had loomed out of the night, brandishing a dagger. He cursed as she ran past then half wished Dorothea had found her first. How the hell can I comfort that he thought, while Celeste ran swiftly back into the studio and put her hands under Tara's arms and tried to lift her again. 'Wake up, wake up, they will take you away. Don't leave me, don't leave me…don't leave me.' Over and over, she begged Death to release Tara and although Death could, it did not.

Padrain followed her quietly, as if he were approaching a wild animal. He cast a casual but narrow eyed glance over the rows of paper and his brow furrowed. His shoulders tensed when he caught sight of one of the headings – Nympts and the way home – though he pointedly ignored them. After, there would be time to pick them up, after, he thought with a heavy sigh.

Celeste screamed at him when he approached her, his hands held before him as if he calmed an anxious horse. 'Don't you take her, don't take her away, please. Mr Al Tine, I can wake her up, leave her be…I gave her too much tea, she's asleep.'

Padrain flapped his hands at her to be quiet. Celeste went back to trying to wake Tara, while he swept past her and into the other rooms. Dagger drawn; he made his way quietly up the stairs. There was nothing and no one there. He came back down just as Dorothea arrived and ran quickly to Celeste. Padrain sighed loudly which earned him a hard frown from his wife.

She pulled her gently away from Tara. 'Leave her be, Celeste. Let Padrain lift her, she's too heavy for you.'

Celeste nodded and made grief noises that sounded like an animal in pain. It made sense that Padrain should wake Tara up. She let Dorothea lead her from the studio, through the kitchen to the sitting room. She cuddled her close while they sat heaped together on the saggy old couch in front of the fire. Dorothea struggled to contain her own emotions and each time she tried to offer comfort the words stuck like hot embers in the back of her throat.

She nodded to Padrain over the top of Celeste's head while she stroked her hair and did what she could to send her waves of soporific calm. 'I'll stay with her tonight. Bring me my apothecary bag, then you do what needs to be done. Get Cissy for me,' she whispered, and her words were short and tense.

Padrain folded his arms across his wide chest as he stared down at the two women. Celeste's head was buried into Dorothea's shoulder where she continued to wail. The fire glowed small in the grate and two tallow lamps burned low under their small glass chimneys on the wooden mantle. 'No, I cannot get Cissy. Have you forgotten that her, Moin, and Abhhain must be away to Lodewick, after Cissy's taken care of the new head? Do you want to send her mad, woman?' Padrain struggled to contain the thunder in his voice. He saw all his carefully laid plans disintegrate with the death of Tara and knew when the change came it would hard to bear. Arianrihod would come, not only for Celeste, but for Dorothea. She would use any excuse to call her back to Romar Ri and they had handed her just what she needed. Over my dead body do they take my wife and leave my people to the demons when the gates of hell open here, and open they bloody-well will, he thought, and his jaw tensed so hard he heard a pocket of air at their hinge crack like a bone breaking. He moved to the front of the old couch and took two logs from the hearth basket, then placed them on the embers. Then he took the small brass bellows and blew air until the logs caught, throwing more heat and light into the room.

'Oh, Pad, I had forgotten. Even with her ability, she could not be in three separate places this same evening. Forgive me, I am overwhelmed,' Dorothea replied, while she took a linen square from her pocket with one hand and dabbed at her own eyes, while still cradling Celeste. 'Which direction should we take? We will send for Ganaim, that will help.' She inclined her head towards the weeping Celeste.

Padrain grunted his agreement while he adjusted the wick of the lamps, then began warming his hands at the fire. 'Aye, I'll see he's back before the morrow if it's possible, an' I'll contact Col. We will have to begin it. Dot…I am so sorry, love,' he choked slightly, but only because he saw how sad his wife had become, like some of her spirit had left her when Tara's own had, 'but it is the only way. I can't do anything more.' He knew he was babbling but the look in his wife's eye, the fear nestling in the pit at the centre of it, was looking toward a future they had both avoided for so long it felt like they had thoroughly escaped that fate. He coughed and cleared his throat. 'Neither of them will be able to return to normal…we will figure something out…on Gaia's oath, we will. What just happened?' He undid his helmet and took it off then he ran his hand through his thick hair and found himself repeating his words. 'What happened to her protection ward, Dot?' He pointed towards the studio.

'I know, I know,' Dorothea shushed in Celeste's hair. Celeste continued to bawl, while Padrain wondered, I should just put an end to it all, bring the shot gun down from the farm and finish it off properly, she will never be right for the job. Tara did nothing to prepare her.

'I did not think Tara would, oh dear me, I thought her safe.' She could say no more when a sob escaped her, but feeling the heat and grief from Celeste, she pulled herself together, while something set deep inside her that had her eyes flashing like a star exploding. 'This wasn't part of the plan,' her eyes narrowed, and her lip curled, 'the trade deal, and the protection? They were complete. This,' she flicked her head, 'has his work all over it, but…oh dear Pad, oh dear…what of my promise to Aindreas, and Henna?'

He shrugged, barely able to hide his anger. 'One missing assumed dead on the work of the wizard,' he screwed his face up in disgust, 'and the other holed up in Lodewick, trapped, ancient, and useless now Aindreas has gone. Do you see other options, Dot? Because I do,' he replied softly, leaving the question hanging.

Dorothea's face hardened. 'You would make yourself like them?' She snorted angrily and continued to soothe Celeste.

'It's an option, and an opportunity, Dorothea, that's all. It needed to be said.'

Dorothea tutted loudly and Padrain shrugged. A missed opportunity if you ask me, he thought while he moved away from the fire. 'I'll pick the papers up and check on her vital signs, make sure she's gone – we've seen them come back before,' he said, and his voice was filled with dry truth. On Earth death had been absolute, in retrospect he found that a comfort.

Padrain kissed Dorothea on the head and squeezed Celeste's shoulder. 'She'll have to go,' he mouthed silently to Dorothea over the top of Celeste's head while she continued to sob.

Dorothea nodded and replied in a voice that was less than a whisper, 'But alive, Padrain Al Tine. Whether that choice costs us or not, the deal was to keep her alive.'

Chapter Twenty

Dark Dreams And A Black Sun Rising

Celeste struggled to keep her eyes open, strained to listen to Dorothea but sleep and despair pulled her between them until she felt wrung out and thinner than mountain mist. Dorothea rustled next to her bed while she whispered oaths of vengeance. 'I will kill you myself for this Yalan, mark my words…'

Finally, her eyes drooped closed, and she succumbed to an escape that at first seemed better than the horror of the reality she left behind. Carried to that shadowy hinterland of her frail existence on a numbing wind of strong sedatives, strange herbal powders, and miserable exhaustion, obtained from the depths of Dorothea Al Tine's leather apothecary bag – a vile concoction that turned nasty in the dead of the night.

'No,' she croaked, 'no,' while she struggled to wake and felt the denseness of the dream world suck and pull at the fabric of her being. Was that Dorothea, asleep in the armchair next to her bed? She pulled herself up into a sitting position and felt the force release her while the room spun violently. 'Dorothea, 'Help me,' she croaked, and her arm shook while she reached towards the soundly asleep woman.

Suddenly, an arm clothed in emerald silk reached through the snaking mass of blanket and sheets and grabbed her around the ankle. It yanked her back to her nightmare. Tara loomed over her. Celeste dropped to her knees and held her head while heavy pressure began to squeeze her ears towards the centre of her skull, finally it popped. 'Where am I?' she gasped and rubbed at her nose. The heat was as dry as a kiln but smelled like hot metal and seared flesh, she gagged and brought her hands to her face, they were spectral while the landscape around her felt realer than life. She was on the edge of the stone circle, Elvan's Barrow, and in its centre, instead of a lumpy hillock of rough grass, a black pool lay. There was a mountain range on the horizon to what she supposed was north and to the south a blue ocean sparkled with diffused light.

Tara lifted her left hand, which was made entirely of silver and held a scythe-like crescent moon protectively above her heart. 'We are in the void. This is my Creation Shard. An island of existence, where I will stay until I can go home, to Earth,' she said defiantly, and Celeste felt an old hatred rise.

Then Tara pointed sharply at the black pool with a large broadsword. It looked too heavy for her to wield, but it was not substantial but made of light, of the same pearlescent radiance that hung like a thin cloud around her hair, it glowed like a numinous energy which was wrapped around everything and there was a sense of newness, of something just created and filled with the light of intent. The jewelled pommel of the sword glistened with a myriad of rainbow colours and the guard was like two human shoulder blades, delicately carved with feathers which began to move. Susurrus wings flapped gently while Tara held the grip and the tips of the feathers like long fingers appeared to feel through the air towards where Celeste stood.

'Where did you get that?' Celeste brought herself to her feet and pointed, the note of accusation clear in her voice. This was her dream, and she would not let her Nana be mad inside her head, it had been bad enough outside it. 'That is the One-God Anuk's sword! Nana, put it back…they will send you to work the wind, put it down,' Celeste pleaded. Then, she reached forward to take Tara's arm.

'Do not reach out for me. Do not wish me back there, not while we stand here,' Tara hissed.

'But the swor—'

'Why do you believe everything you are told, girl?' Tara cut her off angrily although her mouth contorted with the effort to speak. Then she flickered and faded as if the dream were about to break. 'I am not supposed to speak to you thus. I do not have much time, just listen, and believe. Please.' She leaned forward and put her hand gently on Celeste's shoulder.

Icy cold passed through her in waves, as if she had plunged headfirst into a chilly pond, she gasped. The sensation was a hand's span wide, running from her crown, down her back, all the way to her feet, and pinning her to the ground as if a fence post had been hammered right through the back of her body, then deep into the earth below. Celeste's eyes widened and she grunted while she tried to move but found she could not.

Tara whispered, 'It is called the Rod of Power. I have opened the channel for you, my gift – tell no one…' She struggled to finish, and she began to flicker and fade. Her mouth moved but no sound came out and the anger and frustration in her lightless eyes burned with a black fury. She tensed then croaked, 'No one but Cissy Al Tine, only Cissy must know of it.' She gasped while she forced the words out. 'Cissy…Meet her eye to eye when you tell her, it will be enough to begin the activation. Then, she must come here. Cissy Skywalker can take me home.'

Suddenly she began to fracture, then spiral as if she was being dragged back into the void and the large standing stones began to vibrate. Tara took the sword and rammed it into the shore next to the dark pool. 'NO!' she shouted and clicked back into solid form, but Celeste could see the effort it took for her to remain in her dream. The words came from Tara's mouth of their own volition even though it looked like she was trying to bite them back down her gullet. Still, they poured forth. 'When the Black Sun rises, you must trust that you will know what to do. You will have all the things you need, but they will not be what they seem. Your power can only be perfected when you return to earth.' She reached forward and tried to say something else, but she screamed, and was torn away while tatters of black void spewed from her mouth and moved through the air like a swarm of bats.

Celeste felt her knees buckle. She grunted when they hit the ground with a crack. The smell of seared meat had been replaced with something rotten, decaying flesh and spilled innards. The stink of death hung heavy in the air, cloying into her lungs as if she were drowning in a sea of offal. Celeste gagged. The dark pool pivoted, and the flat disc of water became a large black sun that crawled up the distant horizon like a giant black spider scurrying along the wall of a deep red the sky. This is not Elvan's Barrow she thought and nipped herself on the arm, but she was still a ghost and could not feel the pinch nor wake herself from the dream.

The air was hot and filled with the energy of dry storms, thick salty saliva coated her tongue and the tang of metal, copper, set her teeth on edge. The black sun hung in the red sky like a devil's dream catcher, a portent of coming doom, suspended over a terrible landscape filled with mounds of the dead. Greasy streams of putrid run-off meandered through the mounds, red streams flowing sluggishly with water that was thicker and darker than blood. In the distance a river of magenta blood ran straight as a canal, and it flowed to the heart of the black sun, it was brim full of gore, mutilated bodies of animals, humans, and non-humans; some still alive tried to escape the canal, only to be dragged back in by others, howling, screeching, and wailing, as they headed towards the centre of the great black orb.

Celeste's palms erupted. Violent stigmata like sticky red suns bubbled through her flesh. A voice echoed through the screeching horror of her pain, and it cast its curse while it howled with glee. 'Cursed by your blood, marked in the palm of your hands, Spectral Star.'

~ ❖ ~ ❖ ~ ❖ ~

'You cannot reveal these to anyone, child, do you hear me? Celeste, promise me, do you understand, not a soul. Not Ganaim either.' Dorothea held cold compresses around Celeste's hands. She had been asleep in the chair next to her bed when the attack happened and woke up when Celeste started screaming. The black sun was seared across her palms, branded in the waking world as they had in her nightmare.

'I promise, oh dear lords above, what are they? What are they, Dorothea?' She sobbed.

'I do not know, child. Oh, thank the Light they are fading. You must keep this to yourself. I think you have been marked, cursed, and that they will get you killed if you reveal them to anyone. It may be to do with your grief, or it may be to do with what Tara prophesised, or the voice in the dream.' Dorothea wiped a film of dewy sweat from her brow while she checked Celeste's palms again.

'They are gone. Do you feel pain?' Celeste shook her head as she turned her hands back and forth. 'You must excuse me; I must be away downstairs. Here, drink this. Do not worry,' she noted Celeste's hesitation, 'it is not a sedative, you need to wake fully. You must feel the pain in order to begin healing. I will be back up soon.' Dorothea headed to the door calmly although she wanted to run and scream herself. *Light, the entire world has been turned upside down and inside out, in one night.*

'Dorothea…what is going to happen to me?' Celeste sobbed.

'Oh, dear love, I don't know, but you cannot stay here. Those hideous things could be some sort of tracker, I just do not know.' Dorothea hurried from the room wiping her eyes as she went through the door. She was bone tired but hurried all the same. A sudden shaking fit almost upended her, and she fell halfway down the stairs, grabbing at the thick ship's rope Padrain had strung on the wall to fashion a banister. Harrumphing loudly, she pulled herself to her feet and flew down the rest of the rickety worn stairs to the living room. Steadying her breathing, she made her way to the round table and two winged-back chairs that sat before the window. She retrieved a large violet crystal, shaped like an egg, from the bottom of her apothecary bag which rested on the plain dark wood table. There was a good fire roaring in the grate which shared the same flue as the kitchen stove on the other side of the wall. The lumpy old sofa faced the fire, three brightly coloured rag rugs lay over the paved stone floor and created spirals of colour beneath the few items of furniture in the room. Tara's paintings of butterflies and flowers hung everywhere.

Dorothea stopped suddenly, then on the tips of her toes, opened the window and flapped at the space to stimulate the air flow. 'Poor Tara, she's beginning to smell, and it's hardly two days since she went, it is too warm in here to keep a body from rot,' Dorothea spoke softly to herself. She sighed with relief when she caught sight of the low flat wagon, being pulled by Nellie, crest the hill of Long Field. I hope they have remembered to bring me a change of clothes, although I suppose Tara was a similar build, I could just use hers…but dungarees? Dorothea screwed up her face and smoothed her fine wool and mohair dress down; the creases sprang back into the fabric as if they had been pressed there like pleats. She ran her fingers through her white hair, still long and thick although tatted at the back in a way that would require the attentions of Cissy with a curry comb. Grooming had been her last concern.

Cissy walked slowly next to the horse; her head bent as if she listened while they meandered over the brow of the field opposite. A sleek black shape came hurtling after them and jumped on the low wagon; she thought Cissy laughed but could not be sure the distance being too great and her eyes not what they once were. 'At last, they've come for her…' she whispered to the empty room. 'Light, how we'll get her over that hedge…' Dorothea sat at one of the high-backed armchairs on either side of the table; the upholstery beneath the blankets and sheepskins was worn thin, but they were comfortable, and warm, and provided a good watch post to keep an eye on the Long Field and farm beyond. Cissy and Nellie moved cautiously with the low cart which zigzagged across the field, so it did not run away down the slope. The large cat sat on top like a statue carved in ironstone, black but with a deep fiery orange hue that could only be seen in certain light. Its ears pricked up while it cast its gaze toward her. Its eyes were bright green eyes, like saucers of lightest jade laid on smoky velvet. She had not wanted cats, but once she saw how many Fear Me's they caught, she was more than persuaded they were worth the trade with Fairmist Al Mara.

'To be kept, housed in comfort, and fed fresh meat and water. In return they are to be left alone, to clear the shadows as they see fit. We need more of them at the stone compass',' Fairmist had said, 'but they are hard to come by as they are native to the Southern Isles. They are not like the moggies you normally have on farms, Dot,' he had finished just when the great beasts had wandered into the kitchen and sat before the big stove taking up all of the hearth and blocking most of the heat.

Large was not how she would describe them; she had seen big cats before and these cats were more than that. Their illusion rippled around them like clear water over stone, slipping, and running, until she felt dizzy and turned her head away. When she met their gaze, they had looked at her disdainfully, as if they dared her to try as hard as she liked, but what they were, was not for her eye, nor anyone else they had not chosen. Cats looking down their noses at me, she thought. Then she realised the wards she had set about the farm, had been easily breached by the Fear Me's, recently come from the Lake of Unum. My power, like my eyesight, is not what it once was she thought, and a heavy sadness settled in her chest before she turned to Fairmist and said with a little tartness to her words. 'I will not have them sleeping on the beds.'

CHAPTER TWENTY-ONE

The Crone. Arianrihod

Dorothea took the violet crystal and turned it in her palms as if she held a flame. Her hands trembled. *Light, Dorothea Al Tine, Padrain is far too busy to know that you are contacting Arianrihod. Get a grip of yourself, woman,* she exhaled then placed it to her heart. She focussed on an image of the one she needed to speak to. From a distance they could be mistaken for sisters, but they were not; Dorothea was smaller with a heart-shaped face, a tiny snub nose, and large slanted eyes. A smile was never far from her pouting mouth with its pronounced top lip cleft – the "love charm" it was called. She felt a warmth fill her palms then pulse twice, while she whispered gently, 'We are all connected. It is I, Dorothea Al Tine, of the first changeling tribe of the Romarii. Who answers my request?'

'I Arianrihod do. How may I aid you, sister?' A gentle voice whispered and an image of a long-faced woman with a sharp nose and deeply arched brows wavered in and out until it snapped suddenly into a clear connection. Her violet eyes were as large and slanted as Dorothea's own, but keen and hawkish, her full mouth straight and determined. She could be the most beautiful woman on Gaiadon if she smiled but she did not; it had been a long time since she had smiled or felt joy. She was aloof and held herself regally. Before she had taken the mantle of The Crone's Cloak, she had been royalty; she had been the Romaros' queen, but demons and gods, war, and love, had changed all of that.

'I am greatly honoured by our connection, Arianrihod, but dare not linger on gestures of assent, things here move quickly. Are you made aware of the passing of Woman-Tara?'

'You are my equal in all things, sister, we shall drop formalities. Yes. I felt her pass, even here at the caves of Romar Ri. Her time-to-die came far too early, and the vibration suggests without her consent. This abuse of power alone will have consequences beyond our ken, but sister, your news first, if you please.'

'I agree,' Dorothea said gravely. 'Arianrihod, my news would support your fear. Tara's essences remain.' The vision in the crystal egg wavered and Arianrihod drew in a sharp breath. Dorothea continued, 'The body has not evaporated and returned to her own dimension along the axis like humankind should do at death.' Dorothea ran her hands through her hair. Her dress was creased and shabby. She lifted the crystal slightly, so the other woman did not see it, then remembered that her hair was like a crow's nest and her eyes creased from lack of sleep and sunken with worry.

'The tainted humans return so because of a natural activation of their time-to-die, a set law from the dimension below which has transcended the dimension jump and remains in place for humankind. Does this corruption, this murder…cause Tara's body to remain in a dimension it does not belong in?' Dorothea posed the question to Arianrihod although she feared she already knew the answer.

'I know not for certain, not until a rebirth takes place, if one does at all,' Arianrihod replied cautiously.

'My lady Arianrihod.' Dorothea clenched her hand into a fist, Arianrihod annoyed her when she was not forthcoming, she would know. If I were the Crone, I would know she thought then pulled her resolve tight around her spine and replied in a voice that frosted with shards of ice. 'There has been no dispersal of the essences that I can see or feel. We arrived shortly after the death, and I saw no soul bird or spirit animal leave. Therefore, my lady, we have a corpse to deal with. A corpse that stagnates and rots.' It is so unnatural, such a waste she thought and felt a shudder run through her flesh.

'Nothing, not a god, or goddess, or a devil, has come to claim it nor any of its essences. The wizard has cast it aside as if it is less than carrion, whether by accident or design, who can know.'

'You suspect the wizard's hand?' Arianrihod interrupted Dorothea.

'I have no proof either way, but I do have a body that should not be here. I do not know for certain whether Tara's essences, her soul and spirit, have separated. Have they gone or do they remain here, attached to the putrefying physical shell…my suggestion is we put her in the cold store up at the main farm until we decide what to do with the body, but I require guidance from you, from our Goddess Gaia? What does she desire?' Dorothea continued watching out of the window, while she spoke into the crystal, noting the ease with which Cissy communicated with Nellie.

'I feel a quick and quiet funeral. I am almost sure Woman-Tara would want a woodland burial,' the soft voice suggested with a hint of urgency.

'I will get someone to write that down somewhere, the girl may want to see it…conveniently, we will find her final papers up at the house…yes, if we bury her in the woods when the dimension rift is healed, perhaps Tara will be, I mean her body and essences will be returned to her own dimension. Will that be the case, Arianrihod?' Dorothea paused. She sensed Arianrihod hesitate, so she ploughed on. 'I do not wish her to be reincarnated through the Gaia logos, she is not of this dimension and struggled in pain and madness in her last life. She could not adjust to the dimension jump she had to endure. She deserves some peace, but I foresee there is no peace to be had here, only the coming war.' Dorothea held the crystal tightly and hoped her reasoning would be palatable to the other woman, while silently praying that she was wrong about Tara being trapped forever on Gaiadon.

'I hear your reasoning, but I cannot claim that I foresee that burying her will return her to her own dimension in the future, Dorothea…it may be so, but things are changing. It is as you suspect, Gaia may claim her from the earth,' the voice replied hesitantly, although Dorothea suspected that Arianrihod knew exactly what Gaia would do.

'Oh, no, I cannot allow, I mean…my apologies, I made a promise.' Dorothea gasped. 'We need to move the body soon. What do you recommend?'

'You doubt the wisdom of Gaia claiming Woman-Tara? If so, you cannot bury her, you must burn her and pray that her magnetic essences can find their way back down the axis to her own dimension, where she will be born again under the Pistis Sophia logos where she was first created. The risk with this release is that her magnetic essences may be drawn into one of the other dimensions, even the Bardo, and that is too close to the entrance to Umbra Horrenda. The demon may claim her, soul, and spirit, and extract knowledge from her causal imprint.' Arianrihod paused and Dorothea heard her take a sip of tea.

'She may have appeared mad to the casual eye, but we both know she was far from that. I cannot get a shaman to you in time, Dorothea, to guide Tara home.' She sniffed disdainfully then added, 'Unless, you have a fully functioning and well-tutored human there who has the galactic signature ability of Galactic Earth or above.'

Dorothea narrowed her eyes but kept her mouth closed and chose to ignore the other woman's slight. It would be typical of Arianrihod to draw her into a debate, one where she would end up cornered and making promises or trades she did not have the time or heart for.

'Of course, if Padrain had not been so remiss with the information Romar Ri required, and if I had understood fully how the Star had been tutored, how her ability was developing, or not, as the case would seem, would we even be having this conversation? Would The Star not be in my care already?'

Dorothea ignored the last comment and shook her head. 'No. We are a rural zone as you are aware. Only lower powers, Resonant or Magnetic Seeds and Earths, enough to soil sing, to grow crops. We cling to hope that we are remote enough to survive, but that is changing. There is not enough power here to wage a war against the demon-horde, not yet.' She aimed her barb at Arianrihod. Light, she is out of touch with the reality in the zones, she thought and twisted her lips into a tight line when she heard the other woman tut impatiently.

'Therefore, we cannot ensure that Tara's magnetic essence, returns to the planet of origin. If her time-to-die code had been activated when it was her time to die…the return of the magnetic essence, her soul, would have been a naturally occurring phenomenon, bound by the fundamental laws of the universe from whence she came. But now…' she trailed off and Dorothea noted the increasing tension in her voice while she rubbed furiously at her own forehead and a headache that was threatening to rumble to a full-blown storm. She bit her lip but held her tongue, it was the only way to lure Arianrihod into giving her further information.

Arianrihod sighed. 'The sword of souls is missing, Dorothea, despite what Abrecan, the demon Anuk believes – he does not have it. He does not know the myth and legends and the truth hidden therein, not like the wily wizard and our own Aindreas did. What the Demon Anuk has is a thing, it is an object from Talas, a material artefact but it is without its element from Lokas, therefore it is not complete, which is why he still uses blood magic to necromance. To make matters worse, the element from Lokas is missing too. The boundary between the worlds of the living and dead is breached, the axis is compromised, dimensional leaking is occurring along the breaches of the axis more frequently, coupled with all manner of things crawling from the depths of the Lake of Unum. Anyone with a smidgen of magical ability seems to be able to conjure what they will from the waters of the One-Thing. I know not what influences the Lake of

Unum. Something of the shadow must be leaking into it from somewhere. Romar Ri finds it ever harder to patrol the water below. We have many casualties and few new rangers to replace those we lose…'

Arianrihod was building up to something. Dorothea pursed her lips. It will not be long now, she thought as the other woman continued.

'Although…it is my thought that we fight demon magic with rangers and warriors, we fight crystal weapons and lasers with bows and arrows, when we should be asking those who hold vast amounts of wisdom and power, which has been neutralised, for help to fight magic with magic. What say you, Dorothea?' Arianrihod finished coolly.

'I understand what you ask, Arianrihod, but I cannot, we all must do what we can, and from where we have been placed by the wheel as it turns. My power now? It is not strong enough to ward the farm against Fear Me's. I will be no use to Romar Ri unless you need a hedge witch and her apothecary bag of herbs and amulets.' Dorothea smoothed over Arianrihod's barely veiled hint for her to return to Romar Ri, to bring her wisdom with her and regain her powerful magical ability which she had neutralised so she could lead an almost human life. To regain her power would mean leaving Padrain, not just leaving him but severing her connection to him and his human nature, a thing that could have dire consequences for him. They were connected, deeply, and intrinsically woven together so that they could live with and love one another, and create a living being together the way humans do. Dorothea frowned; Arianrihod had just asked her subtly whether she would risk killing her husband.

'I thank you for your answer, Dorothea, it seems love is stronger than magic once more.'

Dorothea steeled herself to continue. 'But the child Tara protected, The Star – can you accept an orphan? She must have guidance. I cannot give her any, not without my full power, and then I fear it would not be the kind of guidance she needs. She cannot…must not stay here, it will interfere with the work Padrain, Cissy, and I do. The trade clearly stated the protection of Woman-Tara and her ward…until such time of change that it was no longer feasible,' Dorothea whispered urgently into the crystal.

'Orphan? She is not an orphan, Dorothea, but I have been made aware of your plight should she remain…you must ensure her departure is clean and final, nothing should remain of them, and the route I suggest is with the Romarii tinker caravan by Ninmah and the canal crossing to Kai; from there, Romar Ri will take her. Tara, I believe, took great pains to ensure the protection was complete when she was in her lucid moments. They were isolated and protected by the elders in the community, but the veil did trouble her so, in and out of reality like that must have been akin to a curse. I have also been led to believe that the child was something of a loner, quiet enough to not have made much of an impression anywhere, but regardless, one of them may have made error somewhere. I send Sonii Romarii to you, even as we speak. The council of Romar Ri requires a full briefing on The Star and her ability. Ganaim shall arrive shortly…Dorothea.' Arianrihod hesitated after the mention of Ganaim, and Dorothea tensed when she heard the sigh in her voice. Not now, please let us not focus on *that* now.

'Ah, Dorothea,' Arianrihod said, then finished with a long sigh she did not try to hide. 'I struggle to find the words to soften what I must say, therefore I will make plain: Ganaim is not Romarii enough to stay with us permanently. I could arrange for a Romarii walk-in ceremony to increase his resonance to our own, but I know he carries too much Fae-light for that, and I cannot waste a changeling on an ill-fated attempt. Yes, he will learn the ways of the Roma Ranger as was agreed in the terms of our trade, but even as I look in the mirror of the water below, his future is unclear; there are many ways he may go, and death waits for him at the end of more than one. If one of those is a path he chooses, and that end is his, he will not even be reborn Romarii. He carries too little of what we are. Despite you being his grandmother, you chose a human life, and he did not enter Gaiadon through the caves but by a human biological birth. I sense he is something new but ancient and expected. I will need to consider what Cassandra Novantae chronicled all those Ages ago.' Arianrihod lowered her eyes thoughtfully while she waited for Dorothea to respond.

Dorothea felt time unravel and waves of doubt uncover every nerve sheath until her flesh tingled, until her skin crawled with premonition while her violet eyes, suddenly a lighter shade of lavender, filled with saltwater and a lone silver tear made its way down her pale red cheek. 'I always hoped there would be enough of one of us in him to thwart that destiny, Arianrihod. I had hoped a walk-in would tip the balance in our favour, but it was only a hope.

'I am aware of what Cassandra Novantae predicted, but why him? Why not one of the crofters from the north? They are as scaled as he, some more so,' she replied, and her tone was full of sadness. I am worse than Tara for not educating those in my care she thought.

'The crofters from the north are maritime people, closer in blood to Selgovae, you know that, and I doubt they have the sire that Ganaim does.' Arianrihod spoke cautiously.

Dorothea remained tight-lipped, and stony-faced, while Time itself drew back from her building anger. No one spoke of Ganaim Al Tine's sire. No one.

Arianrihod waited but she knew Dorothea was not going to reveal the sire. She smiled inwardly. What did it matter? She already knew that Ganaim Al Tine's father was a closely guarded secret; she herself had only just uncovered it, after looking for ways to overthrow the demons, she had found a foretelling in ancient and occult texts, which were part of Gaiadon's cosmology.

'So, it is true, the Keys of Stone were saved and taken to Romar Ri,' Dorothea exclaimed bitterly.

'Not all of the library but books, artefacts, and sacred instruments that could be carried and hidden by the descendants of the Fae made their way here, eventually, and all came with a price.'

Dorothea raised one eyebrow and replied, 'I am sure the trade was equal and fair.'

Arianrihod sniffed then took a sip of her tea before replying, 'Romar Ri certainly thought so. But to Ganaim,' Arianrihod pressed on, 'He may be more human than he looks. Does he have a galactic signature power from his DNA3? If he does, we can attempt the Romarii walk-in ceremony, we have recently completed one, and successfully at that, with the young man of human descent, Raife Oarfish. Then Gaia can decide what Ganaim becomes. Ranger, like Raife. Changeling from your own caste, or Healer. Or something else.'

'No, he does not, nothing has ever activated.' Dorothea sighed heavily and felt her heart hit her knees. It never will she thought morosely, because that is not where his destiny lies, it lies in death, and in fire.

'And Padrain? Cissy?'

'Padrain has a Storm signature, as we suspected when we found him, him thinking that all on the planet could spark fires with their fingers.' They laughed softly at the memory. 'And Cissy is a very reluctant and untrained Skywalker, who uses her gift only when she must to walk the stone compasses, but loses random memories each time she does, because of her lack of knowledge. She has shown no predilection towards the crafts of the Crone, or Changeling caste, despite being my own daughter through human birth.'

'Then that only leaves me one avenue to explore fully, Dorothea.' Arianrihod led Dorothea to her reluctant acceptance of Ganaim's future.

'Do you believe the prophecies relate to him and not to Micah Apollon, now dead, and all hope for the Ningen, and for us, gone with him?' Dorothea could not help the sharpness of her tone.

'Micah Apollon was the Sun in Winter. Despite being the youngest, he was made the heir apparent to the throne at Galay. His Lord Bucky's grief is yet to slash through the land. You must prepare for the worst where that is concerned. A hard rain will fall, and it will keep falling until he is spent. Let me see...' the other woman rustled papers on a desk near where she sat. Dorothea could just make out the glow of a fire behind her.

'Micah will be given to fire on the next available Sun galactic signature which will be eighteen days hence. Bucky will make his way back to his beloved Caislean Gairdin. He will not venture further north to Galay, it will be too much for him to bear, but also, he knows that Caislean Gairdin is more central for him from which to release his wrath. He will call on cardinal energies from The Ice Blight, and the source of Gaia's Howl, and we will know his sorrow, we will suffer his fury. He will spare no one.'

Dorothea nodded. 'We will be prepared.'

Arianrihod continued. 'No, it is not Micah that Cassandra speaks of.' She paused and let her words hang in the air before taking a hard breath and pushing her regret for the other woman aside.

'Solas Nua Novantae, the new sun of the Novantae that rises in the west, Dorothea. The prophecy says this, "Solas Nua Novantae will come set the Ningen free, although he is not born of the seed complete, he will still rise in the West, made from a traditional line and a line that is outside our space and time. A line that should never have been at all but for the giant who roared through the wall, bringing on his wake of death, the grand sire to the impossible sun that will rise in the West. The sun not meant to be, Solas Nua Novantae." The words of the prophecy chimed through the air like a distant warning bell.

'How did Padrain come to Gaiadon? Was it the same as the other humans, was Padrain a part of the demon's harvest when he kidnapped the tainted stream of humans? You must consider this, Dorothea, perhaps Padrain was never meant to be here at all?' She waited patiently and mentioned not that she heard Dorothea sob a little. Arianrihod held back her own tears; if Padrain had not come,

Dorothea, the Lady Aos Si, would still be the Romarii Crone and she would be free to rip the underworld apart while she looked for her beloved husband.

'I…I will, but give me time, please, and accept my deepest gratitude, my lady Arianrihod, for all that you allow.' Dorothea sagged, then said heavily, 'But I cannot answer for sure about Padrain. I fear his reaction to an event he never speaks of. Surely, we took enough information when we found him wandering in Glean Glas? For the rest, you must do what you see fit. I answer to my Goddess Gaia through you, her voice on Gaiadon.'

'I will leave no stone uncovered in my search for answers, but be aware, if he is Solas Nua Novantae, he will quicken. He should not be alone if this happens, he requires a guide, or he will die.' Arianrihod waited while the other woman digested what she said. 'Despite what your human husband thinks,' Dorothea frowned, she made Padrain sound like a shackle, 'does or says, Dorothea, if Ganaim is the sun that rises in the west, if he be Solas, then he must go with his father, or his father's kind. There are many more predictions that follow Solas Nua Novantae, not least him leading decisive assaults in the last battle against the legions of the undead that will rise from the Red Plain of Umbra Horrenda.'

Dorothea groaned inwardly, Light, save them, but hurried to end the conversation, Cissy was at the hedge. 'My gratitude extends from my heart to your heart, sister, thank you for all your portents. I look forward to their meaning being revealed.'

'And my deepest gratitude extends to you, Dorothea. I do not forget who you are, Lady Aos Si, the first of the Changeling caste of Romar Ri.'

The crystal shimmered, then went opaque. Dorothea was glad to release her iron-hard grip and her connection to the Romarii Crone, Arianrihod. The woman who had taken her place when it was clear she had fallen in love with the human Padrain Al Tine, and he with her.

It rankles Arianrihod that she cannot use her power to rescue her husband, which is why she wanted the Cloak of the Crone above all the others who came forward to make claim. How would someone from the Ranger Caste know that the Queen Bee cannot leave the hive? Though she wishes me to believe she set me free so I could love Padrain.

'Humph. Silly woman assumes I have lost my touch and gone soft in the head since I left Romar Ri.' Dorothea's hand trembled while she slipped the crystal egg into a black velvet pouch and placed it in the bottom of her bag.

She began waving out of the window but was not sure if Cissy could see her as she tried to act normally. 'Light! I cannot juggle another ball. Ganaim not Romarii enough, nor human, although that is apparent. I cannot tell Padrain any of it, he will set traps for they will come, they will smell him if he is one of them true, and they will come and make claim. Light on my soul. Was there any good news? If I get my hands about Yalan's neck... Hells what a to do,' she mumbled as she put another log on the fire. The basket was a beautifully crafted weave from Far Falamh and was almost empty. She rose stiffly then went through the door to the kitchen. Will Arianrihod force my return to Romar Ri with the information she has or if she can prove Ganaim is Solas Nua Novantae. The dawn of a new age? Lead us into battle against demon-manced foulness? He can barely look to himself for looking up skirts. Solas Nua Novantae my foot. Poor Pad, all your efforts to protect those you love are coming undone, my poor love.

~ ❀ ~ ❀ ~ ❀ ~

Padrain Al Tine was a young man, and not much concerned with gods or demons, nor any grand design of any kind. He was a farmer's boy and knew the land of his birth and their small holding, all the animals upon it and every crop, tree, bush, wild animal, and secret path through the forest, better than he yet knew himself.

He had told Carter his parents had died in their chairs to spare the man the horror of what really happened when you did not survive the dimension jump. They had died where they stood while he sat at the kitchen table finishing his breakfast. His mother was in the kitchen too, to his left putting dishes in the sink that sat beneath the window that looked down the yard to the barns, the stables, and the setting of suns beyond; his father slightly to his right, was at the back door, pulling on his wellington boots before he headed out for the day.

Padrain took a slice of thick white bread and mopped around his plate, soaking up egg yolk and bacon fat. 'I always say, there's no need to wash a plate after you've eaten, Pad, what do you say, Talam?' His father was pulling a woollen hat onto his dark curly hair, streaks of grey badgered from his temples, and he ducked his head back under the door frame and said, 'Magda, just put it in a trough for the lad, he's not that fussy.'

His red-haired wife, almost as tall as Talam, threw a dish rag at him. 'I'll not be putting my cooking in a pig trough, Talam Al Tine, how dare you suggest such a thing?' Her glacial blue eyes sparked with laughter.

Talam caught the cloth and threw it back. Padrain shook his head at the pair, his thick dark hair was curly like his fathers, his face the same, apart from blue eyes that cracked and flashed as if a glacier floated in their depths.

'I'm only glad I don't have to suffer rations, poor sods in the north and on the mainland,' Padrain said with his mouth full of the last bit of bread.

They all agreed to that. 'Aye, but we'll be sending what we can north and we're trying to get a ship through to Liverpool, lad, if we can avoid the Jerry's. They're shooting even when they see we've marked our vessels as neutral.'

Padrain frowned. 'Bastards, but I've heard it will soon be over.' He pointed to a bank of radio equipment in a corner next to the table. Then they returned to their business.

Padrain pushed his chair out and stood away from the table, taking his plate and mug in hand…The world went black briefly, as if a fainting fit had caught him in its sucking embrace. He shook his head to clear the flapping blackness from the peripheral vision at his left eye. The plate and cup clattered to the table. When he opened his eyes, the day inside the kitchen and the people in it, were moving frame by frame.

His mother Magda was closer to his father; and she had taken a step away from the sink, she paused and moved a step, then another pause, on her way to kiss her husband good day. Still slightly to his left and as each frame jerked past, she dropped closer to the floor while she died a little more.

His father Talam, by brute strength alone, pushed his way through a wall of material that resembled the sheath of fascia that covers muscle; it was pale sickly yellow but translucent, and myriad patterns like distorted snowflakes and scrolls of runes in shades of black, scarlet, and crimson ran across its surface. Talam pushed then taking his knife from his waist he sliced it, put his fingers through and tore it apart. There was a pause, then he hurtled towards his wife. Another pause, while he moved frame by frame, as Magda continued to fall to the floor. He roared in anger, and in fear, and it stretched across his mouth and fled from his throat until the sound was pulled into the other side of the membrane. Pause. Talam reached Magda and got his arms around her before she hit the floor.

Padrain, was only seconds behind his father, the fingers on his outstretched arm determined to grab them and pull them back, passed through thin air above where his father and mother had fallen. They hit the floor and their bodies broke and shattered as if they were made of china before they disappeared in a column of black fog. An oily swirl of smoke that spun quickly back through the membrane and out of the door, then away from the farm towards the North. Padraig turned to follow but the hideous membrane schlepped closed, and even though he knew he was in their kitchen, he also knew he was not.

Padrain fell, stumbled, and crawled after the smoke, but he knew that they were gone as soon as he left the back door of the farm. He knew immediately that he had been trapped someplace else. He only had to smell the air, alive with ozone that sparked like lightning, and feel the spirit of the place, which was filled with a sense of wrongness that made the inside of his mouth taste like metal. High above him the air crackled and hissed as if a great war took place across the dome of the sky. It cracked, and he could see the universe laid bare and a darkness beyond that yawed and seeped through. Arid heat speared like the blast from a forge and a hot metal stink descended when the blackness began to ooze towards the ground. Suddenly a viscous liquid, like slushy running ice, snapped like the fingers of a cat-o-nine tails from the North and filled the fissures. The substance had an energy all of its own and though it was strange it felt right, and was filled with a luminous light.

The sky domed above him, clear as a spring day and he knew in his heart that he could find a way back. He put his hands before him, reaching, searching for the membrane when suddenly, dark coloured runes, and occult shapes rolled across the vast expanse above him. He knew then that a dark magic had been cast across the ceiling of the world and its evil went as far as he could see.

He fell to his knees and covered his ears though that did not make any difference. The screaming ululation tore across the land like the sharpest edge of the most powerful typhoon. It turned his insides to quivering jelly and his marrow to water in his bones while it howled like the first and last agony, and a blast of roiling clouds made of ice and wind hurtled in from the North.

The sun went out, then two moons rose in the sky and all around him reality stretched, distorted, skewed at strange angles, until he could look no more. Then reality snapped back into place with a single cosmic thunderclap around the globe of a world he did not know.

He ran to the fields; scrawny beasts with too large heads and oddly shaped splayed hooves munched on grass that seemed too sparse and dry. He did not need the light of day to see it, he felt the wrongness reach out of the sudden dark.

He lurched at an unsuspecting sheep with a single curled horn in the centre of its head and turned it over. He grabbed a leg, the hoof was not cloven, but split into four, hard, arthritic fingers with blunt talons at their end. This is not Earth, he reasoned, while he wept tears of anguish and anger at the death of his parents.

'My father was not supposed to come here, he bloody well pushed through that thing to reach my Ma, and you are not my animals,' he shouted, and he pushed the sheep away, but the silly beast did not run or walk off, it only stared at him. 'Meep,' it rasped indignantly and began raking at the grass with its strange feet. Then when it had uncovered worms and grubs it began to eat.

He boarded up the farm and freed the small number of animals that had appeared on the land. He was ready to leave by sunrise and when it rose in the East he fell to his knees. 'Thank you,' he prayed while one of the two moons faded away, beyond the horizon. The other was strangely dark and still hung in the sky.

He was followed by most of the sheep, who meeped behind him while he headed across the fields and into the first of the trees at the edge of his father's land. Scrubby bushes led to stands of silver birch then maple, beech, and oak. The sun climbed higher but on he walked. Cedars perfumed the air, normally, and he gulped at their scent, as if he had not found himself on another planet; he lost the corrupted sheep and cows along the way, while he prayed that there were predators who would put them out of their misery.

He ignored biters while they feasted on his flesh, grateful that the midges and mosquitos were the same as those on Earth, although other birds and butterflies were not. He dove for cover when a flock of tree drake landed on the branches of a cork oak, thinking they would set him afire, and he laughed hysterically when they belched stinking pops of gas, which fizzled a little, but they were not the plume of fire he had expected. He watched when they began to roost for the afternoon, like lengths of dusters hanging in the tree.

Eventually, coniferous trees, gigantic and dark, were all that he could see in any direction, his footsteps were muffled by ankle-deep carpets of needles and light and shade fell in a mosaic of muted colour across the golden floor of the forest. His breath became long and slow as he inhaled the scent of the ancient trees – this he knew, he knew the way of the forest. Earth and the tang of pine, antiseptic resins as they ran from trunks, a woodpecker hammering, small birds flitting as green as the needles on the trees, wolves baying, on the hunt, but away in the distance. Wolves? I am far enough away he thought and looked for a place to camp.

He made camp, seeking the right kind of sticks to make a fire; and with fire on his mind, he had clicked his fingers when he remembered cedar was the best for beginning a friction fire. A spark flew from his fingers and ignited the toe of his boot; he studied his finger for a short while then executed the same action, another spark. He aimed at a nearby rock, click, point, a small flame erupted and hit the rock. He sat down and stared at his fingers as if he were seeing them for the first time. He was still sitting there, feeling like a god, when the sun began to lower in the sky. He decided that he would live in the forest until he figured out exactly what had happened but made a promise to be more cautious with his magical fingers, what with all that wood around.

Several weeks had passed when a shaggy haired and bushy bearded Padrain, dressed in animal skins, was stalking a deer he had followed for an entire day when he stumbled upon the creature. It had lambent violet eyes and was bathing in a secluded mountain pool the river had carved from the limestone valley floor. The pool was full of emerald water as it reflected the verdant greenery all around. The creature swam and placed the dead fish it had caught with its own hands on a flat rock next to a small waterfall, which tumbled happily between large boulders come loose from a gently inclined cliff face. He thought her a shimmery red mermaid until she left the water to talk to the animals who had gathered around her. It is a water sprite, Padrain thought while he wondered what sort of world, he had found himself in. Silver white hair tumbled down her back as she conjured magical things out of the very air: a handful of nuts for the squirrels, a soft branch of tender shoots for the deer he had been stalking, a huge beast with knubby wings at its shoulders and a too knowing look in its eye. She sat upon a flat rock, childlike but not – her body was clearly that of a woman. Her green robe and creamy under garments hung on a nearby bush, soft boots beneath. She skinned, boned, and gutted the fish for a fox that appeared with her cubs. The guts she saved for a hawk, a golden eagle, and four crows, who she fed away from the other birds, raucous as they were. She spoke to the crows in a language Padrain did not understand, laughing often, although it seemed as if they were trying to cheer her up, as they strutted about bobbing their heads. The bones she buried beneath a sapling while she sang to it of growing things. She washed the fish blood from the rock and dived into the water again.

The other animals moved away suddenly, the buck snorted and bounded into the forest when a large golden mountain cat came and lay on the rock; it watched the green water intently. Padrain looked at his hunting knife, puny in comparison, and rubbed his fingers together but could not bring himself to burn the magnificent animal so he picked up a rock to throw into the trees away from the pool. It will go and investigate, and I will yell at the water sprite to be away. Just as he was about to launch the missile, a fat river trout came jumping from the water; the mountain cat leapt and caught it, grumbling as it bit into it. It did not move when the water sprite came and lay on the rock next to it, like two animals basking contentedly in the sun.

He backed stealthily away from the scene and made plans to keep watching the creature; it would tell him what had happened, and how to get home. He stupidly thought she was not aware of his presence, although he had wandered like a noisy stampede of horses into Glean Glas, smelling all human, which was a smell as wrong as murder to the Romarii. I will trap her, he thought, and he constructed a snare of sorts which he submerged in the pool. He put out piles of nuts and berries which he thought would lure the creature to the water's edge, then lay hidden beneath ferns and bright green bracken while he made ready for his prey to stumble into his trap. He sighed when the sun mottled yellow and lime-green through the lacey fronds. A pine ladybird, black winged with four red spots, flew lazily away and his eyes grew heavier. A dragonfly as big as his hand buzzed noisily past. Nothing smells as sweet and clean as fern, he inhaled deeply, then yawned sleepily as the earth warmed beneath him and drew his tired soul to her bosom and the deepest of sleeps.

Dawn found him bound with vines, tied to a large strong branch, being carried like a dead stag by two huge men. Their arms were heavily battle scarred, and their eyes were amber but blazed with a fearsome light. They did not utter a word while they carried him towards the mouth of a cave in the mountain side. It was hidden behind the boulders near the pool, although he would swear it had not been there the day before.

~ ❋ ~ ❋ ~ ❋ ~

'My poor Padrain,' Dorothea fretted but smiled at the memory of those little piles of berries and nuts, and her guardians' anger when she told them that the human thought her an animal, to be lured into a trap with titbits. It was all she could do to stop them skinning him alive, them being hell-bent on killing humans at the time, until they realised that the humans were no better than the foul animals that had appeared on their lands. Indeed, they were probably worse off.

She heard the water pump rattle into life as Celeste filled the bath. The oven and hearth had been kept alight since before the Night of the Dead. Deep winter is a moon away, she thought, while she looked at the sky. Arianrihod says prepare for Lord Bucky to unleash his grief in eighteen days. I hope we have enough supplies. I will get more wood put in that shed, but then again, I may need the space for animals and crofters. How bad will it be? She paused and turned her thoughts to how she would feel if someone had murdered one of her family. Light, save us. Bucky has power; the goddess knows how much…but his grief will be relentless. He did love that poor boy so. Though it was only a matter of time until they killed him, him being right in the bloody demon nest and used by Abrecan to taunt his father.

Cissy tethered Nellie at the ancient Blackthorn. The watery afternoon light, a thin reminder that there was a sun somewhere beyond the hazy overcast, caught Cissy's hair, and spun an aura of gold around her curls. She frowned, took an old woollen hat from her pocket, and pressed it angrily on her head.

Such a natural beauty, but too serious by far, although it is hardly surprising, Dorothea thought, while she tapped on the window and pointed. 'We'll need the wheelbarrow from the woodshed, Cissy. I'll be out in a minute.'

'I hope you've laid her out properly and covered her up,' she muttered sourly making her way towards the woodshed. She stopped at the door and sniffed. Then pushing the door slowly open she checked inside. She studied the large pile of logs that covered a third of the floor and were stacked to the rafters. A dark look clouded her eye and her lips set in a white line. 'Francis,' she called, and the large black cat jumped off the low cart and slinked through the hedge. 'I smell Fear Me's.'

The black cat padded into the building and made a circuit around the walls. Standing on his hindlegs, he stared into the shadows between the piles of logs. *Yes, have you used the stone compass? That will attract them. I must inform the others we need to hunt.*

'Not since the night of the dead. Do you think they smell her, Woman-Tara's death?'

I do not know, sad-woman with yellow-fire hair. Francis replied and sent her an image of the name the three cats had given her, which translated as bubbling fire, inside sad sunshine. *I will find the others*. He slunk to the wagon and jumped lightly atop it, then closed his eyes.

Francis had shared his real name with her; it was *Ko tetahi kua wewete i te wha o nga motu o te pourewa wairua,* which was relayed to her in images of imprisonment, a witch, an envious sister, Tuahine Hae he called her, and he showed her in a jealous rage, while she used his blood and his Hun, his psychic power to cast her spells from the Copper Tower, Te Hinu Pourewa, against the Galanglas pirate Silas Al Seamist. Finally, he showed her a rescue on a beach and his freedom. *I am the Free One. I am Francis.* He struggled with how few words were needed to describe such a momentous name.

'How can anyone be out cold for two days, with hardly enough Belladonna to knock out a mouse?' Cissy frowned while she thought of Celeste luxuriating in her sick bed, with Dorothea at her beck and call. Try as she might, she found it difficult to find any sympathy for Tara; she was dead, she was free, Cissy thought darkly. She had even less for Celeste who she hoped would soon be gone. Far away and then some more would do her, far away from them all, especially Ganaim. The whole family were a curse; Aindreas should never have brought Tara to them. She grabbed the barrow and pulled it out of the shed. 'She should've been moved right away and put in the cold store,' Cissy mouthed to Dorothea who was paler than apple blossom while she stood watching from the window, a ghoul trapped behind glass and a mountain of circumstance.

'Give me a minute, I will come and help but I need to check on...' She thumbed upstairs to where she hoped Celeste would stay until they moved Tara.

Cissy frowned, then shrugged and pushed the barrow across the yard and parked it in front of the wide glass doors at the front of Tara's artist studio. 'O thank you, Mama,' she said as she peered through the window at the body wrapped tightly in white sheets, like a mummy laid out on top of the large kitchen table that had been brought through. 'She's done a decent job by the looks of it,' Cissy talked to herself while she opened the glass door and stepped inside, stopped, retched, turned quickly about and back to the clear air of the yard. Leaving the door open until they were ready to move the corpse, she saw the cats coming down the hill at speed and shuddered when a thrill of anticipation coursed up her spine. Now, this was something she could do; she studied the axe which lay on the chopping block outside of the woodshed and smiled.

She called to Dorothea as she made her way back across the yard. 'You may need to keep her away from the windows, there's rats in the woodshed.'

Dorothea nodded while Cissy removed the axe from the block. 'We'll have to take their heads off, I've no arrows with me.' The three cats hurtled past her into the shed. Two Fear Me's raced out of the door and were decapitated by the axe that swung so fast it seemed as if it was a silver wing that slashed through the air; a further four had their necks snapped and were tossed outside, where Cissy removed their heads and picked them up putting their bodies in one trap and heads in another.

Dorothea came out of the studio door and waved. 'No time like now, Cissy.' She pointed toward the studio.

'We're done here,' Cissy replied with a wide grin and wiped sweat from her brow. The cats slunk out of the shed, and she went to one knee before them. 'I'll deal with this, then we will hunt. I need to kill some more,' she said, and the black queen licked her lips.

By the time Celeste had finished bathing and was dressed in her breeches, and her jumper, that Dorothea had cleaned for her, Cissy, the cats, Nellie, traps full of Fear Me's, their bodies twitching as they tried to get back to their heads, and what appeared to be a roll of white laundry on the back of the cart, were almost at the brow of the hill, where the crofters Moin and Abhhain waited.

'After we've finished this lot off, I'm away to bed, Moin, and I'll not be up with the cock crowing either.' Abhhain rubbed at the back of his neck.

'Agreed. What a weekend. You can keep them city dances as far as I'm concerned,' Moin replied dryly, while he watched Cissy make her way towards them.

Abhhain said, 'Aye, but the things them spinners from Juno could do, and that Alcyone Sun? Well, I'm in love.'

'You and several thousand others,' Moin replied while he turned his attention to Cissy.

'I'm going to Elvan's Barrow,' she said.

Moin put his hand on her arm. 'You don't have to,' he replied softly, while his mouth dropped at the corners.

'I do, Moin. Then, I will sleep.'

'I could do with a stretch of my legs. Stiff after all that dancing. Think I'll be wandering up there myself,' Moin said, and Cissy smiled gratefully.

*

'Did I hear Cissy?' Celeste asked dully while she sipped her tea, curled up on the saggy old couch before the fire.

'Yes, she was down to check that the woodshed was full, there's a bad storm coming,' Dorothea replied, and she began to lift out individual bottles of herbs and potions from her bag.

'Ganaim is coming home to tend to you, dear. I will stay another night then I must be away to the farm before the weather breaks. I'm leaving you potions which you know how to mix but you must take them, Celeste, they are to fortify you, and to help with the night, well, you know what I mean.' She thumbed the small vials and shook her head while she thought morosely, it will take more than Valerian to help with what she has. 'I will make sure either Ganaim or Moin bring plenty of supplies. We will not leave you. Do you understand?'

Celeste stared into the fire. 'That's nice,' she replied, and her voice was weaker than vapour while she felt as substantial as a heat haze on a distant horizon.

Chapter Twenty-Two

Saying Goodbye

They pulled up their hoods and clasped their cloaks about them tightly. Breath steamed from nostrils and fell to the earth in curls of white. They followed the small path which had dried out after a spell of hail, until the narrow strip of dark earth faded away; no more than a rabbit track subsumed by thick undergrowth, snarly vines, and ivy. They trod carefully while they made their way towards where Dorothea said Tara wanted her body laid to rest. The sparse group of people, wearing long cloaks lined with rabbit and hoods of dark fur, held them tight against the cold and gusts of icy wind that cut through cloth and skin like swords. They followed a trail of small beeswax candles, resting inside lanterns. They lined the path as it snaked through the woods, following the meandering ways Tara used to walk when she went looking for tree Nympts, and the way home.

Tara had already been given to the earth. Her final resting place was a peaceful clearing at the foot of a large Blackthorn with small clumps of dark purple sloes still upon its branches; the frost had not been harsh enough under the canopy of ivy and mistletoe, to finish the fruit off. Conifers, dark, and straight, with branches stiff at their sides, like sentries, stood further back from the clearing where the deciduous trees had shed their leaves in curling tears of brown decay. The Blackthorn was hung with small, coloured lanterns. It is wasted on the dead, Celeste thought bitterly, then remembered that the Before the Tears ceremony was a celebration of the virtuous deeds and kindly nature of the departed. The lanterns were there to shine a light on the deeds that she had done, that there were so many told a tale of their own and Celeste felt a fleeting prickle of shame creep up her cheeks.

The forest smelled fetid, of humus and decay. Rotting wood, and leaves, had been cleared away for the burial and had released their death scent like bad breath in a too small space. A tiny mound of soil covered with lush greenery lay beneath the lanterned Blackthorn. Celeste stared at it dryly. The forest felt too warm, oppressive, and hungry after the walk that had chilled through her cloak and into her bones, she felt it nestle deep inside, and extend tendrils of ice where her sadness ran through her marrow, until the cold too, became part of her.

Above them, representatives from three tribes of tree Nympt hid in the evergreen branches, their faces cast in shades of sorrow and grief, but their coal black eyes glittered with knowledge of strange places that only they knew, and the deed they had done to aid Tara Silverhair.

In the absence of flowers, Cissy had created a bower of evergreens, cork oak, cypress, and conifer branches, entwined above the mound of earth to create a deathly grotto. On top of the mound, holly, ivy, and laurel tumbled and weaved around bough and branch, as if the forest held her with arboreal fingers twisted and green.

Little Lugh wore a woollen cloak quarter lined with rabbit skin, but with a full hood of black fox. He sobbed all the way through the first rendition of the song of her galactic signature, the Blue Planetary Hand, an artistic and healing power, but the more he sang, the steadier his voice became, and his voice grew on the essence of her song while he lamented her passing. 'I perfect in order to know. Producing healing. I seal the store of accomplishment from the shadow and its taint. With the planetary tone of manifestation, I hold worlds in my hands. I am guided by the power of my vision.'

He sang until his voice became hundreds of voices and a strange vibration came with his words and spun into the air shimmering orbs filled with symbols that were the words of her song made manifest in the language of light. They hung in the air above the mound, and all gathered there, gasped at their beauty.

Then, a column of light lifted from the mound, and Dorothea whispered, 'It is the notochord. Thank the light.'

After this a rose-gold owl spread its wings and they shone like fire and spirit light while it ascended through the chord, which sheathed its body until the Owl tore away. Then ascended like a comet from the mound of earth.

Dorothea sighed so heavily she nearly lost her balance. Ganaim stepped forward then hesitated when Cissy caught his eye and frowned while she shook her head then mouthed, 'It is done, the spirit flies through the notochord and returns to the core. It is intact.'

The departure of Tara's spirit animal left a vacuum of silence, and the temperature dropped. Dorothea took her gloved hand to her mouth and coughed to clear her throat. Her breath froze in tiny crystals like white tears in the fur around the bottom of her hood, but she spoke clearly. 'We give thanks to Lugh for sharing his galactic signature gift with us.' Then she stepped to the head of the mound; the lantern light from the tree streaked her face in shades of purple and yellow-gold. She wore a woollen cloak fully lined with otter fur. Her breath misted when she said, 'Tara would have appreciated the beauty of song made into shape and form that our own Lugh created with his Resonant Wind galactic signature. Her spirit is released; we wish her Goddess-speed on her return home. She would be proud of you, Lugh.' Lugh bowed his head, and she ruffled his hair, while tears streamed down his face. Then Dorothea put her hand on his shoulder. 'Go on,' she whispered while she fretted that she had not seen Tara's Soul Bird. Yes, her spirit animal had flown, and it had been beautiful and majestic, but the golden owl was not her soul bird. Light above, I hope it released at the time she was killed and is already away back to Earth or that spirit bird may fly back to it, wherever it is.

Lugh wiped his eyes on the edge of his cloak. 'She saved me when I was born because she took the cord from round my neck,' he finished on a croak, then ran to his mother, and hid his face in her skirts.

Celeste looked on numbly, barely listening to Dorothea as she continued with the Before the Tears ritual.

'She painted Lavender Lady butterflies for me, and I swear it was like they moved across the canvas.' Dorothea's voice caught in her throat as she stepped aside and let each person share a good memory of Tara and her kindness to them. Tears flowed freely while they spoke because that was the purpose of what they did.

When it was Ganaim's turn, Celeste thought he would struggle to find something to say. She knew they had a relationship based on mistrust but when he spoke, it was quietly and there was dignity there she did not know he had.

'She fed me even though she knew I had already eaten, because that was in her nature, kindness.' People around him nodded and smiled, his own smile was thin and cold, watery as rain, but he squeezed Celeste's arm and she felt like she was further away than the stars and her voice when it came felt strange in her mouth and her words sounded hollow.

'I loved her; she was all I had.' She stared at the small mound of earth and the clutch of people gathered around it. Dorothea, and Cissy, Padrain had not attended he was busy preparing the farm for the coming storm, or so Ganaim had told her. She had replied she didn't give a rat's backside whether he came or not, while she hid her suspicions from him and drove herself mad.

Goodwife Shroude was there, and Carter, as well as Old Muntor, who recalled Tara as a good friend and kind person. Raife Oarfish, a Roma Ranger now, with amber fire in his once dark eyes, stood on the periphery of the gathered folk, next to a large cork oak with his arms folded across his chest and the hood of his cloak drawn over his face. Apart from his fiery gaze, he was invisible while his Roma Ranger cloak reflected and blended into the surroundings. His warm resonant voice like the colour of his eyes had been replaced with something hard and terrible, a blade made of Solais Silver it lanced into the night when he said gruffly, 'I remember that she spoke the truth about many things. Especially, the Acolytes of Anuk. She knew the truth, about it all.'

Celeste knew he was thinking, if only we had all believed her. She met his gaze eye to eye until she felt the heat and anger while they flashed fire. He nodded once before he turned and left the clearing but there was no empathy in his gaze, only hatred and anger. He is here to check that she has been buried, that her spirit left this place Celeste thought and knew in the pit of gut that her suspicions were true even though they sounded mad.

The details of the burial had been expressly requested in her final day paper, although Tara had never once mentioned it to Celeste, which made her wonder why she had one. It was all so precise, not like her Nana at all. She was always far too busy conjuring conspiracy theories and hatching half-baked plans to take them across dimensions to a place and time she made up in her imagination.

No, Celeste thought, it does not fit, she was too determined to leave, to even consider she might die here.

~ ✧ ~ ✧ ~ ✧ ~

Bucky laid his favourite son to rest. Then he took his airship to Caislean Gairdin, his residence above Ninmah and he closed the gates and sent all his staff to their quarters but one, who he sent to Ninmah with a message for his friends and allies there. If you value your life, that of your loved ones, and the life of your animals, get inside and stay there.

Clouds began to gather. Deep pinks, dark blue-black, and vivid purples, like tender bruises on the white flesh of the sky while they rolled in from the sea to the West and the mainland to the East. Clouds like white horses stampeded from

The Ice Blight in the North, their crystalline manes and plumed tails tore behind, and sprayed the air with needle thin ice and a wind that keened and promised of more, yet to come, while they roiled and thundered across the sky.

Serpents with segmented backs coiled and slithered; bright orange, yellow, and deepest red, they roared, and spewed fire as they vortexed from the source of Gaia's Howl in the South. Serpent and snake snarled and coiled as they slid and fought along the horizon, desperate to join the gathering storm while it whirled in a fantastical spiral above the golden spire, on the highest tower, of the castle on Autumn Hill, The Caislean Gairdin.

Dorothea watched the sky every day with her knuckle in her mouth. 'Light of the blasted flame,' she cursed and Abhhain agreed.

Then she said, 'He has called the energy of Eyrie Whorls from Koura Pourewa, and Ice Horses from The Blight. When it comes; it will be relentless. It will be a hard, hard rain.'

She trebled the activity on the farm while shadows grew beneath her eyes and the sky spun like a maelstrom above, yet it did not release. Large herds of animals were brought in from the forest. The woodshed outside had been cleared. The wood was piled high in Tara's bedroom. Her studio housed a small flock of Gaiadon sheep. Nellie and Black were wrapped in blankets and deep straw put on the floor in the woodshed, which was easily big enough for them both, it being an old stable. Their stable at the farm housed more crofters that had come in from the woods, exotically coloured and bumped and barbed like the Selgovae. Cows were in byres, alongside other horses from the forest, with crofters and their curs, and more animals housed in Padrain's garage. Swine had been rounded up and penned inside the factories in the forest with hardy crofters who had volunteered to stay and endure the weather. Campfires burned and crews were selected for duties: clear paths, count heads, prepare food, watch for stragglers, obsidian, and black tourmaline arrows were fletched, spears, longbow, and crossbows made ready. Moin and Abhhain, three cats, and Cissy to patrol Elvan's Barrow; not everything would fear the storm.

When Padrain and Dorothea were happy all was in place and a satisfactory plan to keep the lane clear between the farm and the shed was agreed, Dorothea relaxed. She almost thought she had been too hasty as the sky stopped swirling and the lull seemed to stretch for days. The spiralling colours became less dramatic, colours mixed and faded, then turned grey, to nothing, a thin veil of sadness and many wondered if Lord Bucky had spent his grief. Dorothea wondered if his magic was only powerful for illusion and spectacle though something deep within her told her not to be so naive.

~ ❋ ~ ❋ ~ ❋ ~

Lord Bucky cast his inner eye towards the future. Then he sent his consciousness up and out, off the planet and along the edge of reason, his eye slid along the curvature of Time until he found what he was looking for, a way into The Void. Then he saw it, softly spinning, an oasis of Eleri Imole, potent supernatural light. Then he felt it like a punch to his hear and the great tree An Aon Charobh yielded, then faded in ripples of graceful surrender that wove through space and time. He held himself still while his spine set to steel and all happiness that he had ever held dear, was took from inside his heart and every hollow space was filled instead with rage and grief. Micah had gone, and now he knew she had gone too, and he cursed the path that he found himself upon, and the long, long game he had had to play.

'I loved you, Cass. Why didn't you stay with me?' He asked the Ever-Was and fancied he heard her voice echo from a past moment they had once shared. 'I am a servant of the White Flame, chosen by The Lady Prescience herself, to do the bidding of the Lords of Light, I need nothing more.' He let his tears fall as he had once before. Then, he spun along the curve and tore past the Temple of Time and his gaze, and his consciousness fell from the sky and into his body while he brought his fist to his heart. 'If it takes my last breath, then let it be so,' he growled and thumped on his chest thrice before he took his hand and raised it above his head. He uncurled his fingers in a motion that was sharp and unclenching. 'Let it begin,' he thundered, and his words not only meant the storm of his sorrow.

The translucent clouds whooshed away from Caislean Gairdin, as if he had cast his own veil over the sky, and the mist grew thicker, then thicker still, until eventually banks of grey clouds blanketed the sky above all the north, and the air smelled like cold, wet steel, while an unnatural silence waited patiently beneath his shroud.

'My sorrow is made manifest and my grief a howling lament,' Bucky intoned then fell to the floor. Blackness descended on him, and the wind whispered and sung like despair.

Then, suddenly it began. A howl pierced the unnatural silence as if it contained all the sadness of the world in its mouth, all the cries of grief vortexed in its throat, and all the wailing notes, of the eternal song that sang of the loss of love, blasted forth, and its power flew below the overcast. Tension stretched through the air, hatred upon the rack, all sinuous and raw while it sought revenge and its release.

Dorothea felt it in her insides, an opening of blood vessel and artery, the quicksilver run of fear. 'Tell everyone they must stay indoors, Pad. Quickly now, it comes,' Dorothea shouted, and Padrain, Moin, and Abhhain relayed the message around the farm.

Temperatures dropped faster than a coin falling to the ground. The skies wept hard icy tears of sorrow, longer than a finger, and sharp as a blade, but fragile as glass. They stabbed at the hard ground and shattered, as if to test the land's resolve. 'Are you mourning enough?' they questioned, while they ricocheted off the frozen ground, and tore roofs, forests, and fields apart. People and animals cowered in fear, while Lord Bucky's fingers of sorrow stabbed at the life below and decided that their grief was not enough to compensate for the death of the Winter Sun.

Blizzard after blizzard vented. An unrelenting series of winter storms that spewed snow across the land as if the sky were the ocean laying sand into dunes. Snow, the like of which had not been seen for centuries, did not just fall from the sky, it was dumped.

Celeste gawped out of the window while hellish weeks of Bucky's grief, reflected her own and she wished she had his power for she would not have stopped at the weather, she would have torn Baelmonarchia apart. She spent her days and nights in a frozen daze, her spirit was kin to the temperature outside, broken by feverish dreams; bouts of depression and anger, which came and went with the undulating rage of the winter winds, snow, and ice. 'Sheep in the studio, horses in the woodshed, madness in the attic,' she sung to herself while she put powders in her tea and waited to see who would make it through the storm to see if she were still alive. They had taken all the sharp knives, and the axe, and had left her with Bucky's heartbreak and her own, while people she thought she knew, flitted in and out like ghosts that belonged to her past life.

Ganaim stomping snow off his shoes, a light, and hope, that life would go on at a dark time when her life felt futile. He made his way through the drifts in the lane, with his jaw set rigid, and regret set deep in the pit of in his eye.

Unknown crofters, who were just popping by to see to the horses or sheep, became the things that marked Time passing. Moin studied her and a worried frown crinkled his pale green forehead. 'Here, you read this, it's Meite a Thomhas' Phantasmagoria.' He thrust the book into her hands, and she stared blankly at it. Selgovae, Novantae, Ningen, and other Magical Beasts was gilded on the front cover. She blinked and tried to push it back.

'I don't want it back, it's a common book among my people.'

She nodded mutely, then grunted her thanks like her tongue had forgotten the way to form words. Moin pulled on his furs, then left, shaking his head while his breath steamed out of the breathing hole at the chin of his fox fur hood. His face was a mask of worry beneath the fur, and his thick gloves held the ropes strung along the lane as if they strangled a snake.

The crofters and Ganaim braved bitter weather to carry supplies or herbal medicines, saying the right thing at the right time, but it was only words. His touch, his embrace and his warmth had receded with the Summer. Through her sadness she sensed a distance between them which she put down to the hideous things that grief does. Worse, she had been plagued by the prophetic nightmare and blistering palms. A pail of water and cotton compresses remained close to her bed, with woollen mittens she pushed the compresses in. She refused to house anyone in the cottage with her, folding her arms about her chest. 'No. I have sheep in the studio, which is all the company, and stink, I need.'

Dorothea supported her. 'She needs to mourn, she is in no state to house anyone, anyone at all,' she insisted, much to Ganaim's relief, Cissy's disgust, and Padrain's narrowed calculating gaze.

In her solitude, Celeste started to pay attention to the torment of the thing she had been cursed with, as she sought an end to it, and although the stigmata horrified her, she was determined to find a clue within the nightmare that would help her heal or help her kill herself. She toyed with a pencil then snapped it. 'I will not write anything down. I am not like her, not like her, she was mad in the attic, not mad, not mad,' she repeated, while she banged her balled up hand on her forehead and paced about the cottage.

'The reason the voice has not cursed me again in my nightmares is because it was not part of Nana's message. It was something else, someone speaking outside of my dream. I was taken or pulled somewhere else.' She cried when she realised, she had made a breakthrough, standing knee-deep in snow in the yard between the cottage and the woodshed as one blizzard finished, and another made ready to howl and weep. Her cream nightshirt was wet and dirty at the hem, her numb raw hands were stuffed into woollen mittens, which were wet through with the compresses she had pushed inside, while she shouted at the sky, 'You win, my insanity, but I know I'm not mad. The voice was outside. It was outside of the dream. I was at Elvan's Barrow with her, but they were not.'

Francis, bounded through a gap in the hedge, with a clump of snow stuck to his nose. Nellie whickered. Celeste thought she heard her say, *Thank the Light of Llamrei*, but Francis muzzled her mitten, then nipped the cuff of her nightshirt gently between his teeth and he pulled her inside. He spent the night with her while crofters moved about outside, tending to horses and sheep.

Glassy emerald eyes stared at her while she sipped her tea. He padded after her when she went from room to room weeping. Herding her back to the fire and the saggy old couch. She covered herself in her green wool cloak and slept, while he lay before her on the hearth. *Clearing this space,* he said as he too slept.

Still trapped in her grief, she had begun to look at Ganaim in a different light and had started to question the intentions of the people around her while she sat and listened to the scanner night after night. Sending herself crazy with fear as the protectorate guard launched aerial raids on villages along Kai, terrorising people who were already frozen and starved. Why? she asked herself as she heard the command given. 'Burn Anuk, and everything on it – light up the sky.'

Why is this happening? Is it because of Micah Apollon? She heard he had died on the same night as Tara, news she accepted dryly, just another part of her madness. She had known before it happened. The Romarii seer had told her that the prophet and the crone would die, but why tell a girl with no power, that two people would be killed by a blindman? She did not have the answer, any answers to make sense of a world suddenly turned upside down after her Nana's death.

The raids eventually stopped as the winter of Bucky's grief bit down hard like the jaws of an iron trap and the scanner like an animal spent, went morosely quiet. Though the silence left her alone with the madness that stalked her in her dreams. 'Is this what I inherited?' she sobbed, night after night.

~~ ❀ ~ ❀ ~ ❀ ~

At the Winter Solstice, the wheel still turned even though the world was frozen and stuck fast. Sonii Romarii exited the stone compass, leading Nimrod, with Cissy, three cats and two dozen traps stuffed full of Fear Me's. In the distance orange light domed above the farmyard, next to the longhouse they had built in the summer a fire blazed and tall flames licked towards a sky that was heavy bellied with yet more snow.

'Light, the compass is infested with them.' Cissy's breath purled from her nostrils while she shook her head and stacked the traps on the outside of the stone circle, next to a large standing stone. She was dressed head to foot in skins and wore a fur hat with ear flaps pulled tight to her skull and tied beneath her chin.

'Come, one of the crofters will collect them.' Cissy stroked Nimrod along his sleek neck, and they made their way from the stone circle, following a guide rope suspended next to a small dark path that slashed through high snowbanks on either side. Then they followed the crest of the field into the farm by way of a cleared lane, banked high with frozen snow on either side, behind Padrain's garage.

'You've an army of Selgovae waiting for your catch, Cissy.' Sonii said wryly though his voice was deep and melodious. They made their way past the crofters who waved and pointed. Cissy nodded towards Abhhain who gathered a handful of people to go and collect the traps. 'They think it a game, Sonii, even the children, but it will put them in good stead for when we fight the real demon and not just their fearful illusions.'

They walked slowly up the yard between banks of cleared snow, past the farmhouse. The kitchen as usual was full; huge pans of soup and stew sat atop the range, warm bread smells wafted through the chilly air. The cats pushed their way in and to the hearth in front of the range and Dorothea immediately moved them away.

Sonii did not stop until they reached the gate that led to the lane. Before he mounted Nimrod, he drew Cissy close to him and held her gently as if she were a child. 'My sister, be careful. I would hate to lose you. Do you recall the days and the journey, after what I showed you?'

She embraced him in return. 'I do, but perhaps not fully. I need more practice, but I will use it. I had no idea I had to take a bearing, but it makes perfect sense now. Although it has made it easier to return, I still feel I am missing something, a further technique perhaps.'

He squeezed her. 'It always does when someone shows you how.' He released his grip and said, 'I know only what I know. You have seen inside the compass, it is madness itself, there must be other secrets to travelling it. Still, you must remain cautious. And your promise?'

'Brother, do not concern yourself with my safety, you look to yourself and the burden you must bear.'

Sonii bent down and kissed the top of her head. 'Your promise, Cissy?' He released her and mounted Nimrod.

'I swear by the Lords of the White Flame that I will not hunt and kill Selene,' she replied. 'And your burden, Sonii?' Her eyebrows arched and she folded her arms across her chest.

'I have not decided whether I will bear it yet,' he replied dryly.

Cissy nodded then whispered to Sonii's while he turned away, 'But I will not promise that I won't defend myself if ever my path should cross with hers.'

Nimrod trotted through the gate, then Sonii heeled the horse who tossed his head and jumped forward. She waited at the gate listening to Nimrod build up speed as they made their way down the lane and through a channel dug out of deep snow, it was like a tube of blue ice, the snow having been cleared repeatedly had been packed hard up the sides of the high hedges, although the floor of the lane was clear.

'Easy Nimrod.' Sonii pulled on the reins to slow the horse down as the cottage came into view. 'I would curse Bucky for this weather, but I do not think he has been relentless enough with the demon king.'

Chapter Twenty-Three

Sonii Romarii

Sonii Romarii arrived like thunder down the lane on horseback, made louder by the hushed velvety gloaming and her own anxiousness which held her suspicious, whispering breath, tight and shallow in her chest. She stood behind Ganaim in the yard, silhouetted before snow banked to either side of the paths they had made to the woodshed, and to the rusty old gate that had been taken off its hinges. She held a tallow lamp from the cottage and did her best to illuminate the pitch-dark yard with a pool of greasy yellow light. Ganaim held a hissing alchemical lantern, although its blue glare was stronger than the tallow lamp, its light held no warmth, it was colder than ice. There was no mains rubicity, the snowstorms had seen to that and no light from the night sky while the overcast remained firmly in place. The snow was another tone in a land of dark and shadow that smelled sterile like wet steel and set her teeth on edge. There was no hint of things to come; the thaw and the spring, when all things were held under the thick shroud of Bucky's agony, when all things had succumbed and fled from his sorrow.

'By road? Bloody hell, Sonii?' Ganaim asked and held his lantern aloft.

'Not quite, we came up at the stone compass, but Nimrod here wanted a hard ride, let off some steam. We were told the lane had been partially cleared.' He patted the horse on its neck. 'Oh, the horses no doubt.' Ganaim shrugged. He ignored Celeste when she threw him a puzzled glance. 'I kept the lane clear as it was necessary for me, and Moin, and Abhhain to keep coming back and forth,' Ganaim said, although it sounded like he was explaining something to Sonii that puzzled Celeste. Had to keep coming back and forth, "had to"? I thought you wanted to, why explain that to him she fumed silently.

'Is this her then? By the Mother's breath, she's a child.' The large piebald nickered and bobbed his head enthusiastically. 'He'll need fed and rested.' Sonii nodded towards Ganaim.

'I've prepared the stable, Black and Nellie are in there.' Ganaim pointed to the brick building that had been an old stable before it was used as the woodshed. 'One of the crofters was su—' At that Moin appeared around the gate and said breathlessly, 'You took off afore I could catch you. Go on in, I'll see to Nimrod and the other animals while I'm here.' Sonii nodded curtly to Moin by way of thanks, which Moin ignored while he took Nimrod's head collar. Ganaim frowned at him, but Moin only shrugged; what did he care if it were Sonii Romarii, he had no trade dealings with Romarii, and would like to keep it that way.

Sonii dismounted in a single fluid, oily movement of muscle, black leather, and suede; aromas of patchouli oil, loam and leather, grassy herbs and campfires descended like a wave of aromatic musk. Celeste inhaled quietly, inwardly she felt herself giggle. He smelled, wild and free. At one with nature, animal, passion and fire, his scent said while it knocked her off her feet. She felt a slick heat rise across her cheeks; and was thankful for the dark when her pulse quickened, and her heart leapt. She glanced sideways at Ganaim and was relieved he was not looking at her.

Sonii greeted Black and Nellie, who whickered and snorted and made a show of themselves, overcome with the same sort of excitement she was sure she felt. She put her hand quickly to her mouth while her heart fluttered, inside she chastised herself for being so silly and girlish.

'Are you coming?' Ganaim spoke petulantly, sparks of icy light flashed in his eye, and he muttered something about, 'Bloody Romarii,' turned and stalked away to the cottage.

'Do I have a choice?' she retorted though she was glad of the chance to hang her head while a fresh flush spread from her toes to the roots of her hair.

He strode towards them as they walked slowly back to the shed, he was like Dorothea but did not have white hair or purple-blue eyes. He was strong, she knew that just by looking at him. She also knew instinctively that he was intelligent, a leader just by the way they all seemed to react to his presence without him having done anything. Brave too and there was something else she could not put her finger on. Just below the surface of his quiet confidence, there was something else that mirrored her own broken heart. She sighed and hardened her resolve; it was time for action. She knew if she was to survive, she had to depend on him. Sonii Romarii.

Her survival had become the single focus of her days, since she had convinced herself, she was going outside the box. That Padrain was a killer, she was sure of it – did Dorothea know? And as for Gan, she trusted him less each day. When she had waggled Thomhas' Phantasmagoria at him from her usual position on the saggy old couch, he had hung his head sheepishly and said, 'I thought Tara would have given you a copy. You know I'm not much of a reader.' She had jumped up and threw the book at him and shouted while spittle flew from her mouth faster than he flew out of the door. 'Not much of anything other than a big fat liar.' Then she followed him into the yard and screamed, 'Do not come back here unless you can bring me another book, and it had better be one that Tara was supposed to give me. You, lying bastard Al Tine. You knew she wasn't mad, but you let me think it anyway.'

Sonii pulled her back from her memory when he marched past and put his arm around Ganaim's shoulders. 'We should get on with it,' he said dryly but she heard the hint of resignation in his voice and wondered if he she was a task he would rather avoid, a burden. She followed silently behind, happy to make herself invisible, while she strained to hear.

'Not sure if this area is under surveillance by anything other than Fear Me's, but they're everywhere. A powerful shadow-friend must be mancing them from Unum in their thousands. The weather will hamper other surveillance, that, and Bucky's air embargo in place,' he shrugged, 'but it will come to its end, he will not corrupt the seasons. Winter Begone and First Spring will arrive as the wheel turns.'

Ganaim nodded. 'I can hardly believe Bucky could do this to the weather, the power…' he trailed off.

Sonii added in a hushed voice, 'Not even his full power, the things they could do. He could rip the sky apart, but here on Gaiadon, they are bound by the laws set by An Cloch Cosmai.'

Ganaim mumbled something that Celeste could not hear although she suspected it was about her or Tara. Sonii reached the door first and halted. 'I'll tell you this, The Crone felt Tara pass, she was on the island, she felt it all the way to the caves of Romar Ri. If she did, then so did others. We must move fast, friend, as fast as the weather will allow. I doubt Bucky can hold the…' he struggled momentarily for the word, then smiled at Celeste while she stared at him open mouthed. She blushed and he continued, 'He won't hold the current stasis much longer…soon as this snow retreats back to the north…no more dawdling with her preciousness.' He nodded towards Celeste, and then he stepped back, and half bowed. She scowled at him as if he were a dead rat on her dinner plate, then she pushed past into the cottage. How dare he call me a child, she fumed.

~ ❖ ~ ❖ ~ ❖ ~

Sonii pulled a hard leather case out of his pocket. He extracted a neat piece of red velvet which he placed on the table and unrolled with care, inside was a meticulous array of small shiny tools, scissors, needle and thread, and scalpel. He showed Ganaim a silver vial and said, 'Wound glue. Just in case.' He conducted his work efficiently, while Ganaim fretted about the room, pacing, and rubbing his forehead, blowing air out of his mouth in big raspy exhalations.

'Will you stop that pacing. You are like a stallion wanting to cover a mare, Gan,' he paused then added, 'Bring Celeste a drink. Here,' he threw him a leather bag, 'put some rations in there for me too.'

He studied Celeste while she jumped to Ganaim's defence. 'It's not that…' she trailed off as Ganaim left. Then said quietly, 'It's the blood, he's not keen.'

'I thought he'd be over that by now.' Sonii met her gaze with his own and there was something hard in his eye. They flashed bright amber. He frowned and she said, 'You reminded me of a friend, Raife.' Her throat clammed tight after she spoke, and heat crawled and tingled under her skin and along every downy hair on her cheek and brow.

Sonii replied. 'He was accepted into our tribe with some others. They are doing well.'

She gulped back tears and found a well full of relief that had been hidden in the centre of her chest, a secret place she dared not visit, or hope to ever see again. Out there, somewhere, Raife Oarfish, Margeride Shroude and Sarlat Penroe were doing well. It was all she needed to steel her resolve and she snapped her spine a little straighter when he tapped on her forearm with the tip of a hunting knife. 'The trick' he said, 'is to make it look like it's been there since you were a young; that's why I'm going to cut you here.' Celeste changed her earlier opinion of him in an instant; she was sure he was taking pleasure in making her feel uncomfortable. 'Just under your elbow joint…and push the dud down under your skin, we can't risk a new scar on your wrist. Especially if we want to avoid trouble at the canal checkpoints. The proc guard use visual as well as scanners, best to be one step ahead. Not too many, Celeste, as that would cause suspicion, but one or two steps mean we are just lucky that's all.' He winked at her; she flushed and gulped down a giggle. Until he pinched the skin of her forearm between his fingers, picked up the scalpel and sliced the lump of flesh in two.

She would not give him the satisfaction of vomiting, so she took her thoughts elsewhere, to her newfound friends, the crofters Moin and Abhhain. Because of them she was beginning to understand a little more as she worked her way through Meite a Thomhas' Phantasmagoria. It was so much more than a catalogue of mythological animals, it was the history of a race of beings called Fae and the two tribes they belonged to, Selgovae and Novantae, and the magical animals that were part of their world, part of Gaiadon until they had to leave, because they were full of a magical light, Eleri Imole, although that was not explained fully.

Once she had begun to read it, she could hardly thank Moin enough for the gift and understood why he had given her it. 'I am sorry for being so, dismissive, this is priceless' she said, and her cheeks flamed red.

Moin flapped his green-grey hand at her. 'Don't be daft, it's a history of my ancestors, and the wonderful creatures that shared their world. I's most glad that I could share it with you. Now if you want to know more about the Galanglas Giants, you need to find a copy of Charyia Sea Storm's Captain's Periplus, her being one of them, and if you do, you let me have a read too, as I never did see one anywhere, but heard it sung of more than enough.' He rubbed at his smooth chin thoughtfully for a minute as they stood next to a growing midden heap that steamed in the cold afternoon air. There was a window in the snowstorms which had been filled with freezing temperatures. Moin and Abhhain were down to see to the animals, and Celeste.

'And there's another book you should read too. No, I don't remember the name of it, mad naked Cassandra Novantae's book, she is half in this world and half in the future. You know? When she walked inside Silver Tower. Abhhain, Ab,' what's naked Novantae's book called?' he shouted to Abhhain, and his breath foamed like white waves scrolling through the breath hole in his fur hood.

Abhhain was putting the sheep back in the clean studio. Wrapped in furs himself he looked like a wolf walking on two legs; he closed the glass door and laughed when fluffy white faces stared through the window at him. 'Light, Moin, you'll give the lass nightshades to the end of her days, which isn't far off according to Cassandra Novantae…' he paused, then shrugged and continued. 'You'll never find a copy, love, rare as unicorn dung, but in the common tongue it's called the Chronicles of Cassandra, and in it the white-eyed seer tells of her visions, prophecies, and predictions for the arrival of heroes and demons to mark the end of all time.' He put his head to one side thoughtfully then said, 'When the Winter Sun sets in hell, the eve of destruction begins, or something like that. The other book, Moin the scholar, is referring to is Navigating the Southern Isles by Charyia Sea Storm. Even rarer than Cassandra's Chronicles…which is called,' he paused, and his eyes searched in the middle distance of his memory. 'Got it. In your tongue it's called, The Age of Man and Shadow Yet to Come, but the Selgovae Fae call it, Aois an duine agus an scath.' Abhhain plucked at the air with a gloved hand the size of a giants, just as the first fat snowflake of the next blizzard landed on the dark leather and took far too long to melt.

'Time to make tracks,' he said to Moin while he studied the flake, and Celeste heard the exhaustion and worry in his voice. She felt it in her own water, if Bucky did not stop soon, they were all going to die.

~ ❊ ~ ❊ ~ ❊ ~

Sonii frowned then leaned close to her ear, bringing her back from her reverie. He whispered while he rubbed a stinking ointment onto the small incision at her elbow, which to her surprise had already stopped bleeding.

'Use the crystal, it's part of a violet hatchling shell.' She almost jumped out of her skin, but he gripped her arm until she steadied herself; they could hear Ganaim rattling about in the kitchen, looking for things to eat. There is hardly anything left she thought but said instead, 'How do you know I have it?' She asked hesitantly while she thought about the box Dorothea had given her after Tara had died. It did have a shard of crystal in it, a photo of her parents, rarer than Navigating the Southern Isles she thought bitterly and an obviously fake birth document. She could swear the ink had still been wet and was disappointed at Dorothea for thinking her a fool.

'It will hide the curse when you're on this journey, Celeste. You have been marked.' She tucked her hand between her knees and felt her jaw drop open while he continued. 'Although we don't understand what it is yet. If you are discovered, you will be killed and my people with you. Promise me you won't tell another soul about the prophecy Tara delivered, or the curse you carry – your life depends on it.' He searched her face for acknowledgement while she fought back tears and nodded weakly. 'Doro—' she began, but he held up his hand. 'This I know already, let her be the only other, do you understand?'

She nodded and tears of relief filled her eyes. She knew suddenly that this strange man, his leather clothes stinking of the earth, horse shit and herbs, tattoos of things that should only exist in the book Moin had given her, cavorted across his flesh, so far beyond belief that she could not look at them, his dangerous animal eyes, and shimmery red skin – this man, Sonii Romarii, would help her because he knew how to.

'You can cure me, you can take them away, the pain?' she whispered incredulously while a heavy feeling pushed a wave of blackness over her.

He caught her before she fainted. He supported her against his shoulder until the room stopped spinning and whispered, 'Hush, hush – no. No, we cannot, we can only hide it from others and only while you are travelling…the crystal shard will absorb the vibration. It is a counter to the curse that was cast. I can do no more to protect you other than what I can do with sword and bow. Use the crystal you were given, sleep with it, keep it on your person – it's no good to man nor beast in that box.' He nodded towards the dresser drawer.

'Sonii? You can help?' she whispered furtively, aware that Ganaim may appear at any moment. 'I can feel it…Am I in some sort of danger? Light. What a stupid question, of course I'm in danger, going outside and destined to be working the wind, oh, is that it? Tell me what it is? What's wrong with me?' Her voice hissed and her hands trembled while her thoughts would not form a coherent sentence and she rambled on. Just like my mad nana she thought and took a deep shuddering breath.

'Have they told you nothing?' He leaned forward and taking her chin in his hand he looked intently into her face. 'By the Goddess they haven't! What was Tara thinking?' He looked over his shoulder towards the door that led to the kitchen, heard the water closet door creak further down the corridor, and Ganaim retracing his steps. 'It's not our place to get involved too much in the affairs of hu…in your affairs and for good reason. The goddess only knows why we have agreed to this. The trade must have been beyond compare, and yet to be revealed…I wouldn't have touched it, but…look child, my advice – just keep moving until you get to the people who can help you.' He rose suddenly and his eyes were full of regret. Then as if a curtain had been drawn over his feelings, a cloak of resolve set like ice over a lake leaving the air frigid between them.

'Don't call me child,' she said sharply, annoyed that he would not tell her more, and hating herself for almost weeping, and as for nearly fainting! She rose from the chair at the table and threw herself onto the couch before her legs gave way.

'Perhaps one day,' he retorted quickly, and an angry look clouded his face. 'Maybe one day,' he repeated quietly while he studied the top of her head above the back of the couch with a heavy look in his eye and a perplexed frown chewing at his forehead. But let that not be what Gaia desires. I pray that is not the path we have to tread. He thought better of his rough words and came to kneel before her, his eye level with hers as she sat in her usual nest on the couch. The fire roared behind him, shadowing his face, but not his eyes which were easily as bright as the hottest ember. 'You are so young. So very new compared to my people. You do not deserve it, you do not deserve any of it, Celeste, and I hope that whoever is given the task to take you to safety is the best Romar Ri has.'

It was so final, she almost burst into tears and was glad to hear Ganaim when he pushed the door open. Sonii stood casually and walked to the table where he put his kit together. Ganaim came back through with water and the small leather bag stuffed with dried meats, fruit, and nuts. He passed her a beaker of water and a peculiar look flitted across his face, she mumbled thanks and turned her face away from his penetrating stare.

A dark shadow crossed Sonii's face, he was angry and when he spoke to Ganaim his words were short but full of fire. 'I wish to talk to you, outside?' Then he turned and with a visible effort he kept the anger out of his voice when he said, 'I'll make my farewells…Celeste? The goddess willing, I will see you on the road, if we are destined to meet upon the dagger path once more. Remember what I said.'

Celeste nodded, bewildered, while he bowed slightly then turned to leave. The water was cold, everything was cold apart from the small space before the fire. She sipped at the fluid, it felt strangely soothing as it travelled down her throat; it took her mind off the crawling sensation under her skin, burrowing along under the surface of the subcutaneous flesh of her arm. It did not hurt like she thought it should. In fact, it still felt like Sonii was still massaging it. She shook her head as another flush crept across her cheeks. 'I wonder if they're all like him.' She sighed as she listened to their muffled voices, suddenly a bit clearer when Sonii and Ganaim began to argue hotly, about some misplaced sense of responsibility and what the real responsibilities were in raising her.

She rose slowly from the couch and made her way carefully to the window which was hardly defence against the weather let alone a couple of raised voices. The snow in the yard had been shovelled back and it bordered the edges like high white walls with a gap that led to the entrance to the lane. She sat quietly at the table, being as still as she could, just out of the line of their sight. She could still see the two men, illuminated by the weak glow from the tallow lamp Ganaim held, while they walked towards the stable.

'She thought she could hide her, by the seven hells, that child in there is going to start vibrating like a cosmic axiatonal alignment soon,' his rough voice rose an octave higher. Ganaim shrugged which angered Sonii and he hissed, 'isn't that what she's supposed to do?'

Ganaim mumbled, 'How would I know,' and shrugged off the question. 'The pair of them would not discuss that with me. I was her little guard, nothing more,' he said bitterly.

'You don't know?' Sonii sounded venomous but softened his voice as he continued. 'Well, let me tell you in the absence of information and common sense from Padrain, or will it be too late when half the universe hears her activate, and the last battle pops above our heads, when they start to argue over the harvest – then the demon king rips a hole all the way to the core of this planet in his search for the heart of the logos. None of the predictions mad Cassandra made are come to pass, there is no aid,' he ran his hand through thick dark hair that fell to his shoulders in waves, 'and we are not enough. The Romarii are never enough.' He pointed upwards. 'Juno waits for the attack to come to them. They cannot send us the armies we need, because they have had to close the gate to their dimension, trapping Ten of their best warriors here.' He pointed to the ground and his breath fumed in the air.

'Honestly, Sonii, I do not know everything. In fact, the more I find out the more I realise that I know hardly anything at all,' Ganaim replied sourly. They were further away, next to the midden heap, which was topped with a thick layer of snow, like almond paste on a dark cake.

'You don't know because Padrain as usual keeps his own council, not content with stealing the heart of the most powerful crone Romar Ri had, he will not instruct you in your destiny either.' He stopped suddenly. Celeste heard Ganaim mutter something about weird goings on, then she heard him say quite clearly, 'Airgid and Gaoth, but they said nothing I could make sense of; besides, I've committed to the Roma Rangers now.'

Sonii snorted. 'Have you? Do you think it is that simple? Think hard before you make promises and contracts with Romar Ri. Do you hear?'

'I will, it's just that, well, you know how it is.' Ganaim shrugged and his breath steamed against the air while he exhaled heavily.

'I can hardly recall being your age, Gan, maybe I once was, but it is many, many lifetimes ago. I have not been made that young for as long as I can remember. The goddess Gaia wills what she needs,' he pointed to his chest, 'This. It has been ages since I experienced life through the first summers of my youth like a young buck does. You are a young buck, remember that before you do anything else stupid enough to get you ensnared deeper into somewhere you are not supposed to be.' He stalled while he took dark leather gloves lined with fur out of the waistband of his breeches and put them on. Then he laughed dryly. 'Solas Nua Novantae, I suppose a legend has to begin somewhere, but beware the council of Romar Ri, they might be the death of you and the death of hope for many.'

'I do not feel it, Sonii, not anywhere in me. I feel I am a Romarii and that is where I will make my home.'

'You will find it hard to thwart your destiny and harder still to put roots down in Romar Ri if you are not acceptable,' Sonii replied sadly, and he touched Ganaim on his shoulder. 'We just all want to go home, Gan. It is not right living in disharmony like this…some of our new young, despite the memories they are supposed to retain are beginning to think that all of this is real,' he swept a fur clad arm all around, 'and the stories we tell round the fire? A myth. They hardly remember their past lives. The dimensional pocketing is reflecting our inability to remember our previous existences; that means separation from our goddess, and ultimately, extinction for my people.' He lifted his hand and rubbed his forehead. Ganaim nodded slowly and his own head felt heavier than a boulder. Every time he heard something new the burden increased.

'What's Padrain say about it all?'

'He's…not sure…he thinks Yalan bungled.'

'Bungled, ha,' Sonii said wryly. 'He is not called wizard for nought. His other names are Ancient of Days, Golden Light of the Endless Flame. He is the Will of the Logos, the Sophia's first progeny, and The Lord Death. He fought the Nomos for the Stone and won, not just once either if what Cassandra Novantae said is true. Yalan is the most dangerous Being on this planet. His power is weakened while he is dislocated from his own dimension, and his hands are tied while the demon-horde hold the Sophia captive there. Believe me when I say this, I for one think that a blessing in disguise. Bungled. Is just what he wants you to think.'

'I know, Dorothea explained once, but he seemed so nice.' Ganaim stuttered a little and Sonii guffawed. 'He is charming and bumbling. Haphazard, and accidentally where he needs to be, the unexpected guest but often unwanted, and polite to a fault but as deadly as a hungry dragon above a sheep pen.' He stopped and thumbed to the cottage. 'He kills 'anything' that gets in his way. Get a message to Padrain, tell him the council of Romar Ri says he is to stop stalling. I will need to ask them to convene before we can make any further arrangement for her,' Sonii finished sharply and thumbed over his shoulder.

'What?' Ganaim replied hotly. 'Another layer of trade and dealings, Sonii. Padrain does not care, we have kept up our end, protect Tara and her ward for as long as was necessary. I thought that had been agreed. You need to take it up with her lot if further trade is what you are after. I went like I was supposed to, and I bent the knee to Romar Ri, and Cissy went before me. What else will this cost?'

Sonii sighed while he saddled Nimrod. Then he bent and checked his hocks and his harness. Rising he tilted his head to one side and said incredulously, 'They haven't told you?'

Ganaim shook his head and thunderous look brought a knot to his forehead and set the crystal light beneath his skin pulsating in waves of red and gold.

'Cissy and her Skywalker ability in service to Romar Ri as and when needed, was the trade for Tara and Celeste's safety.' He paused and pointed a gloved finger at Ganaim's chest then said dryly, 'You were the trade for the horses.' He put his hand under his chin while he watched Ganaim's eyes nearly pop from his head.

'Fuck off, Sonii.'

Sonii shrugged. 'Ask them but I tell you this, there is no her lot and my lot, not anymore. It is all of us against the filth in Lodewick. Romar Ri agreed to take into their care a functioning weapon, which we helped create. We expected her to know what she is, and to be able to use her power by now. We did not expect an adept, a master, there is not any who could train her. Light, she is not even fit to be a novice.'

'It's only just activated, and I for one couldn't be sure if it has properly…' Ganaim trailed off. He still blamed himself for Celeste. He rubbed at the back of his neck and played with his pointed ears nervously. If he had not had sex with her, would everything still be the same? Hells, it feels like a million years ago.

Sonii tilted his head while he studied Ganaim. 'I heard you did well recently, very well. You could be an asset, if the crone Arianrihod does not reject you, Solas,' he emphasised the name dryly, 'but Romar Ri will only take risks like that,' he stopped and pointed to the cottage and then Ganaim's chest, 'for an equal trade and a heavily compensated deal. What we have now is akin to us being ripped off – wars have been fought for less. The council will need to convene, and I need to present them with this latest information. What we thought we were getting, is not in fact, what we have. Tara failed in her duty and paid the price, Padrain has been hesitant to share the facts with us, and as for Dorothea...' He raised his eyebrows in disbelief that the Lady Aos Si suffered so much hardship under the control of the human. *Love does the strangest of things to folk* he thought.

Ganaim went to the stall where Black and Nellie were and asked, 'Was it a fair trade?'

Black bared his teeth at him, but Nellie nuzzled him. *Sonii tease you too easy. The trade was simple as Dorothea could make it. Two horses on the farm in exchange for your training in the way of Roma Rangers. If you need be fists or eyes for them, then you be ready for the job. Was never supposed to be for evermore, child. Was supposed to be over and done, and you free by now.* She looked perplexed, and a little disappointed.

Black ho-hummed into his head. *You never be free after what I hear from Niyaha. Rovander take your balls off with her teeth, silly little stallion.*

Sonii laughed deeply while Ganaim blushed. Then he slapped him on the back. 'Come on, there are worse mistakes to make than that, lad, and she may change her mind yet.'

Nimrod nickered and bared his teeth. His breath steamed against the chill air, and he stamped his big hoof noisily, eager to get back on the road as Sonii drew an amber crystal out of a pocket. He wore rabbit skin and leather clothing lined with the hide of miscarried lambs and his boots were lined with beaver fur. Ganaim noticed his cuffs were loose and knew that Sonii had throwing knives concealed there. He reached behind the saddle, loosened a sausage-shaped bundle, and unfurled his cloak which he threw about his shoulders. It had been lined for the winter with a detachable rabbit fur inner and the outside blended in with the night and the snow, leaving a disembodied head floating above the collar. He cast his crystal orb into the air and began to chant softly, then mounted before he turned to where Ganaim walked across the yard.

'Honour the contract you have made if you must, but I urge you to make no more promises, Solas Nua Novantae. Look to Cassandra's Chronicles for the prediction but mark this, in the absence of Akasha, the Selgovae seer, Airgid, is the most accurate oracle in the North.'

~ ❦ ~ ❦ ~ ❦ ~

Ganaim slammed the door behind him and put the tallow lamp on the table. 'Oh well, that's him away,' he said coldly while he pushed his anger to one side. 'Can I have a look then?' He walked towards where she was sitting beside the fire. 'You look a bit flushed, no wonder that looked awful, much worse when you're older, I suppose.'

She narrowed her eyes while he approached and was pleased when his false smile and shallow concern, oiled off his face. She had not heard a quarter of what she would have liked but had heard the name Novantae and knew that there was a book of prophecy that Sonii had referred to, as had Moin and Abhhain.

'You will find me a copy of Cassandra's Chronicles, liar Al Tine' she demanded while she continued to stare into the fire.

Without a word he turned and stomped out of the cottage. I will have that ranger cloak, I bloody-well will. If Raife got accepted, then so will I he thought angrily, and he slammed the door a second time.

Celeste jumped. 'Goodbye, Ganaim Al Tine,' she shouted. Then hugged her knees to her chest while she whispered to the flames, 'I do not know you anymore, nor myself, or what we will become.'

Ganaim Al Tine was gone and in his place was a young man with a heart of stone. Worry creased about his laughing eyes like crinkles in old bark, they sparkled still, but it was with wet regret rather than the mischief and joy that had once been there. Like Raife Oarfish, he had become cold and distant, brooding, and fretful like the winter weather. Whatever had robbed him of his joyful youth and exuberant tongue had been as sure of its success as the march of Time. Her Ganaim had gone, and with him the promise he had made, to love her forever.

Chapter Twenty-Four

Miserable Folk

Celeste paused as she paced before the window, thumbing the crystal shard while the cottage timbers cracked like old hip bones breaking. 'I can't believe it's the sound of her that I miss the most. It's sparse without her, that's what it is.' She stopped pacing, sat in the armchair beneath the window, and talked to her distorted reflection in the glass while the pale winter sun rested on the crest of Long Field, silhouetting the top of the largest of the monoliths in the stone circle.

Ganaim would be here for her soon. She still did not know who was travelling with them and had heard nothing more from Sonii, although she had secretly looked from her window more than she would have liked, hoping to see or hear Nimrod clattering down the lane, the handsome Romarii astride him.

She knew instinctively that she had to trust what the Romarii said. He had revealed more in a single night than anyone had in her entire life. She looked at the crystal shard, a cloudy deep lavender although he had said it was violet, it was not a strong enough shade of purple. According to Sonii, it would hide her stigmata while she travelled. She bit it then tried to snap the shard in two; it may look fragile as glass, but the thing was hard as Solais steel. He was right on one count though: it had started to work, although its effectiveness seemed to be determined by how close it was to her. It worked better when it was under her pillow, near her head, and was no good at all if she left it on her nightstand next to her bed or the floor in front of the saggy old couch where she had taken to sleeping.

Now, when the foul black sun rose, a fox as dark as the sun itself leapt into the sky and tore it from its trajectory, holding it in its jaws as if it had caught a chicken, it shook it into fragments of oily dark. When the stigmata had begun to bubble and rise through her flesh, a golden phoenix flew past, and stole the heat from her palms by pulling it into its tail of fire.

Then her dreams would turn into a chaotic swirl of nonsense as she hurtled from one nightmare dreamscape to another, always with a sense that she was not dreaming but was awake outside of her body.

Recently she had seen a huge man in his middle years, in a dungeon, Romarii, and bearded like Sonii, he was chained to a wall. She hovered near the ceiling while a tall man with brightly coloured serpent eyes said, 'Die here or fight. Show me this fabled Romarii honour.' The large man spat at his feet. 'Take me down and fight me in the ring, Volsunga,' he growled, and the man called Volsunga laughed cruelly. 'That is an invitation I will not refuse, Romaros, but first you will be tested.' He swished out of the dungeon and his robes trailed on the floor like heavy streamers of smoke crawling along the ground. Then guards entered with keys to unshackle the prisoner.

Following this she cartwheeled through a vortex of colour and found herself watching a girl, slightly older than herself, with a narrow red face and Romarii eyes, large and slanted, and a bit too big for her head. She was being plunged into a barrel of water headfirst, her hair cascaded then spiked through the water like shafts of ice crystals while she looked through the roil and said, 'Dreamwalker?' Flawless hands, one on the top of her head and the other on her shoulder kept her beneath the water, and two rings of gold sparkled on each elegant index finger.

Another time, she had woken up coated in sweat and Micah Apollon was sitting cross-legged before the fire, only just fading away while he shouted at her, 'VEIL SLAVE, will you just WAKE UP? The black moon has filled the sky with lies and you are supposed to know how to undo it!'

Still, that was not the worst. The worst was the fleeting image of a young man, thigh-deep in roiling water. His eyes were dark, like ironstone and coal, and she could not find any light in them, they were wide and bulging with blood lust. Spittle flew from his mouth, and he snarled, then bared his teeth while he raised a cruel blade and began to hack off a naked dead man's hand. His mouth was taut, and he howled silent words at the pewter overcast. *I accept your oath*, a woman's voice tinkled like glass shattering in the distance, and she woke with a start and a sharp but fleeting pain across the back of her neck.

*

'It's getting late, where in the hells are, they?' she talked to herself anxiously while the shadows lengthened in the yard. In the garden beyond, snow drops were poking through the thin layer of snow which was cracked and holey like lace where the last of it had thawed in some places, then refrozen. Her hand trembled as it rummaged one last time in the box. Her finger traced the bumpy surface of the burnt words: Be aware, the axis of reality is vertical. 'What does that mean?' she spoke aloud, forgetting that there was not anyone there to answer as she removed the photo, sticky and tatty now, for one last look; it was of her parents. The only image she had of them; pictures like this were rare in rural zones, all the best technology was kept in Lodewick or the manufacturing cities like Nenesh, Yamal, or Shad and Pali, but still it was proof that they existed somewhere, other than in her imagination. They could afford a crystal box, she smiled. It comforted her that they had not been poor. Not like we are now she thought. They were standing side by side on a beach – not a windswept beach which ruled out Eirini, Falamh and Talam Na Soar. This beach was more foreign than that. It looked hot, and sunny. Celeste pursed her lips; it could be anywhere she thought then studied them and their miserable faces again. She sucked air into her cheek. They were not holding hands or embracing, but immobile as statues and looking awkwardly towards the lens.

Celeste thought, not for the first time, Anukssake, what miserable folk. Her father had a wide brimmed hat pulled down over his face, all that she could see was his mouth, set in a grim line, his jawline and broad shoulders, the way he stood, his arms folded casually but with an air of readiness, reminded her of someone, though she could not think who. It looks as if they had a row, I wonder if it was about me.

Her mother's hands cradled the unborn Celeste, tucked away safely inside the bump. A funny sort of half smile that looked like a contemptuous sneer, sourer than Cissy's worst, stole across Selene's lips, taking her beauty with it. She looked down her nose into the crystal box, her eyes stared directly at the lens, haughty, while her hands grasped triumphantly at her swollen belly; they seemed eager to hold the new life. They do not look like hands that would give up a baby. So, why did she?

The door creaked open, and Celeste put the crystal and photo quickly in her breeches pocket. 'Oh, it's you, Cissy. What do you want?' she asked coldly as Cissy made her way into the front room.

'I'm not on my own,' Cissy replied just as coolly while Moin, Abhhain, and the Moema cat, Francis, appeared in the door behind her. 'They have something for you.' She said and inclined her head towards the Crofters.

'Ah lass, you look better by half at least,' Moin said as he slipped past Cissy. His grin split his face in two. Abhhain, his brother, followed. Both Crofters wore thick furs and wore dark boots to their knees; they still patrolled the boundaries of the farm, and both had hunting gear with them. Although all three looked too thin and haggard. Bucky's wrath had been relentless, the damage and the loss of life beyond the count. The storms had decimated the Protectorate Guard barracks, and border posts all around Eirini and the Lake of Unum was still frozen solid. It had been hard on them all, but not as hard as losing a son. Not as hard as the Winter Sun setting for the last time.

Moin and Abhhain were similar as peas in a pod with creamy pale-green skin, that unique sort of skin that descendants from Selgovae Fae had; though their skin was not scaled or barbed, it was smooth as a seal. Abhhain was fond of saying we have Selgovae blood, but it is thin, and I am glad of that. Large dark eyes, almost lidless, and wide kind mouths with laughter close to their lips, reminded Celeste of seals bobbing out of the sea, although their pointed ears did not. 'We brought you some gifts for your journey,' Abhhain said as he put his pack on the floor.

'Aye, so you don't have to enter into trade with the Romarii for anything that we can give you freely. Make sure you do not trade with them, lass,' Moin said as if he were her father. Cissy had taken a seat at the window. The cat sat next to her, and they looked on. A thin smile tried to lift Cissy's mouth, but she cowed it with a stern frown.

'Now we know you is good with a bow and arrow, lass, a good hunter, better than Ganaim, eh?' Moin said as he brought out a leather quiver filled with the silver and black arrows. She gulped back tears; it had been so long since she had hunted, or ran, or laughed, it felt as if they talked about a different person.

'Me and Abhhain crafted and fletched these, so they will aim true and fly fast. The black tips are magicked as well as they can be.' He gave her the quiver and waved his hand to silence Celeste as she was about to protest, her eyes all full of water.

Abhhain came to kneel on the hearth. 'We will not hear any protests from you, Celeste. These are crofter gifts, freely given.'

Celeste looked to Cissy who nodded slightly, her mouth all serious and a cold determined light in her eye. Abhhain took a small spear – although it was more like a polearm in his hands – a composite bow made from yew wood and horn, and a leather arm brace from his pack. 'Now I know you can use these, though you be out of practice after…well, you know,' he stumbled over his words, 'but don't you leave them in the en…I mean in what you hunt, you retrieve them when you can.' He pointed to the arrows. 'They be Solais silver shafts and black tourmaline heads that have been magicked, so they don't shatter, break, nor dull. The spear is made from a branch, all the way from An Crann Amhain, the city the giant's called One Tree in the common tongue. An Crann Amhain is the seed of Gaia's first tree, and we be giving this to you as was told by Cassandra, for you will give it to the wind.'

Celeste looked befuddled, but Cissy interjected, 'I will explain in a moment, Celeste, but know that what you hold there is rare, and perhaps too great a gift.' She eyed the crofters who lifted their chins defiantly. 'You should make your goodbyes. They will be here soon.'

Celeste jumped off the saggy old couch and burst into tears proper while she hugged Abhhain and Moin. 'I am so sorry to have caused you all that trouble…me wandering about in my nightshirt most of the time, mad as you like, and not being able to care for the horses or sheep.'

Abhhain ruffled her hair. 'Ahh, grief do strange things to even the strongest heart, and me and Moin know yours to be strong.'

Moin came and kissed her on each cheek. 'If only we had been here before or even sooner than that, we could have done more, we could have given you some teaching.' Cissy coughed at that, and the two crofters stepped back sheepishly.

'You may have the cottage and do with it what you wish.' Celeste surprised herself at her gift. The crofters nodded thoughtfully while Cissy narrowed her eyes. 'I know…I know, you…light, I know I won't be coming back, not ever.' None of the party in the room corrected her as they knew it too.

'Thank you, Celeste, thank you, sweet child,' Moin and Abhhain said. Then they placed their right hand on their hearts. Following this they turned them towards her and opened them, palms flat and facing upwards – a crofter gesture of deepest thanks, gratitude, and love, between friends.

Celeste returned the gesture; she had read about it in Meite a Thomhas' Phantasmagoria. Then recalling a greater honour, she had read about in the same book, she touched the centre of her forehead with her index and middle fingers, then held her hand out fingers still together but the flat of her palm towards them; I see you, was the gesture. Moin and Abhhain returned the honour, as pleased as a well-fed crofter cur, although their eyes were wet with tears when they picked up their hunting gear and left.

She turned to face Cissy, her eyes turned hard and suspicious even though she tried to put a neutral look on her face. Francis came and sat heavily beside where she stood on the hearth, her weapons at her feet and her hands clenched tight at her side. Cissy pulled the armchair round to the side of the fire. 'You may as well sit, though I won't be long.'

She pulled a bag out of her hunting pack, it moved like the Roma Ranger cloaks did, almost invisible, it was small, no larger than the size of a man's palm, and old, it had a single thick strap that you wore across the body. Celeste sat down reluctantly and waited for Cissy to begin, determined she would not be the first to talk.

Cissy tutted.

'I thought my worst nightmare had happened when you were made, but it seems that I was wrong, that there are worse darker shades than that, that I have to endure losing my son once more, and therefore I am about to do, what I do – for him.' She held her palm up to stop Celeste. 'Please hold your tongue, I do not want to be here anymore than you do. Ganaim is to accompany you with the Romarii, and despite my best efforts to educate him in certain ways, he was ever a poor student of the written word, but you on the other hand devour books, made apparent by your knowledge of the correct ways of gratitude and deepest respect to the crofters. Whether you knew the value of the gifts they gave, you honoured them in the most respectful way.' Celeste shrugged by way of acknowledgement.

'Ganaim said that you were asking for certain books which I assume you have heard someone talking about?'

'Not just talking about, they are mentioned in Thomhas' Phantasmagoria, and I wish to cross-reference them, Cassandra's Chronicles being one,' she watched as Cissy nodded, then added quickly, 'and a pirate's book on navigating the Southern Isles.' She was sure that was where her parents had been. She could get a better idea from the best book ever written on the isles, according to Meite a Thomas.

Cissy retrieved two books from the bag, although once they were out of it, they seemed far too large to be put back in. She passed her the empty bag and pointed. 'What I am about to give you, must be kept in there at all times unless you are reading them. All you need to know is that I am doing this, not for any concern I have for you, but because I love my son. I know you will read them where he will not, and the knowledge you gain may save his life.' Celeste moved to sit on the end of the couch; her eyes glittered while they caught the fading embers in the fire, and she shuddered.

'This was supposed to be Tara's role as part of the trade, but I suppose better late than never.' She handed Celeste the first book. It was deep red leather, the pages were thick vellum inside, and on its cover was a single eye. The indigo iris veined with gold; the pupil was silver-white. The eye sat inside a triangular cave embossed in the leather in silver, with a straight path, which was a daggers blade wrought in gold that led up to it.

'It is my own copy of Cassandra's Chronicles. It is written in the old tongue and my notes are pencilled lightly beside the text, further translations are here,' she passed Celeste one of her handmade notebooks and added, 'this does not require particular care. The Chronicle is what you asked of Ganaim?'

Celeste dipped her head while she hid her embarrassment, not an ask but a demand in a mad rage that he got her a copy. She took it and tried to still her hand but failed, and it shook as she opened those first delicate pages. 'It does not have the account of her leaving over the waters of the Bay of Loka,' Celeste said incredulously.

Cissy nodded. 'No. It does not, and I know that you are aware of what that means. It is a precious thing but not more precious than my son's life.'

Cissy pointed to the front page. 'Read the dedication.'

Celeste gulped and read Cissy's pencilled translation. 'Marama Rawa beware her stare, Hiriwa Pourewa the soul laid bare, Marama Rawa all are equal in her eye, Marama Rawa not even gods may lie, before Marama Rawa,' she finished and closed the book gently then lay it next to her on the couch.

'Make no mistake, Cassandra Novantae was the first to walk the Dagger Path. She was the first to walk inside Silver Tower and the first to be ordained to the Crystal Dagger Path, and the madness that is the paths inside the mind of Time. The wraiths inside the Temple of Time call her sister, and she has walked the curve of reality to the Edge of Reason and beyond. Her visions, while obtuse, are accurate. Moin and Abhhain think a foretelling relates to you and the spear they gave you. It is in the section titled The Age of Man and Shadow. Excuse my translation, but it says, Blood of the Selgovae carry the spear made by Crann

Og Riamh. They will find a star when they turn their faces from the sky and turn their hearts towards life after death for the living. This marks the beginning, of the end, of Time.'

Celeste jumped. 'How do you know…'

Cissy cut her off, 'It is too late for explanations now. I just do. There are references to 'The Star' and Solas Nua Novantae, as well as others. I would like you to study them. Would you do that for Ganaim?'

Celeste nodded while she took another book from Cissy. Fatter than the first, it was bound in midnight blue leather with stars and planets in silver embossed all over its covers and a ship cresting a gigantic curling wave on the front. It was surprisingly light although it was easily twice the size of Cassandra's Chronicles. She ran her hand over the title: Navigating the Southern Isles by Charyia Al Farraige Stoirme. 'Light above, is this real? How are they not rotted to dust?'

Cissy sniffed. 'Of course, they are real.' She pointed to the indigo book. 'In there are accounts of the seven isles and the witch queens who rule them. There is an account of the Witch Queen Mordeana Never Dead and the Never Age spell she used to protect these very books, as well as other things.'

Celeste gasped but Cissy ignored her and continued. 'It is no longer wise to keep them here, times are changing, and it would be unfortunate if they were discovered. Only two others know I have them.' She almost smiled when a faraway look came into her eye, but she shook her head and with a tight frown continued. 'They were a gift,' she said softly, then her old stone-face returned, and she set her mouth into a hard line. 'But that does not matter. Charyia wrote in the common tongue, as pirates do. I give them to you in the hope you will learn something from their pages, and remember this,' she ran her hand through her hair, her face screwed up with concentration and the effort of speaking so much and being almost half pleasant. 'If you can avoid it, do not go to Romar Ri, and make no trade with the Romarii. If you can, get to the Southern Isles, seek out Marama Rawa. She may take pity on you, and my son…Look to the chronicles and my notes. If the worst happens…' she trailed off and her eyes filled with moisture then with a visible effort she met Celeste eye to eye and said in a voice cracked with pain, 'If the worst happens, you must take Ganaim to Taluthaar's Barren Isle.' Her hand fluttered at her heart. 'Do you understand?'

Celeste nodded mutely, although she did not understand at all.

'Good. Now quickly, do you have any questions?'

Celeste looked at the other woman as if she were mad while she wondered where she should start. A million things tumbled about her mind; but of course, the taint she could not get rid of, surfaced first. 'Was my Nana mad?' she asked.

Cissy smiled thinly. 'Only in her defiance of the wizard, and not meeting the terms of the trade. She fell in love with you as a grandmother would her only granddaughter.' Cissy laughed, more of a rasp, it was short and dry and filled with bitterness. 'And none of the fools saw it coming. Though she loved you, she also failed you, Celeste.' Cissy began to stand, and the cat Francis stretched as he made ready to leave.

Celeste blurted out, 'My mother, where is she?'

'Your mother is a dead woman,' she replied coolly, and Celeste frowned.

'I am sure she is not dead,' she said quietly, but on looking at the thunder behind Cissy's eyes, she decided not to pursue it, nor the question she was about to ask about the wizard.

Cissy pointed to the books. 'They must go in that bag for travelling which you must wear under your clothes, also there seems to be some enchantment on both books. They seem as if they will not fit inside but they will. When carried, it is as if they are not next to your skin at all; they are invisible, and light as a feather. Be careful when you come to read any of the charts in Charyia's book, they are much bigger than the book suggests it can hold between its pages.' She smirked wryly.

Francis pawed at Cissy's hunting pack and meowed loudly. 'Of course, against my better judgement, the cat's, in league with Moin and Abhhain, insisted I have this made for you. Though pay attention, a Roma Ranger you are not, do not promise yourself to that path, or to Romar Ri, whatever they may throw at you.' She narrowed her eyes then continued, 'At this very moment, you are almost free. I am sure the deal is off where you are concerned. I have not time to explain now but you may be able to decide your own future. Take what is yours.' She tossed a bundle of cloth at Celeste which unfurled as if a piece of silken mirror glided through the air, almost invisible as it reflected the room around it.

'Don't you want Ganaim to have this?' Celeste exclaimed as she stood and caught the cloak.

'Stupid child, he already has one. It arrived not so long ago, a lure for a wide-eyed youth with romantic notions of a ranger's life, though I know with certainty that the crone will not accept him although Rovander wants him. He will be devasted, and I delighted.' She frowned at Celeste. 'Take no more herbal remedies, lest you befuddle your brain permanently. And leave your grief here,' she pointed to the floor of the cottage, 'Otherwise, it will get you, and my son killed,' she finished bitterly. Then turned and picked her hunting pack up and slid it easily over her shoulders. Her quiver and bow waited for her next to the spilt stable door that led out of the cottage.

Celeste, overwhelmed by events, placed her hand to her heart.

Cissy snorted contemptuously. 'Do not even think of honouring me so, this is for my son. I wish you had never been born.' She turned from her and walked stiffly away.

'Wait,' Celeste said angrily to her back. 'Why now, why tell me how much you love him now, does he even know?' It was all she could do to stop herself from throwing the spear at Cissy.

Cissy did not turn round. 'Of course, he knows,' she spat the words. 'If you have any sense at all, you will not let anyone know what, or who you love. Take heed – that kind of knowledge will be used against you, especially if you bend the knee to Romar Ri.' And with that said she walked calmly through the door, retrieved her arrows, and bow in one easy movement, and slid off into the night. The black cat, Francis, padded to Celeste slowly and nipped her wrist gently, his pale emerald eyes shone like sea glass, then he too turned and left.

Celeste ran to the door. 'Wait, I have a message for you.'

Cissy stopped, turned, and took one step back, her hands rested on her hips and a sneer lifted one side of her mouth. 'Well?' She tossed her head impatiently.

'You have to know of something called the rod of power. You can use it when you travel the paths in the compass. You can use it to travel in the void…I think you will be able to talk to people in their dreams…Tara said you needed to be shown it.' She blurted the words out, not even sure of what she was saying.

Cissy met her gaze full on and though she wanted to, she could not step toward Celeste, although she wanted to give her a good shake. She was clearly as mad as her grandmother. Then, for a couple of heartbeats, their eyes met, black pit to black pit and there was a light in the depth of Celeste's left that rooted her to the spot. Then, a cold sensation passed through her body. A handspan wide, it went from the crown of her head all the way to the ground beneath her feet. She gasped and it felt like a column of ice had wrapped around her spine and she was drowning in freezing water. The rod of power burned like dry ice, old ice that had not seen the sun or the thaw. It ran through the hollow shaft of her spine and its energy filled her gullet, and stomach with ancient knowing and power. Lore that belonged beyond the stars, was gifted and it roared through the centre of her body, then anchored beneath her feet with the force of a meteorite hitting hard ground.

Cissy gasped, then staggered forward. I have been given a gift through her she thought while she pulled herself together. She gave Celeste a hard look then walked slowly back towards her, she did not trust her watery knees to do anything else, then she came to a halt, a single step before her. She studied her face intently before she replied. 'Light, no wonder I did not see her soul bird…the crafty old witch is in The Void, and now she lures me in too…unless Yalan has a hand in this.' Cissy shook her head to clear her thoughts then smiled suddenly and it was full of incredulousness. 'You have no idea what you have just told me?'

Celeste shook her head. 'It's just a technique; Tara said it would keep you safe.'

Cissy nodded sharply. 'Yes, I felt the intention pass from you to me,' she touched her right eye, 'and the rod materialise along my spine.' She paused and her gaze took on a faraway look as if she searched for something in her memories. When she found it, she frowned, and a sadness pulled the edges of her mouth down. Then with a resolute sigh she said, 'When you walk your nightmares next, you must thank Tara on my behalf, but tell her this…the next time she communicates with you from her creation shard in the void. She is not safe there. Her spirit bird flew; she might have retained her soul bird, but without the spirit animal, and the power from Abraxas, her own power will not be strong enough to maintain the creation shard indefinitely. Only Maroke and Rakua Poturi can do such a thing, and that is because they are The Crown, and The Root, she is only one.' She rubbed at her temples, her frown as deep as Celeste had ever seen it. Then with a short bob of her head she said, 'The only way left to her, will be to let Gaia claim her before something else does. You must make this clear to her. She is a hedge witch out of her depth and the Nympts should have known better.'

Celeste was about to deny seeing Tara in her dreams but thought better of it. When she looked the other woman in the eye, they glittered like fire beneath ice with a passion she had never seen before. She dropped her gaze and nodded while she said softly, 'I will do as you ask.'

'One last thing, Celeste, devour the books I have given you, but more importantly, you must guard your loose tongue. That information in the wrong hands would see your journey cut short. I urge you to make your way to Marama Rawa. She will see right through you and make her own decisions. Arianrihod on the other hand will not bother to look and use you however she sees fit.' Cissy placed her right hand over her heart, then extended it forward, palm out; she half bowed, then turned and walked away into the twilight, making no sound but leaving Celeste dumbstruck at the sudden show of honour the other woman had bestowed.

Celeste wiped tears out of her eyes. 'Stupid bloody thing crying over Cissy sour puss,' she said to herself while she heard Cissy say to Francis, 'You are sure the Queen Shabba will share the technique now that I have the gift…'

Walking back into the desolate cottage she sat heavily on the couch, then took hold of the books. They will never fit she thought angrily as tears smarted at her eyes like boiling water. I hate her, being nice for once in her life and making me cry. The books slipped easily and impossibly into the bag, as if on automatic she took her arm out of her clothes and slipped the bag strap under them and neatly over one shoulder. She manoeuvred it into place; the bag disappeared next to her skin, then she pulled her linen shirt and jumper back into place. I do not understand her…absolute bitch has tortured me over the last year and now this…thanking Tara and telling her about birds, when all I do is run, or scream whenever Tara comes to me in my dreams. Oh! That is, it, I need to stand my ground and tell her Gaia will come.

The books and bag weighed nothing at all. She pulled her own pack from beneath the couch, it had her copy of Thomhas' Phantasmagoria inside, it was the only thing she had packed. She threw Cissy's notebook in next to it. The quiver and buckler would fit easily inside, the spear and bow would attach to the outside somewhere, though she may get to wear them, if there was hunting to do. The spear, as beautiful a thing as she had ever seen, caught her eye, the spear tip was more like a dagger blade, made from Solais Silver which was tempered like the hardest steel. She picked it up and tried to read the engraving on its shaft, inlaid in gold or brass the words twisted around the black wood which had not affected the balance or weight. Nuair a choinníonn an ghaoth mé ina lámha. Oscklóidh an ghaoth Geataí Loka. Crann Og Riamh. Everyoung tree…the last few words were all she could translate from the old tongue. She placed it next to her own pack, then picked up the quiver and arm brace, it had been artfully worked in laminated leather and was embossed with runes and dragons in flight. The arrows, though metal, were as light as any wood arrow she had used. The cape she draped over the arm of the couch, marvelling at how it almost disappeared, as she leaned over it and retrieved a large parcel wrapped in a piece of hessian and tied with string.

She opened the parcel slowly: a brand-new pair of breeches, waxed moleskin with many pockets and cuffed at the ankles, her favourite kind – the new boots had arrived two weeks earlier – a leather jerkin laminated to be hard at the shoulder blades, chest, and waist like armour, creamy new undergarments, fresh cotton pads for when her moon-time blood flowed, and socks, a dark green close-knit woollen jumper, all wrapped around a cylindrical tin. The tin held apothecary powders in tiny, waxed papers, bread buns and half of a round hard cheese, a large folded sweet pastry with dried fruit, sticky with honey inside and a note on top.

Dear Celeste, I cannot bear to say farewell. I hope our paths will cross again in better times, though I fear they are a thing become rare. I hold you fondly in my heart always. You were like one of my own, and I trust you feel the same way. Love, Dorothea.

She crumpled the note in her hands and bawled harder than if she were a tired child. If Dorothea had come, she would not have wanted to go, and Dorothea would not have let her.

Chapter Twenty-Five

A Change Of Direction

Celeste splashed chilly water on her face and shuddered. Then wiping her cheeks on her sleeve, she peered out of the kitchen window. No one in sight. She popped her head around the door into the studio. It had never been so clean. It was stripped bare, not even the smell of sheep remained. She walked slowly back into the sitting room; the place smelled musty already, no smell of lilac, paint, or freshly baked bread. Tara had gone; now it was her turn.

Her trail-pack waited by the spilt stable door. She wore the new boots Dorothea had given her, and the leather jerkin, stiff like armour, below the cape Cissy had thrown at her. In her pack was Meite a Thomas' Phantasmagoria and Cissy's notebook, her breeches, jumper, and linen small clothes, all rolled tight around the arm brace and quiver full of arrows. She had unstrung the bow and put it carefully with other rolled strings and flints, inside wax paper in the food tin Dorothea had given her. The unstrung bow and spear she attached to straps below her pack while she hoped Ganaim would have their bedrolls and further supplies.

'That could get me killed, bloody fake that it is.' She held the birth document between her fingers then went to the tallow lamp that sputtered on the table under the window, and lit it, before she tossed it into the empty grate.

'I wonder when I was born if Star was unusual? Light, I don't even know what I'm supposed to do with the damn thing.' The small wad of books beneath her clothing was light as a feather and only noticeable where they rested against her body where the skin was warmer. She cast her mind back to the times she had thought she could manipulate the particles that made up the dark, mould it in her hands, the time in the classroom when reality had taken on another layer of being. She patted the books and released air through her nostrils. 'I will find out because the answer lies between these pages.' She jumped when she heard gravel outside crunch. After the bad winter and the crofters' relentless clearing of the lane, you could get a galleon down there now, but it was Carter's old car that chugged into the yard. She bent in front of the grate and blew on the paper, relieved when it curled at the edges, burned blue, then yellow, finally all that remained was a square of fragile ash.

'You ready, Cel?' Gan put his head around the sitting room door.

'No,' she replied tersely.

'We have to go, Cel, we cannot keep you here anymore. There is more proc activity. It will only be a matter of time until we are crawling with acolytes. It will be a toss-up who is worse. Bled to death into The Chalice or lobotomised at The Wind. You understand?'

She sighed, 'Not really and no one seems to be forthcoming…but I know you're right, I have to go, but that doesn't mean I'm not terrified.'

He came into the room and hugged her, then stood back and looked admiringly at her attire which was not that different from his own. 'Cloak suits you. You know you would make a fair ranger with your bow skills, and you are a decent rider,' he said thoughtfully while Celeste's insides clenched, and she remembered Cissy's warning. *If you can, do not go to Romar Ri, and make no trade with the Romarii. Does that include invitations to become a ranger?* she thought and eyed Ganaim suspiciously.

She jumped when Ganaim put his hand on her shoulder, and she could see the tension in his jaw and something in his eye, a soft flame flickering but too far away like the light he had held for her had been dimmed on love. 'We need to go, Celeste, I am not saying I am not without nerves but once we start, it will all settle down.' He cupped her chin in his hand, paused before he looked into her eyes, then dropped his hand and gave her a friendly pat on the shoulder.

Her face was suddenly overcast with confusion, but she hid it well, while she reasoned they had both changed and now was not the time to dwell on it or discuss why. Instead, she said, 'Well, at least I'll be able to wave the old school good riddance when we pass Mount Wraith.' She only half-smiled and a hard frown lined her brow. 'I used to hate school, now I wish it were all just back to how it had been. Even fighting with Melaine Merilyn was better than this. Better than her being…' she trailed off and studied her boots while water filled her eyes.

Ganaim moved towards the door, his own cloak swishing and changing colour as he moved. The headlights from the car swept across the door like a searchlight as Carter turned the Ensign in the yard. The crystalline light about Ganaim's face undulated like light on water but his brow was low and his eyes fierce when he said, 'We can't reverse it, nor can we stop it, Celeste. Not for all the black eyes, and broken teeth in the world can we bring any of them back.'

She nodded glumly; thinking about Melaine and the others always brought a lump to her throat. 'Light, when did it all turn upside down, Gan? I thought it was when Tara died but it wasn't.'

'I know…our lives and our safety, fragile as that was, have been eroded even further.' He ran his hand through his crest of thick wavy hair, and it caught the light like flames; it was completely shaved around his ears now, revealing more scrolls of fine scales than Celeste remembered him having. He looked troubled when he said, 'About the school…we can't. I mean we are not going that way. The whole of the records room, archives, and library – gone up in flames. There was that much paper in there. Dorothea's been on the scanner since it happened. We must go into the Bloom, Cel. We'll be meeting a Roma Ranger there…somewhere.' Ganaim looked towards the floor, not sure how much to say or even how far he was going on their forthcoming journey.

The Romarii would tell him later. I am so used to always being aware of where she was and what she was doing, protecting her, he thought bitterly, it felt like I was properly free when I left the farm to go with them, he thought while he ran the cloak through his fingers, or am I, he added, and a peculiar feeling settled in his stomach. He tried to smile to make light of the situation, but heavy dread settled around his shoulders. It reminded him of that sinking feeling when he had been called back to the farm after Tara had died. How he had felt the burden she had become increase with each step he took home. He shuddered when he remembered their relationship, and he felt like a coward when he felt the inevitability that it had run its course, while she made girlish plans to get handfast in a year and a day. He had seen it in her far-too-trusting eyes. He scowled into the yard while Carter made the last slow turn while he thought, why should I let her go. Even though I know I cannot have her, I still want her…I wish I had never met women – no, that's silly, I take that back.

He put his scowl to one side when she said. 'That's the opposite way to where we need to be, if we are going over Kai Land.'

'Yeah, it looks that way, but trust me, it probably isn't.' He raised his eyebrows and picked up her pack for her as they made ready to leave. He turned his back so he could ignore her questing look. She would want answers, she always did, and he did not know where to begin.

*

The car smelled of Foss, or was it Cheen? She could not tell, only that it prickled the inside of her nose. She found the thin metal handle between the glass and the top of the door frame and moved it down. It half-opened the window. The night was chilly; freeze or suffocate, she thought. Her trail-pack hit a couple of empty glass bottles as she pushed it across the back seat and a fresh waft of fuel filled the car. They drove along unnamed roads and narrow lumber paths more used to mule-drawn vehicles than cars. The old Ensign puttered away as it zig-zagged higher into The Bloom. She looked back and could see that the sky above Mount Wraith was aglow with muted orange light, like a small sun attempting to rise, somewhere round about the location of the school.

'Will it get put out?' The old car juddered, and Carter changed gear. They had begun their ascent into the mountains proper. 'Depends. If they think there's owt worth saving,' Carter said cheerily as he handed Ganaim a pair of binoculars. 'Have a gander, lad, before we round the shoulder of the mountain.'

'They must do, Col, there's some flyers.' Ganaim turned around in his seat and pointed past Celeste's shoulder. He passed her the binoculars and she turned and watched two flyers, like two small beetles in the distance.

'The beam looks like a gigantic stinger,' Ganaim said, and Carter nodded and replied with a hint of melancholy in his voice. 'It's the future but not the one I thought I would see.' He tossed his head towards them. 'It's crystal tech from Marama Rawa's isle that keeps them airborne, you can't see the beam of light toward the ground but it's there; it repels the magnetic field beneath it.'

'Light,' she said with a startled stare out of the back window. Carter studied her in the rear-view mirror and said, 'They aren't indestructible. They only want you to believe that. All it would take is an alchemist to create something that reverses the polarity settings inside the craft or even a disruption of the local magnetic field. That would bring it down.'

Ganaim shifted in his seat so he could face her, his eyes were set hard, and his mouth was a thin white line. 'We have them Cel. They do not know it, but we have polarity disrupters.'

She nodded and replied in a hushed voice that shook with fear. 'But not here. Not right now.'

With a challenge in his gaze, he replied harshly, 'We aren't in any real danger.'

She lowered her gaze and pretended to study the spear that was strapped below her pack. A spear against antigravity aircraft and laser beams, she fumed silently.

'Ah well, binoculars away and we'll need to knock these off as a precaution.' Carter switched the car lights off while he leaned over the steering wheel, his face peered into the dark and they continued up the steep lumber track and around the mountain at a crawl.

Celeste held her breath. The two men were quiet – tense. The sight of the drones had stolen Carter's earlier bravado and had quietened Ganaim to an almost statue-like stillness. He opened his window to stare into the dark ahead of the car. She fancied she saw his jaw clench and release methodically while she thought, they are holding their breath too, as if that will save us from plunging to our deaths down a ravine or being blown to pieces.

They rounded the shoulder of the mountain and her relief when it came felt like she had shed a second skin. Soon after, they pulled to a halt in a small clearing on the far side of the mountain. The sun was setting somewhere beyond the forested mountain range but had already disappeared behind the crest of the nearest mountain to them. Neither day or night but a time where they were both suspended; not true twilight but something that was made more of shadow than of light or dark. She shivered and pushed an uneasy feeling away.

Carter turned the car around which seemed to take an age driving forward inches, reversing, driving forward, reversing, while Celeste forced herself to remain calm. All the while she wanted to scream while the shadows eventually surrendered to a deeper shade of dark. 'Right, you two, this is where I leave you. I have got to get back to the Nags Head. Ganaim, take the bottles with you, lad.' She jumped; Carter sounded too loud in the silence as he got out of the car and opened the back door for Celeste to get out, taking Ganaim's trail-pack and bedrolls out too. She heard the camp cookpots clink together dully.

He turned and shook Ganaim's hand. 'I'd like to say it'd been a pleasure, but I'm not a liar. Although I owe Padrain my life and sanity for looking out for me all those years; and you, also.' He clapped him on the shoulder while Ganaim nodded all misty-eyed and grasped his hand, thumb over thumb as she had seen the villagers do in Mount Wraith; it meant steadfast and strong, family but not blood. 'Ah Col, it was awful hard sometimes for us young ones…you know we don't suffer from the dimension jump disease, but light was it tough watching our elders struggle.'

Carter hugged him and slapped his back. 'You've grown la…no more lad for you, not anymore.' He turned to the car door then paused while he said, 'You're a man now but even a man needs a blessing or two. I wish you all the luck the goddess can throw at you, and you too, Celeste.' He waited while she exited the car.

'I know, Col, and thanks. I wish it could have been different,' Ganaim replied then shrugged when Carter gave him a wry smile and said, 'I would not have had it any other way. Though the job ahead would be easier if I was a younger man.'

Celeste put her fingers to the centre of her forehead, then turned them around to face Carter. He nodded, then smiled and returned the gesture, 'Ah Celeste…I see you,' he said, and his voice was low with sadness and a note of finality that stabbed her unexpectedly in the centre of her chest and left her suffocated and breathless. Her breath, when it came, juddered against her ribcage, and her eyes were brim full of tears when Carter continued. 'Out of everyone I have taught, Cissy included, you have something that they all lacked, an other-worldliness but I know you will work it out.'

Celeste nodded. She hardly trusted herself to speak, the lump in her throat was as large as a ball of wool. The pain in her chest still stabbed, not sharp and fleeting but an aching, thick pain, as if a wooden stake had been pressed right through her heart.

'Will you be…' Ganaim asked but Carter cut him off. 'I will have been in the Nag all night, don't you go worrying about me, it's all-in hand.' Then he opened the door and took his seat. He wound the window up and headed slowly and carefully back down the mountain towards Mount Wraith and The Nag.

They shouldered their packs while Carter drove the old ensign away. 'We have about three hours trek ahead of us…uphill, mind, towards Eagle Ridge,' Ganaim said while he took a bearing off the stars overhead.

'Tip of the sky sisters' arrow points true north,' Celeste said quietly while she looked at the distant chevron of seven stars. He reached out and squeezed the top of her arm, then they began moving off through the woods. It was past sundown though not late evening, it being one moon until Winter Begone and the first days of early spring. Celeste followed Ganaim's crest of hair, the rest of him was invisible beneath the ranger cloak he wore. She steadied her breath and saved her words, it was a hard trek to Eagle Ridge, a place where they had hunted and camped once or twice before, when they were younger. She grimaced at the thought. When we were younger…light, we are young now, only I feel as old as

Dorothea, but she held her tongue, there was no point spending her breath on idle chatter. They left the lumber path and made their way into the forest; their cloaks reflected the encroaching blanket of the surrounding night, and the shadow and shade of trees beneath a midnight blue sky, until eventually they ghosted away into the Bloom.

Chapter Twenty-Six

Travelling Light

A lone wolf howled in the distance and her heart heard its wild call as something more ancient and primal than the thing she was now, but still it was held like a spark in her blood, and a shard of diamond in every cell, and she wanted to open her own throat and ululate a reply. The Resonant Moon had waned to a quarter, though that shone brightly enough in the thin crisp air. The day was Kinetic Ninety-four, White Electric Wizard, and ice crystals hung in the air as if they were seeds that had been dispersed from starlight.

'You'll need to get your sheepskin bag out.' Ganaim paused while he set up camp and passed her a thick sausage of dark material that had been strapped beneath his own pack. She nodded as she accepted it and took stock of her surroundings. They made their camp next to a clump of evergreen laurel bushes the dark coniferous forest swept away in every direction, but they camped close to the wall of the overhanging cliff they called Eagle Ridge.

Ganaim unstrapped his own bedroll, made from a thin layer of soft waxed material, waterproof in all but the worst downpours; it had a lining of embryonic lamb hide that Tara called Astrakhan fur. Cissy collected the dead or miscarried lambs and being Cissy, she made sure that they were still used. Her sheep stem cell face balm had not really caught on, but her outdoor bedrolls were sought out by Roma Rangers. Expensive by rural standards, the Romarii were her only customer. Stillborn and miscarried lambs were not a guaranteed commodity; their supply was often down to her ability to find the lambs before the mountain cats did. The northern crofters, who were descended from Selgovae Fae, made several things for Cissy, and in return they were sheltered from the encroaching glacier. They were also the craftsmen and women who wove the Romar Ranger cloaks that were the nearest thing to an invisibility cloak outside the pages of a fairy tale. There was mistrust between the crofters and the Romarii; they rarely traded anything with them apart from the cloaks and that was a carefully brokered, ancient deal. The crofters were known for their generosity usually, but not in this trade. That Celeste had been given a Roma cloak by Moin and Abhhain, was testament to how highly they regarded her. The material the cloaks were woven from was hard to come by it being rumoured that it was the hide of rare aquatic animals that resembled squids, which gave the fabric its reflective almost invisible quality.

While Ganaim lit a small fire, he pretended that he was not aware that she was ready to blow. It had been a hard trek to the campsite with her eyes boring into his back. Like two hot pokers he thought and fussed on with the kindling. He had not dared look back for fear he got the tongue lashing that she was chewing over. Light, what for now? How do I diffuse this?

'The forest canopy is mainly coniferous here. It's dense enough to hide the light.' He nodded to the freshly lit kindling catching in the small fire pit he had made.

'What will we do if they see it, just say they see us, Gan?' She sounded small and anxious as she fumbled about with her sheepskin roll. Her hands had begun to shake, and she kept checking her palms, rubbing them on her thighs then tutting and looking down her nose at him as if he were being rude when he stared at her odd behaviour.

He sighed. 'I'm not saying I'm not worried about the flyers, Cel, but there are plenty of woodsmen and hunters in the forest who would have small fires lit in the open – I doubt they would check everyone. You know that there are small bothies dotted about here and there too. We'll put a kettle or a pan above it, that will dim some of the light.' He talked steadily while he watched her out of the corner of his eye. She continued to stare wetly off into space, while she rubbed her palms against the sheepskin roll. It was as if she had been transported elsewhere, the only sense of her being present was the susurrus noise her hands made as they worried at the material – rub, rub, rubbing. It set his teeth on edge he took a deep breath then said, 'Cel, are you well?' He flinched inside, his words had been too sharp, but he remained where he was, reluctant to reach out to her physically.

'What do you think, Ganaim?' Her eyes snapped into dark focus as she spat venom. An automatic response as she continued to process recent events, while trying to keep a lid on the sulphur that seethed under the surface of her skin; she wanted to blow. 'It's been over four moons since Nana died, and I've been left with people I don't know and now,' she looked like she might spit, 'and now…well, I wonder whether I can trust any of you.' She emphasised the word as she nodded curtly in his direction. 'I'm not being told the truth, I'm not stupid,' she hissed across the fire as she stood up with fists clenched tightly to her sides.

'Woah, Celeste, what in the hell, ca—' He was about to say calm down but thought better of it when he saw the waves of rage pass through her body. He knew better than that. It was best to step back and let it run its course – for now.

'I need you to tell me everything you know before the Roma Ranger arrives, never mind what your da or anyone else has said, I need you to tell me everything, Ganaim, or I'm…' she balled her hands into fists and put them on her hips, 'I'm not going another bloody step. AND…and I'll go outside the box right here on this mountain and bring those flyers right to where we are.' Her lip curled while she bluffed at him and pointed to the carpet of crunchy pine needles beneath her feet.

'Celeste, stop. Sit back down…I understand you must be scared.' He raised his hand in a gesture of pacification, then rubbed nervously at his temple and left ear. His scaling glimmered dully in the faint light from the small fire, but his eyes flashed impatiently, ice blue, lilac, and gold. He was as terrified as Celeste, but only because another outburst could result in an episode of vibrations.

Dorothea had warned him that on no account should he allow her to have another attack like the one she had in school. His hand went reflexively to the knife at his belt, his mind to the twist of powdered poison in his pocket. I will not use either, there must be another way. Light, we are nearly at the top of Eagle Mountain, he thought, it will be like a beacon for all the proc in Ninmah to register. At what point do I kill her, what do I use? His tongue stuck to the roof of his mouth and his throat tightened. He could feel sweat slick down the back of his neck. Neither Dorothea or Padrain had been clear on that he thought as he recalled bitterly Dorothea's small heart-shaped face with too-large eyes and a kindly mouth while she patted him on the arm. 'It is a last resort. If she puts you or herself in danger you cannot recover from, you must end it,' Dorothea said, and her words were hoarse and thick with emotion. Then she covered her mouth with her hand and turned from him. He knew she was weeping and wanted to comfort her, but he could not. Inside his guts roiled and fear bubbled, and hatred hissed. How could they ask that of him?

Cissy put her arm around Dorothea and said bitterly. 'We should have killed her the night Tara was murdered. We knew her galactic power had activated and how unstable she is. All it would have taken was an extra dose of Belladonna.'

Then she dropped her arm from her mother's shoulder and stomped to her room leaving him standing in the middle of their kitchen.

A void of loneliness and shame yawed before him, and a storm full of regret hung at his back while he thought, I activated her, I just know it was my fault. Then, where have my family gone, who are these people, these killers who inhabit a space that was once full of love?

'I will not,' he had hissed at Dorothea's back, then turned and kicked the door open, knowing full well that Padrain would find him, and persuade him otherwise.

~ ❋ ~ ❋ ~ ❋ ~

Softly glowing embers were all that remained of the fire once he had finished telling her what he thought she should know. He left out the parts that painted him in a bad light, where he was a spy pretending to be her friend, distracting her with jokes and playfulness whenever she asked too many questions, even taking her virginity. He did not mention his whispered promise to love her forever, or take his own attention to it, how could he? He had known all along he would not love her forever. Then the Selgovae, Airgid and Gaoth turning up and throwing another iron on the forge. I am in a big enough spin myself, he rubbed anxiously at his forehead. He felt like a traitor and worse besides. Now that he knew he could never be with her again, he wanted her, to be as far away as possible. He was sick to his marrow of what he had become: liar, her little guard, toy soldier and now, potential executioner – had he ever really loved her?

After spending time with the Romarii, he realised he could never be with her, not properly ever again. His dream of them staying at the farm, even handfasting, living a full and happy life, had been torn away. He understood why Padrain had told him to not get too emotionally involved. Tara's lectures to Celeste on his wild ways – they were not trying to keep them apart, only trying to avoid the inevitable heartache later, when she had to go. Although, no one had really thought about how she would depart. Murder victim runs in her family, he thought while he felt sick as a pig with a belly stuffed full of rotten fruit.

He told Celeste, that Dorothea had been asked by her elder brother Aindreas Sackeyfio, and his wife Henna, to find a home for Tara. A woman Aindreas knew through the college where he worked in the Capitol, Lodewick. She was a resident artist but one who could remember the time before a cosmic calamity had happened, which most of the elders in the community believed in but was dangerous to talk of; those who had a nano device were usually unaware of the dimension jump. Carter remembered it suddenly though he had never had the implant, the rest of the people Ganaim knew mostly had dud copies anyway. He lied to Celeste when he said he was not sure what the cosmic calamity really was, but thought Tara was half right. He did not think telling Celeste that he had always known about the nature of reality on Gaiadon would be helpful, especially if he wanted to keep her calm.

'Even Foss was easier to come by then, until it started to dry up, siphoned by the elite,' he said bitterly, but then added, 'Cissy says that scarcity drives innovation and that we've found other means of energy production, so two fingers to the elite anyway, but she would say that.' He shrugged but watched her closely for her reaction; when there was none, he continued.

'When Tara moved to the cow shed, I am not sure if Selene was with her at first, maybe she was a baby or Tara was pregnant. Then, when Selene was older, she left to travel with the Romarii. I am not a hundred percent, Cel, but it seems like no one knows where she is. If she's alive even.' He shook his head and ran a dirty hand through his hair before he continued; he did not want to tell her that he suspected the Romarii trade to get them out of Baelmonarchia had involved Selene going with the Romarii when she came of age – like he had to go with them, but then again there were worse trades than that where the Romarii were concerned.

'I think she's still alive, even though Cissy said she was dead. I can feel it, Gan,' Celeste said sadly. 'I used to think it was a dream, but now perhaps it's a real feeling, some sort of connection.' She rubbed her head.

'I heard Sonii say to Pad that the one thing Selene was good at, was disappearing. All they knew for certain at the farm was Selene had some sort of "calling".' He hung his head, poked at the embers of the fire with a stick and avoided eye contact with her – glad that the fire had already warmed his cheeks before he continued.

'She went off travelling on some errand. Sounds like she did that a lot if you ask me. When she came back, she was up the duff.' He shook his head – red and gold curls fell across his face from the front of his crest, tiny scales shimmered the colour of orange sunset on ribbons of cloud, as they caught the last light cast by the dying fire.

'I'm not keen on Cissy,' she said matter-of-factly.

'Few are, Cel, she's prickly as a hawthorn and has a sharp tongue. If it helps, I didn't think she minded you.' He shrugged; he was sure she had been jesting about the Belladonna berries.

'I'm surprised at that. She said some awful things at the Night of the Dead, you know, at The Nag, she was well-away in her cups,' she replied, barely hiding her disgust, but still careful not to bring up the matter of the books she had given her. She would wait until the right time.

'In her cups?' he asked perplexed. 'She doesn't drink, Cel.' He sounded surprised but continued; he did not want to dwell on their apparent dislike for one another.

'Selene and Cissy are a similar age. Years after Tara had arrived, Cissy was pregnant, she gave birth to me at the farm. As Dorothea likes to say, one crisp winter evening, every star in the sky out to welcome me, silly woman. It was Tara who helped with the delivery, you know.'

Celeste looked surprised. 'The more I find out about her, the more I realise she never told me anything. I knew she was a Hand signature, but thought it was artistic expression. I didn't realise there was healing too,' she said weakly but thought about all the times she had closed her ears and her eyes to the ramblings of a mad woman. A small woman, with silver hair that bobbed about when she talked, who always had something in her hands – brushes, paint, or flour…once long ago, a new-born baby who she took from those who she thought would use her.

'Gods, I miss her so much,' Celeste muttered. She just might be right about everything too, she thought, why did I let Dorothea keep all that paper? Grief, and a lack of knowledge had addled me from my common sense. I should have kept the papers, though I suppose Cissy's gifts are equally as valuable.

'We were all in safe hands with her, you know – she delivered little Lugh and a few others in the town too, something to do with her healing and artistic hands. Anyway, it was six moons later when Selene had you, but I don't know where you were born.'

'So, you know who my folks are, where I can find them?' She stared at him, and her fingers found the tatty photo in her pocket, her eyes wide with the effort to process the information he had given her which she was grateful for, but which also raised her suspicions further. Her so-called friend Ganaim Al Tine – liar.

She swallowed bile and a toxic retort as she thrust the picture at him. 'Here, look, do you know who they are?' He took the photo, and a startled look widened his eyes. He looked set to speak but lowered his gaze and studied the image intently. 'I can only tell you what I just have, Celeste.' He gathered himself together but seemed reluctant to pull his attention away from the tatty photo and continued as he stared at it, his eyes cold and distant. 'All I know is what Padrain and Dorothea told me. I asked Cissy and she pretended not to know, clouted me over the ear and told me to, keep my nose out or we'll all be in serious trouble, Ganaim Al Tine, and not from the procs either, there's worse than them out there – believe me or not.' Celeste half smiled at his silly accent and the way he bobbed his head and pulled his mouth into a sour little sneer like Cissy did when she talked.

'It seems like I'm no further forward. There is such a lot missing. Why did they leave me? Where was I born? Did they die? I think they did. No, I must believe she is still alive. Who knows about my father – I can't even think about that, I'm just focussing on her for now?' She took the tattered photo from his outstretched hand. 'Don't ask me how I know this, it's just a feeling, but that person in that photo isn't my father.' She shrugged.

'How do you know, Cel? It could be, but I honestly do not know. Far as I can tell, they were helping Tara, keeping her safe. Selene had gone off…then you came along,' he lied. He knew the person in the photograph was not her father, but why add more confusion to the midden of lies that already made up her life. Let the Romarii sort this out, he thought.

It was times like this when he was disgusted with the lot of them, times like this when he just wanted to take them both far away, somewhere safe where they would not find them. He would be able to tell the truth then – only he knew there wasn't anywhere like that left for her. Would she ever be safe again? When even her best friend had been told to kill her should it become necessary.

He watched while she put the photograph in her pocket. His mother Cissy had a photo of the same man; it was not tatty or crumpled but had been cared for like the precious thing it must be, put away and hidden in a box under a loose floorboard, in her surprisingly warm and comfortable bedroom. A haven where she let her expertise and skill in crafting and acquiring soft furnishings and handmade furniture take precedence. It was a beautiful sanctuary of warm, earthy coloured linens and cottons, beautifully woven tapestries hung on the walls, depicting surreal hunting scenes where elven men rode dragons out of the sea, and intricate rugs patterned with Romarii mandalas, delightful and almost whimsical cushions, embroidered or painted with woodland animals, winged deer and Nymph's dressed in Solais Silver armour. It was completely at odds with how she was on the outside.

The differences in the poses of the people in the photographs were pronounced. In Cissy's photo, the man had his arms wrapped around her and he pulled her towards him, while his hand rested protectively on her swollen belly. In turn, Cissy had hold of the lapel of his jacket while she pulled him towards her, and his fiery mohawk hair whipped away behind him, caught by the stiff Eirini breeze. He could clearly see the intricate pattern of his crystalline scales, coloured lilac, and magenta; they traced along from his temples behind his ears, along the sides of his shorn scalp in an occult language long forgotten by any who walked Gaiadon now. They stood in front of an old wooden gate in one of the farm's far-off fields. The Bloom stood majestic, dark, and foreboding beyond. Their eyes were closed, but it was easy to imagine that before the moment was captured forever, they had looked deeply into each other's eyes. Cissy's belly was swollen with life and his chest was puffed up with pride while he kissed her – full of love, and passion.

When Ganaim was younger, he used to alternate between standing at the gate, the one in the photo, waiting to see if the man with the pointed ears would return and sneaking up to Cissy's room to look at them both in the photo, but it made him sad. Even when his fine crystalline scales appeared through his flesh and the hair above his pointy ears stopped growing and fell out, he was secretly delighted with the scrolls that appeared there – just like the man in the photo – but it was short-lived, and he became sad again. When he had rushed to show Cissy the first bald patch above his ears, the crystal light shining red as a berry beneath, the look on her face told him her heart had turned to lead and dropped out of her chest. Without a word she turned and fled from him, her hand over her mouth and tears streaming down her face. Afterwards, he had sneaked into her bedroom again, he was confused by her reaction, he studied the photo intently. She was happy then, he knew it. What had happened to steal that away?

He gazed at the fire while Celeste smoothed the pocket, she had put the photo in. The man in that photo is my father, not yours, and his name is Balinas, he thought and felt a coldness settle over him.

*

'Then I grew up and started to go outside the box,' she continued, he frowned then covered it with what he hoped was an attentive look when she snatched him back from his thoughts, 'putting everyone in danger. My Nana dies and I must move before the procs get hold of me and I end up working the wind or dead, and all you lot dead with me. I felt it, Ganaim, last year in school when I had that outburst, I felt it and then there's the nigh—' she stopped. Do not tell him about the nightmares and the stigmata, he does not need to know. He is not telling me everything so why should I. She rubbed at a sudden swell of tears.

'Hey! Stop that, Cel, it will be better once we are away from here.' He moved around the fire and came to sit next to her. He wanted to say more but the words would not come so he put his arm around her shoulders and kept his gaze on the fire.

Despite her anger, Celeste leaned into his familiar chest. Glad of the feel of strong muscles and the solid closeness of him, her heart began to skip a little faster as she wondered if she should ignore Sonii's advice and just tell him about the message from Tara in her nightmare, about the foul black sun stigmata on her palms...she would even tell him about the warning from the Romarii fortune-teller, the dark would write across the palms of her hands.

He squeezed her shoulder. 'Less of that talk, you are not going outside the box, Cel, it is something else, but we don't know what it is. Look, I think...' Damn it, he thought, I'm going to have to give her something.

'The reason Tara was hiding you has something to do with how you feel and that Arianriho...I mean the Romarii crone will be able to help. I just feel it – she will be able to help you. I wish I could, but I do not know where to start or what to do – apart from get you to safety. That I can do.' He smiled and squeezed her shoulder again before continuing. 'Mount Wraith will be dangerous for you if you stayed,' he lied; he knew with absolute certainty that Mount Wraith would be fatal for her if she stayed.

'I hope you're right. I don't know where to start either, but I suppose this is as good a start as any.' She relaxed a little and the knot at her heart unfolded like frozen water thawing; he had said the right thing again, put her at ease like he always did. 'Cissy gave me some books you know,' she said casually and noticed that he stiffened, then he replied, 'That's good. You were asking for some?'

'Yes, it was kind of her. Should I tell you anything I read of interest, though I doubt there'll be much mention of underground tunnels?'

'Don't believe me?' he jested, 'You'll see…If you find anything in them that could help us, and I don't mean folktales about some magical hero that I'm supposed to be, load of bloody cow dung. I'll be thinking I'm Micah Apollon before I know it.' He half-laughed at the ridiculous prophecy that Airgid had shared with him. Merfolk, he had heard of, Fairmist Al Mara had talked of them before and it was not like they were even mythological creatures, they were the seafolk who harvested the silicone from maritime forests in the shallow oceans around Kazamuki, a solitary island that was part of The Commonwealth of Turanga.

As for him being a new sun? Solas Nua Novantae, he drew the line there. A Roma Ranger is what he was and what he would be. It was enough for any man, kissed by Fae blood or not. I only hope the Crone Arianrihod feels the same way. She took Raife, she will accept me, she has to he thought while his lip twisted, and he recalled Raife's eyes had changed colour, they were like two hot embers, not red but fiery amber and they were full of revenge, but that was not the only thing that had changed. Raife was a man now, even more than that he was a Roma Ranger. I must have a measure of galactic power in me somewhere he thought, and he knew in his gut that it sounded like a prayer.

Although, they were all Gaia's children, the Romarii were her first, and their walk-in ceremony was not suitable for all. In fact, according to Raife, it was the worst thing that had ever happened to him in his life, and he had lost his twin sister Sirena, and his best friend had killed the girl he loved, a girl he had never told. Hel Croce.

'I will start to read and let you know but I doubt either of us are that important. We're just caught up in something bigger and the real people in charge will show up soon and tell us, thank you very much rural peasants but we have better folk than you to do this job, and they do not smell of pig shit,' she finished with what she imagined an elite accent was.

He laughed aloud roughly, then said, 'I know exactly what you mean, Cel.' She smiled. She liked it when she was able to make him laugh, he seemed more like himself then.

'For now, I just want to forget about it all.' She relaxed, reached up slowly to stroke his hair, then moved her hand, ready to caress the crystalline scales at his temple, hoping to kiss him gently on his neck, but he pulled away, breaking contact with her like he had been burned. He almost jumped to the other side of the fire.

'We had best get some sleep. We are not travelling along the Roma roads without proper rest. It's too dangerous…ermm, that is according to Sonii it is.' He moved off, got hastily into his own bedroll, and turned his back to Celeste.

'What the hells, Gan?' she asked his rigid back.

'Not tonight, Cel. We need to sleep. Trust me, it's not you…it's me…you won't understand,' he replied and hated every word he uttered as much as he hated himself for not finding the right words. *For pity's sake, if I cannot find the right words, I will not be able to tell her in a way that makes it seem like I am in the right…like I did nothing wrong.*

'Oh no. I do understand, you're abandoning me like everyone else has,' she whispered, and gulped at black emotion that was suddenly thick in her throat. *I hate him*, she thought, while she took out her crystal and placed it in the sleeve of her jumper, as near to her palm as possible. 'Well, at least we'll see if this works – I'm now officially travelling!' She wrapped her arms around her shoulders, determined not to weep or give in to the fear that snapped at her heels and bubbled through her palms. She drew her knees up, tight to her chest; but she felt fearful tension crawl tenuously at first but gathering strength like the howling of a storm as it made its way out of the unknown possibilities of her future. *Where is the light, where is the hope, where are the heroes…? I am so afraid* she thought and shivered when fear gripped her body tight. Shadow hands squeezed her inward, until she was left with only her own dark thoughts for company – her own hell. Stiff like rigor mortis, she eventually slept but woke suddenly sometime later. She lay on her back looking at a black sky. The air smelled like hot metal, dry heat from a blacksmith's forge, on a sweltering day. A woman sung in the distance unlike any song or voice she had ever heard; it sounded like a full choir coming from one throat, peaceful and inviting but immensely powerful.

'You just appeared there.' Tara stood above her, resplendent in a green silk gown and pointed to the ground where she lay.

Celeste resisted the urge to scream and run; when she did that, the black sun stigmata would bubble through her palms. She looked at her hands. They were normal. Then she sat up. 'I can't touch you to help you up as you do not belong here,' Tara said, and her eyes twitched towards a large monolith behind her.

'And neither do you, whatever you are. Foul phantom.' Celeste got to her feet and cast her gaze around. 'Elvan's Barrow?' she asked while she pointed at the stones. Lifting her chin, Tara opened her mouth to say something but stopped and nodded instead.

Celeste put her hand on her hips, her mouth turned determined and hard. 'This is my dream, and I will have control of it.' She rubbed at her head and the singing changed pitch, a little more demanding now but just as soporific. 'If you are Tara, you need to know what Cissy said…you do not have the strength to stay on this creation shard. She saw…actually, we all saw your spirit animal fly. It was an Owl with rose gold feathers but made of light. It took something with it.' She stopped and searched her memories. 'Dorothea, said it took the notochord with it when your spirit animal left.'

'Yes, I am aware of that.' Tara twitched her hand to her empty black eyes, 'I am without the sheath, the hollow tube, the spirit needs to enter by.' She looked set to say something, then thought better of it and smoothed her emerald gown. 'Did Cissy understand about the rod of power, and her ability?'

Celeste frowned but nodded. *What is she up to?* 'She did, but I got the impression that she did not know how to use it properly even though she said she received it.' Celeste narrowed her eyes at the other woman and looked at her own clothes, satisfied that she wore what she had gone to sleep in, apart from her ranger boots.

'Then she did not agree to come, to take me from here?' Tara asked and shadow of rage pitted her eyes further into her skull. Until with a visible effort she regained her composure.

'Light, no. Why would you think such a ridiculous thing? Have you forgotten what she's like…are you still a lunatic, even here?' She wanted to shout but ended up spluttering the words in frustration; something about the song in the distance, urgent and compelling now, forbade anyone shout, especially while the woman was singing.

Tara leant forward, her empty black eyes were devoid of the light of spirit now that her spirit animal had flown back to the pleroma, but they still burned into Celeste. 'I was never a lunatic. She is a Cosmic Skywalker and can use the stone compass' like Elvan's Barrow to travel between dimensions…it was a long shot, but still, she may come. You must get a message to her.'

'I'll do no such thing. Why the hells can't you stay dead and leave me alone?' Celeste tried to raise her voice, but it was snatched away by the song which filled the black sky above them. 'She said you are danger, that The Gaia might come claim you or something like that…it might be your only hope.'

'The Gaia might come…? What do you think that song is, child?' It is already here. Her dawn rises at my back, and the devil maws before me.' Tara pointed to the body of water behind Celeste, who turned reluctantly expecting the black sun to rise, but the water was not the same black pool. At the foot of the mound where Elvan's Barrow stood, there was a small ocean, bright like polished glass with crests of golden waves that sparkled beneath a sky that was no longer black, but filled with a misty light, as if the sun were rising behind a piece of fine linen cloth. Tara pointed down the shore to where a range of mountains stood jagged and bare. A wide cave mouth flared red and orange on a rise towards the top of the largest mountain. A blast of acrid air raced across the small piece of creation shard and the smell sent Celeste's stomach reeling.

'Geata de Talas,' Tara whispered. Then said, 'It seems far away but all is an illusion here, distance, and dimension skew to our perception of what we expect to see or what we wish to draw to us. This creation shard is hardly bigger than our old yard, yet the vista is leagues in every direction.' She paused and took a shuddering breath while a sting of regret tightened her chest, she had so hoped Cissy would come for her and take her back to Earth. Yes, she would lack a spirit but so did every other demon on Earth, she would manage without one somehow, but every plan she had made had ended in failure, even this one. Even a manifestation in the nowhere place of The Void was not enough to get her home.

'If you are quite done, I think I will try and wake up,' said Celeste and felt heat sheet across her cheeks. The sting in her words did not sound like her but she could not and would not tolerate a dead woman's madness.

Tara snorted. Then raising her chin defiantly, she said, 'They have gone through already, and Cassandra Novantae waits their return.' She pointed over Celeste's shoulder towards a woman with one white eye who leaned against a stone on the far side of the circle.

Celeste's heart stopped and she felt her mouth drop open before she stuttered, 'Who?'

Tara tutted and cut her off before she could say any more, 'I've told them they cannot use my creation shard for their travel to Umbra Horrenda, but Novantae, over there, told me she would slit my throat if I did not hold my tongue.'

Celeste narrowed her eyes while she wondered if she had made Cassandra Novantae up, she was hell bent on reading her chronicles. That is why she is here in my dream she thought, then took her attention to the woman who wore black assassin clothes and the most disdainful look on her face she had ever seen, she made Cissy seem positively vivacious. The flesh she could see, shone like crystal, and spun gold. She turned her back to her. If I ignore her, she will fade she thought while Cassandra made her way towards them.

Celeste eyed the mountain nervously and a shiver of dread crept along her spine. Oh no. She looked at her palms, but they remained normal, clammy but normal. 'This is my dream,' she said angrily. 'I will control it.'

Cassandra Novantae stood before her and placed her glittering finger on the centre of her chest. 'It is a shared dream, Spectral Star. Our thoughts create our reality in The Void because it is saturated with Prima Materia. That you are here at all means that your power has activated, but are you ready? Are you prepared?'

Celeste felt her bottom lip tremble, but she managed to ask. 'You are like my friend, Ganaim Al Tine?'

What she meant to ask was, will my friend end up looking like you but there was no polite way to say that. The woman was no longer flesh. A strange crystalline luminescence radiated from her skin. One of her eyes was black as the deepest night, the other silver like a full moon. Her fingers ended in nails like talons, and each knuckle was like an embellishment in her skin, and they refracted light like a jewel rested there. She had pointed ears and her scalp was bald around them, a crest of midnight blue, almost black ran across the top of her skull and at the back of her head, thick tresses hung past her shoulders and were braided with leather.

The small crystalline lights beneath her skin told a story as old as Time, in a sacred language she did not know, and Celeste's heart cartwheeled when she felt the future crash through her like an eternal wave. She knew before Cassandra spoke, it would be words she did not want to hear.

Cassandra eyed her with her head tilted to one side. 'Ganaim Al Tine is Solas Nua Novantae. You will go to Glean Glas, there is one there who will teach you the Monas, but do not go to Romar Ri. From there go to Silver Tower. Go save my son.'

'But' Celeste stuttered, and Cassandra cut her off. 'I have seen it. Therefore, it is already so,' she finished dryly, then turned and walked back to the stone she had been leaning against. She took her gaze to Geata de Talas and said over her shoulder in a voice that sounded like a lecture. 'Say your farewells, Tara Silverhair. Time has you in its eye, and Gaia wants you for her womb.'

Pulling her rattling thoughts into her mouth Celeste stuttered,' Why has my nana got Lord Abrecan's sword?'

Cassandra Novantae turned and pointed to the sword. 'That is Lokas, Abrecan has Talas, but it is still a murder weapon non-the-less.' She looked pointedly at Tara. Then turned back to Celeste and said as if it was a waste of her breath, 'Try to remember my words, if you can.'

Celeste groaned. She could see a phoenix, it glinted gold in the distance as it made its way toward them, just as she thought of the fox, a black shape, sleek and fast, ran along the sand, its large tail streaking behind. The crystal ward was working. 'I will be taken from here soon,' she said softly, then pulled her resolve tight. 'I made *you* appear in my dream,' she said in a voice full of confidence while she strode towards Cassandra Novantae, then stood before her with her chin tilted and her arms folded about her chest.

Cassandra turned to her and taking her arm she swept it all around them and said in a voice that could cut diamonds to dust. 'I placed my finger upon you.' Then, quick as a flash she reached out and nipped Celeste on her arm. It was hard and painful, but Celeste pulled away and did not utter a word, it was her dream, it should not hurt, even though it did.

Cassandra snorted contemptuously then said, 'How do you not know any of your Lore? All of this is real. If we die here? We die. Go now, I will not mention that we met. I have not seen it; therefore, it is not so.' She drew two blades from sheaths that crossed the front of her body and began moving them through the air. She stopped one last time and turned her hard gaze on Tara before she said, 'Make haste Silverhair. Make your peace. You,' she pointed one of the blades at Celeste, 'are on the eve of destruction. Are all your family dawdlers, and deadwood?' She lowered the blade, snorted contemptuously, then nodded once while her white eye flashed like lightning. 'I will buy you the time you need, laggard, but know this, the price to be paid is beyond your comprehension but pay the balance, you will.' Without another word she turned and walked off.

'I am caught between the devil and the deep blue sea.' Tara said gravely but the emotion did not reach her empty eyes, and her mouth was puckered into a distasteful scowl as if it was full of the taste of defeat.

'What will you do?' Celeste asked though she found it difficult to be concerned for the creature in front of her, who said she was her Nana, but who seemed nothing at all like her, standing there in fine silks with the light of spirit gone from her eye. As for Cassandra Novantae? She liked her better when she was between the pages of a book.

Tara picked up the large sword and rested her elbow on it. 'I have always found that I am a better swimmer than I am a fire eater,' she replied wryly and tilted her snub nose in the air.

Sorrow stabbed at Celeste's heart like a skewer made of hot metal but before she could say anything more, the phoenix and fox made their way towards them, and their presence closed the door on her dreamwalk.

Chapter Twenty-Seven

Well Met Sonii

Absolute old witch. That is what she was supposed to be teaching me, how to make things out of nothing...I just know it. Her dream flitted away from her in fragments like butterfly wings and autumn leaves. Was there someone else there? She could not recall. Celeste sighed and savoured the wet tickling sensation on her face, like whiskers and a lover's breath as she returned slowly to chilly wakefulness. Hay?

Nimrod snorted wetly into her face before moving his attention to a clump of sparse grass near her head. Celeste kept her eyes closed while they watered briefly then dried. She thought it was Ganaim. Then she pretended she was still asleep. Her face flushed and she scolded herself for thinking that Ganaim Al Tine would even think to wake her with a kiss. He never had, so why start now. She squinted out of one half-open eye at the large piebald horse. It is Nimrod. Sonii Romarii must be close by. Her heart fluttered and she silently berated herself for being such a silly girl.

Ganaim was standing next to two other horses, they grazed on the scrubby herbs in the silver morning light. Where is he? Where is Sonii?

Sonii moved quietly back through the bushes. His cloak blended and reflected the colours cast by weak sunlight that dappled shades of green, grey, and brown through the dark canopy of evergreens, his breath evaporated in small clouds of curling steam. He was part of the forest, she thought, as he approached fastening the front of his breeches. 'You take Aquene, Gan. More of a warrior horse, she likes the open plains, better suited to that than the Roma Road. Celeste can take Niyal, he was born for the Roma Road.'

Ganaim nodded. 'How did you arrive here?'

'Cissy picked us up at the Mobius source compass; it's high in the mountains and barely functions. The winter still has hold up there. The cork oak and stone pine will not survive if the weather does not break soon. Large tracts of trees have split...though it will not bother the Sylvan pine. It was dangerous going, the snow is deep in parts and the higher passes are blocked still, but we followed the river down to Eagle Valley.' He paused and met Ganaim's gaze answering his unasked question. 'We cannot use the stone compass to take us to Gleann Glas I will not risk alerting shadow spies.'

'Cissy, is she...'

'I showed her a way of anchoring herself, and one of the cat's is instructing her in another technique, the rod of power, which will open up more paths for her in the Stone Compass.' She takes a bearing so she can get back to her memories and uses the rod of power like putting a pin in a map.' He put a hand on Ganaim's arm.

'Thank you, Sonii, I thought she would lose herself in there.' He sighed and moved his attention back to the horses. 'What's the meaning of their names?' He stroked the nose of a large but graceful silver-grey mare.

'Aquene means Peace, but she's from warrior stock. Once we needed more of them to fight our clansmen on the plains and tundra in the north, silly little squabbles that were caused by a great evil,' he shrugged, 'but you know all that history. We fought our last battle on the plains at Cale, all our attention focussed there while that demon took our most sacred centre. It should not have happened, but since the corruption, the high meadows and tundra no longer exists – we would need snowshoes if we had to do battle there now. The Winter Lands are skirt the north of Galay now,' he replied dryly while he rubbed the horse's neck.

'Her name was given to her in recognition of her skills in battle – peace is hard fought for, and difficult to keep once it is won. She did something that no other could, she saw something that we all missed, a darkness had come among us, but she saw and acted upon it. Although it was too late to save the day, she did save the Romaros' life. I'll tell you her story, if we have time and a decent place to rest on the way.' He stretched casually. 'Niyal over there.' He pointed at an older chunky gelding with splayed hooves and a huge triangular shaped head. Slabs, and bundles of muscle, and sinew, rippled and bulged. His chestnut coat was crisscrossed by scars on his deep chest. 'Niyal means wind. He has been bred for the road. He is ranger stock, built for stamina, strength, and defence. Not as graceful as our Lady Aquene but just as likely to outpace her.' The older horse shook his head, then whinnied towards Sonii while he bared big yellow teeth and laughed – Celeste could not help but smile.

'What news from Mount Wraith, Sonii?' Ganaim dropped his voice as they moved off towards a thicket of bushes and young saplings. Celeste stretched and wondered if she wanted to leave the warmth of the sheepskin bag. She decided she did not, closed her eyes and fell asleep again. I feel safe she thought as she drifted off.

'There is nothing, but ash left of the school. Protectorate flyers were all over it like a swarm, seems they were getting ready to pay a visit. Fortunately, Col knew it was coming, he didn't trust the new head.' He paused and leaned against a nearby tree. 'They asked your mother…Cissy…to help.' He stopped talking and cupped his chin in his hand while he watched Ganaim digest what he had said.

'So…' He raised his shoulders petulantly, while he pretended not to care.

'It was because of Cissy's actions that we gained vital information; you know when she happened to meet him at The Nag. It meant Col had time to plan and then act. Yes, I had to go on a bit of a detour, and we cannot risk a journey over Kai Land just now, but no harm done with that, perhaps it's what the goddess wants.' Sonii peered intently at Ganaim and waited for his response.

'Is that what I am then, Sonii, the product of a deceitful encounter, with what? And her…a whore, a lady loose-skirt?' he hissed angrily as hot tears welled in his eyes. He felt like that silly little boy again – waiting at the distant gate for a man who never came back, while he felt his mother reject him as she slipped deeper into blackness. She had eventually improved, a little; the sweet open smile she used to possess, as golden as her hair, had gone. Sour and bitter was what was left. He did not know how to undo the misfortune he had caused when he showed her his crystalline markings proud as a peacock, but the damage had been done. Even though he was only small, he knew he must remind her of him, of her pain, so he avoided her, and everyone seemed happier with that arrangement, somehow. He had accepted it at the time and had grown to understand that she loved him but could not show it. She had become his friend in one sense though he mourned the loss of her as the smiling young mother he could only just remember, but this? They had her whoring herself; it was too much. He wanted to kill someone. Why in the Light didn't she tell me what they had her doing? Anukssake.

'Do not dishonour her with that foulness, Ganaim. You might not know the whole truth, but you know that isn't the truth of it.' He placed his hand firmly on Ganaim's arm until he calmed down. 'Not that it makes any difference, but the new head isn't an evil man. He is just an ignorant man, not fully awake, and his nano device is fully functioning like most of them are in Lodewick. He is a puppet of the state, but I assure you, she is safe.'

'I'm sorry, I know, but that might explain her drinking. Celeste said she was well in her cups, she must've been acting merry, or she'd had to get herself drunk beforehand…poor Cissy.' He hung his head, ashamed of his hasty words while he calmed down. 'And what about Carter?'

'He is well,' Sonii smiled broadly and continued, 'Col was in the Nags Head when it was all going down, with more than a dozen witnesses. They are prepared for any backlash but doubt the new head will point the finger in that direction. He's completely enthralled with Cissy – she is an incredibly beautiful, intelligent, desirable woman, you know.'

'Please don't tell me anymore about what she's having to do.' Ganaim turned away sharply and ripped up a small evergreen sapling that was trying to grow on the remains of the trunk of a felled tree, humus now – it had rooted itself in moss and shallow soil below. Thinking better of his action, he replaced the loose sods of earth with his boot and raked angrily at the ground with the sapling's stiff little branches. 'And the farm?' Ganaim bit the short painful words through too-tight lips, aware of a dry sting in his throat that threatened to strangle him. A pinecone fell sharply on his head – it was a perfect shot. He looked up and scowled as he rubbed his crown. Little gets. In that briefest moment of time, he thought he hated Celeste, her mother Selene, and Tara. Why did they ever come to us? Bad luck witches.

'The farm is all quiet and business as usual, but would you believe that ancient cattle shed at the bottom end of your Da's fields burned to the ground. You were in it, smoking oil of the night poppy…it's a bloody tragedy, you will be sadly missed.' Sonii reached forward and held Ganaim's arm firmly above the elbow, while he searched his face. His amber eyes held concern but also command; he would wait for him to process events, but not forever and certainly not if it endangered them.

'I know I can never go back, Sonii…it's, it's just bloody hard to accept…' he trailed off, 'and you're sure it's been done properly, my family will be safe?'

'I would never do anything to compromise their safety and the current life of my first mother, the Lady Aos Si. Your family are strong, resilient – they will survive. Even if I asked Padrain to return to Romar Ri with Dorothea, he would refuse; he keeps the crofter communities alive. Must I tell you how important it is that we maintain contact with the Selgovae now that Talam Na Soar is under

Gaia's ice? If the prophecies Cassandra made, happen, then we have a chance at victory. Slim as it may be, the Selgovae and Novantae are key to that.' Ganaim nodded though his heart felt like lead in his chest while he hoped the prophecies regarding Solas Nua Novantae applied to someone else, anyone really, the further away from where he was, the better.

'We need Padrain to run negotiations with the guild of smugglers and in return they join the resistance. He is a vital part of our network – your whole family are. They are as safe as Padrain keeps them,' he continued his report to Ganaim, 'The horses have been released and have been given a new mission before they make their way home, so there is no connection to us Romarii. You are dead, the factories in the Bloom are running again, and the crofters are back to work. Light, it's been a slow process, but the arrival of Fairmist Al Mara and the true blood Selgovae were the blessing we needed since we lost the Sun in Winter.' He released Ganaim's arm and folded his hands across his waist; the tattoos along each arm moved under the shadow of the canopy. A lion and a bear, a salmon, deer, bats and toads, foxes, chattering flocks of woodland birds, and a winged horse, a frightening Hyenoi hound and a phoenix to name a few – depictions of all the spirit animals who had walked with Sonii Romarii during his many incarnations on Gaiadon. They were there as gifts from the animals themselves rather than by any artist's hand.

'Will they be safe? I got to like Hossy once I could hear him...and Nellie, who wouldn't like her,' Ganaim said sadly. He was surprised at how concerned he felt for them and how stupid he had been with them, always thinking that mucking them out, feeding, and caring for them was a burden – when the opposite was true; it was an honour.

Nellie forgave him first saying, 'Ignorance makes people blind. You were blind and deaf – now you not,' but Hossy took full advantage of his discomfort. 'You owned now, man-child. One day you may be great ranger, but now you wet in your big elf ears. You lower than me, lower than the scrawny demon spawn sheep. You was traded for two horses...two horses,' he whickered, and went on and on whenever Ganaim was nearby. He had eventually come to be more tolerant but remained very dry where Ganaim was concerned. He suspected it had something to do with his relations with Celeste.

'They will be safe with Hossy's strength and Nellie's brains. They have only gone to pick something up for us from the Mobius River region, and as for the shed, even the ash makes ready to blow away. They will move the huge pile of dung from the over-wintered animals. A midden will stand where it once stood.'

Ganaim laughed at that. 'Cissy's idea?'

Sonii clapped him on the back. 'Of course, the fire went completely unnoticed, what with all the action in Mount Wraith. There had been some unrest at the canal too – a bare-knuckle bout between Inola and a number of guards who had thrown their hats in for a go.' He stopped and sighed then said, 'It got completely out of hand – a riot really.' He smiled wryly then added, 'He should retire but he's tougher and more supple than chewed leather.'

'Inola was at the canal district?' he sounded interested.

'They were all there seeking information on the black-hearted fool who is mancing Fear Me's and the goddess knows what else out of the Lake of Unum. They have left now, all were well,' Sonii replied dryly as he continued to wait for Ganaim to be ready to leave.

'Did they find him?' he asked and Sonii made a disgusted noise in the back of his throat and said, 'One of them. Staved and skin hung, before they left.' He heard Celeste rustle in her bedroll behind him. Awake and listening, he thought.

'I'm glad they're away from the proc areas and you are right; who comes to investigate the death of us rural peasants? Now if it was a flock or a herd that had been rustled,' he shrugged before he continued in a hushed voice, 'do not tell her, Sonii, she will be devastated. She gave it to Moin and Abhhain.' He nodded in the direction of Celeste, paused, gulped down a rush of nausea. 'And Tara, I mean the remains…did they dig her, I mean dig them up? You know, burn them?'

'Moin and Abhhain used the flames to activate the essences of dozens of Fear Me's at a single go; the crofters are training hard, you see. They're a suspicious lot, the Selgovae descendants, so I doubt they would have put her remains on the pyre with that lot.' He shrugged. 'I won't mention anything to Celeste and don't know what they did with Tara's remains. If they had any sense, they would have been inside and been burned with the cottage. We can't leave anything behind now, Gan.' He touched his arm and nodded towards the clearing. 'You know she is not going back?'

Ganaim dropped his head, his shoulders felt too weak to support the weight of that knowledge. He shrugged, gathered himself and nodded curtly at Sonii but could hardly meet his eye. 'I know, I have always known – it's what I was bred for, wasn't it?' he whispered shortly at the Romarii and dropped his head to hide his shame while tears prickled in his eyes.

'You understand. Good. We need to make haste.' Sonii ignored his bitter outburst. 'No clues as to where we have been, where we are going. Get this camp packed up, night soil and the remains of the fire hidden, use that,' he pointed to the sapling branch, 'and replace the sod where the fire was…sweep the dirt. I will ask the mountain for a way. Did you brief her?' He pointed towards Celeste while he strode purposefully out of the undergrowth. The tension that he had been carrying about his shoulder eased a little. Ganaim was new to ranger ways and had much to learn. He was even less aware of the ways of the Brotherhood of Morrigan, and to Sonii's mind he had more than just growing into his maturity still to do. Without a walk-in he would have none of the knowledge from past lives, poor as the connection was becoming, it was still an essential part of being a Romarii. He paused his thoughts and studied Ganaim. *If it were my choice, I would not accept him either.* He knew just by looking at him, that his destiny lay elsewhere, and if he could, he would make sure he walked in the right direction when the Dagger Path presented itself to him. The direction that led to Silver Tower.

'She thinks I'm bloody crazy,' he replied dryly.

'My little lady if you are ready?' Sonii walked over to where Celeste faked waking up. She had caught snippets of their conversation, Ganaim had woken her from her slumber, crashing about in the undergrowth, his voice raised over what Cissy had had to do.

'Celeste, time to make your morning water, then we make haste. It is too dangerous to linger here. If you make solid waste, you must collect it and carry it with you until we can dispose of it later. That goes for you too, Gan.' He leaned over her, his back to Ganaim. 'Nod if it worked?'

Celeste nodded as she stretched her stiff cold limbs, but before opening her eyes she had hoped that he would still be there, bending over her, staring intently into her eyes. She paused, wondered if he was as handsome as she remembered. Her eyes fluttered open, but Sonii was already walking towards a cliff face obscured by scrubby dark bushes that grew next to it.

He took an amber crystal from a deep pocket in his leather jerkin, not unlike her own, which he wore underneath his ranger cloak. The crystal was shaped like an egg. Then he brought it to his mouth, closed his eyes and whispered to it before he placed it at the centre of his chest. He took his free hand and placed it on the cliff face and began to whisper softly in a language Celeste could not understand – it was like a song.

Where his hand touched the cliff face, she saw it pulse, fractals of crystalline design swirled briefly across the granite surface in a chaotic pattern of rectangles in shades of gold, black, and silver with iridescent flashes of bright pink and blue. It was beautiful, and for the first time she was not afraid that she could see the small parts that made up the whole. They were different to what she had seen previously. She felt her attention being pulled to them while the rest of the scenery faded into the background. Something deep inside switched on and her mouth filled with saliva, she reached out with her mind and knew intuitively that there were even smaller parts behind the reality of the crystalline matrix of the rock face. She saw them briefly, miniscule spheres that she was able to draw to herself, complex designs, snowflakes inside geometric or spherical shapes, but they whispered away from her scrutiny with a note of hissy dissonance.

They are not mine to meld, they answered him, therefore I cannot interfere – I wonder why that is. How do I know that she thought while she turned her attention to her sleeping gear and began to roll it into a tight sausage before securing it with the leather ties – it was warm and light, beautifully crafted she thought as she recalled snatches of her encounter with Tara. Where is Geata de Talas and is it safe to tell anyone else what she has created in The Void she thought anxiously and touched the centre of her chest. There is something I need to remember from my dream. She paused and reached into her memory. Elvan's Barrow next to the ocean, it made her smile, it was almost pleasant she thought and reached again. Tara, the sea, and the mouth of hell, birds, and foxes. Was someone else there?

Sonii brought her back from her memories. 'It won't be long now.' He turned and smiled. 'The mountain is receptive to my request and will make a winding way for us to follow. Bring the horses up. Ganaim, you take the rear, I will lead. Celeste and Niyal, take centre. We must lead the horses at first and travel in single file until...' he paused and closed his eyes as a ripple of light passed through his body from his feet to his head.

Celeste gasped when she saw a stream of light leave the centre of his chest and enter the rock face like young shoots and tendrils from climbing sweet peas. He hesitated while they faded away then continued, 'Perhaps until we reach the root of the mountain. Following this we should be near the Roma Road.' He sat down quite suddenly and rested his back against the rock while he took a small vial from another pocket. It held a tiny amount of dark green liquid that shimmered with a deep gold iridescence.

'Sonii?' Ganaim asked as he stepped towards him. Sonii waved him away.

'I'm not as young as I used to be and it has been a tough few Moons too,' he nodded imperceptibly towards Celeste who was acquainting herself with Niyal while she gawped at the ranger, 'and this sort of work costs you know.' He smiled at Celeste; she blushed; she had not meant to stare. He pulled a single blade of dry scrubby grass from the earth, dipped it in the vial then placed it under his tongue. He turned the vial around in his hands. 'It all costs, you both remember that.' He pointed to the mountain and waggled the vial. 'Anything that you would claim or name as magic, comes with a price.'

Ganaim caught his eye again and asked, 'Will that be enough? I mean, considering what you've just done.'

'Perhaps. I cannot afford to use more than is necessary. Worry not, I'll recover if I don't have to ask anymore mountains to open up a way for us.' He smiled, not without irony. He had been on the road for longer than he cared to remember and had failed to complete his mission to find a way into Umbra Horrenda, again. He and Nimrod had been in the bowels of the Earth intermittently since shortly after he had implanted Celeste with the fake nano.

He had visited Arianrihod briefly to report on the suitability of Yalan's weapon, the Spectral Star, and had had to sit through several tedious council meetings where blame and suspicions were more prominent than solutions and actions. He had eventually intervened though he hated to do so. He was Brotherhood of Morrigan, free of the manipulations of Romar Ri but still he found himself ensnared. The crone Arianrihod hardly veiled her triumphant smile when he suggested that the faulty weapon be taken and made fit for purpose. The trap sprung when they had all voted him as being the only one suitable to take on the task. But he used their request as leverage for his own deal for more time before he returned to Romar Ri permanently, time he hoped would see him rescue the Romaros and Akasha, thus ensuring he remained free.

Rovander had caught Silas Al Seamist and a creature called a Tree-wish in the ancient Galanglas forests to the east of Serpent Lake, too near to the ruins of Stone. Inola spoke of Lord Cernunnos appearing in his serpent form and he took this as a sign to parley with the smuggler. Although Rovander had been keen to kill the Tree-wish, Inola had volunteered to do it if the parley went badly. They had called him to the parley and while he had not been sure of everything

Smuggler Seamist had told him, about the strange paths that they had walked through the mind of Time, he was no mystic or white-eyed seer from Silver Tower, nor did he fully believe everything he said about where he had been and what he was set to do; but he believed him when he said he had seen Akasha and The Romaros, and that they were being held prisoner at the foundation of the Fifth Tower which was rooted in Umbra Horrenda. Then into the Earth he had gone with Nimrod, more determined than ever to find his way to Umbra Horrenda and rescue the Romaros and Akasha. Only he had not had the time he needed and had had to come for Celeste. He did not share what he knew with Arianrihod, they were not ready for war and that is what she would start if she knew where the Romaros and Akasha were, getting them killed in the meantime. No, it required a much gentler approach, just one or two steps at a time, then he would get the Romaros and Akasha back where they belonged.

Then, Arianrihod could go and sing to the sea for all he cared, he would not be manipulated onto the throne at Romar Ri by that woman, and all on the precis that as the first son the Lady Aos Si, had carried for Gaia, thousands and thousands of years and many lifetimes ago that he was somehow the heir apparent. He snorted and made ready to get to his feet while he noticed the other two watching him suspiciously.

'Besides, the goddess will provide if we need it, although I seem to need more of late,' he said gravely while he pushed the multiple layers of dealings and the trap the crone had laid for him away, before jumping to his feet, but not before Celeste noticed a pained look travel across his face. Which when she thought about it; it looked drawn, and pale compared to the last time she saw him. There were charcoal hollows at his cheeks and shadows beneath eyes that sat too deeply in their sockets. She studied Nimrod; he was a fine horse, well proportioned, sturdy, and flexible, with a deep strong chest and solid legs, easily the best out of the three, but she could see ribs protruding. Compared to Niyal and Aquene who looked in good form, he seemed haggard, tatty around the edges.

'Come on, we've a way to find and a road to follow,' Sonii said cheerfully.

'Here, Celeste, take his reins.' Niyal nudged her shoulder in a friendly fashion, his mouth wetting her cloak while he looked for something to eat.

'Hey there, new friend, I've not got anything for you to eat. We will get to stop later; I will get you an apple. Would you like that, old boy? Would Niyal the brave like a bit of apple,' she continued to talk to her horse and made a mental note to put some pieces of fruit in her pockets for her new friend while she ignored Ganaim and Sonii – and her mounting fear.

Niyal snorted gently into her ear. Reassured, she whispered as she led him forward. 'Good boy, good old Niyal. We are going to be good friends; I can feel it. We will. I had a friend called Hossy Black, you know, and a friend called Nellie.' She continued while fear worried at her like a crofter's cur on a bone. Oh no…what is going to happen now? We are going into the mountain for Anukssake, Gan was not jesting!

Ganaim gave the camp area one last look, brushed the hoof prints away, made sure that no sign of their presence remained, when a slight tremor passed beneath the small group, and the horses nickered, and their ears pricked. Niyal hoofed at the ground eagerly. Aquene bared her teeth, but Nimrod looked sternly at them, blew out of his large nostrils, and despite his slightly tattered appearance he commanded respect. The other two horses stood to attention.

'Is that her moving now?' Ganaim asked while he joined the back of the group taking Aquene's reins.

'Aye it is, she's not doing too badly either. Quicker than I expected. It is a good sign if the mountain wants to help us. The way to the Roma Road will be steep, dangerous, a long journey down before we take rest. It is the dimension rifts, you see, that and his foul reality laid on top of Gaiadon; we need to avoid anywhere the black moon is. Do you understand?'

'I think so,' she replied bravely, though she had no idea what he was talking about. I am not showing myself up for a child in front of him again she thought and nodded her head confidently.

Hot earthy wind gusted from the cliff face as the mountain exhaled, revealing a dark crevice like a distorted horizontal grin in the rock face. Celeste noticed Ganaim brushing away the remaining hoof prints with the sapling, which he brought into the tunnel with him.

'Trying not to leave any signs,' he whispered, though she thought she heard a tremor in his voice. It was the mountain trembling and sighing as it continued to rumble. She heard him fussing with the branch and the smell of horse increased, the rumble receded – rolling like thunder further away in the dark distance.

'Niyal, I hope we're going to fit through there,' Celeste continued to talk softly to her horse, his bulk and strength grounded her in a way that Sonii and Ganaim could not. She felt a connection to him. He emanated a warm safety that enveloped her; it was like he was trying to say that he knew what he was doing; this was where he belonged, and he was not about to let anything happen to her.

She touched the leather bag and books strapped across her body, impossibly small and light; it clung to her skin like a patch of hotter flesh while she sweated with nerves. Niyal whickered softly and stamped his foot, eager to enter the mountain and find the Roma Road. She drew strength from him and was as equally determined to get into the mountain. She would find the Romarii crone, this powerful woman people mentioned, Arianri…what was the name Gan had called her? she thought. How does he know her name? More secrets, more lies. Uncovering another lie only added to her resolution, made her even more determined to find the answers she needed while she thought about the fortune-teller at The Nag. She knew my Nana would die and what else was it, something about darkness on my hands and she knew about this, this strange journey…and the prophecy in my nightmare. What did she say, what is my Nana trying to tell me, why is Sonii asking me to keep it to myself?

The crevice hissed closed behind them, and she jumped as it stole the small fragile light away. She felt a finger press against the centre of her chest and knew she had to remember something but just as quickly the thoughts that jumbled through her turbulent mind were gone. Then there was a vacuum of quiet – inside and out.

They stood with silence, their invisible companion, close to their horses' heads, on a single width track, hewn out of the inside of the mountain. To her right and left, Celeste could feel cold emanate from the granite. The atmosphere was chilly, but not as oppressive as she had imagined it would be, even though she felt that the roof of the tunnel was barely two feet above Nimrod's head. She reached out in the pitch dark and placed her palm against the warmth of Niyal's coat. He smelled of hay and horse manure, earthy warm animal, he was not afraid to be trapped under the stone like she was. She inhaled deeply, felt his steady heart, as it beat a smooth rhythm in his wide-muscled chest, his alert stance reassured her – he was ready even if she was not. Niyal, the wind, would be her horse under the mountain.

Part Four

Troy.

A Galactic Cycle In The Life Of...

Chapter Twenty-Eight

Tranquillity

He paused and felt the blood being drawn from his face like frozen rain slowly melting down a pane of glass, while he forced the words from his too tight mouth. 'Tranquillity what? How did you get my sequence?' he snapped while he ran his free hand over his shaved head. His finger found an almost healed scab behind his ear, rough, and loose at the edges, it was just waiting to be picked; he obliged while he ground his teeth and thought, who in the hells is she?

'Doesn't matter. I've got something for you, belonged to your long-lost friend.'

'Fuck off,' he snarled while he squeezed the silicon mo until it was almost ready to pop its spider web guts into his palm.

The caller tutted arrogantly, then there was a moment of silence, as if she were thinking about her next words carefully. He felt her anger fizzle in his ear and was about to end the call when she said, 'Meet me where I first gave you the finger. Idiot. He's not dead.'

He pulled the mo from his ear and gazed at it as if it were a piece of starlight that had landed in his hand. 'Who, who is this?' he stuttered, but the mo was silent.

Time did not stop, but it hung in the air, suspended, while it watched the very fabric of the day around him pause, as if it too had forgotten how to breathe. The scab came loose beneath his fingernail, pulling at unhealed skin beneath and he felt the fleeting sting of skin tearing, then hot blood well to the surface, but he did not stop to wipe at it, he leapt off the side of his bed.

The finger? He knew who it was and where he had last seen her. This is madness he thought while his feet hit the cold tiles of the dais with a sudden hard slap that sounded like two dead fish thrown on a quayside. He leapt down the steps then raced to his wardrobe for warm clothes, while he ignored the blood that tickled like a flea crawling down the side of his neck.

It had been a long, gibbous, four moons since Micah had died, and he had marked his descent into despair and madness by their baleful light. First, Self-Existing Moon, he could not find a way to exist without him, without the Sun in Winter, he was less than a shadow. There was no warmth, or love, and light, left. He retreated into his rooms and locked his doors. His father left his work for him outside without a word, but his instructions were written in his precise annoying hand. His mother came only once: she did not knock but fluttered about outside, like a trapped bird unsure of where the window and freedom lay, while he sat before his fire and watched her silk slippers pace back and forth, then turn and leave. Servants brought him food, and coal, and wood, he lit his own fire and kept the braziers beneath the tile dais his bed sat atop, stoked, and glowing red. The heat in his room was hotter than hell, but inside he was hollow and dead, and he occupied only the smallest part of himself, while he numbed everything else with droge waere, which Weasel slipped discreetly under his door with his bitter message uttered in a hushed voice, 'Take the fucking lot, Valoroso then choke on your own vomit. You, spineless, privileged cunt.'

Even his grief was ephemeral and weak compared to the rage Bucky unleashed across the land. Dark, and bleak, Bucky vented his grief in shards of sorrow that cut deeper than a blade, and blizzard after blizzard that froze ships in their berths and covered the Ophiuchus in opaque ice that was thicker than two tall men. Then came Overtone, Rhythmic, and Resonant Moons and each of their twenty-eight days and nights belonged to the orchestra of his pain. But now this? Bucky's sorrow had eventually abated, and his icy clawed vengeance was a grey thaw that uncovered a city that had been ripped and torn. Starved corpses, strangely preserved beneath snow and ice, their silent screams caught in open mouthed surprise, were collected by Acolytes of Anuk and carted off to the flame only knew where.

He snorted when he selected the clothes he would wear and whispered while he pulled on the very same breeches, he had worn that fateful night, 'Today is the day of the Self-existing Eagle, Micah. If you are alive, help me soar. Help me find you. I do not normally believe in this bloody rubbish, but if I do, please, let it count.' He paused, just say it is a trap and they are coming to kill me too he thought and began to rummage in the bottom of his wardrobes. He found a set of brass knuckles, a small throwing dagger that would slip inside his boot, and a spring assisted Stiletto. He toyed with the blade, it had been a gift from Micah, from the forges of Cumagh Solais and made of Solais Silver or so he had told him. He held it up to the light while he studied the potent alchemical alloy colours, they oiled down each side of the double-edged blade like parts of a rainbow turned to liquid light, rendering the silver harder than the hardest tungsten blade from Nenesh. Micah had told him it was a magical blade, but he knew alchemy when he saw it. What it was, was a thing of beauty, like the stilettos elite gents and lordlings carried with them when they socialised in places like Boho and the other polite districts of Lodewick.

Once he was dressed, brass knuckles in pocket, dagger in boot and the stiletto strangely cool and a sharp reminder while it rested against the skin of his lower back, that he could be walking into a trap, he walked quietly down the stairs keeping to the carpet that hugged the middle of the marble like a lush green snake, he did not want to risk brushing against the walls, Reynard had all the cunning of a fox, including its large ears. Before he did anything, he needed to check on the whereabouts of his father, and Weasel. Creeping to Reynard's study door he leant forward to put his ear to it when a firm hand took him by the shoulder, and a perfectly polished boot pressed the door open.

Weasel pushed him through and said, 'Troy, as you requested, my lord.' Without another word he went and stood behind Reynard and turned his attention to the informatics monitor.

'What the hell are you wearing?' Reynard slid his gaze up and down his body. A note of disgust put a sting in his words that did not move a muscle on his perfectly neutral face. 'Now.' He clicked his fingers and pointed to a spot next to him. The monitor was warming up and the banks of crystal tubes holding rubidium and copper pipes in the back hissed while they threw off an unnatural light. The air was charged with their alchemical power like the caress of a gentle breeze lifting forearm hair. The heat from the rubicity had the silicone monitor stinking like seaweed.

He flicked his eye to the side, but Leleth hid her face in a large glass of Katharos red, and he knew that Weasel would not come to his aid. Why should he? The suits and jackets Weasel wore were plain, a uniform, which identified him as something other than elite, but also not lower class. What did the most unfashionable man in Lodewick know about anything he thought while he tilted his chin haughtily and took his place next to his father. The game is on he thought and felt the mood in the room, it was heavier than a kidnapper's hood and hung in the air like a threat, a leaden sheet, ready to drop at any moment and deny him his chance of freedom. I will have to tread very carefully, or I will not get to the silk warehouse he thought and pressed his lips into a tight line. He took one hand and deliberately smoothed the front of his dark green, long tailcoat. He knew his father was watching him from the corner of his eye, so he folded his arms across his chest and set a rod of steel in his spine. I will get out, and I will find Micah, he thought and gulped down a wave of fear that filled his mouth with salt.

Following the night of the dead uprising, fashion favoured by the elite youth had suddenly changed. The braiding down the front of his jacket and the glass buttons were like the ribs and jewels on the Spider King jacket he had worn the night Micah died. He knew he was protesting; he knew they all were, but this was as far as they dared go. He even had the same breeches on that he had worn that night. It felt appropriate that he should, although they were not as tight as they had been, but just as warm, and he had taken to wearing black leather ranger boots. Other's favoured top hats and canes with silver animal heads. He had resisted the temptation, although now he regretted that when all he could count on as weapons were brass knuckles, a throwing dagger, and a silver stiletto. He doubted any of the fops he knew could use a staff, Micah could and so could he, but not like the rebels from the Night of the Dead.

His father pointed to the monitor and his voice was a low angry snarl. 'Do you know any of these peasants?'

He coughed into his hand and replied. 'What do you take me for?' He feigned disgust while he watched the recording. The Fae-eared Abhhain twirled through the grey day, the cane in his hand was a blur like dragonfly wings while he engaged protectorate guard in close quarters until their faces bloomed and their blood sprayed. Moin, had obviously disarmed one. Most of the sugar skull make-up had gone, apart from the black around his eyes, his face was ashen, paler than the dust of dead embers, but he still stabbed daggers of green fire, which volleyed like arrows made of light at the fists of guards. He flipped and somersaulted between, and over debris. It was like watching an acrobatic skeleton go on a psychotic murder-fest. He slid his gaze quickly to the side and studied Weasel, who had his arms folded about his chest and a look of pure admiration on his face while he nodded his head respectfully. He was behind Reynard he could afford it. Though he noted quickly how the tiniest of veins pulsed at Reynard's temple and felt a small wave of selfish joy rise when he thought, I wonder if he knows he has a tic.

The two men reminded him of seals, it was their strange eyes and flat sort of noses, though the similarity ended there. They were sugar-skulled, decorated death, and whirled as if they were made of leaves and air, a swirl of energy picked up by the White Lunar Wind and hurled against Lodewick; two typhoons wreaking havoc while the grey overcast flowered in fiery shades of orange, and glistening blood red. He felt a rush of adrenaline that nearly sent a cheer catapulting out of his mouth when the ground trembled and a great beast roared when Athanasius Blood's warehouse went up in a column of greasy fury. It was, he thought, the most magnificent bloodbath I have ever seen, and I was glad to be there, proud to be the fuse.

He steadied his breath, took a shaking hand, and wiped a dew of sweat from his top lip. He suddenly felt tired, heavy. Then he reached up and rubbed another almost healed razor scab at the crown of his head. Others dotted his bumpy skull like resinous moles, but he refused professional grooming. He liked how it disgusted Reynard and took pleasure in the horror that crept across his mother's face whenever she saw him. *'You will be no good unless you keep yourself as well as you were made. You know what happens to useless things in Lodewick?'* Her thin hand had fluttered at her long, elegant neck like a frightened butterfly, her tilted dark eyes, seductive like his own, were wide with an anxiety she knew intimately, but could not share.

He tried to keep his thoughts reasonable, but a deep unease settled on him like a shroud of sad and before he could stop himself, he said bitterly, 'Is this what it looked like without the fake Micah running around carrying that dwarf, you know, the one you dressed like a child?' He imagined he saw his father's hair stand on end and could have sworn he heard him growl in the back of his throat. Out of the corner of his eye he caught Weasel bite the malicious grin from his bottom lip while he continued to look studiously at the uprising on the screen.

'Why couldn't he have become The Lord of Galay? Just take what was his by birth right; it was the only place in the world where I saw him be genuinely happy.' He turned his attention to Leleth, but she studied the bottom of her glass and would not meet his eye.

'Why would Lord Abrecan place a king of Bucky's making to the North, Troy? Bucky's popularity is already hard for him to stomach, he would not tolerate The Sun in Winter on the throne at Galay.' Reynard dismissed him with an arrogant snap.

'Why are you quoting a mad woman's prophecy as if it were true?' He raised his voice. He did not want to let this go, not this time. He met his mother's eyes over Reynard's shoulder, and he could see a plea in them. Though it only served to fester his hatred to boiling point.

'Have you been in my study, Troy?' he asked suspiciously.

He saw his mother's hand flutter to her throat. She twitched her head, and he took a deep breath before he replied with all the disdain he could muster, 'No, why would I want to bore myself with what you read when I can visit a poet in one of the salons in Boho for fantastical adventures. Now, he makes claim that he is inspired by the chronicles of a mad seer of old. His work is romantic, imaginary of course, but hardly thought-provoking.'

Leleth visibly sagged and gulped at her wine as if it were the last water on the planet.

Reynard's lips curled into a condescending snarl. 'This is not wise,' he snapped while he took his index finger and stabbed it in the air above Troy's chest, pointing to the green tailcoat. 'He is Conquest, and if he thinks you and your sop friends' clothes are a new rebellion, he will quash that too. He will grind it under the heel of his contempt. Not you, you understand. It is never *you*,' he spat out the words, 'but every tailor, mender, textile merchant, and button maker. He will take them all, and he will name them insurgents.' He paused then pointed to his own chest and thumbed towards Weasel while he said in a voice that was no more than a whisper, 'He will leave it to us to clean up your mess.' He left his sentence hanging in the air, they all knew what that meant, and Troy dropped his head when a sheet of red hot shame swept across his face.

Reynard studied him, as if he were a carcass he had been asked to marry, before he turned to Weasel and said coolly, 'Rodney, you will drive me to the Fifth Tower. Leleth.' He strode over to Leleth and air-kissed the top of her head. She rose gracefully when he took her offered hand and replied, 'I will be in my sitting room should you need me.'

'Have you finished the maintenance plan? I cannot keep the large sewers closed forever. You might want to live in shit like the swine that you are, but the rest of us…' he barked at Troy over his shoulder, his words fading while he escorted Leleth to her sitting room.

'I've been too busy fucking pigs in the mire,' Troy shouted back. Then added, 'I will do them now, just leave me alone, do you hear. All of you, leave me alone.' He tried to slam the huge wooden door and failed, so he faked stomping away and returned up the stairs with so many airs and graces he almost flew. He hid at the top of the stairs and took sharp gasps of air to steady his nerves. He put both of his shaking hands under his armpits and nursed an oily ball of seething emotion in his guts until it was calm and set like a layer of grease on top of freezing water, while he watched Weasel and his father leave.

He resisted the urge to run when he returned to his rooms, if the caller were so desperate to talk to him, she would wait, he felt certain of that. He closed the door and locked it, then turned his attention to the maps that he had laid out on his desk, a wry smile twisted his mouth. He had been given a mountain of paper, and maps to work through. Boxes of the stinking stuff, which mapped the sewers of Lodewick as if they were diagrams of the snarly intestines and belly of a great beast, but inside a worn leather tube rolled within two maps was a tissue thin piece of yellowed paper. Sketched in charcoal were the chaotic angles, twists, and turns of deeper levels of tunnels. The labyrinth ways of secret places hidden beneath the monolith, Lodewick. A map, which had been hastily drawn, and titled *The Well of The World* in spidery writing, noted "dead end," "deep water not accessible," "lost a man here, no body found," "dangerous levels of Ectoplasm," and finally, "beware Bloodgita's bitches."

He ran a finger over it and imagined that if there was anything else down there it was sealed like a tomb, crushed beneath the metropolis above. But why map it? Why hide the map? It was intriguing and he liked to imagine that there was somewhere below Lodewick, The Well of The World, a better place. Studying the maps and imaging secret underworlds had helped him to hide from the horror of Micah's death. It was a place to escape to, even if it was in his head, while his mind unravelled, and he sought solace in droge waere. Sweaty, gibbous addiction, droge waere that burned, droge waere that numbed, droge waere that stole his mind. The worse was the Memorigi oil and the places it took him inside his head, while he marionetted through his shadow-life, stiff and frozen like a puppet all the way to his core. His usage eventually reached an alarming high, as he sought to join his friend in the hereafter but like the maps he studied, he could not find the way in, and eventually even Weasel refused to sell him enough night poppy to help him on his way and his words when they came had a stab of truth to them. 'You're a craven hearted fuck, Valoroso, but you've stared at the stars too long and the flame knows why, but it's hurting Lady Leleth.'

*

I will meet her, then I am going to ground, he thought while he folded the map carefully and put it in his inside pocket. He waited another quarter before heading back down the stairs. Weasel is a sneaky runt. It would be just like him to come back to see if I were in my room.

He put his head around the large door into his mother's sitting room. Before he could ask, Leleth said, 'Rodney will be quite some time at the castle with your father, and Lord Abrecan.' She lifted her head from a book she was reading, and he frowned while he thought, this is unusual. Why is she reading philosophy, morality, and ethics? Books she hid from his father. She closed the book quickly. Her knees were drawn up beneath her, making her seem smaller than she was. Her crimson gown pooled across the powder-blue silk sofa as if an oil slick of blood had leaked into a lake. She wore her hair curled and tied in elaborately weaved patterns on the top of her head. A large, red topaz teardrop, hung in the centre of her forehead, attached by a fine silver ring to silver diadem. Imperial jewels, for one from an imperial line, she told him once, when he was small enough to believe everything, she said. When he was small enough to believe that everyone had a cold heart, and empty stomach.

She played with the jewel between her thumb and forefinger then said, 'Do you recall the first thing you ever stole?'

He dipped his head to hide his blush but when he looked at her, she was amused rather than angry. He pointed to the red topaz jewel and said, 'It looked like a berry. I wanted to eat it.'

'I am glad you did not,' she replied, and he almost heard a laugh in her words. She smoothed her skirt as if she played for time. 'I recall I said it was your first grand theft, The Tear of Blood, and that you would go on to steal many souls.'

'Surely you meant hearts,' he replied. Then he folded his arms over his chest while he thought, what is wrong with her, she never speaks of my childhood. He studied her until she picked up her book and began flicking the pages back and forth impatiently.

'Your secret is safe with me,' he said dryly and nodded toward the book.

She half-laughed, not a full bellied laugh, she had never had one, but dry and arid. A starved laugh as if she were unsure what to do with the warm feeling of mirth she had suddenly found in her stomach. She looked set to say something then thought better of it and said instead, 'And yours with me.' Then she lifted the book slightly and added, 'He keeps the best ones in a secret compartment under the window seat in his study. You may find them interesting.'

They shared something then, for what seemed like the first time ever. It was not love, but a kind of understanding. One where they both knew where the invisible bars of their prison were. A solidarity between two inmates, both as foul as one another, but still not as foul as their gaoler, and none of them worse than Lord Lucas Abrecan.

'You won't be…' she trailed off and a puzzled look crossed her thin perfect face. Her eyes pooled, suddenly illuminated against her milky white skin and she gasped and patted her heart.

Troy paused and narrowed his eyes. He wanted to ask her what was wrong, but he could not find the words and was afraid of her answer should she tell him the truth. Instead, he said, 'I won't be whatever it is I should not be, and I will be careful.'

She nodded and spoke in a hushed voice that held a note of fear. 'Yes…you should be. Be incredibly careful.' She patted the centre of her chest again and a look of complete consternation fled across her face, then with a look of utter confusion she began thumbing through the book furiously. Clearly dismissed, he closed the door and left immediately for the silk warehouse.

~ ❖ ~ ❖ ~ ❖ ~

He ran skinny fingers over his shaved head, sluicing off the greasy wet and regretted not having enough hair to at least absorb it as he peered cautiously down the derelict street. It was so cold the air purled from his mouth like silver smoke and had dewed on his crown from the heat from his skull. The silk warehouse was in the Copa Nordende quarter, the northern district for silk and textile merchants. It still looked like a war zone even though the silk warehouse had been tiers away from Athanasius Blood's slaughterhouse. When the night of the dead went up, it had truly gone up. Light, I was lucky he did not kill me. Why didn't Abrecan kill me? He killed anybody else he could get his hands on, including Micah.

What was left of the silk warehouse was skeletal, empty, and abandoned. Its roof and face had been blown off, finding their way to the bottom of the quarry behind the building. The remaining wall where the painted doors had been, were jagged and ruinous. The doors had been ripped to shreds. Troy sighed and wiped at his eyes. He was half expecting to see him, that grotesque portrait of King Micah, the flaming Sun in Winter, Lord of Galay, gigantic and smiling beneficently while his eyes were afire and harder than anarchy. He was half glad he had died at the tribal; if Abrecan had gotten hold of him, he would have ripped his heart out of his chest and ate it whole.

'There's nothing bloody left, all dead or derelict. Like my heart,' he whispered, then jumped when a soft voice said, 'Ah there you are, sweet thing, thank you for meeting me.' Her arm threaded its way through his and she guided him away from the alley and the destroyed building. To anyone who observed, they looked like a young couple on a romantic rendezvous, though there was something hard and cunning about Tranquillity that set his teeth on edge. Is she going to kidnap me he thought, and a sting of fear passed quickly through his gut? He could not put on his brass knuckles. Would I want to hit her he thought? Then felt the throwing dagger at his ankle rub like a stick against his skin, far away from his hand, and only good for causing a blister on his ankle. Likewise, the stiletto down the back of his breeches, if he made a move for it, he suspected it would be his last.

They walked slowly along the deserted road, moving through clouds of stinking greasy vapour that rose from iron vents. Heat and fumes hissed as if a beast was trapped in the bowels of Lodewick, and fluorescent shrooms bloomed in shades of vomit green, sulphur yellow, and Tuatahi pink, so named for the colour of the porcelain made on one of the southern isles. They grew from the walls like rounded steps, garish, and vile. They grew all year round and had survived the winter of Bucky's sorrow, when other plants, animals and people had not. Slimy rivulets were frozen solid and encrusted with lurid green minerals, which ran back towards the vents as if the walls had snotty noses. Troy shuddered and brought his neckerchief up around his mouth and nose; shrooms were thought to be responsible for yellow lung and proliferated in the poorest areas of Lodewick, but then again so did a lack of food and physicks. He was not about to take any chances; if he died, it would be as a hero, in a blaze of glory all hot and dry, not bed-bound, soiling himself while he coughed yellow mucus and his innards up.

'We should watch our tongues, and our behaviour here…we need to get off the streets. They have eyes everywhere, as you know.' She squeezed his arm.

'Where then?' He mumbled through the material around his face. He resisted the urge to pull his arm away, but he knew better than to cause a scene on a street in Lodewick. There were eyes everywhere, especially after the Night of the Dead uprising. His own gaze casually traced the line of the eaves of a nearby building.

They were heading away from the front of the cliff buttress. Most of the routes towards the hairpin bends that led to other tiers were still impassable to vehicles and dangerous for pedestrians. Ah there, he thought as he spied the globe of the eye and the faint halo of its strange blue alchemical light, just under the eaves of a wooden warehouse and above a large painting of his Divinity Lord Abrecan. He shuddered and hurried on; Tranquillity took his lead. It was not the sort of area you would want to be found in after curfew siren without the permits to be out. 'We'll pick up a rickshaw at one of the Cheapside markets,' he said quietly and turned his head slightly to Tranquillity.

'We'll head to SoSo,' she replied, and her voice sounded determined.

He groaned inwardly, he hated the municipal nature of the central entertainment and pleasure zones. They were usually full of merchants or guild apprentices, too much carnival and not enough culture, he thought dolefully. There were much nicer areas to hang out in – the artisan district of Little Bohemia where artists, poets and musicians lived. It was one of Micah's favourite zones. According to Micah the whores there were honest, not like the loose legs in the Bliones Tun. Although they still called themselves courtesans and muses, their trade was honest flesh work, not loose-lipped, secret-spilling. He felt his throat tighten. It was always an unexpected memory that stabbed him in the heart, a sharp fleeting pain like a rapier had been pushed through his ribs then pulled out quickly. Micah fondly called the zone Boho. He was about to protest but held his tongue when he recalled that Tranquillity would not be allowed in; it was only accessible by two fortified bridges, it was only for the elite. The bridge that led from the west and the docks, was wider and made for the transportation of goods and wares. It spanned a deep shaft of a shadowy circular ravine with raw sewerage running from open drains down its sides, precarious ledges jutted like ragged shark teeth, they were where Fire Drake raised their whelps in the Summer. The Merewif bridge, was adorned by the Sisters of Bloodgita with bodies hanging by their necks from its balustrades, it was commonly called the witch's bridge. The Merewif was the name also given to the pit of water below it, that sprung up through the rock from the sea. The Merewif was rumoured to be bottomless, and lightless, an abyss of watery matter, blacker that the surface stone of the bridge which spanned it. The black granite bridge had checkpoints at portcullises set in the abutments at either end. A crenelated citadel squatted at its apex. The Black Bridge was the domain of the ochre robed Sisters of

Bloodgita The Effusive. A particularly vicious band of Acolytes of Anuk who venerated the feminine aspect of the One-God.

From the east, Boho was reached by a Whitestone bridge called Silver Seaf, its elegant arches spanned a reservoir of fresh water called Seaf Lake. The Silver Seaf bridge was guarded by proc city guards, from a single checkpoint at its eastern entrance which led to the Elite residential areas. Boho, he decided was not for her kind. He studied his own wrist and wondered whether it was for his kind anymore, while he imagined a sister of Bloodgita chopping off his hand when he failed to pass their scan.

Her arm felt like a shackle while it threaded through his. It was warm and muscular, a fighter's arm, not a goodwife or a domestic. She was not humble or invisible enough for that; a servant would never have dared call him, using a stolen mo that had belonged to Micah, she was clearly on a death wish as great as his own. His tongue stuck to the roof of his mouth, and he thought suspiciously is she a Romarii! Light, am I really being kidnapped? Death wish be damned. He did not want to die under an umbrella of festering shrooms, robbed blind, and lords only knew what else down a back alley in the Cheapside. He coughed, then he spluttered, and her arm tightened on his own. 'Come on, we can ride the pipe. We'll head over the Dyer cat span.' She paused, then said softly, 'I take it you aren't afraid of heights. Then we'll take the pipe from Breakers Yard.'

She will either kill me or take me to Micah, if, he is still alive he thought while his gut clenched and something icy and sharp raked along his spine. 'Am I being kidnapped?'

'Breakers Yard stop is just around this corner, fuckwit.' A huff of steamy breath clouded out of her hood then she tilted her head forward and grimaced while she looked at his tailcoat. 'Here, you'll need to wear this.' She took off her top cloak and gave it to him. It was brown, rough homespun, beneath it she wore another one, exactly, the same. He brought it to his nose instinctively. She screwed her mouth up and huffed down her nose sending her breath curling from her nostrils like dragon smoke. He put it on without another word.

Outside the station several bodies hung from a wall, their heads were covered in cloth bags and their hands were in baskets beneath them with a placard that said 'Thief' and one that said, 'Liar.' Beneath it someone had added, 'False and cultish claim to Worldbridger power,' another said, 'Removed Nano to hide Storm power.' They did that to avoid deportation to one of Volsunga's factory cities he thought, while he glanced quickly at a clutch of Acolytes of Anuk, dressed in the purple robes of The Brotherhood of Perpetual Pain. They waited with their meat barrows while two Merchant Guild Guards took the bodies down. They were fresh hangings, and the corpses would be taken to the Temple of Perpetual Pain, their organs would be harvested, and the bodies bled there. Troy pulled up the hood of his cloak and lowered his gaze, noting the metal cuff that gave them regular rubicity shocks, wrapped around each acolyte's ankle, while he shuffled past with the crowd. No one stopped to look and when he sought Tranquillity she had disappeared, she had blended invisibly into the crowd of brown cloaked drudgery.

They will be making their miserable way back to hovel-town, he thought and kept his kerchief over his nose. She materialised next to him when he was eyeing an almost empty merchant-class carriage, well-lit with lamps that glowed with alchemical blue light, softened by viridian glass shades. Small booths that lined one side of the carriage were attended by servers with silver coffee pots and fancy cakes on shining trays. Troy cursed silently and whispered, 'Why couldn't we have pretended to be merchants on our way back from the Cheapside docks?'

'No permits, that's why.' She bundled him along and into the domestic carriage. The train ran on animal waste fuel; it was raw. Sometimes they ran on charcoal or water hyacinth briquettes, but this was not that train, it was not that time of night. Tranquillity looked down her nose at him and wondered when he would hurl.

The lowers' carriage had a roof and seats, cheap seats, but was open at the sides and he spent the whole journey covering his mouth with a silk neckerchief while smoke that stunk like silage curled thickly alongside the carriage and invaded the space like poison mist. He tried to study Tranquillity Maegdelan, through the smoke and stink but she breathed normally and studied him right back, all the way down her slightly large nose. Infuriating, Troy thought, she knows I am about to vomit.

~ ❀ ~ ❀ ~ ❀ ~

'Here, this is on me.' Tranquillity pushed a steaming mug of Chib toward Troy. He studied it and said, 'What is it?'

'It's made from chicory and barley. Chib,' she said and raised her eyebrows. It was dark and bitter, not like the coffee he was used to drinking which Reynard had imported from the Southern Isles. It came in hessian sacks, all aromatic and smelling of the sun. 'My father had coffee at dinner once that had been shit by a cat or something like that.' He paused while she guffawed and he added quickly, 'I didn't try it.'

Tranquillity put her head to one side and said, 'No matter which way you look at it, if it came out of an animal's arse, then it's dung.' He grunted his agreement and lifted the drink to his mouth while he imagined it tasted just like the Chib. The only difference he thought, is the price vanity places on something.

'Are you from round here?' he asked while he held his mug between his filthy hands and wondered where the conversation would go.

'Once, but no...' Her dark optics were pushed back on her head, and she studied Troy through narrowed eyes. They gleamed like cool green glass. A ring of fiery amber ran all the way around the edge of her pupil. It was so unusual; not beautiful but strange, as they mocked him over the top of her mug of Chib. 'I'm deciding how much I can trust you, how much I can tell you, Troy Valoroso-Wyburn.' She slurped at her Chib.

No manners at all he thought and shuddered but said, 'You can't trust me.'

Tranquillity snorted. 'That's good. As long as we understand each other.' She ran her gaze over the young man before her and could not help but feel for him, a little. His friend's apparent death had been hard on him. He was skeletal, his eyes were bruised and hollow, and his head was like a slashed giant fuzzy fruit that rested precariously on top of a stick thin neck. 'Dobrogost!' She raised her hand politely.

He studied the sweaty chib and bun shop while she called to the owner. They sat in a rectangle of a room at the front of the building, it had a high vaulted ceiling. A bakery stood beyond a strange glassy wall at the back of the Chib shop. A blackboard next to the door held a list of items available and the coppers needed to purchase them. There are no nano device transactions here at the end of civilisation, he thought sourly and rubbed his wrist.

A huge man, who he had noticed standing behind the tall wood-panelled counter when they entered, nodded. He had been so still until that point, as if he needed to compensate for the oppressive nature of his bulk, a difficult thing to ignore, but it was not what he had noticed first. It was the way he held his head – at a very slight angle like he was thinking about a great mystery that only he could solve. Despite his size, he walked lightly over to take their order. His eyes were obscured by a low brow that resembled a cliff edge.

'Yuh?' His mouth hardly moved.

There was too much muscle on his forearms and beneath his shirt, slabs of it rippled and twitched beneath skin that was patterned by ugly scars, silvered with age, but some resembled claw marks. He had his sleeves rolled up and wore an apron that was dusty with flour. What an unlikely baker Troy thought, then shuddered when he glowered at him.

'Couple of sweet bread buns would be nice. Thank you.'

'Chiko…Chiko, couple of sweet buns over here.' He returned to his position behind the counter and began polishing cutlery. A girl with skin like hazelnut shells and a fizz of curly blonde hair, brought over two bread buns and refilled their mugs from a steaming hot jug of Chib. 'Anything else, Tra—'

Tranquillity cut her off, 'No thank you – that will be all.'

Troy took a bite of the bun and leaned against an ornate metal pipe. Thicker than two men, it protruded from the thick glassy wall next to his seat. It felt surprisingly warm. 'What's this for?' he asked while he stroked it. It looked ancient. The metal was so distorted and lumpy it was like it was made from pewter scales.

'Don't know, old pipes, who cares?' She shrugged coolly, and he pulled his eyes away from it. The pipe reminded him of an animal, a serpent, but Tranquillity tapped him on his hand before he could follow his train of thought.

'Can I trust you?' Tranquillity whispered and her voice was serious.

'Probably not,' Troy whispered back. 'Though that may depend on what you want.' He raised his eyebrows.

'You're making this difficult. Here, take this.' Tranquillity pushed a mo over the table.

He picked it up, inspected it, then put it down and pushed it away with his finger. 'So, what? It's a model from about what…ten, maybe twelve moons ago?'

'Yes, it is.' She smiled and tapped it with a finger. 'It's Micah's old mo. Check the contacts. It's how I got your sequence.' She leaned back on her chair, her cloak lay across the back, and put her hands behind her head and stretched. She pushed her chest forward while a triumphant look filled her gaze.

Troy gulped and tried not to stare when he saw the shape of her breasts beneath her linen shirt – the small bump of her nipples. He pulled his gaze away then searched through the contacts; she was right, it was all there. His sequence, Weasel's, Micah's father, Lord Bucky who he had entered as, Favourite Bastard's, Father. Troy smiled, then shook his head sadly while he scrolled quickly through the numbers. What he was looking for was not there. He was looking for Daboath. He was clutching at straws.

'It's under C…if you are looking for,' she shrugged then added, 'He's under C for Crow. The sequence is corvine.' She reached across and held Troy's wrist. He felt her gently massage the area where his implant was. 'Now, can we talk?'

'How much do you want for it?' Troy checked under C. Crow. Two sequences, one a sequence of runic symbols that represented corvine, the other he could not work out. I will try them later. She might be messing with me still, but it is worth a try.

'We'll come to that later. Troy, my name is Tranquillity Maegdelan. I work in service at Lord Bucky's with my friend Homily, who…who Micah…' she trailed off, lost for the words that would describe what Micah had done.

'I know, I saw – I remember that bit, but how did you get this? Did you steal it?' he asked with more interest as he tapped the phone with a thin finger.

'No, we did not, well, not at first. I will try to keep it brief…I am a room maid at Bucky's city residence. Homily is in the kitchens. We get all the rubbish jobs no one else wants, including cleaning and keeping the candles lit in the room where he was brought to.' She paused and took a drink.

Troy nodded. 'Go on.' Though I do not believe you he thought, while he tried to imagine her with a duster and mop.

'They brought him back to the palace. Bucky was out of town; he had been celebrating the joyful harvest after the Night of the Dead, in his province Eirini, at the Caislean Gairdin, but was coming back to Lodewick.

'I was ordered to his room and antechamber to clean and make it presentable, light the candles – the usual stuff that needs to happen for the Before the Tears, and the After the Tears ceremonies. My friend Homily was obsessed with him, I'm sure that's why she took a job there in the kitchens. We share quarters, you know, so I can tell you there wasn't anything she didn't know about Micah.'

He held his urgency in check although he wanted to reach forward and shake the information from her.

'Homily begged me to let her in, to see the body, grotesque and weird, but that's a fanatic, I suppose. I agreed, and we snuck down in the early hours; there wasn't a soul about. We went to the kitchens first, you know, on the pretence of lighting more candles and filling the lamps with oil. She walked behind me carrying an armload of flowers of the sun that had arrived earlier that day. She was determined she would be the one to lay them around his body first and get all maudlin, no doubt. She hadn't stopped her howling since we'd heard.'

'He was my friend,' Troy said sharply.

'Oh sorry, I'll keep it respectful then, shall I? I filled the lamps, scattered scented oils, relit candles, and Homily went to the bier where he was laid out. He looked like a god. They had put a circlet of gold around his head with this large bright jewel at the centre – worth a small fortune no doubt.' She paused when she noticed Troy tense. 'And he had the most beautiful white, gold, and yellow silk robes on. Open at his chest, they flowed like liquid solar light down each side of the bier. He glowed, truly he did.' She dropped her head, and a small frown wrinkled her brow. Troy tensed again. What had happened to the pendant and the data?

Tranquillity continued. 'He had been dusted with gold and treated with oils too, he was aglow in the soft light like the sun was inside him, but when Homily finished laying the flowers around him, she went to kiss his forehead then shrieked. "It's not him Tranquil, this isn't him." Well, I nearly…'

He reached over the table slowly. He held Tranquillity's gaze and his dark eyes glittered like two tilted shards of malevolence, flashing with red like only ironstone can. Swift as a blade scything grass, he grabbed both of her wrists and pulled her towards him. 'If you are lying to me, I swear, I will kill you.'

'Get off, why would I, you bloody psycho. Let me finish…it was the tattoo on his chest. She had a good look at it that night when he got close to her. She had gotten over her shock at her encounter with her superstar and was back in love with him by the time we had walked a few miles, knew that tatt in the greatest of detail and went on about it all the way back. It was a tri-fold heart, designed around an accurate tatt of an organic heart – never seen anything as beautiful, she said.

'She took me to the body. I had not seen the original and to be honest, I did doubt her at first. She was very grieved over him, but according to her, whoever had done the tatt, had missed one of the hearts. It wasn't tri-fold, just a double around the organic one at the centre of his chest.'

'And you believe this? Is she absolutely sure? Where's the proof?' Troy asked sharply. Tranquillity shrugged and took another sip of her Chib while Troy resisted the urge to throttle her. What in the hells is she playing at?

'Look here, I remember the tatt myself, so you better not be bluffing me. What proof do you have anyway?' He felt disappointing bile rise. Micah was dead, and he was trapped in Tota Zone with the crazy accomplice of Micah's super fanatic. Are they going to kidnap or kill me? he wondered as he tried to look around without raising suspicion. Everything looked normal. The chib shop was empty. It was getting late, and it was dark outside, the thick glass of the window was misted with steam inside and outside slushy rain fell against it and silvered down like starlight shedding tears. The giant behind the counter was cleaning the work tops; the pipe he leaned against groaned, an empty sort of reverberation, just like his heart.

'Here,' Tranquillity tossed him a folded piece of expensive paper with Bucky's crest on it. 'When we got back that night…you know, before the body arrived…she sketched it out, wanted to get one for herself, but how they'd get that delicate design across her big brown tits is beyond me. But I am telling you this, Homily was a bloody expert on him. Paper's a perk of the job,' she added before continuing, 'I am not being gross, but we checked whether the tatt was freshly done, but he'd had that much oil and gold dust applied, we couldn't tell, then…' she trailed off looking for the right words, 'we, ermm.' She paused and took a gulp of her chib then said quickly, 'We took them after the fact. Right. Before I show you them…we did not go in with the intention of recording his dead body; I'm no weird super fan, despite what this looks like, but look in the gallery. I lifted the mo, from his personals in his room.'

Troy narrowed his eyes. She looked slightly abashed which did not suit her he thought. His hand started to shake while he picked the mo up. His mind reeled with possibilities; what if I look in the gallery and I just know it is really him. Despite what she says, I know he is dead and never coming back? Just say I look and know that he is not dead at all but was carried away by a flock of gigantic horrors. Hell fire…will this nightmare ever end? His breath sounded ragged, and he had to breathe deeply past a lump in his throat. He found the crystal pip on the side of the mo and pressed. Then taking his thumb he pushed it into an indent at the bottom of the mo, the alchemical charge needed to release the images from the recordkeeper crystal would have to be taken from his princeps pollicis artery. They were a new alchemical invention, no more than a decade old, and had been called portable mouths at first, but that had soon been replaced with, mo. Although Micah had insisted on calling them potty mouths for longer than was necessary, even after it should have stopped being funny, he had still laughed. His eyes stung with the memory, and he blew air through his lips until they vibrated, until he was sure he was not going to weep.

Tranquillity continued talking as if she were aware that he was struggling with some inner conflict, which she needed to get him past; much depended on this going well. 'Micah was laid out in the antechamber. I trust Hom enough to know that something was wrong, so I slipped into his chambers…and well, you know…people buy information. I knew you'd been with him that night…so, I rummaged in his drawers, found the mo, and took that image, and well…you know the rest.' She shrugged and ignored Troy's look of utter repulsion while she thought, he needs to give himself a good look over in the mirror and get himself dried out before he looks down his wonky nose at me, that is why he can't smell himself, lucky for him. 'He was dead, he didn't mind that I looked through his personals. Actually, I reckon he didn't give a fuck about his good side and the lighting.' She raised her eyes to the ceiling and resisted the urge to give him a good slap. Sensitive bloody elite.

Troy struggled to analyse the possibilities; hunger and thirst and grief had numbed him. He stalled for time…finished his Chib slowly and took a bite out of his sweet bread bun – it was good, he thought – while he waited for the image to flicker then take shape on the blue screen.

Homily was right, even though his skin shone with oil and gold dust, the tattoo was different. They had missed one of the hearts that enclosed the organic heart at the centre of his chest. He looked closely; was the design just covered in gold? No. Whoever it was, looked exactly like him – facially, hair, weight or lack of it, all angles and slat ribs, jaunty hips, soft full lips, and good cheekbones. He had been oiled and dusted with gold and that was what had helped with the disguise. It had been good enough to fool everyone at his Tears Ceremonies, including Reynard, who never failed to spot a flaw or an opportunity to fall further into Abrecan's good graces. How hadn't Bucky known? he wondered while he checked the image of the corpse again. suddenly he knew deep inside his heart that Bucky had known. He had to.

'If it hadn't been for the tatt, would you and your friend have known it wasn't him?' He asked Tranquillity while his dirty fingers caressed the screen, his thoughts felt like they had been sucked into the vacuum of the blackest night, difficult to see or order, while he tried to analyse the information he had. It was proving to be troublesome, especially with those judging, green-glass eyes staring at him, down her slightly long, but I suppose elegant nose, he thought.

'No, definitely not. Whoever that is in the picture, they were exactly like him.' She pointed at the mo.

Troy struggled to accept that it was not Micah. The corpse was his double, although he could not see what colour the eyes were, they had been closed, but the truth of the tattoo could not be denied. He picked up his mug, not sure what to do, but then stopped – it was empty. 'If that is not him, then who is it? Poor suck…' he said almost to himself while he wondered whether it was another of Bucky's bastards or perhaps a vanity modification. Lords of the Light Flame, help me he prayed when he realised deep in his gut that if it was a vanity mod then it had all been planned. Just like the final act he thought, and his heart caved in. All he had the energy to do was continue to study the photo and push away the wasteland that his life had become.

He massaged his temples again and his attention was drawn to the large yellow and gold striped petals of the gigantic heads of the flowers of the sun, special flowers for a special person. The centre of the flowers were shaped like a heart, full of round black glassy seeds that looked like beads made of jet. They were used to make one of the most expensive oils on the planet. They surrounded the body, in an explosion of yellow, gold, and black, around the shimmering golden corpse. 'When did you say the flowers arrived, Tranquillity?' He reached up and scratched his head, felt another scab come away under his fingernail – he hoped that it was healed underneath.

'Same day he came home, but earlier that afternoon. He was released soon after Reynard Wyburn identified him, prepared somewhere else, then brought home maybe just after lunch time, but certainly before afternoon tea and put on the bier in his antechamber. It was that afternoon when the flowers arrived; we got them out of the cold store in the cellar that night. Why?'

'Because who orders funeral flowers for someone who is still alive. These are extremely rare flowers, you know, from overseas. They take an age to get here, even by airship. Longer by sea.' Troy continued to analyse the situation. 'Why would his father order his funeral flowers, say what…two or three days before he died?' he asked Tranquillity.

'Oh, they weren't from Lord Bucky, not from his father,' she said matter-of-factly, the orange nimbus around her green iris flared and she added coolly, 'Troy, they were from yours. They were from Fox Enterprises, isn't that your dad's operation?'

'How do you know that?' he gasped while his heart hammered against his chest. Anukssake, who and what was she? Suddenly, she was more dangerous than he had ever anticipated. Fool that he was, he was being interrogated, interviewed, but for what. Did they know about the data? Why in the hells had this happened? Where was Micah? Who was that in the photo? What had happened to the pendant? He felt a wave of giddy dizziness push against him but grabbed the edge of his seat – he was not going to pass out in front of her. Lords only knew, she would rob him blind and take an image of it.

'Two thumb presses,' she said and waited while he pressed, and the image changed. It was an image of Homily. Her soft brown skin looked like it had been dusted with ash, such was her pallor. She was red eyed, and her face was streaky with tears. She held a document. It was an order reference and invoice. He studied the area around her. She stood just inside a huge cold store, typical of the type in the kitchens of palaces and grand houses – there was one in his own mansion. Behind, he could see rows of food, fruit, cheeses, and vegetables – what remained of a crate of flowers of the sun. The order had been raised by a certain R.W, on the evening of the launch party.

He read the slip of paper Homily held. 'Invoice R.W. of Fox Enterprises.' RW? Reynard Wyburn? Rodney Weaselton? Bloody Weasel, but why? Because I hate him more than Father? No, he thought, I hate them both equally.

'Flowers of the Sun from the Commonwealth of Turanga. Shipped from the Isle of Kazamuki, YCS, EM 13,' Troy read aloud. 'It's Yellow Cosmic Sun, Electric Moon, 13, the night of the launch party. Light, the commonwealth is the most easterly of islands in the Southern Isles. I have not even heard of Kazamuki. Whoever RW is, they ordered these while Micah was still alive,' he finished flatly and the silence between them stretched on until he said, 'I need your help. I need to disappear, Tranquillity.'

'Please call me Tranquil. As do we, Troy. What can you get Homily and me? No silly offers, I know what this is worth,' she tapped the mo, 'and…' she stared hard at Troy, her wide mouth narrowed into a thin humourless line, 'also what you're worth.'

A sudden chill spread up his spine which terrified him and excited him more than any droge waere he had ever taken. She is dangerous he thought, I was right, and I am also right not to trust her fully.

'We've got papers and passage on a ship out of here, it leaves in the small hours, and we need to be on it.' She pulled the mo back towards her.

He slid his eyes towards the door. He had already marked the exits: one at the front of the shop, another behind where he sat in front of the pewter piping which encircled the wall of opaque glass – through its whorled surface, he could just see the exit to the street, blurred through the thick glass wall, but it was there, standing slightly ajar. The tradesman's entrance for the bakery in the back of the building.

He would need to push her out of the way, feign towards the front exit but take the door near the counter through to the bakery and then out of the exit there. His eyes slid here and there, marking time and passage, while he wondered if he should just reach across, take it, and run. He favoured the back exit as they would not expect that, it was closer, it was free of tables and chairs blocking the way. Sweat beaded across his forehead.

Rasp, shuwsh, rasp, shuwsh, rasp, methodical metal being run against stone, the sound of a knife being expertly sharpened towards his left shoulder made him hesitate. He did not look around; he did not need to. The tiny downy hairs at the nape of his neck stood up and they were all the warning he needed. A slick of sweat oiled his palms. His breath became shallow. His hand twitched involuntarily. 'Fair enough. Leave it with me. I will get you the equivalent of an elite's ransom.' Troy shrugged casually as he hatched another plan that did not involve a knife in his back in a chib and bun shop in the rear end of hope. He leaned over the small table, then whispered the amount he was willing to pay. Tranquillity put her hand on his arm and Troy prepared himself for her to whisper her agreement.

'You will bring me a king's ransom, then you will ensure you do not insult me ever again with such a stupid offer, or I may take one of your body parts to compensate for your lack of understanding.' He was about to protest but she squeezed his bicep hard until he almost yelped. 'This trade is for your friend's life, how dare you cheapen it so…As I said, I know what you are worth, and you will bring it all…Do I make myself clear?'

'Who in the hells are you?' He hissed while he pulled away. 'I will bring the amount I have in the Merchant Bank, which is what I assume you refer to?'

'Perfect. Make sure payment is in Baelmonarchian Crollar from the Temple of The Needful Scrip. No silver bars, or gold regals, vellum only.' Tranquillity smiled thinly.

His knees had turned to water, but he decided not to get to his feet, while he stole a glance at the enormous bulk of muscle behind the counter, the baker she had called Dobrogost who stood in graceful repose. Rasp, shuwsh, rasp, shuwsh, rasp, his head slightly to one side. Beneath the cliff of his eyebrows, he stared back at Troy without blinking, cold and hard as he lifted his chin and grunted. A knowing look passed between them, and it ripped Troy's elite veneer away and bared his shady soul.

In Dobrogost's mind, Troy was an open but thin book, easily and quickly read, every ill deed that was recorded there, had already been executed by the man with the knife, and many more besides. It was as Dobrogost had thought, no surprises; he would not have made it to either door, not without two or three knives in his back.

He is listening. Somehow that brute can hear...vaulted ceiling...of course, and that does not look like a bread knife either. Troy frowned. *Who in the hells are these people?* he thought while he took out his mo and called the Merchant Bank of Baelmonarchia, never closed to the elite, who never knew when they might need a large withdrawal.

'It will take a few horas; I have to collect some things,' he spoke softly to Tranquillity, aware of Dobrogost's flapping ears.

'I cannot miss the ship at dawn. It is an old steamer that carries animals. It will be in and out with the tide. They will not want to pay extra if they miss the tide. Here is the berth number, it's docked at Livestock Wharf.' She passed him a slip of paper. 'Show that to the wharf master, he will let you pass,' she smiled sweetly and thumbed to herself then said, 'And Troy, you will have to be quick if you want this.' She took the mo and pulling the neck of her tunic down, she deposited it between her breasts.

Troy gulped. 'I will have to get back on the pipe. I cannot risk calling for a car,' he said while he kept his eyes firmly on her chest; well, it was his soon-to-be property that she had down there, he had a right to keep an eye on it.

Tranquillity nodded nonchalantly. 'Well, don't let me keep you.'

He rose and bowed his head slightly, more than a gesture of politeness from him to one from her station. *She should be honoured and impressed,* he thought. 'If you'll excuse me.'

She tutted and flapped her hand at him while not meeting his gaze. He turned and left, avoiding eye contact with Dobrogost. His knees felt stronger now and he had no desire to undo that. *At last, he was going to get Micah and the data back...and there are some things I want from Reynard's secret little stash too* he thought as he oiled out into the night.

Chapter Twenty-Nine

Bon Voyage

Troy met Homily and Tranquillity at the farthest-away part of the docks. Where the river gratefully ran out of filthy dockland as it sought the part of itself that had been separated during the great calamity, when the demon had triumphantly punched his way through the Heartland of Gaiadon and split the great River Sulis in two, renaming the once silvered water, Ophiuchus, dirty brown and riven, called in the common tongue the Serpent Bearer.

Produce went up the western River Ophiuchus by barge to Plantation – a city, built around the need to grow and harvest wood, likewise wood, and coal cargos and the goods made from them were sent south to the capitol Lodewick, or south down the Ophiuchus then west on the huge freight canal to Malice. Horses were small and used as work animals, mules were used in Plantation. Only the extraordinarily rich possessed horses to ride; only those who wanted to draw unwanted attention to themselves had Romarii horses. No produce was sent up or down the eastern branch of the River Ophiuchus. It was a pleasure area for the elites. Abrecan kept it free of all trade traffic. It was one of his main routes to the north. He was so powerful, he had command of a whole river for his own use and the use of his elite governor generals. Bucky used it to travel to Galay, and Volsunga used it to inspect the mines on the boundaries of the Flat Lands, which Lord Dolmen said was an excuse to spy.

Following the city of Plantation, the River Ophiuchus could be traced to its source in the Iron Hills, Lord Dolmen's province and the home of Dolmen's Eyrie, a fortress castle carved out of a mountain which Lord Volsunga coveted. However, before this, the main tributary of the river joined the Blood River in a confluence of water which was wide, deep, and strong. The Ophiuchus flowed southerly from the confluence while the Blood River flowed through the gorges past the Iron Hills to Wolfsea in the north. Minerals and ore from the Iron Hills often turned the water deep red, giving it the name the Blood River, which was very confusing in dry weather or the summer months, when the water was as clear and blue as the northern skies above Galay.

~ ❦ ~ ❦ ~ ❦ ~

'That's all I have in my account,' Troy said.

Homily frowned. 'All? Disgusting. Sitting in a vault when people starved or froze to death,' she huffed at him, and her breath clouded out of her nose like silver steam threading its way through the predawn light. 'Here, Tranquil, we need to half it, separate it about our persons.' Homily thrust a duffle bag at her.

Troy narrowed his eyes and studied Homily, there was just something that did not sit right with him, but which he could not put his finger on. Tranquillity was dangerous, he could feel the warning like a hot stab of adrenalin that set his nerves on edge. It excited him. He would not run from Tranquillity. He wanted her badly. She was so alive and lately he was heartsick of death, but Homily was…invisible, he thought suddenly, she is invisible to my senses – why? It is like something slips beneath her skin constantly but when I focus on it, it is not there. I cannot get a feeling, a connection to her. Every time I try, the sense I am using slips past the thing she is. Even those soft brown eyes, full lips, and big chest, am I getting a sense of an attractive woman? I should be…but she is closed he thought and frowned while he focused on Homily. Tranquillity stepped in front of him and said over her shoulder, 'You start doing it, Hom, I'll need a word with Troy.' She moved off taking Troy by the arm. 'Come with us.'

'Where to?' he asked full of curiosity but with no intention of joining them. He needed to find Daboath first, then Micah and the stolen data. Finding out Micah was not dead, well, not the dead person in the image, had created an altogether different type of mess, the type of mess that would not just disappear. He had to find him and get the data.

'Suppose there's no harm in telling you, you'll never believe me anyway. We are heading North towards Eirini. A storm is brewing Troy, a war is coming. There are places there that are safe for people like us.' She nodded towards Homily, who had stuffed the duffle bags full and was waiting patiently in the shadows of a warehouse.

'I can't, I need to find him, Tranquil. I'm really sorry you both have to go, leave here and your families…will you be safe?'

'Families?' she seemed puzzled. 'We never leave our fam—' she cut off as she shrugged. 'Don't be, it's the best thing for us. We can both see "things," and this won't protect us for much longer.' She wiggled her wrist at him. 'You'll need to be careful of your own too, their tech will eventually be able to detect fakes.'

He gasped. 'You could tell, is it that obvious?' Troy replied, worried. Curse Micah and that bloody night.

'No, not obvious at all, but I avoided checkpoints earlier, just in case yours was not as good as it should have been. Especially, the Merewif, the witches of Bloodgita would have had your hand off and you swinging from the bridge faster than you could have shouted Anukssake.'

He replied, 'I know but a slip off the Dyer cat span would have had much the same affect.'

She snorted and said, 'Try to recall all the old cat span bridges, the planks and ropes, the ones that are closed or have fallen into ruin, they are the secret routes round the city. They cannot post sentries on them all. Some are controlled by apprentice gangs, but coin always ensures safe passage. I promise you they are not interested in scanning wrists.' She paused and tapped the bangle on her wrist then said, 'This crafty little device, is made especially for the job of reading nanos...I mean to those who made it, it's not much more than a toy really, considering what else they make.' She showed him her wrist cuff. He had thought it a piece of jewellery but when he looked closer, he could see the alchemical formulae etched in the surface and the lay and type of crystals was precise rather than ornate. He paused, then took notice of her optics currently, resting on top of her head. They had several embellishments that he now suspected were not for decoration. Small dials sat innocently, like tiny golden doughnuts wrapped around the arm, no more than a half a thumb's length away from the lens, her earring, curled and looped, nestled against a messy tumble of dark hair, but he noticed how it cuffed her ear at the back then disappeared where it looked like it could be connected to her optics. He had not practiced alchemy for so long it took all his concentration to study the optics. Finally, the tiny etchings on them revealed themselves in almost invisible pale blue light. Hells, he thought, that is some serious kit.

'Troy, your friend Micah, he was a prophet you know...' she snatched him back from his reverie, 'to some folk. He was not just Bucky's favourite bastard either, he is more than that – so much more. Bucky...' her eyebrows wiggled on her forehead as she struggled to assess what information she should share, while Troy looked on and thought. Is she going to go all misty-eyed on me? But she continued, 'Bucky and his mother put a "lot" into Micah.'

'Tranquillity, hurry up, you said enough to your friend,' Homily whispered gruffly from the shadows. 'Best be careful, he's right from the rat's nest and may yet return to it.'

'I am offended, Homily, I am right here, and can hear you!' Troy hissed back towards the shadows. He thought he caught a flash of unusual violet light, two lambent jewels that soon disappeared, but pushed it to the back of his mind with the thought that if she had not made her whereabouts known by talking, she would not have existed to his senses at all. He felt his flesh creep with unease but put it down to the bone-sucking cold as the night retreated. 'What can I say, she's right,' he shrugged, 'but you already know that don't you? You know what they are like? What motivates them, how foul they are?' he asked Tranquillity.

Tranquillity nodded. 'I do, but do you fully? You a bio, Troy?'

'Why? Isn't everyone?' he asked while a perplexed look creased his brow. People could not reproduce naturally, everyone knew that; they were all bios, the mother and father's reproductive material selected and mixed externally from the host – some mothers carried their own offspring, but he had been surrogated or tanked, he was not sure and cared less, all he knew was that his mother Leleth was too thin to carry a baby.

'You'd be surprised at how some people are conceived and born, Troy…anyway, what's your signature?' Tranquillity pressed on and ignored his frown.

'Not sure, Red Hand or something,' he lied. 'But you know how it is – people think it fortuitous to have certain signatures for their offspring. Look how lucky Micah was.' He gulped past a sudden lump in his throat.

'Fortuitous? Your parents are not the type to leave such things to fortune, Troy, nor is Abrecan. Your signature, the day you were born, was chosen for a reason as was Micah's. You should think on why they were.'

Troy shrugged then continued, not wishing to be diverted any further; he still had plenty to do and could see the watery winter sun lighting up the distant horizon while mist ribboned away over the brown estuarial water. 'I might. Are you sure you'll be safe?' he asked again, surprised at how much it would mean to him if he knew for sure she would be.

'Of course, we are made of strong stuff us domestics, you know.' She gave him a peculiar look then reached into a pocket and pulled out a piece of paper. 'This is for you, you said you needed to disappear. It is a contact for the nightcrawlers. You need to talk to Eschamali or Elgenubi Zuben, no other from that tribe or you will not get in – they move about, see. I am not saying they are beyond the law, but if you keep moving for now, you will be harder to find. I mean, that's if you really need to disappear.' She looked enquiringly into Troy's eyes.

'I do,' he said with conviction. Thinking about the stolen data he had given Micah, worried him constantly. The hack had not been mentioned by his father or mother which was strange and had him wondering if he had stolen anything at all, apart from the last few decades of his best friend's life.

He shrugged. 'A dead man who is now maybe alive told me to come find him, it's time I heeded his words. Best of luck to you both, good journeying and may the sun be on your face, so the shadows fall behind,' he said softly with what he hoped was conviction and bit of romance.

He had heard Lord Bucky say that to Micah once when they were young, off to the Palace Galay, Micah's inheritance in the winter lands, to hunt and play – to be happy. Then Bucky had embraced Micah and kissed him. He had hung his head, afraid he had interrupted an intimate moment between father and son, but Bucky had come to him too, had lifted him off his feet, embraced him, kissed him on each cheek. 'You won't get any love off those parents of yours,' he had bellowed. 'Call themselves parents – Reynard more likely to rip your throat out, and stiff Lel? More likely to drink your blood, then spit it out, than give you a hug and kiss…that is what children need, hugs, love, and kisses. By the seven hells, they do not deserve you, lad, none of them do. Do you hear me? None of them do,' he shouted, and his voice was filled with such strong emotion, Micah stared at him in horror and said sharply, 'Father, you go too far.' Bucky had huffed and gusted when Micah chastised him, but he had enjoyed it all, the embrace, the kiss, the terrible behaviour. He loved Bucky and hated to think how broken he must be now. Do I tell Bucky what I know? If I tell him, I may as well sign his death warrant myself. If he had a part in it then it is a secret that he could not tell me, Micah could not share it with me. I am on my own, but where should I start?

The sun rose into a cloudless sky and the smoky cloak of the remains of the night retreated to the west. The light brushed over Tranquillity's cheek and whether it was the energy of the day of Yellow Overtone Warrior, he suddenly felt renewed, he bent forward to kiss her on the cheek. She turned at the last minute and kissed him full on the mouth. Not lingering, but he had time to feel her soft lips and taste what she had had for breakfast that morning – spiced bread and cheese with chib – before she whispered, 'Luck won't come into it. We've more money than enough, Homily has super tits and I've got this.' She took his hand and pressed it against her buttock; he squeezed it. I knew that I liked her, he thought while he enjoyed the wash of sensation tingle through his groin, she took his hand to her outer thigh.

'You know how to use it?' He laughed raising his eyebrows.

'Had lessons from the best knife-thrower in the business, 'course I do.' She only had to reach up a little way and tweaked his cheek, then she turned and walked gracefully into the shadows. 'C'mon, Hom.'

They linked arms easily. Homily seemed taller and thinner somehow. The slightly lumpy duffle bags were cast casually across their shoulders as they walked towards Livestock Wharf where the steamer was berthed. Both padded softly away with an agile grace, and an alert demeanour. Did I miss that earlier? They are like mountain cats – and as for that bump at the nape of Homily's jacket, it is a throwing knife, he thought. Not the kind of knife you get from working in service.

'Goodbye, ladies.' He waited until they looked back, then flicked his cloak out of the way and bowed elegantly, like the elite gents in Lodewick did. He heard Homily call him a 'gigantic tit-head,' and then they laughed all the way to their ship, a dual steam and sail, goods freighter, which stunk of animals. The plimsoll line nestled just above the water. She said animal cargo, but there are no noises…possibly carcasses he thought while he sniffed the air. The Elleadern Weatende, the west end quarter where the tanners, knackers, and leather craftsmen worked and lived, was close by.

He turned from the ship and began to walk back along the wharf as if he were making his way to the quayside. Why would they be taking animals back north to Eirini, such a lie, and why do I suspect they are on a smuggler's ship? He smiled and whispered, 'I really did like her – she was just my type.'

*

'Dobrogost's daughter, you're expecting me,' Tranquillity said as she alighted softly on the deck and Troy slipped back into the shadows. He heard a small plop in the water; that will be the money-case from the bank, I hope. Good, it will look like I cleared my account and disappeared at the docks, mugged, suicide. My last journey will lead anyone looking for me to wherever that case washes up. If it does at all.

He took the mo and a wad of crollar from his tailcoat, stuffed some into his breeches pockets, not tight like Spider King – he had changed when he got back to the mansion – but sensible, with many pockets and cuffed at the ankle, not as baggy as some of the sailors wore their breeches, but just as comfortable, more like the protectorate guard wore, although cut from finer cloth. He untied his ranger boots and lined the inside of his socks at the ankle with more notes which cushioned his ankle from the throwing dagger. He contemplated throwing his tailcoat into the dock. It was exceptionally fine wool and expensive. Should I keep it he thought while he ran the material through his hands then with a sigh he added, it is the most impractical thing I ever wore, and I will never get the stiletto out of that sleeve. He threw it as far as he could into the oily water of the dock and watched while it was sucked out to sea. He still had the rough homespun cloak and had a thick woollen cowl around his neck instead of his silk neckerchief, and a dark fustian jumper on beneath what he thought was a craftsman's or smith's leather doublet, which he filched from one of the servants. That would have to do until he could replace them with something better. In a fit of guilt, he had left a silver bar where the clothes had been, more than enough to replace them and it was the type of money the lowers used. If he had left crollar they would not have been able to spend them, paper money was the currency of the Elite. It was highly decorative, and the paper notes were large and made from vellum. They were designed and printed by Acolytes of Anuk from the fortified Temple of The Needful Scrip.

Finally, he checked the small money pouch at his belt where he had put some other silver bars and two gold regals he had found lying about in his suite of rooms. No one used money anymore, it was all being filtered through the nano, everything is traceable, he worried. 'I'll get these notes traded for bars and regals the first opportunity I get,' he whispered as he watched the steamer rattle to life and make its way out with the tide. The captain was sure of the deep channels that ran between mudflats and hidden banks at the middle of the river, and he watched while the craft wove and meandered away.

Gathering his pack, he checked inside and smiled thinly while he thumbed the spine of Meite's Phantasmagoria, Cassandra's Chronicles, and Navigating the Southern Isles. *Dear me, naughty Reynard, you must not value your incredibly vain head.* None of them were original, and the Southern Isles book was only part of a book, and very tatty at that, but all of them were forbidden by his uncle, the Lord Lucas Abrecan.

'Eirini? Who in their right mind wants to go there? It's full of peasants and filthy Romarii.' He spat into the water then shrugged when he looked at his own dirty hands when he pulled the woollen cowl over his head. *The filth is not on their skin but in their blood* he reasoned.

~ ❈ ~ ❈ ~ ❈ ~

'Did he follow us?' she asked as she pulled the cabin door gently closed.

'Yes, of course he did. You like him, Tranquil?' Homily placed her duffel bag carefully under her bed. Her shoulders felt too high and tight when a sudden wave of tension set them rigid. She paused but did not turn while she waited for the reply.

'He wasn't as bad as I thought he'd be. Nice soft lips, more bearable than these damn eye lenses. Here, give me yours, I will clean them. You ready to use your crystal, Hom?'

Soft lips, and soft in the head Homily thought while she said, 'Don't put them away, we may need them again in a hurry. I'll contact the Lady Arianrihod shortly, tell her we're on our way, though,' she paused, and a worried frown creased her brow, 'I wish we had found a way into Abrecan Castle and the location of the entrance to the Fifth Tower.'

'I hope it's a decent port this time,' Tranquillity said, barely stifling a laugh.

Homily smiled sardonically. 'Yes, we are lucky like that, aren't we? We go north from here to Shad, offload the animal products and buy weapons and information. Best be careful with our latest heist – we will need it. Crollar from the needful scrip will get us what we need in Shad, no questions asked.' She allowed herself a giggle, as she took her cloak off and loosened a surprising number of concealed weapons from about her person. She began polishing them and said softly, 'There are no decent ports where we're headed.'

Tranquillity nodded then said, 'I told him we were going to Eirini. I hope the elite dope doesn't get himself caught. I wish we'd been able to get the location of the Fifth Tower too, I hate failing,' her mouth set in a thin frustrated line. 'I would give my life for that.' She paused, then took some food from a chest that was next to their small beds – bread, cheese, and apples with some weak wine in a ceramic urn. 'I'll miss the luxuries at Bucky's, mind. It's a shame we couldn't get a transfer to Abrecan Castle.'

'Do you think he knows it wasn't Micah?' Homily asked.

'Does a father know his own son?' Tranquillity smiled thoughtfully. 'Although, I can't say whether the others bought it. I think they did, it was very convincing, an exact copy if you ask me – if it hadn't been for you, I wouldn't have known. You informed the Lady Arianrihod?'

'I did, but if Bucky did know and I'm not sure he did, Tranquil, look what he did to the weather…but if he did, he's a brilliant actor, that's what Lord Bucky is.' Homily replied while she began to get undressed. The whole affair had left her wondering just how far the mummery went. Who was involved and why? It was clear Micah was on his way to work the wind, but whoever had faked his death had saved him from the very same fate.

'His life probably depended on it, Hom,' Tranquillity replied as she took a large drink of wine. 'How I'm going to miss Bucky.' She pulled a face while she investigated her wine.

'You mean how you're going to miss the larders, pantry, and vast wine cellars.' They collapsed in fits of laughter, relieved that they were leaving Lodewick, but also a moment to relax before they headed out to the Sea of Shad and up the coast to the city of the same name. They had been left merchant sailor garb at the foot of their beds and some scissors to cut their hair.

'We'll need to bind your big tits flat, Hom.' Tranquillity ripped some strips of linen from the end of her sheet, and began passing them to her friend, who was already cutting her hair.

'The sacrifices I've made for the resistance, no one will know the half of it,' she replied with mock seriousness as she finished the last of the cutting and began binding her chest.

'I'll let them know. They will sing songs about your mammoth efforts all over the Southern Isles. You will be more celebrated than the witch queens themselves,' Tranquillity teased, not even bothering to suppress her laughter.

'Well, that would be amazing – and I hope they do,' she said dryly. 'Especially as I'm from Arid Falamh, my parents are Fala, and they took me to the Mobius River at Rodinia and threw me in the water there, when they discovered that the Hyenoi Hound pup in my cot hadn't eaten me but was actually me.' Tranquillity guffawed even though she had heard the tale a thousand times. 'Poor things thought it was bad enough when I had the recessive shifter gene, I half believe they wished a consciousness carp had not shown up and that I had drowned...but I did enjoy my time under the water, got to meet some Selgovae too.'

'The things we put our parents through...well, not me but you.' Tranquillity pulled her boots off. 'How in the seven bloody hells did I get stuck with you?'

'Really? Did you forget nobody else wanted to pair with us at Glean Glas?' Homily put the scissors down and smiled fondly at Tranquillity.

'You the smallest there, half Rodinian and half Romarii changeling, after what the crone did, so you could get the egg.' Tranquillity paused while she nodded towards the crystal egg, then shuddered. It was called a walk-in. When you were not fully Romarii, but Gaia chose you and you swore yourself to her. The Crone Arianrihod accepted you into the tribe, but to become Romarii you had to accept a Romarii changeling walk-in. She caught Homily studying her and she waved her hand at her. 'I'm fine. You know me, Techie Tranquillity – what a bloody pair.' Tranquillity sighed.

'Come on, they were all big brutes, warrior-rangers, or healers and clairvoyants.' Hom's voice thickened, and she said softly, 'Or changelings.'

Tranquillity passed her the wine and said, 'They didn't appreciate our subtle arts. We were the new wave or supposed to be. Light knows why Gaia chose us; it took everyone by surprise, even The Crone. Though it didn't stop her carrying out the changeling walk-in ritual.' Tranquillity frowned; she had not liked that one bit. Although she was honoured Homily had asked her to be the solitary witness to the ceremony, she just hated what some of the changeling children had to do, even though that was what they were usually birthed for.

'I've asked you not to dwell on that day. We are one now. It was only the changeling body that died, I am me, and him, I have his eyes which I cannot change, nor would I. I honour his sacrifice. We are two consciousnesses in one, all his past lives are ours to access, and because of that I can be reborn through The Gaia Logos. We will all be reborn together. Who better than a Rodinian shifter, who trained with Ri Fiali for that task?' Homily leant forward and kissed Tranquillity's forehead. 'Enough worrying, you're the best spy out here, as you don't look fully Romarii apart from your amber eyes, and look at the tech you've designed, those optics, that bangle – it's amazing stuff, and you'll know what we need at Shad and the price to pay too.' She turned back to the small mirror and made some final adjustments while Tranquillity marvelled at how fluid someone's skin, flesh, and bone could be.

'We don't need me at the dealers asking for green death rays, now do we?' She removed her breeches.

Tranquillity replied, 'Quite.'

'Well, what do you think?' She pointed to the bandages across her flattened chest. 'They'll eventually disappear by morning – I hope. I am not as quick nor as skilled as some of the full Rodinian shifters, it is to do with the Romarii changeling, its presence has blocked my full ability. A cocoa skin boy with dark stubble at his chin, muscular but lithe, with a broad chest and ready smile, stood in front of Tranquillity.

She looked her friend up and down, her eyes lingering on the soft linen underclothes. 'Impressive as always, Hom.'

The transformed Homily grinned cheekily at Tranquillity and got on the bed next to her; he pushed her gently back onto the rough blankets. 'Did you say the elite boy had soft lips?' Hom raised his eyebrows playfully.

'Come here you…I love it when you do this…I think we have time for a little relaxation before we reach Shad, young sir,' Tranquillity whispered as she pulled the rest of her clothes off.

'Yes, let's make the best of it while we can. You know I'll revert to my true form after Shad, although I know how you like that too,' Hom whispered playfully in Tranquillity's ear.

'I can't recall what your true form is, and neither do you, Hom.' She sighed, then stopped. 'Was the corpse of fake Micah a Rodinian shifter?'

Hom continued to kiss her neck. 'No. When we die, we cannot hold any form. We change…completely.'

~ ❈ ~ ❈ ~ ❈ ~

'Pass me my optics, Hom.' Homily reached across to where they lay on the chest next to the bed and passed them to Tranquillity.

'Is there something amiss?'

'I need to check the illusion meme flow. It's been stable for ages; nothing new, I mean nothing newly false, has been downloaded for a while which makes me nervous,' she trailed off as she started to move dials on the arm of her optics, 'it's worth a check before we reach the lovely city of Shad.'

Homily made a disgusted sound while Tranquillity put on her optics and began to adjust the dials until a curtain of data waterfalled down the lens.

'Oh no. The evil cunt, what's he doing that for?' She tensed. 'Get ready to contact the crone, Hom, this is dire indeed.'

'What's he doing?' Hom dressed quickly and pulled his violet crystal orb from his jerkin pocket.

'More blood temples at the main cities, Yamal, Shad and Pali, slave sacrifice to appease chaos. Guratt's to be repaired and reopened. Oh lords, it is beginning – he is going to shed as much as he can for the blood magic before attempts Juno Seven, which means he can feel the Spectral Star. The Star has activated, it must have!' She held each arm of her optics gingerly as she read the data inside the lens.

'In that case, the Romaros and Akasha are in grave danger wherever they are. Keep interrogating the data flow, Tranquillity, I'll contact Arianrihod now – our mission may change course yet.' Hom held his crystal to his chest then blew gently on its surface as he envisaged the being who he wished to communicate with.

'We are all connected,' he whispered.

Chapter Thirty

Nightcrawlers Remixed

He wandered along a waterfront that was just coming awake. The wind was gusty and frozen, thin, and sharp as a blade it found its way through fabric and skin, shrinking blood vessels until it felt like it had severed the circulation to his cheeks, nose, and ears. He walked quickly past breakers yards that stunk of tar and timber. They had begun their own dawn chorus with each rattle and ring, which lifted through the chill air to meet the rising sun. In the distance work had begun to reclaim marshland from the estuary but as far as he could tell, all that had been achieved was another lake of water behind the stockade. Though he could see the gigantic wheel that would be used to power the pumps and wondered who would have to tread the splintered boards inside it. The wharfs at the far end of the docks were wide and made of old timbers and chunks of quarried stone. They stank. At the shore end of Live and Dead Stock Wharf, empty pens waited hopefully for livestock. There was a heap of rusty shackles next to one berth. He dropped his head rather than stare. Slavers? he thought and moved quickly on. He passed Textile, Flour and Grain Wharfs with massive tithe barns at their ends and guild dockmasters with flinty, hungry-looking eyes, smoking pipes outside their offices. Then through a small market with a couple of shops and two taverns huddled at the shore end of the wharf where bulky cargo like sea coal was brought ashore.

Wedged between a currently closed brothel whose alchemical lights were turned low and sickly, and a tavern with a picture of a charcoal burner above the door, was the smallest shop he had ever seen. It looked like it had been built across the narrow alley. A red tin roof squatted at an angle above the wooden structure. It had an air of abandonment about it but painted on a wooden sign above the door was a picture of a single eye. On the door, lettering in dulled and flaky black paint said, *Euphemia Eye, white-eyed Seer. Silver Tower trained.*

'She's took off with her fancy-man.' A voice that sounded like a seabird screeching, informed him.

He turned, and found a small, fat woman, standing next to several braziers that cracked like dry knuckles while they burned bracken faggots and sea coal. She stared at him through narrowed but beady eyes, behind her were her wares; hot pies, chestnuts, ale, and chib, waiting to be purchased from a brightly coloured but shabby stall.

'I did not want,' he cut off his words, and finished by saying, 'A meat pie, and a beaker of chib, if you please.'

She nodded her approval and waited for him to come over before she said, 'What about a clanger? Pork one end, apricot and nuts the other.' She pointed to a long oblong pastry, a favourite of dockworkers and sailors.

He studied it and wondered where her apricots had come from. He could smell sweetened turnip and lord only knew what her pork was. Freight had been getting through to Lodewick, slowly, but he doubted it had been apricots! He shook his head and replied, 'Just meat. Real meat.' His appetite was scarcer than his hair, his stomach was shrunken with droge waere use, and that clanger was larger than his shin. Best left to larger appetites than mine he thought but felt a pang of hunger all the same while he sucked saliva from the pits of his cheeks.

She sniffed disdainfully at his refusal of a clanger, and said with a loud tut, 'I only sell real meat, and sugar's extra.'

'I'll have two sugars,' he replied and felt a wave of tiredness creep into his bones, it had been a long night. 'Make that three. Large,' he added while he felt the coin in his money belt. There were several copper bits in there, he did not want to risk bringing out a silver bar or a gold regal. He was not a wealthy merchant, if he had that kind of coin he could easily be accused of stealing it, he did not have a guard with him either and he quite liked his throat uncut. He paid for his pie and warmed himself at one of the braziers while he watched the stall holder heap three spoons of deep brown sugar into his beaker. He took it gratefully and drank his chib slowly, savouring the warmth while it oiled down his gullet and almost thawed his chest and stomach. Tastes better loaded with sugar he thought.

'Euphemia took herself off with Athanasius Blood. And' she paused for emphasis and widened her currant eyes while she nodded toward the shop, '*HE*, left in a hurry.' She brought her apron up to her mouth and coughed into it then dropped her voice. 'You know who I mean, it was his warehouse that had all the rebels in it, afore it went bang.' She tapped her eye then pursed her lips into a disgusted scrunch and said tartly, 'Euphemia thought herself something special with her one silver eye, but if you ask me, she was nowt but an old whore, like the rest of the old whores on Coal Wharf, sucking cocks in there for coppers. I saw some strange folk going in and out. Not the types who would give a dollop of drake shit about their future either. Reading fortunes! My left tit.' She flapped her hand at him and pointed to the beaker of chib. He finished the chib in several gulps and was glad it was only lukewarm; he could hardly wait to get away. Then he returned the clay beaker with a mumbled, 'Terrible carry on all of that. Good day.'

He ate his pie while he continued walking, glad to be away from the woman, she had put him on edge. He did not want to be dragged into any conversations about rebels, or Micah's death. He only stopped to spit out a knuckle of gristle. So, Athanasius Blood had fled Lodewick before the night of the dead, I wonder who paid him to do that. Should I leave too, should I have gone with Tranquillity? No, he thought, that would take me further away from finding Micah.

Eventually he found himself pushing through the crowds at the docks where the wharfs berthed the vessels that brought in finer goods, and people. It was still the Cheapside, but what silk merchant wanted their wares dropped in animal dung or coal dust? What genteel passenger wanted to share their wharf with lines of shuffling slaves. He clenched his hands into tight fists while he thought, Rubric Volsunga takes them, I just know it will be him. They will come here and be kept like animals then they will be transported to Shad or Pali, and then to the forsaken Wind. He recalled the humod sniffer with a shudder and a feeling of utter despair settled in the pit of his gut. I need to find Micah and that data, if what he says is true, we need to take that abomination out of the sky. He did not look for the black moon, he did not need to, it was ever present and hung above Lodewick without orbit or phases. Why haven't we questioned the unnatural nature of it? he thought, while he rubbed the fake nano at his wrist and swallowed bitter bile. He knew that the desire to ask about it had been eradicated from anyone who had been implanted with a fully functioning nano device.

His legs felt leaden, a burden he dragged beneath his too tired body. What he had eaten of the pie sat like a lump of grease in his roiling gut. He tried to push thoughts of Lord Abrecan and Volsunga away and took his attention instead to the unimaginative names of the wharfs. Rum Runner Wharf, People's Way Wharf, and the well-guarded, Jewels and Precious Metal Wharf. After this the docks ran into rubble, the water was full of rocks and fallen debris, dangerous to navigate. Even for a small craft the shore was inaccessible from the river, if he went any further, his way would be blocked by the headland, the Tiers of Lodwick, and the disused proc sentry post that was built into the buttress there. The merchant ship The Silken Sea was berthed at Sugar and Silk Wharf and was unloading spices, silks, and coffee. Too busy he thought while he walked past and thumbed the piece of paper Tranquillity had pushed into his hand and hoped that when he opened it, it was not blank, that she had not written drop-dead or some other pleasantry. He hoped that inside those grubby folds she had given him something that would save his sorry skin. He walked on until the crowds thinned and the headland wind picked up, sharp as an icy blade but still stinking like a sailor's shore-leave breath, beery, and fishy, at the same time. He found a squat mooring post that was drake shit, and ice free, then tucking his cloak beneath his backside, he sat down, and was about to read his instructions when he felt a finger tap lightly on his shoulder and a rough accented voice ask, 'You ready for business, sweet lips?'

He did not turn but slid his eyes to the side. The hand was plump and tanned, and every finger wore one or two rings. Like an additional digit, a silver bar was held between a fat index and middle finger. The merchant smelled of spice and lemon oil. 'Nah,' he said in a gravelly, tight voice, and watched while the silver bar disappeared as if I magician had spirited it away. Then he added, 'I've a throat full of sores. A good sucking will have 'em weeping like rotten mangoes.' He paused for a breath then said in a forlorn voice filled with regret, 'Again.' He coughed and spat into the filthy water for good measure and did not bother to look round; he knew the merchant had gone.

After a moment or two he bent forward and casually adjusted the cuff of his trousers while taking a quick look around. The dock was getting busier, a passenger Ketch, with the rusty red, square sails, typical of the Eastern cities, Shad and Pali, was docking, and several acolytes dressed in ochre robes waited on the quayside, their prayer bead held in their left hand, and their hoods pulled over their heads against the brisk frigid wind. He frowned while he tried to place the order then thought, the sisters of Bloodgita. With a sigh he sat upright and took out the note. He paused before he read it while a sudden thought crossed his mind, there are no silver-eyed seers. Not just Euphemia Eye. Usually, the wharfs would boast three or four one-eyed fortune tellers, swapping prophecy for alms, but he did not have time to think on it too long. Bucky's winter of grief had changed a lot of things in Baelmonarchia and not just in small ways. Most of the wharfs had sustained damage, and one or two of the wooden ones, where the timber river barges from Plantation docked, had been swept away when the Ophiuchus thawed. The smaller ramshackle cockle-fisher wharfs had fared better, like the cockles they were named for they had clung on to the rocks and had survived.

He unfolded the paper and read her words, then laughed but cut it short, when one of the acolytes looked his way. Inside Tranquillity had written, *The Zuben's hire suicidal maniacs all the time, but you must be a special sort of psychopath to fit in with them. You will be perfect. Follow my instructions to the letter, otherwise you will get your throat slit. Call this sequence, -∴-∵∴-⁞~, then say these words exactly; "Tranquillity Maegdelan was sorry to hear you lost your little birdy, she sends you a spider instead." No more than that, idiot. T.*

He pulled out Micah's old mo. The most expensive mo on the planet he thought wryly, and it is not even new. He pressed his thumb into the indent at its base and waited until he felt the tingle of the alchemical transducer when it took the charge from his princeps pollicis artery, then he pressed and rotated the crystal pips to select the sequence. There was no sound, but he knew his call had been answered. He read his lines and waited, while the wind whipped his rough woollen cloak around his legs, and overhead seabirds screeched while they followed a fat bellied, filthy ship, up the river to the livestock wharf. The ship was from the Copper Isle and made of dark timbers girded in red metal. Just behind midship, it had a three story tower, with a chimney that belched alchemical smoke and fire. It was where the captain and crew had their quarters but below decks it would be crammed full of flesh. He turned on the mooring post, he did not want to follow its journey, nor see what it unloaded. Though he thought bitterly, they must have bled the North dry if they need to import flesh.

He pressed the mo to the side of his head. No one spoke and the silence rushed and pumped in his ear. The words he had just said, and his hope slipped into a vacuum, but he knew someone was on the other end just by the silky texture the silence held, it was too full of potential for it to be completely empty. Then a woman said, 'The Tanner's Apron.'

He felt the line go dead, then pocketed the mo and with his lips twisted into a disdainful sneer, he said quietly, 'Not the leather guild apprentices watering hole.' Then he ran his rough woollen cloak through his hands and felt the lumps of scabs on his badly shaved head. With a loud snort he set off. I will fit right in he thought and made his way through the nearest network of alleys, avoiding the livestock wharf and moving away from the Cheapside docks and back into the city by way of one of the shadiest parts of Lodewick, The Shambles.

The Tanners Apron was several tiers above and sat with other inns of ill repute in the greasy and smelly Beamhouse Square. On foot it was best reached by the permanently closed, shoulder width, and crumbling cat-span Dyer Bridge. To the west of the Dyer Bridge, the Wet White Bridge spanned a deep ravine, and was used for heavier traffic that brought skins and chemicals to the Elleadern Weatende, then the tanned leather went to the warehouses for export. He gave silent thanks to Tranquillity for showing him the route earlier and wondered if she knew he would be asked to meet the Zuben's in Beamhouse Square. Feeling more confident he set off, he would avoid the Wet White, the bridge was fortified, and had a guarded gate tower set in the abutments at the dockside entrance. I will risk life and limb on Dyer-death-Bridge instead he thought while he threw the remains of his pie at a hungry looking Fural. It was scratching about in the alley he was skulking through on his way to the Snide. It had been wily and feral enough to survive Bucky's winter and the ravenous empty bellies of Lodewick, at least it deserved to eat whatever the pie vendor had stuffed the pastry with and called meat.

Lodewick was laced with alleys, gulley's, ravines, cuts, and cobbled roads that meandered where they could across the lumpy, pox ridden rock of the metropolis. The Snide was where gold, precious metals, the latest crystal and alchemical wares, maritime silicone, grain, and finer goods, had their value marked in ledgers by tight skinned men with bony knuckles, and thick optics resting on hawkish noses. It bristled with merchants, money lenders, scriveners, and scribes. Pawn shops, and avarice, congealed on each side of the wide cobbled road that was teeming with rickshaws. Rumour had it that you could buy anything on the Snide and have it sent anywhere in Gaiadon, If you were sure, you knew what you wanted, and your purse was bottomless. The Snide was the spine of commerce in Lodewick, but the streets, alleys, and cut throughs, which led to and away from it were the bowels and bladder. The Shambles tumbled towards the docks and the Ophiuchus but leading away from the Snide towards the plateau was the area known as Sceatta Sceat, commonly pronounced seegda seed, and fondly called the seedy seed, an oily sounding name that perfectly fitted the district where all manner of dubious thing that was not recorded in ledgers, were bartered, and sold. The Temple of the Needful Scrip, where Baelmonarchian currency was minted, behind walls smoother than glass and darker than obsidian looked down on it all, and Matriarch Goldweard took Anuk's Cut from it all. It was true that the citizens of Lodewick were chipped and controlled, but every city had a seedy underbelly and it wrapped itself around the Snide like a second skin. Assassins for hire, the offices of the Apprentice Guild's, guarded by menacing men with thick arms and low brows, muscle for hire, who would, if you had the money, fashion you a nice piece of leather, forge you a weapon, or set a fake jewel in a brass ring as well as wallop your enemies, rob your competitor's barge or caravan, and even, if you had the coin, set something afire and slit a throat or two. Black Alchemists, blacker apothecaries, Silver Tower Seers, Usurers, speculators, gamblers, and whores, all of whom had a keen but subtle eye turned towards Lord Lucas Abrecan's pennants. They were everywhere, crimson like blood, his pentagram black sigil tattooed onto the fabric as if it were flesh cut through with a knife; they snapped in the wind from the Ophiuchus, and if you knew where to look, the metallic spy eye hidden beneath them, blinked and turned.

There were few motor vehicles, but rickshaws creaked past like old bones rubbing together, pulled by sinewy men and women, pools of alchemical light bounced blue off the cobbles underneath their axles. Strong or not, it took more than flesh, muscle, and bone to pull some of the fattest merchants from their respective wharfs to the Snide. Lines of solars waited expectantly for the sun to hit their black glittering wings, some had already started buzzing and the strange sound rubicity made rose like a swarm of metallic insects about to take to the wing, but he knew he was not going to walk along the Snide, there were too many spy-eyes.

His heart hit the inside of his chest like a mallet against wood. Weasel was walking out of Scriveners Street. He turned eastward along the pavement. No, not walking Troy thought and felt bile rise. Skulking and sneaking, every movement he made a carefully constructed act to make him look like a man about business. Or is he? Troy thought and waited until he had moved away and the roil of greasy pie had settled in his gut. Then, he slipped out of the alley and walked quickly over the road, using the rickshaws as cover. He slipped into Scrivener Street and before taking the first cut through he pulled his hood up and leaned against the wall of the offices of Oliver Sudden and Company.

Shortly, two apprentices appeared with Anuk's Cut in two fat purses, to be taken to the Temple of The Needful Scrip. Their top hats were deepest blue, and their overcoats were plain but made from good, boiled wool. They each carried a court sword, and he wondered if they could use them as well as they could a pen. He felt the press of the stiletto at his back, the dagger in his boot, and the brass knuckles in his pocket. He slipped them onto his left hand and flexed his fingers against the metal. If they saw him and thought they were going to be robbed, then they would kill him. There were no excuses or absences when it came to Matriarch Goldweard taking Anuk's cut. They will be able to use those swords he thought and felt his mouth go dry. They reminded him of the rebels at the night of the dead and with a lurch in his stomach, he fell in behind them, and made himself invisible, just another tattered piece of debris being blown about the streets of Lodewick.

'What was Master Weaselton about?' The taller of the two scriveners asked.

'A release, relating to the employment of Master Valoroso. You know his duties with Lord Abrecan, to appease the masses. Why do you ask, Endwine?'

'I thought it would have been the obituary piece I constructed several years ago, you know after…' he trailed off.

Endwine snorted before he replied, 'Remember? I recall working night and day to clear up the shit storm those two idiots left in their wake. Though, Lendric, I would still blow the dust off that.' He slowed his step, turned to the other man, and tapped his nose while his gaze slid around the street to check for eyes. Then he said in a lower tone, 'I have heard Master Valoroso is on the run, and that is what we are hiding, but we all know what that will mean when he is caught.'

'The perpetual brotherhood?' Lendrick hissed and Endwine shushed him with a flap of his fingers. 'I can construct an accidental death,' he finished quickly.

'Good, good,' Endwine replied, 'but where?'

'We should work together. You ensure his duties are inspection. We could say the mines in the Flat Lands. I will organise the explosion, casualties, his corpse should we need it.'

'Agreed,' Endwine replied. Then added thoughtfully, 'Hopefully, he will be found before we have to sign off on a mass killing.'

Troy fell into the first cut through he came to after that and emptied half the contents of his stomach onto the icy cobbles. Well now I know the lies they set their pens to writing he thought and belched up another frothy mouthful of vomit. He spat it out and taking a deep breath he turned westwards and upwards to Elleadern Weatende and Beamhouse Square. So, Master Weaselton, the sneaky prick, is trying to pick up my scent, and they have already arranged my new life and sudden death, should they need it. He felt a sudden stab of regret. I was that disposable he thought and quickened his pace.

~ ❋ ~ ❋ ~ ❋ ~

He toyed with his mug of ale, it was the vilest thing he had ever drunk, it tasted bitter, and salty. Just like chewed leather he thought while he put the pewter mug to his lips but did not drink. The stench from the tanners hung in the chilly air like steamy tendrils from a pan of thick, bone-glue-soup. I will never wash the stink off. He pulled a face while he rubbed at the back of his hand with the edge of his cloak and imagined a layer of grease coating his skin. He pushed all thoughts of the scriveners away, it had only made him more determined to survive, to get away. I need to focus on this meeting, on surviving. It was quiet in the tavern, and he had taken his seat in a corner furthest from the bar. He watched out of the frosty windows and kept an eye on the door and bar at the same time. He had been waved across Dyer Bridge by a cloaked and hooded, skinny woman, whose words slipped through her missing teeth with a fine shower of spittle. 'Ice on the bridge, mind how you go,' she said and flapped her hand at him when he made to pay. He thought her an unlikely toll keeper until he saw the glint of an arrowhead poking through the filthy mesh of a window three stories up, at the other end of the span. The bridge was not just icy, but its surface appeared to be made of glass, and not content with that it appeared as if someone had then poured oil over that. He pulled off his boots and tucked them under his arm then made his way across in his stocking feet. He felt them stick to the icy surface and welcomed the cold when it started to eat at the tips of his toes. He heard the woman behind him titter her approval and say, 'That's the way to do it.' After his run-in with the scriveners, her encouragement bolstered him, and he shuffled along the span while he recalled Micah's words about the dagger path. Is it as slippery as this he thought and felt a fleeting wave of joy – Micah could still be alive.

The tavernkeeper had the tell-tale signs of a previous existence in the tannery, his skin was pockmarked, one hand looked all but useless and the skin was thin and withered close to the bone. One of his eyes was cloudy white, though the other was shrewd, and darted quickly from side to side. A fire was set in the grate, he looked longingly at it while his breath fogged the air, and his toes tingled with returning circulation, but he knew it would not be lit until noon.

Next to the fire was an ancient Falamh Grass basket of tightly woven bracken faggots and a scuttle full of sea coal; it washed up on the black shores south of Shad and a whole industry had risen from it. Though it was greedy coal, hard to burn and not forthcoming with its heat. The bracken faggots were sold at every market you happened upon in Lodewick and were the copper-bit industry of urchins and goodwives. The smell of pies in the oven, butter beans, and salted peas on the hob was unmistakable and he wished he had not bought food at the docks. The tavernkeeper wiped tables half-heartedly with a grey leather cloth, and when he came to his table he said in a hushed voice, 'We're serving food in the back room.' He inclined his head to the right.

Troy replied, 'I think I will have a bite to eat.' While he hoped that he did not have to eat anything, and that his rendezvous was in the back room.

It was, and she was called Elgenubi Zuben.

'Follow me, spider.' She said quietly and nodded to a back door. Then she pulled the hood of a long, boiled wool cloak, over a snarl of amethyst and platinum locks. She left two silver bars on the table, next to a half-eaten bowl of salted peas and a plate that was scattered with black breadcrumbs and the remains of a pat of butter. Far too much money for the food he thought and wondered if she had a stomach lined with lead. He was about to say something to that affect, but she stopped suddenly in the doorway, and he ran clumsily into her back. She tutted and cut him short. 'You follow me, so that I do not know that you are there. So that the spy eyes do not know we are together. You do not say a word. You show me that you are a good spider.' With that said she set off at a quick pace, oiled over Dyer Bridge like a tightrope walker, and made her way further up the tiers and into Lodewick proper, skirting on the edges of districts they should not be in, weaving through temple squares, and pleasure parks, stepping lightly across rope and rung bridges, while he trailed in her wake, a distant ragged shadow.

Show her, he fumed. Prove to her, he thought and frowned. I will prove myself, all right. He felt the long dagger, pushed hastily into the front of his waistband, and smiled.

Then, he stalked her through the fortified Square of Severed Souls. It boasted several gibbets that were strangely empty, they creaked in the frigid wind, a high and plaintive call like an animal squealing for food. They had been picked clean during the winter of Bucky's grief, and it had not been by the crows. They had been picked clean too, along with anything else that flew or swam, cats, rats, furals, and mules. There was an executioner's blade with a blood trough and channel below which led to the temple, and a newly installed laser wall. Though the crowds tended to prefer a traditional execution, the acolytes favoured a river of blood, but he was sure the condemned would prefer the sudden, dry death, and oblivion, of laser fire.

Red pennants with embroidered severed hands in gold thread, snapped taut, then bellied in the sharp chill wind that raced off the Ophiuchus, a remnant of the winter and Lord Bucky's fury. The red marble floor tiles and parts of the temple walls were scored in places as if they had been hit with the edge of a broadsword. They still felt smooth and slippery beneath his feet like a coat of ice remained, even though the hard winter had almost gone. The market before the temple, bizarrely, sold jewellery, it specialised in rings, bracelets, and bangles, although he wondered what use they would be to someone without hands: and fancy goods, made by the temple acolytes. As usual there were plenty of hot food vendors mixed between.

All the large Temple squares were mini fortalice's, small, fortified settlements of Acolytes, their lamasery buildings, and the quarters and establishments of the serfs who served them. The square was surrounded by castellated walls with temple guards on top. He oiled his gaze over them casually while he thought what is different about them. The guards were not really watching the crowd but were talking in groups, many had their backs turned toward the square, they wore black batons at their waists as well as swords strapped to their backs. There was no sign of compact or crossbow, weapons that were usually trained on public places, especially during executions or blood lettings. The eyes above the temple moved jerkily back and forth scanning the crowds, but only two were working. They are getting lazy he thought, relying on the lasers at their waist, putting their faith in crystal and alchemical weapons.

At the centre of the square was the usual statue of the One-God Anuk, defeating a version of Gaia's consort, this time it was Spider King, sometimes it was a crowned serpent, other times a snake, winged deer, or a man with horns or fanged teeth. He did not stop to admire the statue. Spider King, it all started then. When I put on that damned costume and stood at the Sun in Winter's right hand. He noted quickly that the statue had been damaged by the hard fingers of rain that had been named the Shards of Bucky's Sorrow, the scoring in the marble floor was caused by them too, he realised. They had ripped the city apart, and the storm of Bucky's grief had taken out every holo-clock, they had ripped tiles off roofs and render off walls, they had shattered the glass in every un-shuttered window. Then after they had finished, the blizzards began, the temperature plummeted, and Lodewick froze.

He skirted around the statue with a grim look in his eye and a fist of resolve in his gut while he wished Bucky's shards of sorrow had been aimed truer, he wished they had killed Abrecan and Volsunga. He wanted to spit but walked purposefully past, a man about business, not a shadow following a rebel, and certainly not an elite on the run.

Anuk was always wrought in the best metal, and he was always resplendent in white armour, and wore a crown like the rays of the sun while he took the head off the beast with a silver sword with a winged handguard. Above the statue the holo-clock had been repaired and spun the galactic cycle in different holo images each day. The galactic cycle was two hundred and sixty days of different energies. They were four moons into the year of the yellow cosmic seed, four moons since the night of the dead and Micah's disappearance. It was a vanishing act, he is not dead, not yet he thought while he noted the clock. It was the twenty fifth day of the Resonant Moon, and the energy for the day was the Yellow Overtone Warrior. It is a good day to meet with a band of renegade warriors he thought, just as he spotted a trio of Acolytes of Anuk. Tomorrow was the twenty sixth day of the Resonant Moon and it was a Red Rhythmic Earth day. A day for soil singing in rural zones, and a day for bloodletting in Lodewick. That is why the gibbets are empty, and the blade rusting in the chilly breeze, why the fat bellied slaver is docking at the wharf, he thought while he took the mark of the acolytes. They are preparing the square for tomorrows sacrifices.

The acolytes wore blood red robes lined with ivory silk, beneath them they were dressed entirely in black breeches and tunics, with leather jerkins above, they wore knee length boots with a soft sole and a split toe. Around their necks a dark leather thong hung, it had a braided length at its end, and attached to that was a fist sized prayer bead. Every fool who had ever had a run in with an acolyte knew that the leather thong and bead were no more than a decorative cosh, but the acolytes, when in public at least, had to hold the prayer bead as if their life and their salvation depended on it. He also knew that they were thirsty for blood, and greedy for gold. He felt in his money belt and found a gold regal, it was fat and warm, oily like only pure gold can be. It would make a sound like only gold could when it hit the red marble tiles before the steps of the massive Temple of Anuk. It was run by the biggest bastards in Lodewick, The Brotherhood of The

Unhanded Revenge, so called, because they were the acolytes who freed people from the burden of their thieving hands. Then not content with that, they took every drop of blood they held in their bodies too.

Elgenubi was a thick cloud of boiled wool making her way across the square before him. There were several portcullises around the walls, but she was headed towards a timber framed postern between a tavern and shop that sold wine, holy he assumed. Though, he had never met an abstinent acolyte yet, no one had. He marked the alley at the same time he flicked his coin before the acolytes, he heard it ring when it hit the cool red marble, a rich golden chime, not thin like tin, and not a pitchy ping like iron and copper, but a luxurious purr of an oily gold chime. He smiled when he saw the glint of honey light as the coin spun on its end, the invitation, the lure. Then, the rustling of robes, while the acolytes fell forward. He did too. Slipped his dagger out of his boot and fell heavily against one of the acolytes but was pushed out of the way by a pair of strong hands, accompanied by the pious words, 'Fuck off, filth.' He stumbled backwards then twisted his body until he was in a crouch and from there, he slipped his dagger in his boot, stooped low and drew his cloak about him while he took the first few steps forward. He continued quickly, only a fool hung around to witness the results of their work. He disappeared through the crowds then through the postern and into the alley he thought she had taken.

She was not there! His heart clattered around his chest, a tiny piece of undigested pie that he had not vomited, snaked heavily in his gut, followed by a frustrated narrowing of his throat. He had to spit to clear it. He had lost her. The alley ended in a rough wall of natural limestone pocked with green lichen and running with tendrils of frozen green slime. It stunk of piss, and rot that was festering beneath the ice, waiting to release its odour as soon as the temperature rose. Damn I was sure she would take this alley he thought, while his breath purled out of his nostrils in thin streamers of white. It was freezing. Leeching cold that felt like another presence behind him, of the type that could only be found lurking in filthy shady alleys, when you were up to no good. He felt the warmth drain from his face until only a tingle at his nose and ears remained, but he took his time while he walked slowly along the centre, studying the icy dirt, frozen rats, human excrement, and debris beneath his feet.

There were no doors or windows to either side, just high smooth stone walls and flat tile roofs that backed onto the rampart and crenelated wall above. He made his way to the end and ran his hand over the rough wall until he found what he was looking for, a still wet, greasy scuff mark, which had tiny ice crystals trapped in the dirt, right on the edge of a protruding rock.

She had climbed the wall.

~ ❖ ~ ❖ ~ ❖ ~

This is the only way she could have gone he thought anxiously, while he breathed in, and turned his face to the side, then he slipped into the crevice. His cloak felt too thick, and the hood was caught on something, he could feel it pulling the neck of the cloak tight around his throat. He exhaled but there was no more space to be had. Then he felt the rock push into his flesh and compress his bones. He inhaled slowly though he wanted to gulp at air. I am stuck he thought, and a cold sweat greased across his skin, but not enough to birth him from his stony tomb. I will starve to death wedged between the riven cliffs of Lodewick he worried while he wondered how long it would take, when a hand grabbed him at the back of his cloak and yanked him out by his hood. She did not say anything but held the alchemical lantern she had in her hand up to his face and pulled what he could only describe as the most disgusted expression he had ever seen. Then she pushed him through a labyrinth of chilly tunnels, half a dozen had rough walls and low ceilings, tight spaces to wriggle through. Others were too square and neat to be anything other than hewn by people. They crossed several rope bridges, and up more rungs than he cared to count, then forward into a damp torchlit cave that stunk of green slimy things, salt, smugglers, and his freedom.

'Tranquillity send us a spider,' Elgenubi said, while she looked down her nose and pointed.

'Spider? It like a cracked egg. What's its name?' Eschamali replied while he pointed to Troy's head.

Before Elgenubi said she did not know. He jutted his chin out and said with all the bravado he could muster. 'Marcus. My name's Marcus. Tranquillity sent me.'

Eschamali leaned against a large crate, two lit torches guttered and smoked behind sending strange alloy colours in sheets across his mahogany skin. The wall where they were placed, ran with moisture. Eschamali curled his top lip into a contemptuous sneer while he studied him for what seemed an age and a half, until Troy felt his skin being stripped from his bones, and even though he thought himself tallish, he felt diminished and shrunken, before his gaze. Then Eschamali said in a voice that sounded like gravel being chewed, 'Marcus? I don't believe you, kid, but I need runners. They burn out, can't keep up with the party. You not built like my kind, kid. You, soft of flesh, weak of mind. Not built for the night.' He grunted in amusement. Then he turned his attention to Elgenubi.

He could not see her, but he heard the fabric of her clothes shush when she shrugged and said, 'We desperate after Birdy got it in the neck.'

Eschamali folded his arms about his chest and replied, 'You trust him?'

'No,' she said shortly, then added as an afterthought, 'Inside his dark slanting eyes I see a thief, and a liar.'

Eschamali frowned then said, 'I not take Romarii cast offs. How do we know if he any good?' He eyed Troy while he stroked a black dagger at his waist, his eyes did not blink, and the lens across them was strangely silver-cast like a shark swimming through the greenish half-light of the cavern. Elgenubi tutted behind him, and he knew she would not speak for him while he hid his surprise. Tranquillity was Romarii!

Eschamali's hand tightening on the hilt of the long black dagger at his waist, soon brought his attention to a razor-sharp edge. I am going to die he thought and gulped while he put one hand up in a gesture that said, wait. Then he took the other slowly into his cloak with the words, 'I got a nice dagger for you.' Putting his hand to his waist band he pulled out a long Solais Silver dagger, with beautiful scrimshaw worked into a grip made from sea elephant tusk, and handed it, hilt first, to Eschamali.

Eschamali took it and guffawed while he turned to Elgenubi and asked, 'You felt him take this?'

'I thought he was feeling my arse,' she huffed. Then strode over and snatched her dagger back.

Just then the wall behind Eschamali moved and the largest, ugliest man he had ever seen peeled himself off the rock face. Or at least that is what it looked like. His skin was not just craggy, it was segmented like parched brown earth, and he wore dark clothes that barely fit him, and a cloak that did not reach his knees. 'You come steal something off Homan Wind. See if I can feel it,' he bellowed, and moved forward like an avalanche.

Troy put his hand up and said while he pulled the bead out of his robe, 'I just took this off an Acolyte of Anuk, a brother from the temple of the unhanded revenge.' Out of the side of his eye, he caught Eschamali raise one eyebrow. Then he held out the prayer bead on its length of severed braid. Walking forward and praying that his knees did not turn to water, he put it in Homan's hand and said, 'I'll show you how to do it if you like?' When Homan's gaze left his own, and he turned the bead over in his massive hands, Troy took a step back and held up a simple leather cuff. Homan lifted his empty wrist and laughed, then slapped him so hard on the back he became airborne, and any clever words he was about to say were catapulted out of his mouth when he landed with a thud and began to cough.

Suddenly, something washed over him. To begin with, it was a shiver caressing every hair on his skin erect, then it went deeper. It seeped at first, like ice forming on the surface of smooth water, it stole oxygen and light, then it burrowed through to bone. The sensation was heavy inside, and painful, as if his marrow had turned to lead, as if even the fabric of his bones and the stuff he was made of were dull and lacking in light. The dread wrapped around his heart, and he knew, with absolute certainty, that he was worthless. He tried to push the feeling away when the hollow voice of the son of the abyss said behind him. 'It is a pocket's trick, Homan. A child could do it, so it should be perfect for you.'

'You want me to show you what I can do, son of a librarian?' Homan growled and Troy felt a whip of air flash past his cheek and the flesh upon it burn as if it had been wind chapped. The solemn voice disappeared as if it had been absorbed by the shadows in the cave.

He turned around quickly and felt his knees give way, but Elgenubi saved him from falling when she pushed him in the top of his arm and said, 'It is El Nath Night, he cast The Dread at you, and you nearly piss your pants.' She put her fists on her hips and snapped, 'You weak in the night. Birdy punch him in the lights for less.'

'He weak in the night, but good thief.' Homan thumbed to Troy, then folded his huge arms across his chest and waited for Eschamali to reply.

'Good thief, just what we need. You double-cross me, and I rip off your arms – you got that?' Eschamali brought his arms before his body and clacked his forearms together and bellowed, 'You want arms like mine, minnow? You need chitin for that, you got none, you weak in the flesh. You not even got crystal face like the lost warriors. Like Sun in Winter.' He turned his lower arms back and forth to show off his arm braces which were the same colour as his skin; they were part of him, angled, shiny mahogany like laminated and polished leather. They ended in a mitred point at the back of his wrist and similarly below his elbows.

Troy nodded, then gulped down the frothy prayer for his survival that was half-formed in his gut and tasted of dead pig, and chib. 'I will never have arms that big,' he said, and Eschamali snorted his agreement. 'What happened to Birdy?' he asked quickly, hoping to take attention away from his weak flesh and whatever the hell else they had said he lacked.

Eschamali pointed a finger at Elgenubi and the dragon that was inlaid with red and gold jewels, set right into his skin, glittered, and the light from them radiated and danced like small fireflies across the wet ceiling of the cave. Then he drew his finger across his neck and said, 'Elgenubi end it for him, before Velig the Butcher carve him up. He got caught and we could not rescue him. We not a charity for weak in the flesh waifs, and piss-pant minnows.'

He was glad when Elgenubi interrupted when she said thoughtfully, 'He is skinny like a minnow. Little fishy can wiggle through the sky-window at Volsunga's warehouse. Then we decide if we keep it or kill it.' They both roared with laughter while he stood with his mouth gaping and thought, that is not funny. Not just the joke but the thought of wiggling into one of Volsunga's warehouses filled him with dread. He groaned inwardly while he imagined himself being caught robbing Lord Abrecan's righthand man, before he had even left home properly.

He did not know where he found the courage from, but find it, he did. He rubbed his hands together theatrically and replied while he wiggled his fingers greedily in the air. 'Snake-eye Volsunga has more than enough to spare. When do I start?'

Homan put his fat fingers on his shoulder and gave them a bone crunching squeeze while he beamed and said, 'Soon as I find rope long enough.'

Elgenubi added, 'Hope you tired kid. We been Nightcrawling in the caves at Tota, the first since the thaw. Now we sleep.' She lifted the alchemical lantern and pointed through an opening into a small dry cavern. Several huge shapes that resembled gigantic black pea pods, were suspended from the ceiling. Eschamali and Homan were already making their way towards two of them.

'I could sleep,' he replied, dryly. While he thought he heard every aching bone and jittering eyeball weep with relief.

She nodded, then thumbed over her shoulder. 'There is blankets and a pallet, suitable for your weak flesh, but do not touch the pods. They, not for you. They burn.'

He wrapped himself in his blankets and used the rough woollen cloak Tranquillity had given him for a pillow. The straw mattress on the pallet was lumpy, the air was cold, he was not sure he was free, but he was sure the pods were alive and the Zuben's were mad, but none of it stopped him falling into a deep dreamless sleep. He supposed he had made a first impression on them, whether it was a good one or not he did not know, but it was the right one. They needed a thief, and in him they had found one.

~ ❋ ~ ❋ ~ ❋ ~

Homan woke him with a fat, wet finger, pushed into his ear and a bad breath whisper. 'You ready minnow. We off to rob a snake.' He sat back on his haunches and waited for him to wake. Then put his finger to his lips, 'They still sleep.' He stood and walked quietly back to the other cavern.

Troy untangled himself from the blankets and pulled his creased cloak about him. Then stretched, accompanied by a quiet groan and several cracking bones. Then he followed Homan through to the other cavern where he stopped short. The cavern had been emptied during the day and he had not heard a thing. Homan pushed half a loaf of black bread at him and a flagon of warm milk. 'We shit and piss in a gully two turns back that way,' he said while he thumbed back the way he had come with Elgenubi earlier that day. Then Homan sat back on his haunches and continued while Troy ate and drank. 'We need medics, dog soldier supplies, and clothes, but not so it looks like he been robbed.'

Troy paused mid-bite and thought, they are mad, but said instead, 'How?'

'Guards all-round the perimeter, two at the doors, so we go over the rooftops, and in that way. El Nath wait for you in the shadows, you give him the scatt, he brings them back here. No lights, no noise. Here, take these,' he paused while he passed over a pair of optics, like Tranquillity's, 'they night eyes.'

'Why can't El Nath just get the scatt? I mean contraband.' He asked then drained the last of the warm milk.

'Take too long, and he not able to read. We in, we out.'

He smiled inwardly, the voice of doom could not read, the knowledge filled him with a strange sort of power, though he knew he would have to keep it to himself. 'Right,' Homan put the empty flagon down, 'clothes, big sized clothes to fit you all, medics, dog soldier supplies,' he paused while Homan nodded,

'Wound glue, adrenaline, night poppy, marching powder, coms devices, and black laser batons?'

'No laser weapons. They drain life force from here,' Homan replied seriously while he pointed to his right-hand side. Then he added while he pointed to his massive feet. 'Get me biggest boots. El Nath have water dancer's feet, he needs baby boots. Now, go shit and piss, Marcus. I not got all night.'

~ ❊ ~ ❊ ~ ❊ ~

He had returned to that cave only once. It was five moons after his first meeting with The Ten. Summer had come early and sweated like the chaffing inner thighs of a fat whore, and it stunk just the same. The sun shone white overhead, hard and emotionless like Micah had not died, like the winter of grief had never been. It was Kinetic Two Hundred and Twenty-three, Blue Lunar Night. He was there with Elgenubi, and El Nath Night, to help a girl of no more than thirteen summers give birth to her baby, naturally. The Acolytes of the Unhanded Revenge had been using her since she was a child and whether it was fate or destiny, she had seen Elgenubi, and himself, disappear into the dead-end alley where only rats and shadows ever went. Elgenubi had found her hiding in one of the secret tunnels with a basket of rotten inedible food, a stolen blanket, and a small urn of holy wine. Natural births were forbidden, acolytes were supposed to be celibate, and she was as good as dead. Half-starved and fully pregnant, Hydra the Cup had healed her as best she could but predicted that the birth would fall on a special day and that El Nath should be present just in case the baby fell into a shadow and was lost.

'The babe will be a Night power when it activates,' Elgenubi whispered. 'They shadow walk, which is why El Nath is here. It could turn up anywhere.' She thumbed over her shoulder and dropped her voice even lower. 'There have been others like her, but the acolytes kill, then burn them.'

'How is she even pregnant,' he replied in a hushed voice and pushed a wave of revulsion back down his gullet. She was so young, a child, biting on a piece of leather, while El Nath was chanting and had his hands placed lightly on her stomach. He was not sure whether the fear in her eyes was due to the impending delivery, or the sight of El Nath, the son of doom, turned midwife.

'It happens sometimes. Not everyone infertile, not every birth made in one of Volsunga's tanks, or implanted in one of his brood-wombs.' She replied quietly, while she guided him out of the chamber. He felt icy hatred emanating from her like the sharp edge of a tongue turned to steel.

She left him guarding the entrance to the makeshift chamber they had made for the girl and returned to help El Nath. Before she went, she said, 'He will appear to be an old gentleman, but he is not. Then, you say, Captain, and he reply, Stonewall. You got it?'

'Yes,' he replied and felt apprehension's caress like a cold breeze against his skin. It tasted of lead in his mouth, and its pressure was dispersed, like the weight of a crypt and the slow erosion of its stone trying to mark the passage of Time, and something absolute, that was owed, that had no price that could be measured in gold, or blood, or sorrow. Pressing, not piercing. He knew, though he did not know how, Death. It was a whisper which he brushed aside while he nodded and turned his attention to the dark tunnel.

The girl and her baby were not going to stay with The Ten. They were going to be taken by Captain Stonewall to what he understood to be a tribe of some sort. A tribe of vagrants, vagabonds, and the dross that was regularly culled from Lodewick. It was not the tribe from the Shanty. Whoever these people were, they lived in Lodewick, they lived underground, and as far as he could tell were ruled by someone called Sewer King. He thought about the maps Reynard had given him, and especially the thin bit of parchment. Was that what the mapper had been looking for? A way into this Sewer King's realm. A loud groan behind him stopped his train of thought and he heard El Nath say, 'Remember, I am here for the baby.' Then there were several grunts, the sound of the child exerting herself way beyond her capability, or strength. Then there was silence.

Was it alive, had the girl survived? He heard a slapping sound then a plaintive weak mewling. A baby! Not mixed in a petri-dish. Not grown in a tank as fodder for Rubric Volsunga's manufactories in the desolate cities of Nenesh and Yamal. Not bought by the Elite, to be born on a certain or special day. He wanted to see it, this real baby, and turned from his post when he heard soft feet pattering along the tunnel and a young voice say, 'Is done. I feel it.' Then an older voice said, 'You wait here, Noctis. No further, you hear.' There was a moment of silence then a huffed, 'Not fair.'

The old man shuffled up the tunnel. He pushed a wooden wheeled chair before him with an alchemical lantern swinging from one handle. He stopped before Troy and waited.

'Captain?' he asked.

'Stonewall,' the man replied, and pushed the wheeled-chair past him with the words, 'Best be about it, son. Those that dawdle, die.'

He waited at his post and screwed his eyes up while he looked down the tunnel. He could swear there were two pairs of eyes down there. One taller than the other, but both strangely aqueous in the pitch dark.

It felt like an age, but finally he heard the wheeled chair squeak behind him, and he turned to help. The girl was wrapped in blankets and her body tremored despite the humidity in the caverns. She was paler than milk and her stick thin arms held a bundle to her chest as if she carried her heart in her hands. Her eyes were wide and stark, and the abuse she had suffered was a dullness in the dark pit at their centre. All the cruelty inflicted on her had eaten a hungry hollow in the dip beneath her cheekbones, and the witness she had borne to the sins of Anuk's acolytes were burned in charcoal shadows beneath her too knowing eyes.

He felt a well of emotion push into his throat and his eyes stung momentarily, and when he said, 'Can I look, please?' the tremor in his voice was hard to hide.

Elgenubi lifted a torch from the wall and held it carefully above the mother and babe. 'Can he, Lolade?' she asked gently, as if the young girl would suddenly bolt like a frightened animal, but she nodded and pulled back the swaddle the baby was wrapped in and showed him the new-born. Compared to her it was a rose bud, with fat cheeks, and pink lips that sucked at the air. It was as if she had flowered and had gone to seed in the time it had taken her to give birth, as if she had given her vitality to the soft lump of flesh she held in her hands.

'It is beautiful,' he whispered, and everyone made pleased sounds.

Lolade said hoarsely, 'I will do my best by the bastard, but if it so much as looks like one of them cunts, I swear, I will drown it.'

Stonewall made a placating gesture with his hands and said gently, 'Lolade, you only have to feed him, just at first. We have a 'firmary below, and many healing hands to see to you both. Then, if you still can't bear to be near him, there's plenty of nannies who will see to him.'

Troy studied the shrunken girl, then caught Elgenubi's eye. Something peculiar and sad shone in its depth and a fleeting stab of sorrow hit him in his chest like a hot needle. It is so unfair he thought, and turned his attention to El Nath, who met his gaze fully until he saw something yield behind his usual impenetrable black stare. Then he knew deep in his gut that she would not survive. He rustled in his money belt and pulled out his last gold regal and thrust it at Stonewall. 'Here. For whatever she needs. Whatever it takes.' He wanted to say whatever it takes to save her, but he did not trust his voice not to falter, and for all her bravado, Lolade looked frightened to death.

Stonewall took the coin then said to El Nath. 'We have already been paid for this rescue.'

El Nath shrugged and replied in his cold flat voice, 'It is a gift borne of guilt and shame.' He looked pointedly at Troy. Then taking his gaze to the top of Lolade's head he added. 'It is appropriate, is it not.'

Troy wanted to thump him in his hard, angled jaw. Why does he always see through me, shadow dancer he thought angrily, and stomped into the makeshift chamber. He heard the party trundle off down the tunnel and Stonewall say over his shoulder, 'I would like to promise that what we use it for would make amends for that, but wash away the sins of devils, it won't. Till next time you need us, we will continue to watch the water.'

He waited inside the chamber until Elgenubi came in. 'El Nath has shadow walked,' she said, and her voice was heavy with grief, while she began to bundle soiled linens into the centre of a relatively clean sheet.

'She was so quiet,' he said, then lowered his gaze, he could think of nothing else to say.

He heard Elgenubi take a deep snotty breath before she replied, 'She learn to suffer her pain in silence. Those that didn't got killed first.'

'Why do they watch the water?' he asked but could not meet her eye. Then he attempted to help by moving blankets and stacking basins in one corner while his guts roiled. It stunk like a slaughterhouse. There was a lot of blood, even in the poor light from the torches, it was bright red and spotted with faeces that stunk of rot. The placenta sat like a black jellyfish amid it all, impossibly large to have come from Lolade, but it had, and he only had to look at the carnage spread across the floor to see that it had brought the end of her days with it.

'They put them in baskets and give them to the river,' she said, and her voice sounded forced through a grief narrowed throat, and her knuckles were whiter than chalk while she knotted the heap of soiled sheets together.

He did not have to ask who 'they' were, and what was in the baskets.

~ ❋ ~ ❋ ~ ❋ ~

Nine moons had passed since his meeting in The Tanners Apron. It had taken him four of those to recover from the birth in the cavern. Elgenubi Zuben stood behind him with her hand cupped under his chin. She lifted it and held her favourite dagger, the one he had filched, and the one she alleged had been forged by Crann Og Riamh from magicked Solais Silver, firmly against his throat. He gulped. The year of the galactic seed had flowered into the year of the red solar moon, and if he was truthful, he had grown, but he was still no closer to finding Micah. Although, he knew that would soon change. She had offered to get him in the neck if he were ever caught, but he had declined and said he would take his chances with Velig the Butcher, but he knew deep in his gut, that if he were ever caught, he would be dead before he drew a single breath as a captive.

'There…all done,' she said while she trimmed the excess hair from his beard. 'You look much better now, eh, Mar-cuss, not like the scrawny cracked egg we first took on. You, almost a man now.' She laughed softly while she wiped her dagger on her breeches, then flipped it into the ankle sheath inside her boot. Following this she sauntered gracefully towards a bank of shelves that covered one wall. They were laden with jars that contained honeycomb, bee curd, several coloured liquids, animal parts in brine, and an array of other weird and wonderful potions. She sighed heavily and whispered, 'Cracked egg, his head was like a cracked egg,' while she began stirring a solution in a bowl.

He did not understand their sense of humour, but he knew the state he had arrived in was a source of amusement to her, Eschamali, and the rest of The Ten. They had arrived at various times to study their new runner, the one with the head resembling a cracked egg. They found it hilarious, but it felt as if they were just learning how to make a jest. It was silly and childish to him when they were anything but. Then when he told them he had willingly shaved his hair, Eschamali Zuben howled with laughter. 'Best poke your eyes out too, fool. You blind as a man looking into the sun.' He had not understood that at first, but now he did.

Eschamali Zuben was a meathead, and he knew there was nothing he could do to impress the man. He was a weed compared to him, and Eschamali did not understand the sciences, so his alchemical and crystal craft knowledge would be wasted on him. Although he was careful not to reveal too much about what he knew, he was supposed to be a down and out. But Eschamali knew how to fight, and he knew how to spin. He used his holo-cast device like a man operating a machine without understanding the cogs, wheels, and inner workings, and that was enough for him. The rest of The Ten had various functions as far as he could tell, but Eschamali was the lead warrior, and he was the minnow, or the kid, or the cracked egg. He sighed, it was frustrating not being the one who everyone knuckled their forehead to, but being Marcus, meant that he lived another day. Being someone else meant that he was another day closer to finding Micah.

'Here, crush this poison, it is the last batch. And do not breathe too heavily near the powder,' Elgenubi chastised him while she put a pestle and mortar onto the wooden desk behind where he sat.

'I am not about to poison myself,' he replied irritably, then added, 'Again.'

She snorted and said, 'You mean, again this week, Mar-cuss.'

He ignored her, then got to his feet and pulled on pigskin gloves that fit like a second skin. He flexed them into place over his fingers; they had had a lot of use. Then he lifted the hemp cowl from around his neck and brought it around his mouth and nose. He secured it around his ears then fastened it with a silver clasp at the back of his head. She threw him a clean pair of goggles and he grunted his thanks then began crushing the dried leaves into a powdered fish gill secretion from what Elgenubi called a Weaving Fish. She caught it straight out of the filthy water of the Ophiuchus. Under her tutelage, he was becoming quite the apothecary, botanist, and purveyor of all the nasty things nature hid behind innocent eyes, bright berries, colourful flowers, and sticky gills. He wanted to impress her, and the others, tell them that he knew science, that he was an adept at alchemy and crystal craft, but he held his tongue. Vagrant's called Marcus, who came looking for dead-end jobs did not know alchemy and crystal craft.

'You learn fast. You make assassin one day. Then you challenge one of us to fight, and join The Ten, eh?' She leaned against the shelves, her gaze was casual but direct, and agile as a spear to the heart.

'Eschamali will not want The Ten to become eleven.' He mumbled through his cowl and continued pressing the leaves and powdered fish gill together.

She gave him a peculiar look and said, 'The Ten, always The Ten.'

He gulped, a fight to the death for a place with them he thought, light of the flame I am out of my depth. He steered her towards his failings and said with some confidence, 'Besides, he thinks me weak, not built for the night.' He pressed the pestle hard against the side of the mortar and ground his frustration into dust.

She strode towards him and folded her arms across her waist, while she met his gaze fully. Then she made a loud tutting noise, and said seriously, 'He is quite correct. You weak and not built for the night. We are all of us amazed you are not dead already, Mar-cuss. I myself have lost wagers to Himalia Skywalker on this matter, thinking you the worst runner we have had, and we have had unbelievably bad runners. Very weak and stupid…and you the worst…now crush.' She waggled a long finger at him then swung round and returned to the shelves where she checked the contents of another bowl. She took a pair of wooden tongs and lifted a length of her own silver hair, entwined with fibres she had taken out of her sleeping pod, then inspected it with her eyes narrowed. 'This lock ready to be weaved, Mar-cuss.'

'You're sure I will be able to sense all the way to the Shanty?' he said while he studied the contents of the mortar. He had ground the ingredients to a powder that was finer than pollen. Taking a square of soft silicone sheet, he placed in on top of the mortar and wrapped it around the bowl and the end of the pestle. The powder would need to settle; he knew that from experience.

Elgenubi had been weaving his dreads since his hair had been long enough. They were not like hers or Eschamali's though. His hair was thick but not coarse enough for the salt-locks they had. Their hair like their skin was chitin but a finer composite and it shone too. Elgenubi's locks shone like lengths of amethyst and platinum, they looked alive, because they were. She had woven her own hair into his along with pod fibre. He had agreed to it because he desperately wanted The Ten to treat him as an equal and he was proud of what he had grown, not to mention that when they were close to him, he could feel a connection to the others in The Ten through the lengths of dreaded hair; and he knew that he was almost unrecognisable. He belonged to this strange family, yes, it may be as a kind of pet, but never far from his mind was his real goal: find Micah and the data.

'Yes, Shanty no worries. Be easy for you now, you have my locks and pod fibre. Given this time, kid, not filched by your sticky little spider fingers.' She raised a pale eyebrow at him, and he winced inside, while a knot of dread set in his gut. Whenever she called him spider he wondered if she recognised him from the Night of the Dead.

'I didn't know any better, Elgenubi.' He felt a sheet of heat prickle up his neck and sweat form behind his ears and was glad he still had the cowl over most of his face. It was a stupid and disrespectful thing to do, but he had been too much like Troy Valoroso-Wyburn still. Too entitled, used to getting what he wanted, taking what he was denied anyway, not giving a damn about anyone else or their possessions. He had given a damn about someone once, and he had died, and he still was not sure whether that had been his fault. He had known in his gut, and his inner voice had shouted, go home, but still he had escorted his friend to his fateful end. Even now he had no guarantee that Micah was alive, he only knew that the dead body had not been him.

She tutted and said, 'Cracked egg, and spider fingers, you a crazy thief Mar-cuss,' while she rolled her deep indigo eyes upwards, and extracted the hair and fibre out of the solution. Then she began to roll it in a linen cloth before she bound it with silk thread and strips of thin leather. It was no thicker than a man's thumb, but it was long, and it moved as if it was alive while she cooed over it.

He watched her from the corner of his eye while he waited for the powder to settle. He had hardly been there a moon when he tried to steal the pod fibre. He lifted his top lip into a half smile, sometimes the advantages of being with Elgenubi far outweighed the dangers of having his arms ripped off by Eschamali. One evening, Elgenubi had emerged from her huge black sleeping pod, naked. They both had no shame in their nakedness, and she moaned frequently that there were too many layers of clothes for her to wear and that her skin could not breath. He had seen her hold up underclothes and fall about laughing on more than one occasion. The fashions in Lodewick baffled her. *Where do you carry your dagger, how will I be able to spin and kick in this? There is too much fabric, I could hide Mar-cuss under here but there is nowhere for a sword, my throwing knives are stuck in my sleeves. I am not wearing a dress.*

She liked to be free to fight she said, and it was on her orders that they broke into the warehouse that Volsunga owned, which held military-issue combat wear, destined for the dog soldiers in the north. To be fair, it was the only place they found anything large enough to fit Homan Wind. He checked on the silicone sleeve on top of the mortar. There was a fine layer of dust caught beneath and he tapped it with the pad of his index finger and smiled when he recalled it was Homan who lowered him from the sky-window by a rope. Light, his heart was thudding so loudly that he felt sure he would set off the alarms, and his blood felt like hot oil in his veins. If Volsunga caught them, he would have them beheaded, but he had taken a huge breath and set his stomach to ice while he hung on to the thought that he hated Rubric Volsunga, and the robbery would be a small revenge. Then he had taken his hatred and turned it to a sharp cold edge which he placed with his resolve along his spine, and a cold determined light set in the pit of his eye while he had whispered, 'Let's do this,' over his shoulder, and with trembling hands took hold of the rope. He looked back at Homan, for further instructions while he was being lowered into the warehouse, but the big buffoon's face was puffed up with mirth and he whispered to him. 'Homan caught a little minnow on a line, wiggle, wiggle.'

'For lights sake,' he hissed, and Homan replied, 'No, no lights. Look to shadow for El Nath, quick now little fishy.'

He snorted at the memory and Elgenubi glanced up and said impatiently, 'I be there soon as dread is ready.'

He nodded and tapped another film of powder from the inside of the silicone sheet. He had hardly been with them a moon when Elgenubi pointed to her sleeping pod and said, 'Not for you Mar-cuss, it will burn.' Who tells a thief something is not for them? Unable to resist, he stole fibres from her pod. He took them on the end of his knife, he believed Elgenubi, and did not want to risk being burned. Then he hid them in a glass jar at the bottom of his bedroll, also filched from the dog soldier stores. Which according to Elgenubi, meant that they were still functioning biologically; they needed sleep…which meant they were still alive. 'They not been made undead.' She told him and looked relieved.

That morning after their night-crawl had ended, they made ready to sleep for the day. She did not look at her pod nor attempt to uncurl it for the day's rest but walked purposefully towards him and held out her long pale arm, her palm opened while her eyes narrowed. 'Mine.'

'How did you know?' he asked and blushed while he retrieved the jar from the depths of his sleeping bag.

'If I snapped your finger off now, would you miss it?' She folded her arms crossly over her chest. 'If I called for Eschamali and asked him to rip off your arms, would you know they were gone? Do not deceive me, Mar-cuss, I am your only ally here.'

'It smells funny,' he replied petulantly.

'So, do you, Spider.' Her eyes flashed silver and indigo, ablaze with cold light that he now knew, was her temper.

~ ❋ ~ ❋ ~ ❋ ~

Satisfied that all the powder had settled, he removed the silicone and rolled it up carefully. Then he opened one of the drawers in the desk and took out the small oblongs of waxed paper the poisons would go into, and the small silver scoop used for measuring, followed by a delicate brush made from beaver fur, that he would brush off the residual powder with. 'This is the last batch of the Weaving

Death powder, Elgenubi. Will it be boxed soon?' he asked quietly through the cowl while he took the silver scoop next to the mortar and began to carefully fill the waxed papers.

There were a lot more boxes on the shelves behind her, full of various poisons and powders they made. Weaving Death, put in a drink left the unlucky recipient wobbly-legged, as if drunk, until they fell into a deep sleep, then a four-day coma, then the arms of death. But unlike a drunken stumble, Weaving Death was easy to spot if you knew what to look for. The poisoned person would walk, turn, walk, turn, walk turn, three times, stumble and fall to sleep for a few seconds, then try to regain their feet, only to repeat it again – narcoleptic cycle poison Elgenubi called it, with a studious look in her eye. Widow's Kiss was always put into tiny glass vials and best applied on the tip of a needle or dart; the very brave painted it on their lips, keeping the antidote handy after they had kissed their victim. Lovelock to stop the heart, went into tiny pike-skin canisters that were sealed with wax; it was popular with thwarted lovers who wanted to punish but not kill their passionate others, as the remedy was easily enough administered. A good thump to the chest to start it ticking again. She muttered about getting a Never-Age Anemone and a trip to the Southern Isles, for a giant cat of all things, but only after she had killed the dark lord.

Elgenubi finished her invocation and gave the linen cloth a final squeeze. 'They are to be hidden in the cork oak bark, for transportation by Lady Dorka. Weaving Death and Widow's Kiss is much sought by the Kanohi O Te Wai Pango…The Turanga's assassin spies. You know them?' she queried. 'The Eyes of The Black Water.'

'An apt name for the delightful girls from Ara Pourewa, I'm sure,' he replied sardonically and Elgenubi snorted. He had almost said that Bathory Dorka was not a real lady and had nearly bitten his tongue. The last thing he needed was to raise a suspicion that he did not want to deal with. The small twists of paper suddenly held his full attention while he wondered how under the Lords of the Light Flame, he had gotten away with his pretence so far. He was the sheep in wolf's clothing, hiding in the middle of the hungry pack. Light almighty, I should be bloody dead already he thought and twisted the end of the paper tight.

'Himalia wants two boxes of Widow's Kiss,' she said casually.

He felt a wave of unease like a premonition of dreadful things to come grease over his soul, but he could not fathom why. 'Himalia?' he asked puzzled. Then added, 'It is not like The Ten to use such a lot of the kiss.' He turned to meet her eye and there was question in his own. He knew she was reluctant to share something with him. He frowned and said impatiently, 'If I am on a need to know only basis, then so be it, but if not, do tell, Elgenubi.'

Her brow bunched into a snarl of knots, then she lifted her top lip in a sneer. 'Spider now has tongue sharp as a blade and oiled with bravery.'

He turned his back on her and continued wrapping poison until she said, 'It is no secret. Himalia wants them for the Mother Runga of Hiriwa Pourewa. We will exchange them for laser weapons.'

He felt his heart slow, then stop, then start again with such a kick he could not draw breath. 'You can't use them. They will take your energy and kill you,' he blurted out before he could stop himself.

She walked slowly toward him and there was something written in her face that was far too knowing, but she hid it quickly, then said, 'You know too much Mar-cuss. You watch your big mouth where the others are. These are weapons from Silver Tower, the crystals are different, they do not deplete your life force.'

He was going to challenge her but when he saw the sadness in her eye and the look of concern that had turned her lips down at the corners and had aged her a hundred years in one moment, he dropped his head and whispered, 'I am sorry.'

She put her hand on his shoulder and met his gaze fully, then said heavily, 'So am I.'

He put his hand on top of hers and held her gaze. He would not look away, he felt that she knew something but had not revealed it to the others. He was still alive, so his secret or whatever Elgenubi knew must be safe with her.

She surprised him by taking his hand and squeezing it. Then she said, 'The shadow has stolen the sun, and the great tree has fallen. Alnilam is distraught, and Himalia prepares the path in the Willow Wilds for he who walks the paths inside the Mind of Time.'

He nodded and sighed with relief but held it inside. Then said calmly, 'Have you shared it with the others?' While he thought, thank the light she does not know anything.

'Yes, it was Alnilam who felt the tree fall and I always knew the sun would set in hell.' She paused and studied him intently, then said harshly, 'Mar-cuss it is written in your books. Children know it. Why do you not?'

*

Their latest hideout was a warehouse belonging to the self-styled Merchant Queen, Lady Bathory Dorka. Troy wondered how she got away with giving herself a noble title. Lord Abrecan must be too busy to care or too busy planning an horrific end for her he thought then paused, or she is cleverer than she looks.

The apothecary was a squared off corner on the top floor. It was dry and airy, and that suited the cork oak she prepared there for export to the wine making regions in the southern isles. Two outside walls of the apothecary were red brick and lined with shelves, the other two were half-timber and half-glass. Outside of the apothecary an area was kept clear. This was where the Zuben's practised their combat and martial arts. It was where Elgenubi practised with him, and where Eschamali fell about laughing when he watched. According to Eschamali, he was a girl, or sometimes a librarian, and therefore he should fight with girls. Although Eschamali always shut his mouth when Elgenubi asked if he would like to spar with her.

Beyond this area, rows of disc-shaped cork oak bark, threaded on lengths of rope, and suspended from the ceiling to the floor, dried in neat columns as if they were a forest of gigantic strings of beads, all reds, browns, and mellow gold. The Weaving Death powder as well as other poisons they made to generate an income would be hidden in the crates of bark. Troy checked that the box was full, wrapped it in plain wax paper, then sealed it with red wax. Then he went to the shelves and counted the vials and pike-skin canisters, ready to be boxed and hidden too. We'll have to be out of the warehouse soon he thought then asked Elgenubi, 'Is the bark dry enough for crating. You know before we begin to put the merchandise in?'

'I check with flour, it fine, no dampness. Put two boxes,' she paused then said, 'best make it half a dozen Widow's Kiss for Himalia.' Before he could protest at the quantity and value of such an amount, she waggled the wrapped length of hair at him and said, 'Now, Mar-cuss, are you ready?'

Elgenubi brought the weave and another wooden chair over, which she placed in front of his. She carefully lifted the last box of poisons from the desk and put it onto the shelf next to the others. Then she brought a damp cloth and watched while he put the pestle and mortar in a bowl filled with a neutralising solution, then he wiped the desk, then his hands. Although practice had ensured he was extremely careful with the powders, that, and one or two accidental doses, was enough to ensure caution – not deadly doses but enough to lay him flat and amuse Eschamali no end. *'See, my prediction is already come true, weak and stupid, like them all,'* he said while he stood over Troy and marvelled at the froth coming from his mouth. To which Elgenubi had replied, *'You are right, did you wager much on his death? I have lost a considerable sum to Himalia; if he pulls through, I will owe her again this week. She sees something in him we do not.'* Eschamali had cupped his chin in his massive hand and snorted. *'She sees a way to make money, and knows we are desperate for runners. Contact her and inform her if she wishes to make good on her wager, she will need to bring Hydra the Cup. The minnow has swallowed poison without making the antidote first – again.'* Elgenubi had toed Troy with her ranger boot and her mouth puckered while she said, *'Stupid as well as weak, you are right, brother.'*

Troy sighed he was only glad he was not conscious when he overdosed on the poison, but Homan always filled him in on the details afterwards. *'I seen many men piss themselves before, but you pissed and pissed like a hot spring, just when we thought it over, away it went again. We never thought it would stop.'*

He undid his cowl, then removed it carefully and placed it in a linen bag, he took his gloves off inside out and deposited them in the bag too, he placed the lot in the neutralising solution with the mortar. Then he went to a bucket of the same solution and taking a damp shamy he wiped his face and hands. The antidotes to the poisons were on the shelf. He had eventually learned to make them first. Weaving Death's antidote was made from the foul excretions from Shroom fungi, but only the lurid yellow ones would do. Widow's Kiss was made from a precise concoction of different berries, steeped in urine and vinegar, then fermented, it was the foam that was the deadliest. The Widows piss liquid as Eschamali called it, was only good for the trots, but the antidote, was made from the bark of Sylvan Pine, and not just any. Only the variety that grew in the far North, in The Dark Forest. It was hard to come by and Acumen Sting brought their supply from the Shanty. Lovelock antidote was an accurate thump to the chest, but the poison itself was what Elgenubi called, the dust in the bottom of a hedge witches' bag. There we just so many things that Lovelock could be made from and most of them grew by the road, or in the hedge, or hung from branch or bough.

'We be on the move soon, Mar-cuss. More action, less apothecary…this suit you better, I think.' Elgenubi sat before him with the lock of hair in her hands. Loose pod fibres tendrilled through the air.

'Yes, I suppose. I have been missing the night…we have been too quiet of late. Though, I like the apothecary too.' He nodded to the undulating dread. 'Whereabouts will it go?'

'The last of the six portals around your crown. Just do the same as before.' She reached forward and patted his knee while he took a deep breath and began to visualise a hole at the top of his head with six smaller ones around it. As soon as he took his attention there, he could feel the empty space, like a small patch of numbness, different from the other portals, where the other dreads made of pod fibre, his own hair and hers had attached themselves. He tipped his head forward and Elgenubi guided the dread; it tickled as the pod fibres connected to the portal.

'There, it is attached. Give me your hands.'

He steadied his breath and thanked the light that Eschamali, the great lummox, had not insisted that he watch. He had for all the others, noting vocally every tremor, every drop of sweat, or film of dew on top lip, commenting that he was weak in the night, and the same colour as a librarian, which had him slapping his thigh and roaring with laughter.

With his eyes closed and his hands in hers, he opened the all-seeing eye at the centre of his forehead and cast his gaze outwards and into the thing Elgenubi called the Ever-Was. He felt the world peel away, and his sense of self expand, and become thin. It was something she called his diamond or astral body. He could only manage it when she was beside him, although with the sixth lock attached to his crown, he felt the difference immediately.

Her galactic signature power had an image, and a resonance that he could not see with his actual sight but when he used his inner eye and his diamond body to peel away the dross of physicality, he could see her, fully, and it always filled him to bursting with awe. She was a silver-violet flame atop an ornate bridge made of smoky platinum light. Eschamali relaxed on an old chaise at the far end of the warehouse. His signature was brighter and harder than a diamond, multifaced and strong, immovable and at its core 'The Warrior' stood. Suddenly the sixth lock crackled, and he felt a tingle pass thought him in waves. Beside him he felt Elgenubi nod, then squeeze his hand. 'Cast your sense a little further upwards,' she squeezed his hand again and said urgently, 'Not along the curve of time, or you be lost Mar-cuss, and we won't be changing your pissy pants for you when you stuck there. Hydra does not bring you back from that place. No one can.'

He nodded and taking a deep breath he pulled his sense of self back, reluctantly, from the golden arc that oiled seductively into the future. He felt her exhale with relief and the steady stream of her hot breath whispered across his face a waft of honey and lavender. Then she said, 'Outwards, over the water. Who do you sense?'

The Ever-Was, rolled in every direction like banks of different coloured dark cloud. The water below was another shade of smoke, pewter but tinged with green, sluggish, and thick, like the Ophiuchus sometimes was, while he was naught but a thought, encased in a body made of light, and his sense of self was held in his expanded sight. His connection to his physical self was through Elgenubi's hands, placed firmly on his wrists, her voice, and the steady measure of his breath. He did not expect to see anyone's image, he had not been able to before, but the thought had hardly taken shape when a shimmering blue hand jumped into focus; from it extended wave after wave of joy, health, and vitality. 'Hydra the Cup,' he said surprised.

'Good. You will pick her up easily...she has healed you often enough.'

He frowned and concentrated, his head tingled pleasantly although he could feel his brain beginning to push against his skull and he had to suck saliva from the pits of his cheeks once or twice. It felt like alchemy when he used his dreads to try to connect but Elgenubi would have none of it, reminding him it was not science or magic, but his inner eye was his birth right, as natural as the two eyes on his face. 'She is deep in the bowl of the Shanty...at the edge of the Bayou with...' Suddenly a bright yellow sun, almost green, flared then dimmed, followed by a rose gold orb that was fluid and contented. It emanated peace, where Eschamali had been hard and faceted, fury. 'With Alcyone Sun, and Acumen Sting.'

Elgenubi squeezed his hands. 'Good, continue.'

He withdrew his inner eye from the Shanty and soared. The shaft of light caught his heart and his mind, but he pulled his attention away from the hypnotic golden arc and imagined that he felt his diamond body turn northward. 'In the Willow Wilds, Alnilam Seed, his signature is a gigantic tree with roots as large as the boughs,' he paused and said hesitantly, 'It is raining tears from its branches.'

'Yes,' she said in a hushed voice, 'it is.'

He wanted to open his eyes and ask why she was so sad, why Alnilam was, but knew if he did it would take him an age and a half to reconnect. Instead, he said, 'He is with Markab Storm, a pink and magenta vortex and, and…' his head felt as light as a feather, and the arc of time slipped through the mist towards him, but he was determined he would find and name all The Ten. 'He's with a red sword or is it a staff, Himalia Skywalker. Ouch, what the…? Light, she saw me watching and slapped me. I felt that…they are hunting things through the trees. They are like scarlet shadows,' he paused and though he thought he imagined it he said, 'they smell funny, rancid and sour, but they have no images.'

He stopped and opened his eyes, then rubbed his cheek. It had been Himalia that he had seen in the Wild's the night Micah died. It had been Himalia who had lifted him to his feet in Athanasius Blood's warehouse, but he had looked like Spider King then. Now, he was Marcus, a minnow. If she recognised him, she did not say, nor show it in her eyes. He had gotten into the habit of avoiding her if he could, and she had no reason to seek him out. Himalia was the equivalent of a ranger, a scout for The Ten; she was hardly ever in Lodewick.

Elgenubi studied him carefully and looked set to say something but instead she laughed. 'Ha, it is the rod of power. She has anchored it…you see it, this is exceptionally good, Mar-cuss, particularly good. No one can sneak up on Himalia, whether in person or in the Ever-Was. I have lost yet another wager to her. I bet that I would use you to take her by surprise today.' She clapped her hands, delighted that she had lost the wager and that he had had his face slapped. Then she hesitated and flicked her fingers with her thumb and said, 'The scarlet shadows are just that. They are shadow spawn. Demon beasts or drudges gone into the Willow Wilds.'

So that is what Himalia killed. That was the monster I saw the night Micah died he thought and formed a question to ask her, but the words set like ice on his tongue, and the hairs all over his body stood on end. Then a great weight fell across his soul, and the light was sucked from him, and every bit of sorrow he had ever felt rose to the surface. He did not need his other sight to know. 'El Nath Night is here,' he said flatly while his eyes fluttered and watered.

Elgenubi took his hands again and said, 'Close your eyes and connect to him. He will think you weak if you do not.'

He gulped, closed his eyes, and opened his inner eye, he could feel the locks on his head roil greasily, and reach toward El Nath's image, the signature of his power, while he, and his common sense, wanted to flee the other way. It was an absence of light, and life. A pit of soul sucking despair one moment, the face of death in all its guises the next, then a shadow and a suggestion of something waiting in the dark. A terrible thing just out of reach, which needed to be discovered, if you dared. He hated El Nath for what his power drew forth from his own shadow. El Nath Night was a shadow-walker, not all Nights could do what he could. Most were lucky if they could see in the dark or hide themselves in a shadowy corner, but he was a master, a Cosmic Night, the top of the range of power. He had transcended the shadow, he used the absence of light, and dark energy much the same as people used alchemical batteries to move rickshaws. 'You do good. Look at it,' Elgenubi encouraged him. 'The shadow there for us to use, Mar-cuss. In the dark we grow; in the light we grow. Both the same. Both are power.'

He whimpered and almost fainted. She tutted loudly and said, 'Will you not let him do that to you, Mar-cuss? Erect your shield. Reject the Dread-cast as a thing of fantasy that he has made. He walks the dream and dances with shadows, he a master, and now he throws all your nightmares at you.' He felt the warmth of her hand about his wrist which suddenly felt too thin, and too sweaty, and he thanked the light that at least Eschamali was not there to mock him for his fear. Then he imagined his dreads coated with sheaths of iron and his diamond body was a mirror and a shield. He felt a wave of something from El Nath, and if it could have had words it would have said, *better*.

He opened his eyes with a start at a sudden bellow, and the racket of massive feet pounding on wooden floors. Eschamali burst through the columns of drying cork oak just as El Nath Night stepped out of the shadow in the corner. Then they began to fight.

'Son of a bloody librarian,' Eschamali roared as he reached El Nath and delivered a killing blow to the other man's skull.

'Your mother wanted a daughter, and she got one when she had you,' El Nath Night replied coolly, while he let the shadows pull him back and to the side. His skin was thick with chitin too and shone like an aurat beetle as it angled over the planes of his face like armour, in hues of gold, with alloys of green, blue, yellow, and red. He poured out of the shadow and delivered a bone-crunching blow to Eschamali's ribs, then disappeared again, while Eschamali roared like a hungry Eyrie Whorl.

'You shadow dance because you are weak, you are a water dancer.' Eschamali spat while he searched in the shadows for El Nath after offering him a great insult, another one that was completely lost on Troy.

Elgenubi groaned and turned to him. 'And the other idiot?' she asked, then waggled her fingers to indicate he should close his eyes again.

The distance will not be too great, he thought and sought Homan in the near vicinity. Where El Nath was, his sidekick Homan, would not be far behind. They were a very odd pair. 'Coming up the side of the building as if he were a spider walking up a wall,' he replied dryly, and his eyes popped open. He almost laughed but the remainder of the Dread-cast El Nath had thrown at him had emptied him of joy. Massive twit he thought and pushed the last wave of fear away.

Elgenubi harrumphed. 'Well, I for one am not contacting Hydra to come fix them.' She rose with a swing of her dreads that hissed through the air like a whip. Then stomped off to the shelves where she began to count the poison and tally up what Bathory would need to pay.

'I will do it,' he offered, and closed his eyes. Then he cast his awareness back towards the Shanty, just as Homan Wind came through the window and was immediately caught around the neck by Eschamali, who threw him towards the office. He slowed himself down enough to not break the windows, but his big ugly face squashed flat against the glass. Troy opened one eye and lifted his hand by way of greeting while Homan's wide nose and dark resinous flesh peeled off the glass. His skin was lighter than El Nath Night's. It still planed over the angles of his face, but it was cracked like parched earth. His alloy colours were earth red, ink blue and lichen green. Elgenubi said a pod malfunction caused their skin to harden and Homan's pod was not doing what he wanted it to. When the pods were healthy and happy, they kept their skin soft which was better for their disguises when they were in Lodewick.

Surely, they can see we are busy making coin. He opened both his eyes and gave Homan a hard stare, but the mammoth idiot lifted his hand briefly, and smiled showing teeth like tombstones. 'Minnow, you want to fight?'

He shook his head and said,' Too busy.' The columns of cork undulated and shook while Homan sped like a typhoon through them to seek Eschamali. He winced when several rows of suspended cork oak bark collapsed to the floor and fragments sprayed everywhere. They spattered the window as if someone were throwing a volley of solid wood at them. That will need paying for he thought, and probably when the time came, it would be double, or treble. Bathory Dorka as well as being greedy, was also extremely cunning, and The Ten? For all their supernatural power and strange ways, were terrible at some things, money, and jests especially. He sighed and thought I will need to check the invoice for the assassin powders too. Lords only know how she will have tallied it up this time. They charged what they needed at that time, it was always in multiples of ten, sometimes it was far too little like ten tens of silicone sheets, and sometimes far too much like the time Elgenubi had asked for ten skiffs and he had explained to her that she could have five skiffs or half of ten, which meant that each skiff could have two people in it. He had earned a thump on the arm for that and the tart reply that if they were putting two to a skiff, then there was no room for him, and he could swim. She finished by telling him that nine of the skiffs were going upriver and she would charge whatever she wanted to. Bathory, he suspected, kept her own tally, in case she ended up out of pocket.

He closed his eyes and let the locks at his crown guide him. He easily found Hydra's spectral blue hand, shimmering, and moving through the Bayou, by skiff. His forehead creased while he constructed the image, then projected what he thought was a good mental picture of the three buffoons fighting next door. The blue hand stopped, then balled into an angry fist.

'She's got the message, Elgenubi,' he said with his eyes still closed and his dreads tingling like frost forming on water. 'She seems…irritated.'

Elgenubi grunted and Troy heaved a sigh of relief. He felt more like himself, the iron shield had worked. El Nath Night was not a pleasant person to be around, he always felt like prey near him, while his flat look of disdain weighed him up and found him seriously lacking. There was a heavy thump from the warehouse, followed by a crack that sounded like a whip passing through air. Homan was weaving wind, and then a yelp from El Nath Night, good, he thought. Dorkus, he imagined himself saying that to him even though he knew he would not dare. At least the noise had kept his attention away from the golden arc and he found he hardly had to concentrate to avoid it. Then he took his consciousness and hovered over the bowl of the Shanty, then rose a little higher. Himalia flickered and reappeared close to where he had left Hydra the Cup; there was a stone compass in the Willow Wilds and there must be one in the Shanty too for her to have travelled so quickly he thought and stored the information. That was the advantage of being with the Zuben's, they had opened a whole new world to him, not just the heightened senses he felt through his dreaded hair, which was something to do with the pod fibres, but also things like stone compasses, merchant smugglers pretending to be ladies, a tribe that lived below Lodewick and their lord, Sewer King, the level of resistance that was growing against Abrecan…and this, the thing he was doing now.

Consciousness is mobile, you only think it is not because you have yoked it to the vessel. It was one of Elgenubi Zuben's first lessons. He was bringing his consciousness back to the heaviness of the shell of his body when he saw it. The beast wrapped around Lodewick, a gigantic serpent with stubby clawed legs, wingless, and yellow bellied, it had orange and black scales along its body. He knew it was a galactic signature image, but it was enormous. The taste of blood filled his mouth, a dark power radiated from the serpent that made El Nath Night seem positively sunny.

He whimpered, then the beast turned its eye towards him, and crimson and black runes flew like spears and daggers in his direction. They hissed towards his inner eye, and he could not tell whether they had hit him when suddenly he fell off his chair and blackness took him completely.

He woke to find Hydra the Cup holding his hand. Her storm-cloud-grey dreads were fine, like a bunch of silken rope twisted into a bun that she wore caught in a net at the nape of her neck. She patted his wrists, then looked into his eyes, kind as a grandmother. 'Oh, dear me, love, what did you do this time? Was it the Weaving Death powder, again? I dare not give you the antidote, Elgenubi insists it was not poison, and I agree, I can feel no trace of it in you. You are improving, just as you make the last batch.' She looked over his head at Elgenubi and said, 'At last I have won. Himalia owes me.' Then she took her attention back to Troy. 'I said you would not make it to the end without another incident.'

Elgenubi tutted. 'I should have refined my wager. I have been betting on the week he will die.'

Hydra laughed gently while she held a damp cloth to his head, hardly necessary as he had felt the jolt of her healing wave pull him back from his nightmare, as if someone had taken hold of the tail of his spine and flicked it like a whip. 'You test my skills, Marcus, that you do.'

Eschamali stuck his head around the door. There was no sign of the others, and he looked as if he had been healed – no blood or broken bones. 'You were screaming like an elite lady who saw a spider on her leg,' he bellowed. 'We all stopped fighting to see you being weak in the night.' He tapped the side of his head and crossed his eyes, then lolled his tongue out of the side of mouth. Elgenubi frowned at him and flapped her hand to shoo him away; he walked off laughing. 'Weak…like all of your kind.'

She pursed her lips, then helped him sit. 'That was worry itself, Mar-cuss. You have been away from yourself for a long time and far away at that. It is the final lock; it is powerful, yes?' She tapped his chest with a long finger, and genuine concern made her eyes soft and her face beautiful.

Hydra patted her on her shoulder. 'He is back now and will need some nourishment before he goes running tonight.' Elgenubi nodded while the older woman gathered her things. Even though Hydra was smaller than Troy and comfortably round, she waddled when she walked, she sat on her haunches as most of The Ten did; when she rose, it was with effortless grace. He had seen her cuff Homan Wind about the ear before. It was fast as a frog lashing out its tongue to catch a bug. She may be a healer and spent a lot of time with the lowers in the Shanty, healing them, and talking with their witches and shaman, but he did not doubt for one moment that she was as deadly as Eschamali Zuben.

'I wish to speak to Eschamali before I go. Himalia waits for me at the Wilds. This is getting too dangerous. They are warriors, not children of barbarians. I will put a stop to their foolishness this time.'

'They bored, but yes, it is time for us to move Hydra, I have seen it,' Elgenubi stated sadly. Then she said in a quiet voice, 'There are six boxes for Himalia. For her to trade with Pouri Hikoi.'

Hydra met her gaze, and something passed between the two women. He felt sure it was a look of grief or fear and he felt his own insides flip and turn, what under the sun would Elgenubi be afraid of.

'Then it is agreed, I will make plans with the clan chiefs who control the Bayou,' Hydra replied. Then taking her attention back to Troy, she ruffled his hair and said, 'Eat, now.'

Then she walked to Elgenubi and put her arms around her and gave her a hug while she drew her head onto her shoulder. He saw Elgenubi's shoulders shake and heard her breath draw snot back into her nose. She had never been upset by the meatheads fighting before, so why now he thought, and continued to listen to them while he pretended to get something to eat.

'I cannot believe she is dead,' Elgenubi said hoarsely into Hydra's shoulder.

Hydra released her and taking her wrists in her hands she held her at arm's length then met her gaze full on, and said with a note of ice in her voice, 'Is she though? I for one smell a plot, within a plot, within a plot.'

'What did Mother Runga, Trathul, say?' she asked Hydra quietly while they walked to the door.

'Trathul is as two-tongued as any of the adepts from Silver Tower, indeed she has more than two, because she has been there longest, and is not the Highest Mother because of her reticent nature. But she tripped herself up, whether it was deliberate or not, I cannot say. She was making plans for Pouri Hikoi, when Cassandra Novantae was still The Eye of Hiriwa Pourewa. When Pouri was still a Kanohi and deeply in love with Raiona.' Hydra paused at the door and put her hand softly on Elgenubi's arm. 'It was not an emergency replacement because Cassandra had suddenly disappeared, but a carefully wrought strategy.' Hydra touched her eye and said dryly, 'Cassandra Novantae will have seen it, she will have made sure her replacement was just so. That he was ready, with whatever means she had at her disposal.'

Elgenubi nodded and replied, 'You are right. It was unexpected…' she trailed off and sniffed, then added quietly, 'I thought her indestructible.'

Hydra snorted, stood on her tiptoes, and kissed Elgenubi on the forehead then turned to leave. 'So did she,' she said over her shoulder while she made her way through the door and into the forest of cork to find Eschamali.

What? Cassandra Novantae is at least three thousand years old, Troy thought while he remembered where he had left his books. As soon as I get time, I will read them. How is it that she has just died?

~ ❊ ~ ❊ ~ ❊ ~

Elgenubi watched Troy out of the corner of her eye, she knew he had been eavesdropping, and while he was a good runner, and she liked him, she did not trust him. He be like a frightened librarian if I push too hard. How to get him to spill his secret words without him bolting. 'Mar-cuss, what happened? Where did you go?' She put concern in her voice and hoped it sounded genuine while she took his hand and led him to the old leather couch that rested against one wall. Next to it was a small table with his precious books on. She smiled inwardly and pointed to the books and said, 'You need to seal them in silicone sheets before they are too damaged to read,' while she went back to the shelves and poured two beakers of water. She liked that he read, but Eschamali and Homan took it as proof that he was a librarian, and weak in the flesh like all librarians were.

'I…I'm not sure, he replied, and she almost believed him. He was not good at remote viewing and was only just learning to connect to the others using his locks. She nodded her encouragement and he continued. 'I just collapsed.' He paused while he gulped at the water.

'Go on, Mar-cuss, I must know if this affects our decision to contact Murzim.' She pulled the chair over from the apothecary table and sat before him.

'That was all,' he lied.

She narrowed her eyes, it was going to be harder than she thought, like catching the wind of his breath with her fingers, then separating the truth from lies. 'What made you pass out? It cannot have been the weaving death.' Her hand wove in the air as if that would help explain one of the deadliest poisons they made.

She could see he was reluctant to answer and knew he did not want to jeopardise the plan to meet Murzim. They had all been in better moods the last few days and it had lifted his spirits too. It was a hard, nomadic life with The Ten, she understood that it did not suit everyone. Though he had adapted to it well, he had been a scrawny down and out when he came to them. Now, he was anything but. While he was not like them physically, not as quick, not as strong, he was the best runner they had ever had. For his kind, he was tough, strong, and a good fighter, but there was something more to him, that was too genteel, a softness at his centre that would not set, she knew he would not kill, but she hoped he could if his survival depended on it. Soft like a librarian she thought and took her attention back to him. She always felt he was temporary, and though she knew he liked her, he had made no attempt to show his feelings. He was terrified of Eschamali but that was not the thing that held him back, it was a decision he had made. He was with them because he was hiding, not surviving, not like Birdy had been, and he would not stay because the line of fate on his hand told a different tale, and the light of destiny in his eye told her he had hidden something inside his heart. She dropped clues and probed to see whether he would reveal more but he was adept at lying, always changing the subject or spidering his way out of things. It worked on the meatheads, he was always ill whenever he was in Hydra's company, hiding behind his weakness, and as for Himalia, he avoided her but not obviously, and now he had lied to her for the last time. I have had my fill she thought.

'You forget I was looking into the Ever-was with you, Mar-cuss,' she hissed indignantly and met his gaze full on.

He brought his beaker to his mouth and pretended to take a good long draught while he thought, light she was too. But when? I cannot remember. He did not want to lie to her but was not sure how much to reveal. If they did not like what they heard or saw, they would kill him. He put the beaker down and exhaled while he tried to calm his heart. It was pattering like the sound of feet, running away. 'I saw a snake…more like a serpent. It felt wrong, evil…wrapped around Abrecan Castle. It was attached to the black moon by some sort of a leash, and there were lots of other leashes that came from the moon like threads and were attached to,' he paused, and his forehead bunched into tight knots,' like strings attached to the holo-clocks above the statues of Anuk. I think, I'm not sure.' He faked a shaking fit to distract her, she was staring too intently into his face, and he knew she could read a lie a hundred leagues away.

'It is the king of the shadow spawn, stronger on its nest, holding the black moon in the sky. I do not know why the moon is joined to the holo-clocks.' She flicked the nail of her right thumb across the pads on the tips of her right fingers, a gesture of rejection or protection. He felt his world skew violently. Micah was right. Abrecan was manipulating reality through the black moon. He wanted to throw up. Instead, he pointed to her fingers and said, 'I tried that with El Nath Night,'

She frowned and thought, he is trying to distract me? Why? But said instead, 'Did it work?'

'No, he said,' he took a moment to lift his top lip into a disdainful sneer and put his best voice of doom on, then said, 'I do not understand why you ward me. I am not evil.'

Elgenubi snorted and said, 'He is not.' Then she narrowed her eyes thoughtfully, and with her head to one side she said quietly, 'But the serpent is. Why do you think you saw Lord Lucas' galactic signature?' She frowned as if trying to puzzle something out. Then with a shake of her locks she said, 'You think on it Mar cuss, then you tell me.'

'I will,' he replied, and made ready to rise, but she held him with a contemptuous look and said, 'I have not finished with you.' Then waved him back to his seat. 'Prepare to view again,' she said, and he heard a note of anger in her voice and felt dread settle in the pit of his stomach while he thought, she knows who I am, I can feel it.

It was not long until they were both disembodied, but this time, she did not hover behind him but floated by his side, sometimes she even merged her energy with his, but he could not tell, and she felt a little guilty at the pleasure she took from feeling him deeply without his knowing.

'Why does it feel different this time?' he said.

'We are closer together, melded,' she replied and was glad that both their eyes were closed. She was sure she felt blood flush her cheeks. 'Now, show me where?' Elgenubi felt a swirl of motion when Troy turned his astral form to the East. 'There,' he said, and she heard the fear resonate through his words.

She squeezed his wrist and said, 'We are in the Ever-Was in our astral form, it cannot see us. Physically, we are safe in the warehouse, our nano devices are duds, remember.' She took her own gaze to the beast, and he felt her physical frown reach even as far as the Ever-Was. The serpent was colossal, and its power emanated in a wall of dark waves that pulsated slowly across all the lands where the people were implanted with a nano device and held enthralled under the false light of the black moon. It moved sluggishly as though holding the moon in the sky was an effort. On the index claws of each front foot, it wore a ring and the alchemy within each band sparkled in blue rune light upon their surfaces.

She whispered, 'It has much power now. From death and blood, you understand?' He did not reply, and she continued. 'Imagine we connected by a rope.' She smiled when she felt his concentration and a tightening around her astral form. Then she said, 'Look at the curve of time with me?' She felt him flinch and the rise of his fear, but she pulled him with her until the swirling shades of black, brown, and grey parted, and they saw the golden arc spin away into eternity. 'It is the arc of the spine of the Ouroboros,' she paused while she heard him grunt and felt the tightening in her own gut and a surge of nausea, not her own, but his, as it passed to her through their connection. 'Ah, I knew it. The Star has activated.' She pulled Troy's astral form round further to the West and heard him clear his throat. Then he said, 'Light of the flame, I was so busy concentrating on finding The Ten and avoiding being pulled into the future, I did not see it.'

In the northwest of Eirini, a yellow star like a ghostly apparition glowed softly and flickered in and out of substance. He wondered if the serpent could see it. It looked like the beast was looking for something, but its eye slid over where the Spectral Star was, and whenever it looked to Eirini a dullness came across the lens of its eye. While they watched the Star suddenly blinked out, and he gasped, 'Where did it go?'

Her grip tightened on his wrist, and she whispered, 'It has returned to earth.' When he did not reply she said, 'It is a prophecy in Cassandra's Chronicles. Its power will be perfected when it is returned to earth. You must read your books

Mar-cuss.' Her voice sounded as if she was shouting through a wall and he felt his astral body float away when she pulled him back with a thought and said, 'You were off along the arc, stupid. What other lights do you see. Begin in Lodewick.' There was a sharp note to her voice that cut through the swirling mists, and thickness of the Ever-Was. Suddenly he felt her share something with him. It was an intimate melding of consciousness that was so different to his own it stole his breath from his chest, and he could not subdue the sudden excitement he felt when it pulsed through his blood like desire.

'Is this how you see?' he asked in a too throaty voice.

'Yes, it is clearer in the Ever-Was for me, but I have never seen the serpent, even though I am medial woman, and been viewing into far off places for long time.' She felt his desire and knew she had spoken too harshly, but she pushed his thoughts and feelings away. He was so loud. It was not unusual for him to project desirous thoughts, feelings, and energy towards her, it amused her that he was usually unaware of it. Although, Markab Storm had once whispered to her, 'You have the minnow cunt-struck, Elgenubi.'

Troy took his attention to the ghostly galactic signatures that bobbed and weaved around Lodewick. Compared to The Ten, they looked weak and sickly. Once or twice a bright signature would flare, but the serpent took its attention to it and as far as he could tell, it fed off it somehow and the image turned to crimson or black. He shuddered and felt revulsion crawl beneath his physical skin as if a layer of his subcutaneous fat had melted then reset. 'It is feeding off their power and somehow subduing their light,' he whispered.

Elgenubi tutted angrily and said, 'Conquest subjugate and grind all to dust and shade. He is the great devourer; the nano device alerts the beast to when it is dinner time, then it serves the serpent the power. Now, view the Shanty.'

When he took his inner eye to the Shanty all he could see were swirling thick fogs and dense brown matter, although he knew that there were hundreds of refugees hiding there. 'I cannot see anything. They are obviously without galactic signatures and any power.' He heard the disdain in his voice after it was too late to hide how he felt about the lowers who lived in the filth of the swamp.

She snorted and said, 'Their light hidden from you by their shaman, Mar-cuss. Lord high and mighty, with his nose stuck in the air.'

A sheet of anger burned across his cheeks, and he made ready to release her grip and open his eyes, but she hissed, 'Do not.' The heat in those two words was enough for him to know that what she meant was, *do and I will kill you.*

He snapped, 'Well hurry up, we have other things to do.'

'Take your view to the west. What do you see?' she bit off her words impatiently.

He felt another elevation of her power through their connection and suddenly a rainbow of galactic signatures popped like a scattering of different coloured blossoms, like lamps had been lit through the swirling fogs that covered Lord Bucky's zone, Eirini. 'There are hundreds,' he ran out of words while his thoughts reeled. There were Storm galactic signatures, many Earths and Seeds, Monkeys, and Eagles, Hands, and dozens of Mirrors. Briefly he saw a rod of red power. He took his attention back to where he had last seen Himalia Skywalker, she was still there. That meant there was another Skywalker, in Eirini but to the south of where he had seen the Spectral Star.

Elgenubi interrupted him when she said in a hushed voice, 'They are the human resistance, but he cannot see them with his serpent eye, their nano device a dud like ours. The Romarii implant a nano that makes it appear as if they have not activated when they have.'

'I thought I would only be able to see The Ten. How can I see all of them?'

'I do not know,' she whispered, and he heard fear and a strange curiosity in her voice.

He dropped her hands suddenly. And taking his own hands he covered his eyes while he opened them. His head was thumping, and his brain felt too large and too oily, his physical body was too heavy, and he longed to be out there again, slipping along the arc of time, to a future where the monster serpent who ate energy, and the light of the living, did not exist. With a deep shuddering breath, he curled his unease into a tight fist deep in his gut but there was hardly room for it there, not when the knowledge that there were not enough people in the resistance, not enough power to challenge Abrecan, sat there like an undigestible brick. He had not studied the images for long, but he knew that there were no Dragons, Suns, Wizards, or Warriors. They will all be found and killed he thought while he took his hands from his eyes and wondered if he would ever be able to see as clearly again without her aid.

Elgenubi was studying him intently, with a calculating look in her eye and her mouth drawn into a thin hard line. After a short while, a look of knowing set on her face, she nodded as if to agree with her inner thoughts, then rose. 'I must speak to Eschamali. It will not affect our contact with Murzim, but we will ask The Ten to shield us when we go to the meeting. The serpent is a fat, hungry beast, with a piercing eye, here, in Lodewick.' She rummaged in her pocket. 'Eat this.' She pressed a hard lump into his outstretched hand.

He put the lump of what looked like a huge scab into his mouth and gagged; it was bitter as hell. 'What is it?'

'It is bee glue, bee curd, the thing they repair their hives with.' She made kneading motions with her hands. 'It is made from their saliva, wax, and botanical sap.' She nodded enthusiastically then turned to go with a few final words thrown over her shoulder. 'It is good, it protects us from your diseases.'

He waited until she left then spat it back into his hand. He would do almost anything to please her, but he was not swallowing bee spit. Unless she is trying to poison me for lying, he thought, while he frantically went over the afternoon's proceedings. What does she know? What does she suspect? He leaned back with a groan and the books on the table caught his eye. What did she say? Its power is perfected when it is returned to earth.

He walked to the store of silicon sheets and picked several out. Then he returned to the couch and individually wrapped Navigating the Southern Isles. When he picked up Meite a Thomas' Phantasmagoria it fell open on a page that began with, *'Does your eye slip and slide over that which stands afore you? Man, woman, child, fish, bird, or beast. It is all of them, and none besides, when your senses fail and your eye oils across the water babes of Ri Fiali. The Rodinian Shifter.'*

'Anukssake, Homily shifty-skin is just that.' He could hardly wrap the book and kept thinking, a skin changer, a shape shifter. He lay Meite's book on top of Navigating the Southern Isles. Once another silicone sheet had enveloped the two books, they were impermeable to dirt and water. He put them carefully back on the table, then he took his tatty copy of Cassandra's Chronicles and began to thumb through it, he had more things to learn than he had time to cram into his head. Just then he heard footsteps approach, but he had nothing to fear, no one had keys to the small door they used to enter the warehouse, four floors below, and all cargo left the building by boom and winch through cargo doors high in the walls. It will be one of The Ten he thought just as a knuckle rapped on the glass of the apothecary.

*

'Is it any wonder they call you a librarian, if you always have your wonky nose in a book.'

'Markab! I saw you in the wilds.' He put his book down and leapt to the door. He greeted Markab with an arm clasp and a wide grin. 'Librarian? It should insult me more, but I do not understand what's so bad about librarians.'

'Then I will enlighten you while I get something to eat for myself and Alnilam,' Markab replied then moved like a dancer over to the counter and started rummaging about in cupboards, looking for bread and cheese. 'Are you sleeping here tonight?' he asked over his shoulder and Troy replied, 'Yes, loose ends with Bathory, then the meeting with Murzim.'

There was a clatter of plates and earthenware beakers while Markab said, 'You want a bit of fun tonight?'

'I am not going whoring with you in the Tun if that's what you mean.' He replied while he started clearing some space on a low table before the couch.

'Tut, tut. Marcus the Kid could earn a fortune if he would only follow my lead.' He paused, then with a wicked grin he said, 'Or are you still cunt-struck with one amethyst-locked lovely?' He leant against the counter like grace itself was taking its ease.

Troy waggled his arms and said, 'I love them more.'

Markab guffawed then said, 'Kid, for what you lack in the night, and in the flesh, you make up for in jests. And, I will have you know, I am gainfully employed, and while I enjoy my employ, it is not without its drawbacks.' He paused while he carried over a stack of plates, heaped on top with bread, cheese, pickles, fruit, nuts, and a pile of mint leaves. Putting the pile of crockery and food carefully on the table he said with a sigh, 'I'll need more Neemna seed, half a dozen fine silicone sheaths, and mild sleeping draughts. Oh, and we need flower of the sun oil, keep our skin smooth and soft.' He paused when Troy inhaled sharply. 'Our pods will not tolerate any other oil. I'll give you the regals myself.' Markab flapped his hand at him.

'It's not the cost, well it is actually, but I'm not sure there is any to be had.' He said to Markab's back while he returned to the counter.

Markab paused while he thought for a moment then said, 'Bathory will have some. Just pay the greedy crone double.' He returned with water, and wine, held by the necks of the clay carafes they were in, and three earthenware beakers tucked under one arm.

'Best get him a dozen sheaths, and a mild aphrodisiac too. He has a busy night ahead. Slits to fill, and rows of sticks standing to attention like fat sausages hanging in a butchers window,' Alnilam said while he made his way through the apothecary door.

'Anything for you Alnilam?' Troy replied as he rose and grasped Alnilam's arm in greeting. It did not take long for his spirits to rise when he was in their company, and the serpent around Lodewick was soon forgotten, and El Nath's dread-cast no more than the memory of a fretful headache.

'A couple of earplugs. Being the pimp for one of the most sought-after benedicks in Lodewick is proving to be a duller song than I had ever imagined. It is the same tune, night after night, and how those lovely elite's like to sing and dance to the tune from Markab's flute.' He slapped Troy on the back and they both headed to the table. Troy sat on the couch while the other two sat on their haunches before the low table.

Markab passed the plates around. 'Last night, though. Thank the flame for that. I did not think I would ever tire of it, but if I get another hard-on after tonight, someone throw a bucket of freezing water over me,' he said, and the edge of exhaustion was a droll note in his voice.

When not spinning holo-casts to gather information at tribal gatherings, he and Alnilam worked the Bliones Tun, the pleasure gardens. They did not speak or act like the other Ten, they had refined their language to suit the palates of the most expensive whorehouse in Lodewick. Although, to call the Bliones Tun a whorehouse, was akin to calling Bucky's winter residence, The Palace Galay, a shack. The surroundings were fantastical. Pavilions, coloured alchemical lakes, fountains and falls; woodlands with modified men and women, satyrs and nymphs, Fae, and Dryad, and Drus, mock castles with dungeons well stocked with the tools of the cruel prince's trade. Alnilam, and Markab, rented a suite of their own pavilions, used in rotation, in the most private part of the gardens. The part where supposedly celibate people came to be serviced. The pickings were rich, keeping a secret like that cost, and Markab had earned himself a reputation as the most experienced, and circumspect benedick in the Bliones Tun. The Lothario of Lodewick. Strictly by appointment, whereby Markab choose who he would pleasure from a long waiting list, the clientele was escorted, bound, blindfolded, and masked, to and from the pavilion by a silent and menacing Alnilam, always in disguise, which all added to the subterfuge and the cost of a hora or two with the Lothario. The collected information was priceless while it slipped over the tongues and teeth of the rich, like the expensive oils Markab massaged into their yielding flesh.

'But first a lesson in librarian's,' Markab said and pointed to Troy's pile of books.

'That first, then an invitation to join us.' Alnilam added while he piled his plate with cheese and fruit.'

'Where to?' Troy asked.

'We're off to blow up the dam at the new flyer base,' Alnilam said, and his grin split his face in two, and the light in his eye was hungry for action. 'It will, of course, look like an act of nature. They have alchemical orbs and antigravity flyers there, and I would prefer it if they had none.'

'What about the pump-wheel slaves?' Troy asked while he poured wine and water into the beakers. Markab put his hand on his and meeting his gaze he shook his head then said quietly, 'Gone to the witches bridge, or the salve.'

Troy nodded and his mouth turned down at the corners, while his forehead bumped into a tight frown, he did not have to ask for an explanation. The slaves had been used, and now they were bags of blood for sacrifice or flesh and bone ready to be modified.

'That reminds me,' said Alnilam through a mouthful of bread, 'You are entertaining one of the delightful sisters of Bloodgita tonight.'

Markab groaned and said, 'It will be their Aldhelm, she has the coin and the appetite. Best make it a strong sleeping draught. They have incredibly loose lips when they are almost comatose. I'll need to get as much out of her as possible now that The Star has come to its power.'

'I did not think they were fuckable flesh, and blood,' Troy said bitterly.

'Quite the contrary. I put on my Lothario costume and mask, fill her full of holy wine, then punish her for some misdemeanour she has committed, a sin against the One-God, which she confesses to, spilling her guts and secrets while I tie her to the rack, she keeps her robe and mask on, and her pleasure sounds like a little pig feeding,' Markab replied, then lifted his nose up with his index finger while he pulled a pig face. He continued in a bored voice, 'Then I say, I give thanks to Anuk's little whore's for bestowing their blessing on the Lothario of Lodewick. Of course, by this time she is away in her cups, and I can say anything I want. Indeed, I usually give her arse a good hard slap with a wooden paddle when Alnilam picks her up to carry her to the recovery pavilion.' He caught Troy giving him an odd look and put his hand up and said, 'It is what she pays for. She likes to feel the bruises long after I have gone. Here,' he pointed to his groin and said, 'She wants not to be able to sit down for days. She pretends Lord Abrecan sent the Lothario to fuck her senseless as a punishment.' Then he looked longingly at the pickles, while Troy and Alnilam wiped tears of laughter from their eyes. With a theatrical shrug he pushed them away and took a pat of plain soft cheese, vinberry, and mint instead. He poured his wine back into the carafe and said, 'The Lothario of Lodewick is oiling a pig tonight, and a little mint sweetens the pork,' while he filled his beaker with water and crushed mint leaves into it.

Alnilam did no such thing and after gulping his bread and taking a long draught of wine and gathering his mirth back into his belly, he said, 'Librarians are a pale-green fleshy grubs, almost taller than you. He pointed to Troy then said, 'They are the immature form of an insect that stores knowledge like a library in the silk of its cocoon. They are extremely slow and studious, ponderous, and philosophical, and inhabit catacombs where they are cared for until they pupate, usually when they are stuffed full of knowledge. According to librarians the knowledge is given to them by the salt and minerals of the rock itself. They hatch, then the silk from their chrysalis is taken and woven into reams of data that can be read by the adult librarians,' he paused and ate a handful of nuts.

'Are you making a jest,' Troy said while he wondered if the creature would be mentioned in Meite's Phantasmagoria.

'No jest, and the adults are a large, humanoid creature, with armoured chitin body panels and huge colourful wings that hang like a cloak when not in flight. They have oval shaped eyes, a small nose, and mouth, and feathery antennae coming from their eyebrows, they are called Keeper of the Mysteries, and are extremely pacifist.'

'Well, I'll be damned,' Troy said and sipped his wine. Then he added, 'El Nath should not call me a librarian to insult me if he cannot read himself.'

Markab put his beaker of water down and carefully asked, 'Who told you El Nath cannot read?'

'It was Homan, on the night we went to rob snake-eye, Volsunga.'

Alnilam guffawed and sprayed the table with half chewed nuts. 'Light of the flame, crater face made a jest all on his own. If you had said to El Nath he could not read he would have had the dread on you that tight, you would have been glad to hang yourself from the Merewif Bridge.'

'The crafty, clumsy, lump of turds,' Troy said and took some bread. 'I still can't understand why El Nath just didn't get the scatt himself then.'

'Was a test,' Markab added. 'They wanted to see if your balls had dropped.'

He laughed. Then asked, 'How long will it take?'

Alnilam rose effortlessly and gave him a squeeze on the shoulder. 'I knew you would come.'

'I haven't said yes yet. I've had a big day,' he protested while Markab began picking up the dishes. He balanced them in his hands and slunk toward the counter while he replied over his shoulder, 'We heard all about your big day already. Elgenubi will like it, and we will have you back before bedtime.'

Troy snorted then said, 'I was coming anyway, even before you said that about Elgenubi. Right?'

'I believe you,' Alnilam said, then added, 'We will fill you in on the way there. We have a skiff waiting.'

'I will pack the supplies first,' he said, and Markab and Alnilam smiled while they passed him their packs. They were narrow and long and were worn strapped to the front of their bodies, so fighting staffs, swords, other weaponry and cloak or coat would not be affected by bulk at their backs. He began to pack Markab's supplies, sheaths, aphrodisiac, and sleeping draught. He picked up the last precious bottle of the flowers of the sun oil, it was half full and no bigger than two of his fingers put together, he put that in too, then said, 'I'll put you some Widow's Kiss and the antidote in, Markab, you never know it being the last night and all.'

Alnilam said, 'Now you are like us, kid' while he patted his own pack, which doubled as a black leather, segmented, and laminated, breast plate, 'Always prepared for the Nightcrawl, always ready to run.'

He nodded and collected his weapons, nothing fancy, just the ones he had carried with him when he left home, a brass knuckle, a throwing dagger, and a Solais Silver stiletto. Then he went back to his stack of books and picked up the night optics Homan had given him from the back of the table. He turned to others and asked, 'You have some?' They nodded. Then with a wide smile and a surge of adrenalin that set his heart racing, he attached his own pack. His desire for action was a hot and quick thrum in his veins and he said with mock theatrics while he tapped the hard shell of the outer wall of his chest pack, 'Then let the Nightcrawl commence.'

Markab asked, 'Cloaks or coats?'

'Coats, there will be no city gents, in fine cloaks where we are going tonight. Only guards, slaves, and the soon to be damned, we need to blend in,' Alnilam finished dryly.

~ ❋ ~ ❋ ~ ❋ ~

They landed the skiff at a dilapidated and disused cockle fishers' wooden jetty and made their way along the edge of the marsh to the hinterland of the docks. Once or twice savage howls floated through the trees from the Willow Wilds, and Alnilam said, 'Himalia is hunting with the Volpi.'

Troy gulped but held his tongue. Volpi, according to Meite a Thomas' Phantasmagoria were a cursed tribe of Fae, called Novantae.

~ ❋ ~ ❋ ~ ❋ ~

It had happened too quickly. He had killed an outer patrol guard with his throwing dagger but had not even had time to stop to consider what he had done. He had never killed before, not a person, but the adrenaline, and Markab's and Alnilam's determination to get to their destination had swept him forward without pity for the loss of life, or shame for what he had taken. He was a shadow in the night, and they were crawling, belly down, across a field of scrubby willow and coarse long grass. Markab slithered next to him and passed him his bloodied dagger. 'In the heart, quick kill,' he said in a voice that was softer than a summer's breeze.

He did not trust himself to speak, a strange feeling, like a wad of cotton stuffed into the back of his throat held his words and his feelings prisoner. Instead, he nodded and put the dagger back in his boot, where he could swear, he felt the heat of his crime burn a hole in his ankle. I have never killed before he thought, but the emotion he sought to berate himself with was strangely absent, suffocated. The blade was hot at his ankle, but his crime had passed, and he felt only layers of the now. The warm air floating above the cooling ground was condensing into a thick mist, the smell of the earth beneath the grass stung his nostrils, while the Ophiuchus to their right stunk like the bottom of a brewer's barrel. To their left the city loomed like a bejewelled brown mountain in all the shades of tile red, tarry brown, marsh gas yellow, and tallow lamp gold. Blue alchemical lights flared at temples, and rich merchant guild houses like the rarest of scattered sapphires in the mud; at their backs they felt the menace of the wilds, reaching, clawing.

They paused. Alnilam crouched on one knee, with one palm on the earth while he faced the wilds. He chanted slowly under his breath in a guttural language Troy did not understand but its tone and texture moved something primal inside him, until he could bear it no longer and he put his hands over his ears. Markab did the same while he mouthed silently, 'Powerful.' He nodded and was glad when Alnilam drew his chant to a close and said, 'Ready?'

Troy was about to ask for what, when Markab whispered, 'We will use the day of the resonant serpent to make our strike.' Then with no word of warning, only a sudden and strange charge in the air that pushed his breath back down into his lungs, Markab blew the dyke sky-high with a sizzling bolt of white lightning. It forked when it hit the metal girders in the dyke and from there the power shafted into the row of copper coloured, city orbs. Their round metal bodies exploded like seed pods in blooms of alchemical and crystalline light that burned a bank of river fog away. The antigravity flyers went next and their passing into oblivion left a strange metallic taste in the air.

'I borrowed it from the sky,' Markab whispered to him, and his grin lit up his eyes, and the pleasure he took from his work was an infectious madness that made Troy smile and clap him softly on the arm. 'Spectacular,' he said and wondered why he was with them.

Alnilam had incanted the roots from the scrub willow to a kind of life that was wild and gnarly, it walked in the dead of night, through swirling skirts of thick mist upon the marshy land as easily as he walked on the ground. The strength and flexibility held like muscle and stringy tendon in branch, bough, and root, had made his heart hammer in his chest while he thanked the flame that trees were benign. 'My incantation is not a spell to do my bidding,' Alnilam said in a hushed voice while he thumbed over his shoulder and the strange alchemical light pooled and flashed along the neatly plaited shafts of his grey hair, 'but a call to the trees to save their home.'

They answered, and then they pulled apart what Markab had not blown up. The filthy river water returned to the marsh with a rush of wind that sounded like a gigantic sigh, while Troy turned to Alnilam with his mouth gaping open and said, 'How?' While he thought, what would Micah be able to do if Alnilam can make trees walk.

'We are at the top of our power, all of The Ten are, but it does not come easy. We have to master the Monas,' said Alnilam while he pointed at Markab while they ran, doubled over, through thickly curling fog, while they made their way back towards the first dilapidated buildings of the city. Alnilam asked, 'Youth of seventeen summers?' While they threaded through the first alleys between coal and timber warehouses, drawing mist and smoke with them and only just avoiding the crowds that spilled out of the quayside taverns. They oiled further into Lodewick, always one step ahead of the crowds who were pouring towards the docks, while they ran like rats along every filthy cut and gulley they knew. Troy shrugged and nodded. Markab, the self-styled Lothario of Lodwick, was a full lipped, topaz-blue-eyed, pale honied youth, with tight black curly hair pulled into a top knot of locks. He was muscular but lithe, vital, and handsome in the way that youth on the cusp of its prime is. He looked about seventeen summers, one or two more. Then Alnilam said, 'Is four hundred summers. I, am much older than that.' He pointed to his chest and said, 'Spectral Seed,' then to Markab, 'Solar Storm. No higher power than that for seeds and storms.'

He had felt useless and stupid, until Alnilam called a halt just south of the Snide and put his hand on his shoulder while he met his gaze fully. There was kindness in his green and gold eyes when he said, 'Your turn now, kid.' He thumbed upwards and said, 'The net is about to drop. How do we get away without being killed?'

He felt a sense of pride and a rivulet of fear run like ice through his veins. 'Hold your noses, and tuck your breeches into your boots, it's down the sewers for us.' As if to confirm that was the only way to go the sky was suddenly illuminated with the blue alchemical light from a dozen copper orbs. 'Quick, this way,' he said in a hushed voice and led them into the warren of alleys that ran like tree roots from the wide cobbled road. First to the Elleadern Weatende and the ravine beneath the Wet White Bridge. A huge sewer emptied into its North end, and another lay to the South. All the sewers shit their waste into the many ravines, rivers, disused quarries, and gullies, on the Cheapside of Lodwick. He knew for certain he could take them from there, past the Merewif, then he would lead Markab and Alnilam to the tunnels and pipes beneath the Seaf. From there it was a slink along the lake shore, to the Bliones Tun which bordered Boho to the North. He knew the way. He had spent what had felt like a lifetime studying the damn maps.

*

'We need to do what?' Markab asked with a look on his face that said he would not.

'All the shit of Lodewick and now drake shit too?' Alnilam complained while he popped his head out of the culvert. The jagged tooth of rock that sat before the drain that led from the leather workers district to the Merewif was littered with drake debris. Across the vast circular ravine, the sewer that led from the Merewif to the Seaf, rested like an open but inaccessible invitation right beneath the arc of the witch's bridge.

'I cannot find my way round,' Troy huffed and ran his hand through his locks. He adjusted his optics then said, 'They are all closed or blocked. Someone has not been maintaining them,' he finished on a wry note. Then continued. 'It is the only safe way.' He turned to Markab, and with a shrug he said, 'I will get you to the Seaf, then from there to a culvert in a gulley at the perimeter of the Bliones Tun, but I did not say it would be easy.'

The sky above was cut through with crystal laser beams, orbs thwucked and whipped the air into unnatural vortexes and their lasers pierced and stabbed through the dark like rapiers hungry for blood. Pockets of resistance had erupted as soon as the proc came down heavy, and Lodewick, as usual, had responded in riot and rage. Its hidden fury was a hard fist in the gut, and an eruption of hatred tore through the night in pockets of fire and flame, which had the aerial units scattered before its blast, like whirling seeds as they tried to catch the wind and failed. The flyer base burned, and the curfew sirens wailed.

'It's not that far,' Troy grunted over his shoulder while he eased his body out of the sewer grid and began to climb around the slippery, shitty, stinking wall of the Merewif chasm.

Alnilam pushed Markab forward, 'Follow the spider, he won't fall.'

Markab pulled a face while he adjusted his night optics and eased his body out of the side of the rusted grille. He whispered gruffly, 'I hope Spider is as difficult to kill as his namesake, and as for tonight? I will be fucking stinking, Alnilam.'

Alnilam levered the grille further from the wall then squeezed through after. He paused for a moment to study the sky. The orbs had drawn everyone's attention upwards, and he felt a wave of something that felt like good fortune wash over him, it was icy and sharp like the rising gyre of wind from the black watery eye of the Merewif, while it roiled and champed below. The witch's bridge was over a quarter of a league long and almost half that wide. Fortunately, they had come out of a sewer gate that was close to where they needed to be. The Temple of Bloodgita at its centre, was a closed fortress silhouetted against a sky alight with the alchemical glare from orb rubidium engines, while they made their way to the river. They had heard the portcullis' chains creak into action, and the huge iron gates squeal shut while they hunkered down on the ledge and decided what to do. A typical strategy when riots began, and although the black steel gleam of its guards were blurred from the unnatural light above, he knew that their eye was not cast toward the deep throat of the ravine. Who would be stupid enough to be down here, Alnilam thought? Then said in a hushed voice, 'Your first client is a maiden rescue scenario, from the Lilac Lake. I will bundle her into a swan boat without oars and a long rope. If we hurry, you can wash your cock in there while you pull her from the water, fuck her on the shore, that will buy me some time, then bring her back to the silver pavilion.' He heard Troy snort above them while he held his own laughter in check.

Then Markab said, 'The spider has big balls after all. Everything had better be ready for me when I arrive with her. I have two fat noccs to deal with after her, then the sister of Bloodgita, I cannot afford to make a mistake tonight.'

Alnilam whispered, 'Do as I say, a thorough doing over beside the lake will give me time to beat up the first sausage in the red pavilion, get her to the silver pavilion for a large draught of sleepy wine. Your clothes and sword will be waiting for you, then tidy yourself up and come rescue the fat merchant from his sewer stinking, drake shit covered, dock-rat assailant. Leave your dirty clothes lakeside, she will faint with desire if you carry her to your abode naked. I have the mask in my bag.'

Troy heard Markab tut, then reply softly, 'Well if you put it like that.'

He wondered at the precise nature of the lothario's comings and goings. He and Alnilam had it off to a well-practised art, a master mummery, although to him it sounded mechanical, a work undertaken in shifts like the scenes from a play, and he wondered if their clients had any idea. 'Follow my lead, but watch out, the Drake lime will be slippery, but they are long gone at least.'

Markab said in a hushed voice, 'Do you recall any plant growth or roots here? Alnilam may be able to create a rope to aid us.' He heard a shrug in the near dark and Troy replied, 'The drakes will have stripped anything like that bare to make their nests, but their ledges and nooks are like gigantic steps round the throat of the Merewif.' He paused, then said quietly, 'We have to go down two ledges to the right, five across, then about twenty up. The drain we want is just under the Boho edge of the bitches bridge.' He paused while they nodded their agreement and in that moment of silence the ever-present wind, which wrapped around the throat of the chasm like the first note of a song, seemed to sing to him in voice that was full of salt and sadness.

'Did you hear that?' he asked, and Markab pulled a face.

'What?' Alnilam added, but he had a peculiar look in his eye.

'It sounded like a song,' Troy said over his shoulder but said no more when, Markab laughed. 'A song? It will be piss-poor takings for any Minstrel down here tonight.'

They laughed quietly at that, then moved silently to the edge of the lip of rock and dropped quietly to a ledge that was four paces below them and jutted like a ragged tooth above the maw of the Merewif. The ledge was littered with fish remains, sticks, and ragged bits of cloth, as well as brightly coloured half eggshells the size of a large fist. 'I'm glad the drakes are away South,' Markab said while he kicked the debris over the edge. 'They would have attacked us this close to their nesting site.' Then they descended once more to their right and rested for a short while on the apex of a huge arch. Just over one hundred feet tall, large chunks of sandstone had fallen into the pool at its base, and the water of the Merewif roiled over them, then disappeared under its span and roared away into the depths beyond. Troy led and Markab followed, and they began the arduous climb to the circular culvert below the Boho portcullis. Above them, the city festered and burned, but behind them, Alnilam paused.

Only a fool would be down here but a wiseman would look into the eye of the Merewif given the chance Alnilam thought and recalled Euphemia Eye, and a prediction she had given him before she fled Lodewick, with a wry lift of his brow. He waited while Markab made the ascent before him, then he adjusted his optics and peered into the black water. The old prune was right he thought, when he saw the alabaster shape glide serenely beneath the choppy water below. A Ningen! But a small one and hunting in the labyrinth bowels below the city.

~ ❦ ~ ❦ ~ ❦ ~

Sometime later Troy brought them out at a wide, deep, culvert that ran alongside the strangely opaque and turreted walls of the pleasure gardens known as the

Bliones Tun. Running through the alchemical glass were rippling patterns of coloured light. A wide band of pure Solais Silver wrapped around the walls of the pleasure gardens, and along its surface blue alchemical runes chased one another without beginning or end.

Alnilam thumbed a sequence on his mo and said in a hushed voice, 'El Nath, will you kidnap Lady Swealve for me? Then dump her in the silver swan boat at the jetty on Lilac Lake. Give it a good shove into the water.'

Troy felt his breath catch in his throat and made sure he did not meet Alnilam's eye. He knew Swealve, her father was governor of the population bureau and was close with Volsunga. Then he heard El Nath's deep voice of doom reply. 'I do not care for the Tun; it reeks of genitals.'

They bit their lips or put their hands over their mouths, until Alnilam said in a hushed voice, 'That is the stink of life El Nath. Just dress as Volsunga and pick her up from the south promenade inside the gardens.' He pulled the mo from his ear.

'Will he?' Troy asked and Alnilam replied, 'Yes, but I'll never hear the last of it. Now to the pressing matter of getting you out of here. Lodwick is alive with proc.' They climbed the storm drain incline and used the cover of ornamental bushes and trees while they made their way towards a narrow wooden postern door that looked more like a supporting timber than a door. It shone like spun gold. 'It is memory wood,' Markab said and pressed his hand to it. 'Its cost would have your eyeballs falling to the floor,' he added, and the gate swung silently open, 'but a lordlings ransom, is merely insignificant change to the Lothario of Lodewick.' They all passed through the gate sideways on, and he suspected that most of The Ten had not been in the Bliones Tun, well not by this gate at least. Before Markab could say anything further Troy asked, 'Why does Lady Swealve come here? She is from one of the richest families in Lodewick.'

'It has nothing to do with riches but to do with pouring a salve on an unhealable wound,' Markab said, and suddenly the vitality of his seventeen summers fell off his face. 'Volsunga took her to his bed when she was a child of ten, and for all their money and power, there was nothing her family could do to stop it. Tonight, the masked Lothario will rescue her, and the love we make will be romantic and gentle. I will promise to marry her and take her away from here, from Volsunga.' He sounded weary while he put his optics in his pack. Meeting Troy eye to eye he said, 'It is what he does. Rescues. The merchant? Rescued in fantasy from a very real threat in his life, one which excites and repulses him in equal measure. The sister of Bloodgita, rescued from her sins when she is made to atone on the rack. And her reward is a forbidden fruit,' he pointed to his chest and winked, 'one she has sworn under oath, and signed in blood, that she will never eat.' He shrugged then turned and said finally, 'I would rather do that than mix powders in the black apothecary.' He took Troy by the arm and clasped it in a gesture of comradeship. 'Thank you, for tonight, Mar-cuss.' He said his name like Elgenubi did and he was about to laugh when Markab leant forward quickly, and kissed him softly, full on the lips. Troy pulled back with a start, but not before he felt something stir and heat rise through his body in a pleasing wave.

Alnilam laughed and intervened. 'Markab or should I say the Lothario of Lodewick has a way with energy because of his storm signature. He can go on long after he should have collapsed, and he can…how do I say it? Ah, get a rise out of the dead.'

Troy laughed, though he felt a sheet of heat prickle up his neck and flush his cheeks. Then he said, 'You stink of drake shit but at least your breath is minty,' while Alnilam retrieved a piece of shimmering fabric from his pack. It was the mask, and it had been alchemically wrought to become a second skin on the wearer. It was finer than gossamer and moved like liquid in his hand. Markab turned his back to Troy while Alnilam slipped it on for him and fastened it behind each ear.

'It's in place,' Markab said, and he jutted his jaw out a little while he felt it meld to his face. Then he turned and flourished a theatrical bow. He rose with a with a cheery, 'Until we meet again, I must be off to work, and a wooing.' Then turned and made his way towards the far end of the gardens, where his first job of the night waited, bound, blindfolded, and lightly gagged, in a silver swan boat.

Troy staggered backwards and felt the edge of the postern stop his fall. 'He's Micah. He's Micah Apollon,' he stammered, and his heart shattered so hard he could hear the shards of ice, he had encased it in, crack and ring while they fell through the air.

Alnilam studied him thoughtfully. Then said carefully, 'If you think the memory wood is a lords ransom for that thin sliver,' he thumbed to the narrowest door in Lodewick. 'The price of that mask makes it look like the price of a bit of reclaimed wood. Anyway, Kid, who better to rescue Lady Swealve? Who better to play the Lothario of Lodewick? It is why he is so expensive and kept like hidden treasure in the hearts of his clients. He is adored like the golden mouthed prophet himself, in minds that ought to know better, but do not, while they empty their purses, open their legs, and spill their secrets.'

'I, I,' he stuttered then pulled himself together. 'I had no idea,' he finished and took a gulp of moist misty air. Light of the flame, the dead Micah he had seen had been wearing a mask. 'It looks exactly like him. Not that I ever saw him close, but light of the blasted flame!'

'The mask is one of a kind,' Alnilam said, and Troy felt his world cartwheel on its axis while he thought, it was their mask...they used that mask on the fake body. Alnilam brought him back from his thoughts when he said, 'I apologise, we did not return you to Bathory's warehouse like I said we would. I can offer you a pavilion to sleep in as recompense, but you will have to help me, ermm, gently rough-up a merchant first.' He smoothed a weathered hand along his grey beard, which had been plaited and weaved with platinum wire that was finer than silk thread, while he waited patiently for Troy to reply.

Troy took a moment to study him. Alnilam was non-descript and grey. Ephemeral like a cloud, he blended in to wherever he was. He had seen him dressed as a merchant, and an acolyte of Anuk, male and female, and once or twice he had even thought he had bought food from him at market. 'I'll pass, I don't think the Tun is for me either. It's the reek of genitals,' he said, trying to lighten the mood but Alnilam did not laugh. He paused and took another gulp of air to steady his voice. 'I can find my way back to the warehouse by sewer from here, easily,' he said, and shook the other man's hand. He did not want to be pulled into any further questions about his reaction to Markab's disguise, or sudden shows of emotion. Though he suspected Markab often took people by surprise like that for no other reason than having a laugh about it afterwards.

'You know the sewers well?' Alnilam asked while he steered him to the shimmering memory wood door and placed his palm upon it.

'It's where spiders thrive,' he replied cryptically, and hoped that Alnilam thought he meant that that was where, Marcus-the-made-up-Kid, was from.

Alnilam studied him thoughtfully before he said, 'I must away attend Markab. The merchant and the sister of Bloodgita must be handled carefully. We have lost our intelligence from the Southern Isles,' he paused then said, 'The silver-eyed seers returned to Hiriwa Pourewa recently, they are a great loss to us. A terrible thing happened, and we are left without any concrete knowledge about the future, about the eve of destruction.' The note of desolation in his voice was clear, and sorrow sagged his jaw and etched lines around his green-gold eyes.

Troy nodded then said, 'Euphemia Eye. Her shop was abandoned.'

Alnilam replied steadily, 'She saw many things. She told me a spider would lead me to the eye of the Merewif where I would behold a child of Time, and after that we would leave the city.'

'I hope she was right,' Troy replied with a courteous bow. 'Farewell, Alnilam,' he said, and the other man replied, 'Farewell, Spider.'

Troy turned and left. It was always difficult to dupe a mummer and the look in Alnilam's eye had set his nerves on edge. When he reached the storm drain and slid down its sides towards the sewer gate, he knew that Alnilam had watched him all the way.

He traversed the sewers, drains and culverts like a marionette and it was not until he exited them, in an alley that led from the dockside end of the Shambles to Bathory's warehouse, that he realised he had walked them with the same sort of familiarity someone taking a stroll in a well know garden would. He opened the small wooden door with his key and closed it gratefully behind him. The warehouse was cloaked inside with cool quietness that calmed his heart rate to something like normal; even the orb activity had died down and the incendiary nature of the night had blown itself out. There will be no flyers patrolling the river he thought and wondered what the real reason for the attack on the base had been. He could not get the image of Micah out of his mind and his hands shook while he stripped naked and put his dirty clothes in a large stone sink. Then he showered off the filth from the sewers at a pump hose on the ground floor and scrubbed his hands and nails with a cake of Elgenubi's, Janome linden soap, and a small brush, until they were red and sore. The water came from a spring rather than the filthy river and he was grateful for that. He took the stairs quietly, every step an effort while his legs trembled and his head swirled with a vortex of possibilities, none of which he could ask about. He made his way wearily towards the apothecary. The black apothecary Markab had called it. He snorted; it was exactly that. All was in darkness and four sleeping pods hung between the rows of cork oak like gigantic black chrysalis'. The first light of dawn was several horas away. Sleep, first I sleep he thought, while he pushed open the apothecary door. Elgenubi was before him before he knew she was there. She put her palm on his heart and he felt waves of heat and something else pass from her to him. Then she said, 'I am glad you are returned.'

He did not know what to do or say, he was naked, and wrung out, so he put his hand on hers and said in a voice choked with emotion, 'I killed a man.'

'I know,' she whispered, 'Alnilam says it has...' She trailed off and he gave a heartfelt whimper of gratitude that sounded like a sob, but at least his odd behaviour at seeing Markab in his Micah mask, would be written off as delayed shock, because of his first kill. She led him to the couch and pushed him gently into its saggy folds, then covered him with several blankets. He thought she would leave him then, to his grief and sorrow, to his relief, and the thudding pain at his temples where waning adrenalin had sucked his arteries dry, but she did not. Instead, she lay next to him and put her arms around him until he fell into a deep, dreamless sleep.

Tears pooled like melted ice in the corners of her eyes. 'Now you are a killer, as well as a thief, and a liar, Troy,' she whispered, and stroked a lock of damp hair from his face. Then she made sure he was deeply asleep before she made her way back to her own sleeping pod with a heavy step, and a resolute look set like granite in her indigo eye.

Chapter Thirty-One

Elgenubi Zuben

What in the hells was Violet doing here, Troy thought while he slipped between the columns of drying cork oak. They had slept for most of the day and were making ready to go to the meeting with Murzim. It was the last thing he needed, someone recognising him, and he knew deep in the pit of his stomach that Violet would. He calmed his breathing and ordered his thoughts, although the nights events had left him reeling, but only confirmed to him that The Ten were key to finding Micah. The problem was, how to ask the question.

He slipped further into the shadows. Violet? From the night of the dead. She must be part of the finishing crew, Bathory's people, who come in and clear the warehouse or she is here to pack the poisons he thought, then added, and clear up the fallen cork oak. The cork oak was dry and smelled like a forest in the height of summer, dry and woody, but with a faint aroma of the cleanliness of tree sap and bark. Although, he thought the smell comforting and out of all the places they had stayed he had liked the cork loft and the black apothecary best. Let Bathory not show, he prayed. He had changed. Was it enough to fool Violet? On the night of the dead, she had looked him in the pit of his eye with a knowing that had turned his insides to water, and then she had spat at his feet. Abrecan had killed her parents and she knew that he was his nephew, she would only have to look in his eyes again, and she would know him, because he knew he would not be able to hide his shame. As for Lady Bathory Dorka. The woman had made a career out of knowing who was where on the slippery pole of elite social climbing in Lodewick.

'Elgenubi dahhling…' Her voice was sharp, like a leather whip tanned in lemon juice. He shuddered and slipped further back between the lengths of cork and crouched next to the window Homan had been dragged through, a good place to spy on the proceedings.

'My Lady Bathory.' Elgenubi came out of the office and embraced Bathory, it was warm and friendly but then again, they were smuggler friends.

Bathory Dorka, was slender as a willow switch and wore a long gown of emerald velvet, high at the neck, with long sleeves cuffed to the elbow with rows of jet buttons. Elgenubi looked over Bathory's shoulder while she hugged her and shook her head when she saw the bustle of material that was currently in fashion with the elite ladies of Lodewick. Violet stood quietly beside Bathory, her hands covered in silk gloves and clasped before her, in a similar cut gown though it was made from deep brown velvet and trimmed with creamy seed pearls. Expensive gowns for a rich lady and her... Troy studied them, what is Violet doing? he thought while he strained his ears and Elgenubi released Bathory and opened her arms wide. 'Do not stand on ceremony with me, Vee child. I must hug you. How you have grown.'

Vee paused and he could see that she tried to be ladylike but then she leapt into Elgenubi's arms. 'It has been too long, and I have not grown a single bit.'

Elgenubi put her down, then held her hands while she bent forward and studied her small face. 'On the inside, where it matters the most.'

Bathory nodded, her dark hair was steaked with wings of silver and caught in a bun at the nape of her neck then encased in a silver net. Similarly, Violet's hair was caught in a bronze net. They could have been mother and daughter or granddaughter. Violet was still small and even though he knew she had a mouth that would make a Cheapside sewer seem clean, she looked like innocence itself. A fleeting memory of Lolade holding her baby pricked at his consciousness, she had had a mouth like a sewer too, but unlike Violet she had not looked like innocence, she had looked like death, wearing a too tight skin.

'Violet has spent her time wisely with Turanga's Eyes...' Bathory noted Elgenubi's frown and continued quickly. 'Marama Rawa insisted she went there first. It is part of her Dagger Path. Then she must decide if she wishes to give herself to Silver Tower.'

That is why I did not see her after the Night of the Dead, Troy thought. Even though he had been part of many more tribal gatherings in the last year, and he did all the disc running for the Zuben's, he thought he would bump into her and when he had not, he thought she had been killed and had spent more than a moon blaming himself for her death. Lumping her corpse with Micah's, Lolade's, the people who had been executed outside Abrecan Castle after the Night of The Dead, and anyone else he could think of.

'How did you find the training with the Eyes of the Black Water?' Elgenubi asked while she released Violet's hands from her own.

'I found it enlightening, but I must say I preferred what they wear to what I am currently attired in.' She shrugged and pointed to her bustle.

Elgenubi laughed, then said, 'I thought it was your sleeping pod back there.' Then when Violet had to hide her laugh behind her hand, and Bathory tutted impatiently she said, 'Yes. Their breeches and shoufa make for good combat wear, especially for martial arts.'

'It is a necessary disguise, Violet. You must convince people you are my niece, and a lady yourself. Ladies in Lodewick follow ridiculous fashion and therefore so do we. We do not act like little black-eyed assassins,' Bathory scolded, then turned to Elgenubi. 'Violet was doing extremely well…well enough that she was asked to remain with the Kanohi at Ara Pourewa by the Turanga herself. She is so well educated, you see, some of the girls they get from the Commonwealth…lack the, ermm, finesse, Violet's parents insisted on.' Violet scowled but Bathory ignored her and continued, 'Unfortunately, Tuahine Hae heard of her exceptional skills and made an assassination attempt. Hence her early return, but she will return to Ara Pourewa with this shipment,' Bathory explained dryly, while she pointed at the apothecary.

'You learned to oil your tongue in the halls of the elite, and now you are fit for the court at Ara Pourewa,' Elgenubi said and grinned. 'And how did you counteract the attempt?' Elgenubi asked and the note of curiosity in her voice was plain.

'I rooted out and killed Tuahine Hae's plant in the Kanohi. She had ingratiated herself to me; we shared a bed occasionally. It was easy to end her using Widow's Kiss, then I set a trap, with some other Kanohi I trusted, for the assassin crew Tuahine Hae sent. We lost two that night but only one of hers returned to tell the tale. It was an extremely good education, and I thank you and Eschamali for arranging my adoption by Bathory.'

'Not really us, but Acumen Sting and Hydra the Cup. You impressed them when you played for them.' Elgenubi put her hand on the small girl's shoulder. 'You, very lithe,' she finished and raised one brow.

'But without you, where would I be, a whore, or dinner for Abrecan, or a refugee with the tribe below. She meant to capture me and put me to use in her pleasure rooms rather than kill me outright.' Violet shrugged.

'You would have been a great prize for her to own, especially as The Turanga merited your worth highly. Are you still playing?' Elgenubi said as she turned to the office and the two ladies followed her.

'Yes, though it saddens me to my core.'

Elgenubi put her arm around Violet's shoulders, and they paused at the apothecary door. 'Keep it up. It is a good thing, if we ever need to send you with Fairmist Al Mara, or Rowa Hellfire. Did you know that Silas Al Seamist, Fairmist's distant cousin, is Marama Rawa's coddle?' Violet giggled into her gloved hand. 'Now to business, Lady Bathory.' Elgenubi turned to Bathory who tutted and shook her head, she found the Zuben's more than a bit rough around the edges but had given up trying to oil their tongues many moons ago.

'Where is that runner of yours? Marcus the Kid, he is getting quite a reputation for himself in the shadowy underbelly of this shifty city. I would very much like to meet him?' Bathory asked.

'I too would like to thank him personally for his Widow's Kiss potion and antidote, they were sublimely blended,' Violet added, and Troy froze. The window to his right suddenly looked very inviting though it would be a straight drop onto the tithe barn roofs of the tier below. Bathory's cork warehouse squatted right on the edge of a cliff, sixty feet above the next tier. I wish I were really a spider he thought.

Elgenubi snorted and said, 'Thank the Lords of the Light Flame he is not here to hear that sort of praise. His raggedy head would not fit through the door. He is out doing what I pay him to do, running errands.'

The women laughed as they entered the office. 'We must make haste…The Star has activated…and I have heard she has not been prepared properly and is called to Romar Ri to face Arianrihod,' Bathory said.

Elgenubi paused and a faraway look came into her eye while she replied softly, 'Then what has been seen, is so. The Ten go must go North, Bathory. Our destiny lies there.'

Bathory nodded and said with a sigh, 'I will miss you, and the excellent wares from your black apothecary,' while she closed the door.

*

The day had drawn to a wet and windy close and he felt his exhaustion like a blanket of confusing thoughts stuffed in his too full head. Though he would never admit that he was tired or out of sorts to The Ten, he just gave thanks that he was now fitter than the rebel Moin, and that deep inside he had the stamina and strength to endure. I must find some more energy from somewhere he thought and wished he could draw it from the sky like Markab. Then he took his attention to Elgenubi when she said quietly, 'Our barge is here, Mar-cuss.' She pointed to a freight barge tucked alongside the rest of the flat self-propelled craft, currently moored against the slime and filth of Coal Wharf. They jumped into the barge that had been loaded with wood waste briquettes that had come down from Plantation and were destined for Shad. It smelled of fresh resinous wood and charcoal, warm smells that reminded him of heat and fires blazing. The Winter of Bucky's grief had been harsh, the summer had been too short and now the sky was leaden with pewter ready to weep Autumn in shades of misty grey, pissing down brown, and freezing cold silver. They sat on the deck and took shelter under a tarpaulin while they rested against the sides of the coaming. He sniffed loudly and said, 'The Shanty stinks.' He felt her bristle beside him and knew he had said the wrong thing.

'Some of the best intel we get, come from there, kid.' She pointed in the general direction of the Shanty. 'There are some of the finest musicians, minstrels and troubadours in the Shanty, but their music is not for the refined palates of the city, nor are their tales of the horrors they've seen on the journey out of the Flat Lands to the north.' Elgenubi paid the skipper while he checked the tarpaulin where they hid without a word and shortly afterwards, they set off at a sedate pace that only increased his temper. He was irked with Elgenubi for calling him out on his assumptions, his ignorance. 'I know about Baelmonarchia, you know.' He sounded like an irritated, tired, child. A last volley of hard rain twanged against the tarpaulin and echoed his irritation.

'You know nothing about anything, Mar-cuss Spider…that is also another fault of yours,' she said coolly while she checked her hidden weapons.

He screwed his face up, glad of the dark so she could not see his lips had twisted, and his mouth was full of sour disdain. 'Anyway,' he began spitefully, 'Why doesn't Abrecan just have the minstrels killed?'

'Because' she sighed in exasperation while she pulled the tarpaulin back, 'he is afraid of the Poets Curse. I have heard the Copper Tower witch has been afflicted with it.' She smoothed down her trousers then said, 'Gaiadon has magic in the strangest of places. One of them being in the mouths of minstrels, poets, and bards.'

He had heard of the Poet's Curse; it was mentioned in Thomhas' Phantasmagoria. 'They should all just get together and curse him,' he said thoughtfully, while he wondered if that would work and imagined legions of minstrels cursing the foul serpent that he had seen wrapped around Abrecan Castle. He knew they would not be enough either. Just like the scattered lights of the resistance, in Eirini, would not be enough. As for the tribe that was somewhere below Lodewick, he knew the sewers, and if his escapade with Alnilam and Markab was anything to go by, he wondered if there was only shit, and rats down there. There were no people, and no Sewer King. He recalled the old man who had come for Lolade and her baby, pushing a squeaky, wooden, wheeled chair, with a weak alchemical lantern swinging from its handle. Abrecan is undefeatable, he thought morosely, and welcomed a blast of icy wind when it hit him full in the face like a hard slap.

'Each time they utter the curse, the price to be paid is the loss of a song, a story, or a poem, but they never know which one it will be. So, the curse is never used lightly, it does not kill either. They never know what the cursed one receives, only that they will lose words, and rhythm, and rhyme from memory. It could be the greatest spell ever made, alchemical formulae, a sorcerer's worst, or best invocation, or a child's nursery rhyme,' she said in a hushed voice, and there was a note of sadness there. Then she clicked her fingers and said, 'Gone.'

'What did the Copper Witch lose?' he asked, though he was only half interested.

'Rumour has it, it was her youth and beauty, but I don't know. We don't have that magic where I am from.'

There was a break in the overcast and the night was suddenly clear, although the water still smelled like a latrine pit, undercut with the brackish salt smell of estuary water and marshland. He promised to read more of Thomhas' Phantasmagoria when he got time. He lifted one corner of his mouth wryly, when I get time he thought and asked, 'Is that where you're from, you know, The North?' He pointed vaguely over the river towards the Shanty which was more north westerly than truly North.

'I'm from up of here,' she pointed above her head, 'but Eschamali orders me not to share that with you. He, not trust you.' She shrugged and her eyes glittered, lambent indigo, and gold.

'He, not trust anyone,' he replied, and tried to hide the irritation in his voice. She was right, the great big lummox did not trust him, and he felt his fate and the hand of death moving closer every day.

~ ❊ ~ ❊ ~ ❊ ~

He still thought she meant The Ten came from the North. There were exotic and magical creatures aplenty there, well according to Meite's Phantasmagoria there were, and he suspected the fantasy woodland in the Bliones Tun had been created, and the creatures within it, populated from a reality that was closer than myth.

He had been to the Palace Galay, taken Bucky's barge up the Ophiuchus, not on the filthy side but the other river, the blue and white Ophiuchus that smelled of ozone and sea salt, not sulphur, and sewage. The river wound East then North as it skirted the riven lands, and the vast forest called The Willow Wilds. North of this The Ophiuchus became one again and they had continued upriver, under solar sail, past the massive wooden city called Plantation. The docks and jutting wharfs along the river were busy with barges carrying freight, but the city itself was a smouldering dark smudge on the horizon to the northwest. After that they sailed along the western edge of Lord Matthias Dolmen's province, through the stark beauty of the Iron Hills and deep valleys of the borderlands to The North. At the confluence of the Blood and Ophiuchus Rivers, they took the Blood and followed its flow while it ran to the ocean at Wolfsea Crossing. Then they were met by Bucky's household guard from Galay. Mounted on the finest white horses with golden manes. The guards were resplendent in uniforms of red fustian with creamy tabards embroidered in gold, and silver thread. The Winter Sun emblem was set above their hearts in seed pearls and clear white crystals, at the centre of their chest a white stag was set in white sapphire with peridot eyes. They escorted them in a royal procession through the garrison town of Wolfsea Crossing and over the triple arched Whitestone bridge called Winters Way.

Before they crossed Bucky dismounted and gave out red purses to the old, and the poor, with the promise that no one on his doorstep would ever be turned away from food, shelter, and the warmth of an embered hearth. Lord Bucky loved the pageantry. Both Micah and he knew he would have armed men hidden in the crowds, with laser batons under their clothes.

He remembered the peasants he saw – they had fair hair and skin dotted with fine crystalline lights that shone like fish scales under water but in earthy colours, which looked like freckles when they were dim. A few had more elaborate patterns about their faces, like Micah's, a secret language written in scrolling runes. He shuddered when he recalled Micah sitting on his fake throne outside the old silk warehouse, and to distract himself from his morose thoughts he asked, 'Wouldn't it be easier to make our way back along the river then over the edge of the marshland and up into Tota Zone. We could take the pipe?'

The barge heeled when a current with a strong undertow caught it and tried to spin it onto a sand bank. His stomach lurched and he decided to stand. He made his way out from the cover of the tarpaulin and leaned against the gunwale while he studied the lower tiers of Cheapside while they passed by in soaking-wet shades of brown and grey, scattered with coloured lights. Blue alchemical lights pierced through the drudgery-brown smoke, but their expensive light glowed on the walls and in the windows of the merchant guild houses. The black temple of the Sisterhood of Bloodgita the Effusive, sat atop the witch's bridge and blazed, well-lit after the attack on the flyer base. He smiled and studied Elgenubi out of the corner of his eye then said, 'Thank you, for last night.'

She flapped a hand at him and replied, 'Alnilam speak to me on the portable mouth, said it was delayed shock. I did what any of the others would do.'

He did not reply but laughed inwardly when he imagined El Nath comforting him in the same manner she had. She calls mo's portable mouths he thought and wanted to hug her, like she had him. A warm feeling flushed him with a sense of belonging and he took his attention back to the glittering pile of dung that was Cheapside with a new set of eyes. It was where she belonged, and he knew that because of that he could belong there too. A fleeting image of Micah on his makeshift throne pricked his conscience but he pushed it aside. 'It is almost beautiful, in the dark,' he said softly and flushed when Elgenubi snorted in reply.

Lower down the metropolis was lit by nimbuses of tallow light, and the sickly yellow-green hue of marsh gas streetlamps. Warehouses and dockside offices, with small markets at the lower levels were closed or packed away. Dockside taverns were shuttered against the blade of a piercing wind, and the sting from squalls of driving rain. Slats of light, shone like yellow ribbed openings from the corpse of a choking, charcoal-night. Occasional noise floated over the water, swollen like the sound of ale and bravado, on arrows of heart-felt desire, which sought the solitude of the other shore, but the wind pulled the notes to pieces, and cast their song out to sea. Then the heat, and the passion of their lament, became like dead leaves sundered from the tree; and the truth of a rebellious heart, that filled a mouth with freedom, was suddenly doubting, and forlorn; and its throat was devoid of moisture in a city that ran with tears. And freedom's white words were naught but a dry echo, slung low, until they kissed the tops of the cowling waves, and the Ophiuchus, the serpent bearer, was at least, appeased, while the Tyrant King sat atop his throne, and squeezed every drop of blood from flesh and bone.

Large machinery, winches, booms, and pulleys rested skeletally, and their angles glistened like waxy skinned elbows in the poor light. The crenelated walls of the fortified Temple Squares were rows of teeth chewing at the tiers above. The debris from the night of the dead uprising cascaded down the side towards the jutting cliffs. It was an ugly wound across the face of the city, a slash with a sword that revealed not bloody flesh but rock, rubble, and stone. Guild houses and then the lesser merchant houses ascended towards the flat level of the city. Towards the top, black and grey monstrosities loomed, cold dark buildings that withstood the headland winds like stones in a graveyard tried to withstand the erosion of time. The rich always believe they can cheat death by buying the trappings of a wealthy life, he thought and wondered why he felt so philosophical. He felt the energy of the day like a cowl of lead around his neck that suddenly released when the energy of the Red Resonant Serpent slipped toward midnight, and the mystery and power of the day of the White Galactic Worldbridger made itself known.

'It was the day of the red resonant serpent,' he said quietly, while he watched the city disappear behind a bank of cloud.

Elgenubi put her hand on his arm and said softly, 'I know.' Then she coughed and said, 'We cannot venture too close to the wilds side and to Tota, demon beasts are killing people in Tota. I for one, would not like to be with you if we were attacked.'

They both heard the hiss through the air before the arrow shaped yellow craft appeared through a bank of cloud, the pale green light from its undercarriage was like a tail of ice against the overcast. The unmanned flyer glided past to scan the bayou. 'We should have done more,' he said while he studied the flyer. It was not a good sign.

Elgenubi narrowed her eyes thoughtfully and said, 'You did enough.' She pointed to the flyer and added, 'They had to have two flyers sent from the base at Malice and have taken over a breaker's yard to house them. That thing is looking for something, or someone.'

'I hope they fail,' he said quietly and deliberately took his attention from the sky.

Sensing his mood, she changed the subject and said, 'Better to try to bribe the proc guard on the stairs on the Side of Light or slip past them or….' Elgenubi trailed off with a shrug then began to check her weapons again.

He did not have to guess what the "or" meant. He had seen her slit a proc guard's throat before; it was a casual action, polite, and discreet. As graceful as the martial art called Monas, she practiced every day. She had not seemed too bothered by the killing afterwards. He on the other hand, had been shocked; beautiful, graceful Elgenubi, had killed a man before his eyes as casually as she had shaved his face. It was the reason he had never been caught in those early days; he nearly had that once, but she saved his life. Afterwards, he saw the sorrow etched in feather lines of pain at the corner of her mouth and the memory of Birdy burned cold in the sad light in her eye. It was one of his first times running, and he vowed then, never to put her in danger or cost someone their life because he had been sloppy when he planned his escape routes out of the tribal, and sloppy in taking care of himself. It dawned on him that he was running with the Zuben's, not acting up with Micah. He gave up droge waere, and dealt with the painful, sweaty, gibbous torture like the fop he was. He was afraid when claws clenched at his guts, and fingers of ice raked up and down his spine, and invisible hands cramped his muscles into slabs of acid pain. He had begged her, 'Get Hydra for me, she can stop this.' Elgenubi had folded her arms across her chest and tutted disdainfully. 'I will not, Mar-cuss…this you must feel, this you do alone. To defeat this is to regain self-worth. The thing your addiction stole from you, it must be recovered, numbskull.' She frowned while she pointed at his trembling hands. 'Weak,' she snapped in a louder than usual voice, while he continued to vomit in a bucket he could barely hold. Eschamali, his ever-present judge and jury, added in a mock serious voice with a smirk on his face. 'You, not burnout, kid, I was wrong. You turn stomach inside out instead. Weak of flesh, weak in the night.' But with her help he took better care of himself. A moon or two after she began to dread his hair, he felt himself grow into Marcus. The tendrils of her hair and her pod fibre, along with his own locks, as she had promised, connected him to The Ten. 'Even for your kind, you have a strong connection. You allow the Ever-Was to be in your heart, and in your all-seeing eye, and The Ten be there too.' She patted him on the head, as if he had done a good trick, then kicked his feet from beneath him. 'Pay attention.' She laughed and retreated while she waited for him to regain his feet. Crouching like a tigress there was a hunger in her eye that set his teeth on edge and sent tremors of fear running along his spine like a dagger of ice being pressed into every vertebra. But he knew better than to show his fear, and with cool determination and a neutral face, he launched at her. He aimed his kick high, then at the last moment he twisted in the air and let gravity drop his body while he swept his legs into a wide scything arc. She fell on her backside with a thud. His moment of triumph was short lived when she flicked into a handstand, and he felt her feet on either side of his neck. She turned and used the weight of her body to pull him to the floor, where she proceeded to strangle him, until he hit the floorboards twice, a sign that he had surrendered.

~ ❋ ~ ❋ ~ ❋ ~

'Side of light, here we come.' he smiled thinly at her while they turned from the gunwale and sat back down. He risked moving himself closer to her in the dark. Recalling their combat bouts always filled him with warmth and a desire to be close to her. Alone and naked would be best but he knew that could never be, and he poured a bucket of chilly water on his desire but not before he recalled Markab Storm saying, 'You, cunt-struck, Kid, but you take her, and…' he had paused and pretended to pull off one of his arms while he made squelching noises.

He moved his body away from Elgenubi. She gave him peculiar look, then said, 'You know what they call the Cheapside? Side of shi—'

She laughed when he interrupted. 'I know what they call it, Elgenubi.'

She pushed him on the arm and said, 'Your mouth too oiled, like Lady Bathory Dorka.'

He snorted and said, 'Oiled with vinegar and other people's money.' He waited until she stopped laughing then said, 'It's not just because of the sewerage from the city being run out of Cheapside, it's because of the sunlight. When it rises in the northeast, on the Elite side, it catches the small particles of crystal in the granite of the lower tiers, and the pink crystal caught in the sandstone of the uppers, the water falls and pools are clear water, even the marble and granite Temples on the side of light throw tiny rainbows from their surfaces. They reflect off the water, the buildings reflect it again and it just creates a nimbus of perfect crystal light.' He paused.

She nudged him in the ribs. 'Go on, it fills the journey, take our mind off the ascent into Lodewick. May distract us from the aroma of the water.'

'Cheapside faces towards the nor' west and the sun does not catch it the same way. As it sets, the whole area looks like it is awash with dirty reds, oranges, and browns, even the buildings on the Cheapside are made of wood, brownstone, and tile, and of course then there is the colour of the river water. Then,' he waggled his finger in the air, 'If the brackish estuary water is not bad enough, we also have the sewer drains emptying out their contents like a loose-arsed merchant with a bad case of the trots. Oh, and let us not forget the smell from the marsh gas.' They grinned at each other, and their teeth sparkled like two crescent moons in the dark. The shape of mouths that could not share how they felt, and the light in their eyes was of the same intensity and knowing, a mirror of their love, and their barely hidden desire. She squeezed his arm, and they held back their laughter with their hands over their mouths until she said quietly, 'It was named justly, eh.'

~ ❦ ~ ❦ ~ ❦ ~

Ahead, peaks of white water frothed and chewed against the headland where the river forked. The skipper had weaved his barge through channels close to Cheapside, testament to his expertise as the channels, called Wyrms by captains and skippers alike, threaded through the Ophiuchus like intestinal parasites. Constantly changing course, while they pushed through the silt and shit to find new ways for the filthy water to find its way to the sea. There were harder sandbanks and rocky ledges, but they edged the Inawyrm Channel, the deep wide river of fresh water in the centre of the estuary. Large beds of seaweed tumbled past like green and brown fingered hands trying to seek purchase on the slimy shore.

'You know what they say about this river, Mar-cuss?'

'I read in Cassandra's Chronicles that one day the River Ophiuchus would crawl on its belly like a brown snake. Then run clear beneath the hooves of white horses, and on that day, things would change when the face of a red goddess would be revealed beneath the clear water,' he half-quoted from Cassandra's Chronicles.

Elgenubi whispered, 'Terrible in her fury, she will send a catalyst into Lodewick and place a baleful star in the sky, their destinies intertwined, until one perishes at the hands of the other,' she paused and added, 'But only if the brown water run clear.'

He shuddered though it felt as if it had come from within rather than the cold. 'I prefer the story at the front, you know, naked Cassandra,' he tried to lighten the mood.

'Hmm, you would,' Elgenubi retorted dryly. 'I do not know what poet made that tale, but her breasts were not that large, nor was her rear end so peachy. Cassandra Novantae was hard as granite, and slim as a reed with slabs of muscle that were harder than ebon wood. Her crystal lights here,' she tapped her forehead and pulled at her ears roughly, 'brash, and she had too haughty a chin if you ask me, not to mention her mouth. She talks with two tongues, and both sharper than a rapiers blade.' She huffed and lifted her chin while she turned her face from him.

He stuttered, 'It's only a story.' He was not sure where her irritation had come from.

'You think they let soft fruit walk Marama Rawa's Dagger Path. You think they have a dainty maid caretaking Silver Tower and skipping along the paths inside the mind of Time. The Eye of Hiriwa Pourewa is harder than the mountain itself. You are a bigger fool than you look,' she said with a snap of her fingers, and got to her feet. He followed, chastised, but not sure why or what he had done.

'I see the stretch of shingle. Light, it's no more than the width of my arm, Elgenubi.' He pointed to the thin sliver of shingle, glad to change the subject while he calculated how he was not going to get his feet wet. The tide had pushed up the estuary against the swollen river water. The snow from Bucky's winter was still a thick layer on top of the encroaching glacier on the highest ground to the North, still melting and filling the river to bursting. Powerful undertows pushed and swirled; swells of pregnant water buffeted the barge. The wind whipped up foaming scrolls of white and cast pieces of dirty sea foam on the wind like gobs of frothy spit as the river continued to make its way to the sea. He studied the flow, judging the suspended fingers of seaweed and the *slap, slap* of water against the shore, the tide was full now; and would soon turn.

The barge chugged against the current while they made ready to jump ashore, staying expertly close to the tips of two submerged fingers of black granite that raked arthritically towards the face of the cliffs and the buttress' that locked onto the front of Lodewick. The cliff was uninhabitable and formed a natural barrier that kept the two sides of the city apart. He shuddered when he thought of Violet's mother throwing herself off the cliffs of the headland into the Ophiuchus and hoped she had not landed on one of the fingers, he hoped that she had been dead before she hit the water.

Elgenubi jumped softly onto the shingle, and he followed. He winced when his feet crunched heavily against it…like an army had just landed in the gloom. 'Shush your big jiggers,' she whispered. The nearest sentry tower was only a short distance away; the square window was dark, and the place had an air of abandonment about it. 'Sorry,' he hissed back.

Suddenly, the engine cut, and he turned to watch the skipper navigate his way around the dark fingers of granite, using the pull of the hidden Wyrms to continue his journey downriver towards other small harbours nearer the sea. 'It might be called Cheapside, but it is not cheap to moor there,' he said quietly, and tried to sound light-hearted while they made their way to the slimy green wall next to the shingle.

Elgenubi frowned and dropped her hands off the top of the wall. Then she turned to study him. 'A lesson in commerce, Mar-cuss?' Concern flitted across her face. 'I know most freight gets in and out quickly.' She paused, perplexed. 'Are you well Mar-cuss? Is it about…' she trailed off, and he knew she was about to ask about the man he had killed? He met her gaze full on and shrugged as if he did not know what she was talking about. A steely look came into her eye, and she said in a hushed but stern voice, 'I cannot have you jittery as a water dancer. You must concentrate.' She put both her hands back on the top of the wall and pulled herself gracefully over it, easily avoiding the stinking slime. He scrambled after her, then wiped the green jelly from his hands on his trousers. He did not want to discuss what he had done. How the knife had been in his hand and hissing through the dark before he had even been aware of drawing it. How he had felt the guard's heartbeat in the centre of his own chest and tasted salt and copper in his mouth. It had all happened so quickly and the saliva that filled his mouth was wet with hunger, it had revolted him, afterwards, but at the time he had not felt that at all, only desire for death and the taste of blood. The guard had a nano device like everyone did, but because of his lesson with Elgenubi and the last weave at his crown, he knew the guard's galactic power was Eagle, but it had been drained dry by the Serpent wrapped around Abrecan Castle and the image was ghostly and weak.

'We'll take the service steps.' He jumped at her words, and she pulled him close to her and whispered. 'The mansions here are deserted.' She shrugged then said, 'There will be skeleton guard only above.'

He nodded while she pointed along the wet causeway. 'Along there, where the rich have their yachts and ships. It is always patrolled. They are afraid of the people from the outers coming down here. Come – be careful, the stairs are slippery, these are not cleaned, they are too close to the headland,' she cast her head towards the distant marina, 'and we cannot take the cable. That would be asking for trouble.' She smiled broadly.

He sensed she was trying to reassure him and took a deep breath before he said, 'What if we are stopped and I, and I' he stammered, then finished quickly, 'If I have to kill someone?' He felt the dagger at his waist and the throwing knife at the nape of his neck. He was precise with both when he practised on a cork target, he had made for himself. It was round. Even though Eschamali had told him to make it man-shaped, he could not, but what had that mattered. He could have made it any shape he wanted because now he knew that when the desire to kill came upon him, he could feel a heart fifty paces away in the dark, he could put his throwing knife in it, if it was in range.

'We have done everything we can in planning this route to avoid people stupid enough to be in our way. It should be deserted here, in this weather.' She tilted her head. 'If we kill, then fate has decided it be so. We made every effort to avoid it.' She paused then said with a note of resignation in her voice, 'Markab should have taken care of that guard. He would have, but he said you were too quick.' She waited for him to reply but when he did not, she tutted then added, 'We have done all we can, Mar-cuss. Pull yourself together, connect to the Ever-Was. Master your breath.' She reached forward and yanked one of his locks then turned and strode towards the stair.

~ ❋ ~ ❋ ~ ❋ ~

The stair felt greasy beneath his feet and water ran down it as if it were a salmon ladder. The run-off had saturated his black leather gloves and his fingers were numb, the muscles in his thighs had set like slabs of granite and the ball of his right calf ached. Under his clothes he felt unnaturally warm while the steady rain soaked his breeches, and when the wind whipped at the fabric, it leeched the heat from his body with all the effectiveness of poultice applied to a fevered brow.

Ornate floating buttresses anchored into the rockface to their left, the maintenance stair was hidden behind them. Small square platforms, welcome rest places, were situated at regular intervals to their right. Short wide flights of stairs left the rest platforms and led onto cobbled roads, avenues and warrens of streets, alleys, and bridges. Empty palaces and deserted gardens, lakes, and aqueducts, arched bridges, and tunnels hidden by tumbling vegetation, all awash with silver water that fell like grief, while it made its way to the churning river below. There is less life here but more wealth he thought then said, 'This is probably unused most of the time.' He pulled himself up the ladder of stairs, repeating what he already knew just to fill the place in the pitch black where he thought her back might be. The dark, the wet, the climb, and especially the silence had his nerves on edge – he knew it would not be long until he made a mistake. He was bone-weary and chilled to his vitals.

'All of this beauty and grandeur, all of those empty places and yet your people live in squalor in the Shanty,' she muttered under her breath.

He replied, 'Please, not "the people" again.'

She stopped suddenly. He heard a velveting noise in the dark as her long arm unfolded. Her hand was over his heart in an instance, a warmth above his chest in the chill dark as she leaned toward him and whispered, 'They are your people. They are not "the" people, they are yours.' She paused then hissed, 'One day, they WILL be your people, stupid Mar-cuss who knows nothing.' He heard her voice break, a tremor of raw emotion that took him by surprise, but he ignored it and pushed away the sense of unease that had travelled up his spine like an icy finger. 'Should we use a spider now?' he croaked and felt her shake her head.

The stair ended in a small square landing to their right. From there a narrow flight of slightly better maintained steps led out from the well of the landing and onto a wide cobbled section of road. A lamp mounted onto the wall hissed and its flame burned low, the smell of marsh gas wafted heavily through the drizzle. He peered over the edge of the top stair. Across the wide expanse of cobbled street, he could see the sweep of the tight narrow chicane where the road curved up the monolith then disappeared behind the walls of another mansion. The streetlamps burned blue with alchemical light but even that was weak and turned low. They were in Estmere Scir, the district where the Patriarch's and Matriarch's of the Temples of Anuk resided, leaving the day to day running of the temples to their Aldhelm's, their first Bishops. It was quiet and he knew that they had been called back to their temples following the attack on the flyer base.

He smiled but felt it slip off his face when a chill shiver crept along his spine. They will make the streets run with blood he thought just as he spotted a dark arch hidden behind trailing vines. It felt like a million leagues away and was almost invisible, just another part of the craggy side of the headland but through that arch, the stair continued upwards. Troy narrowed his eyes; the sentry post below them was unmanned but the road was too exposed. 'We need to use a spider?' he whispered. 'I can't see properly to the right, there are buildings opposite, perhaps with alleyways between, there,' he pointed. Elgenubi nodded and he continued, 'On this side, roof gardens, terraces, the rear gardens of the mansions that face the river. Spider?' he asked again and put his hand to one of his pockets to retrieve the small metal eye that was mounted on eight legs.

'No, it's too wet and they are too valuable. We may need them after the meeting,' she whispered.

They slipped out of the stair quietly and turned the corner onto the street. Anticipation and fear oiled out of the shadows with him. He could see clearly now; thirty or so paces after the gardens that backed onto the street, it led onto a wide plateau to the right, then ornamental gardens beyond – deserted now and hidden behind a sheet of soft drizzle. They made their way across the shiny cobbled stones to the small sandstone arch. Head down, he pulled his collar up to protect his ears from the chill. I just want to get to the meeting, he thought wearily, while the wind pressed his damp clothes to his stiff, aching legs, and his heart began to beat erratically, drawn to something just out of sight. He balled his hands into tight fists and shoved them into his pockets.

They almost ran into them as they came around the corner of an alley one building away from the sandstone arch, silently, staring straight ahead like marionettes. They hesitated, and he felt his breath catch in his chest and the oily taste of desire fill his mouth with salt and copper. He and Elgenubi were wearing stolen dog soldier clothes, military fatigues in dark colours. We may get away with it he thought just as Elgenubi threw a dagger into the throat of one and leapt like a tigress on the other – his neck creaked and squelched. He tried to see the guard's galactic power but there was nothing there.

'Don't just stand there, help me get them over the side,' she ordered while she lifted the smaller of the two, put him over her shoulder and made her way back down the stairs they had just come up, then through a crumbling gap in the wall where the flying buttress was anchored to the cliff. There was a small wiggle space which led out onto a natural ledge on the cliff face. He was still staring at the prone body of the other guard when she returned. 'Hurry, Mar-cuss, the tide takes the bodies,' she hissed.

'I think this one is still alive,' he whispered while he used the toe of his boot to point to the body on the floor. The dagger was lodged in his throat and dark liquid bubbled from it then spilled down his chest.

'He is still alive,' he repeated numbly and realised that his own throwing knife was in his other hand, but he had no recollection of pulling it out of its neck sheath. He put it back quickly.

'Yes. You are right, Mar-cuss.' She drew the dagger out of his throat, took a handful of his hair, exposed his throat, and sliced it across his neck. 'Will you help, Mar-cuss, or there will be blood everywhere,' she ordered. 'I do not know if their nano is activated for tracing their whereabouts and life beat, hurry up,' she hissed impatiently.

'Did you have to?' he whispered. 'We could have bribed them. I know I could have done something,' he retorted sharply and pushed the image of the knife in his hand away while he turned and spat his disgust onto the road.

'They were not for bribing, Marcus, look.' She lifted the wrist of the guard and showed him what was in his hand; it was an illegal weapon called a wire.

A wire thrower was a disc-shaped device that released a length of copper wire that was weighted at each end. It garrotted the intended target. They seldom missed as they were a weapon designed to lock on to the target by isolating the pulse of the jugular vein of the victim, followed by a rapid swoosh as the wire ripped through the air and wrapped itself around the neck. It was quiet, an assassin's weapon really, considered a bit old-fashioned now.

'Light, I thought they had been made illegal after that elite child caught it in the neck.' Troy nodded to the guard's hand; the strap was still about his wrist. Elgenubi threaded her arms under the guards, and he took his feet. They carried him to the entrance to the cliff face.

I am no closer to finding Micah and recovering the data he thought while he studied the guards face as she pulled him through the wriggle hole. He was young, and thin, and pale. I doubt now that I could take the data back, apologise, pretend it was all a prank that went horribly wrong. I will be killed; my parents will be killed he thought while he wriggled through the space on his belly. A wave of nausea roiled greasily in his gut, and he felt his knees turn to water so instead of getting to his feet, he pretended he was resting on his heels while he watched her tap the wire on the guard's wrist. 'They were banned. These two, rogue proc, on the lookout for sport. No bluffing them, they would have tied us up and took us there,' she nodded in the direction of the sentry tower. 'We would have been used for days. You understand, they not men anymore, they not animal…smell them. They were demon drudges become men, now they demon sleek. The Estmere Scir full of their kind. Living like small gods in palaces, harvesting blood when they need it.' She paused and ran her fingers over her thumb making a flicking sensation to ward off evil. He felt like joining her but took a shaking hand and wiped misty rain from his forehead and replied quietly, 'I could not see a galactic power image. The other guard was…the one I,' he stuttered…' he used to be…it was an eagle.'

'They do not have one, but they be pumped. We blew the flyer base and now it's only a half moon away from the Night of the Dead.'

'Two and a half weeks won't be enough time to plan the tribal.' He pushed the corpse's feet away gladly; urine and who-knows-what else had started to run down his legs. She was right, he did smell funny like rancid almond paste, sweetly decaying, the greasy smell clung like death in the insides of his nose. Elgenubi took the guard under the arms, half stood him on the side of the ledge, then pushed him out, he tumbled through the air like a black crow flying and into the dark seething water below.

'There will be no more gatherings,' she said thoughtfully then added, 'It's why we go to meet Murzim tonight. I will use the White Galactic Worldbridger energy.' She sighed and continued while they made their way back through the wiggle hole and onto the stairs. They slid across the street and through the arch and began to climb again. 'Remember it is the energy that makes a gateway, and roads lead to and through gates. White Galactic Worldbridger, it is a road I can follow, a channel I can use.'

They had climbed the height of another tier when she paused and said, 'C'mon, we waste time. We will use the Houses routes now.' He followed her off the stair and along a natural ridge in the rock, from this they dropped onto the roof of another abandoned sentry station. 'Just what I want to do, Elgenubi, scramble through wet gardens, alleys, and shady secret steps cut in the cliff, so elite ladies and gents can be serviced by, ermm, the gentle folk of the night.' He jumped from the roof lightly and followed her over a wet shining road towards a fair-sized mansion to their right. They had entered the Bealdras Landar, the district where lords and ladies had their summer palaces and mansions. His parents had one, but they never used it, they preferred living at the top of

Lodewick, in the clouds, and in the vicinity of Abrecan Castle. Bucky and Micah each had a mansion in the Bealdras, but Micah's was closer to the Silver Seaf. The Estmere Scir was grand he supposed. Elgenubi thought the temple Patriarch's and Matriarch's lived like small gods, but their mansions were carefully not as grand as the palaces on the Bealdras Landar. The land of those heroes, Micah had said it was called, but when he had asked what heroes, Micah had replied that there were not any, it was all made up, a lie like the rest of Baelmonarchia.

They waited until two more guards walked to the end of the chicane then turned and walked away before they slipped down a service alley, and over a high wall. Then they headed towards the gardens at the rear which meandered towards the lush vegetation, rock, and cliff. 'You could get work in one of the houses. You pretty like a courtesan. Even Markab say so.'

He thought he heard something different in her voice, a compliment. 'I say, Elgenubi,' he growled quietly in what he thought was a seductive voice, 'are you flirting with me?'

'Silly Mar-cuss, my brother have your arms off.' She giggled and he smiled. Was she softening? At long, bloody, last he thought and wondered if losing his arms would be worth it.

Chapter Thirty-Two

𝔐urzim

The tension along his jaw had set off a pulse in his temple that throbbed and pounded. Blood rushed in a dizzying vortex that set his head reeling while he tried not to look troubled, while he tried to act confident and made plans to gather what information he could. The run-in with the guards had left him unsettled, he had been stupid to go with Markab and Alnilam, as for killing a man, whether he had been a demon or not, it had set something off inside of him, something he knew he had no control over. He tried to put his thoughts into a stream of words he understood, but he could not push his sense of unease away. He knew that something lurked at the boundary of his mind, waiting, and watching, and it had a voice that said, it is time to move on, before you are killed, or caught.

They were contacting Murzim tonight because it was Kinetic Eighty-six, White Galactic Worldbridger. *I am medial woman, a bridge, and she who swims the channels of space and time.* He had lost count of how many times she told him that and he was still uncertain as to what it meant. He knew the image of her power was an amethyst jewel on a platinum bridge, but lords of the flame only knew what her actual power, her gift was. It helped if he thought of their strange powers as gifts. It was easy to say that Hydra the Cup was a gifted healer, that Eschamali was a warrior blessed by some force they could not name or understand. That El Nath's shadow walk was something that had been bestowed on him, a gift that looked like a curse and made his flesh crawl every time El Nath appeared out of the shadows. But Elgenubi? He did not know. Worldbridgers, not real ones, but the freaks who created weird and wonderful cults, were never conceived in Lodewick, he doubted that they were anywhere, but whether they were false or true he imagined their fate to be the same as the bodies swinging from the wall outside Breakers Yard station. Worldbridger? A bridge between worlds. He could say the words, and reconjure the image of her power but he could not imagine what it was or how it worked.

'You sure you got her supported, kid?' Eschamali asked while he glowered at Troy over the shoulder of a seated Elgenubi.

'Yes. Comfortable, Elgenubi?' he tried to ask softly, but his mouth felt too tight and his teeth bit at the words until they sounded half-said and strangulated. He had stopped his hands from trembling by sheer force of will, but his legs and arms still ached from the climb, and muscles twitched sporadically in his thigh. It had been a long, long day, and he for one could not wait to get out of Lodewick and find somewhere to sleep.

Elgenubi sat on a meditation chair, it had a cushioned seat and a high back, and her legs stretched along the thick matting of the studio floor. A control room with a wall of long, fat, glass tubes, full of bubbling rubidium and copper spirals sat behind a glass wall. They generate their own power, he thought. Strange clusters of anemone-shaped tendrils covered the walls and ceilings like tiny stalactites. The sound was condensed and flat, like what they said was being heard in a secret cave, deep underwater.

'It's our equipment, kid,' Eschamali explained. 'This is sound, and sonar proof, otherwise the proc will use their wave disruptors to locate us when we begin to transmit. We used it after you report on the Serpent. Was a decent job.' He inclined his head slightly, the equivalent of a heart-warming hug of deepest gratitude. 'Is she comfortable?' He nodded towards Elgenubi while he retrieved several types of crystal and resinous silicon shapes from his pack.

'Yes, stop fussing, Eschamali. Keep my spine straight, Mar-cuss, and do not let me fall to either side. Oh, and do not piss your breeches either when I go under – you got that? Promise?'

'It is not a thing to make a jest on, Elgenubi,' Eschamali scolded her.

He was taken aback; it was exactly the sort of thing that Eschamali would normally jest about. She turned and squeezed his arm and he nodded, still unsure as to what was going on, but determined to meet Murzim. He had a question ready. Damn it if it got him killed but he was going to ask their leader for help. He was going to say aloud and to his face, I know you used Markab's mask on a dead body to make it look like Micah Apollon and now I want to know where he is. He groaned aloud and wondered who would kill him first. Eschamali, he will take off my head, probably with his bare hands.

'Mar-cuss,' she whispered, 'I need you to be strong – for me.' Her gaze pierced him to his core, and he knew she was asking him to put aside his anxiety about the man he killed. If only she knew that was one note in an orchestra of his lies and shame. He nodded and the light in her eye softened.

Then she took her attention to Eschamali and said, 'I give you all the time you need, brother, even if it seems too much, you take it.' Something passed between them and Eschamali shook his head, but she reached forward and put her hand on his arm, then said in a hushed voice, 'Last chance. It could be our last time.' Eschamali took her hand and squeezed it but did not speak and he could see the lump at his throat work up and down while he gulped. He dropped her hand and turned while he reached for his pack. The muscles in his back were bunched into slabs of tension and a vein throbbed at the side of his neck.

He is upset, really upset Troy thought but he held his tongue and waited while Eschamali brought out a long, thin, clear tube, and beaker, then a vial of blue liquid, easily recognisable as essence of night poppy, and a proc military adrenaline pen. The pen contained three five hundred mcgs of adrenaline and a huge needle; one shot was more than enough for a normal adult. There were three shots in the pen because Baelmonarchian dog soldiers were not normal human adults. It had come from the robbery on Volsunga's warehouse and had earned him a hearty clap on the back from Homan Wind who had said, 'Minnow got eyes like a hawk, and sticky fingers like a yegg.'

'What the hell's that for?' he half-shouted, not able to keep the fear from his voice.

'Hush, Mar-cuss, no talking from now on. We have done this before; it is what I am able to do – it is part of my own galactic signature.' She frowned. 'I have discussed this with you. I am medial women.'

You have, he thought and wondered when. Then he frowned while he tried to recall if she had ever told him she was going to kill herself. It would be the sort of thing the Zuben's would do. Eschamali, the suicidal, meathead maniac, regularly tested poisons, and their antidotes on himself. He said he liked to kiss the arc of time and spit in death's eye, but he was sure he did to scare him silly, but this was different, there was a lot of night poppy, and although there was a lot of adrenaline, he wondered if it would be enough.

'Ready, Elgenubi?' Eschamali passed her the tube, and she fed it down her throat, leaving one end of it in the beaker by her side.

He passed her a vial of blue liquid. 'Will you take all?' he asked. Troy tensed and thought, for pity's sake, what is she going to do to herself?

'No, not all, I need only travel…two thirds of the way. They are waiting for us to contact them, half only this time.' Despite the tube sticking out of the side of her mouth, she drank half in a single delicate gulp. There was enough to kill a horse. Two he thought and sat in stunned silence. Every bone in his body wanted to reach forward, he wanted to take his hand and swipe it out of her grasp.

Eschamali caught his eye and imperceptibly shook his head, but not before Troy noticed a sheen of silky moisture dew suddenly on his dark forehead, and alloy colours he had not noticed before oiled across his skin, bronze, flame orange, and a sickly pale ochre. He fancied he heard a tremor in his otherwise gruff, steady voice when he said, 'The count is sixty-five…keep her upright, Marcus, and wipe away any sweat or vomit, she must not choke. Once she starts to rattle here,' he tapped the top of his chest, Troy looked startled, but Eschamali continued, 'Once that starts, you siphon off the death slime. You understand?' He inclined his head towards the tube.

Troy nodded automatically and began to gently sponge Elgenubi on her face and neck as he listened to her breath become shallow when the night poppy began to work, but also partly induced by herself.

He had seen her enter meditative states before and he clung on to that memory. She knew what she was doing. *'I embrace The One, Mar-cuss. Come join with me,'* she would say, and he always declined and pretended to be busy doing something else while he watched while she sat immobile for ages. He studied her skin which glowed like spun silver, and her long neck which he always imagined kissing. He knew beneath her snarl of dreads every bone along her spine was raised and looked like embellishments on silver armour. He watched while her consciousness flitted elsewhere, he watched and studied every part of her. Long graceful fingers folded together on her lap, the curved bow of her top lip and how the light angled off the planes of her face. He may as well have joined her but that would mean he would have had to close his eyes too, so he kept them open, and through them he knew her beauty and strength. He knew every line that pain had etched into her perfection, every crease of joy which were too few, he watched, and he fell in love – but this was different. How could he? He had already seen his friend die and now this.

He knew when the drug had taken hold. Her beautiful silvery skin turned to ash, then a sudden release from her chest shuddered violently and he jerked with fright while she began to fall towards her death. Eschamali met his gaze full on and mouthed quietly over her head, 'She strong in the night. You hold her fast.'

'Who are you?' Eschamali asked roughly.

He almost jumped out of his skin, and his eyes darted towards the door. Does he know who I am he thought, and panic sheeted through him like waves of shock. Then Eschamali said, 'Where are you?' Her eyes flickered open but were distant and milky.

He sponged her forehead gently with a wad of cotton pad and moved her limp body, so it rested more firmly against the back of the chair. Her jaw at her mandibles had begun to vibrate with the effort of breathing, and a mucous rattle had begun in the back of her throat.

Eschamali nodded. 'The siphon,' he said softly.

Troy took the other end of the thin tube and sucked gently until he saw a yellow liquid begin to flow like lazy honey down into the beaker.

'Nuru-Sha-Shutu…I am asleep in my pod in Juno Seven.' It was a child's voice speaking through Elgenubi, clear like a small bell. He wiped saliva from her chin, rubbed balm on her dry lips and gently set her head straight.

'How goes it on the surface?' Eschamali asked.

'Another moon has arrived, but it is not solid, as was predicted. He not able to lock the nodes because he does not find the centre.' Troy heard pride in the small reedy voice. 'Our Worldbridgers have surrendered their knowledge, they have given the keys to our Lord Juno, not like the traitorous pretender Worldbridgers of Gaiadon.'

'You let ego determine the contents of your mouth,' Eschamali scolded, as he pulled discs from his pocket. 'Do you see the discs?' he asked as he lifted the first disc and slipped it into a small silicon cube, resinous, and fluid-like it pulsed. A beam of light projected from the side of the cube onto the centre of Elgenubi's forehead.

'Yes, I see them and the patterns upon the beam.' The child sighed, and a spiral of coloured snowflakes and geometric mandalas spun out of the cube along the beam of light in a tumble of ultra-radiant, holographic colour. He gasped and hid his surprise quickly. They were the same as the ones that had left Micah when he pulled his nano out of his wrist. How long ago? Not just a lifetime but a whole different world away he thought then licked sweat from his top lip, and felt moisture run down his spine like hot oil, and the delicately placed talon of a massive serpent.

'Do you see anything different in them? Look carefully, child. We need your rhythmic tone to organise the parts into a readable sequence. It is scrambled, as you can see,' Eschamali instructed Murzim. Then catching Troy's eye, he said quietly, 'The proc use wave disruptors to scramble the intel.'

Murzim replied, 'I see that, but still, I see nothing fresh. Scattered incoherent thoughts, Anoia, and sequences of radial plasmas, but there is nothing concrete there. No intelligence we can use.'

'We remastered discs from the Night of the Dead?' Eschamali nodded towards the glass window. A shape moved behind the glass, then a door hidden behind susurrus anemones shushed open softly.

Troy wiped sweat from Elgenubi's brow. The secretions had begun to taint with specks of blood – he prayed it was not so. 'I will try,' the small voice replied, and something softened in Eschamali's eye while he took the discs from an elderly man with thick dark optics that fit close to his eye socket. Troy kept his attention firmly on love while it died in his arms, and the bespectacled man slid past without a word or a look. Sweat leaked from his forehead and stung his eyes with salt. *If she dies*, he thought, then realised he did not know what to do, where to go. He wiped his eyes on his shoulder before dipping the cotton pad in the bowl of water and sponging Elgenubi down. *How is she so cold, but sweating too? It is like the world knows she is dying and is taking back its water.*

'Thank you, Crow' Eschamali said quietly without taking his eyes off Elgenubi.

The man did not speak, merely inclined his head, then left silently, invisibly, while Troy's heart jumped in his chest, kicked him in the hollow of his throat cutting off any words he had ready. Elgenubi slipped from his hands, and when the choice hung in the balance, he chose her, and grasped her to him then put her upright again. The door shut with a final click that felt like a boot to the gut.

Eschamali scowled, then snapped, 'Do not let her move or we lose the connection; worse, we lose her.' He changed the discs and projected the beam onto her forehead again, while her breath continued to rattle like dry weak ivy leaves scratching against a wall, and her wet clammy flesh grew cold beneath his hands. 'What do you see?' Eschamali prompted and he heard the urgency in his words and felt tension emanate from him like a hot wind.

'It is jumbled, but I see some signatures – Lord Lucas was there, as was his heir; the serpent be disappointed as their signatures are not the same, much remains in the unknown. The Memitim stole the sun in winter, the spider wept, and the white wizard danced while his manifold plans unravel with no end – oh, the things he has done.' The small voice had taken on an unnatural metallic vibration like something else was talking at the same time, but from a vast distance away.

'That is enough, neither of you must enter the oracle this night, I forbid it.' Eschamali thundered an order, but the metallic voice had gone.

He thought Elgenubi had opened her eyes, but when he looked again, she had not. He mopped her face and felt the vibrations at her jaw pulse and ripple through the flesh of his fingers. She laboured for each breath, and he felt his own lungs constrict and his own heart weep. He felt useless and could do nothing more than adjust the siphon, the yellow honey secretion was spotted with red but when he tried to catch Eschamali's eye, he shook his head and growled 'Not yet.' Then, an opaque body, vaporous as marsh mist, begun to rise away from her physical body. It lifted a thumb's length away with each exhale, then was drawn back down with each strained, ragged, inhale.

'What in the hells is that?' He felt his locks snap with a sudden rush of electricity and the air around them became charged and thick with power while they tried to weave towards her, and he wished that they were his heart and that he could give it to her, that she could share his life force with him.

Worldbridger, she is a death walker he thought and wanted to pick her up and run from the room. His hand tightened on her shoulder, if I can just get my other arm under her legs, I could lift her away from this horror.

Eschamali said 'Stay strong, she is getting close to death now, her bodies begin to separate, the physical and magnetic body remain there,' he pointed to her prone form, 'the astral body is there,' he pointed to the ghostly apparition, now a handspan above her physical form. 'I terminate or lose her.' He reached for the adrenaline pen.

'Wait,' Murzim interrupted sharply, her little voice high with excitement, 'Data for the black moon, it was there – a remnant of the blueprint in the formation of the radial plasmas…someone was carrying coded data for the dark moon.'

He felt his heart flip into his mouth. It landed in the back of his throat and closed his airway, he could taste the blood, and feel the throb, throb, throb of fear pounding on his tongue. He tried to swallow it down and gagged but kept his hands on Elgenubi's shoulders, while he lowered his head and kept his gaze on her. He knew if he looked at Eschamali he would not be able to hide the guilt on his face the message surfacing inside the pit of his eye…I know it was there. It was me; it was all my fault. I killed Micah Apollon because I stole it, and now I am going to kill her.

'I must terminate,' Eschamali shouted, and spittle flew from his mouth.

Just then Elgenubi's astral body sat forward and separated from her physical self. She rose from her seated position like a silver spectre, made of naught but moonlight and the radiating beauty of stars. His breath caught in his chest; she was the most beautiful woman he had ever met but nothing prepared him for the sight of her soul. Her power ran through her astral form in waves of crystalline light, her locks lifted and spread in an invisible wind. Emanating around her was a violet light, numinous and mystical it was the same as the jewel on the platinum bridge. She is the jewel; she is the gemstone he thought and felt a surge of emotion sting the back of his eyes. He wanted her to see him, because he felt something inside himself see her, but she did not look. She pointed first to Eschamali and shook her head vigorously, then she pointed to her almost dead body and mouthed, 'Go on, you must – I order it.' She held a shimmering cord in her left hand. It sparkled like star dust and moved like quicksilver as it snaked through her fingers. It twisted from the left side of her physical form and into the left side of her apparition body. Making a cutting motion with her fingers, she indicated it was still complete, it had not been severed.

Eschamali caught his eye and said, 'Notochord, is loosening.' Then he said in a voice edged like the rough side of an old sword, 'Murzim, Elgenubi is separate from herself. She not got long until Gaia come claim her. Pass the intel to Lord Juno.' He smiled proudly while he rushed his words but the worry on his face had aged him a million years and his hands shook uncontrollably while he kept the projection running into Elgenubi's forehead.

'Let her live…let her live…let her live…' he pleaded under his breath while he fought against the horrible realisation, the crushing disappointment, that he could have been so wrong about their leader. Elgenubi would die without knowing how he felt. The man Eschamali called Crow had walked away without knowing he sought his friend Micah, and Murzim? Murzim was a child! Who knew where she was? He had not heard of Nuru-Sha-Shutu, but the certain knowledge that the Nightcrawlers did not have the numbers or the power to help him find Micah weighed on his mind like a dead animal and the stink of failure, his failure was just as foul. He had done everything wrong – everything! – and now Elgenubi was separated from herself and was about to die, and he could not stop any of it and to make matters worse his heart had begun to thud with an unnatural rhythm and his mouth was full of saliva that hungered for death and blood.

'Father, there are to be no more collections. You come home.' The little voice stifled a yawn as Elgenubi stirred. Her rheumy eyes flickered into the back of her head while a tremor passed through her physical body as if a wind had rippled under the glassy surface of a clear lake.

'Gaia comes. We cannot let her soul be absorbed here; it belongs to Juno,' he whispered gruffly to Troy, and he knew in the centre of his chest that Gaia was singing to him too. He held his breath and steadied the thump at his heart and took his attention to the astral Elgenubi who mouthed, 'Continue – it is an order,' while the physical being breathed her last few breaths.

'The Khronos Portal has been disabled. The silver cord that holds her weakens, my little Murzim. Quickly, tell me – what are you about?'

'We are learning about them, in case they come here, in case we need to fight.' She yawned loudly.

'I will be home before then. I love you, Murzim.' Eschamali choked on the last words, wiped his eyes on his arm as he dropped the projector box. 'And I, you, Papa.'

Troy hardly had time to digest that the huge brute in front of him might be a father who loved his child, that someone in the universe got to call him Papa, and still lived. The connection faltered as Elgenubi spasmed. Her astral form looked sad while it held out the shimmery, crystalline cord. A single tube made of molten platinum and sparkling shards of glass that somehow connected her to the stars. 'We're going to be too late,' Troy shouted as Eschamali drove the adrenaline pen into her heart; it clicked twice – the amount a dog soldier would need.

He was terrified but worked on automatic while he pulled out the thin tube and put his finger in her mouth. He retrieved her tongue and pushed the sponge pad on top of it to stop her swallowing it, then wedged the rest of the sponge between her teeth while Eschamali rolled her onto her side.

'You do well, kid. Elgenubi is right, you the best runner we ever had.'

He passed no comment but grunted instead and did not meet Eschamali's eye, he could barely see for the tears. If he faltered. If Eschamali gave up now? What was left? Where was their strength and spine?

Guffawing sobs racked his own body; the only thing that kept him upright was the need to be there for her. She had told Eschamali that he was the best runner they had ever had…she may as well have told him that she had fallen deeply in love with him, and that Eschamali wanted to take him for his son.

~ ❦ ~ ❦ ~ ❦ ~

Afterwards Elgenubi rested. Eschamali said, 'You will wait here with her, kid. I must be away back to the warehouse, to check the work Lady Bathory's crew has done. It is two, three horas before sunrise, it will be light if the sky is clear of cloud. We move. I shift the gear. Elgenubi will bring you to the docks. Then once we are away from here, we sleep. Here,' he pointed to the adrenaline and essence of night poppy, 'put them in your pockets and make sure she finishes all of this.' He passed Troy a pack of food: grilled sea mushroom – they grew on the edge of the docks, like stacks of yellow and green plates sticking out of the green slime. He thought they were poisonous; indeed, they made a poison out similar green shroom plates, but the Zuben's loved them – slices of parsnip that had been cooked with honey and wrapped in chicory leaves, a large lump of bee curd and a flask of water. Troy's stomach rumbled when he realised the honied parsnip was for him. Light, Eschamali Zuben had brought him food! There was no meat, The Ten never ate it.

He grabbed the pen and essence of night poppy, shoved them in his breeches pockets. 'I need to talk to you, Eschamali, about the man you called Crow, who is he? Is he still here?' he could hardly control the quake in his voice. The unnatural rhythm that had assaulted his heart had died down when Elgenubi came back from the brink of death and presence they called Gaia had faded away.

'I, not have time, kid.' He paused at the door and pointed at him. 'Elgenubi, you answer the kid's questions. Tell him whatever he wants to know – no more secrets, eh. He our best runner, a family pet now. Pet…' he guffawed, 'Pet Spider, Juno would laugh until his eyes leaked.' Then he smiled broadly, and though relief was written across his face there were other deeper lines that had not been there earlier. 'Later' he nodded towards Elgenubi. 'Our pet spider, eh.' He barked a rough laugh. Unlike Elgenubi, he looked like he had aged a century.

Elgenubi nodded. 'Eschamali, there was a vision too. I saw blood-letting…on a massive scale,' she said in a weakened voice then took a gulp of water while she waited.

He scratched at his locks as he assessed the information. 'Blood? When we are away from the spawn pit, you may meditate on this, but waste no energy on it now. No distractions,' he chopped the air with the side of his hand, 'our escape and survival depend on us being strong in the night.' He tapped the side of his head and Elgenubi nodded her assent. 'I for one cannot wait to get out of hell,' she said, and he replied, 'From hell to ice. We go North.' Without another word he turned then closed the door.

She waited until the door had closed before she spoke, and he could feel her eyes on his back. When he turned to face her the tight line of her mouth and the cold glare of her anger told him all he needed to know.

'All you see, and you ask about a man who was a shadow, here, and then gone. Mar-cuss spider, with all his secrets. Even his name not real. Is it Troy?' Elgenubi chewed the bee curd and took huge gulps of the water while she waited for him to answer.

It had not been the sudden plunge off a cliff type of shock he had expected the discovery of his identity to be. Instead, he felt diminished and ashamed. He paused and took a deep breath. It was Elgenubi, if it had been any of the others, he would be dead or in chains in a dank cavern somewhere. 'How long?' he asked and shrugged. It was over if they knew who he was.

'I did not know, not at first, but then I suspect. Your face is unique,' she said and lifted her eyebrow while she twisted her top lip into a scornful curl.

'I, I' he stuttered.

'Save it,' she flicked her thumb over her fingers, and he felt shame draw colour up his cheeks. She was warding herself against him. Then she said, 'The serpent around Lodewick, hiding from Lady Bathory and Vee, avoiding Himalia. Then the shock Alnilam said you felt after you had killed the guard, but I knew it was strange that it only happened when you saw Markab disguised as Micah Apollon.' She paused then held out her flask. 'Here share some of my tonic, it will restore you too...and...only one of us knows Troy. You still got your arms; if Eschamali knew, well, then you would not.'

He sat before her and took a moment to gather his thoughts. When he spoke, his voice was filled not with remorse but a steely resolve. 'I will not apologise, because that too would be a lie. I am not sorry for trying to find my friend. Instead, I will tell you the truth.'

She snorted and replied with a note of accusation that cut him to the quick. 'You a liar. I knew it first time I look into your slanty lie-eye. Just like your mother, just like your father.' She finished with a loud tut then waved her hand at him to continue. He was sure if she had been strong enough, if she had not just almost died, he would be eating dirt of the floor.

He nodded and shuffled towards her slowly. Then he put out his hand and took her own in it. She flinched but did not pull away when he met her gaze fully and said, 'I'll talk first, then you must tell me everything too. Please do not ward against me, I am not evil.' He paused while she snorted and wondered why she had not spat in his face, the look on her own was sheer revulsion but still she did not shrug him off and let him continue holding her hand.

'Why haven't you told him?' He studied her face intently and was surprised at the strength and command in his voice. How not having to lie about being Marcus had returned to him some of his nobility and bearing, his confidence. He was Troy Valoroso-Wyburn, he had stood at the Sun in Winter's right hand, and it had felt like all the world had bent the knee to them. That they were the future, a better place that was in the making, and that was why Micah had been taken he realised, not because of the stolen data but because of their relationship. I was not supposed to like him or Bucky he thought when he quickly recalled all the times he was supposed to go with his tutor and mentor Rubric Volsunga, and all of the times his mother had stopped that happening, all the times he had conveniently been at Galay instead. He took his attention back to Elgenubi.

'Eschamali would have killed you or worse, tried to barter with your life. Also,' she flicked her head to the side as if she did not want to meet his gaze, as if she was afraid of what she might find there. Then she said, 'I like broken things – some say I'm broken.'

She turned her attention to him fully and a knowing smile teased the side of her mouth but there was something else in her manner and a look in her eye that set his pulse racing. Then when she spoke, she put the invitation she knew he wanted to hear in her words and took his hand and placed it above her heart. 'Secrets for secrets, spider?' she asked softly. 'My secrets make you mad, here, in the night.' Something set deep in the cavern in the centre of her eye, and it was a light, and a promise that theirs was a secret she would keep. She leaned forwards and whispered, 'In the night,' while she pressed her finger gently to the side of his forehead. Then keeping eye contact, she took her finger and brushed it over his lips.

'Willing to risk it,' he replied and leant forward.

'As am I,' she whispered thickly, and felt the heat of his body when she drew him to her, and the honey and parsnip scent of his mouth when she placed her lips over his.

CHAPTER THIRTY-THREE

Worldbridgers Are A Funny Old Lot

Elgenubi tilted her head to one side. 'But you do not know where the Sun in Winter is?'

'No, like I said, we were at the night of the dead tribal. I lost him, and he died. The Memitim took him, but then Tranquillity got in touch and sort of proved he was...' he paused and helped her tie her locks up and smiled when he felt his own crackle with a deeper connection to her. 'At least the corpse I saw in the picture...well, it was not him, but was wearing the mask Markab uses in the Bliones Tun. I knew I wouldn't be safe, so I disappeared, but I need to find Crow.' Troy talked softly while he retrieved their dog soldier fatigues. Elgenubi's were still a heap of black and grey damp, but she had brought fresh with her in her pack.

'The mask came from the Wizard. Eschamali call him Crow,' she replied, and there was a note of confusion in her voice. 'But Markab only start working the Tun dressed like that after Micah Apollon died. It was when the white-eyed seers returned to Hiriwa Pourewa, we needed more intelligence, and the Tun is full of secrets.'

'Another dead end, until I find this wizard,' he said and could not keep the disappointment from his voice or the flutter of a memory from surfacing. A hand upon his back, propelling him forward, the touch paper that lit the Night of the Dead rebellion. He pushed the memory away, they started to get dressed. He had not told all, he never did, but the secrets had had to wait. He turned to her and felt his heart soar, she was intoxicating, and it was all he could do to tear himself away. Though it had been her who had ended their embrace and he knew in his gut that if he reached out to her again, she would reject him. He knew in his mind that she was forbidden fruit, deadlier than droge waere, and that she would eventually kill him. 'Are you sure you are well enough to move, Elgenubi?'

She shrugged and replied, 'I almost died, true, but the best way…no, the only way to recover is this – the first act of life. Do you understand this was the first act? Love, and life.'

He nodded but he did not understand. At first it had felt like sex to him. Although she had been different. Vastly different and everything he thought he knew was of no use to her or to him. Her scent was overwhelming, sacred, and more powerful than any droge waere he had ever taken, he had lost himself in it, and she had taken him past the edge of sweet surrender, it was then that he realised that she had taken him, and that was when he felt the hidden thing within her. It was better than him in every way, but it did not cause him to feel weak even though it was stronger, and its Will was diamond hard and resolute. It was the many faceted violet jewel that she was part of, a thing that was beyond his comprehension and when he pulled back afraid of that knowledge, he felt her give him permission to stay, though he did not understand that either, only that he would never feel it again and that felt like homesickness, a longing, and a hunger inside him that no other woman would ever satiate.

Small lines furrowed her brow while she studied him. Then she said, 'White Galactic Worldbridger was right for our union. This day sacred, and the only way for me to safely complete this act with you.' She paused but he could think of nothing to say but sought instead that light in her eye. A reassurance that she at least felt the same.

She narrowed her eyes and tutted loudly. 'Do not go lovesick on me, Troy, this was not about that. What I do, I do for the higher good, for the Lords of the Light Flame. Not for us.' She paused and a faraway look came to her eye and her mouth turned down at the corners. Then she said in a voice tinged with regret, 'In the future there are things I must do that...' she trailed off and added sharply 'They are not for us but for the greater glory of the Light over the Dark…you understand?'

He did not.

'Hurry or we lose our chance to enter the Shanty.'

'How do I find Crow?' Troy asked as he pulled on his boots.

Elgenubi shook her head and said, 'Eschamali or El Nath Night know, but how you ask without losing an arm.' She waited until Troy finished scowling. 'El Nath throw the dread-cast at you because you let him. Challenge him. He thinks you not built for the night; you not strong enough here.' She pointed to her head. 'He is an excellent teacher for you.'

He nodded. He understood what they meant – finally. When any of The Ten slept, they called it night, regardless of where the sun or moons were in the sky. They were recharging inside their sleeping pods and their eyes were closed, and their consciousness was cast to where they wanted it to be, which took great mental control. They were strong in the night or in his case not built for the night…weak. Eschamali, Homan, and El Nath all had skin that had more chitin than the others. He was not sure whether it was because they were male, or whether they had chosen to produce thicker skin naturally, although Markab, Alnilam, and Acumen did not. The chitin looked like arm braces on Eschamali. Homan was segmented like a dry lakebed, El Nath Night looked like he wore armour plates on his face and the rest of his body. Even Elgenubi's spine was slightly raised like embossed armour, likewise the other women in The Ten, Hydra the Cup, Alcyone Sun, and Himalia Skywalker; all had parts of their body that was covered in thicker skin, chitin, which shone like armour. He did not, therefore he was also weak in the flesh. He scratched at his dreads – water dancer? Who knows, he thought.

'What was Homan Wind's signature? When you received your final dreadlock, you saw us all, but never said what his was,' she demanded, and he jumped back to the present moment.

'It was the head of a flower, but one that had gone to seed, like a large ball made of wings…a fairy flower. They grow everywhere, bright orange weeds really, but the seeds have tiny gossamer wings and when they take flight they look like hundreds of small fairies in flight.'

'Do you know why?'

'I don't, though it was unexpected, him being the size he is, it should have been a maelstrom, a tornado, even though he made scaling that wall look like a fly crawling up it, delicate.'

She half-laughed. 'He is master of wind. He not just weaving the wind as some do but is the wind. He merged with his power. The fairy seed head is fragile. A passing butterfly beating its wings can set the seeds floating. The sun warming a blade of grass can cause the smallest vortex to rise, that set those fairy seeds flying. This he knows and through his knowledge of the wind he keeps the seed head intact. You saw him climb the wall using only small pockets of air he had commanded…he could have fallen and broken his neck. I could have succumbed to the pull of Gaia.' She stopped and searched his face, 'You felt her too?

He dropped his head rather than let her see the lie he was about to utter, but she snorted contemptuously and continued, 'It matters not. Both are ways to die, but they are ours. We are not afraid of them. Find your power…know the ways you can die; you need to know this. Soon.'

'I do not have any power, Elgenubi…you know that, how many times must we go over it?' He lowered his gaze and pushed aside the memory of salt and copper in his mouth, the unnatural rhythm while his heartbeat connected to his victim, then the overwhelming pull when he knew he had connected and the engine that pumped their blood was in his sight and their life was his for the taking.

She harrumphed and snapped, 'You biggest liar in the universe, though I have not heard of that power anywhere else but in the mouths of the two-tongued, white-eyed seers, inside Hiriwa Pourewa.'

He changed the subject. 'Tell me what you can…all of it, I'm listening.'

~ ❋ ~ ❋ ~ ❋ ~

'I am the mission's Worldbridger, a medial, I bridge dimensions if I have another of my kind to communicate with. Tonight, I speak with Murzim, Eschamali's child.' Elgenubi waited, but he did not interrupt as a multitude of questions poured through his mind. He stilled them and nodded that she should continue.

'Murzim is on, Juno Seven. Inside the city of Nuru-Sha-Shutu. I speak with my own kind, but it costs. The bridge I walk, is the frequency of death. To enter the channel, we be the same resonance. Some do not survive the near death that is required. If I speak with Murzim and she only a few thousand light years away, then I meditate deeply; if I speak across the planet, then I use my locks, next room,' she paused and nodded her head behind her, 'I shout…but to another dimension…' she trailed off and studied his face which was as blank as new parchment. Sometimes she wanted to shake him he was just so stupid, and she wondered if the seed he carried in his sex would be stupid too. With an exasperated sigh she continued. 'Murzim is a Rhythmic Worldbridger, I a Cosmic Worldbridger. Murzim organises chaotic patterns of thought on the discs into a song she understands. I cannot.' She tapped her head. 'Up here, people are never quiet – chatter, chatter, chatter – tumbling's of this thing and that, even if they were interrogated, we would not get from them what we do during the Nightcrawl. The Nightcrawl is a sequence of movements that brings stillness of mind. Most not aware of what they think, even fewer of what they have seen. When they give themselves to the manifestations we spin, they become an open book. Nothing is hidden.'

'I understand,' He recalled the emo-manifestation Himalia had spun at the Night of the Dead tribal. It was not just knowledge they harvested, but also what people had seen and not registered consciously, on top of that, they harvested emotions. It made sense, though he had never come across the alchemical formulae or the crystal grid matrix that would conduct such a deep mind sweep, he did not doubt that they had the equipment, they were extraordinary people who had done amazing things. Just look at the modifications they have carried out on their bodies he thought because he believed that they had, that what he saw before him was not natural, but a bought and paid for physical enhancement.

'Where was Murzim's mother, why didn't she do it? Why use a child?'

'It our curse, to know death intimately and recognise the channel we need to use. When we born, our mother dies, the pattern is established. Worldbridgers never give birth to another Worldbridger, we are like mules. Medial is a mutation. Eschamali lost Nuno, a Crystal Warrior like he, when Murzim was born. Before this, I kill our mother when I was born.' She paused and her head drooped while a look of utter devastation fled across her face, she shook herself but not before he saw. He leant forward and took her in his arms then held her against his chest.

'Light, no wonder he looked so angry. He almost lost it, Elgenubi. He could not bear the thought of another loved one's death.' Troy shook his head incredulously. 'His own death wish makes sense I suppose, his insistence that he test the poisons and antidotes personally and as for the combat with Markab and El Nath…they should know better.'

She pushed Troy away. 'Do not judge him. I weep. I grow soft, it is this place. Death is the way of the world as it ever was.'

Troy scowled while he wondered how fit for the job a suicidal warrior was, and to be the leader of The Ten, though he knew he would not challenge him over that – ever.

'Murzim cannot bridge the distances I can. The practice we carried out tonight is strictly forbidden by the principles of my order, the Monatha, but I have dispensation to use it on this mission.'

'What? Killing yourself should be forbidden, Elgenubi, unless the wound is fatal, and it would be cruel to let a person live.' Troy shrugged. He tilted his head thoughtfully. 'Are you ever going back, or is this a one-way mission? Is that why you all came here? To die?' He ran his hands fretfully through his dreads and picking up a thong from the floor, tied them into a snarl of black, amethyst, and platinum hair. He ignored her while he picked up their fatigue jackets. Light, The Ten are as vulnerable as I am he thought and could feel the tension knot his back into ridge and bump.

'Your irritation, it smells like fear,' she accused him, and he could hear the unsaid, weak in the night. 'We have done this kind of work before, that is why Lady and Juno selected us for this mission. We have no fear of death,' she pointed around her and said, 'This is death, this is sleep, all illusion and pain, greed and hate, though you think it real and that The Ten are on a death wish, because they cannot live through this hell, and wish to be reborn sooner than fate will allow, you know so little, Mar-cuss.' Her eyes flashed blue and gold. Her hands balled into tight fists at her hips. 'You have made me angry, Spider, with your foolish ignorance. How can I help you if you have no ears?'

'I do not want you to die!' He shouted while a look of surprise passed over his face and his cheeks flushed red.

She frowned at him; then her face hardened and something in her eye said she was not likely to be receptive to clumsy declarations of love. 'We all die when fate and the prophecy held in our souls as destiny utters its final word. Sit down and listen, please.' She pointed to the floor as if he were a child. He narrowed his eyes but loosened his tense shoulders and sat down heavily.

'There is never enough time,' she said with a weight in her voice that sounded like destiny and an echo from the future; his future, slipping away to the lords of the flame only knew where. He steeled himself and waited. 'We do not know where our journeys will lead next, whether we remain together…it is not clear…but you must have this knowledge, even though it may be the death of me.' She reached out and took both of his hands in hers. 'We are currently on the planet Gaiadon. Below this, there is a planet we call Pistis Sophia after the logos who created it out of the void. 'The logos are Celestial Being's…it an energy, and a design, they are demi-gods. Gaiadon it is Gaia. On my home world, the logos is Lady. They are accompanied by their evolution engineer; they too are small gods. It is the first thing they do on arrival in the part of the void that has been designated fit for dimensional evolution. The engineer is birthed for he does battle with the Nomos to gain The Stone, and the laws and lore, which define that dimension.' She paused to finish off the water and he studied her and knew in the twisting labyrinth of his innards; they would never be. When she spoke like she did now, it was in another way to the one he was used to. Her tone and her language were alien and the Elgenubi he knew, the one full of joy and excitement at discovering a new poison, or laughter at the ridiculous fashions in Lodewick, disappeared, and in her place was this creature, an otherworldly crone, death-walker, ancient, and stuffed full of knowledge she did not speak about often, because no one would accept it to be true, no one could understand it.

He wondered how long it would be before they were torn apart and felt a stab of fear in his heart that cut like the blade of truth. She would not appreciate him maudlin over her, so he said, 'Actually…that makes sense, and it is what we are taught – the One-god Anuk defeated the chaos beast on the Plains of Cale with its Romarii allies and he placed the black moon Lilith in the sky to heal the rift between worlds. It is also thought that when people go mad, outside the box, it is because some sort of evil energy attacks the brain and nervous system, a thing left behind by the dark magic the Romarii used in the war.' He nodded, pleased with himself. It made sense and would explain how demons had come to be in Lodewick, surely, they had not all been conjured out of a cauldron.

'Oh, is that what you are taught…and no one questions that?' She leant forward and tapped the device in his wrist while she shook her head uneasily and frowned. Then she said, 'The defeat of the Romarii on the Plains of Cale is not ancient history, it is hardly more than half a century ago. Captain Stonewall, was there.'

'Ridiculous,' he replied, and flinched at the flash of cold fire in her indigo eyes.

'I will tell you ancient history,' she snapped. 'The engineers must defeat the Nomos to gain possession of The Stone which is the thing that anchors the laws of that first planet to the axis of reality. Pistis Sophia has Yalan. Gaiadon has Cernunnos. Lady has her Lord Juno. There are other anchor planets like beads on a string all along the axis of reality both above and below where we are, and their galaxies spin and turn around them.' She stopped and nodded at Troy. 'You understand?' her eyes were wide with anticipation; she had kept it as simple as she could.

'How does he fail to find the centre?' It was something that Murzim had mentioned, that and the North and South Nodes that interested him while he tried to recall what Micah had told him about the moon holo-cast and how it was being held in place.

'The planetary centre is the Stone, it can be mobile, they all are. We know that Ningen are here, Alnilam has reported that he saw a child of Time. They are creatures of space and time from The Void. They stink like red-hot, forge-seared, metal. It is faint but if it is here…we know that an aspect of the great beast must guard a sky portal here in this city.' She rubbed at her temples.

Troy reached forward and touched her lightly on the arm. 'We should get out of Lodewick. I do not want to put you in any further danger, Elgenubi.'

She nodded. 'You are so kind, considering…and a good heart. I wonder if he knows. It is such a flaw in your design…but never mind that,' she blabbered. He noticed her thumb rubbing over her fingers, her ward against evil and wondered if it were still directed towards him, if she would ever consider him untainted by whatever evil she thought his parents kept in their skinny bones and behind their perfect faces.

'Your books, the Phantasmagoria, the Chronicles, what do they tell you? They are the most accurate record of the ancient history of Gaiadon.'

He rubbed at his eyes and sighed, he was bone weary and wanted to sleep. He was not a Zuben, he did not have their energy. I am weak in the flesh he thought while he got to his feet and began putting on his jacket; he handed Elgenubi her own. 'The Chronicles are written in the old tongue and have been challenging to translate but if I correctly understand them a Lord Bucky, a powerful magician collaborated with a white wizard, and they used a sky portal made from a space snake to begin the exodus of magical power and a supernatural light, Eleri Imole, from Gaiadon.'

He paused and Elgenubi nodded. 'Your translation is fairly good. This happened two Ages ago. Continue.'

'There were two tribes of Fae, Novantae and Selgovae and their creatures, they were in grave danger if they remained here as the Shadow Yet To Come, would consume their light and their magic. According to Cassandra, the Ningen were lost under the sea and failed to answer the call to leave as they had their own destiny to answer on Gaiadon. Long before this, another Age before, a ship of Galanglas giants left the Bay of Loka, captained by Crann Og Riamh, considered a giant weakling – a runt if you like, but a warrior-smith who had been God-touched or blessed with magical ability. They were left behind, but it seems not by accident, and that is as far as I have gotten with the Chronicles. I am still trawling through her predictions for The First Age of The Stone. Thomhas' Phantasmagoria tells similar tales in the common tongue, and the copy I have of Navigating the Southern Isles, is by a woman who claims she is descended from the giant Charyia Sea Storm. They are quite new copies, maybe two, three hundred years old, considering the myths they tell of are thousands of years old.'

'There is truth in myth. That is where you may find the help you need, in the Chronicles especially,' Elgenubi replied mysteriously. 'The Ten came here,' she reached her hand above her head and clicked her fingers, 'through the ripped membrane. We used the rift to travel down the axis and have been here as long as the Lord of the Dark Flame, Conquest. We are a species who lives an exceptionally long time, five score years is a heartbeat and a breath to us, but never-the-less we are marooned here until we find a Khronos Portal. Himalia has tried to use the stone compass here, but the gates have been blocked by Gaia, and are overrun with Fear Me's. But the Khronos Clock. We think it is disabled and until we locate its whereabouts, we will head north and join the Romarii resistance.' She pulled on her boots and fastened the buckles at the sides.

'If I had not seen it in the Ever-was, and if Micah had not tried to warn me, I would have thought you mad. I suppose that is why Abrecan's galactic power is so strong. He is descended from the One-God Anuk.'

'By the bloody light of the one true flame. THE ONE GOD ANUK IS NOT REAL!' she shouted.

He jumped, and felt his bones slip upwards through his skin. What have I done now? he thought but held his tongue when he saw her white hot rage flash in the pit of her eye.

'Nor are his children…It is him – he is Anuk. He is Bael. The so-called sons and daughters are his elite inner circle, the bloody demons are the temple Matriarch's and Patriarch's that crawled out of the lowest hell with him. After ravaging Pistis Sophia, he brought chaos, war, famine, and death, to the doors of Gaiadon, then he kicked them through.' Her voice screeched, 'Anuk is the name of the Demon Lord of the Dark Flame, Conquest. Anuk is the chaos beast… Anuk "is" your dearest uncle, Lord Lucas Abrecan.' She gasped but continued, 'Anuk is every evil, he is Bael, self-anointed king of the demons, he is the tyrant king behind every act of conquest…' She began to calm down; her right thumb flicked furiously across her fingers.

'I, err, I'm not...are you lying?' he sputtered and stuttered, then backed away. She was almost catatonic with rage and a finger of fear stabbed him in his spine and he felt a knot of knowing, deep within him, unfold slowly like hot liquid pouring.

'It is part of his corruption. He spews chaos wherever he goes...it is all upside down.' She made a twirling motion with her hand. 'He drops his illusion memes from the black moon. He uses the serpent in the Ever-Was to watch the population, and he consumes their power through that,' she tapped his wrist.

He groaned and massaged his wrist, 'It's a fake,' he said weakly, and she snorted then replied, 'Clearly it is. You still have your hand. If that had been real, I would have hacked it off the moment you walked into the Tanner's Apron.' She finished her laces, reached out and almost squeezed the blood from his hands while she studied him intently and prayed that he would wake up before she really did strangle him.

'I, I don't know.' Troy blurted and felt his world drop away. 'He doesn't look like a demon. He is quite an attractive man some would say. I have read the stories on how his ancestor Anuk defeated the demons and well...how can he be Anuk? Demon or god, it must be Ages old?' He was startled by her passion and found himself stuttering out questions as he tried to make sense of it all while he knew with a twisted sort of certainty that the last thing it could be, the impossible horror, was what it was.

'Why is it too far for you to believe? I speak truth. I gain nothing from lying.' She stopped. 'No, I have not made myself clear. Anuk, the demon, is the Lord of the Dark Flame, Conquest, who calls himself Lord Abrecan now, and he is as old as the celestial being who first cast him into the Void. The reason he does not look old is,' she paused and nodded her encouragement.

'I don't know, Elgenubi. He has a secret potion; he drinks from a devil cup,' he replied quickly and hated the petulant ring to his tone. He shrugged and tried to pull his hands from her grip.

'Almost...he uses blood magic to...' She waited expectantly.

'I do not understand, though some of it makes perfect sense but Abrecan is not eternal, he is a man like any other, Elgenubi. Will you just hurry up? It will be dawn soon, you know you hate the light,' he said, trying to mock her. His mood had turned sour.

She sighed and finished buttoning her jacket. 'Our mission is complete. We have not been successful, but must return to Juno Seven if we can, use what we can of the information Murzim has seen in the remastered discs and somehow disable the false moon. It is unlikely it will be destroyed here.' Her words sounded leaden, and her shoulders sagged while her chest sunk.

He had never seen her look so defeated, or old. 'What do you mean, destroyed here? Can it be destroyed?' he asked as his interest grew alongside his pressing need to find Micah and the pendant. Do I tell her about the data on the pendant he thought briefly, but something held the words and the secret firmly inside his mouth? He knew they could not help him and if he told her, that he would lead her to her death. I will not have your blood on my hands he thought and took his attention back to her.

'Yes. He will align the axis on a massive scale, not the whisper of a death channel for him. To take Juno Seven, he will need to move armies across dimensions. He cannot use his anti-gravity fleet, Juno is an interior World, so he will need to bring his best soldiers through a portal of his making. There is no rift,' she said and answered the question he was about to ask. 'Not anymore. It suits him to tell everyone that is what the black moon is for, but Gaia closed the dimensional rift with her last breath. He will need a special ability to open another.' She paused and snapped back the words she was going to say. He will need a Spectral Star to open the membrane between dimensions she thought and felt the pull of destiny draw her North, to the weak and feeble radiation of the Star she had seen in the Ever-was. She put her fist to her chest and her voice was filled with pride when she said, 'We warrior, he cannot defeat us, and he knows that what he has is not good enough. He must create super strong warrior-castes before he challenges us.'

He suspected she told the truth but wondered how much more of it was yet to be revealed. A sneaky fear crept upon him, not unlike the dread – and a sly voice whispered insidiously, hissed like a snake when it said…Did you choose the right side? I can make moons appear in the sky; I can march armies across dimensions, while you play at "rebel" with a bunch of dislocated, suicidal aliens. Who has the power?

He jumped when she asked, 'Are you sure you cannot help us, Troy? If Eschamali finds out who you are, he will hold you hostage, an attempt to stop your uncle?' She spat the words and her thumb ran along the back of her fingertips flicking away an evil she could not see.

'Then he would fail, Elgenubi, my uncle cares little for me, for anyone.' Their eyes met and he held the secret of the pendant with data on it, hidden in a black place deep inside his mind. She reached forward and brushed away a dread that had fallen across his eye and made it water. He returned the gesture and caught her tear on his fingertip. Then rested his hand gently on the top of her arm.

'Then Eschamali will kill you. He does not understand like you do not understand; your uncle cannot kill you,' she finished on a whisper and shrugged him off while she turned from him. 'Come, we must go before we are discovered. Before the sun rises, we must be in the Shanty.' She pulled the door, and it whispered softly open.

'Will you attempt to stop him if he tries?' Troy whispered.

'Stop Eschamali?' She seemed perplexed at the question. 'He, Crystal Warrior.' She pulled him through the door. 'It will be quick for you.'

'Then I need to make sure he doesn't find out,' Troy replied as he followed her out into the pre-dawn, grey world of Lodewick. They headed silently towards the nearest whorehouse; it was well-lit, muted conversation and soft music, harps, and piano, could be heard, laughter that tinkled and sparkled through the night. They sought out the stairs that would take them to the first of the tiers on the Side of Light and the Bealdras Landar. It was an ornate wooden door in a wall towards the back of the beautiful gardens, dotted here and there with private pavilions, some glowed with lights from fires and braziers within. They inched their way along the wall of one and heard a short sharp slap, an experienced hand on flesh, and a man groaned inside. The inky grass sparkled with dew, but the overcast hung low, a cloud of despair waiting to descend that mirrored his mood exactly.

'Will we retrace our steps?' Troy whispered and his head hung like it was stuffed full of lead. That was what her words had been, heavier than lead, and he could not digest them nor pick the part where he would survive. Where any of them would survive. She reached out and touched his arm. 'Only to the ledge where we threw them off. I noticed it almost goes straight across to Cheapside, but it is no more than a hand-span at that side, then a crack that we will be able to get our fingers in.'

He picked the lock. The door opened onto a small sandstone landing. An alchemical lantern hung from the wall, its light was cool and eerie. Next to it a bundle of unlit torches sat in a wrought iron basket next to a lit torch in a black metal sconce. She put her hand up indicating that Troy wait. 'The floor is dusty. I see a set of prints that go only to the wall to keep the torch lit. Make no more, we will climb around the inside of the wall. Do not touch the floor. Take no torch, they will be counted, and make haste they will come to retrieve the lantern at dawn.

'No lantern means, shop's closed,' she said as if she shared a great secret. Then added, 'Markab told me that. Come, I will lead, you follow. You have the night optics?'

'I do,' Troy replied dully as he pulled out a pair of round optics with dark lenses and put them on, adjusted the small pips at the top of the arm where it met the lens. I wonder where Tranquillity went, he thought wistfully. Light, I wish I had gone with her.

~ ❈ ~ ❈ ~ ❈ ~

Elgenubi was quiet while they made their way along passages and secret chambers, some natural and others cut out of the rock. He followed her sullenly out of another garden and over the cobbled street. He was glad that their way back was uneventful. Although, he thought, if a guard steps before us now, I will rip out his throat with my bare hands. Hard rain volleyed against them and the cold and wet chewed at his fingertips while his head still reeled, and he looked at Elgenubi with something other than love in his eyes. Fear he thought, and knew it was not for her but for himself, he was trapped with The Ten. He was the sheep in wolves clothing and now one of the wolves knew who he was. He pushed an image of Markab crushing mint leaves aside.

They slunk across the street and onto the landing. 'We will have to hang off it and use our hands to move across – it's not far, a couple of swings ought to do it,' she said with forced cheer as she looked through the gap in the stone buttress at the ledge beyond

'Two for you, probably four for me.' Troy shrugged.

'Look, kid,' she sighed and the note of impatience in her voice stabbed him in the gut, 'you've got the strength and flexibility from our training, but you lack mental control. You do not notice what you should because your mind is not still. Connect to the Ever-Was. Control it, Mar-cuss, or it get you killed.'

'I'm Marcus again?' A smattering of rain stung his face like tiny knives cutting.

'If you want to live,' she said over her shoulder, but her words were snatched away by the wind.

'Talking about living…' he paused while he tried to gather his thoughts, he could not think straight, tiredness gnawed at him, and his mind was a pool of roiling dark. I will never control it he thought then said, 'Why do you think Lord Abrecan won't kill me, Elgenubi?' He waited for her answer while the image of his father, Reynard, surfaced from the chaotic roil of his mind. 'Not you, never you,' he had snarled, and at the time he had just brushed it off, but now he wondered, why?

'You tell me, Mar-cuss, you must have worked it out for yourself by now,' she talked while she eased through the crawl space in the buttress that led to the ledge.

'Because if he is a de…no, not just any demon, he is the Lord of the Dark Flame, Conquest, born at the same time as his dimension was evolved out of The Void…according to myths and legends,' he felt her shake her head, 'then he is old, really old.' He paused and Elgenubi looked back and nodded at him to continue.

'He's so old that whatever physical body he once had, is long since gone. I have seen the history books, representations of the chaos beast…losing that body can only be a good thing. Therefore, he needs new bodies. You said he had crawled his way here, so he does not control the bodies from his demon throne in hell or something…he is, physically here.

'So, if he is not controlling bodies, then he must make himself new bodies. And that is what he is doing up at The Wind. Making himself an army of new bodies,' he finished on a triumphant note.

'No, you, total numbskull, he needs only one, and it must be perfect for his design. He has failed consistently for scores of years to produce what he needs. He has always been the thing that crawls, slithers on its belly, spineless and flexible. On the planet below, he existed for millennia, until he was trapped in the jade coffin. His brethren, worked out how to free him while he waited for the technological advances he needed. Always causing war, collecting blood and death, always the same creature in different bodies. The acts of his ancient evil captured in myth and lore; his modern atrocities recorded in the histories of the wars of men. The evils that he and his fellow demon horde created were legion there. They ruled the planet, enslaved the people by creating cyclical patterns of chaos. Always War, Famine, Conquest, and what can Death do but follow in their wake. He had to choose his host from human stock, but here,' she raised her arm, 'Here on Gaiadon, fertility and DNA are different. There is less natural fertility and more active DNA3.' She did not laugh at her own joke but grimaced and something hard set behind her eyes.

'In this dimension, even with his blood magic, he desires something more…his next host must be a direct blood relative of his body now, and a galactic signature close to his own serpent kinetic.' She waited.

'He does not have an heir, Elgenubi – thank all the gods and goddess that ever were or ever will be. Imagine that? Poor sop.' Troy replied and his words were bitter on his tongue.

'He has an heir, Troy,' she stated flatly, and he felt icy cold creep under his flesh and maggots of fear burrow into his marrow, while a strange lurching sensation untethered him from his body until he felt himself pivot away from her words.

'He used blood magic to make an heir with Leleth, your mother, in his own laboratory; a bio which they grew in a tank, but he did not want a Snake for his next host, always the snake, so many serpents in so many different guises. This time he needs a Dragon. You.' She tapped him lightly on the chest.

You, you, you – her voice echoed, and it felt like the hard little hammer inside a bell that was tolling in the future, and its sound washed over him and through him, until he could taste his own death, and it was copper on his tongue, until it congealed like black blood in his mouth. He felt her heart pumping; life blood, and her galactic power, rushing through vein and artery, and he wanted it, to stop it, to consume it, to grind it to dust.

'Help me,' he whimpered, and his voice was tiny and far away while something that was too large for his frame, older than the stars, and filled with hate and vengeance tried to oil into his being, but every muscle in his body resisted, every cell shouted NO, and his knees turned to water while he slid down the cold hard cliff face.

Then everything fell into crystal, clear, place.

'Now,' she said efficiently, 'Do – you – understand?'

He could not feel his face. His eyes had turned into two pools of vitreous vacant ironstone glass. Moisture from low cloud stung their lens while he stared out from the headland and watched mist roll above the bowl of the Shanty like a shroud. Small lights wove about like will-o-the-wisps then went out and he wondered if he would be extinguished too, though he knew he would not. He would be pushed to the furthest part of his himself while the lord of the dark flame, occupied him. No, he thought, I will not call him that. He is not a lord; he is a foul demon.

'Abrecan will not subsume me, my consciousness completely.' He said in a hushed voice that trembled with fear. Elgenubi crouched next to him and put her hand on his back. He felt a small patch of warmth emanate from it, but it was a drop of comfort in an ocean of turmoil, shock, and fear. He blew air out of his mouth and inhaled until he felt his nostrils pinch together before he continued. 'He will make me watch while he takes his foul pleasure on the woman I call mother. He will make me watch while he tortures, rapes, and kills people I know and love. It will be my hand the blood is on and my eyes that witness it, but I won't have any control.' He took another deep breath and pushed away a deep sense of unease and the memory of the guard he had killed. 'He will even make me kill Reynard.'

After a moment that seemed to stretch to the horizon and back, where he waited for Elgenubi to offer some comfort he said in a voice filled with disgust. 'He will make me watch, and I will be present when he carries out the foulest of his desires. I will eat human flesh, until eventually I will desire no other kind of meat.'

Elgenubi sat down, then pulled him to her, and without a word of comfort or any other thing that would sound feeble and wasted on the moment, she held him. Their feet dangled over the edge of the narrow ledge. Wind pushed, then tried to pluck them from the cliff face, rain pelted them with volleys of hard drops that felt like pebbles being thrown against their skin, but he paid it no heed and let everything unravel like intestines unfolding from a man who had been sliced in two. When he breathed, it felt like a demon raked its claws down the inside of his throat and squeezed his larynx tight. His words would not come, then he hacked and coughed, retched, but found his voice and in it his strength.

'It's all perfectly clear, they knew – Micah and Bucky knew, especially Bucky.' He stopped and retched and gulped the taste of parsnip in the well of his throat back down his gullet. He will kill Bucky and I will have to watch, trapped inside my own body, my actions not even my own.' He shuddered and continued. 'No wonder he was forever insisting I stay with them. By the seven hells, Bucky was afraid he was going to occupy me without any notice. The hunting and fight training, sword play, the many forms of fighting…I mean so many, Elgenubi. Not that I am violent, I am not – he was preparing me, so I could defend myself. Worse,' he paused and let his tears fall, 'If he had possessed me? Micah or Bucky were going to put me out of my misery. Weren't they?' He turned to her, but she did not reply, although the answer was written in the inky knowing in her eye, and the hard line of her jaw.

'I've never felt any connection to Reynard, no love, nothing – poor twit, does he know? He must. And Mother? Leleth? Who the hell is she really?' he babbled while Elgenubi rubbed his back.

'It's genius. How was I ever going to know? It was hidden in plain sight – the money, the privilege, extravagance after grotesque extravagance, getting away with anything short of murder anyone else would have been corrected for. Brainwashed with wealth – Anukssake.' He raked at the wet granite with his fingernails while the wind pushed salt spray and icy water into his mouth. 'I'm no better than a slave, no, hang on...I am less than that, less than human...just an object. I am a thing he made.' A sob racked painfully through his body. A strong gust of wind buffeted against his legs and tried to lift him off the cliff. He felt ready to let go...that would show Anuk.

'Please, Troy...do not be weak in the night...do not go to the dark place inside, it is where he waits for you.' Elgenubi placed her arm around his shoulders.

'I'm nothing more than a bloody vase waiting to be filled. I am done for, aren't I? He must have made more. Elgenubi, tell me I'm not the only one?' he rambled on until the contents of his stomach entered his mouth. He leaned precariously over the ledge, not caring if he fell. Elgenubi held on to the back of his fatigue jacket while he sprayed hot liquid into the wind. Partially digested parsnip floated away on a pale ribbon of mucous and acid.

'Pull yourself together, please...we must be away.' She pulled him close while she rubbed his back again and whispered, 'I will protect you, Troy. I will get you away from him...but you must try too. Poor spider, come with me. Are you able to move now?'

'I had better be able to move my sorry carcass, that bastard is not occupying my body.' He got shakily to his feet while he gathered his resolution. No, he will not take me. I will kill myself before he uses me that way. I will not bed the woman I think is my mother, I will not wait until he possesses me, then watch while he takes over my body and kills Bucky, Reynard, Weasel. Even Weasel does not deserve to die.

'Perhaps he will not, Troy,' she heard the lie as she said it, 'but from now on you will need to be careful. Yes, I can help you, but do not rely on me, only on yourself. Remember the training Bucky gave you. You must learn what Abrecan is about, his strategy – your own must be better, not just to survive, one day you must stop running…to survive, you will have to kill him or be subsumed by him. He is the Tyrant King, Lord Conquest. If he enters you, it will take everything you have to beat him – no man has, ever. He is ancient evil and would be best defeated when he is in his current body.' She stood when he did, then looked into his eyes, she nodded, then sniffed. Satisfied he was able to move, Elgenubi began inching her way across the ledge with her chest and cheek close to the cliff face.

'It couldn't be any bloody worse, and here I was thinking the stinking Shanty was going to be a shitty experience. Is there anything else I need to know about my impending doom?' Troy followed Elgenubi. He looked forward to the climb across the cliff face now – anything but think about it. It was going to send him mad.

The ledge was beginning to run out as Elgenubi reached out and found the thin fissure in the rock face, slipped her hands inside and eased her weight slowly off the ledge. 'It's safe to follow, hurry, there are a couple of toe holds.'

Troy huffed as he followed Elgenubi's lead.

She said, through clenched teeth, 'Look to the Shadow Yet to Come, for your answers.' She moved slowly onwards; the wind snatched her words away while rain pelted their backs. Troy found the fissure and readied his body which felt like it weighed four times what it had earlier. He knew he lacked the strength, even though he was fitter than he had ever been. Even her combat and mind training has been to aid me he thought and stepped lightly off the ledge and into the most uncertain future he had ever imagined. Light, poor Leleth, no wonder she did not want me to go to work with him. Hells, is she a demon too? Why does she have feelings? From reading a book on morals…? This is madness he thought then added, no not madness this is ancient, and evil, and it wants to make a house out of my body and steal the light from my soul.

Chapter Thirty-Four

The Ophiuchus

Rain lashed, so hard it hardly felt like water at all, it felt like fingers of ice raking the face off Lodewick, as if the elements knew he was a foulness, a disease, that needed scratched from the surface of the world.

'Will you hurry up, Mar-cuss? It will be dawn soon.'

'It's pissing down, Elgenubi, it'll be dark for ages yet,' he snapped, and heard anger and fear in his voice. She paused just inside the hole in the buttress that led from the cliff. Then she turned and looked back, her face and her worry lines were deeply etched and the look in her eye was stark. Framed in the narrow hole just so, she looked like a portrait of sorrow.

'I'm sorry,' he said quickly when he saw how concerned she was.

'Come, let us get to the skiff, Mar-cuss. Eschamali waits.' She waited until he had pulled himself through the hole then put her hand to his chest and met his gaze fully with her own. With a defiant tilt to her jaw and her top lip curled she said, 'It will be dangerous, but not impossible – nothing ever is. Where there is a will, I know there is a way.' She turned and moved off quickly, then climbed over the foundation that held the buttress to the rock and waited for him in the shadow of the curved structure. He scrambled after. They were at the East end of the Snide, the long wide road that led to the offices of money lenders, and gem dealers, pawn brokers, and fat ledgers stuffed with the value of immoral gain that passed off as trade and commerce. There were no buildings or people at this end of the Snide, the ground was too unstable and riddled with crevice and crack where it had been quarried for stone. Three tiers below Athanasius Blood's warehouse exploding had loosened even more rock and large square chunks lay at the bottom of quarries that were full of shadow and filthy water. 'I know a way from here to the docks,' he said through chattering taut lips while he stuffed his hands under his armpits. The sodden coat clung to him, and he crouched like a winter tree on wind-blasted moorland while he turned and slunk towards the Greystone quarry to their right. The culvert he sought was still covered in dripping vegetation but inside it was dry. The rainwater is still being channelled down the other side, it will back up and fill the Merewif to the brim if they are not careful, he thought and snorted aloud. It seemed no one had taken on his drains and sewers, or they had not been able to fully unravel the complex labyrinth of underground waterways, culverts, sewers, and storm drains after he had left. They eased the curtain of vegetation to one side and slid into the drain. It was large enough to walk upright in and he paused while he adjusted his night optics and waited until she had put her own on.

They made their way further into the rock and ruin of Lodwick, always heading towards the left and the direction of the Merewif. They were wading in waist high water that was pulling their legs from beneath them when they heard the thunder and rush of run-off as it emptied into the dark pool of the Merewif. Elgenubi raised her voice over the roar of water. 'We will be drowned.'

'No,' he shouted back while he kept hold of the rough stone wall with one hand and adjusted his night optics with the other. 'This is as far as we go. We head up a rope ladder three paces down from here, then take another channel that leads to a small gully just behind the Shambles, we avoid the Merewif,' he paused and pulled her out of the current when a load of vegetation and the lords only knew what else tumbled past. Then he said, 'The Merewif overflows into the ravine beneath the Wet White bridge, then out into the marshes from there. Assuming the outlet culverts aren't closed or blocked.'

'You know the sewers?'

'Rats always do,' he replied, and felt her tense, but he did not want to talk with her, he wanted out of Lodewick. Then, he would decide whether he stayed with them or whether he would be safer if he struck out on his own. His mood was darker than an executioner's hood and his will to survive hung by a thread. He had toyed once or twice with the idea of returning home and confessing to the crime of stealing the data, claiming some sort of madness had assaulted him or even blaming it on Micah, but now he knew if he returned then he was walking into a fate worse than death.

'To the Shambles then,' she snapped and pushed past him.

'It's the other way, Elgenubi.'

The Shambles was the warren of alleys, cuts, and secret shady places directly behind the docks. They came out of the sewers into the disused cellar of a dilapidated tithe barn, then made their way towards the wharf where Eschamali would meet them. 'Try the sequence again…it may be the last chance you get for a while,' she whispered, and he could see the plea in her eye and felt a wave of shame course through him. Pull yourself together it said. They were sheltering under the eaves of old dock buildings that leaned towards one another like gossiping goodwives, leaning their ample bosoms over the alley.

'Yes, you keep an eye out for Eschamali.' He forced aside his unease; he could imagine no future where Eschamali did not kill him, or a demon king did not possess him. Then he nodded towards the entrance of the alley and slipped inside a doorway. He pulled the mo, out of a pocket and thumbed the second sequence listed under "Crow." He watched the thin rivulet of sewerage run down the centre of the street and nodded; he was right they had not opened the main sewers yet if it was still running down the streets. It was all a lie he thought and suddenly felt something set inside him. Everything before was a lie and now, I can make the rest of my life the truth, my truth. If I want to be Marcus the Kid, the Zuben's runner, then that is what I am. I will grow into it, and I will leave Troy where he belongs, like a bloody rat hiding in the sewers.

His fingers were purple, and bleeding, they clutched at the mo, while an agony of razor-sharp pin pricks coursed through them when his circulation returned. The mo felt thick and slimy in his hand, and he almost dropped it when a voice said, 'Micah. You have escaped? We were betrayed.'

He stuttered and his words caught in the hollow at the bottom of his throat. His head was reeling, and he whispered angrily, 'This is not Micah. Where is he?' The call ended with a click and Troy studied the mo in his hand as if it was a gold bar. The voice had been polite, but somehow bumbling, and a bit flustered. He jumped when Elgenubi whispered, 'Eschamali is here. Did you get anything?'

'No, nothing – as usual,' he lied, and slipped the mo back in his pocket.

Everything has changed he thought while he wondered who Crow was. He had not heard him speak at the studio. Did the voice fit the man he had seen when Elgenubi was dying? Whoever it was, thought Micah was still alive. You have escaped, he had asked, but more than that he said they had been betrayed. By whom and why? he wondered then felt each layer of his being freeze until the cold reached right into the very last corner, of the last cell in his blood and the pattern in its ice wrote on the wall of his soul. Memitim. He shuddered and pushed down a wave of sickness that oiled from the pit of his fear. I am a vessel for a bloody demon. Not just any demon but a lord of the dark flame, I should not be afraid of them, but he knew he was. He had no proof that they had betrayed

Micah, only a feeling that they had, and as for the man on the mo. The voice was familiar. He itched between his shoulder blades and felt a pressure like a large hand pressing and pushing, while a memory fluttered just out of reach. He shuddered and rubbed at his arms they were stiff as a puppet.

He spied Eschamali sail the skiff inelegantly towards the quayside and deliberately walked slowly so that he could process another stream of questions he had no answers to. Though, truth be told, he wanted to jump in the water and swim to the other shore, such was the fear in the pit of his stomach, but he was determined not to show that before Eschamali. He had accepted him, finally. He was no water dancer, whatever that meant but he slowed his steps even further when he realised that he was their prisoner, and that Eschamali would use him to lure the demon to a fight. He had never seen him cast magic, like El Nath Night cast The Dread, and he wondered if the huge warrior could. While a sinking feeling told him that Eschamali's magic was held in slabs of muscle, sinew, and tendon, he was a fighter, a warrior. Whereas, Abrecan had blood magic, by the bucket full.

He checked his pockets, while he took one anxious step at a time – night poppy, adrenaline pen, mo, stickle bug, he pulled his optics off the top of his head and put them in his pocket too, next to a couple of spy-eyes shaped like snails. Then he checked again – night poppy, adrenaline pen, mo, stickle bug, optics and a couple of eyes shaped like snails. He patted another pocket; oh, and a small spider. 'Better,' he sighed and thanked The Ten for their thorough training of their pet runner, Spider.

There was a snarl of unease he kept pushing aside, not just fear of the Lord Conquest or the Memitim but something else...I am a hostage, and we will never maintain the lie he thought while he studied Elgenubi. Someone, somewhere, will eventually recognise me. Will we be able to hide our attraction? No, not with another nine Junonians travelling with us. He squeezed his hands into tight frustrated balls and thought, I am already a dead man. Why am I following them? Elgenubi turned and waved him on, her hair and skin were silvered like they had been misted with dew, as if she was made of diamonds, and ice, and starlight, and his heart knew it was because he would follow her to hell and back.

The skiff was flat-bottomed with a small sail and some oars. They made their way cautiously down the slimy ladder and took positions in the boat. It was cramped once they were all aboard and had strapped their packs on. His bedroll and their black pods rolled up like sausages, some camping gear and an assortment of weapons, spiders for surveillance, stickle-bugs for throwing and blowing, most were Romarii designs stolen then copied from the proc military. He reached for his optics; the night lens might be useful he thought then changed his mind when he noticed the overcast greying toward dawn. It was his least favourite time of day or night. It was airless, a nothing place made of grey, birds were still asleep, the river was too quiet, and even the most experienced of shifty folk, tread carefully through the translucent curtain that hid nothing and revealed all. It was a vulnerable moment that stretched too far, that sliver of time between night and day. He slipped the night optics back in a trouser pocket and felt them rub against the vial of night poppy. 'Night poppy, adrenaline pen, mo, stickle bug, optics, a couple of eyes shaped like snails – and a small spider,' he whispered.

'Are you well, Mar-cuss?' she hissed quietly. He heard the warning in her voice and shrugged while his eyes darted about manically, searching for a demon. If I finish the poppy essence, I will die, he thought, then it would all be over.

They slipped silently away from the dock. The water was shallow, exposed banks of silt stunk like rotting vegetation and cloying death; not the best time to try to row across the estuary but they had no choice. They rowed quietly onwards. Traders beginning to set up market stalls echoed strangely across the water, their voices disembodied in the pre-dawn. They met each other's gaze and knew to keep their own voices low. They caught a current in a narrow but deep Wyrm and let it pull them towards the Inawyrm Channel. It was a few miles to the opposite side and the sheer cliffs of the basin where the Shanty lay. He shook his head when Elgenubi indicated that he could stop rowing, he let his thoughts come with each pull on the oar and hated himself when he realised, he was why Micah had to disappear. Abrecan was going to kill Micah because Bucky was hell bent on helping him escape his impending demon possession. Then Bucky must have faked Micah's death, but how, and with the help of who? Not The Ten, thank the lords of the light flame. They had not acquired the mask until after Micah had died. Crow, The Wizard, he wondered and pulled the oars through the brackish water with a grunt. He honestly could not believe any of the elites would dirty their hands. One thing to pretend Micah was a king on a fake throne, another to plot against Lord flaming Conquest himself. His head was reeling as he struggled to recall who had bent the knee to Micah outside the silk warehouse, but he could not recall any names, they had all been dressed for the Night of The Dead. Who had been present at his Tears ceremonies and cremation…Lord Yew Drydanward, Lord Matthias Dolmen, Lady Bathory Dorka, and an envoy from the Southern Isles…a Witch Queen, perhaps? He pulled the oar through the water and inhaled deeply, the smell of salt and rotting seaweed filled his mouth and his lungs until he felt the tips of his fingers tingle and a sense of clarity lift his confusion. Of course, Tranquillity Maegdelan, and shifty-skin Homily were there, he thought acidly, one a Romarii and the other…Light, what was the other? He cast his mind over Meite a Thomhas' Phantasmagoria…by the light of the flame, Homily was a Rodinian shapeshifter.

'This way…over to this side, there is a sand bar ahead,' Eschamali whispered back to Elgenubi who had taken the rudder. They headed in the opposite direction. The skiff bumped about against the current as it tacked towards the sand bar, bringing him back from his thoughts while Elgenubi failed to tack using the wind. 'Have you done this before?' he asked and put up his oars, glad of the distraction. Her mass of platinum dreads shimmered like an enchanting lost cloud of ghost, beautiful, against the leaden overcast.

'No. Others sail the water courses of Nuru-Sha-Shutu.' She moved indicating that he should take the rudder. 'You will be better than me.'

He took his seat with a feeling akin to relief and did not look back as he left Lodewick behind. Lord Bucky had some heavyweight support there, he thought while his confidence grew. I am away from the demon nest, and just maybe Bucky has enough to overthrow Abrecan, the dark lord, Conquest. If anyone can take Lodewick it would be Bucky. Light of the flame no wonder they watch him like a hawk watching its prey. His thoughts were spiralling out of control, so he put the rudder under one arm and squeezed it against his flesh and focussed his mind there. Suddenly, a tight shivering fear spread along his spine, and he felt he needed his books on his person; they had too much information in them that he needed to know, to treat them so casually.

'Can you pass me the books out of my pack?' Elgenubi looked puzzled but left the question she going to ask in her mouth, while she shrugged and indicated that he should turn about while she reached into the top of his pack and passed him his books. They were not large, them being copies, and he suspected they were not complete. She motioned he wait, then rummaged in her own pack and brought out a sheet of silicone.

'It's just a precaution, I could easily lose my pack, or they could fall out, and I don't want to lose them for the sake of taking a moment to carry them on me.'

He explained himself and felt like a fool, but she nodded her approval. 'Now you think like one of The Ten. This craft will sink after this mission rather than let it be traced to us or its previous owner,' she replied as she wrapped the books tightly in the silicone sheet. 'It is the best I can do. Here.' She passed Troy the pack and he opened the military fatigue jacket and put the wad inside the jerkin he wore underneath it.

'I do not want to lose you, I mean them,' he said in a hushed voice, glad that the dark hid his red face.

She scowled. 'Keep your mind to your job in hand, do not be a stupid blind librarian, Mar-cuss.' She scolded loud enough for Eschamali to hear.

'Reading, like a librarian!' Eschamali grunted in disgust.

Holding the rudder, he found the torque against the current and took them portside just skimming around the end of the sandbar Eschamali had pointed out and into the dark fast water of the Inawyrm. He adjusted the small sail. 'There.' Eschamali pointed from bow of the skiff, his eyes focussed on the wall of cliff they sailed towards. A white rock glistened wetly, alone on a narrow shingle beach. 'The tide will soon turn, make what haste you can.' He continued watching the cliffs as they slowly grew larger.

'How old are you?' he spoke softly and Elgenubi turned towards him carefully, keeping holding of the mast where she stood. He smiled inwardly; it was the type of thing he should know he thought while relief washed over him; they were out of Lodewick. He would do whatever it took to survive.

'Five thousand Juno years.' She frowned and her gaze pierced his. I hope he is not becoming attached to me she thought. Then she set her mouth to speak but the words would not come, and she felt her tongue cleave to the roof of her mouth. She would tell him it was not love when they reached safety, he reminded her of a water dancer, wobbling at the knee and sad in the eye, knowing that death was waiting, whichever way it jumped.

The flyer rose out of the night behind her, while he gawped and thought five thousand years old. The malevolent-yellow metal skimmed above the line of the cliff like a gigantic beetle; its crystal power burned cold like the blue inner tongue of a flame. He saw Eschamali slip quickly into the river at the same time it shot an acidic green beam that would have taken his head off, but instead it ripped through the bow and kept coming. It blew the small mast apart. The boat fragmented and they were tossed like discarded scraps of garment into the air. Part of the rudder was still in his hand as he hit the water and sank.

He bobbed to the surface, rasping for breath, gulping freezing water, choking, while the trapped air in his backpack kept him afloat and the world rang silently all around. The sky stunk and when he closed his eyes, they still burned green behind his lids, and when he opened them, he was flash blinded with green light. It felt like an eternity until he heard her voice, distant and distorted, while his ears still rung thickly from the shock of the blast. 'Do not attempt to swim, Mar-cuss, fight your instinct and float until the water shock has passed.' She had him by the pack and was pulling him towards a sliver of sandstone that looked vaguely like part of a gigantic, submerged wall, suddenly revealed by the lowering water.

'I can't see, Elgenubi, and I've been hit by something, it's in my side,' he groaned as she loosened his pack and let it float away.

'It is flare blindness it will pass. The pack will sink, was there anything in it…?' she trailed off as she reached the ledge of sandstone and held on to it with one arm.

'No, all of value in my pockets, and the books still in my jerkin,' he chattered through clenched. The flyer disappeared into the night towards the cliffs of the Shanty, scanning. They were out on the water without permits, and the flyer did what it was programmed to do, eradicate smugglers.

'You received the full impact as the mast broke. I have some small splinters in my side, but will be fine, let me feel.' His vision was blurry when it returned but he could see that it was worse than that. She had a gash that ran from her right temple to the bottom of her jaw, and her jacket was shredded on that side. The rest of her was submerged but he guessed it to be no better than his own injuries. A thin trickle of blood ran from behind her ear and down her neck.

She ran her hand gently along the front of Troy's body, then stopped when she felt the piece of wood. 'It's penetrated the right side beneath your lower ribs. You may be lucky – I think it too high, too shallow to have punctured your vitals, but it needs to come out. I need to get you out of this filthy water and on to shore.'

Eschamali swam silently through the debris, pushing the two rolled-up pods before him, slick and oily like two seals; they looked like his prey, while his eyes were wide and cunning like a shark. They scanned Troy and Elgenubi. He had a deep gash across his forehead. The skin was peeled back, ragged, and thick, as if it were made of gelatinous shell rather than flesh, but still the wound showed white bone underneath.

He listened while Elgenubi gave him her damage report while she kept Troy afloat next to the stone wall, and the skiff wreckage was slowly sucked out to sea on the undulating back of the Inawyrm. 'We keep to the mission. People wait for us, we cannot lose this opportunity, Elgenubi, they will wait. Hydra will expect us to survive, she will feel it.' He paused and scrutinised Troy. His eyes glowered and the skin above his eyebrows bunched into a knot that set blood running from his wound. Something passed between them, a peculiar look, and Eschamali grunted and said, 'Let him go.' He nodded sharply.

'I can swim with him, Eschamali. We will both use my pod. He has been a good runner, too good to lose,' she replied dispassionately, but Eschamali was her kin, and she could not hide everything from him.

'What? Since when, did you care?' He swam up to her and glared from beneath his lowered brows directly into her eyes while he searched them for something. He snorted then barked, 'That's an order. My order…I followed yours without question. NOW, let him go, he slows us. You would risk the lives of The Ten for that?' He thrust her pod at her and without another word he swam away.

'Let me go, Elgenubi,' Troy whispered through lips that were pinched and blue. His teeth chattered, and he could feel the icy water seep through his flesh and begin to gnaw at his bone. 'It's all right, the water chill has gone, let me go,' he lied, and his voice sounded distant to his own ears, and everything was awash with too many shades of grey.

She reached beneath the water and retrieved her blade. It glistened like a silver fish from a sheath at her calf. She pushed it down the front of Troy's trousers.

'Remember, do not swim – float. Keep your mind clear,' her voice broke, but she took a deep breath and continued, 'I go north. The Straits of Loka.' She kissed Troy softly on the mouth. Then pulled away and her eyes were set, and her mouth was tight, determined, and her words when they came were laden with truth when she hissed. 'All I told you…it the truth. You in great danger.' She paused while he grabbed her hand and whispered, 'What can I do? I will hide.'

She shook her head and felt a sharp stab of regret pierce her, but it did not deter her from what she had to do. 'He will find you,' she said slowly and met his eye fully while the water slapped around them, and he felt his life ebb away with the tide. 'You feel him as doubt at first.' She used her pod and the current to move away from the sandstone wall, dragging Troy behind while she sought a smaller Wyrm current, if he stayed in the Inawyrm, he would be sucked out to sea and drowned.

He had lost all will to protest. Eschamali was right, he would cost them their lives. He grabbed at her wrist and whispered hoarsely, 'Go, now.'

She pulled him to her and nodded once. She was ready to let fate and destiny take him. Then she said, 'He will prepare the ground before he enters.' She held his face while the brackish water slushed about them and small waves sloshed into his mouth while he lay on his back, already like a corpse. 'Listen…remember this, insidious and slow will be his way…you not even realise he there, until it is too late. Be careful of the deeds you do – do not forget this – the deeds you do. Ask always, are they mine?'

He met her gaze one last time and said in a voice racked with emotion until it sounded hoarse and raw. 'Let me go.'

Elgenubi's eyes sparkled like small embers of gold in the greying light. 'May the Lords of the Light Flame guide and protect you.' She pushed Troy away from her and into the current that would return him to Lodewick. She did not stay to watch or wonder if he would survive, she knew that he would. Then she turned and kicked after Eschamali, her pod kept her afloat and lent its warmth to her.

Eschamali had been swimming slowly and turned when she swam beside him. He grunted, 'Best put injured pets out of their misery.'

She nodded but did not trust herself to speak so she kicked on furiously and let the pain of her injuries flay her cowardice from her, until she had put some distance between them. Eschamali brought up the rear and wondered at the strange things a heart wanted.

~ �֍ ~ �֍ ~ ✳ ~

'Books,' he tried to shout but his teeth chattered and bit at the words until they were naught but ragged whispers, 'night poppy, adrenaline pen, mo, stickle bug, optics, a couple of eyes shaped like snails and a small spider.' A madman floating down the river while it seeped dirty brown chill further into his bones. He could feel fingers of ice wrapping greedily around his marrow and the leaden feeling of a man being drowned. The ache in his side became a distant earthbound torture, while the sky changed colour, and his life waned with the rising stony-grey clouds.

'Books, night poppy, adrenaline pen, mo, stickle bug, optics, a couple of eyes shaped like snails and a small spider,' He forced the words past lips that grimaced like death while his heart bled and he knew that when he saw her again, he would not be the same. How could he.

He watched himself separate and his other-self hovered above his body while he resisted the urge to just close his eyes and let go. 'Books…' he shouted then thought better of it and whispered to the salty water that whipped across his face. 'Bucky is a sorcerer. And I, am the devil's spawn.'

He repeated the list of the contents in his pockets like it was some sort of prayer while he reached into his breeches pocket where the adrenalin pen was, retrieved it by the sensation of it shape rather than anything he felt, and with clammy fat fingers wrapped around the barrel of the syringe, he found the distribution button. Then with all the clumsiness of the walking dead, he drove it into his thigh and pressed. 'Books, books – the answer is in The Shadow Yet to Come – night poppy, adrenaline pen…adrenaline pen…adrenaline pen.' His astral body shrugged, and he fancied he heard it say, you really cannot drown a spider. He put his hand around the wooden stake in his side and pulled, and screamed silently inside, while his adrenaline-full eyes bugged from his face.

Sculling and kicking through water that felt colder than the surface of the moon, and thicker than treacle, the books felt heavy as a brick, but he would not let them go, his salvation could be in one of them. He kicked towards the headland at the front of Lodewick and the dark granite fingers that raked against the grey dawn sky. Adrenaline coursed through his veins and gave him a jolt of life that shuddered in waves through his stiff body. Will it be enough he thought and kicked harder?

'If there is a goddess beneath this river, please help me now – I will repay you one day; if you help me now, one day my life will be yours.' He shouted the words to the dawn, then screamed like a madman when tendrils of seaweed wrapped themselves around his neck. He imagined it was Lord Conquest strangling him, but the wind howled louder, while the filthy river roiled and chopped all around.

If the tide had been in and the water higher, he would have floated on past the smallest of the fingers that raked at the headland, and out to the open water of the Sea of Shad and his death. But he sculled to the finger and held onto it while he brought his legs painfully underneath his body. He leant against the finger of granite and tested his weight. He could walk, but only just, and he made his way through dirty waist deep water, bent double, holding his right side as if a precious baby rested on his hip, his life blood felt warm while it leaked though his fingers and into the Ophiuchus.

The fingers of rock pushed out of the river like a clawed hand. The tide would return soon, but the water level was low, much lower than when the barge had brought him this way…a lifetime ago. He struggled waist-deep in water along a ledge of partially submerged broken rock. Finally, he reached the middle finger, he rested on an exposed bank of dark stone that was creased with lines like the palm of a gigantic hand. The current where the two rivers met seethed and frothed behind; the headland of Lodewick towered above, ominous, and dark. The top obscured by thick cloud.

He fell to his knees behind the cold stone while it pointed to the sky like a beacon, like a plea, and he prayed. 'Please, please help me – I am not expecting a miracle, just something. Anything you have.'

The wind stopped howling and a lonely beam of light cast a thin thread of cold warmth into the desolate day. It shone bravely down, illuminating a sorry pile of black rubbish caught against the crook of another finger. It was the last guard they had tossed from the cliff. He was caught like a dead animal behind the next finger along, though dangerously close to floating away. 'Thank you whoever you are – I owe you,' he chattered and made his way into the water.

His breath came in short painful gasps that jabbed inside his chest, and his heart hammered unnaturally, but he knew it was different. Not like when he had killed a man. There was no pull from his chest to the life pulse of the other man. The guard was a shell, his light, and his life, had gone out. It was adrenaline that had his heart thundering, but he knew the adrenaline would not last much longer and dared not think what would happen then. He was injured, badly, although he could not feel it. He was hungry and empty, and his heart was sundered. He dragged the body back and began to strip the uniform from the guard. He was deceptively heavy, saturated with the water he had taken into his body. The wound from the knife throw had stopped bleeding and it lay open and clean like an accusing eye but surprisingly close to his jugular. She just missed it, he thought, while he rolled him onto his back. He did not want to look at the wide slash across his neck but needed to get his jacket and shirt off. His own clothes were in tatters. 'Books! Where are my books?' he screeched then took them out of the leather jerkin and placed them on top of the dead body. 'I must keep them dry, commander,' he spoke to the corpse and knew he had gone mad. Then was thankful, would Lord Conquest want the mind of a madman. No, he thought, he will not but it does not matter anyway, he only wants my body, he will bring his own mind, his own thoughts, and a vast library of all his ill deeds. 'Night poppy, adrenaline pen, mo, stickle bug, optics, a couple of eyes shaped like snails and a small spider. No, shut up, that's not right, you used the pen,' he muttered while he checked the guard's pockets. He found what he was looking for, wound glue. Then he stripped off his shredded shirt and squeezed the tube over the raggedy puncture wound, which was already red around the edges with the first blush of sepsis. He watched the glue set with grim fascination while it sealed the hole in his flesh with a blob of silver-grey resin. He peeled off the remains of his ragged breeches. The proc uniform was soaking wet, and a little too long in the leg. 'Night poppy, check.' He put it in his new breeches pocket. 'Adrenaline pen, empty, mo, check, stickle bug, check, optics, check, eyes shaped like snails, check, and a small spider – check.' He patted the full pockets, rolled the extra length of the breeches up as best he could and adjusted the sodden wet shirt. The shirt was stained with a bib of blood, but it was a dark stain on dark fustian fabric, it would pass. They will have to do he thought as studied the rips in his jerkin then threw it into the water. Then he picked up the guard's jacket, it had inside pockets, and he stuffed the bundle of silicone wrapped books inside and prayed that the wet had not leeched through. He was a badly turned-out protectorate guard, he knew it. His heart sank, the disguise was not going to fool anyone, but…he eyed the guard's wrist…then, his own.

He sliced his wrist with Elgenubi's dagger, just like Micah had done it all those moons ago, and dug his fingers in, and removed the dud nano. There were no trails of light and geometric shapes, there was barely any blood – it was a dud, which held the minimum amount of information. Then he bared his teeth and snarled aloud, while he kicked the dirty brown water and tried not to look at the wasted naked body before him.

'Come on, come on, you can do it, filthy devil's spawn, just take it out…' he hesitated and closed his eyes. Then he growled, and snarled, like a rabid beast while he brought down the dagger and hacked at the guard's wrist. He felt the dagger slice through gristle and the resistance when it hit bone. He had done it too quickly and with too much force but could hardly remember lifting the dagger. 'Not a demon, not a demon!' he shouted, then vomited empty air followed by filthy river water that had been caught deep in his belly. 'I am sorry, I am so sorry for it all. I did not know – I will stop him if I can.' He cried while he took the nano and placed it in his mouth. It set his teeth on edge and coated his tongue with the taste of copper and salt. He pushed the guard into the flow of the river and watched his waxy body be taken by the brown waves.

He wept even though Elgenubi had told him he was not a real man but a drudge who had evolved and looked like a man. Another kind of demon, but he looked like a man, and he had not deserved to die or have his wrist hacked off by a madman. He took the guards nano between his fingers and pressed it into his wrist, then he squeezed wound glue over the cut and nipped the edges together until they stopped bleeding. His body was racked with jittering shivers, and pain coursed from his side in waves of fire.

He did not weep but accepted his fate, his rejection from The Ten, with a sense of detachment that seeped from the deepest part of his soul when he took his hands to his hair and felt his locks. He cast his attention out and he knew that Eschamali and Elgenubi had made it to the Shanty, her violet flame was weak and wavering, the faceted jewel was red and crackling like molten fury. Hydra was there, a pulsing blue hand, and the red rod of power that belonged to Himalia Skywalker. He felt her hand caress his cheek. *Do what you must to survive, and take a care who you kneel before*, she said into his head, and he did not need to tell her he was going to cut off his connection to his strange new-found family, she already knew. *I have not lost a wager on you yet. Do not let me down now*, she spoke softly as if she were beside him, as if she were his mother, and he wept as if she was just that. *I will meet you on the Dagger Path when the time is right*, she said finally, and he knew it was the truth. With lips pulled back into a snarl that was only half to do with the adrenaline, he sawed at his hair.

He left the six portal dreads, but cut them short, a round cap of fuzz like some of the mendicants and beggars wore theirs and hoped that he had not killed the pod fibre too, but he knew the connection was gone when the world took on another shade and it was not in any colour he knew, but it was the nothingness of twilight, and it was silent. Then shaking violently, he waded out into the water and lowered his snarl of hair into the swell. They came alive in his hands and curled around his wrists and fingers as if they were saying goodbye. He pushed them gently away from him. 'Thank you,' he croaked, and they snaked away on the surface like silver, black, and amethyst fish. He stared after them, long after they had gone but his mind was empty, and he felt his heart palpitate like a totem drum calling for war, insistent, and faraway, and it felt like it belonged to someone else. Then suddenly he tried to smile but it was a grimace and it looked like hell had come to live in his eyes when he said, 'It worked, Elgenubi. I know what I must do.'

He slipped her dagger into his boot while he cast his mind back to when he was hanging off the ledge high above. He had seen a large drainage culvert below him. The culverts were not being used because he had not given his plans to Reynard. Then he remembered he had put the old tissue thin map inside Navigating the Southern Isles. A new light set behind his eyes, and he thought this fight is not over. Not yet, Conquest. I will not let you down, Elgenubi.

'Attend to the most immediate danger first,' he heard her whisper, *'the wound before it goes bad.'*

He waded into the foaming water at the headland and crabbed along bare rock until he reached the culvert. Every step was a blazing agony, every pull of the water was a fight he thought he would lose while his fingers clawed at the slime and filth of the dock wall.

It would be so easy to let go and float away he thought, but he clung on until he felt a ledge, a fabricated construction beneath his feet. In his mind he had half a plan, and deep inside his chest he knew he had been left with half a heart, but he was alive, and he knew he would survive. I wonder if I am indestructible, does he have that kind of power he thought, and felt a sliver of hatred run along his spine and nestle in the centre of his chest. I will not be afraid, if I am, I may as well invite him into my body. He put his shoulder to the metal grille that covered the culvert, and it screeched open. Something in an eddy of dirty water beneath it, caught his eye – it was the wire.

'I may not be indestructible, but I do believe I have the luck of devil,' he said in a voice that was quiet and dry, while he bent down and groaned when a sheet of pain coursed through his body. He held his breath and taking the wire in his hand he squeezed it until the pain passed and he was able to stand up. He stepped inside the large circular pipe and grimaced as he slid towards a labyrinth of passages and pipes that were not on any map Reynard had ever seen.

He felt the adrenaline ebb, and his pain increase to a white-hot throb, round about the same time he realised he was out of danger. The culvert was part of the cross-drain system, and it ran under the docks, where it followed the course of a natural stream, long since built over.

Eventually, he exited the system at the roaring chasm of the Merewif. He stood on the narrow ledge before the dry culvert he had followed and watched while silver water thundered out of scores of the sewers and culverts that lined the throat of the massive sink hole, then waterfalled hundreds of feet into the dark pool below, its surface was ribboned with tatters of roiling froth of creamy white. Rain hammered down in a torrent of weeping grief and despair, a release that matched his own, the sky was still thick with heavy clouds. The witch's bridge was a black blur and the temple of Bloodgita the Effusive at the apex of its span was hidden behind a curtain of water vapor.

Water snaked, fast and thick out of a wide gap in the wall of the chasm directly ahead of him as it sought its own level in the marshes and then the sea, but that was not the way he wanted to go. To his right beneath the witches bridge, the way to the Silver Seaf was an open gullet that spewed white water, it churned the Merewif below to a frenzy when it punched into the surface of the pool. Just behind the column of water there was a large arch; he had rested at its apex, not so long ago with Alnilam and Markab. Large enough to sail a ship through, once long ago it had had steps that swept down one side and led to the pool, but now, they were crumbled to huge lumps of half-submerged red stone. The waters of the Merewif had risen, the lower culverts were all submerged, but the water had found its own way out of the sink hole chasm and poured under the gap in the arch. It rushed onwards, a thick black Wyrm, to only the flame knew where.

He brushed a sheet of wet from his forehead and out of his eyes, then brought his hand to his face. He watched it shake and acknowledged the sinking feeling in the pit of his stomach with a grunt. Waves of pain crashed through his side and his wrist ached like he had tied a tourniquet too tightly about it. He calculated his route, along the ledges of culverts that were not pouring with water, then several scrambles and climbs up the natural rock steps that jutted around the throat of the chasm. He dropped his hand; then paused and took a deep breath while he took one last look at the towering majesty of the chasm. It rose above him hundreds of feet high, the massive span of the black bridge was no more than the pulley and crank, used to lower a bucket into a well. Below the water was a black mirror that was being broken by spumes of hard water that fell like crystalline spears, piercing through its surface until they disappeared in froths of white that looked like clouds of scattered stars. He knew with a mathematical certainty that he did not have the strength left for the climb.

With a sudden realisation he pulled his gaze away from the vista before him, and whispered, 'I am at the edge of The Well of The World.'

He checked the contents of his pockets once more and felt the hard reassuring press of the silicone wrapped books against his chest. Then with a loud sigh he said in a voice that was strangely strong and inviting but hard at the edges with pain. 'I made you a promise.' He paused, while his words were snatched away by the wind and vapours that rose from the Well, he felt his jaw go slack with disappointment when no answer came. Then he heard it, that strange song he had first heard when he had passed by the Merewif with Alnilam and Markab and it pulled at his heart, stronger than the pull of the vertiginous invitation to fall. In that strange guttural song, that had no words, nor rhythm he understood, he knew that there was a power beyond his understanding.

'I am nothing but a vessel,' he yelled into the maw of the Merewif. 'Currently vacant, and awaiting immediate possession…First come, come claim me,' he shouted, then jumped off the ledge into the roiling water below.

~ ❀ ~ ❀ ~ ❀ ~

Outside, the sea had drawn the river water back faster than it could flow, exposing mud flats and architectural shapes jutting beneath the dark wet sand, fountains, bridges, buildings, and statues, all torn asunder. Moored boats suddenly found themselves marooned on silty banks that had not been exposed for many years, others toppled and crashed into their neighbours – waking dockmasters from their slumbers – they rang the alarm bells that jolted the guild guards awake.

'Abandon the docks, abandon the docks,' jack tars shouted, and they knew as they fled from their whores and their inns, that the old saying was come true. Though none dared stay to check the water. They were joined by their captains, who would not stay with a ship in the way of The Great Wave, and the docks emptied like ants running before the scald.

Then her fury came. Heralded by clouds of birds lifting away, screaming. More flew up the estuary, a hard rain of black and white spears hurled on the wind from the heart of the sea. They spun like tattered feathers before a wall of water hundreds of feet high that foamed at the top with white horses stampeding.

And she roared, and the cliff dropped its loose rock like massive granite tears falling. Her voice ran before the wild wind, and her song pierced like fingers of fire and ice, through flesh, blood, and bone. She ululated like a mother in pain, and she howled like every widow in her grief. A sister full of sorrow, and a woman filled with fury on her way home, to take her revenge, while the filthy brown water, retreated like a brown snake on its belly crawling back to hell.

Gigantic white horses spumed from the base of the wave, unbridled they galloped on, and on, until the water ran clear like a dawn full of white frost and the palest blue sky.

Then her face was revealed. Gaia.

Glossary

Abhhain and Moin: Two crofters from Talam Na Soar who come to stay and work at Al Tine Farm. Descended from Selgovae Fae and adept at seeking the rare aquatic life form that Roma Ranger cloaks are made from. Also, keepers of Riamh's Spear.

Abraxas: In the context of this work, Abraxas is the power of creation beyond the pleroma, the power at the core, the Godhead.

Abrecan, Lord Lucas: The demon lord of the dark flame, Conquest. *Abrecan*, from Old English, to conquer, conquest.

Acolytes of Anuk: A common name for anyone who is a member of any of the religious orders that preach about or support the One-God Anuk.

Aindreas Sackeyfio: Dorothea Al Tine's brother, but as far as Romarii kinship goes, this does not mean brother in the sense we would understand it.

Airgid and Gaoth: Pure blood Selgovae Fae minstrels.

Amnasia: The advancing glacier is the physical consequence of the planetary consciousness (Gaia) rejecting the demon invasion by entering stasis to protect itself from exploitation. The ice that Gaia uses to freeze the planet is ectoplasm, a universal glue that the demi-urges and their evolution engineers use to bind their creations.

Anoia: The word and meaning of Anoia was inspired by the word "Noia" which means thought and Anoia which means mindless thought. "Paranoia" which means outside thought and "Prenoia," the impulse before thought (Greek).
Anoia is the stream of mindless thought which includes all the unrealised potential for ideas, inventions, and creation, which in the fourth dimension,

humans process through their DNA3. Waves of Anoia also activate Galactic Signature Power in humans. The Demon, Lord Abrecan controls thought/Anoia waves by implanting humans with a nano device, thus stealing all their potential ideas, and disabling their "galactic power." The Ten have devices that read Anoia.

An Biseach Naofa: The Sacred Spiral. The Galanglas name for the village of Stone. Or Tearmann an Cloch Cosmai as named by the Romarii which means sanctuary of the cosmic stone.

An Crann Amhain: The One Tree, the forest city of the Galanglas Giants so named for the gigantic tree that stood at the heart of the city, which was not used for habitation like the other trees, but for dream-walking ceremonies, and journeys led by Tree Nympts, Dryads, and Drus. An Crann Amhain was the first tree grown from seed from Gaia's first tree, An Aon Charobh.

Anuk: The northern region that borders the Lake of Unum. Also, the name used by the being masquerading as Lord Lucas Abrecan when he possessed the body of the man who invaded Gaiadon, shortly after WW2 on earth. Because Abrecan has control of reality, the people of Gaiadon think the battle between the One-God Anuk and the Romarii took place thousands of years ago, and that Lord Lucas Abrecan is a descendant of the One-God Anuk, when in fact, Anuk and Abrecan are one and the same being – the Demon Lord of the Dark Flame, Conquest, and the battle between Anuk and the Romarii is approximately half a century old.

Arid Falamh: A section of the province Far Falamh which faces the western seaboard but is arid and dry due to a wind anomaly called Gaia's Howl, which originates in the Southern Isles and keeps the barren rocky land hot and dry for most of the year. Searing temperatures during the day and freezing cold at night. Thunders Head is a headland on Arid Falamh so named as legend says that all the storms in the world are made off the coast at Arid Falamh.

Athanasius Blood: A purveyor of blood and meat products. His warehouse was seconded by The Ten for the Night of the Dead tribal gathering. Athanasius left Lodewick with Euphemia Eye when she returned to Hiriwa Pourewa.

Bad Lands, The: High altitude land north of the Demon Mountains.

Balinas Amu Novantae: A Fae of the tribe Novantae.

Baelmonarchia: The realm of the Demon King.

Bathhory Dorka: A salt and lime merchant. Self-styled merchant queen of the almost uninhabitable Empty Isles; The isle named Lime being a gigantic quarry and the isle Salt being predominantly salt pans where conditions for the manufacture of salt is almost perfect due to Gaia's Howl. Her permanent residence is in Bathory Vale, in a mountain retreat overlooking Blood Lake, at the south end of the Cliffs of Maw, a gigantic cliff created at a destructive plate margin. Behind the cliffs are the Impenetrable Mountains.

Bathhory Vale: An exposed sea plate consisting of mainly low-lying land, wetlands, and lakes at the foot of the Cliffs of Maw governed by Bathory Dorka. Apart from the area around Blood Lake which has unusually high hills, and semi-tropical forest in comparison to the rest of the land which is below sea level.

Bealdras Landar: The district where elite residences are. *Bealdras,* noun, plural, lord, masters, heroes, from Old English. *Landar,* noun, property in a landed estate, from Old English.

Beamhouse Square: A large square and surrounding industrial area in Elleadern Weatende where hides are prepared for tanning and leather goods are produced.

Buralo Bay: Wolf Bay eventually leads to an epeiric sea, moving inland past Wolfsea Crossing but the actual bay is the stretch of sea that separates the Winter Lands and Galay from the correctional colony, The Wind.

Black Apothecary: A place where illegal potions, spells, and contracts, can be bought.

Black and Nellie: Romarii horses involved in a trade deal with Padrain Al Tine.

Bliones Tun, The: A huge, enclosed pleasure garden on the plateau of the city of Lodewick. It is surrounded by alchemical glass walls with a band of Solais silver running through their middle, etched with rune, and ancient alchemical symbols. The walls are like a medieval castle and have turrets and crenelations, the glass is opaque and changes colour in waves of rippling light.

Blue Planetary Hand: Celeste lies about her galactic signature because her nana has asked her not to tell anyone what it is, and at the entry point to *Shadow on the Other Shore*, it is through her becoming more aware of the anomalies in her life that the reader is able to imagine the reality of life in the rural zone Eirini.

Bran Muntor: A young man from the rural community Mount Wraith who took the Dagger Path to seek Hiriwa Pourewa, the Silver Tower, after mercy killing his betrothed, and her friend.

Celeste Melsie: A girl with the galactic power of Spectral Star.

Captain Charyia Al Farraige Stoirme: The whirlpool captain of the stormy seas, gained her name for her bravado, piracy, sea-witchery, and devil may care attitude to high-risk activities. Charyia is the daughter of Crann Og Riamh and his navigation officer, who died aboard the Sea Song during childbirth. Although Crann Og Riamh was considered small for a Galanglas Giant he was blessed with super almost God-like strength and is remembered as the Warrior-Smith who wed Mordeana Never Dead. Giants have an incredibly long-life span, but not as long as the remaining true Witch Queens of the Southern Isles. He and Mordeana Never Dead have a son called Athas Orga.

Copa Nordende: The silk and textile quarter to the North of the docks. Not quite in Elleadern Weatende but close enough that leather can be bought and transported easily.

Cosmic Warrior Memes: The ten spinners, from Juno Seven, a planet in the fifth dimension are masters of eidetic memory projection/manifestation which means that during the dance they cast psychotronic meme's, in the case of Eschamali, his were cosmic warriors. While they engaged with the crowd, they recorded the data/thoughts/Anoia the revellers are processing subconsciously through their DNA3. The spinners then upload the data captured by the visual Meme's onto their discs for analysis later.

Cyclic law: The ever-turning cycle of creation can be understood at the microcosmic or macrocosmic level, from the cycle of re-birth, life, and death of an individual to the same law that governs the creation of galaxies. It can be broken down to decades or yearly cycles for individuals, or even how the cycle of hours passes differently for us individually, the daily (diurnal) rhythm.

Crystal Box: Recording devices like cameras.

Crystal orb (Romarii): Can be used for communication and is a remnant of the Romarii birth process. They all have one and are an instrument for magic. However, the magic that is wielded through them comes from two sources. Firstly, it is permitted by Gaia and uses some of her essence; secondly, it uses the life essence of the Romarii who wields the orb, because all magic comes with a price. Gaia will replenish the life essence of the user by providing an elixir which means that the Romarii life essence is protected, but only if they operate within her jurisdiction. If the Romarii do not act in the best interests of their own people or the planet, then Gaia will not replenish their life energy and they will have to resort to darker means of sustenance. On their death the Romarii return to Gaia which maintains the balance of that which is given. The Romarii trade because a fair deal should keep all things balanced, although the recipient of the trade deal may not feel that way.

Day and Night of the Dead: A celebration like All Hallows Eve.

Droge Waere: Drugs in general. *Droge*, noun, excrement, from Old English.

Dyer Bridge: The almost derelict cat span bridge that leads to Beamhouse Square and is subject to an illegal toll payment taken by the Tanner's Guild Apprentices.

Cale, Plains of: The site of the last battle between, Anuk and his legions of the dead, and the goddess Gaia, her Lord Cernunnos, and the Romarii.

Charcoal Burner, The: A dockside inn at Coal Wharf.

Claiomh Cernunnos: Cernunnos' Sword, a large scimitar shaped peninsula to the far North. Covered by the glacier Amnasia. The towns of Claiomh Solais (sword of the sun), Cumagh Solais (eternal/everlasting light) and Riamh's Forge were to be found there, with mixed populations of Romarii, Fae, and Galanglas.

Compass, Stone: A forgotten means of travelling, both over distances and through time, but only by those with a Skywalker power or a blessing to do so. The compass stone is like a stone circle.

Dolmen, Lord Matthais, and Dolmen's Eyrie: Lord Matthias Dolmens mountain fortress in The Iron Hills province. A mining province between The Flat Lands to the east governed by Lord Rubric Volsunga, and Plantation Province to the west governed by Lord Yew Drydanward.

Dimensional splicing: Tara thinks she has been spliced or split between dimensions and she refers to the concept of the totality of our consciousness existing multi-dimensionally.

Drydanward, Lord Yew, and Drydanward Castle: Lord Yew Drydanward's castle in the north of Plantation province. It is remote and hidden deep within a large tract of forest and is remarkably close to a fully working stone compass.

Eidetic: Relating to or denoting mental images having unusual vividness and detail so that they seem real. Therefore, an eidetic manifestation would be to imagine something and make it so in the reality you and others occupy. This is the power of the demi-urge when they are creating worlds; they use chaotic thought (Anoia) alongside glue (ectoplasm), building blocks (radial plasma's), and solvent (Alkahest) to bring into reality their eidetic or mental images.

Eirini: From the ancient Greek word Eiro which means to connect. A fertile land exploited by Lord Abrecan.

Elgenubi Zuben: Galactic Worldbridger of The Ten.

Elleadern Weatende, The: The West End of Lodewick above Cheapside Docks. It is the quarter where tanners, knackers, and leather craftsmen work and live. *Elleadern*, adjective, plural, wholly of leather, from Old English. *Weatende*, noun, the west end of anything, from Old English.

Endwine and Lendrick: Scriveners for Oliver Sudden, Scribe and Scrivening Services. A place where false information is created.

Estmere Scir: Named for the clear bright water that runs through it, rather than the creatures who live in the mansions there. *Estmere*, freshwater lake, from Old English. *Scir*, feminine noun, an ecclesiastical district, from Old English.

Euphemia Eye: A white-eyed seer from Hiriwa Pourewa (Silver Tower). An intelligence source for The Ten.

Fae: The two tribes of light – Novantae – inspired by a border's tribe from the Esk region circa 6000bc and Selgovae – a border tribe from the Esk region circa 6000bc. In this work, Selgovae are traditionally a maritime race, their land is called Talam Na Soar, land of the free, but is being subsumed by the glacier Amnasia.
The Novantae are mountain Fae from the area known as The Plains of Cale and the Straits of Loka, but not exclusively.
Other tribes of Fae live in the Bad Lands, but they have become separated from their roots, and from Gaia, and worship the god of hard places.

Feill Sgaoilte: One of Lord Bucky's sons, murdered by Rodney Weaselton in the Inn called The Well Met Stranger.

Gaia: The living planetary logos currently in stasis, the planetary consciousness of Gaiadon, a demi-urge. Her evolution engineer is Cernunnos Lord of the Wild Hunt. Their planet Gaiadon is in the fourth dimension and is the higher aspect of the Earth. It is The Other Shore.

Galactic Signatures and their power: Based on the Solar Seals and Tones depicted in the Tzolkin/Mayan Calendar.

Geata de Lokas: The gates of light. The entrance to the higher realms.

Geata de Talas: The gates of hell. The entrance to the lower realms.

Hel Croce: A girl with a Seed galactic signature.

Hyenoi Hound: Or Falamh Grass Hound. Large dog-like beasts that hunt in the Falamh Grasses which is why Falamh goats sleep in the trees. Hyenoi Hounds are not canine, and many believe that they were taken by demons and subjected to genetic experiments. The Hyenoi beasts the demons developed are larger and can be controlled by a master though they are rare and are known as Hell Hounds. The Witch Queen Tuahine Hae has hell hounds, and their riders are Demon Sleeks.

Far Falamh: To the west of Eirini and the birthplace of Rodinian shapeshifters. Areas of the province are the Falamh Hills, Grasses and Dunes; all as inhospitable and empty looking as one another. In contrast to Arid Falamh whose rocks, shores and thin soil is as black a charcoal, Far Falamh seems as if it is made of gold which is the colour of the large, thick Sere grasses that almost cover it entirely, it has rocky outcrops and stunted trees, water is largely found underground, and Gaia's Howl is more of a scream, pause, scream. Wares made from Falamh grass are said to be exceptionally durable. The King of Falamh, missing for some time, is said to have taken to the seas in a coracle made from gigantic Sere grass in a quest to find Cassandra Novantae. The people are elegant, dark honey brown, with green or brown eyes and hazelnut coloured hair. They are divided into clans ruled by clan chiefs. The clans are nomadic apart from when they have produced a shape shifter then they make their way to Rodinia. They are known collectively as The Fala and are Gaia's children in much the same way as the Romarii are.

Halcyonic Bird: Mythical bird identified with the Kingfisher that has the power to calm the elements.

Henna Devine: Aindreas Sackeyfio's wife.

Inola: Roma Ranger. His name means black fox (native American).

Jiggers: Feet.

Kinetic: Like kinetic energy. It is the power humans possess because of the activation of the third strand of DNA3. Their power depends on the day or the galactic signature day when they were born. The demon lord, Conquest, harvests their kinetic power or corrupts it to his own ends. For example, soil singing in rural zones uses the power from Earth kinetics while he also bleeds the people who carry out that activity. Other tribes on Gaiadon do not possess the ability to channel kinetic power as they are indigenous to Gaiadon. They are not human and do not possess the same DNA.

Kinetic 128 Yellow Spectral Star: Celeste Melsie's galactic signature.

Kinetic 200: The energy at the time Micah Apollon was born was Kinetic 200, he is known as The Sun in Winter, and his galactic signature is Yellow Overtone Sun.

Lemegeton – *The Lesser Key of Solomon:* Also known as ***Clavicula Salomonis Regis*** or ***Lemegeton***, is an anonymous grimoire (or spell book) part of which deals with demonology. It was compiled in the mid-17th century, mostly from materials a couple of centuries older. It is divided into five books – the *Ars Goetia*, *Ars Theurgia-Goetia*, *Ars Paulina*, *Ars Almadel*, and *Ars Notoria*. https://en.wikipedia.org/wiki/Lesser_Key_of_Solomon

Librarian: A large sickly green coloured larvae, and the immature form of an insect on Juno Seven that eats the salts from the ancient rock of the planet. In the salts are the answers to all mysteries. It stores the knowledge in its silk. They are extremely slow and studious, ponderous, and philosophical, and inhabit catacombs where they are cared for until they pupate, usually when they are stuffed full of knowledge. They hatch and the silk from their chrysalis is taken and woven into reams of data that can be read by the adult librarians; a large, humanoid creature, with armoured chitin body panels and huge colourful wings that hang like a cloak when not in flight, it has oval shaped eyes, a small nose, and mouth, and feathery antennae coming from their eyebrows and pointy ears. They are called Keeper of the Mysteries and are extremely pacifist.

Llamrei: A horse deity worshipped by the Romarii Horses. Llamrei, a white mare, was also the name of Cassandra Novantae's mount, and Merlin too.

Lolade: A temple girl for the Brotherhood of The Unhanded Revenge.

Lord Bucky: Governor general of Eirini and of the Winter Lands, he has seasonal palaces. Namely, The Palace Galay, Caislean Gairdin on Autumn Hill overlooking Ninmah, Summer Hill at the entrance to The Bay of the Sun and his city residence in Lodewick.

Lord Yew Drydanward: Governor general of Plantation Zone.

Lord Lucas Abrecan: The self-anointed, divine protector of Baelmonarchia and the Demon Lord, Conquest. Also known as Anuk, and Bael.

Lord Matthias Dolmen: Governor general of The Iron Hills, usually at loggerheads with Rubric Volsunga about mining rights and land boundaries. The whole of The Flat Lands can be viewed from Dolmens Eyrie using a secret device called Lamina Oculus.

Lord Yalan Daboath: The Sophia's evolution engineer and a demi urge, known as the White Wizard.

Luna and Lilith: A natural moon, and a demon made device.

Mearberig: Marrowberry, fist sized fruit that resembles a huge plum full of red pulpy fruit.

Memorigi: Memorigi is a purple fruit. In Lodewick it was called, Seofonstierre, but the Fae called it Seachd Rionnagan, the Galanglas; Seacht Realta. In the Southern Isles it was called Seven Stars in the common tongue, and the starry-eyed users who sought the door to the heavens in its smoke, were referred to as those who sleep alone.

Merewif, The: A super massive sink hole that has created a huge circular chasm with a bottomless pool of black water in its depths, known as the Merewif. The enormous black bridge that spans the chasm is known as the Merewif Bridge but is more commonly called the Witches Bridge because of The Sisterhood of the Temple of Bloodgita the Effusive, that sits at its apex.

Nano Device: A small micro-chip, like a lemon seed, inserted into the wrist.

Navigating the Southern Isles: by Captain Charyia Al Farraige Stoirme. Is a book of maritime charts for navigation, recipes, spells, and other miscellany, it is rumoured that the fabled grimoire, mentioned in Charyia Sea Storms Shanty, is hidden in the original copy of Navigating the Southern Isles?

Nightcrawlers: The name given to The Ten and anyone who attends their tribal gatherings.

Ningen: Mythical Sea giants that inhabit the cold dark seas of the north.

Ninmah: is the agricultural administration centre for the rural zone Eirini and is also a semi-garrison town that protects the canal barrier that separates Eirini from the land bridge Kai.

Niyaha: Rovander's mount. *Feather*.

Noble, Captain: Commander of Aerial Orb-unit One.

Nomos: A mythical space-time dragon. Nomos, the concept of law – from astronomical, or nomos meaning the laws attached to something. When a demi-urge and evolution engineer wish to manifest a world or system in the Void, then they must face the Nomos and win The Stone which holds the lore and laws for their creations before they begin to evolve them. They are creatures of Abraxas and are used to test evolution engineers.

Notochord: Defines the longitudinal axis of what will become the spine on a physical level, on a metaphysical level it is an important part of Metatron's Cube. It is also referred to as the primitive streak, further reading can be found in research on the mystical kabbalah, the Rosicrucian knights templar, and sacred geometry. For the purposes of this work, the spiritual significance of the notochord is that it is the etheric channel or tube where the spirit bird or animal enters and leaves the body. When the person dies, and the spirit leaves it takes the etheric notochord with it and the trail of light from that action is like a comets tail or a streak of light (see Black Void for further instances of this phenomena).

On the other hand, the soul bird enters and leaves by the causal chakra located 3 to 4 inches behind the back of the head.

Nuair a choinníonn an ghaoth mé ina lámha. Osclóidh an ghaoth Geataí Loka – **The inscription on Crann Og Riamh's spear:** When the wind keeps me in his hands, the Gates of Loka will open.

Nuru-Sha-Shutu: is the city of light inside Juno Seven. Nuru-Sha-Shutu is also called The Southern Light.

Margeride Shroude: A girl in Celeste's class with a Resonant Hand galactic signature who went to the Acolytes of Anuk at Ninmah to help her friend Melaine Merilyn. The Acolytes used her nano device to corrupt her true galactic signature so that she could be used in the blood-letting ritual called "soil singing." A ritual invented by the demons so they can collect human blood under the pretence that they need it to feed the crops.

Molly: The name "Molotov cocktail" is derived from Vyacheslav Mikhailovich Molotov, a Soviet politician (circa WWII). Which is still true in this work, only no one can remember where the name came from, only that an incendiary device made with Foss (fossil fuel) or Cheen, is called a Molly.

Outside the Box: The name that is given to the symptoms people experience when their galactic signature power activates or when they recall the dimension jump from Earth to Gaiadon. The symptoms are vibrations that resemble fits, then the person's galactic signature power is activated by spasmodic influxes of huge quantities of Anoia.

Prophecies of the Age of Man and Shadow Yet to Come, The Chronicles of Cassandra, The First Age of The Stone: Cassandra was said to be the last pure blood descendant of the Fae tribe Novantae, and to have lived in a cave that overlooked the Straits of Loka. She was reputed to be four thousand years old but looked no older than thirty summers. Some claimed this was because she had been a novice, then an adept of Marama Rawa's, and had intimate knowledge of the Crystal Cathedral, the chamber inside Silver Tower, before she mastered the paths inside the mind of Time.

Raife Oarfish: A human with the galactic signature power Eagle, accepted by the Crone Arianrihod into the Romarii tribe at a walk-in ceremony deep in the caves of Romar Ri. His twin sister was Sirena Oarfish.

Reynard Wyburn and Leleth Valoroso Wyburn: Troy's parents and part of the inner circle of elite who surround Lord Lucas Abrecan.

Rodinian shifter, Homily: Half Rodinian, which is a place in Far Falamh, and half Romarii changeling, after a ceremony conducted by Arianrihod to give Homily a changeling "walk-in." These are the characteristics Homily projects to others, but she is neither really. Homily is a "polymorph," a shapeshifting being from Far Falamh.

Roma Rangers: Romarii who range areas of Gaiadon on horseback, they seek out and kill shadow spawn, chimeras, and Demon Beast.

Romarii: A tribe of indigenous people who live in harmony with the planet Gaiadon.

Romarii Crone, Arianrihod: A woman who has attained great spiritual power through the trails she has undergone to become The Crone.

Roma-Red: A resinous product made from mysterious herbs by the Romarii.

Romaros: The Romarii King.

Rovander: Roma Ranger Captain. Her mount is Nlyaha.

Rubidium: Soft, silvery white, alkali-metal that ignites spontaneously in air and reacts violently with water. It is used alchemically to produce Rubicity, an alchemical energy which is a lot like electricity. It is mined from the Flat Land region and the mains energy is produced from powerplants to the South of The Wind. Rubidium can be bought freely but at a cost from black alchemists and apothecaries.

Sarlat Penroe: A girl with an Earth galactic signature.

Scatt: Stolen goods, derived from, *Sceatt*, noun, property, goods, treasure, wealth, from Old English. Pronounced in Lodwick as Sc-att.

Sceatta Sceat: The less reputable area that borders the Snide and leads towards the top of the plateau of Lodewick. Sceatta, noun, tax, bribe, tribute, rent, from Old English. *Sceat*, noun, nook, area, region, from Old English. Pronounced Seeg-da Seed and commonly called the Seedy Seed.

Scrag and Scrap: Two demon beasts who remind The Romaros of two Dire Wolves he once had. He is fond of them and has made them loyal to himself by naming them.

Scrid: An oval shaped car, which can be driven in any direction, it runs on rubidium, which charges its alchemical engine.

Seaf, and Silver Seaf, The: The Seaf is a body of fresh water in the elite district of Lodewick. The many arched Whitestone viaduct that spans the lake is called the Silver Seaf. The bridge takes traffic mainly from elite areas to the Bliones Tun, the fabled pleasure gardens of Lodewick. *Seaf*, noun; reservoir or lake, from Old English.

Seeds for seeds, earth for earth: A common saying in Eirini. The population and fertility are controlled through the nano device so much so that certain births and their galactic signatures are prevalent in certain zones, in the rural zones the predominant signatures are seeds and earths. Hands are the healers and artists of Baelmonarchia and would be found throughout the country; Nights would work in the mines and Storms would be prevalent in the technological zones, whether the galactic signature power is active or not, the energy of the person is used by the demons.

Seft: Monkey in Captain Nobles orb-unit.

Selgovae, Novantae, Ningen and other Mythical Beasts: Meite a Thomhas' (myth weaver) *Phantasmagoria*. A compendium of Monsters, Myth and Legend, thought to be by a group of artisan scribes from Talam Na Soar. Most certainly a copy of earlier manuscripts before all were destroyed by the demon horde.

Shambles, The: The labyrinth warren of alleys, cuts, culverts, and hidden squares behind Cheapside Docks.

Sidhe Draio: Handed down to druids by the ***Sidhe Draoi*** were the magical secrets of the trees and the ***means*** to learn the arts of astral travel and divination. It has been said that while there is no harm in following the ***Sidhe Draoi's*** music it may be wise to not stay too long for one may be tempted to stay in their astral realm. (paganpages.org). In the context of the story when Tara tells Celeste that they must make plans to return to Earth, Celeste thinks she is mad, but Tara knows that the Bloom Nympts could help her because of the secret arts of astral travel, which is a form of dimensional travel that they know.

Silent Thing, The: Is an entity, a consciousness that exists in the realm of Gaiadon. In itself, it does not communicate with the horses but has layers of energy and channels (part of the Ever-Was) that can be accessed by certain species if they have telepathic ability.

Siursach: Whore.

Soul and Spirit Birds: The soul bird is the entity that lives at one of the spirit doors of men (in the Gaiadon Universe the soul bird spirit door is the causal chakra between the back of the neck and the base of the skull) and is 3 to 4 inches away from the head. The door and the bird are the guardian of free will and the thing that helps record our actions in the causal body (the soul).
The spirit bird is the entity that belongs to Abraxas (the Godhead) and is our guide and a source of higher power, like a spirit animal totem, it enters and leaves the body by the etheric Notochord tube.
The soul bird is always a bird; however, the spirit bird or animal can often change to other kinds of animals depending on what we need at the time.

Southern Isles, The: An archipelago of isles spread over thousands of miles. Not all islands are known or charted, some are even rumoured to appear and disappear at will. Infamous for being the home of the Seven Witch Queens and the source of Gaia's Howl.

Spider King: Is an aspect of Cernunnos that has been demonised by Lord Abrecan. The last battle on the Plains of Cale portrays The One-God Anuk/Lord of The Dark Flame, in a good light when he defeats Spider King, the form Cernunnos took when he defended Gaia against hordes of the undead.

Snide, The: Extremely large road and surrounding commerce and business district.

Swealve, Lady: The daughter of the Lord Governor General of the Population Bureau.

Talas and Lokas: There is a vast amount of theory and research on this but for the purpose of my writing I have kept the meaning simple. Tala is the inferior world to that of Loka (Sanskrit).
However, in this story I use Tala to describe a metaphysical object that is made manifest or material, it can be seen felt or touched etc. Loka then, is the higher aspect or spiritual power of the object which is less tangible.

Tanner's Apron: A tavern in Beamhouse Square.

Tara Melsie: Celeste's guardian who has failed in her duty to inform Celeste of the true nature of reality.

Tearmann an Cloch Cosmai: The name given by the Fae and the Romarii to the sanctuary of the Cosmic Stone. A secret village hidden deep in the giant woods, called Stone, in the common tongue. The Galanglas call it The Sacred Spiral.

Temple of the Brotherhood of Perpetual Pain: A series of smaller temples known for organ harvesting and secret rituals. Not run by demon elite's but governed by Gumrice Begalan a human sorcerer, masquerading as a demon elite, who recruits humans into the order, including recruits from the protectorate guards, scriveners, and merchant guilds. Their pain bands are wave disruptors that interfere with the nano device, protecting them from demon scrutiny. (From Old English - *Gumrice*, the power to rule over men. *Begalan* to sing incantations over, to enchant).

Temple of the Brotherhood of the Unhanded Revenge: Huge temple complex known for relieving thieves of their hands. The Patriarch is Hergend Unbealu. (spoiler of innocence).

Temple of the Needful Scrip: A place where Baelmonarchian currency is minted. Located above the Sceatta Sceat region and controlled by Matriarch Goldweard. *Goldweard*, noun, keeper of gold (dragon), from Old English.

Temple Matriarch's and Patriarch's: Cardinals of the highest rank from the Acolytes of Anuk who live in large mansions in the area known as Estmere Scir. Their nominated Aldhelm's (bishops) run the temples on a day-to-day basis.

Temple of The Saviour's Salve: A temple complex where Volsunga carries out modifications on human thralls when he is in the city. Probably the place where Troy was conceived. The facilities, alchemist's labs, and birthing vats are used by Lord Abrecan to artificially create thralls with powerful galactic signatures, but with limited success. The Matriarch is Slifan Smite.

Temple of the Sisterhood of Bloodgita the Effusive: Built at the apex of the Merewif bridge, the Sisterhood takes toll from those passing over the bridge into Boho district and hangs blood drained corpses from the sides of the bridge. The Matriarch is Hyngran Slyppe.

The Calling and The Becoming: Romarii rituals that ensure the tribe's survival by carrying on the stream of consciousness that belongs solely to them, which means that all Romarii are connected to the goddess Gaia, have conscious rebirths, and remember their past lives.

The Lake of Unum: The Lake of the One Thing.

The Lady Aos Si: This was Dorothea Al Tine's first incarnation among the tribe of Romarii. On falling in love with the human Padrain Al Tine, when he arrived on Gaiadon as a young man, she surrendered her title and her power.

The Son of Sophia: Is an alter ego of Micah Apollon's, his other being Veil Slave.

Thrall: A demon slave.

Tree-wish: A form of Dryad or Drus.

The Sword of Souls: Is a dimensional anchor device used to lock the anchor planet onto the axis of reality.

The Tainted Stream: A group of human beings who have a certain thing in common.

The Tiers of Lodewick: The cliffs and plateaus of the city.

Time-to-die code: Coded information held in our astral field (soul body which surrounds the physical body). The code may activate certain diseases or even certain events that lead to death.

The Ten: Alien spies from Juno Seven sent to Gaiadon to gather intelligence on Lord Abrecan and to destroy the Black Moon Lilith. Eschamali Zuben, Elgenubi Zuben, Acumen Sting, Hydra the Cup, Alnilam Seed, Alcyone Sun, El Nath Night, Markab Storm, Homan Wind, Himalia Skywalker.

Torus: Is a surface or solid formed by rotating a closed curve, especially a circle, about a line which lies in the same plane but does not intersect it (e.g., like a ring doughnut). The Torus Vertex is the hollow centre of the doughnut and is a zero-dimensional point which in the story refers to a non-place, time, and space. A paradox that operates outside of the normal laws associated with the dimensions in the story.

Troy Valoroso-Wyburn: Was created so he could be birthed on the Night of the Dead, under the auspicious galactic signature day of Kinetic 241, Red Resonant Dragon.

Umbra Horrenda: Land of horrible shadows.

Velig The Butcher: A demon sleek who specialises in torture.

Vinberry: A grapelike fruit. About the size of a chicken's egg.

Violet: A girl from a family of troubadours. The demon sleek, Velig the Butcher killed her father, her mother threw herself off the cliffs at the headland of Lodewick.

Water Dancer: Graceful and elegant, long-legged water insect that dances from lily-pad to lily-pad and stone to stone across the waters of the lakes of Nuru Sha Shutu. It must decide if the stone is a stone or if it is a Croaker, a large toad-like creature. The Water Dancer's knees knock together each time it decides to jump, either to gain height or because it is afraid, a source of amusement to Junonian's. Water Dancers are considered extremely stupid because they have wings and can fly, there is no need for them to water dance at all.

Well of the World: The chasm that the Merewif Bridge spans.

Wet White Bridge: Used for heavy traffic to and from the Elleadern Weatende.

Working the Wind: Local talk to describe when someone has disappeared or has been taken by the Protectorate Guard on the orders of one of the Baelmonarchian Administration Bureau's. The Wind is a correctional colony located to the North of Baelmonarchia above the area known as the Flat Lands. People are modified at The Wind.

Witch Queens, The: Of, The Seven Isles of The Towers. Nga Motu e Whitu O Nga Pourewa.
Each isle is governed by a witch queen who is either drawn to the light or dark or is indifferent. The Witch Queens are fallen goddess' sometimes called Sky Sisters, who sought sanctuary on Gaiadon after rejecting proposals from the Lords of The Dark Flame.
Witch Queen 1. Turanga, of Wairua Tuatahi Motu (the first spirit isle) and Ara Pourewa (the Lead Tower).
Witch Queen 2. He Waimarie Pai, of Tuarua Wairua Motu (the second spirit isle) and Te Pourewa (the Tin Tower).
Witch Queen 3. Pakanga Te Hika, of Tuatoru Wairua Motu (the third spirit isle) and Pupuhi Pourewa (the Iron Tower).

Witch Queen 4. Tuahine Hae, of Wairua Tuawha Motu (the fourth spirit isle) and Te Hinu Pourewa (the Copper Tower).

Witch Queen 5. Moe Moema, of Wairua Taurima Motu (the fifth spirit isle) and Hiki Tere-Tere Pourewa (the Quick Silver Tower).

Witch Queen 6. Marama Rawa, of Te Wairua Tuaono Motu (the sixth spirit isle) and Hiriwa Pourewa (the Silver Tower).

Witch Queen 7. Mordeana Kaore I Mate, of Tuawhitu Wairua Motu (the seventh spirit isle) and Koura Pourewa (the Gold Tower).

Worldbridger: A galactic signature with the power to communicate across dimensions, but only to another Worldbridger, using the frequency of the death channel or a higher state of being induced by meditative near death, which is a vibration of 32hz and which is why Elgenubi's physical and astral bodies started to separate.

Yegg: An old English word for sticky fingered safe cracker.

Yumni: Inola's mount, *Whirlwind* (Lakota).